THE PERFECT GIRL

GILLY MACMILLAN

piatkus

PIATKUS

First published in Great Britain in 2016 by Piatkus
This paperback edition published in 2016 by Piatkus

1 3 5 7 9 10 8 6 4 2

A CIP catalogue record for this book
is available from the British Library.

ISBN 978-0-349-40642-8

Printed and bound in Great Britain by
Clays Ltd, St Ives plc

Papers used by Piatkus are from well-managed forests
and other responsible sources.

MIX
Paper from
responsible sources
FSC® C104740

Piatkus
An imprint of
Little, Brown Book Group
Carmelite House
50 Victoria Embankment
London EC4Y 0DZ

An Hachette UK Company
www.hachette.co.uk

www.piatkus.co.uk

Gilly re and
lived s. She
studied History of Art at Bristol University and then at
Courtauld Institute of Art in London. She worked at
urlington Magazine and the Hayward Gallery before
ng a family. Since then she's worked as a part-time
rer in A-Level Photography.

y lives in Bristol with her husband and three children.
debut novel, *Burnt Paper Sky*, was published in 2015
iatkus.

Visit Gilly Macmillan online:

www.gillymacmillan.com
www.facebook.com/gillymacmillanauthor
www.twitter.com/gillymacmillan

Praise for Gilly Macmillan:

One of the brightest debuts I have read this year – a
visceral, emotionally charged story' *Daily Mail*

'A pacy, twisty thriller' *Independent*

'Heart-in-the-mouth excitement from the start of
this electrifyingly good debut ... an absolute
firecracker of a thriller' *Sunday Mirror*

'If you love *Gone Girl* and *Before I Go to Sleep*,
you need to read this' *Closer*

'A very clever, tautly plotted page turner'
Good Housekeeping

'What an amazing, gripping, beautifully written debut'
Liane Moriarty, author of *The Husband's Secret*

'A tremendous debut novel' Mark Billingham

'Tightly focussed and fast-paced. You won't rest until you
really know what happened' Lisa Ballantyne

'A beautifully written, deeply probing psychological
thriller' *The Huffington Post*

'Every parent's nightmare, handled with intelligence
and sensitivity … I found myself racing through to find
out what happened' Rosamund Lupton

'A powerful page-turner' *Woman's Weekly, New Zealand*

'What an exciting debut! *Burnt Paper Sky* kept
me up until the small hours' Charity Norman,
author of *After The Fall*

'A nail-biting, sleep-depriving, brilliant read'
Saskia Sarginson

'Deft, tense and utterly gripping, *Burnt Paper Sky*
stays with you long after the final page has been turned'
Tim Weaver, author of *Never Coming Back*

To my family

'We dance around in a ring and suppose,
But the secret sits in the middle and knows.'

Robert Frost, 'The Secret Sits', 1942

'My mother died today, or maybe it was yesterday.'

Albert Camus, *L'Etranger*, 1942

SUNDAY AND MONDAY

An Evening of Summer Music

Sunday 24 August, 2014

7 p.m.

Holy Trinity Church, Westbury-on-Trym, Bristol

Zoe Maisey and Lucas Kennedy

play

Brahms, Debussy, Chopin, Liszt & Scarlatti

'You won't want to miss these two precociously talented teenagers making their Bristol debut – this promises to be a very special evening.'
– Bristol Evening Post 'What's On'

In Aid of the Family Bereavement Society

Tickets: £6 for adults, £3 for children.
Family ticket £15.

Please contact Maria on maria.maiseykennedy@gmail.com for bookings and details of future performances.

SUNDAY NIGHT

The Concert

ZOE

Before the concert begins, I stand inside the entrance to the church and look down the nave. Shadows lurk in the ceiling vaults even though the light outside hasn't dimmed yet, and behind me the large wooden doors have been pulled shut.

In front of me, the last few members of the audience have just settled into their places. Almost every seat is full. The sound of their talk is a medium-pitched rumble.

I shudder. In the heavy heat of the afternoon, when I was sweaty and tired after rehearsing, I forgot that it could be cold in the church even when the air was oven hot outside, so I chose a little black dress to wear this evening, with skinny straps, and now I'm feeling the chill. My arms are covered in goose pimples.

The doors to the church have been closed, sealing out the heat, because we don't want outside noise to disturb us. This suburb of Bristol isn't known for its rowdy inhabitants, but people have paid good money for their tickets.

And it's not just that. The thing is that this concert is my first performance since I left the Unit, and my first perform-ance as part of my Second Chance Life.

As my mum said, only about a hundred times today, 'This performance must be as perfect as it's possible to be.'

I glance at Lucas, who's standing beside me. Only a milli-metre or two of air separates us.

He's wearing black trousers that my mum put a crease in this afternoon, and a black shirt. He looks good. His dark brown hair is just about tamed into neatness, but not quite, and I think that if he was bothered to, he could make those girls who are still lame enough to read vampire romance stor-ies wilt.

I look good too, or I will when the goosebumps subside. I'm small-boned, I have pale, clear skin, and my hair is long and very blonde but thin: cobweb-caught-in-sunlight hair, which looks amazing against my black dress. In the right light my hair can look white, and this gives me a look of innocence.

'Like a baby deer, fragile, delicate' was how the prosecutor described me, which I thought was quite nice, though it still hurts me to remember that she added 'but don't be fooled'.

I flex my fingers, and lace them together to make sure the gloves I'm wearing are fitting extra snugly, the way I like them, and then I put my arms to my sides and shake them, to get my hands moving. I want my fingers to be warm, and flexible. I want them pulsating with blood.

Beside me, Lucas shakes his hands too, slowly, and one at a time. Pianists catch hand shaking from each other like other people catch yawns.

At the far end of the nave, in front of the altar, the grand piano stands on a low platform, its hammer and string intes-tines reflected on the underside of the propped-up shiny black lid. It's waiting for us. Lucas is staring at it, completely focused, as if it represents a vertical glacier that he has to ascend with his bare hands.

We have different approaches to nerves. He becomes as still as possible, he starts to breathe through his nose, slowly, and he won't respond to anybody.

In contrast, I fidget, and my mind can't rest because it has to run through the things I have to do, in the order I have to do them in, before I begin to perform. It's not until I play the first note that the concentration I need, and the music itself, will wrap around me, pure and white like a shroud, and everything else will disappear.

Until that point, I'm sick with nerves, just like Lucas is.

Beside the piano, a lady has been introducing the concert, and now she gestures towards us, and then sort of scrapes and bows her way off the stage.

It's time for us to go on.

I pull my gloves off quickly, and drop them on to a table beside me where the coffee and catechism leaflets are, and Lucas and I walk together down the aisle as if we're play-acting a wedding. As we do, the heads of the audience turn to look at us, each row triggering the next.

We walk past my Aunt Tessa, who's in charge of a camera that's been set up to record our performances. The idea is to replay them later, to analyse them for imperfection, and identify areas where improvement can be squeezed out of us.

Tessa is squinting a bit nervously at the camera as if it might turn round and lick her face, but she gives us a thumbs-up. I love Tessa, she's like a much more chilled-out version of my mum. She has no kids of her own and she says that makes me all the more special to her.

The other faces in the church smile as Lucas and I walk between them, creasing deeper into expressions of encouragement as we approach. I'm seventeen now, but I've known this look since I was a little child.

Mum describes these sorts of people as our 'supporters'. She says they'll turn up to watch time and time again if we play well, and they'll tell their friends. I don't love the supporters, though. I don't like the way they come up to you at the end of a concert and say stuff like, 'You have such a gift,' as if piano playing isn't something that you work on day in and day out, if you want to make it perfect.

You can almost see the word 'genius' flashing up like a neon sign in their minds, temptingly bright. Beware that sign, I would say to them, if they asked. Be careful what you wish for, because everything has a price.

In the front row of the church, the last pair of faces I focus on belong to my mum, and Lucas's dad. Or, to put it another way, my stepdad and his stepmum, because Lucas and I are step-siblings. As usual, they're wearing the too-bright expressions of parents who are disguising a level of ambition for their children that could choke you.

Lucas is ahead of me by the time we get to the end of the aisle and he's already taking his seat as I step up on to the platform where the piano sits.

We're going to start by playing a duet. It's a crowd pleaser, the brainchild of our parents. Plus, they think it'll help us to calm our nerves if we play together at the beginning.

Lucas and I would both rather play alone, but we humour

them, partly because we have no choice, and partly because we're both performers at heart and a performer wants to perform, needs to perform, loves to perform.

A performer is trained to perform.

So we'll do it, and we'll do it as well as we can.

As I sit down at the piano, I keep my back straight and I'm smiling for the audience even though my insides have constricted and twisted so they feel like a ball of elastic bands. But I don't smile too much. It's important that I look humble too, that I get my performance face just right.

There's a bit of faff while Lucas and I get settled and adjust the piano stools. We already know that they're perfectly positioned, because we tried out the piano before everybody arrived, but still we fiddle about with them, the spacing of them, a tiny height adjustment. It's part of the performance. It's nerves. Or showmanship. Or both.

Once we're both sitting perfectly, I place my hands over the keys. I have to work hard to control my breathing because my heart is hammering but my focus sharpens on to the music that's ahead, all of me waiting to hear those first notes now, like a starting gun at the beginning of a race.

The audience is hushed. Just a cough from somebody, that echoes around the vaults and columns. Lucas waits for the sound to disappear and, in the absolute silence that follows, he first wipes his palms on his trouser legs and then he positions his hands over the keys.

Now, that smooth run of black and white stretching out beneath our hands is everything and I watch his hands as intently as an animal ready to pounce. I mustn't miss his cue. There's a beat or two more of perfect silence before he arches his palms and his hands bounce lightly: once, twice, three times.

Then we're off, in perfect synchrony.

We dazzle when we do this; everybody says so. The energy two players produce can be electrifying when it's right. It's a tightrope act controlling the power, the tone and the dynamics, because all of it must be perfectly balanced, and it wasn't so good this afternoon when we got tired and cross with each other while practising in the heat, but tonight, it's brilliant. It's seamless, beautiful, and we're right in the music, both of us, and I'll admit that doesn't always happen. Mostly doesn't happen.

In fact, I'm so into it that at first I don't hear the shouting, and not hearing the shouting means that I don't realise that what's just begun is the end.

But I wish I had realised.

Why do I wish that?

Because, six hours later, my mother is dead.

MONDAY MORNING

SAM

At 8 a.m. Tessa still hasn't stirred, but I've been awake since dawn.

I'm a criminal lawyer, with a heavy workload. I often work late and usually I sleep heavily until my alarm goes off, but today I have a hospital appointment that's been burning a hole in the page of my diary for more than a week, and it's on my mind the minute my eyes open.

The curtains are drawn at my bedroom window, darkening the room, and light filters round them in lazy, unpredictable curves as they move with the breeze from the river. If I opened them, I would see the wide expanse of the floating harbour outside, and the colourful mixture of modern apartments and old warehouses and boathouses that bundle together on the bank opposite.

But I don't.

I stay where I am and I notice that the breeze is so soft that it barely disrupts the stillness of the room. They promised us a storm last night, but it never came. There was just a short, violent rain shower, followed by a dusting of drizzle, which offered a brief respite from the heat, but only brief, because now it's thickening again.

Tessa arrived in the rain, in the middle of the night.

11

She apologised for disturbing me, as if she hadn't just made my evening. She said she'd tried to phone. I hadn't noticed because I'd passed out on the sofa in front of the TV, with the remains of a special chow mein on my lap, and the letter from the hospital on my chest.

When I opened the door to her, I noticed dark smudges of exhaustion on the damp skin underneath her eyes, and she stood very still when I embraced her, as if every muscle in her body was stretched too tight.

She said she didn't want to talk, so I didn't press her to. Ours is a quiet, respectful affair; we don't ask for or expect a comprehensive emotional download from each other. We're more in the business of providing refuge for one another, and by that I mean a strong, safe place to reside, a place where we are almost certainly what two less reserved adults would call 'in love', though we would never say that.

I'm a shy person. I moved from Devon to Bristol two years ago, because it's what you do if you want to avoid spending your whole life and career amongst the same small circle of people, in the area you grew up in. Opportunities in Bristol are much greater, and I'd cut my teeth on Zoe Guerin's case, so I felt ready for a change.

But it hasn't worked out too well for me. My cases are more varied, and the workload is more intense, that's true, but new friendships haven't come easily because I have to work all hours, and you don't meet too many potential partners when you're doing prison visits and court attendances. So when Tess and I ran into each other, just in the street one day, it felt like a godsend. She was a familiar face, we had shared history, however difficult, and we slipped quickly into a pattern of snatching time with each other, just coffees and drinks at first, and then more. Tessa is married though, so that's where things have sort of stalled. We can't move on unless she leaves her husband.

Last night, after she arrived, she flopped on to my sofa as if the stuffing had been knocked out of her, and I brought her a cold beer and discreetly slipped the hospital letter into a drawer on my way to the kitchen, so she wouldn't see it. I didn't want it to mar things between us, not until I was sure. Not until I'd got through today's appointment. It was fairly easy to disguise the numbness in my left hand. Nobody at work had noticed it either.

She sipped her beer and we watched a Hitchcock film, in the dark, and the black and white images on the screen made the room flicker as if it was animated. Beside me, Tessa remained still and quiet as she watched, once or twice rolling the cold drink across her forehead, and I snuck a glance or two at her when I could, wondering what was wrong.

Tessa doesn't share the white-blonde hair, pale skin and refined features of her sister, or her niece – her looks have none of their hauteur – though she does share their sharp blue eyes. Tess mostly wears her thick, silky strawberry-blonde hair tied back, and the open features on her heart-shaped face and her lightly freckled skin make her look approachable, and kind, and her eyes often dance with humour. Her figure is athletic, her attitude is practical and no-nonsense. For me, she is beautiful.

As I look at her now, in the warm darkness of my bedroom, she's lying with her hands on the pillow beside her face, fingers curled in beside her lips. Only the sight of the tarnished gold wedding ring on her finger spoils the picture for me.

After a while, I ease myself out of bed, because I want breakfast. So I'm riffling through a pile of laundry on the floor to locate something to wear when my phone vibrates.

I snatch it up quickly, because I don't want it to disturb her.

The screen tells me that it's Jeanette calling, my secretary. She's always at her desk early, especially on a Monday.

I go through an internal fight with myself, wondering whether to answer it or not, but the truth is that I'm a conscientious chap so the battle was really lost as soon as the phone started buzzing. I answer the call.

'Sam, I'm sorry, but there's a client turned up for you here, at the office.'

'Who?' I ask, and I mentally shuffle through the deck of some of my more notable clients, trying to guess which of them might have pitched himself or herself off the good behaviour wagon and back into the mud this time.

'She's only a girl,' Jeannette tells me this in a stage whisper.

'What's her name?' As I ask I think, It can't be, can it?, because I've only had one client who was a teenage girl.

'She says she's called Zoe Maisey, only you knew her as Zoe Guerin.'

I take myself out of the bedroom, into the en suite, shut the door and sit on the side of the bath. Here, the morning light streams in through the frosted window, yellowing the room, assaulting my dark-widened pupils.

'You are joking?'

'I'm afraid I absolutely am not. Sam, she says her mum was found dead last night.'

'Oh dear God.'

Those three words express in only a paltry way my utter

14

disbelief, because of course Zoe is Tessa's niece, and her mother, Maria, is Tessa's sister.

'Sam?'

'Can you put her on the phone?'

'She's insisting she wants to see you.'

I calculate that because my appointment isn't until late morning, I probably have time to deal with this, at least partly.

'Tell her I'm on my way.'

I'm about to hang up the phone when Jeanette adds, 'And she's with her uncle,' and my insides take a swan dive yet again, because Zoe's uncle is Tessa's husband.

SUNDAY NIGHT

The Concert

TESSA

When you don't have kids of your own, people have a tendency to give you things to look after. I think they assume that you're lacking in outlets for any nurturing instincts that you might have.

On the night of Zoe's concert, the child substitute that I've been given to be in charge of is the camera. I'm supposed to be looking after it throughout the duration of the performance, so that I can record it in its entirety. It is, I'm told by my sister in a pedantic way, as if I'm lacking in mental capacity, an important job.

Shall we deal with the reasons for my childlessness straight away? Let's do it. In spite of the fact that I'm a successful professional and happy in my skin, it's what people always seem to be most curious about.

So here goes: 'Unexplained Infertility' is a thing. It's an official thing in spite of its unofficial-sounding title, and I have it. My husband Richard and I didn't discover it until we were in our thirties, because we left having kids until after we'd gone travelling, and established our careers.

After we found out, we tried IVF and went three rounds

16

before we gave up. Surrogacy: I didn't fancy it; not brave enough. Adoption: same reason. They'd never pass us now anyway, not with Richard's drinking.

As for being somebody who's lacking in nurturing instincts, I could snort with laughter over that, because I'm a vet.

My practice is in the city centre, lodged where several of Bristol's most contrasting neighbourhoods meet. On an average day, I probably see between twenty and twenty-five animals who I prod, probe, stroke, reassure and sometimes muzzle in order to treat their health and sometimes their psychological problems. Then I might reassure, or advise, and very occasionally stroke their owners too if there's bad news.

In short, I nurture, all day, most days of the week.

But you know there's a bit of irony here, which never escapes me when I'm with my little sister, especially when I'm roped in to help with her family, as I am tonight.

You see, when we were growing up, Maria was the naughty girl, compared to my Perfect Peter. She had lots of potential as a child, especially musical potential, which got my parents excited, but she never met their expectations.

From a very young age she was feisty, and funny, but when she hit fourteen she began to run wild. While I burrowed into my bedroom in the evenings, swotting away, my heart set on vet school, her desk, on the other side of our bedroom, would be covered only in make-up she'd discarded after getting ready for a night out. She stopped studying, she stopped playing classical music, and she had fun instead.

She didn't see the point of the rest of it, she said, in spite of the fact that my dad's eyes bulged when she spoke like that.

Boyfriend-less, much plainer and less socially adept than

17

my beautiful little sister, I loved living vicariously through her and I think she liked that too. She whispered her secrets to me after she got home in the small hours: kisses, and drinks, and pills taken; jealousies and triumphs: adventures, all of them.

But then, to all of our surprise, aged just nineteen she met Philip Guerin at a music festival. He was twenty-seven, and had already inherited the family farm, and she just took off and went to live with him there, and shortly afterwards she married him. Just like that. 'Living the dream,' my mother said sarcastically, as she actually wrung her hands.

Zoe followed soon afterwards. Maria had her when she was just twenty-two, and I think it was after that that the reality of life on the farm with a small child began to rub the shiny edges off her a bit. But she didn't quit, to give her credit. Instead, she began to put all her energies into Zoe, and when Zoe's extraordinary musicality presented itself as plain to see when she was all of three years old and began to pick out tunes on the piano at the farm, Maria made it her mission to nurture that talent.

That was before the accident, of course, when things went very wrong for them. But my point is, that, in the meantime, having done everything right all my life, and studied hard, and followed the rules, I am married, sure, but I've ended up with no children. I've come to terms with it, but Richard isn't coping so well, especially after a dramatic professional disappointment, which coincided with me refusing to go for IVF round number four.

So here we are tonight. I'm helping my sister and Zoe, which is something I love to do when Maria will let me. I'm looking forward to the performance, because Zoe's playing has almost regained the standard it used to be, before she went to the Unit, and I'm sure she's going to blow everybody away tonight, and I'm hoping I won't mess up the job of recording everything.

I've had a meagre thirty-second tutorial from Lucas, the son of my sister's newish husband, on how to operate the camera. Lucas is a film and camera buff, so I was in good hands, but the tutorial wasn't really enough, because by instinct I'm a bit of a technophobe, and even as Lucas was saying them, I felt his words swimming uncontrolled around my head like a panicky shoal of fish.

I could do with my Richard being here to help me, but he's let me down again.

Just an hour ago I went to find him when it was time to get ready for the concert. He was in the shed at the bottom of our garden, supposedly working on building a model aeroplane, but when I got there I found him squeezing out the dregs of his box of wine from the shiny bladder inside. He'd ripped the cardboard away and he was massaging and twisting that silvery bag as if it was a recalcitrant udder, holding it over his tea mug.

As I stood watching in the doorway, a few pale drops of liquid dribbled from the bag into the mug. Richard drank them immediately and then he noticed me. He made no apology and no effort to hide what he was doing. 'Tess!' he said. 'Do we have another box?'

Even from the doorway I could tell that his breath stank and his speech was slurred, and although he was trying to behave like a civilised drinker, somebody just enjoying a glass of white on a Sunday afternoon, shame wandered across his features and exaggerated the tremor in his hands. The balsa wood model he was ostensibly there to make lay in its box, all the precision cut pieces still in perfect order underneath the unopened instruction manual.

'In the garage,' I said. And I left to go to the concert on my own.

So now I'm here with a camera that I'm not sure is working properly, a pounding head and a disappointed heart, and I'm telling myself that I mustn't, I must not, give in to temptation and go and see Sam after the concert tonight, because that would be wrong.

SUNDAY NIGHT

The Concert

ZOE

Lucas hears the shouting before me.

He stops playing first, but I don't notice immediately because we're in the middle of a complicated passage of music that always pulls me through it with the unstoppability of a freight train.

When I realise that his hands have stilled, and that I'm playing on my own, I keep going at first, glancing at him because I wonder if he's forgotten his part. We're playing the duet from memory, and that happens sometimes: your brain just freezes.

So I'm expecting him to pick up the melody at any moment, I'm *willing* him to remember, because this concert must be perfect, and I'm doing that right up until the moment when I work out that he's properly stopped, because a man is standing in the centre of the aisle.

So I stop playing too and, as the last vibrations from my chords die away, I look at the man, and I think I might recognise him.

The expression on his face is smudged out of normal. It's in no way appreciative of our playing, it's red with rage; the tendons on his neck are straining so much that they look like extra bones.

'It's a travesty!' he shouts. 'A travesty! It's disrespectful!' His words ricochet around the space, and one or two people stand up.

He's staring at me and I realise that I do know him.

I know him because I killed his daughter.

The piano stool makes very little noise when I stand up, because even though it tips over, it's on a square of crimson carpet that breaks the sound of its fall so that it's a dull thud only.

My mother rises from her seat. She knows the man too.

'Mr Barlow,' she says. 'Mr Barlow, Tom, please,' and she starts to walk towards him.

I don't stay. I'm too afraid of what he might do to me.

I leave the stage, my hip clashing painfully with the edge of the piano, and I flee towards the back of the church, away from him, to where there's a doorway behind the altar that takes me out of his sight. I shove through it, then clatter down slippery stone steps into a tiny room where there's just a sink draped with stained cloths and I crouch in a corner, shaking, drenched yet again with the cold sweat of my remorse, with the impossibility of this life of mine, of second chances or fresh starts, until eventually my mum finds me.

She says words that mean nothing but are an attempt to make me feel better. She says them to me in a hushed voice, and her hand smooths the hair on my head, smooths it lightly down my back. She says, 'Shush now. Shush,' but I'm not sure if that's because she wants to comfort me or because she wants my sobbing to quieten down so nobody else can hear me.

Fifteen minutes later – it takes that long for us to be sure that they've got rid of Thomas Barlow and his raging grief – she leads me out of a back door, through the graveyard, and towards the car.

There's no question that I'll perform now. I'm still shaking, and the notes are all jumbled in my head anyway.

Outside, I take in the fact that the night is deeply dusky and warm, and that feels like a balm after the cold air inside. I notice a strong smell from the glowing white roses that hang over the churchyard gate, and the dark fluttering of bats that swarm from a high corner of the church tower. Around us, as we walk in the tired grass, gravestones whose cadaverous foundations have failed them lean against one another for support. I see a Celtic cross, the contours of lichen-covered stone mounds, writing everywhere, words of remembrance, and, above us, the dark, pointed leaves of the yew tree greedily sucking away the last of the light.

From inside the church we hear the sound of Lucas beginning his Debussy. The show must go on. The sound is a warm bath of notes at first, then a river flowing. It's something beautiful, which I wrap around me to shield me from what's just happened.

It diverts me from looking down at the edges of the path where there's a plaque that has been recently laid. 'Amelia Barlow' is inscribed on it. 'Aged 15. Beloved by family, cherished by friends. The sun shone brighter when you were alive.' There are freshly tended flowers planted around it.

We didn't know that her family had laid a plaque for her there. We would never have hired that church as a venue if we'd known, never in a million years. Continents would have drifted and reformed before we'd have done that.

For the whole drive home my mum says almost nothing, apart from, 'It doesn't matter. We can reorganise the concert, and you'll be ready for the diploma. You're already ready.'

My mother: who never talks about what really matters, and who is trying to reassure me, because although public musical performance at the child prodigy level was my downfall tonight, she believes it's ultimately going to be my salvation. She believes that it was the catalyst for our second life, and that it will also be the fuel that will propel it into a stratosphere that is a gazillion light years away from our life so far.

And perhaps I should have listened harder when she spoke because it was the last time she ever truly reassured me, the last time I felt the frustration of our inability to connect with each other prickle the air between us.

Perhaps I should have emerged from the cocoon of my own misery to ask her if she was OK, even though that was the one thing we hadn't been for the past few years. We hadn't been OK.

But I wish I had. Asked her, I mean. I wish I had.

MONDAY MORNING

SAM

In the bathroom of my flat, after ending the call with Jeanette, and feeling a coruscating dread at the thought of having to break the news to Tessa, I sit for a moment longer and remember when I was first introduced to Zoe Maisey, or Zoe Guerin as she was known then.

My first encounter with Zoe was over three years previously, when I lived in North Devon, and the introduction came in the form of a phone call from the Defence Solicitor Call Centre, because I was the solicitor on duty when she was arrested.

The call came in at nine-thirty in the morning, about eight hours after the accident had happened. They described Zoe and her situation as follows:

'Juvenile, appropriate adult present, charge is death by careless driving, two fatalities, another critically injured, ready for interview at Barnstaple Police Station and your Duty Solicitor number is 00746387A.'

I phoned the custody suite at the police station right away, identified myself, and asked the custody sergeant to put Zoe on the phone.

'Hello?' she said.

I introduced myself. 'Don't tell the police anything about

the accident,' I said. 'I'm on my way. I'll be about forty-five minutes. Don't start any interviews without me.'

And in reply she said, 'OK,' in a voice that sounded quiet with shock, and she had not a single question that she wanted to ask me.

I drove through the countryside to get to the police station. It was a beautiful, cold morning. I passed white frosted fields bordered by hedges that were a couple of feet thick, sturdy and sinuous at once as they partitioned off the surrounding fields, and stripped of leaves by the winter but so dense that the shadows they cast were deep horizontal bands. The blue-grey ocean, surprisingly calm, was visible here and there where clefts in the landscape revealed it, and Lundy Island was clear as day offshore, peaceful, ancient and cold.

In the custody suite in Barnstaple the sergeant handed me a charge sheet.

'She won't have her mother with her,' he said. 'She refused, even though Mum's here. Social worker's just arrived. She didn't want a brief either but the social worker overruled her.'

I scanned the charge sheet. It wasn't quite as they'd said on the phone. The charge was: 'Death by careless driving' but there was an addition: 'whilst under the influence of alcohol'.

It was a shocking charge for anybody to face, but for a fourteen-year-old, whose life had been stretching out lazily before her just hours earlier, still packed with potential, it was nothing short of horrific.

'Has she been interviewed?'

'Not yet. Social worker just arrived.'

The police weren't allowed to interview Zoe without an 'appropriate adult' present because of her age. If she'd refused to have her mother with her they would have had to wait until a social worker came on shift this morning.

The custody sergeant wore a tight black police top with a high collar and short sleeves that gripped muscular arms, and literally talked down to me from his desk, which was on a raised platform. As he spoke, he tapped efficiently at his keyboard, eyes glued to the screen of his computer monitor.

'I've just had handover so I'm acquainting myself with the details, but she was brought in at about four-thirty after a couple of hours at the hospital.'

I pitied Zoe her hours in the cell. Even my clients who'd been to prison said that they hated being in police custody more than anything. There's no routine, just four walls, a mattress on a shelf, a toilet that may or may not be properly screened, and a pair of eyes on you at all times, either directly or via the camera.

'Why didn't she want her mother?' I asked him. I was wondering if this girl had been in care, or lived with her father, or was bereaved.

'We're not entirely sure. Best guess: ashamed.'

'Ashamed?'

He shrugged his shoulders and spread his hands wide, palms upward. 'Mum's been sitting in reception since Zoe arrived.'

There had been a lone woman sitting in reception on my arrival, with white-blonde hair and fine features. She was huddled in a corner, and shuddered when the electronic doors ushered in a cold draught with me, and met my eye with the clear gaze of somebody who's waiting for nothing good at all to happen, and has had no sleep to speak of.

It was a common expression in the waiting rooms I

frequented: at police stations, in courtrooms, nobody's looking forward to what's going to happen.

That nice-looking woman, who'd been shut firmly out of her daughter's life at that moment, was my first clue that this case was going to be far from straightforward.

I had no picture in my head of Zoe before I met her. I'd had enough experience by then to know that criminality takes all kinds so you could never predict what your clients would be like, though if I'd had to hazard a guess I might have told you that the girl I was about to meet would be a mature fourteen-year-old, probably a bit rough round the edges, probably a seasoned drinker, maybe a dabbler in the local drugs scene, definitely a party girl.

The girl I met wasn't like that. The police had taken her clothing at the hospital as evidence, so she was wearing an outfit that the A & E nurses must have had to cobble together for her: oversized grey sweatpants and a blue zipped-up fleece top. She had a dressed wound on one temple and long, white-blonde hair, a shade paler even than her mother's, which sparkled with tiny, glittery fragments of glass from the accident.

She sat in a moulded plastic chair that was bolted to the floor, her feet were drawn up and her arms were wrapped around her knees. She looked dishevelled and very small. Her cheekbones were fine, her eyes were a bright, clear blue and her skin was as pale as the frost outside. Her hands were tucked into the sleeves of the fleece, which looked grubby on the cuffs: stains from another life that the hospital laundry hadn't been able to get rid of.

Beside her sat a woman who wore the stoic expression of a seen-it-all social worker. She was middle-aged, with hair cropped short and sharp, and a face that was deeply grooved and greyish from what I would have guessed had been twenty cigarettes a day for twenty years. She had deposited a neat pile of gloves, hat and scarf on to the interview table.

I introduced myself to Zoe and she surprised me by standing up and offering me a timid handshake. Unfolded, she revealed herself to be of medium height and very slight, totally swamped by the borrowed clothing. She looked exceptionally fragile.

We sat down opposite one another.

It wasn't the beginning of her nightmare – that had happened hours earlier – but it was the moment when I had to begin the delicate process of trying to help her to understand precisely how grave her situation might be.

SUNDAY NIGHT

The Concert

TESSA

I'm feeling pretty certain that the camera is actually filming when Zoe and Lucas start playing their duet because there's a red light flashing on the bottom right-hand corner of its screen and a counter appears to be frenetically keeping track of the seconds and milliseconds that are passing.

Zoe and Lucas look great on the podium, as ever: a sweet vision of teenage perfection. They are yin and yang, blonde and dark, an ice princess and her swarthy consort.

I'm one of the first to notice Tom Barlow because the camera tripod and I are positioned just at the side of the aisle, quite near the entrance, so that I can stand up and tend to it without blocking anybody's view.

I don't recognise him at first, and by the time I do it's too late to do anything.

Later, I wonder what might have happened differently if I'd acted at that moment, whether I could have stopped him, and changed the course of things, but it's pointless speculation because, like the rest of the audience, I do nothing more than watch, open-mouthed, as he shouts, his spittle flecking the air in front of him.

Zoe is the last person in the church to notice him and, when she does, fear jerks her limbs like she's a puppet on strings, and she scrambles to get off the stage. I don't blame her. Tom Barlow looks like a man possessed, and he's a big man.

When Maria stands up and makes a feeble attempt to pacify him he's having none of it. 'You have your daughter,' he says to her, and the words seem to strike her like blows. 'Don't tell me what to do. You have your daughter.'

'I'm so sorry, Tom,' she says, but he scythes her down with his reply: 'It's your fault,' he says. 'It was your fault.'

And then there's a muddle, as people begin to leave their seats and surround Mr Barlow, and he sinks to his knees and begins to sob, and it's an awful, wrenching sound, a sound to make the hairs on the back of your neck stand up.

I know who he is, because I recognise him from the trial, of course. Zoe's trial took place in a closed court, because of her age, so I never went inside the actual courtroom but I was still there every day, in the waiting room reserved for families of the accused, and I saw the families of the victims outside the courthouse in the street, day in, day out, huddled in groups.

We kept our distance, to avoid any scenes, but I'm certain I recognise Tom Barlow because his face was in the local paper too. He and the other parents were pictured prominently, black clad and riddled with grief at the funerals of their children.

In the mayhem at the concert, Maria follows Zoe off stage, though before she does there's a tense exchange between her and her newish husband Chris, during which he seems to question her and she shakes her head vigorously. Maria meets my eye as she goes, she looks stricken, and I mouth, *Do you want me to come?* She signals that she doesn't, so I sit down where I am. I'm keen not to draw attention to myself. Others are kneeling beside Tom Barlow, looking after him, so I don't need to. Best if he doesn't see me at this point. There's a possibility that he might recognise me.

I wonder how Tom Barlow knew Zoe was here tonight. Since leaving Devon, she's changed her surname, broken links with the families, with everything. We all thought she'd left Amelia Barlow's family a hundred miles away.

If we're unlucky enough that Tom Barlow and his wife and their remaining children have moved here too, it won't be long before people make connections. Bristol, it seems, might not have been far enough away for my sister and Zoe to move to escape the tragedy, and Bristol is a place where news travels fast. Within certain circles, there are often only a few degrees of separation between anybody in this city.

Chris Kennedy doesn't follow Maria and Zoe. Instead, he goes to stand beside Lucas who's still sitting at the piano. Both of them watch the dying throes of Tom Barlow's meltdown with shock and disbelief on their faces and I feel leaden as I think of all the stories that are now going to have to be told, all the truths uncovered, and I think sadly of the impossibility of my sister's shiny, happy new life continuing as it is.

Zoe, our dear Zoe, has caused domestic bliss to implode yet again.

When Mr Barlow has been cleared away, mopped up off the floor like a spilled drink, it's decided that Lucas will continue to play alone. As the audience settles into this news I double-check that the video camera is still recording. In the screen, I can see Lucas, and I think I've framed him quite well. I can also see Chris Kennedy in profile and he sits completely still, staring front and forward. Only a small fold in his forehead and the utter stillness of his features betray the incomprehension that he must be feeling.

SUNDAY NIGHT

After the Concert

ZOE

The thorny, spiky, typical silence in the car as Mum drives me home means that I get a bit of a chance to pull myself together, because my mum doesn't like crying. It's the kind of silence that we often share, Mum and I. She grips the steering wheel with white knuckles while she drives. When I try to talk to her, she shushes me, and tells me that she needs to think.

I stay quiet, but the silence is demolished when we pull up in the driveway, because the stone walls of our big, grand house are thumping with the kind of sounds that me and Lucas can pretty much only listen to surreptitiously on our iPods.

It's popular music, the kind that the kids in the Secure Unit listened to. Here, in this house, it's usually a treat that's severely rationed so that Lucas and I don't break our diet of classical repertoire, which allows us to 'develop our musicality'.

Mum hurries into the house and I follow her. The volume of music means that Katya, the au pair, is oblivious to us and she doesn't notice us until we're in the sitting room, standing right behind her.

She's on our sofa, with my baby sister Grace on her knee, and right beside her, so close it looks as though he's stuck to her, is a boy who I know from school, called Barney Scott. Grace is laughing loudly because Katya is holding her arms and bouncing her up and down, but when she sees us she reaches out to my mum, and Katya and Barney leap up off the sofa and they stroke down their rumpled clothing and make a totally impressive recovery.

'Hello, Maria, hello, Zoe,' Katya says, and hands over the baby.

My mum is speechless at these blatant transgressions of the rules of the house: the music, the boyfriend, the baby downstairs after bedtime. She clutches Grace as if we've just heard that a landslide's about to sweep the five of us and the descendants of all mankind into the ocean.

'I hope you don't mind me asking Barney here, but his dad is a doctor and Grace was very unsettled,' Katya says. Her full-on Russian accent and her deadpan face, cheeks like slabs of limestone, both give the sentence instant gravitas.

I look at my mum. Even she's not insane enough to fall for the dad-as-doctor line but I can see that Katya has scored a big, fat bullseye with the 'unsettled' comment.

Grace is the Second Chance Baby, the Miracle Baby; she is A Gift to Us All. She is half of Mum and half of Chris and therefore a product of what Lucas calls their Perfect Union. As Chris said at her naming ceremony, she has 'a lovely, sunny disposition' and is a 'joy', and she 'helped us all to start again'.

What this means is that Katya's comment has adeptly manoeuvred my mum's psyche down the path it most likes to travel, which is to exist in a state of fear for Grace's health.

So my mum ignores that fact that Grace looks ecstatic, and is shiny with a sheen of overstimulation, and she takes her immediately upstairs to settle her, with Katya in her wake, and I'm left in the room on my own with Barney Scott. It's weird for me because we would never normally be alone together, absolutely no way. This is because, at my school, he's a Popular Boy.

Barney Scott scrunches his face up and I think that he's trying to smile at me. It makes me wonder what he and Katya thought they were going to get up to because surely only guilt would make him do that.

'Hey,' he says.

'Hey,' I say back.

'Back early then,' he says.

'Obviously.'

'Huh.' He's nodding his head like a plastic dog on a dashboard. 'Did you ... ah ... did you play well?'

Barney Scott is not interested in how I played, though I suppose I'm impressed that he's making the effort to ask. He's the type of boy who posts things online like 'On the Downs. 8 p.m. BBQ, Booze and Bitches' and thinks that's hilarious, and he's probably right because girls like Katya, or the Popular Girls at school, then actually turn up wearing microscopic shorts with the pocket patches hanging out over their foreign-holiday-tanned thighs so they can get drunk and be groped.

'It was OK,' I say. Barney Scott doesn't need to know what happened, and I want him to go away.

36

He obviously doesn't want to be with me either. 'I'll wait outside,' he says, waving at the door to the hallway like I don't know where it is.

'OK,' I say, but, as I watch him go, what I'm desperate to say to him is that I kind-of-sort-of-maybe had a Popular Boy in love with me once, or at least in lust, so I'm not as stupid or pointless as they all think I am, I'm not.

My very own Popular Boy was called Jack Bell and he acted like he liked me. A lot. Unfortunately, there were obstacles to us going out, and the biggest one was Jack's twin sister, Eva, who was the Most Popular of All the Girls at school. Eva lost no time making it clear to me that her brother was not 'in love' but was 'playing the field' instead. The girl he really liked, the one he wanted instead of me, Eva said, was her best friend Amelia Barlow.

And even though the word of Eva Bell was God for most of the people around me at that school, I didn't believe her, because I saw the way Jack Bell looked at me and even now, when I think of that, I get a dissolving feeling inside me. I might be socially awkward, I know I am, but I'm not stupid.

But what I have to do is to shut that dissolving feeling down quickly, because Jack Bell, like Amelia Barlow, is buried now, and the ache of that is too sharp for me to bear.

The sitting room window has been thrown open but the heat inside is still stifling. I hear Barney Scott crunching on the gravel outside and see him leaning against our front gate, waiting for Katya.

I want my mum to come down, but I don't want to disturb her while she settles Grace. I'm starting to feel sick with fear thinking about what will happen when Chris and Lucas get here, because they're going to want to know what the hell Mr Barlow, back there in the church, was shouting about, and if nothing is to ruin the Second Chance Family then me and Mum need to work out what we're going to say.

MONDAY MORNING

SAM

I have to wake her, because I have to tell her about Maria and Zoe, yet no part of me wants to.

'Tessa,' I say. 'Tess.' There's a thin sheet covering her, and its sculptural white folds describe the lines of her body so closely, it's as if somebody had carefully laid it there, like the first damp bandages of a plaster cast.

She's alert quickly, eyes wide open; she's heard something in my voice.

'What?' she says, and it's a whisper; she hasn't moved yet.

I want to swallow the reason I've woken her up, never speak of it. I don't want to do this to her.

'I'm so sorry,' I say, and the words make me feel terribly, throat-clearingly formal. They steal an intimacy from us.

And in the moment after I tell Tessa that her sister is dead, and she sits up, her eyes searching mine for confirmation of the truth of what I've said, I have the strange realisation that she resembles Maria more closely than I'd ever noticed before.

And after a time where I hold her tight while shock takes hold of her, and I experience what I can only describe as an ache in my heart, in spite of the clichéd awfulness of that phrase, I have to let her go.

And that heartache, that hard pinch of a feeling, is not

something I can indulge. It's a shallow, oil-slicked puddle of self-indulgent emotion compared to the oceans of grief that Tess's family have been through, and will now go through again. Just to totally overkill the metaphor: their grief could fill the Mariana Trench.

I gather up Tess's clothes for her and she dresses silently. When she's finished, I ask: 'Do you want to come with me? To see Zoe? And Richard?'

His name seems to me to hover bulkily in the air between us, but it's the least of her worries at this moment.

'I should go to the house first,' Tess says. 'I need to see … and the baby …'

She can't finish her sentence; her words are choked with shock and incomprehension. We have very little information, just that Maria died at the house, but we don't know how. I understand that it's up to me to look after Zoe for now, who-ever she's with.

'Shall I drop you there?' I ask. I'm worried about her driving.

We're standing on the communal landing in my building now. It's a small, bright space, with floor-to-ceiling windows over the busy commuter road below, no lift, just a functional metal staircase that winds its way down to the ground floor and the car park, and it's airless and stifling.

'No,' Tess says. 'You need to go to Zoe. I'll come later.' And then she's gone, sandals clattering on the steps.

SUNDAY NIGHT

After the Concert

ZOE

Lucas's Debussy piece lasts for fourteen minutes, and his Bach is nine minutes. If you add to that the time he'll need to mix with the audience afterwards, and then the drive home, and assume that since Mum and I took the car, Aunt Tess will be bringing them in her VW bus, which doesn't go above 36 mph without belching out black smoke, then I think Mum and me originally had about an hour and ten minutes to talk before Lucas and Chris arrive, minus the time it took discovering Katya and Barney on the sofa and the minute that Barney could stand to be in the room with me afterwards, leaving us about fifty-eight minutes.

I wait on the sofa, stretched out, while Mum is still upstairs with Grace. My hip aches painfully from the bang against the piano and I pull up my dress to examine it and see a dark bruise forming there already. It's tender to the touch. The sight of it makes tears spring to my eyes and I shut them, and lie back down, and try to breathe, the way I've been told, to blank my thoughts, to focus just on the sensation of inhales and exhales instead.

It's hot. Our Second Chance House is a big old Victorian

41

pile and it usually feels damply cold to me, whatever the weather, but this summer's been so hot for so long that the heat's gradually built up and tonight feels like a culmination of that, as if the house has finally reached a rolling boil and the air inside is hot like jazz music bouncing off a dripping ceiling in a packed-full club, or like the picture of a red sun pulsating over shimmering orange ground in the portfolio-sized photo book about deserts that my dad gave me when I was little.

From upstairs I can hear the sound of the musical mobile that hangs above Grace's cot being wound up, then its tinkly noises begin, repetitive and familiar; soul-destroyingly plinky.

Katya appears suddenly in the doorway and looks at me without saying anything.

'He's outside,' I say.

'I know. I just texted him. Your mother is settling Grace.'

'I know.'

Katya stands in the doorway for longer than I'm comfortable with and I lie there silently willing her to go away.

'I tried to be your friend,' she says and I just don't, utterly don't have time for this right now. She has no idea.

'Thanks, Katya,' I say. '*Spasiba*.' I say that because it really annoys her when I try to speak Russian. I get out my phone and scroll around it and try to look like I'm actually expecting to get a message from a real person.

'Zoe, you are your own worst enemy.'

'Original,' I say.

'Excuse me?'

'I saw what you were doing.' I suddenly feel vulnerable in my prostrate position – it's funny how one moment you can feel glamorously hot and worn out like a panting diva in an old film and the next you realise you probably just look stupid – so I sit up and look properly at her over the back of the sofa. 'With Barney. I saw where his hand was.'

She makes an expression that mixes disgust and sadness at my amoeba-level of existence.

'Inappropriate,' she says. 'Totally. Ugh.' She has a habit of using Americanisms, which makes her sound like she's hosting the Eurovision Song Contest.

And I'm about to say how I'm not the one who's inappropriate and what she did was inappropriate, and has my mum even said that she's allowed to go out with Barney tonight anyway, but her phone pings and we're both trained to be silent when a phone pings – this is a Major Characteristic of our Generation my Aunt Tessa says: the veneration of the ping of the phone – and so we're both silent while she reads the text.

'Barney's waiting,' she says, and she turns so fast that the wispy ends of her hair fly out in a fan shape and she's disappeared before I can organise my riposte.

I lie back down. I'm happy she's gone. From upstairs the circus mobile is still crunching out its tune and I know what my mother will be doing. She'll be sitting on the floor beside Grace's cot, being as still as possible, and stroking the baby's forehead. She can do that for ages, and tonight it makes me feel super tense because I feel like the time we have left before Lucas and Chris get home is on one of those kitchen timers that click madly like a bomb that's going to detonate until they make a screechy buzz that Lucas says sounds like a small bird being strangled.

And then I notice a thing. I notice that my phone browsing,

which I basically did for show when Katya was looking at me, has actually turned something up. I have a notification and the sight of it makes my stomach ball up prickly and tight like a hedgehog, because there it sits, just like it used to: a number one, in a red circle, on the corner of the panop app.

It's an app I shouldn't even have on my phone. It's forbidden, because, it was, according to Jason, my key worker at the Unit, and I did have to agree with him, definitely part of my downfall, because Eva Bell and Amelia Barlow and their cronies used it to torment me.

So I should have stayed away from it, but when I came out of the Unit, I couldn't resist downloading it, just to have a look, because I was curious about what happened to the people I used to know. I left one life when I went into the Unit, and when I came out I had another life completely, in another place, and nobody would talk about the old one, and panop was my only way back there. So I downloaded the app, and sometimes I sneak a look to see what people are doing. It's anonymous you see, if you want it to be.

Grace has gone quiet upstairs, but I estimate it'll be another ten minutes at least before my mum appears. With my heart pounding, I click on the app. A question fills the screen:

Did you think you could stay hidden for ever?

44

SUNDAY NIGHT

The End of the Concert

TESSA

At the end of the concert, the crowd has an edge to it, an atmosphere, like a kind of low-level static. Lucas's performance hasn't succeeded in washing away the unease caused by Tom Barlow's scene.

As Lucas takes his bow I check my phone and I have two texts:

Maria: Don't say anything

Richard: Where are you?

I reply to neither of them. I'll do as Maria says, she knows I will, and Richard can wait. I imagine he'll have made it out of his shed and back into our house, and suddenly worked out that he's alone.

When I look up, Chris is by my side.

He's brusque: 'Maria's taken the car and I want to get home, but I think I need to stay for at least a few minutes. People will be expecting me to.'

He's probably right so I say, 'I'll wait. I'll give you a lift whenever you're ready.'

He makes no direct reference to Tom Barlow's outburst.

We don't know each other very well, Chris Kennedy and I, because Maria has always kept him to herself, like a piece of treasure that she'd found, and no wonder really, because she'd been through hell.

When Zoe was convicted Maria's marriage fell apart and she was left on her own to pick up the pieces. Zoe spent eighteen months in jail and in that time Maria had to cope with the transition from farmer's wife with a talented, beautiful child, a musical prodigy no less, to single mother with a teenage child with a criminal record.

She moved from Devon to be near me in Bristol, settling into a rented flat in the only area of the city she could afford, and starting work as a secretary at the university, a job that Richard got her, and that she could barely hold down at first, so powerful was her depression.

It was the piano that changed everything, as it always had done throughout Zoe's life.

Zoe's father would have none of it; he blamed her piano playing for much of what had happened before. He said it had led to her being different, being above herself, and that had in turn led to the bullying, and the accident.

The rest of us took a different view: that piano could help Zoe rediscover herself, repair her self-esteem and provide her with a path for the future. Her talent was so ferociously strong that none of us could bear to let it rest, and, after all, what else did she have left apart from that and her intellect?

On advice from Zoe's therapist at the Unit, we encouraged Zoe to start playing again when she came home, and after a couple of months of practice on a keyboard that

Richard bought for her, and the shlonky pianos at her new school, and with the help of some lessons from a teacher that Richard found and I paid for, Maria entered her tentatively into a low-key, local competition to help her recover her form.

It was a repertoire class that Zoe entered. It was non-competitive, and there were only two entrants. The other was Lucas.

Zoe played brilliantly that day, considering. She rose to the occasion.

I sat with Maria and Chris Kennedy sat just a seat away from us. We were the only people watching, apart from the adjudicator, who would not declare a winner, but would give feedback to the players.

After Zoe's performance, Chris leaned over to us and asked who Zoe's teacher was. Maria answered him, and it wasn't long before I felt like a lemon and took Zoe to find a cup of tea while they chatted intensely in the corridor outside the performance hall, and Lucas skulked around the perimeter.

Chris and Maria exchanged phone numbers that day, ostensibly to share information about Lucas's piano teacher, who Chris declared to be 'the best in the south-west, and the only teacher for a talent like Zoe', and they met up soon afterwards.

It became apparent very quickly that Chris was extremely good for Maria. She began to dress better, and to take care of herself. She smiled. She moved Zoe to the new teacher, who cost Richard and I twice as much, but we were happy to pay. When Maria finally declared that they were in a proper relationship, it felt a little bit as if Chris had saved her.

However, in spite of all that, and even though I've met him on numerous occasions for social events, Chris still feels like a bit of a stranger to me. The only semi-intimate conversation I can claim to ever have had with him was when we met on the train to London once, by accident. It was just after Grace was born because I remember the way he seemed to glow when he spoke about her.

Chris was on his way to be the key speaker at a back-slapping networking lunch for successful entrepreneurs, millionaires who want to be gazillionaires. His description, not mine, and delivered with a healthy dose of irony. I was on my way to a conference about feline hyperthyroidism.

After we met on the platform at Bristol Temple Meads, he kindly bumped me up to first class where he laid his business tools out lavishly across the table that was between us: *Financial Times*, BlackBerry, iPhone, laptop, speech notes.

While he made a business call during which he stared out of the window and said things like, 'Well, as soon as it gets to market it's a matter of how I judge that,' and, 'Yup, yeah sure, indeed. This all plays back to … yes, well, it'll raise hairs, won't it, but it is the fact we've got to get into it,' I sat in front of him feeling intimidated and not daring to eat the flaky sausage roll I'd bought for breakfast, or to get out my *Hello!* magazine.

Still, I didn't need the magazine, because after the call Chris and I chatted all the way, about my work, about his, and about baby Grace, who'd just been born. 'Maria is such a natural mother,' he said. 'I'm a lucky man, after everything.' And I'd felt happy for my sister, because who would have believed that she could have had this turn of fortune after Zoe's trial.

'Do you know what I loved about your sister, when I first met her?' he asked.

I shook my head. When Chris first met Maria she'd been a shadow of the girl who boys trailed around after when we were at school.

'She's a beautiful woman, obviously,' he said, 'but what I noticed most of all were extraordinary qualities of sweetness and poise, as if she just knew who she was. She was like a fine piece of porcelain; I couldn't believe my luck.'

I smiled at the fondness in his words and the emotion, but my first thought at that moment was that Chris didn't know Maria very well; that he'd met a version of her that was coshed by antidepressants and shock and he'd mistaken those qualities for frailty and composure.

Obviously, I kept that thought to myself at the time, but it did make me wonder whether Maria had since concealed what I thought of as her true personality traits. Had Chris ever got a full, no-holds-barred view of her robustness, her intelligence, or her humour, the qualities that were innate to her, that would surely reappear even a little bit once she and Zoe began to recover? Or had she kept those under wraps purposefully, not wanting to spoil the dynamics of this relationship, or the good fortune of this second chance?

I was brave then. I asked Chris about his first wife. Pure nosiness, but who isn't curious about the uncommon circumstances of a man bringing up his son alone? I'd asked Maria about it, of course, but she was either badly informed on the subject or incredibly discreet because she said very little except that Lucas's mum had died from illness when he was ten and that it had shattered him and his father. Chris had

49

apparently not had a significant relationship between Julia's death and meeting Maria.

In the train, emboldened by a surfeit of caffeine on an empty stomach, I said, 'Has it helped Lucas get over his loss, to be part of this new family?'

'Very much so.' Chris's answer was swift and sure.

'How did his mother die?'

'She had a terminal brain tumour, a particularly savage one.' He spoke in quite a clinical tone, but his hand twitched on the table and he began to turn his BlackBerry over and over in his palm.

'Oh. I'm so sorry.' And I was. I felt a blush creeping up my neck and across my cheeks. 'I shouldn't have asked.'

'I don't mind. Lucas was devoted to her of course but it wasn't easy towards the end. She wasn't very stable. I, we, Lucas and I are so very grateful that Maria agreed to marry me. She's a wonderful woman, your sister. I'm a lucky man.'

That day on the train I wondered if Maria had done the right thing keeping Zoe's past from Chris. Surely, I thought, that can't last. I resolved to advise her to tell him, when the moment was right, when he would surely understand. But the conversation never worked like that, because when I brought it up Maria was appalled. I was not, ever, ever to consider interfering in her and Zoe's life like that, she told me. She had found her soul mate and she was going to do everything she could to make it work for her and for Zoe. I was to keep quiet about their past and keep my nose out of their business.

And so I did, but in the concert hall on this stifling night I wonder again if that decision isn't destined to bite us all.

I dismantle the camera and tripod set-up clumsily, and when I join everybody who's enjoying a post-concert drink I notice that the atmosphere still isn't quite the usual one of satisfaction, where the audience appears to bask in the pleasure of exchanging opinions about what they've just heard. Tonight it seems more conspiratorial. People are huddling, and some are discussing Lucas's performance, but most, I can tell, are talking about the outburst.

I strip the cling film from two plates of food that have been laid out on a trestle table at the side of the room. Each has a selection of little snacks on them, which Maria made herself.

Lucas appears beside me, and he looks white. 'Well done,' I tell him. 'You played beautifully.' I say this even though it isn't entirely what I believe, and I touch his arm lightly because he's a nice kid and I always seem to have this urge to reassure him even though he's incredibly composed; maybe because he's incredibly composed.

'Is Zoe all right?' he says.

'I think so. She's with her mum. I'll call them in a minute.'

'Should we go home?'

'I'll drive you and your dad back very soon.'

'Do you …?' He wants to ask me about what happened, I can see that written all over his face, but I say, 'Let's talk about it later, OK?'

He looks at me, and now he's wearing that inscrutable gaze of his again, and after only a fraction of a pause he begins to help me.

Chris peels away from the crowd discreetly after about twenty minutes, and we find Lucas sitting in a pew in the church, doing something on his sleek little tablet, which he hastily slips into his music bag.

In my VW bus, they both seem huge: all knees and hunched shoulders.

We travel mostly in silence.

MONDAY MORNING

SAM

Zoe and I didn't talk for long that first time we met at the police station in Barnstaple. I mostly wanted to introduce myself, to reassure her as much as I could, and explain to her that I was there to help her. I wanted to try to gain her trust before detailed questioning began. And I didn't want to start that until I'd spoken to the officer on the case, to get disclosure.

I met him in the custody reception area. After a brief handshake, we took a seat in a room similar to the one that Zoe was waiting in. He had a broad, whiskery face and Punch and Judy red cheeks. His uniform was tight around the belly.

He handed me the charge sheet and told me that he was going to make an audio recording of the disclosure too. That's sensible, it's a record of what's taken place so there's nothing to argue over later, because that's my job, to find holes in the evidence: procedural or actual, it doesn't matter, either can serve my client.

He told me what they had, all of it. The police don't have to do this, they can be slippery, and disclose in stages, drawing the process out if they're inclined to. I've had disclosures that dribble out over hours, interspersed with exhausting client interviews where we're forced to run a 'no comment' defence because we don't know what they're going to pull out of the bag next.

Zoe's disclosure was forthright, succinct and the content was as depressing as possible.

When you get a good, honest exchange with an officer in this situation, normally it restores your faith in your profession, gees you up for the daily grind of criminality, because that well-behaved, professional exchange between you both feels like an honourable thing; it pushes away the thoughts of the shysters and the ambulance-chasers, the doughnut-munchers and the baton-wielders. You become two men, in a room, upholding the law, and there's a purity to that, a kind of distinction, which is a very rare thing on a day-to-day basis.

In Zoe's case, it only made things slightly more bearable, because the facts of her arrest were so unremittingly grim.

'She'd got herself out of the car when we got there,' he said. 'But she was definitely the driver. We breathalysed her at the scene, seventy-five mg.'

My heart sank because that reading was well over the limit. She must have consumed a great deal of alcohol to be that drunk, even given her small size.

'Three passengers in the car,' he continued, deadpan, though it was tough stuff to read out, even if you're a professional. 'Front passenger dead at the scene, rear left-side passenger dead at the scene, rear right-side passenger transferred to Barnstaple Hospital.'

He caught the question in my gaze but shook his head.

'Died half an hour ago. Massive bleed to the brain. Family agreed to turn her off.'

'Christ.'

'I've seen some scenes, but this was really bad. And there was music pumping from the car, you could hear it on approach, made for a strange scene, spooky.'

I imagined the black night, starlight above, headlights parked at a crazy angle, a steaming engine, crumpled body-work, shattered glass and the stereo still blasting out a loud driving tune to the broken bodies inside, only two out of the four of them producing wisps of misty breath in the cold darkness.

'She consented to a blood test at the hospital,' he continued. 'Confirmed she was well over the limit.'

'Zoe consented?'

'And the doctor.'

I might have had something to work with if Zoe alone had consented to a blood test, because of her age. It was another situation where she had to have an 'appropriate adult' advising her. I was pretty sure the police had this one taped, but made a note that it was something to check.

'Road traffic report?'

'Ordered.'

'How long for that?'

'As quick as we can make it – end of the week probably.'

At this early stage in proceedings, part of my job was to be sure that the police had the evidence they needed to prove all the elements of the offence that the prosecution would present at court. We would need all the test results and paperwork in before I could make a proper judgement on that, but the heaviness in his voice and the apparently rigid adherence to protocol told me that as far as this area of the investigation was concerned, things weren't looking good for Zoe. If I was going to find a defence for her, I suspected it was unlikely it would lie in the procedural detail, or the facts of the accident or the quality of her treatment afterwards, because, so far, the police appeared to have done everything by the book.

'You're going to have to bail her. You can't keep her in, she's too young.'

I wondered if he was going to argue this, because of the severity of what Zoe had done, but he didn't.

'We're probably happy with that, subject to conditions of course.'

'Good. We can discuss conditions. So you're charging her with "Death by careless driving whilst under the influence".'

'Sorry,' he said, but he meant 'Yes.'

We stood. Our chairs didn't move because they were bolted to the floor. A firm handshake and he said, 'It's a bad one this. It's a shame. She's just a kid.'

I nodded. I agreed with him, but I wondered whether the families of the children who died would feel that way.

Before I left the room, I said, 'Does she know? About the fatalities?'

'She knows about the first two, but not about the girl who died at the hospital. Sorry.'

That word again.

SUNDAY NIGHT

After the Concert

ZOE

I shut the panop app and my hands are shaking, because this is what used to happen, when it all began.

In rehabilitation sessions at the Unit, Jason, my key worker, liked to stress this, and liked to make me go over and over it until he'd satisfied himself that I understood:

'What must you avoid, Zoe, when you leave here?'

'Social media.'

'And which social media in particular?'

'All of it.'

'And especially?'

'Well, that question doesn't make sense if we've already agreed that I'm avoiding all of it.'

'Humour me.'

'Panop.'

'Well done.'

'Can I have a gold star?'

'Don't be cheeky.'

Jason was, basically, mostly awesome. He didn't take any crap from anybody.

My IQ has been officially measured as 162. This puts me

in the category of 'exceptionally gifted'. It means that I beat Einstein and Professor Stephen Hawking who scored 160.

But the problem is, a high IQ doesn't necessarily mean that you're clever enough to avoid being a massive teenage cliché. Which is what I was, or what I became. Before my descent into 'teen tragedy', that is.

When Jason looked over my case notes with me, at our first ever session, this is what he said: 'For somebody with a genius level IQ you've made some pretty interesting decisions haven't you?'

At that point, I didn't know that he was going to be as close as I would get in that place to having a knight in shining armour, because I'd only been at the Secure Unit for a week, so I said, 'Screw you,' which was a phrase I'd already learned from the kids on my corridor.

I didn't like the look of Jason with his film premiere facial hair, or the sound of his voice, which was boring and nasal like he had an adenoidal cold, or the stewed tea he put in front of me in a stained mug. I thought 'Screw you' was a good response, but it turned out that Jason had a bit more life experience than me. Go figure.

Panop is an app where you can anonymously ask questions of others. This is what you read on the page where you can register for an account:

> Hey! Welcome to panop!
> We hate to do it, but we need to start with a word of caution . . .
> We know that some people can sometimes get ugly and transform into trolls when they get

online and we're asking you nicely: if you sign
up, don't troll up. Don't do it. Ask anybody a
question, but keep it nice. If you can't be nice,
don't sign up.

And if you sign up and you get asked a nasty
question, don't answer it! In fact don't respond
at all. Panop people (ppeeps!) should know their
own minds, and they should be nice. We're all
about amusement, entertainment and good
times online!

Happy asking . . .

After I signed up to panop, aged thirteen, a brand new
pupil in Year Nine at Hartwood House School, do you want
to know what the first question I received was?

It was this: R u a hore?

I thought it was a mistake. It even took me a few hours to
work out that it was a spelling-challenged attempt to write
the word 'whore'. I was that naive.

I didn't realise that I'd been seen talking to Jack Bell the
Popular Boy, who was supposed to be the exclusive property
of his sister Eva and her posse of Popular Girls at my school.
I didn't realise I wasn't supposed to talk to Jack Bell, because
nobody had explained to me that by virtue of his parents'
money and his boy band hair and low-riding jeans, Jack Bell
was Social Gold Dust, and that, as a recipient of the Year Nine
Hartwood House School music scholarship, I was automatically granted the status of Social Pond Life.

Being a music scholar meant that my parents could not
afford the school tuition, so I was not part of the Entitled. I

wasn't much better than a beggar. Everybody knew that I paid for my schooling with my piano playing, and it subsidised my ugly uniform too. I had to turn out at every concert and open evening, and be in every brochure, hands poised over the keyboards, and smiling serenely as if the very act of being a pupil at Hartwood House School had bestowed me with any talent and opportunity that I might be so lucky as to have.

I know by now that it's possible to overcome the status of Social Pond Life if you work very hard and are prepared to make a multitude of fundamental compromises of the soul, but at the time I wasn't sharp enough even to recognise that possibility.

So I found myself talking one day, during the first few weeks of term, to Jack Bell. And Jack Bell and I got on well, or I thought we did. I didn't realise that other people were watching, and judging, and testing me in fact. I didn't realise that Jack Bell was nothing more than a bright white lure dangling in front of me, blinding me to the dark, wide, gaping jaws of the beast behind, and that those jaws were lined with stiletto-sharp teeth.

There was so much I didn't realise then. 'You couldn't have,' said Jason. 'You were naive, that's all, and probably a bit unfiltered too.'

Jason, bless him, was the master of the understatement, because I was just as dumb as Forrest Gump, dumber perhaps, because I didn't even work out that what I should have done was run.

But, while I'm sitting there with my phone in my hand, remembering all of this, what totally blows my mind is that I get a text from Lucas right then. This is the most activity I've had on my mobile for days, weeks, months even. Check your email, is all it says, and although he's not exactly the master of sensitivity I thought Lucas might at least have asked me how I was, or something. But I do check my email anyway, and there is one from him.

The only thing the email message says is 'Please read this,' and then there's just a PDF attachment called 'What I Know'. The title of it freezes my blood for an instant, but I try to stay calm, because there's no way he could know about me, is there? It's probably just one of those lists of stupid or funny things from the Web, which is the kind of thing he usually sends me and which makes Mum and Chris annoyed because I laugh out loud unexpectedly when I read them and that is apparently 'very rude to the people around you'.

I open the attachment. It's a script, written by Lucas. Lucas is obsessed with film. He's not really allowed to watch any of the films he wants to in our house, but I know he's built a proxy website so when he's at school he can bypass their internet security and watch films on his tablet there. I won't tell, but I know. Lucas is clever in his quiet way.

I start to read.

'WHAT I KNOW'

A SCRIPT FOR FILM

BY LUCAS KENNEDY

Dear Maria and Zoe

**I'm sending you this to
explain a bit about how things
were before my mum died.**

**This is a film script I wrote to
tell the story of what happened to me,
my mum, and my dad, before we met you,
and I hope you will read it.**

Please read it.

Love from Lucas

ACT I

**INT. PRIVATE HOSPITAL ROOM. VERY WELL
APPOINTED. NIGHT.**

A woman, JULIA, in her early thirties,
but looking much older due to her
condition, lies completely still in a
hospital bed. She was clearly beautiful
once, and there are traces of this in
her fine, symmetrical features and long,
dark hair which spreads out over the
pillow, framing her face.

We might see a vase of flowers, and just
one or two get-well cards around the
side of the room, which is immaculately
clean, extremely well appointed and
brightly lit. JULIA is getting the
finest medical care available.

Beside her bed sits her son, LUCAS, 10
years old, who is holding one of her
hands in both of his. He is a lovely,
wide-eyed, dark-haired little boy.
Mostly, his head hangs low, though at
times he looks up and pulls her hand
carefully to rest on his cheek, and
when he does that we might see a tear
fall. As her voice-over (V.O.) begins

he raises his head to look at her, and
adjusts her hair on the pillow so that
it looks nice.

When JULIA speaks her voice is warm. She
sounds like somebody who you would like
to have as a friend.

> DYING JULIA (V.O.)
> This is not how I would have
> liked to meet you. I would have
> liked to have been on my feet,
> with my hair brushed, and at
> least a little bit of make-up
> on. And I would have preferred
> not to be wearing a nightie.
> If you had come to our house,
> I would have invited you in and
> offered you a cup of tea and a
> biscuit, or maybe even a fresh
> muffin if Lucas and I had been
> baking that day. We could have
> chatted in the sunlight at my
> kitchen table, and it would have
> been nice.

The camera is travelling around the bed
so we see JULIA's frailty, her pale skin
and the stillness of her body. She's not
breathing independently.

DYING JULIA (V.O.)

The end isn't far away now, as
you can probably see, and a
big part of me is desperately
grateful to have Lucas here with
me, because I never want to have
to leave him; but I will admit
that there's another part of me
that's relieved that it's nearly
over, because what I can't stand
any longer, is watching Lucas
watching me die. It's been a
brutal, lingering process, in
spite of my efforts to hasten it.
But we're nearly in the closing
stages. I've already had one
massive heart attack you see, and
I'm about to have another, which
will be fatal.

We see a 'Do Not Resuscitate' order
pinned to the end of JULIA's bed.

DYING JULIA (V.O.)

Is that a heartless thing to do?
Lucas wept when they explained
what the DNR order meant, and
he screamed at the doctors. But
it's necessary, so that things
don't drag on, and so that my

boy doesn't suffer more than he
needs to. You see, I had an idea
that in spite of my best efforts
to leave him cleanly, my lovely,
intuitive boy might find an
excuse to come home from school
early on the day I did it, that
he might beg for me to be saved,
whatever state I was in.

**INT. CHRIS AND JULIA'S BEDROOM. DAY. A
FEW HOURS EARLIER.**

JULIA lies on her bed in a sumptuous,
tasteful and beautiful bedroom. She's
already unconscious. Beside her lie
multiple bottles of pills, all empty.
One of her hands is loosely draped over
a bottle of water. An envelope is on
her chest. 'To whom it may concern' is
written on the front of it. We hear
frantic knocking on the bedroom door.

> LUCAS (O.O.S.)
> Mum? Mum! Mummy! Are you in
> there? Mum!

We hear the sound of the door being
kicked in an increasingly frenzied way,

and then a different kind of thudding,
as if somebody is throwing their entire
body weight against it. After that,
silence.

> LUCAS (O.O.S.) (CONT'D)
> Yes, hello, ambulance, please,
> yes, and fire brigade. Please
> come quickly. It's my mum.

**INT. PRIVATE HOSPITAL ROOM. VERY WELL
APPOINTED. NIGHT.**

We find JULIA and LUCAS in exactly the
same positions as before. We also see
a younger CHRIS standing on the other
side of the door, looking through it,
at JULIA and LUCAS. He has the palm of
his hand on the glass. He looks full of
despair.

> DYING JULIA (V.O.)
> That's my husband Chris. He's as
> distraught as our son at this
> moment. He wants to be with me
> too, but he's allowing our child
> time to say goodbye in his own
> way.

The camera has made a full circle
of the room now, and we see JULIA's
monitoring machines, slowly beeping. One
of the readings seems to falter, before
settling back into a steady rhythm
again, and LUCAS stares at it, alarmed.
He gestures to CHRIS, who calls a NURSE.
She bustles in, checks things, then lays
a hand on LUCAS's shoulder to reassure
him. He sits back down and now CHRIS
sits behind him. It's a vigil.

>   DYING JULIA (V.O.)
>   No, don't worry. It's not quite
>   time yet. There are a few more
>   moments, and while I have them,
>   I want to tell you my story. It's
>   the story of Chris, and me, of
>   our life, and the baby we had
>   together, who we named Lucas. And
>   I'm going to start the story when
>   Chris was just fifteen years old.

INT. A YOUNG MAN'S BEDROOM. NIGHT.

A teenage CHRIS is sitting at a desk
surrounded by books and papers, and
he's working in longhand on a pad of A4
paper, writing furiously, only pausing

to check facts in a textbook, or cross-reference some notes. We might see that the room is quite dark apart from a single lamp illuminating his desk. A bare bulb hangs from the ceiling, but it's broken. The room isn't quite squalid, but it's not comfortable either. We might see that a clock on CHRIS's desk shows that it's past midnight.

> DYING JULIA (V.O.)
> Christopher Kennedy was an only child, in a family where he had a mum and a dad, but where crack cocaine was sometimes the third, and always the most unpredictable, parent in the house.

We hear violent shouting coming from outside the room, and the unmistakable sound of somebody being struck. CHRIS winces, but keeps working, he's used to this. Seconds later, a door slams and the sobbing we hear is a hopeless, defeated sound, like the whimpers of a beaten dog. Then we hear CHRIS'S MOTHER call to him.

>   CHRIS'S MOTHER (O.O.S.)
>   Christopher darling, come and
>   help me. Please, come and help
>   me.

CHRIS pauses to listen, we see various
emotions working across his face, and at
first he puts his pen down and appears
to be about to get up, but then his
expression changes to one of resolve. He
reaches for a pair of headphones, which
he puts on before resuming his work.
With him, we hear piano music soaring,
and the sobbing is drowned out. CHRIS's
expression changes to one of calm focus.

>   DYING JULIA (V.O.)
>   Chris knew, from a very young
>   age, that the only person who
>   could help him get anywhere was
>   himself. So he became self-
>   reliant, and he put in hours of
>   work.

**INT. THE WILLS MEMORIAL BUILDING,
BRISTOL UNIVERSITY. DAY.**

CHRIS is attending a graduation
ceremony. We hear his name called and

see him walking up on to the podium to collect his graduation certificate. The large audience applauds.

> DYING JULIA (V.O.)
> Chris's hard work paid off. He graduated with a first class degree in computer science from Bristol University, at age 19, one of the youngest ever to do so. And after that, he kept his head down, and things continued to go well for him.

INT. CHRIS'S OFFICE IN THE COMPUTER SCIENCE DEPARTMENT AT BRISTOL UNIVERSITY. NIGHT.

We might see city lights sparkling outside, through a small, high window. It's a poky space, with a desk and a very plain student-type sofa crammed into it.

> DYING JULIA (V.O.)
> The University of Bristol gave him an office all of his own to develop his ideas in. If he stood in the right place, he could even

see a view. And he didn't rest on
his laurels, because before long
Chris had an idea that made some
other people very excited indeed.

We see Chris staring at his screen. He
writes an email and we can see the text:
'I think I've bloody done it.' He clicks
the 'send' button.

**INT. AN OFFICE IN THE HOME OF AN
INVESTOR. NIGHT.**

An older, and wealthy-looking man sits
at a desk in a room that looks the way
you might imagine a gentleman's club to.
He receives Chris's email. He smiles
when he reads it, and composes an email
in reply. It says, 'WE'RE GOING TO MAKE
A KILLING.' He presses 'send'.

**INT. CHRIS'S NEW OFFICE AT THE
UNIVERSITY. DAY.**

CHRIS's new office is bigger and
lighter, and the view of the city is
extensive and impressive. The only thing
that remains the same is the sofa,

looking a little older and scruffier,
but still there.

CHRIS lies on the sofa, he's wearing a
headset, and is on a call.

> DYING JULIA (V.O.)
> Chris got upgraded to a new
> office by the university, and
> deservedly so. His business idea
> was a good one. In fact, it
> was a great one, and he got a
> particularly tempting offer from
> an investment fund to turn it
> into a business.

CHRIS is speaking on the phone via his
headset, and, as he does, sitting up in
excitement.

> YOUNG CHRIS
> An order for 5,000? That's good.
> That's very, very good, a great
> start, solid ...
> > (listens)
> Sorry? Fifty thousand? Are you
> joking? I thought you said ...
> > (listens)
> Fifty thousand? That's, well
> that's just incredible.

> DYING JULIA (V.O.)
> And the business began to do
> so well, so quickly, that he
> didn't need the support of the
> university any more. He set up
> on his own, and the investment
> fund gave him enough support that
> he could even afford to hire an
> assistant.

INT. A COFFEE SHOP. DAY.

CHRIS is sitting at a small table with a
sheaf of papers in front of him. A young
woman, JULIA, enters and approaches the
table.

> JULIA
> Hello? Are you Chris?

> CHRIS
> Yes! Hello! Julia?

> JULIA
> Yes. It's me. Should I?

> CHRIS
> Yes! Sorry! Please! Take a seat.

CHRIS jumps out of his seat and pulls
out a chair for JULIA. It looks like
a bit of a hasty gesture from a man
who perhaps isn't used to displaying
polished manners, and is clumsy enough
that people at other tables notice, one
or two maybe smiling discreetly at his
display of keenness. CHRIS and JULIA sit
facing each other and he stares at her,
forgetting to speak.

                    JULIA
        So ...

                    CHRIS
        Yes!

                    JULIA
        Here's my CV.

                    CHRIS
        Right! Yes! Thank you.

CHRIS skims down the CV quickly, it's
only one sheet.

                CHRIS (CONT'D)
        Looks great. Perfect. Do you have
        any questions?

JULIA

Oh! Me? OK, well, I was wondering
if I was experienced enough for
the position?
(realising)
Oh, gosh, sorry, that's such
a stupid thing to say. I'm so
sorry.

CHRIS is jolted out of his infatuated
stare, and bursts out laughing.

CHRIS

That is the worst interview
technique I've ever heard!

JULIA

I should go. I'm sorry. This is
the first job I've ever applied
for. I don't know what I'm
doing.

CHRIS

No! No — sorry I didn't mean to
upset you. Stay, please. Let's
talk about the job. And I should
probably ask you some questions.
Before we start, would you like
something to drink?

> DYING JULIA (V.O.)
> I had a hot chocolate. With cream
> on top. And so did he.

**EXT. A PRETTY STREET. A FINE, COLD
EVENING.**

The camera moves along the time-worn
slabs of a fine, old pavement towards
the well-lit window of a restaurant.
It's a small place, and at a table
tucked into the window we see CHRIS and
JULIA, one each side of an intimate
table, both noticeably better dressed
and less awkward than they were at their
first meeting. Candlelight glints off
the wine glasses they're sipping from,
and they both lean back as the waiter
arrives with plates of food, though they
don't take their eyes off each other.
They look warm, cosy and very happy.

> DYING JULIA (V.O.)
> And it wasn't too long before
> Chris was having to interview for
> a new office assistant, because I
> was promoted to the position of
> fiancée. He swept me off my feet.
> He expressed feelings for me that

were so intense they were like
nothing I'd experienced before.
It was intoxicating. And with
all the optimism of young love,
we felt that we owned our lives,
and our city, and that anything
was possible, and that a future
without one another would be
impossible.

Inside the restaurant, once the waiter
has moved away, CHRIS takes a small box
from his pocket and hands it to JULIA.
She opens it and it is, of course, a
ring, a beautiful diamond ring. We see
her delight, and how much this moves
her as well. We see her mouth the word
'yes', and then the camera moves away
from the restaurant window to show the
street once again, and this time we
might notice pretty Christmas lights,
before the camera moves out further
still, up and over Clifton Village to
show us the Suspension Bridge, lit up
spectacularly, and looking ethereal as
it hangs over the deep gorge. It's a
romantic, gorgeous scene and we might
even see a full moon hanging over it
too, looking crisp and hopeful in the
winter night.

DYING JULIA (V.O.)
It was one of the happiest nights
of my life.

**INT. GOLDNEY HALL ORANGERY IN CLIFTON,
BRISTOL. DAY.**

CHRIS and JULIA are standing in the
middle of a fine, Georgian room lined
with floor-to-ceiling sash windows
overlooking a beautiful garden.
Chandeliers hang above them and under
their feet the floor is made from slabs
of soft, golden stone.

DYING JULIA (V.O.)
Chris and I arranged the wedding
together, every detail. He wanted
the very best.

JULIA takes CHRIS's hand.

JULIA
Do you think it's too big?

CHRIS
I think it's perfect.

And we can see from the excitement on
JULIA's face that she does too, but she
wanted him to say it first.

INT. GOLDNEY HALL ORANGERY. DAY.

The orangery is lavishly decorated for a
wedding ceremony, and a modest number of
people are gathered at one end, seated
around CHRIS and JULIA, the bride and
groom, who stand before them and hold
hands as they face each other and say
their vows.

> DYING JULIA (V.O.)
> Of course the room was too big
> for our little ceremony, but
> Chris invited a lot of colleagues
> to make up for the very small
> number of family both of us
> had. His parents weren't there.
> He said that his family meant
> nothing to him, that he didn't
> want to talk about them.

We see the crowd consists of a large
posse of well-dressed professional folk
watching the ceremony.

81

                    DYING JULIA (V.O.)
My mother came. Alone, because
since my father abandoned us
when I was a baby, she said she
preferred it.

We see a rather lovely woman, JULIA'S
MOTHER, sitting at the front where she
has a good view of her daughter. She is
dressed extremely plainly, wears only a
little make-up but has beautiful flowers
in the lapel of her jacket and wears a
carefully positioned hat.

                    DYING JULIA (V.O.)
She was grateful to Chris for
paying for the wedding, because
her budget wouldn't have run
much past two dozen sausage rolls
and a cash bar at the social
club, and it made her proud to
see me entering a marriage that
had so much more hope than her
own, because, if truth be told,
I had figured prominently at her
wedding, in the shape of a large
bump, and was a source of shame
to both parties. But we'll gloss
over that. And I was glad she
came, because I loved her very

much, and sadly she died shortly
afterwards, but it meant the
world to her to know that I was
happily married before she went.

We see a smile creep across JULIA'S
MOTHER's face and then the camera swings
around to show us what she sees: it's
the bride and groom leaning in to kiss
one another as the crowd claps.

When they break away from each other
CHRIS stands with his arm around JULIA,
squeezing her tight and smiling broadly.

                    CHRIS
        My wife! I've got a wife!

And everybody laughs while JULIA looks a
little embarrassed, but very happy.

SUNDAY NIGHT

After the Concert

ZOE

I stop reading because I hear my mum coming down the stairs, finally. The script is quite interesting but it's mostly just a love story between Chris and Julia so far and it's told in the voice of Lucas's dying mum, which I find really weird, so I'm not one hundred per cent fully interested if I'm honest, also because I don't see what it's got to do with me.

Really, I'm not exactly sure why Lucas was so keen for me and Mum to read it.

I put my phone down, in fact I push it down the side of the sofa cushions because the panop thing is still making my palms sweat a bit so I don't even really want to look at it, and I go and wait in the hall for my mum as she comes down the stairs, her hand trailing on the polished banister. When she gets to the bottom, she first puts her finger on her lips to keep me quiet so we don't wake the baby, and then beckons me to follow her into the kitchen.

I follow her in there, and she gets a wine glass out of the cupboard and pours herself a hefty slug from a bottle that starts to drip with condensation now that it's out of the fridge. I wait, listening to the glass chinking on the granite, and I straighten my dress, because since we've been in the Second Chance Family she likes me to look nice, and I think I'm probably a bit mussed up from lying on the sofa.

She drinks deeply, twice, then she says, 'Zoe,' and I say, 'Yes,' and I'm full of fear because this is the moment that she and I have to come together, so that we can decide what we have to do. From the railway-station-sized clock on the kitchen wall I estimate we have about seventeen minutes left to do it in before Tessa and the men get here.

'I think …' Mum says, and with her fingers and her palms she makes a motion that smooths her cheeks up; it's a temporary facelift. And in spite of everything, a tiny part of me glows, because I feel a little bit happy that we're going to do this together, that we're going to do anything together in fact, because that hasn't really happened for a very long time.

And my heart's pumping like the loud techno music beats that make cars shudder, because now's the moment, but then she says, and her tone is as bright as Grace's mobile: 'Do you know what I think would be nice? I think we should make some bruschetta for the boys.'

MONDAY MORNING

SAM

At Barnstaple Police Station, when I returned to talk to Zoe after the disclosure, I found her in exactly the same position as before, curled up in her plastic chair, social worker sitting silently beside her.

Zoe watched me come in and sit down, hungover eyes following me like a cat's under that glass-spangled hair.

'Hello again,' I said.

'Hello.'

'Now. Have you let anybody know that you've been arrested?'

'They phoned Mum.'

'Would you like your mum to be in here with us?'

'No.'

The social worker's lips pursed, but she remained quiet.

'Can you tell me why?'

'I didn't want her to know.'

'She's outside, Zoe, she knows you're here, and she knows why. You're not going to be able to keep this a secret from her.'

An immediate firm shake of her head, so I didn't push it. A fragment of glass fell out of her hair and on to the table in front of her and she put a finger on it, curious, almost hypnotised by the sight of it. It looked like a small diamond.

'Don't,' I said, but I was too late. The glass cut her finger and she pulled it sharply away and put it into her mouth. The little shard skittered away across the table and onto the floor.

'I'll get the first-aider,' said the social worker.

'It's OK,' Zoe said. 'It's nothing.' She held her finger up to show us just a tiny bead of blood welling there, then she sucked it away.

The social worker rummaged in her bag and handed Zoe a tissue. We both watched her wrap it tightly around her finger until the tip went white.

'Well, if you change your mind at any point then we can call Mum in. What about your dad?'

Another head shake, even firmer this time.

'Do you feel well enough to talk to me now?' Close up, she looked worse than I'd thought. They told me that she'd puked at the hospital.

'Yes.'

'Your welfare is important to everybody here so you must let me or ...'

'Ruth,' said the social worker.

'You must let me or Ruth know straight away if you're too unwell to talk, or for any other reason. Ruth is here to support you, and I am, as I've told you, a solicitor, and that means that I want to make sure you get the right advice to help you in your situation and also to help you understand anything that happens this morning or that happened last night. And, most importantly, and this is why you need to tell us if you're not coping at any point, I need to make sure that you completely understand what effects any statements or responses you give to the police might mean.'

'I'm OK.'

I wondered where this stoicism came from. I didn't yet know about the piano, about her capacity for discipline and self-control, and her hunger for excellence, but the intelligence was beginning to emerge. There was sharp clarity in those eyes.

'Do you live locally, Zoe?'

'Between Hartland and Clovelly, at East Wildberry Farm.'

'Near the Point?'

'Yes. That's where we were going.'

'In the car? To the Point?'

'To the lighthouse.'

'Why?'

'Because Jack said I could use his dad's car to drive Gull home, but only on condition we went to the lighthouse on the way.'

I thought of Hartland Point lighthouse, because I knew it well. To get to it you had to sneak past some locked gates and descend a rubbly, steep cliff path down to the shore, where black rocks lined the edges of the tide line like shark's teeth and the lighthouse sat on an outcrop which was fortified by a sea wall, to save it from being beaten away by waves. It was no longer occupied and the light was about to be decommissioned entirely. There were empty buildings beside it, where the lighthouse keepers used to live.

Four drunk teenagers planning to go down there on a dark, cold night sounded like a bad business to me.

'Why did Jack want to go to the lighthouse?'

She calculated something behind those eyes before she replied. 'I don't know.'

I changed tack. 'How do you know how to drive?'

'My dad taught me, on the farm.'

'Why were you driving when Jack was old enough to have a licence?'

'Jack was pissed. He was too pissed to drive.'

'But you were drunk as well.'

'I wasn't. I only had a spritzer.'

'According to the police your blood alcohol level was twice the limit.'

'I wasn't drunk.'

I left the denial for now. I'd tease that out later. If she somehow didn't know she was drunk, we might have a defence to build there.

'Why did Gull want to leave the party?'

'Because she got sick, and she wanted to go home.'

'Sick from drinking?'

'I think so.'

'Were you with her?'

'She came to find me when she got sick.'

'Are you friends?'

'She's my best friend.'

'And where were you when she came to find you?'

'With Jack.'

'Where were you and Jack?'

'In the bedroom.'

I wrote this down while the social worker shuffled in her seat, and I wondered if it was defiance that I heard in her tone. I was going to need to know every detail later, but for now I decided that I wouldn't push her, because when I looked at her I could see that she was fading, and I thought she might throw up.

'I think we should take a break, because I don't believe you're well enough for interview this morning. But before we stop is there anything else you want me to know, Zoe? We're going to talk lots more, but is there anything you want me to know now?'

'It's Gull's birthday today,' she said, and she began to cry.

SUNDAY NIGHT

After the Concert

ZOE

'Bruschetta?' I ask Mum. This is a perfect example of why she's insane to deal with sometimes. We all ate before we came out, so nobody will be hungry when they get back from the concert. I'm one hundred per cent sure that Key Worker Jason would say that making bruschetta at this moment is a classic example of displacement activity.

'Yes, I think we will,' she says. She's not actually listening to me at all; she's just answering herself. She crosses the kitchen, her shoes tapping on the stone floor. She's still wearing her heels from the concert. She heaves open the door of our fridge. 'Now let's see …' she says. 'Have we got what we need?'

My mum has a very big fridge. It's big enough that you could stuff a body inside it. Lucas says that. He once said, 'Do you think if we put Grace in the fridge she would stop crying? Or at least we wouldn't be able to hear her.'

I laughed really hard at that, partly because Lucas doesn't often make a joke when we're all together, so I thought it would be good to laugh, to encourage him, and partly because I pictured Grace in the fridge in a Tupperware box, just like my mum stores all the leftover food. And I don't mean that in a morbid way – everybody always thinks I mean things morbidly – it was just funny.

'Black humour,' said Jason the Key Worker to me once, taking off his glasses and massaging his frown lines so deeply it was like he was looking for something lost in there, 'can be a tool to deal with your emotions and you'll hear it a lot while you're in the Unit, but you have to be very, very careful, Zoe, about how you use it when you're back in the outside world.'

Mum went white as a Mini Milk lollipop when Lucas said that, and even whiter when I laughed ultra loudly. At the time, Grace was so tiny that she just spent most of her time draped over Mum's shoulder with slimy bubbles popping out of her mouth.

Chris went ballistic, which isn't really a good description of him being cross. When my dad used to go ballistic he would shout, and his hands would fly everywhere, and once he threw a baked potato on the floor and it exploded everywhere, and him and Mum and me killed ourselves laughing.

Chris isn't like that, he's far too polite. His version of ballistic is that he just went a bit rigid and said to Lucas, 'Could we have a little chat?' and they left the room and I heard the sound of them talking on and on in Chris's study down the hallway. In the kitchen my mum put on Radio 3 and said, 'You didn't need to laugh like that,' and I felt ashamed. When Lucas and Chris came back in, Lucas said, 'Sorry, Maria, what I said was inappropriate,' and Mum said, 'I understand it was only a joke, Lucas, but I appreciate the apology. It's fine,' and Chris pointed out that if he wasn't mistaken that was Barenboim playing Beethoven on the radio so we all listened to that.

Mum has pulled a packet of small, plump tomatoes out of

the fridge. They're the size of big marbles. 'Please can we talk about Mr Barlow?' I say to her. She begins unwrapping the packet and pulling out the tomatoes; they're blooming with redness and still attached to their stalk.

'Yes! OK, yes!' she says, but then, 'I think these are small and sweet enough that we won't have to skin them. Pass me some garlic will you, please? We're going to need, let's see, probably two large cloves or three small ones.'

In the pantry, I find the garlic, a chunky plait of fat papery bulbs, hanging from a shiny metal hook. It's cooler than the kitchen in the pantry and I feel like staying there, resting my head on the marble surface where there's a chocolate fudge cake in a tin. Quietly, I open the tin and stick my finger into the icing in the middle of the cake, where I won't leave a trace. I scoop deeply and it's productive. I suck the chocolate off my finger and then smooth the icing over so nobody will notice. Easy.

I try to think of ways to talk to Mum about Amelia Barlow's dad.

When I come out of the larder I push the garlic cloves (two big ones) across the granite island towards her. It's a large island, and the granite is a dense, polished black. Chris and Mum spent three weeks choosing it. Chris brought loads of samples home and he said it was her choice, but I know she would have preferred something lighter, like the one where the pattern looks like grains of sand, in beiges and whites, with just a sprinkle of black in there. She went for the ebony granite to please him, for sure, because they always try to outdo each other to see who can please the other one the most. Lucas says they're probably eternally trapped in a cycle of mutual congratulation now, that they'll be doing it until death does them part. He says it's because they're both afraid of being alone.

When I went to Gull's grave it was black granite too, but it had silver shreds speckling it. I think Gull would have liked that; she loved a bit of bling, and definitely not in an ironic way. The churchyard had a view of the sea. Gull's grave was black sparkling granite against the so-green fields and the freezing grey ocean, which, on the afternoon we went to visit, was churning out huge, violent waves like a warning, and the wind was so strong we had to turn our backs to it.

The headstone would have cost a fortune, my mum said. More than Gull's family had, because she was a scholarship girl at Hartwood House School like me. The only difference was that she won her scholarship because she was good at sport. We bonded over it. It meant we could be Social Pond Life together.

I wanted to spend more time at Gull's grave, but it was important that we mustn't be seen, because people would have been angry. I had to wear a beanie hat to cover up my ice-maiden hair. I had to wrap a scarf high up around my neck.

Mum is holding a large knife and she's sawing at a baguette with it now using precise, quick diagonal cuts. I'm looking for an opening in her activity so I can say something but I don't think I'm going to get one so I just say, 'Mum.'

'This is yesterday's,' she says, 'so it's a bit stale, but that's fine.'

'Mum.'

'It's probably better actually. For bruschetta.' She says it the Italian way: *brusketta*. Chris would like that. He took her to Italy for two weeks before Grace was born and when they came back Mum pronounced everything the correct Italian way. She had lots of time to read the phrase book, she said, and improve her Italian, which was the silver lining of twisting her ankle on her fourth day there. My mum puts a lot of store in silver linings. Go figure.

I estimate that there will be three more noisy crumb-scratchy slices to cut until she's finished. Then she'll have to acknowledge me. The sawing sound is relentless but finally the knife goes down on to the granite with a clatter and the serrated edge catches the light as it falls. There are crumbs everywhere and a neat, stacked pile of bread, cut on the diagonal like in the magazines.

'Mummy,' I say again. I know I'm too old to call her Mummy, I know that, but she's not listening to me. 'Mummy. What will we tell them?'

She swallows, and does multiple blinks, which is a sign of tension for her, and begins to brush the crumbs off the granite, cupping one hand at the edge and sweeping the crumbs into it with the other. Her movements are fast, but not as efficient as usual. She's being hasty, and crumbs are falling on the floor. I notice she's drunk two-thirds of her glass of wine already; she must have had a good slug when I was in the pantry. The glass is sweating so much it looks thirsty itself.

'We're going to tell them it was a mistake,' she says brightly. 'That we don't know the man and that he made a mistake!' I can see small patches of damp under each armpit and a single lock of hair that's fallen on to her forehead, and looks greasy, from the heat. She'd hate that, if she could see it.

'But you said his name.'

'Don't argue with me, Zoe. Just! Don't! I need to *think*!'

Her voice is shockingly shrill and it makes my spine snap straight.

She blows at the greasy bit of hair, she can feel it, and it rises, and then falls back on to her forehead, right where it was before.

'God, it's hot!' she says, and she gets a fresh tea towel out of the drawer where they all sit perfectly clean and pressed and folded, and she dabs her forehead with it. Her hands are definitely shaking, and I'm suddenly suffused with the loneliness that's been my real punishment since the accident. I'm riddled with it. It eats me up like a cancer; it spreads into my brain and makes me feel as though I'm going mad. I'm lonely because I'm never allowed to talk about it in the Second Chance Family, even though it happened, and it's a part of me, and I can't change that. I'm so freaking lonely, it's even worse than it was before it happened. But on the subject of loneliness it's best to be absolutely silent.

So I sit on a stool on the other side of the kitchen island from my mum, and watch while she starts on the tomatoes, chopping them into tiny, tiny little pieces, minuscule pieces that she heaps up into a moist fleshy mountain on the edge of the cutting board, and then she grabs handfuls of basil from the plants she has in pots in the middle of the island, and she starts to rip them up, and the little shredded pieces tumble into a white bowl.

'You see, you always *rip* basil, Zoe. You never cut it, because that crushes its edges. Tear it to let the flavour out gently,' she says. But the tearing she's doing is not gentle, it's rough, and I can see that the torn little leaves are bruised.

She never did this kind of cookery instruction before we

lived with Chris, but she never seems to stop doing it now. I think it's because he loves it when she does it. He says it's 'part of a proper upbringing' and he can't wait for Mum to teach Grace the 'alchemy of cooking' and he says that Lucas should listen when Mum is sharing her knowledge.

But I don't want my mum to talk to me like this when it's just me and her and so I can't help it, as she gets started on the garlic, unwrapping the nubbly cloves, starting to chop them in half, I get tearful again. I have to breathe deeply because I know she won't want me to cry because that's against the rule of Preferably No Crying (sub genre: especially when Chris might be on his way home), but I'm overwhelmed with it and I have to start breathing through my nose to try to stop it, but that doesn't work so I'm silently convulsing when I hear the knife stop after just a couple of firm chops. The smell of the garlic is pungent.

'Sweetheart,' she says and for the first time since we crouched together in the room at the back of the church I think I might be able to hear a bit of warmth in her voice again, and I look at her, and her face is worn out, the way mine feels, but then we hear two little beeps from a car horn, which is what Aunt Tessa always does when she arrives at our house, and I see in Mum's eyes that she's as aware as I am that time has just run out, because they're back.

'Leave it with me,' she says. 'Just don't admit to anything. *Nothing at all.* Promise me?'

Her chin goes up and I can tell she wants to go and meet them at the door, but she's waiting for me to agree.

I nod and then I say, 'Wait!' and she turns back to me. I come towards her, where she's hovering at the entrance to the hall, and I tend to the front of her hair so that the little greasy strand is hidden, and she looks smooth and lovely, just like Chris will want her to.

'Thank you,' she says, and she adjusts the strap of my dress on my shoulder, tucks my hair behind my ears and I reckon we might, maybe, just still have a second or two to talk, but then she says, 'Go and wash your face. Quick as you can. And when you come down, you can oil and toast the bread slices.'

SUNDAY NIGHT

After the Concert

TESSA

I park on the street outside Chris and Maria's house. There are so many beautifully manicured shrubs in their driveway that I always avoid parking on it because I'm afraid my VW bus will cause them fatal damage if I have to perform any sort of reversing manoeuvre when it's time to leave. There are also two stone pillars to avoid, which grandly frame the entrance to the drive, chipped and old in golden stone, and I don't want to be the one to topple them.

The gravel crunches as we walk across it, three abreast, and Maria opens the door as we get there. She shares Zoe's ice-maiden looks only her hair's much shorter than Zoe's, cropped into a bob. Considering everything, she looks reasonably composed.

She focuses her attention on Chris, stepping towards him in a light movement.

'Hello, darling,' she says and she places the palm of her hand on one of his cheeks and plants a kiss on the other, which he offers with a practised motion, though it looks, tonight, as if it might need a little oiling. Maria and Chris are always dancing around each other like this, their actions reminding me of choreographed mime. They're somehow able to fit an appropriately socially smooth movement to almost any situation. If I tried to kiss Richard like that one of us would somehow be in the wrong place and there would be an awkwardness of some description. Sam might be a different matter, though I can't know that because our relationship has never been for public consumption; we've never had to present a face to the world because anything to do with us is an entirely secret, private thing.

I wouldn't have got out of my car at all, except that I thought Maria might need some solidarity tonight. Normally, I would have just dropped the boys off and legged it.

Chris says nothing, once he's taken receipt of his kiss, but he looks at her carefully.

'How was the concert?' she asks, as if nothing untoward had happened at all.

Chris looks at Lucas who clearly has to scrabble around mentally for an answer, because his mind is elsewhere.

'Fine,' is all he comes up with.

'Bit of work needed on the Scarlatti, I think, but otherwise not too bad,' says Chris, and Maria says, 'Well, I'm sure you did brilliantly,' and when she turns to go into the house Chris steps forward quickly and follows her with his hand on her lower back, as if guiding her in.

Lucas gives me a 'ladies first' gesture, but I hate that kind of formality. Instead, I link my arm in his and I say, 'Help an old lady in would you?' and he doesn't smile but nor does he protest, and I hope he doesn't notice the deep breath I'm taking as we cross the threshold and the heavily glossed door clicks shut behind us.

101

Ahead of us, Chris is saying to Maria, 'Darling, could we have a quick word?' but she's ready for that.

'Can it wait?' she says. 'I'm afraid I've got to see to the bruschetta.'

SUNDAY NIGHT

After the Concert

ZOE

I wash my face, and I'm careful not to get my hair wet. I reapply a little bit of make-up, then I brush my hair until it's silky. I want to shower and change my clothes, to rid myself of the concert, and of Tom Barlow, of Katya and Barney and the message on my phone. I want to curl up in my bedroom, which is my refuge, my nest, my safe place, but I know I can't.

In the mirror I look like I always do: white hair halo, blue eyes, skin like wax. 'Like a princess,' Jack Bell said, as he held my chin, and gently tilted my head up towards his. People always say I look like a princess. Lucas refuted that when I told him. He says it's a white middle-class fantasy (sub genres: Northern European and North American) that princesses are small, blonde, pale creatures with barely formed features.

Jack Bell called me a princess at a party he had at his house, on the night of the accident. Then he pulled my hand to him, and put it on his stomach.

'Zoe Guerin,' he said. 'Why's your name French?'

'My dad's family was French about a hundred years ago,' I said.

'I bet you know the exact date, don't you?' He was mocking

me because I always had my hand up to answer questions at school, but I didn't mind.

I could feel under my palm that Jack Bell's stomach was muscly. Even though it was so cold outside that the fields were beginning to glow white with a night frost, he was just wearing a T-shirt. I'd been watching him shed layers of clothing as he danced, waiting for the looks to come my way. And they did: a look, and then a smile, and now we're close enough that my hand is on his stomach, my fingers splaying a bit wider.

I liked Jack Bell, even though he could be mean sometimes, like when he ignored me at school if he was in a group with his friends. In spite of that, I really liked him. If I'm honest I thought about him all the time.

Jack Bell played the male hero in every fantasy I had. In my mind, we were husband and wife, friends for life, we were a perfect cadence at the end of a piece of music: harmonious, satisfying, whole, meant to be.

I think that's why it shocked me in a way the actual touching of him, because Jack Bell was so much in my mind then that the real feel of him was strange. His breath smelled of alcohol and his skin was sweaty, and I wasn't sure I liked it but still my fingers widened on his abdomen.

'Come with me,' he whispered into my ear.

I looked for Gull. She was across the other side of the room, talking to one of Jack's friends, laughing at something he'd said.

Jack took me into a room just down the corridor. It was a bedroom. He shut the door, and put his hands on my waist and then ran them up the sides of me, crinkling the folds of my dress. It felt like hot water was pouring through me. The intensity of it made me push him away a little.

Jack Bell smiled and took me to the bed. 'Sit with me,' he said and so I did, and we were side by side on the extra-bouncy mattress. I tried it out, laughing as I bounced higher. 'Come here,' said Jack and we kissed for a minute all awkwardly because we were sitting next to each other. It was my first ever kiss. His hand touched one of my breasts and I jumped. Jack said, 'Where's your drink? Let me get you another drink.'

I'd had one spritzer already, and I knew I couldn't have any more alcohol. That was essential because I wasn't even used to it, and I shouldn't have even been at the party because I had a piano competition the next afternoon so I said, 'Just a Coke, please.'

'Are you sure you wouldn't like something stronger?'

'Coke is good.'

'Sure?' That smile tempted me to say yes, but I didn't.

'Just a Coke.'

'You always know what you want, don't you, Zoe? Did you want me to notice your figure in that dress?'

A little thrill of guilt passed over me when he said that, because I did want him to notice me, but I also thought he was wrong in a way, because I was never *sure* what I wanted, never ever. I'm still not.

'Will you check on Gull?' I asked. 'She might be wondering where I am.'

'Yep,' and he stared at me for just a moment before he left the room and the door shut softly behind him. I fell backwards on to the bed, and stared up at the ceiling and wondered why, if this was one of life's moments, it felt bad and good all at the same time.

And just the memory of that moment still gives me a powerful sensation of falling, even now.

I'm pulled away from it though, all of a sudden, because I'm distracted by movement. Something is flying around the bathroom.

At first I think it's a moth, and I turn off the bathroom light quickly, because I don't want it to bombard the light and flap around me, but as my eyes adjust to the darkness I'm surprised to see that it's a butterfly, because they don't usually fly at night. It seems to like the darkness because it settles on the edge of the mirror and closes its wings.

The reflection of the butterfly in the mirror transfixes me. Its ragged-edged wings look as if they're made of striated layers of dark iridescent powder, which reflect and absorb the light from the chandelier in the hall in uncountable numbers of tiny, unreliable glimmers. It's like a living shadow.

I stand very still and it rewards me by opening its wings wide, just for a second, revealing brilliant colour – a flash of deep red and patches of blue, black and yellow – and I know at once it's a peacock butterfly. When I was little my dad and me would watch out for butterflies in our fields, and we would name them all. We had a book, so if we didn't know what one was we would try to remember it and look it up when we got home. I was obsessed with them, I thought they were the most beautiful creatures in the world, and it's why my nickname is 'Butterfly' though Mum doesn't call me that any longer.

After the butterfly closes its wings again, I stand and watch it for a few moments more, hoping it'll give me another glimpse of colour, but it doesn't. Sounds drift up through the open window, from the garden, and remind me that I need to leave the butterfly, and the mirror, and the room, because I need to rejoin my Second Chance Family.

A final check in the mirror shows me that my eyes now look dark as pools of oil, and again the shoulder strap of my dress has slipped. I pull it up and I make my way back downstairs.

The chalk-cool tiles in the hallway feel lovely again, but I need to put on shoes because bruschetta usually goes with other Italian dishes and sitting down at the table, and Chris prefers that we're not barefoot at dinner.

What would he have thought of my dad, I wonder, but I never dare to ask Mum. What would Chris have thought of my real dad, who couldn't have cared less about formality; who sat on rugs with his back against the sofa and watched TV with me, fish and chips on our laps; who made us toasted sandwiches so we could eat them over the Monopoly board, who never cared what you wore on your feet when you ate. 'Her father never had any boundaries,' my mum said in a family reintegration meeting at the Secure Unit, 'and look where that got us.' Her mouth was drawn tight but uncertain like zigzag patterns on a line graph, and I wanted to say, 'But you never minded that,' but I didn't dare.

When I get down the stairs, I find that everybody's in the kitchen. My heart has begun to pound again, and I don't have the courage to go any further than the doorway of the room. Everybody has their back to me apart from Mum.

'Zoe!' she says and she reminds me of the open-winged butterfly, twinkling bright, sharp and pretty. 'Could you toast the bread?'

She's holding a crystal glass tumbler, which is Chris's Tom Collins tumbler, and there's ice in it, which chinks against the sides, and an inch of clear liquid, which I know is gin. My mum adds club soda and it fizzes. A Tom Collins is what Chris always drinks before supper at the weekend.

'Hi, sweetie,' says Tess, as she turns round, and she gives me one of her huge hugs and while she's doing that she whispers into my ear, 'It'll be OK.'

Over Tess's shoulder I can see Lucas is at the table. He mouths some words at me and I think he's saying: *Did you read the email?* I kind of shake my head, because obviously I didn't finish it, and I don't know why he's so obsessed with it all of a sudden.

I look at Chris last, but he's busy opening the bi-fold doors so that one wall of our kitchen is thrown open to the garden, and he's putting on the garden lights.

They throw up great yellow beams from the base of the trees that are out there. There's a young silver birch that he and my mum planted – a crane had to lift it into the garden – but my favourite is a big old cedar tree whose trunk is huge and grey and forms chunks of dry bark like scabs which you can pick off.

My mother pours olive oil into a small, white round dish. The green-gold ooze reminds me of petrol. She hands me a brush.

'Just on one side,' she says. 'Not too much, not too little.'

I'm concentrating so much on the movement of the brush, the initial resistance of the bread, then the soaking in of the oil, that it makes me jump when Chris puts a hand on my shoulder.

'Zoe,' he says, and his voice sounds extravagantly rich and wrap-around as if we were shut together in a confessional, he behind the screen in robes, me about to unplug the so-long-repressed words to purge my disgrace. I sense his body behind mine, and I feel myself straighten up. I don't think Chris has ever touched me before. He's careful, careful around me like he's read a how-to manual on being a non-creepy stepfather. 'Now tell me,' he says, 'are you all right?' His hand falls away practically before it's landed.

Across the island, over the sea of stripped basil, I meet my mother's eye, but she looks away. Her earring swings from her lobe – finest pieces of gold interlinked. From behind her, Lucas is staring at us. In front of him, in a row, are little tea-light holders that I suppose he's meant to be filling, and a bag of candles. Aunt Tessa isn't meeting my eye; she's busy adding oil and balsamic vinegar to a bowl where the chopped tomatoes and pummelled basil wait damply.

'I'm sorry,' I say. 'I don't know what came over me.'

'Did you know that man in the church?' Chris asks me.

'No,' I say to the baguette slices.

'I beg your pardon?'

'No,' I say it more loudly. I shake my head.

'Did you know him, Maria?' Chris asks my mother.

She turns on her heel and gives Chris full, bright eye contact, just like she did with Jason the Key Worker when she had to explain to him why my dad wasn't coming to family reintegration meetings any more. My mum is a brilliant actress. She could give Meryl Streep a run for her money.

'I thought I knew him, darling, but I don't think I did,' she says. 'I must have made a mistake. Would you like one of these?

They're from the deli.' She puts a small plate of shiny green olives on the island.

'I'm not hungry,' says Chris. 'I have no idea why you're cooking at this time of night.'

'I'm hungry,' says Tessa, who's using Mum's femur-sized pepper grinder to season the bowl of tomatoes. 'Starving actually.'

'But you called that man by his name,' Chris says to Mum and I feel as if his words somehow have substance in the heat, that they're glutinous like the dregs of the oil in my bowl. I keep my head down and I finish brushing the oil, in slow strokes, and then I start to place the bread on the oven tray.

'I thought he was somebody I knew.' My mother has turned away; she's getting another wine glass down, pouring some for Tess. 'But, on reflection, I think I was wrong.'

She glances at me. 'Olive oil side down,' she says, and I start to turn the bread slices over, one by one, so they look untouched again, as though there's not a drop of oil on them.

SUNDAY NIGHT

After the Concert

TESSA

The glass of wine that Maria pours me is tiny, because she knows I'm driving. I'm grateful she's remembered, in spite of what's going on, because it's not the sort of thing you can easily bring up in front of Zoe. I take the glass from her and reach for one of the olives.

'It would be lovely to eat.'

I am hungry actually, but I'd be saying it even if it wasn't true. I don't know what Maria's playing at exactly, but she's definitely buying time.

Chris, for the first time in my experience, looks lost. Their kitchen is vast, cavernous compared to the small space that Richard and I share at home, and he stands in the middle of it, glass in hand, lit up as brightly as our surgical theatre at work by the halogens, and somehow wrong-footed by Maria's unexpected assertiveness.

Light glances off every surface in this room, all of them shined or polished or brushed, and I understand why my sister always looks so put together. There's nowhere in here where you won't see some version of yourself reflected back at you, nowhere where others will be able to watch you in any way other than forensically.

When I look at Chris, who I've always thought of as a benign king of his castle, I can clearly see that he's wrestling with a dilemma.

I recognise this easily because I see it frequently in the owners of pets I treat. The biggest and trickiest dilemma that many of them face is whether to continue prolonging the life of their animal, or to end its suffering. Some people want me to make the decision for them, though I can't do that. Some break down, others wrestle silently with it, faces contorted by the effort of not showing emotion in public, knuckles white around a limp dog lead, or on the handle of a cage, objects that might soon just be mementos, and this is what Chris looks like.

Chris's dilemma is this: to assert himself, or to back down for now, to play a longer game. He has this dilemma because I don't think he believes Maria.

I wouldn't.

While he cogitates, Maria takes the lifeline I've thrown her.

'How hungry are you?' she says.

'Absolutely bloody starving,' I say. 'I could eat a horse.' This is the kind of joke we unashamedly make at the clinic. Amongst the vets and support staff we have a competition to use as many animal-related sayings as possible.

Chris takes a long sip of his drink and walks over to gaze out at the garden. It looks magnificent. It's a huge plot for the location, with a couple of fabulous mature large specimen trees and a view from the end of it across the city.

'I'll lay the table out here shall I then?' he asks Maria.

'That would be lovely. We could use the new lights.'

Chris says to me, 'Would you like to phone Richard? See if he can join us? That would be nice.'

I'm surprised by this because Chris is well aware of Richard's proclivity for drink. It's an open secret in the family. His question gets Maria's attention too. She looks at him, and then she says, words crisply clear: 'Richard's got summer flu. Best let him sleep it off. I don't want Grace to catch anything.'

Chris's eyes narrow because all three of us know that the chances of Richard having summer flu are very, very small. I'm sure I'm not the only one amongst us who is imagining Richard right now, passed out somewhere, stinking of booze, and depression; catatonic with it.

'What about me?' We all turn to look at Lucas because it's not often that he addresses a room full of people. Lucas is a one-on-one person. He's only usually comfortable with an audience if he's sitting at a piano, insulated by his performance.

'Doesn't it matter if I get flu? Or Zoe?' He says it really deadpan. He has a surprisingly deep voice.

Maria's eyebrows raise and she exhales sharply.

'That's very rude!' Chris snaps.

'No, no, it's OK. It's a reasonable question,' Maria says, her hands up, palms outwards. 'I thought it would go without saying that we don't want either of you to get sick. Of course we don't.'

'Apologise!' Chris crosses to the table where Lucas sits and leans over it, head hovering closer to his son than it needs to. In the civilised confines of this room, with the smell of oil-brushed baguette toasting and the drifting scent of somebody else's barbecue through the open doors, this stands out as a gesture of aggression. Lucas's head jerks back. He reads it the same way I do. There's surprise on his face.

'I'm sorry, Maria,' Lucas says it to her nicely enough but drops his gaze quickly afterwards, and turns his head away from his father a little, and begins to insert candles into their holders, each one making a small sound as it lands. I'll admit, I'm shocked. Zoe has her back to them at the grill; she doesn't see it. Maria has been watching with eyes that look blank.

'Sweetheart,' Maria says to Lucas, and for the first time I see her composure wobble. Her voice rattles like pebbles in a jar. 'It's fine, really. Could you possibly pop those out on the garden table for me when you're done? It might need a wipe first. And if you're starving, Tess, I could whip up some chicken Parmigiana? If you'd like that?'

Two things strike me. Firstly, nobody whips up chicken Parmigiana. It's a beast of a recipe, involving breadcrumbs and eggs and dunking and bashing of meat and then sauces and grilling and baking. It's a labour of love, to be prepared starting at five in the evening, not late on a Sunday night. I wonder if my sister can really be trying to cook herself out of this situation, because it's surely a doomed effort; she can't keep cooking for ever. My second thought is, it's my favourite dish, and Maria knows that.

'That would be amazing,' I say and she gives a small nod.

'Great! I hoped you'd want some! We can have an impromptu supper in the garden!'

It's strange, because I'm not normally the focus of her hostess-charm. It's a new skill, which she's developed since being with Chris, and usually I watch her from the sidelines, exempt from being its target myself. The pre-accident Maria ran her household as a 'take-us-as-you-find-us' affair, with a shoe-strewn hallway and a kitchen where you'd have to shift the Sunday supplements to find a space to sit. It was relaxed and informal.

It was everything that Chris, bless him, isn't.

SUNDAY NIGHT

After the Concert

ZOE

I can't handle raw white meat. It's to do with the accident, and the things I saw, and Mum knows this so she gets Lucas to bash the chicken breasts flat.

While he pounds them in a crashing slow-motion rhythm that I'm guessing would equate to about forty beats per minute on the metronome, I lay the outside table with Chris. He wipes it down and I set out shiny cutlery and wine glasses and spread Lucas's tea lights out along the length of it so they look pretty.

There are also wide terracotta bowls on the table, containing yellow citronella-scented candle wax and Chris lights the thick wicks with a long, chunky match that flares in the darkness. The candles smoke blackly at first but then give off a scent that prickles my nostrils in a nearly nice way. Chris looks at me across the table and more or less repeats the question he asked earlier, only he says it slower, as if he wants to give his words more meaning.

'Zoe, are you absolutely sure you didn't you know that man?' he asks me. 'In the church?'

I look him in the eye; both of us lit by the flicker of the

candles, and also by the aqueous blue sheen of the swimming pool lights, which somebody inside the house has just turned on.

'No,' I say. 'I don't think so.' If I know anything, it's that I must do as my mother says. She's basically a human shield between the world and me. But I'm tempted to tell him the truth; I can't deny it. There's a part of me that wants Chris to know, but only if he could handle it. My real dad couldn't.

'Are you sure?' Chris's voice isn't pressing, and there's an encouraging elasticity to his tone of voice that almost coaxes the truthful answer out of me, but the impulse goes when he adds: 'You reacted very strongly,' and that sounds sharper.

'I was afraid of him,' I said. 'He looked crazy.'

In the silence I can still hear the steady pounding of Lucas's meat tenderising and I'm not sure if Chris's breathing is actually audible, but I feel like I can hear it as loudly as if his lips were centimetres from my ear. For a moment he studies me like I'm the *Mona Lisa* or something.

'You would tell me the truth, wouldn't you, Zoe?' he asks. 'You know it's important that we're all honest in this family?'

'Of course,' I say, and I know I should keep my eyes on him, that's the kind of thing you talk about in the Unit, how you should keep your eyes on people so they don't think you're being shifty, but I can't help it, I let mine slide away a bit, because Chris's voice is like caramel and sometimes I want to feel his arms around me in a hug, just like my dad used to do. The urge to tell can be strong.

But Chris turns and strides towards the kitchen. 'Lucas!' he calls out. 'Isn't that done yet? Are you trying to give me a migraine?'

'How flat does it have to be?' I hear Lucas ask my mother. Inside the kitchen, framed by the huge rectangular door opening, the scene looks like something out of an advent calendar window: people preparing food together, talking together. Lucas holds up a bit of roadkill flat chicken for my mother to inspect and she says, 'That's fine, darling. Perfect,' and I have to look away.

I don't like the pool lights being on at night, because it becomes a death trap for insects. I think of the butterfly I saw earlier and I wonder if it's still on the mirror and why it didn't fly towards the light like the moths out here are doing. They're diving like kamikaze planes towards the candle flames and spinning in circles on the lit-up surface of the pool. There are midges out here too, I can feel them nipping at my arms, and making my scalp itch.

I slip off my shoes, and sit on the edge of the pool and let my feet hang into it.

I'm not happy about the lies I've told Chris, but they're just the usual ones so they create a low-level unease that's manageable because it's nowhere near becoming what my mum would call 'an incident'.

Around my shins ripples shoot off towards the pool edges, distorting the light and creating shadows and dancing shapes within the water. A small bird dives down and takes a mouthful of water right in front of me, or maybe it's an insect that's drowned. The bird is gone before it arrived; its flight is the most elegant thing to watch.

'Did you see that?' I say, because I can hear somebody coming out of the house, and yet more lights come on, this time a string of bulbs that hang over the pergola that our table is under. They cast a soft white glow into the leaves that cluster above it, and show up the delicate yellow roses that my mum insists on pruning herself twice a year. She's pleased with them this year because they're managing to repeat flower after what Chris called 'a truly fabulous display' in June, and I think of them as trying very hard to please.

It's my mum who's coming now and she's carrying a plate of bruschetta and a pile of napkins.

'Paper napkins, I think, for a garden supper,' she says. She hasn't heard what I said and I don't repeat myself.

We sit around the table and Chris pours wine: a full glass for him and Mum, but just a half for Lucas and me. Tessa covers the top of her glass. 'Water for me now I think,' she says. 'It's so hot.'

You'd think I'd steer clear of alcohol, wouldn't you, but you see Chris insists that Lucas and I get use to 'being around alcohol in a civilised way', so for us to be offered half a glass of something fine that he's selected is not unusual. Only half, mind you, because anything more would be 'excessive'. Not something he has to spell out for me, but he doesn't know that.

'Tuck in,' says my mum and all our hands reach out towards the bruschetta apart from Chris's.

'To you, darling,' says Chris, raising his glass to Mum, 'the only woman I know who can whip up a feast like this on a Sunday night. What a treat.' He's sitting at the head of the table so all of our heads turn towards him as he speaks.

'Thank you,' she says. 'Won't you have a bruschetta?'

'I'm saving myself for the chicken,' he says. 'As I said, I'm still full from the concert.'

'Of course,' says my mum and she breaks a tiny bit off her bruschetta and nibbles at it. She raises her own glass. 'Can I just say how lucky I feel that we can all be here together tonight. It's very special.'

We all drink. Nobody speaks. Beside my mum on the table is Grace's baby monitor, the green light steady like a snake's eye.

'So,' says Aunt Tess in the silence that briefly follows, 'guess which animal I treated for the very first time this week,' and she's about to elaborate on this, but she's interrupted by the doorbell.

Only it's not just the doorbell, there's also a pounding on the door, as if Lucas were still bashing the chicken breasts, and then the bell rings again urgently. All of this noise registers on Grace's baby monitor; it sends the lights shooting off the scale and back down again, and then we can hear the unmistakable sound of her snuffling.

'Who the hell can that be?' says Chris. His chair squeaks as it drags across the pressure-washed flagstones. 'I'll get it.'

Mum is up too. 'I'll get it,' she says, 'you relax,' but she's too slow off the mark because Chris is already marching into the house and the hissy intercom is telling us that Grace is revving up for a full-blown yell and he says to Mum, 'See to the baby.'

MONDAY MORNING

SAM

Right after the car accident, Zoe remained on bail for a couple of weeks, while the police gathered evidence. I met with her and her parents during this time to discuss strategy for what might happen next. I hadn't yet had sight of any of the papers that the Crown Prosecution Service was preparing, but it was important to get Zoe's story complete.

The family came to my office in Bideford one morning, dressed smartly. Sometimes families hold hands with one another when they arrive; sometimes husbands pull chairs out for their wives or children to sit down on. Zoe and her parents weren't distant with each other exactly, but nor did they seem close in that way.

It was my first meeting with Mr Guerin, Zoe's dad, and he was clearly very uncomfortable. I imagined that he was more used to being out on the fields than in an office, dogs and livestock his usual companions. He looked older than his wife, though perhaps that was because he was weathered.

'We were away that night,' he said. 'We went to my sister's house near Exeter because her husband was just back from a tour in Afghanistan, and they were having a party. Zoe told us she wanted to stay with Gull for a sleepover, for Gull's birthday treat, you see. That's all we knew of it. First we heard was the phone call from the police when they got her in the hospital. We didn't know Gull's parents were away, see, and they didn't know we were. The girls lied to us.'

Zoe's head hung down as he spoke, though I noticed that she snuck one or two glances at me, watching my reaction to her father's words.

'She'd never even been to a party that we knew,' he continued. He was warming up, almost as if he couldn't stop speaking now, as if he'd been waiting to unburden himself of this story. Beside him, his wife and daughter sat silent as his words filled the space between us all. 'She had trouble making friends at the new school, some girls weren't very nice to her, internet bullying that's what she's told us. She was bullied, Mr Locke, and we want to know if that can be a defence against what she's done.'

So this was what he'd been working up to, a spark of hope that the family thought they'd discovered, and which they were sheltering and nurturing with cupped hands.

'They sent her messages through an app, called panop, they bombarded her with awful, vitriolic stuff,' said Maria Guerin. She sounded instantly more articulate than her husband, and I could tell she wasn't born and raised round here. I wondered how hard it had been for her to manage as a farmer's wife, because the rural community can be a difficult one to find acceptance within if you're an outsider.

'We didn't know about it.' Mr Guerin added this.

'What kind of messages?' I asked Zoe.

She looked at me, holding something back.

'Give him your phone, Zo,' said her dad. 'You can see it all on her phone.'

122

She pressed a button or two on her phone and pushed it across the table. It was such a typical young teenage girl's phone: metallic pink, with stickers on the back of it, musical notes.

On the screen I could see the messages that Zoe had received. The content of them jolted me. They were nasty, taunting, shocking messages. They oozed with clever, calculated malice, and targeted every aspect of her figure and her personality. They left me momentarily speechless.

When I looked up, Zoe had her eyes on me, but she dropped them and a flush crept up and over her cheeks.

'Who sent these?' I asked.

'They're anonymous,' Maria answered me.

'Do you know, Zoe?'

'I don't know.'

'You must have some idea,' said her dad. I could tell this wasn't the first time he'd said this to her.

Maria put her hand on his. 'Don't shout. There's no need to shout. Not here.'

He pulled his hand out from under hers and ran it through his hair in frustration. He had proud aquiline features, which lent dignity to his weather-beaten skin. Maria withdrew her hand to her lap.

I wondered what Zoe would tell me if it were just she and I in the room. I wondered what she hid from her parents.

'Do you feel that these messages affected your behaviour on the night of the accident?' I asked her. This was important, because it could lead to a possible coercion defence.

'I didn't get any that night.'

'Which tells me,' her father raised his voice again, 'that

somebody there that night was sending them. It's not rocket science. I might not have degrees coming out of my ears but it's common sense, isn't it? Common bloody sense. They lured her there, and they bullied her into doing something she wouldn't have done otherwise.'

'They didn't.' Zoe's voice was soft and quiet.

'What?' he said to her.

'They didn't bully me into it! I decided to drive. I chose to drive. You taught me, Dad, you taught me yourself. I decided to drive but I didn't know I was drunk. I swear it.'

Both of Zoe's parents were about to speak, but I raised my hand to silence them. I had to intervene because we needed to make rational, careful decisions; the law doesn't legislate for feelings.

'Tell me about that, Zoe,' I said. 'Talk to me about that, because that can be a valid defence.'

SUNDAY NIGHT

After the Concert

ZOE

It's just me and Lucas at the table after everybody else has gone; we're sitting opposite each other, candle flames and a pile of bruschetta between us. There's a scratchy noise still coming through the baby monitor so I turn off the sound.

'Did you read the script?' says Lucas.

'I read a bit of it, but I only had time to look at the beginning. It was sad.'

I think of my phone tucked under the sofa cushions, and I wonder if I can expect more panop questions when I retrieve it. Before, when things were at their worst, the messages used to come through all the time, question after question, sometimes I could get ten in five minutes, each one shovelling away at my foundations in a different way.

Who do you think you are?

Are you sick you filthy bitch?

Crying yourself to sleep yet?

How does it feel when everybody hatehatehate-
hatehates you?

Do gay bitches cry gay tears?

Actually that one really didn't make sense given that the
basis of what they were accusing me of was prostituting
myself to Jack Bell, but it was miserable to read anyway. And
ironically, because I've got what Jason the Key Worker called
a 'finely honed sense of irony', it was the panop messages that
made me so keen to go *that* party: the one where I became a
princess for just a moment or two in the hands of Jack Bell.

The messages were supposed to put me off going near
him, but they didn't, because I'm also what Jason described as
'stubborn' and 'driven'. You don't win piano competitions at
the level I play at unless you're both of those things.

So when Jack asked me to his house party just a few weeks
before Christmas, and grudgingly invited Gull too because
I said I couldn't come without her, especially because it was
her birthday the next day, there was a part of me that thought,
Suck on that Eva Bell and Amelia Barlow. Because I was pretty
sure they were sending the messages, them and their minions.

I take a sip of my wine and say to Lucas, 'Shall we top up,
while they're not here?' It feels like a daring thing to say, and
I should know better, of course I should, but I say it because
I want to jolt Lucas out of his flatness, and get him to joke
around with me a bit. I want to do something that'll make the
memory of the church go away.

Lucas gets the bottle and refills our glasses, but no higher
than Chris originally poured them.

'Will you read the rest of the script?' he says.

He dips his index finger into his mouth and then begins to run it around the rim of his wine glass. A note, high and pure and piercing, sings out from it. I do the same to my finger and my glass.

'I will,' I say, so he doesn't feel bad.

The sound from the glasses has momentum now. Our fingers scoot round and round. He's chewing his lip, and he doesn't answer right away, and I don't want him to cry or anything like that because the script makes him think about his mum.

'Does this count as a repetitive noise?' I ask him. Repetitive noises are irritating to other people, I'm told, if my foot gets the urge to tap up and down on the stone floor of the kitchen, or if I click my fingers in time to some music that only I can hear in my head.

'Nah,' Lucas says. 'It's C sharp.'

I have perfect pitch so I know that his glass is making C natural and mine is making E flat, but I don't correct him because nobody likes a smarty-pants.

'What's in the rest of the script then?' I ask him.

'It's just ... You need to read it.'

'It was quite hard to read on my phone.'

He stops with the glass abruptly then, and the whining note dies away slowly. I stop mine too and clamp my hand on top of my glass, to stop the vibrations instantly. Then the sound of the greedy, flapping filters in the swimming pool becomes our soundtrack. Lucas is passing his finger through one of the candle flames now, and I can see the edge of it blackening.

'Can you show me on your iPad? After supper?' I ask him.

Lucas's eyes look artificially twinkly because the fairy lights are being reflected in his dark pupils. Usually they're flatly dark; unknowable vats of Lucas thought.

'Maybe,' he says. 'But you could just read it on your phone, it's not that hard.'

It's a bit weird to be here with Lucas, with wine, just us two, because there are rules about us in this house.

We first moved in to the house right before Grace was born. Mum and me lived in a scuzzy flat before then, where she survived mostly on Prozac, and Lucas and Chris lived in a different big house. We could have all fitted into their old house but then it wouldn't have been 'a fresh start'.

What I'm remembering now, though, is the talk that Lucas and me had to have with our parents when we all moved in together, which was unbelievably excruciating. The gist of it was – can you guess? – that me and Lucas were not under any circumstances ever to consider starting a relationship with each other because above all we had to 'respect the new family'. The only practical result of this was that we had to agree not to go into each other's bedroom unless an adult was present. I had a fully hollow internal laugh when they said that because it was so like the Secure Unit it wasn't even true.

Afterwards, when we were alone, Lucas said they were hypocrites, and controlling, and didn't trust us. Then he asked me if I'd ever thought about him in that way and I said I had, and he stared at me like he wasn't expecting that answer at all. So I added to my answer, I said Only Once. He never told me if he'd ever felt the same, maybe because I was too nervous to ask. He just went to do his practice and, while I listened to it,

I thought about how some people could rape you with their eyes in the Unit, even if they never touched you at all.

'I sent it to your mum too,' Lucas says. 'The email.'

'Why don't you just tell me what's in it?'

'I don't know how to; it's best if you read it.'

When he says this, his voice is so unexpectedly strange and serious that it makes a shudder run through me, deep and cold.

SUNDAY NIGHT

After the Concert

TESSA

It's Tom Barlow at the door. I hang back in the hallway, by the door of the coat cupboard, and watch Chris greet him cautiously.

Tom Barlow is highly agitated, just as he was in the church: face and neck red, emotions burning him up with the intensity of a forest fire. Chris stands in the doorway, blocking it mostly, and gently tells Tom Barlow to calm down and that he's certainly made a mistake, and come to the wrong house. Chris's voice is calm and measured; he's very much in control.

I stay in the shadows, watching, and I sense Maria upstairs, trying to listen as she soothes the baby. I'm pressed up against Chris's fishing rods and his winter work coats: great swathes of cashmere, smelling faintly in the heat despite being wrapped in dry cleaner's plastic.

Chris remains patient even when Tom Barlow refuses to listen to what he's being told. Chris doesn't invite him inside, but asks him if he'd like to take a seat on a bench that is just beside the ornate front porch, overlooking the driveway.

'Perhaps,' Chris says to Tom Barlow in a tone that's calm but which I think could be dangerously patronising, 'I could fetch you a glass of iced water?'

Tom Barlow is having none of it.

'She needs to answer for what she did,' he shouts at Chris, and then, just like in the church, his phrases seem to circulate on a loop as if the energy that's driving him to these desperate acts is taking so much out of him that he can do nothing more. He repeats it. 'She needs to answer,' he says, 'she needs to answer for what she took from me.'

'Who?' says Chris. 'To whom are you referring?'

And Mr Barlow rocks backward and forward on his feet, disbelief etched more deeply on his face every time I can catch a glimpse of him. He practically spits out his reply. He says, 'Zoe Guerin, I'm referring to Zoe Guerin. Who the hell else would I be referring to?'

These two sentences seem to paralyse the air around Chris and Mr Barlow, and the two men remain standing face to face, speaking not at all. I imagine that Mr Barlow is watching a variety of emotions, and, most importantly, realisations work across Chris's face, because right at this moment Chris must be coming to the conclusion that Mr Barlow has indeed come to the right house and that Maria has lied to him.

From upstairs there's absolute silence. Maria has stopped shushing the baby, and I wonder if she's heard what I've heard because if she has, then she'll know that the game is up.

When Chris moves again his actions are swift. With both of his hands, he shoves Tom Barlow backwards violently and, as Tom Barlow staggers across the gravel, stones crunching, Chris says, 'How dare you?'

I emerge from my nook then. I run down the hall towards them, and I step out on the front drive.

'Hey,' I say, as gently as possible. Tom Barlow has recovered physically and is standing and staring at Chris with intense hatred and not a little disbelief. I put a hand on Chris's arm.

'Hey,' I say, 'Chris, stop, it's OK.'

Chris's jaw is clenched and rigid and his arm is solid with poised muscle. Tom Barlow is breathing through his nose, nostrils flaring and jaw set, squaring up to this threat of violence, this added outrage, and he looks as if he might charge Chris. It's scary, primitive stuff, dogs with hackles up; a hair's breadth away from turning into a nasty fight. I step right between them, my back to Chris, and I say to Tom Barlow, 'Would you like to talk?'

His eyes flick across my face and I think he recognises me.

Behind me, I feel Chris move forward and I put my arm out behind my back until my fingers make contact with him, telling him that I want him to stay there. 'Talk to me?' I say again to Tom Barlow, and I keep my voice soft.

For a moment longer he glares over my shoulder, chest heaving, unable to take his outraged eyes off Chris, but then a sort of collapse takes place within his eyes. Tears well, huge droplets that flatten on his cheeks, smearing them. 'Come with me,' I say, 'we'll talk about it.'

I take his arm, slowly, because dogs can still bite even after their hackles have gone down. I look at Chris. 'Go inside,' I say and I'm shocked at the anger that's on his face, but my priority is to move Tom Barlow away, to prevent him from confronting Maria or Zoe, and from making things any worse than they are already.

Chris doesn't move.

'Go. Inside,' I repeat.

He takes one small step backwards, his gaze still locked on Tom Barlow, and he says, 'I will phone the police if I see you on my property again.' Even then Chris doesn't go in. He stands, long arms by his sides, in the middle of the elegant circle of gravel that shapes his driveway and he's framed by flowerbeds full of manicured topiary and shrubbery, beneath which the shady undergrowth hisses with a discreet watering system to ensure that nothing dries out.

Above him, in an upstairs window I see Maria, with Grace in her arms. She's holding the blackout blind aside, and gazing down at us, but then, as her husband finally turns and enters the house, she drops the blind and is invisible to me again.

SUNDAY NIGHT

After the Concert

ZOE

Lucas notices my shudder. His eyes pass over my bare shoulders.

'Do you need a sweater?' he says. 'I can get you one.'

'No thank you.'

'Are you sure?'

'It was just a little breeze.'

There's a tiny bit of movement around us now, though it's hot, velvety air that arrives from somewhere unseen in the darkness. It doesn't refresh.

'Someone walk over your grave?' he asks.

'Probably,' I say, but that's the kind of comment that I have to work hard to keep my composure in the face of.

I put my finger in the candle flame to distract myself, and because I want to do what he's been doing, but it hurts immediately, and I pull it away. Lucas laughs and then we're silent again and I think about how much I couldn't bear it if he wasn't in this house with us. My mum's not warm any more, not since the accident, and Chris isn't warm. Grace is warm but in a fuggy, baby way, so it's only Lucas who feels truly personality-warm to me, who seems to see things a bit the same way I do, even if he doesn't say much.

'Lucas,' I say, but he's begun to talk at the same time as me.

'Do you ever think of giving up piano?' he says and that is such a totally, unbelievably, jaw-droppingly, incredible, unexpected, shocking thing for him to say that even I'm lost for words.

'Why?' I ask. I can't conceive of giving up piano. Piano playing is like an addiction for me. It's a path I have to walk down, water I have to drink, food I must consume, air I need to breathe. It's the only thing that can take my head somewhere safe and everybody tells me it's going to give me 'a bright future'.

'Don't tell my dad I said that,' he says. He sees my surprise and it's made him nervous, but I'm a loyal person.

'I won't.' I put those words out there quickly because I want Lucas to know that I'm on his side, but I have to ask again: 'Why?'

'I didn't say I was doing it.' He's backtracking.

'But why are you thinking about it?'

He tips back his chair. 'Because it's part of what's not right.'

'Piano?'

'No.'

'What's not right?'

'This. Any of it.'

'What do you mean?' I can't believe I'm hearing this, because Lucas practises longer and harder than me on the piano and he never complains.

He's holding up his fingers now, making a rectangle shape and looking at me through it. I know what he's doing; he's framing me for a shot, because he's obsessed with films. He does it a lot, and it really annoys Chris.

'Is it because you want to do films?' I ask. I know he does, we all know he does, but he doesn't talk about it because Chris says it's not a proper career.

He drops his hands. 'I do want to make films; it's not only that though. Sometimes piano feels like it's just a cog in a machine. Like it doesn't mean anything for itself, it's just for appearances. I hate that. Don't you hate that?'

And those words make me actually gasp, as though the air I've just breathed in is scorching hot, because they really, truly shock me. I would never give up piano. I just would never give up, because we have to move forward.

I have an urge to get up from the table and turn away from him, because I don't want him to see my eyes go filmy with tears about this, so I stand up sort of awkwardly in the way you do when you're rushing but your knees are a bit stuck under a table, and as I do that I manage to flip up the plate of bruschetta with my hand.

So it rains bruschetta. Gobbets of chopped tomato and basil and oil splatter the tablecloth and Lucas and the floor. It's all over his black concert shirt and it's on his face and hair. I couldn't have done a more efficient job of spreading them everywhere if I'd used a spray gun. And because I don't know what else to do, I laugh. I'm bad at laughing when bad things happen. It's just a sort of reaction that I can't help. It got me into trouble in the Secure Unit once, because that's the kind of place you really don't want to laugh at people. I won't tell you what they put in my bed that night, and the night after.

Lucas looks me right in the eye, and the super-serious expression he had a few seconds earlier stays there for just an instant before it dissolves into a nicer one and he laughs.

So I laugh again too, really loudly, like 'that's hilarious' sort of laughing, which means that when Chris speaks from the doorway it's the most massive shock ever because I didn't hear him coming, and it makes me scream, short and sharp.

'What are you both doing?' he says. He's using a voice that I've never heard before. It's icy cold.

Lucas says, 'Sorry,' and I say, 'It was my fault. I'm really sorry,' and I have one of those moments again where one minute you're all standing there laughing in your dress, and you feel good because you're having a nice time with somebody and the next minute it's all back down to earth because you're still just you and you're worthless, and probably worse too.

Chris sees it.

Chris, who's never said a bad word to me, though I suppose he's never really said much.

To Lucas, Chris says: 'Get yourself cleaned up.'

To me, he says: 'Stop behaving like a slut in front of my son. Don't think I don't see you doing it.'

The silence that follows those words makes my skin crawl in cold, fluid patches, as if somebody was moving around me and blowing on it, because I don't know what to do. I stay really still and I focus on the slap, slap of the water in the pool against the filters, and I crunch the skin on the back of my lips between my teeth. My nose tingles with the early warning signal that tears are coming and once again I fight that urge, as silently and as discreetly as possible.

Chris looks as though he's expecting me to answer, but I can't think of a single thing to say, because my brain is confused by the uncertainty of it all. I didn't know I was behaving like a slut, or perhaps I did know, and I've therefore purposely done something shameful, but if that's true then I wonder, should I admit to it?

I feel like I'm naked. Chris's words remind me of the panop messages I used to get, they remind me of the girls who used to bait me, and they remind me of the Unit. Those words don't belong in this house. I say, 'I'm sorry, Chris. I didn't mean to. Truly, I didn't.'

'You're on thin ice, young lady,' he says. 'Go and look after the baby and ask your mother to come down. I need to speak to her.'

I walk past him and Lucas without looking them in the eye at all, and I try to keep my head straight up and make sure that my walk isn't at all like a slut's walk, and when I'm inside the house I start to run and I don't stop until I've pounded all the way up the stairs and I'm standing on the landing outside Grace's room, where I stop.

SUNDAY NIGHT

After the Concert

TESSA

'I know you,' Tom Barlow says. 'Don't I?'

'I'm Zoe's aunt. Tessa Downing.'

'You were at the court.' He recognises me, even all these years on.

I nod.

'I'm so sorry for your loss,' I say. The words are hollow with my inability to make things right for him. My only hope is that he can hear my intention.

We're standing on the street outside Maria's house, but I want to move him further away. It would be too easy for him to walk back into the house from here, or to go around the back and find Zoe in the garden. Now that the secret's out, I think my greatest fear is that he could do her some harm. It's an exercise in damage limitation at this stage.

'Would you like to talk?' I ask him. 'We could sit in my car? Or walk?'

I'm trying to remember what I know about this man, to separate the descriptions I read of him in the newspapers from the other families. As far as I remember, Tom Barlow is, or was, in property. In fact, his profile wasn't all that different from Chris's. He was a self-made businessman, and proud of it. If Chris and Tom Barlow had met under other circumstances they might have got on well. Amelia, who died in the accident, was not the Barlow family's only child but she was their only daughter. I remember photographs of two young boys, the image of their sister, clutching the hands of their parents in the photographs of the funeral.

'I need a smoke,' he says, and he sinks down on to the stone wall that borders the front of Chris and Maria's garden, containing the dense foliage at their boundary. It's not as good as moving away from the property, but at least if we sit we won't be visible from the house.

He pulls a cigarette from a packet and offers me one, but I shake my head.

'Do you mind?' he asks me, and the question, in the midst of all this, almost makes me laugh. How is it that manners are so strong that they pervade all situations? I've lost count of the times that people have apologised to me for crying when I've just euthanised their pet.

'Not at all,' I say. 'Of course not.'

Tom Barlow leans forward and hangs his head. His hands clench between his knees and his cigarette dangles from between his knuckles, the rising smoke making him turn his head a little to the side, away from me.

I notice that he has a monk-like area of thinning hair on the crown of his head that he's tried to disguise with careful use of hair product of some sort. It tells me that he didn't start his day thinking about Zoe, that what happened has probably been as much of a shock to him as it has been to us. You almost certainly don't take time with hair product if you're consumed with rage and indignation.

We sit in silence because I don't want to inflame him again by saying the wrong thing, and after a few minutes, when the cigarette is half smoked, he reaches into the pocket of his shorts and hands me a crumpled piece of paper.

It's a flyer, advertising Zoe's concert.

'Through my door,' he says. 'This morning. Through my front door, on to my doormat, in my house. In my own home. I only came because I couldn't believe it actually would be her.'

I hold the flyer in my hands. I have no idea who distributed it, but my best guess is that it was one of the busybody organisers from the church.

'If we had known,' I say carefully, 'we would never, ever have let this happen. Please believe me.'

'We came here to escape from it,' he says. 'We sold everything, we moved the boys, we lost money, we started again. It hasn't been easy.'

His voice cracks and I think how the same words could describe Zoe and Maria's flight from Devon to Bristol, but of course I don't say that.

I want to put my hand on his back to comfort him but I'm not sure that's a good idea, so instead I say, 'I'm so, so sorry.'

'We buried her in Hartland,' he says, and I think again of the newspaper pictures, where the backdrop to the black-clad processional figures was the tiered grey stone spire of Hartland Church, built toweringly tall to act as a landmark for sailors, to save lives centuries before the lighthouse at the Point ever existed. 'So we couldn't bring her with us when we moved,

141

but we had a plaque laid, at the church in Westbury. We chose a plaque with the boys.'

And so I understand the awfulness of it now. Zoe has played a concert at a church where one of the victims of the accident she caused has a memorial plaque. Zoe has tried to rebuild her life on the site of her victim's memorial.

'Mr Barlow—' I say. I try to choose the words I'm going to say next extremely carefully, but he cuts me off.

'Who is that man?' he says. 'That's not her dad.'

'No. Maria's remarried. That's Zoe's stepdad.'

'Does he know? Does he know what she's done? What she is? Does he know that and still treat me like shit on his shoe?'

He studies me as I try to word my answer, try to work out what is the least incendiary thing I can say, but I'm too slow and he sees the truth.

'He doesn't know, does he?'

'I think—' I begin, but he interrupts me.

'I feel sorry for your family,' he says. 'Living with a murderer.'

He stands up and I do too. I feel things slipping out of my control again. 'Please know that we are truly, truly sorry,' I say.

'People should know. She needs to pay.'

'She has paid for what she did,' I tell him. 'She's a changed person.'

'What? Twelve months in a cushy detention centre some-where doing her GCSEs? How does that make up for what she's done?'

He gestures his hand at Chris and Maria's house, at its immaculate grandeur, and disbelief at the injustice of it all runs rampant in his expression.

'We have nothing!' he says. 'And she has all of this. She shows off with her piano still and she lives in a mansion like nothing ever happened.'

'That's not true,' I say. 'She's been punished. This destroyed her life too. Be fair …'

But that was the wrong thing to say. 'Be fair?' he asks, and he snatches the programme from my hand and reads from it: ' "You won't want to miss these two precociously talented teenagers making their Bristol debut – this promises to be a very special evening." '

There's nothing but disgust in his tone.

'People need to know,' he says, 'and I'm going to make sure they do.'

'Is it so wrong for her to have a future?' I ask. I'm desperate now. My ability to remain calm is slipping through my fingers.

'Why should she have one, when we don't?'

He screws the paper up and hurls it at my feet and then he turns away and begins to walk down the street, away from the house, shoulders slack and head bowed, towards the street light that's making the top of the postbox at the end of the road shine a slippery red.

'What are you doing?' I call after him. 'What are you going to do?'

He disappears around the corner.

I look at the house, and I wonder what's happening in there, and I look at the corner that Tom Barlow has just disappeared around, and I decide to follow him.

SUNDAY NIGHT

After the Concert

ZOE

Chris's words have made me shake. I'm used to being called bad things, but not by him.

On the landing, I notice the butterfly again. It's come out of the bathroom, and now it's high up in a corner flapping uselessly against the walls. I don't like it doing that, because I imagine the sparkling dust on its wings being dislodged every time it makes impact, a microscopic shower of iridescent powder falling like sand through an hourglass, weakening the butterfly little by little, until it won't be able to fly any longer.

It makes me think of my life, and of the damage I've done, and I think that I've been lucky so far, because when things have gone wrong, and when the sand in my hourglass has run through and time has run out for me, I've been able to pick it up, turn it over, and start again. But I wonder if that's ever going to be possible now. I wonder how many chances a person can get.

I ease open the door to Grace's bedroom. My mum is lying on the bed that's in there, on the other side of the room from Grace's cot. Grace is lying with her. As I adjust to the darkness,

I see that they've turned their heads towards me, that their eyes are darkly reflecting the light from the hallway.

'Mum,' I whisper. 'Chris wants to talk to you. Shall I look after Grace?'

I don't mention what he's said to me because I don't want anything else to go wrong for my mum today, especially not if it's my fault.

Normally, Mum would leap up if I said that. She always goes quickly to Chris. She's super-attentive to him. Chris gets first-class service, because the Second Chance Family is a First Class Operation, just like Chris's business, and just like my and Lucas's standard of performance. Chris and Mum set a lot of store in that.

Mum doesn't leap up though. As I walk through the inky darkness of the room towards them, I see that she and Grace are lying together like a bear and its cub. My mum isn't trying to get Grace to sleep; she's playing with her. Mum runs the side of her finger down over Grace's temple, and Grace reaches for Mum's hand and holds it in front of her face. Mum uses a fingertip to dab Grace lightly on the nose and Grace giggles.

I approach them quietly because I want to be on the bed with them. There's a little space just below where Grace is lying and I perch there cautiously. Mum is against the wall. Grace kicks me gently with her feet. The room's hot and she's just wearing a nappy and I feel her warm toes on my bare leg. I move them a little because that's near where the piano bruised me earlier.

'Chris wants you,' I whisper to Mum.

'Lie with us,' she says.

My heart begins to beat so freaking loudly when she says that that I feel like I might hyperventilate. Mum shuffles over towards the wall and pulls Grace gently with her, leaving a thin sliver of space along the edge of the bed. I lie down, my head beside Grace's, and she celebrates with some monster kicking, and then by taking a hank of my hair and giving it a pull. I don't mind though, I'm used to it. Grace tries to sit up but my mum whispers, 'Gracie-girl, lie with us, come on,' and, miraculously, Grace does.

We lie for a minute and then Mum says, 'My girls,' in a voice that's warm and sweet like hot chocolate, and she nestles her head into Grace and reaches across her to put a hand on my cheek and her thumb runs down my temple too, and for the first time in a gazillion years I forget all the things that have gone wrong, and I just relax and lie there and feel her hand on me and Grace's wriggly body between us and if I couldn't hear the butterfly still flapping on the landing, reminding me of my hourglass life, it would be just like heaven.

SUNDAY NIGHT

After the Concert

TESSA

What are the odds that Tom Barlow would be living only a few miles from Chris and Maria's new house? Long. Just as the odds are that Zoe would be playing a concert at the very church where Amelia is remembered.

But if you work in the business that I do, you know that long odds don't always make any difference at all. Somebody always makes up that small percentage of people to whom unlikely or desperate things happen, and there's actually nothing to say it can't be you.

Tom Barlow doesn't jog for long. He gets in a car around the corner from Chris and Maria's house and when I realise that I still have my bag over my shoulder, and my keys are inside it – Maria's hostess skills have failed her tonight, my bag wasn't taken from me on arrival – I turn back swiftly and get my car, even though I fear that I'm going to lose him. But I don't. When I trundle around the corner, his car is only just pulling out, as though he's had to sit in there for a few minutes and pull himself together before leaving, or perhaps make a phone call.

We leave the wide, leafy, sedate lanes of Chris and Maria's

neighbourhood and drive further out into surburbia, retracing some of the route back from the concert. On a long street in Westbury, which seems to go on for ever, Tom Barlow pulls into the driveway of a modest semi-detached house that looks as though it was built in the sixties, and I'm able to park in a space opposite. I keep my head back so that he can't see my face, but I have a view of his house.

It has a large picture window to the front and through it I can see the sitting room. There are two sofas and a TV, plus some gaming equipment. The walls are painted a plain magnolia. There's not much else, apart from a poster-sized family photograph on the wall, where the kids are small, and Amelia is sandwiched between her little brothers, who appear to be twins. The sparse furnishings make the room look more functional than loved.

Tom Barlow stays sitting in his car for a good few minutes before he gets out. In fact, he stays there for so long that a woman, who I recognise as his wife, opens the door and looks out enquiringly.

He gets out of the car and holds her in a long, tight hug.

'I thought that was you. Are you all right?' I hear her say. 'What's wrong?'

I can't hear his reply, but he shakes his head as if to say 'Nothing's wrong' and then she pushes him away from her so that she's holding him by the shoulders, and she smiles at him. 'I love you too,' she says. From the doorway, one of their boys watches, bare-chested, wearing just pyjama bottoms. Tom Barlow puts his arm around his son on the way into the house and, as the door shuts, the child starts an explanation about how it was too hot to sleep.

On my way there, I thought I would ring on the doorbell and try to speak to the family, to convince them that Zoe should be allowed a chance to rebuild, that she and Maria are entitled to their privacy, and entitled to move on. But I can't do that now because I'm pretty certain that nobody else in his house knows what Tom Barlow has been doing that evening. Not yet, anyway, and I don't want to be the one to tell them.

SUNDAY NIGHT

After the Concert

ZOE

The light that's been gently creeping into Grace's bedroom from the hallway suddenly disappears. Mum and me turn our heads towards the door to see why. A man-sized silhouette blocks the doorway and at first it's hard to tell whether it's Lucas or Chris. He steps away after a small pause, without saying anything, but it's enough to rouse my mum. She lets out what I think is a quiet moan, and then eases herself up off the bed. Gracie-girl doesn't want Mum to go. She gives a bit of a whimper herself, but I distract her by making my fingers flutter right in front of her face and she grabs for them.

You never know when Grace is going to accept me as a Mum-substitute. Sometimes she's happy to, other times she just yells blue murder until she gets Mum back. It's the same with Lucas. And even with Chris. Mum is definitely Grace's favourite. Oh, and Katya. But, to be honest, I'd rather gloss over that because it massively annoys me.

When Mum has left the room, she pulls the door softly behind her so that it's almost completely shut but not quite, as if she wants to keep us both just the way she left us. Grace is sort of sleepy now. She turns her body to me and I put my arm around her so that her head can nestle into the side of me, and I sing to her, a little tune that my dad used to sing to me when I was little.

I think about my dad a lot. He's a farmer. He couldn't cope after the accident, because he said it was Mum's fault, that she pushed me too hard with the music, that it had turned me into somebody I should never have been trying to be. He said that I should never have gone for a music scholarship in the first place, because it wasn't for people like us. I should have stayed at the local school and grown up just the way he did: safely, at the farm, at the heart of the community.

'But you *love* listening to Zoe play,' my mum said in the last reintegration meeting at the Unit that Dad ever attended. 'You always said I was right to push her.'

'Not at this cost,' he'd replied, and he put on his coat and said, 'I'm sorry, Zoe,' and then he left, even though Jason asked him not to and talked to him in the corridor outside for ages.

I didn't see my dad for nine months after that, the time it takes to make a whole new human being. I went back to see him at the farm when I got out of the Unit, but only once. We had an OK day and Granny Guerin came round with some scones, but Dad was mostly sad and awkward, and when he went out to see to the cattle Granny Guerin said he never did know how to put a feeling into words and that was just the way he was, but she knew for sure that he loved me and he always would.

I wanted to tell him that I was still the same girl as before the accident, I was still his girl. I wanted to say that I wasn't a bad person, I'd just done a bad thing, by accident, but on that day his silence meant that I found it hard to put anything into words too. Perhaps it's catching.

Granny Guerin saw that I had a lot of words stored up in me, and she said, 'I know your mother thinks I've abandoned you both, but he's my child and I must protect him. I'm just doing the same as what your mother's doing for you. Know that he loves you, Zoe, I can't promise anything more than that now, so I won't, because I don't like to raise expectations. But time can heal things, my darling.'

But on the train on the way back to Bristol I also thought about how time destroyed everything on the farm, how part of my dad's life was just keeping things fixed that time had broken. And I imagined Dad, with his red farmer's cheeks and furrowed brow, and I thought how everything about him looked more or less exactly the same as it did before the accident, except that now the farmhouse didn't feel cosy like it used to, and his eyes were full of sadness. If I was going to be über-dramatic (vampire-romance fans: be alert! This is your moment!), I would say that his eyes were wells of tears.

I don't know exactly what happened to my parents when I was in the Unit. I only know that they found it too difficult to go on together. Jason said that a traumatic event within a family can make it very difficult for a marriage to continue, and that was something I might just have to accept. Cracks in a marriage, he said, can become chasms if they're shaken by trauma. I told him he was almost sounding like a poet. He told me it would benefit me if I could learn to take things seriously.

By the time I came out, Mum had moved all our stuff from the farm and found a flat in Bristol, and started a job that my aunt Tessa got for her through her wunderkind husband Richard the Rocket Scientist, who's fond of a tipple.

We weren't going to dwell on the past, Mum told me, we were going to look forward, to try to start something fresh. My dad would be OK, she said, I could go and stay with him in the holidays. But she cried every night, and she was crying when she woke up some mornings too, until she met Chris.

SUNDAY NIGHT

After the Concert

TESSA

When the door has shut behind Tom Barlow and his wife, I don't hang around for long. I put the bus into gear and trundle off down their road, but I park again when I'm round the corner, out of their sight, because I want to think.

Once I've turned the headlights off, I notice that the darkness is musky and thick with humidity. I can smell barbecue smells from somebody's garden, and a cyclist whizzes past me on a road bike, making me jump.

My phone's in my back pocket and I squirm to get it out. Richard has tried to ring me again so I phone him back. He takes about half a second to answer.

'Tess!' He knows it's me because nobody else phones our landline.

'Hi.'

'Where are you?'

I try to judge the level of his intoxication from the extent to which he's slurring his words. I figure that he's close to being blotto, and he's clearly feeling paranoid.

'I was at Zoe's concert,' I tell him. 'And then I went back to Maria's house. I had to give Chris and Lucas a lift.'

I don't tell him anything more about the evening. Richard's not good at absorbing other people's problems when his own have swelled up enough to fill his mind entirely. His response to what I've said will tell me precisely what his mood is like.

Richard is either a self-hating drunk or an overambitious drunk, but I'm never sure which I'm going to get when he hits the bottle. Neither option thrills me. The self-hating is profoundly tedious because it's a circular, defeatist state of mind, but then the overambitious is bad because it's simply delusional, consisting as it usually does of a series of promises that Richard will never keep.

'I've let you down again,' he says, and I get my answer right there: tonight, Richard is suffering from a case of drunken self-hatred, and he would like me to shore him up in this.

'It's all I ever do,' he says. 'Why don't you leave me, Tessa? Just leave me.'

It's a good question, that, and it's one I've asked myself on numerous occasions, and in fact Sam has asked me that question too. 'Why don't you leave him?'

The answer is that I like Richard, even now. We've been together for many, many years, and I loved the man I married.

We first met when I was doing my large animal placement as part of my training, and Richard was doing his PhD at the university engineering department. It was the gentlest, easiest start to a relationship you could imagine. We just got on as if we'd always been friends. We laughed together; we discovered we liked doing the same things. I loved his gentle intelligence, the way he thought before he spoke and was never mocking or snobbish.

We moved in together into a tiny attic flat, which nearly had a view of the Clifton Suspension Bridge, only four months after meeting, and we both studied like mad and made each other cups of instant coffee and lived on vats of chilli con carne and baked potatoes that we took it in turns to make.

Our flat was an unfurnished place, and we slept together on a cramped futon and sat on deckchairs to watch TV because we didn't have enough money to buy a sofa. It was good practice for the travelling we did after we'd finished studying. Richard and I went around the world with backpacks for a year, and then lived for a time in Kenya, where we both managed to get work.

We married when we got back to the UK, and had our reception in the Clifton Pavilion at Bristol Zoo. It was still a happy time for us then, because it wasn't until a few years after that, after we'd got ourselves properly established back in Bristol, with new jobs and a new house, that things began to slip and slide, almost imperceptibly slowly, into something much less than what we had dreamed of.

So now we find ourselves a somewhat sourer version of the couple we imagined we would become. Richard has no work, and we have no children, and the resulting bitter disappointment has mostly turned him into a depressed, drunken, foolish version of my beloved bridegroom. However, there are hours, days, weeks, when the man that I loved re-emerges, and I find that these are enough to keep me with him. To part would be to acknowledge that alcohol has managed to destroy us, and I'm just not ready to do that yet.

To Sam, I just say, 'I can't, not yet,' and as I say it I feel like a clichéd cheating spouse. But it's not to do with wanting to keep the status quo; it's to do with not being able to let go of what Richard and I had, the perfect idea of us, even though our reality has fallen so far from that.

To Richard, on the phone, I muster all my reserves in an effort not to lose my temper, and I just say, 'Did you find the lasagne? Because you should eat. I'll be back later.' Then, before he can suck me further into his misery, I hang up and start the engine.

SUNDAY NIGHT

After the Concert

ZOE

Beside me, really peacefully, Grace falls asleep. I love her when she's asleep because she looks perfect: all that energy tucked away temporarily inside her silky smooth exterior, recuperating, so it can explode out of her when she wakes up later. Grace has such simple needs. Wake, give love, receive love, refuel, expend energy, sleep. I love that about her. Her energy is monumental though; she could power the Hadron Collider.

I want to stay on the bed with Grace, and sleep with her for the whole night. I've done that sometimes. If I've heard her wake up in the night before Mum or Chris do, I've gone in and taken her into the bed in her room with me. It gives my mum a break, and in the morning when Grace wakes I just get up with her before it disturbs Mum, and I change her and quickly make up the bed, because sleeping with her would be frowned on as 'deviating from the routine'. When I've done that I take her to Mum and go downstairs and start to get her bottle ready. Grace loves to go in Mum and Chris's bed. It must seem as big as a football pitch to her, and she spreads her arms and legs out and nuzzles her head down into their duvet and then looks up to see if anybody is laughing.

Once I heard Chris say to Mum, 'She's energetic, isn't she, for a girl?' as if he was a bit worried about that, but Mum said, 'They all are at that age, that's nothing to worry about.' I didn't hear the rest of the conversation because they kissed and I slipped away.

It would be a burning apocalypse, a red-rimmed sunset and the horsemen pounding so fast that they were almost on top of me before I watched those two snogging for longer than I had to, one of his hands all tight on her hips, puckering her silky pyjama bottoms, the fingers of the other running down to find the place where her buttock meets her thigh.

I might have just stayed there with Grace that night, and things could have gone somehow differently, but Lucas is in the doorway making the same dark shadow as his dad did earlier, and he says, 'Zoe, you need to come.'

I pick Grace up as carefully as I can. Her limbs are warm-heavy-floppy and I cradle her head on my arm, and then lay her carefully in her cot. For a moment it looks like she might wake up again, because she tenses when her back settles on to the mattress, but then she relaxes and her head falls to one side, and I pull the thin cotton sheet just up over her legs because I don't want her to get too hot. Her chest makes tiny rise and fall movements, which I can just see in the darkness and her lips are puckered as if she's expecting a kiss from a prince.

Lucas is waiting on the landing. He's noticed the butterfly, which is still flapping in the high corner, and its wings have reached a pitch that are as fast as the fastest trill I can play on the piano. I wonder how long it can go on.

'Can you save it?' I say to Lucas.

'It's too high up.'

'Why doesn't it fly to the light?'

'Only moths do that. Butterflies don't like artificial light.'

He reaches out to turn off the light switch and in the darkness the butterfly's wings hush, as if it feels relief.

I look at Lucas and smile, but he's looking at me in a really intense sort of a way, which isn't that unusual for him, but what he does next is.

He kisses me.

It's especially clumsy at first, because I'm so not expecting it. He puts his mouth over mine and kisses me like I've never been kissed before, not even by Jack Bell, because it's fearsome, super-hot kissing, like in films.

It only lasts a few seconds and then he pulls away from me and I don't know what to say.

'Zoe,' he whispers. 'I know about you. I've known for a long time, but my dad doesn't. We need to stay with him, and stay with your mum, we mustn't let them be alone, do you understand? They mustn't be alone. And listen, this is important, you need to get your mum to read my email.'

'But we're supposed to look after Grace,' I say.

'This is more important. Come on ...'

He starts to walk down the stairs, but then he turns and looks back up at me because I'm still standing at the top, understanding nothing.

'Come on.' He offers his hand to me, palm open and ready to be held.

'Why can't we leave them alone?' I ask him.

'Because.'

'Because what?'

I can't see the expression on his face so I don't know what

he's thinking in the few seconds before he answers. 'Dad can be mean sometimes.'

And I don't know what to say to that, so I take hold of his hand, and squeeze it a little, and follow him down the stairs.

We find Mum and Chris in the kitchen. They're standing with the island in between them. Chris has his hands on the granite as if he's about to try to lift it up. On the other side, Mum is stuffing hunks of white bread into the top of her food processor, which is whirring and rattling at top speed and pulverising the bread into fine crumbs.

My mum has been crying. Her mascara has smudged a bit around her eyes.

'I thought I told you to look after Grace,' Chris says to Lucas and me.

Obviously we're not holding hands any more. Lucas dropped my hand before we got to the kitchen door. We've got the usual six feet between us.

'She's asleep,' I say.

'Where is she?' Mum asks, fluttery-panicky, as if I'm stupid enough to leave Grace on the bed on her own.

'I put her in the cot. On her back. I put the sheet just on her legs.'

'Oh! She might be too hot like that. Where's the monitor?'

I fetch it. It's on the table outside, amidst the debris of the bruschetta, which hasn't been cleared up yet. I wipe a bit of tomato off it and turn the volume on. Grace is quiet. Inside, Mum takes the monitor from me. 'It's nineteen degrees in her room,' she says to Chris. 'Do you think a sheet is OK?' Grace's monitor tells you practically everything about her bedroom, although it does stop short of videoing her.

Chris hasn't moved. I've barely dared to meet his eye but I can see that he's moving his jaw a bit, clenching and unclenching it.

'I don't know why you're asking me, darling,' he says, and he sounds mean. 'Because, it seems you don't even respect me enough to be honest with me about who you and your daughter are.'

My mum detaches the lid from the blender very slowly and decants the breadcrumbs into a wide, shallow dish. She takes a very deep breath in, she practically inhales a reservoir of air, and then she lets it out through puffed cheeks. All the time, she's smoothing the breadcrumbs flat with the side of her hand, so they're ready for covering the chicken breasts.

'Here's what I suggest,' she says, 'I suggest that we sit down, with some food, and talk about this as a family. There is something that Zoe and I would like to explain to you both, but I would like to do it properly, the way we always do things.'

'Isn't it a bit late for that?' says Chris.

My mother straightens her back and walks to the fridge. She hefts open the dungeon-sized stainless-steel door, and takes out a box of twelve organic, free-range eggs. Her lip wobbles as she walks back to the island and when she gets there she raises the box of eggs high into the air and slams it down on to the island, hard.

'Only,' she says to Chris, facing him over the denuded basil plants, the egg box in front of her looking as if it's been crushed, oozing egg white and yolk in every direction, 'if you don't care about these two children, about that baby upstairs and about everything else that we have built up together. Only if you want our lives to end up like this!'

162

And she opens the lid of the box. The slimy, shattered carcasses of eight or nine eggs lie within it, and I have to look away because I don't like to see things all smashed up.

'Is that what you want?' she says to him. 'Is it? Is this what you want?'

She's scooping her hands into the egg now, dredging up bits of broken eggshell and showing them to him on fingers that are dripping with the slimy insides. It's disgusting. Some of it has fallen down the front of her silk shirt.

'Have you gone mad?' Chris asks her. 'Look at yourself. Have you gone totally stark raving mad?'

They face each other in silence, in a kind of still, mute combat.

Lucas steps forward and starts to take the egg box away, but just as he's got it in his hands Chris says, 'Leave them,' and Lucas does. He slides the box back on to the counter in front of my mother, and steps away, his movements as careful as if he were performing an operation.

My mother says, 'Mad? Is that what you think this is?'

The wrecking of the food isn't something that makes me think my mum has gone mad, because that's the kind of thing my parents used to do when they rowed, before the accident. Food got thrown, maybe a mug, there was shouting, then it was all over, all cleaned up, all settled back to normal, hugs on the sofa.

What's freaking me out now, apart from the obvious, which is that Chris is about to know all about me, is that Mum never behaves this way around Chris. Around Chris she's like the butterfly. When it's appropriate she sits, wings closed tight, demure and tidy, patient, twitching almost indiscernibly until the moment when he's ready for her to spread her wings and show how beautiful she is, and then she's gorgeous, admired. But only when he wants her to be. And that's it. She never, ever gets out of control. The Second Chance Family is not like that.

'Do you know what mad is?' my mum says. Now she's leaning forward with her hands on the granite, and she's fully facing up to Chris. The greasy lock of hair has fallen back over her forehead and the only kind of butterfly she looks like now would be an injured one, circling on the ground, wings shredded and useless, waiting for a foot to put it out of its misery.

'Mad is this! All of this!' She gesticulates theatrically, spreading her arms wide.

Chris looks at her, and then at us, and then at the used, empty wine glass in front of my mother on the granite, which narrowly escaped being knocked over by the egg box.

'You're drunk, Maria,' he says to her. 'It's not attractive.'

'I am NOT drunk,' she says.

Chris raises his eyebrows slightly. 'I think we both know that you are,' he says.

'Don't patronise me!'

'I'll take you upstairs,' he says. 'We'll talk about this in the morning.'

'No!' Lucas says, and that gets all of our attention. 'Where's Tessa?' he says. 'Isn't she having supper?'

Chris and Mum stare at Lucas for a moment as if they're only just remembering that he and I are here, then Mum says, 'Tessa popped out for a few minutes, but, yes, let's have our supper.' She runs her forearm over her forehead and then looks at her hands as if she can't understand why they're covered in gunk.

'Dad?' Lucas says to Chris, who's still staring at my mum.

'Out,' he says to me and Lucas. 'Out of this room. Now!'

And he bellows that in a way that makes my hands go up to my ears and makes me feel like the world has turned dark and I'll never be able to see again, and I open my mouth because the only thing I know to do now is to scream.

SUNDAY NIGHT

After the Concert

TESSA

When I get back to Maria and Chris's house I park on the street again and then I let myself back in, and the first thing I hear is a scream. It's long, and high-pitched, and it makes me hurtle down the stairs into the kitchen.

Zoe is screaming. She has her hands over her ears and her mouth open wide and she's screaming as if something's unbearable.

Maria stands at the island and says, 'Stop it, Zoe, stop it! Stop it! Will you stop it!' but it's not until I have Zoe wrapped tightly in my arms that she does stop and I feel her body go limp against mine. Lucas hovers beside us, anxious. Chris looks on aghast.

Something's gone wrong; that's obvious. I think Chris has confronted Maria. She looks awful: smudged eye make-up, a dirty shirt, red eyes, and there are eggs smashed on the counter.

'Come with me, honey,' I say to Zoe, and I usher her towards the door, and upstairs into the sitting room, which is decorated as if the family regularly entertain minor royalty, which, for all I know, they do. I sit her down and, although it's too hot for hugs, I keep my arms around her for all the long minutes that it takes for her body to stop shaking.

Zoe's a convicted killer. There are no two ways around that. Tom Barlow would probably qualify that further by saying that she is a murderer. But she's still my niece. She's the baby I visited within hours of her birth all those years ago, a scrumpled-up scrap of a thing, at that moment full of all the potential in the world. She's the toddler I took to the beach and made a sandcastle with, she's the girl I took to the zoo and helped to be brave when she wanted to feed the lorikeets but was afraid of the feel of them when they landed on her hand. She was the nine-year-old I cheered on when she made it to her first regional piano final in blinding style, making me swell with pride even though I'd bitten my fingernails to the quick.

She was the child I loved and thought about and took an interest in.

And so, in spite of what she's responsible for, I love her still. Zoe made a stupid mistake one night of her life, which has had the most terrible consequences. But I will always love her. Somebody has to.

I know Maria loves her too, but Maria is closer, obviously, and the fallout from Zoe's actions has fractured Maria's life before and might now fracture it again and that, however much you love somebody, is complicated. They are tied together too tightly for their love to be easy. But I think Zoe has a good heart. I believe her story about what happened all those years ago, on the night of the accident, and I want her to know that somebody loves her after the accident just the same way they did before it. I think she deserves that.

And so, as my body gets hotter, and damper, from the close

contact with hers, I wipe her tears gently as they fall, and I just hold her, and I whisper to her that I'll always be there for her, no matter what, and that I love her to bits, and when she's calmed down enough I encourage her to lie down and I slip back downstairs to see what's happening.

SUNDAY NIGHT

After the Concert

ZOE

When Aunt Tess has gone downstairs I'm alone in the sitting room once more and I think about everything, mostly about how I've stuffed things up again because you shouldn't just scream.

'Screaming might feel like an outlet to you,' said Jason, 'and of course it is in a way, but there are other ways we can channel feelings. We can leave the room, we can ask for a timeout, we can point out that what's being said is making us feel very uncomfortable or anxious rather than just displaying it. These are better strategies than screaming.'

'What about howling like a wolf?' I asked him.

Jason smiled but he didn't run with it, not that I thought he would, but I liked to try to make him smile.

'Let's talk about what you could do instead,' he said, and he started to try to teach me, yet again, how to be a functional human being.

It's funny, I thought I was one before I went to the Unit, but by the time they've counselled the hell out of you, you understand just how freaky you are.

The night I went to Jack Bell's party I didn't feel freaky,

I felt as though I was about to enter the realms of the Popular.

What happened in the bedroom with Jack is something that I've had to talk about a lot with Sam, my solicitor, and at the trial, but that was really all about alcohol levels and issues of (new word I had to learn) culpability.

I didn't ever get to remember that bit of the party as something that might have been nice for me.

When Jack came back to the bedroom at the party, he brought me a pint glass full of Coke, which I told him was overkill and that made him laugh.

Jack handed me the glass and I took a big long drink, swallowing and swallowing until I made bug eyes and the bubbles tingled my nose, just to make him laugh.

'You never do anything by halves, do you?' he said.

'Is that Diet Coke?' I asked him. 'It tastes funny.'

'What are you?' he said. 'Some kind of Coke connoisseur? Yeah it is, so it tastes different. Do you want me to get you another one?'

'No,' I said. 'It's fine. I like it.'

He sat very close to me, and he put his hand over mine, and pushed his fingers between mine.

'I've never heard you play piano,' he said. 'I should one day.'

I didn't really know what to say to that. Piano is, and always has been, a private thing for me, although it makes me a public person, and the sight of his fingers on mine suddenly brought to mind my mum's hand, placing my fingertips on the keys, pushing them down, in the days when her hands were much bigger than mine, when my hands were far too small to stretch to an octave.

Jack interpreted my silence as coyness, as flirtatiousness. 'Perhaps I'll come to a concert next time,' he said, 'sit in the front row …' He leaned towards me and ran his fingers from just under my ear all the way down my jawline to my chin. 'Or would that put you off?' he asked, and he leaned in even further then, and put his mouth on mine and his hand dropped to my chest.

I pushed him away a bit, because the intensity of the thrill was sort of frightening, and Jack was older than me and bigger than me.

'I heard you play like a demon,' he said. 'Like you're possessed or something.'

That made me laugh. 'I don't know about that,' I said, but inside I thought that maybe I did, sometimes, when I was really into the music. You don't really know how you look when you're playing well, because the concentrating and listening are everything.

It's a hard thing to explain to somebody without sounding weird, so I drank some more of my Coke to cover up how awkward I was feeling, and Jack's eyes were on me all the time, even when he downed his drink all in one go.

'What are you drinking?' I asked him.

'Cider. Do you want to try? I can get you some.'

I shook my head.

'It's good,' he said, and he took my Coke from me and put it on the bedside table, and put his drink beside it, and then he sort of climbed on top of me a bit and pushed me back on to the pillows, ever so gently, and he started to whisper something into my ear, words that you dream of, when there was a knock on the door.

'Shhh,' he said.

'Zoe?' It was Gull.

'I have to,' I said.

'Don't,' he told me, 'I want you.'

But I couldn't abandon Gull; it just wasn't something I could do. Jack saw it. He rolled away and on to his back with a grunt of irritation.

'Gull,' I said.

I went to the door. It was locked, although I hadn't noticed him do that, but the key was there so I opened it, to find her slumped against the wall.

'Where've you been?' she said. 'I couldn't find you anywhere.'

She looked disorientated and her voice was slurred.

'Sorry,' I said, as she leaned heavily on me. 'Gull? Are you OK?'

And she puked, all over the floor.

'Oh fuck!' said Jack. 'Get her to the bathroom.'

He kind of manhandled Gull down the corridor. I sat by her as she threw up, again and again, into the loo. Jack went to clear up the mess on the floor, and I realised quickly that I should have locked the door to the loo because before I knew it Eva Bell was standing in the doorway, shoulder to shoulder with best friend Amelia Barlow, and both of them were looking at us with absolute disdain.

'Should have stayed in the library, girls,' she said, 'if you can't take your drink.'

I heard once that Eva and her friends bought mixers to drink while they were getting ready for parties just in case there's not enough alcohol when they get there.

'Shut up,' I said, but my heart wasn't in it because Gull was puking so hard it was making her cry.

'My mum's going to kill me,' she said, and I gathered her hair up and held it back from her head.

'She doesn't have to know,' I said.

'I want to go home,' said Gull. She grabbed hold of me unsteadily. 'I need to go home. It's my birthday tomorrow.'

'What have you been drinking?' I asked her. I didn't tell her it was so late that it was already her birthday, because that probably would have made her more upset.

'Somebody spiked my drink. I swear, somebody spiked it.'

We had cycled to the party, sharing Gull's bike. It was four miles, mostly downhill. The plan had been to walk home with the bike but I could see that that wasn't going to happen. Gull was pulling herself up on me now and I didn't think she could even manage to walk.

Jack said, 'I can drive you home.' He was looking a little nervous now, as if vomit and neediness weren't on his agenda tonight.

Amy was right beside him, hanging off him a bit like Gull was off me only her body was pressed against his, and when he said this her eyes and Eva's shot lasers at me. Amy was not very drunk, or if she was, she was holding it well.

'How much have you had?' she asked Jack. 'Why don't you let them walk home? She lives nearby, doesn't she?'

Amy was right. Gull's family had a small, modern home in Hartland where the washing-up was never done and even the dogs didn't bother licking the grease off the floor. Her mum and dad were the warmest people you could meet, it's just they didn't care about that kind of stuff. They cared about

Gull. Every penny they had, every ounce of love and effort, went to her.

'She runs like the wind, our girl,' her dad would say, 'like the wind,' and my dad would mutter, 'He used to run like the wind too, Gull's got it from her dad.'

Gull's real name was Linda, but her parents, surprised by a baby when they'd given up hope of having one, began to call her Gull when, as her dad said, 'She squawked like a gull at all hours, what else were we supposed to call her?' 'We used to laugh,' he said, 'she squawked so loud. You'd have thought we was throttling her, not getting her a meal and cleaning her ladyship up.'

Gull didn't like people to know where she lived, because of being a scholarship girl like me. We didn't live in big houses like Jack and Eva Bell and Amy Barlow and the other kids at our school. We lived in normal houses where there was mud, and stuff was old, and animals lay beside fires and there was single glazing.

'She can't stay here,' Jack said. 'My parents are coming home first thing in the morning.'

'I'm not drunk,' I said. 'If I can borrow a car I can drive her home.'

'You can't drive,' Amy said.

'My dad taught me how.'

Jack had a look in his eyes suddenly. 'We could drop Gull home and then go to the lighthouse,' he said, 'have you ever done that?'

'No,' I said, but I was suddenly seduced by the glint in his eye, and I said, 'but I'd like to.'

Amy said, 'That's a stupid idea, Jack. Let her drive Gull

174

home and bring the car back. Then she can go home on the bike.'

Jack ignored her. 'It's very cool,' he said. 'You can climb up to the top. I know a way. We could take my dad's car.'

And I got this incredible idea of the lighthouse, with its strong beam of light raking the waves below, and I heard powerful music in my head, classical music, rising like the spray on the rocks. I knew there was a shipwreck there too, which you could see when the tide was low, basking on the stony shore like rusted orange skeleton bones abandoned after a violent death.

'You should go with them, Ames,' slurred Eva. She was drunk, definitely. 'Make sure Jack doesn't cop off with piano girl. He's pissed enough he just might.'

'Shut up,' said Jack.

A boy called Douglas appeared behind Eva and slipped his hands around her waist and buried his head in the back of her neck.

'You coming too then, Eva?' Amy said to her.

'Somebody needs to hold the fort,' she said, 'if Jack goes off. You go, make sure he behaves himself.'

She turned to Douglas, and her body seemed to slide up his and they kissed so long and hard that I was totally embarrassed, and in that moment it seemed that it had been decided that I would drive Gull home.

And I remember finishing my drink while me and Gull sat on the bed waiting for Jack to find the car keys, one arm around her and the other holding that pint glass of Coke. And I remember Amy glowering as if she would rather be anywhere else but with us, but didn't know what else to do.

And I remember helping Gull to the car, and helping her in, and then getting into the car myself and starting the ignition, and I remember how it felt powerful and smooth, quite unlike the truck I'd driven on the farm.

But I shut down the memories there, because this is the bit where it gets painful for me.

I think about how I'm in the sitting room on my own, again, and I wonder if I should go downstairs and apologise for screaming like I did, because 'apologies are always good and always necessary', but I think my mum might want me to stay away so she can keep things smooth.

Lucas lingers in my mind: the kiss, the fact that he knows. How does he know? I wonder. Why hasn't he said? His request that I read his email comes back into my mind. I remember where my phone is, and I dig down under the sofa cushions and find it.

MONDAY MORNING

SAM

The choice that I gave to Mr and Mrs Guerin and Zoe, when we met to discuss her case on that freezing cold morning in Bideford, was a difficult one.

Zoe could go to her initial hearing at court, and plead guilty. The court would look favourably on this, as it avoided a costly trial, and was an admission of culpability. It would probably keep her sentence to a minimum, though she was unlikely to avoid something custodial.

Or, Zoe could turn up at her initial hearing and make a 'Special Reasons' plea. She would have to admit that she drove the car, and caused the accident, but could ask a judge to decide whether she was guilty of knowingly driving when drunk. If you accepted Zoe's explanation, it would appear that somebody spiked her drink at the party, most likely the boy she was with, Jack Bell, who was also one of the victims. We would have to prove that in court though, and that would be a tough call, especially as three of the key witnesses were dead.

'Well, we'll do that then,' says Mr Guerin when he heard this option. 'That's a plan then.'

People who are in the system for the first time are always tempted to mount a defence, because it feels like a chink of light, a way of minimising the damage they've done, the guilt they feel, and the harm to their reputation and that of their family.

Maria could see pitfalls: 'Well, wait a minute, what if they don't believe her?'

'It's the truth, isn't it?' her husband said.

Maria didn't speak; she was waiting for my reply.

'If the court doesn't accept that defence, then Zoe risks a tougher sentence than she might have got if she pleaded guilty.'

'But it's not on her conscience then, is it?' said Mr Guerin. 'If she pleads guilty it's like telling the world that our daughter accepts that she murdered those children. Murdered them, Maria.'

Zoe was shrinking into her chair.

Maria ignored him. 'It's a gamble, then.' She directed this at me.

'It would be a gamble, yes.'

'Would she have a chance of getting less of a sentence if the judge accepts the plea, than if she pleaded guilty in the first place?'

'I doubt it, no.'

'But we wouldn't have it on our conscience,' said Maria. 'It would be a similar sentence but it would be proven that she didn't know she was drunk, that it was just a normal accident.'

In my view, this is what you call clutching at straws, but this family was obviously trying to clutch at anything.

Mr Guerin was on his feet now, standing at the window of my office, which had a view of the waterside, where the tide was low that morning, leaving the boats mostly stranded on the mud. A low, immovable grey sky waited patiently above the scene while this family considered their options, and it dulled and flattened the landscape across the harbour. Below it, seagulls hovered and circled, just as they did every day.

Mr Guerin had his back to us but when he spoke his voice was firm, and it was clear that he'd made a mental U-turn.

'It's not worth the risk,' he said. 'What if they don't believe her?'

'I'll tell them the truth,' said Zoe.

'You've killed people, Zoe,' he said. 'Who's going to believe you?'

Quite apart from the hopeless resignation in his tone, and the effect it had on his daughter, this statement got to me because Philip Guerin was exactly the kind of man who was likely to be on a jury in this part of the world, and while I knew that there would be no jury in a youth court, where Zoe would be tried, it was an attitude that could well be shared by the magistrates, or judge.

'They'll believe her.' Maria was suddenly adamant. 'We can coach her. They'll feel sorry for her, she'll be a good witness, and perhaps we can get some of the other children in the witness box.'

'No,' said Mr Guerin. 'I'm fed up with you coaching her. You've coached her enough, Maria. We wouldn't be in this mess if you hadn't coached her so she got a music scholarship. She'd be at the local school, which was good enough for me by the way, but not good enough for your daughter. If she'd gone there none of this would have happened. It's going to that jumped-up school and trying to keep up with the kids there, that's why this has happened. No. I won't do it. She should plead guilty, and take the consequences for what she's done, pay for it, and then perhaps we can get some forgiveness one day.'

'I don't agree,' said Maria. 'Think of Zoe. Think of us!'

'I am thinking of her. And of the other families. I grew up with Matt.' His voice choked. I recognised the name of Zoe's friend Gull's dad.

'I know you did,' Maria said.

'I won't put him and Sue through a trial.'

'We have to give Zoe a chance to clear her name.'

'No! Gull was their only child, you know that.'

'I'm not willing to jeopardise Zoe's future to save the feelings of the other families.'

'Sometimes, Maria, you have a hard heart,' said her husband. 'What future does Zoe have now anyway?'

I wanted to jump in and defend Zoe, but Maria was on her feet now too, and both of them were seemingly oblivious to Zoe.

'How is it having a hard heart to protect your daughter?' Maria spoke quietly but with a vehemence that was startling.

'And what if it doesn't protect her? What if it goes wrong and she goes to jail for longer than she would have if she pleaded guilty?'

They were facing each other across the table, although it was hard to see Mr Guerin's expression because his back was to the window now.

'Zoe,' I said, because it was definitely time for me to calm things down and I wanted to remind these two adults that their child was listening to them. 'Do you understand what the decision is here?'

'I don't want to go to prison, but I don't want to make it worse for the families,' she said. 'I'll say I'm guilty.'

As there was a sharp intake of breath from Maria, Mr Guerin came around the table and put his hands on the back of Zoe's shoulders. He had huge, red, dry, calloused hands, and they made Zoe look smaller and more fragile than ever.

'Well done, girl,' he said.

But I looked at Maria, and at Zoe, who watched her mother anxiously, and I didn't think this decision was made yet.

SUNDAY NIGHT

After the Concert

TESSA

When I get back downstairs, there's nobody in the kitchen. On the island, the box of smashed eggs lies untouched, and the mess from it drips silently off the side of the granite down on to the golden stone floor.

I go outside. Lucas and his father are standing at one end of the swimming pool, their faces washed blue and yellow by the lights, and at the other end of it, sitting on the end of the squat diving board, is my sister, the tips of her toes in the water.

Maria's breakdown after the accident was a slow burn. It began when Zoe was sentenced, and taken to the Unit, which was when Maria stopped having a purpose, and when the adrenalin that had taken her through the trial, and the months leading up to it, crashed. She'd been closely involved in every detail up to then, liaising with Sam, and with the rest of Zoe's legal team, discussing defence strategies. Adrenalin fuelled her. She lost weight, she more or less lost her husband because they disagreed so strongly, and still she focused only on the case. She continued to be a tiger mother.

But the minute that Zoe was taken down, Maria ceased to cope, because suddenly there was nothing to do. There was just an empty farmhouse, a husband who slept in another room, and a silence that sat with them, twiddling its fingers, looking from one of them to the other, whenever they were in a room together.

'Philip couldn't bear it,' Maria told me. 'It shamed him. He felt he'd failed her, failed at making a family.'

I think she was right. Philip Guerin had been a doting father, while the going was good, but nothing in his life had prepared him for what Zoe did, and while Maria became a dynamo, he retreated, shut himself down. Perhaps it was because he, like the families whose children died, had been rooted in that community for decades. Perhaps that meant he felt the loss of those three young folk more than Maria did. Perhaps it was because he was weaker than she was. Whatever the reason, it was shocking, his inability to cope. He didn't even protest when Maria moved out, and came to Bristol, to be near me, to make that fresh start with Zoe.

In the dense night air, on the end of the diving board, Maria has pulled her skirt up around her thighs. Her shoes have been discarded and lie poolside, one on its side. Her legs are bare, and thin. Her toenails are painted a deep black-red.

When she sees me, she calls out to me, in a voice that I barely recognise, so strained is it.

'So,' she says. 'I've told my husband what happened to Zoe, his stepdaughter. I've told him that Zoe has been convicted of a crime, and do you know what, Tess: I think he's going to dump us.'

Chris turns to me.

'She's drunk,' he says. 'She's totally lost her mind. I can't get any sense out of her.'

I start to walk around the edge of the pool and Maria struggles to her feet. I can't quite understand how Maria could have got so drunk so quickly, because I reckon I've only been out of the house for about forty-five minutes, an hour tops. Though perhaps, as she says, she isn't.

'Don't come near me!' she shouts. 'Nobody come near me!'

I almost laugh at that because the diving board is not high and the tone in which she says it makes it sound like a threat, as if she were teetering on the edge of the Clifton Suspension Bridge, hundreds of feet above the Avon Gorge. But I don't laugh because Maria looks like a broken puppet, and Chris looks desperate, and I don't want to do anything other than help them to get through this evening, in the hope that once they do, they'll find that they still have a future together.

'Maria,' I say.

She staggers to her feet, skirt tight around her thighs, making her wobble. 'Don't come near me!' she repeats.

So I stop, halfway around the pool. I wonder if in fact Chris is mistaking instability for drunkenness, if the real explanation is that years of ghastliness have just reached their peak, and now threaten to topple her sanity. When she got pregnant with Grace, I did worry about her, that she might not cope with the pressures of starting all over again, but she seemed to sail through that, just as she'd sailed into her new role as Mrs Christopher Kennedy, mother to Zoe, stepmother to Lucas, and now I'm wondering whether that was a plaster, masking wounds that I know run very deep.

Chris says, 'Maria, come off there, please. Let's talk; let's eat. Like you wanted to.'

'No,' she says. 'Because the eggs are broken, so I can't get the breadcrumbs on the meat.' She sounds pathetic now. She looks at me. 'I'm sorry, Tessa,' she says.

'It's fine,' I say. 'Of course it is. Don't be silly.'

Teetering now on the end of the board, Maria has noticed the stain on her shirt and she starts to rub at it, and when that doesn't work, she begins to unbutton it.

'For Christ's sake, Maria!' Chris's voice explodes around the pool. 'What are you doing?'

Lucas turns his head away because before we know it she's pulled the shirt off and is standing there in just her skirt and bra, a complicated, lacy bit of apparatus which holds her breasts firm and pert. Her body is perfectly taut. I think that her bra probably cost more than my entire outfit.

'Oh, I'm so sorry!' she shouts at him. 'I'm so sorry that I'm not perfect.'

Chris marches around the pool towards her.

'What are you doing?' she calls and she's taunting him. 'Coming to tell me off? Coming to tell me to behave like a good girl? Coming to tell me I'm useless?'

He pauses at the end of the diving board, unsure what to do.

'Maria!' I call. 'For God's sake!'

And Maria, in a gesture that's at once melodramatic and extraordinary, turns around, pinches her nose and lets herself fall back into the pool, and, for a moment or two, we all just watch the splash subside, and see that she's sunk to the bottom, where she floats for a second or two, eyes shut.

It's Lucas who gets her out. He jumps in fully clothed and pulls her up to the surface, and they both swim together to the side, where he helps her up the steps, and she's gasping and coughing, but by the time they're both out Chris has gone indoors. Turned, and walked away, as if he's too disgusted to deal with her at all.

I take her sobbing, wet body from Lucas and send him inside to change, partly because he needs dry clothes, but also because I've got to strip her out of her sodden skirt and I don't wish her humiliation to be any worse.

I hold her, just as I held Zoe minutes earlier, and I'm persuading her to try to get out of her wet clothing when Chris reappears. He has a large towel with him, and a change of clothes for her. He holds the towel open and Maria looks at it for a moment before walking slowly towards him and letting him envelop her with it.

He wraps the towel around her and holds her tight in his arms. The water from her soaking skirt still swarms down her legs in rivulets. She's shivering.

'Maria,' he says. 'My Maria. Come on. Let's get you in the shower.'

She looks up into his face and nods. 'I'm sorry,' she says, 'I don't know what came over me.'

'Let's talk about it,' he says. She shuts her eyes and leans against him.

'I think it's probably best if you go home now,' he says to me. 'We're all right. We'll be OK.'

'Are you sure?' I say. I want to get Maria's agreement but she's huddled into him, shaking, seeking the warmth from his body, because the air around us is beginning to lightly shift and buffet.

'I'll look after her,' he says. 'Are you OK with that, honey? If Tess goes?'

He puts a finger under Maria's chin and lifts it gently and she looks up at him and nods. Her smile is hopeful but precarious, threatening to break into pieces like the paper napkin that's fallen into the pool, and floats there, slowly disintegrating into many different pieces in the softly eddying water.

SUNDAY NIGHT

After the Concert

ZOE

When I get my phone out, I see that panop has notified me again. It says:

> How could you think you could keep it a secret?
> I've known all along.

And I understand suddenly that it has to be Lucas sending me the messages, because who else could it be? It's Lucas and he's known for a long time like he said, and he's kept that totally secret from me. And in a way that's a relief because it's not somebody from back then, but it's frightening too.

I'm confident enough that I'm right to send a message back:

> How do you know?

I want to know how he found out and I want to know what it means to him, because I didn't get the chance to ask him. I want to know why he kissed me. Was it real? Or did he just want to find out how it feels to kiss a killer. Lots of teenagers get off on that kind of stuff actually, and although I don't think Lucas is that kind of boy, you can never be really sure about anybody.

I also want to know why he's using panop to contact me, because that's horribly, awfully freaky, but Lucas is a super tech computer person so I suppose it's not that surprising that he's found out about me. I close panop, because I'm still curious to have another look at Lucas's email I open my inbox and I find it, but I can't read the attachment straight away because for some reason I have to download it again as my phone is always such a fail and needs upgrading.

While I wait I try to control my breathing, which has become fast and shallow. To distract myself, I scroll around my phone, and I see that his email is surrounded by about twenty other unread emails, none of them personal.

The only one that interests me is a Facebook notification, where I can see what Katya is doing. When she first arrived, Katya was really friendly to me, like a cat rubbing up against your legs, and she wanted us to be friends on Facebook; that was before she worked out that I was Social Pond Life and had no proper friends, either online, or in real life. What being her Facebook friend means is that I can see when she changes her profile picture, and in fact she's just done that. She's just changed it from the vampy Kardashian pout that she put up last week and now it's a picture of her and Barney Scott together, all nostrils and foreheads and sunglasses, all teeth and chins and my heart kind of sinks because they look sexy and funny and cool like teenagers are supposed to look.

There are no photos of me online from the trial because the press weren't allowed to report my name or publish photos of me, which was a saving grace, as my mum said at the time.

The only photos of me online now are from a stupid website that my mum runs to manage my profile. In those photos, I'm always groomed and wearing a concert outfit. I'm never drunk, or stoned, or sexy, or funny or wearing sunglasses. My tongue doesn't loll out rudely like a pop star. The only prop I have in any of my online photos is a shiny silver trophy, which my mum will soon be snatching from my hands so that she can take it away and get my name engraved on it, for perpetuity, just like my criminal record.

I can hear somebody coming. Chris takes the stairs up from the basement two at a time, passes the sitting room door, and continues up to the first floor. 'Sshh,' I want to say, 'don't wake the baby,' but I would never dare. That phrase is in my head because it's what he and Mum say all the time to me and Lucas, and once somebody has said something one thousand times it's in your head for ever. I just let my mouth form the words silently instead. He reappears again quite quickly, holding bundles of things, heading back down. He doesn't look at me, he doesn't know I'm watching and I wonder what's happening.

I think it's best if I stay away from downstairs, though, because I'm messing everything up tonight. So I close the Facebook email and go back to the one from Lucas.

The attachment is downloading so slowly, which is incredibly annoying. I think about the title of it, and it makes my heart start to beat a little faster because now I wonder what 'What I Know' is referring to, and if the script is going to be about our life now, after it's talked about his mum, and if it will tell me how Lucas knows about me. I kind of take a mental deep breath because I'm always wary now of people turning on me and I wonder if Lucas is about to. People can, even if they've kissed you, even if they've kissed you deeply.

'It's complicated that,' Jason told me once when we were talking about what happened with Jack Bell, 'because you'd be surprised how easily people can mix up feelings of love and hate. You wouldn't think they can, but they do, and it's because they're both strong and sometimes frightening emotions.'

I had to agree with that, because although I've never told anybody about it, I fully remember what happened in the car right before we crashed, right before they died.

We argued. I was driving super slowly, and I mean super slowly because it was icy out and I was still struggling to handle the car. In the rear-view mirror I could see Gull's head lolling and Jack said, 'Come on! Let's go to the lighthouse now – all of us – you can look after her, Ames – you won't mind, will you?'

'No,' I said, 'I think I need to get Gull home.'

I felt odd then suddenly, queasy and dizzy, and the road ahead seemed to have a life of its own like a ribbon twisting in the wind. I blinked and it steadied. Ahead in the lights I could see frost-tipped hedges and I knew that around the corner, just after the junction to the lighthouse, was the lane where Gull's parents' house could be found.

I clasped the wheel carefully, hands at ten to two, and in the back Amy said, 'For God's sake, Zoe, you're driving like such a girl.'

'She is a girl,' said Jack. 'She's doing fine,' but then he leaned over to me and whispered in my ear, 'Though you could probably speed up a little bit.'

He turned on the car stereo and cranked up the volume until it was blasting out. '"Highway to Hell", ACDC,' he said and he gave me a massive grin, which I just loved. As the music pumped around the car I put my foot down a little. Jack peered into the back seat. 'Gull's asleep,' he said. 'Come on, let's just go to the lighthouse.

'No, no,' I said. 'We should take her home. Actually, I don't feel so good myself.' In fact I felt disorientated and strange and uncertain, because suddenly the hedges we were driving between somehow didn't look familiar and I wasn't sure where I was.

'Oh relax,' said Jack. He was thumping the tops of his legs in time to the music. 'You won't believe how awesome it is at the lighthouse, honestly, I'm telling you.'

Amy said, 'What are you planning to do with her there anyway, Jack? She's just a pathetic little slut you know.'

I heard that loud and clear and I turned around for just a second to say something to her, to tell her that her comment proved that she was the bitch who was sending me the panop messages, but as I did Jack said, 'Zoe! You're missing the turn,' and I looked back round at the road to see the turn to the lighthouse but as I did I hit the accelerator by mistake and the car surged forward just as Jack reached out to turn the wheel away from Gull's house and down the lane which led to the lighthouse, and it was only a millisecond before there were no memories any more because there was only blackness, until I woke up to hear somebody phoning for an ambulance, and then the rest of my life started.

I remember all this like a slow motion film as I'm watching

the attachment trying to download, achingly slowly, like death by volcanic ash burial, when Tessa comes upstairs.

'Hey,' she says. 'Mum slipped into the pool. She's fine, but we're not going to do dinner because it's getting a bit late, so I'm off home.'

'Did she go for a swim?'

'No, it was more of an accident.'

My mum is clumsy like me but I think that this really takes the biscuit, as Jason would say.

'Do you have to go?' I ask.

I don't want her to go. I really don't. Aunt Tessa is sort of my best friend these days, and it's like she can read my mind because she says, 'Do you want to come and stay the night with me?'

And I do, I really, really so badly do, but I know that Mum might need me here and I don't want her to be alone if there's going to be an argument or 'a talk', so I say, 'I'm fine. I'd better stay.'

She hugs me again, warm and lovely, and pats my back while she's hugging me in the way that she's always done. I feel a tear slip down my cheek. Just one.

'I'll call you in the morning,' she says. 'Be strong, Butterfly, you've nothing to feel bad about. Nothing. Remember that. You've paid for what you did and you have a right to a life.'

I stand behind one of the heavy drapes and watch from the front window as she crunches down the drive. She turns once to look back at the house before she disappears from sight.

MONDAY MORNING

SAM

Zoe did not plead Guilty. Against her father's wishes, and guided by her mother, she pleaded Not Guilty and went for the Special Reasons defence instead. It was an unusual defence – I had repeatedly warned the whole family of that – but, at first, it seemed that we might be successful.

Zoe went into the stand and presented herself fairly well when speaking about the events that had taken place that night. She showed that she had terrible regrets, and she admitted her guilt by accepting that she had been the driver, but assured the judge that she wasn't knowingly drunk. She agreed that she'd had a drink when she arrived at the party, a spritzer, but insisted that she'd asked only for Coca-Cola after that, and repeated her conviction that her drink must have therefore been spiked.

It wasn't until Eva Bell, Jack Bell's twin sister, and a witness for the Crown, took the stand that any chance of success we might have had was ruined.

The Crown called Eva Bell to give evidence that Zoe knowingly drank an excessive amount of alcohol, and Eva couldn't have been a more successful witness.

There were a minimum of people in the courtroom, because of Zoe's age, and we'd been there for a week already hearing testimony from experts about the site of the accident, the condition of the car and blood alcohol levels, so some of the tension had left the proceedings to be replaced by boredom. The walls of the courtroom were clad in wooden strips and there was no natural light so it felt a bit as though we'd all been buried underground for a week. Zoe had agreed to her mother attending but didn't want her father to be there, because she was embarrassed that she'd ignored his preference for an early Guilty plea. If she'd done what he wanted, there would have been no trial.

Eva Bell arrived with her own mother. They were ushered into the court from a separate waiting area to Zoe and her mother, a service the court provided to minimise ugly scenes. They sat alone on a bench across the aisle from the prosecutor.

In contrast to how Zoe had described her, which was as some kind of tormentor, Eva Bell presented as demure, intelligent and, most of all, incredibly sad. Her mother sobbed audibly as she gave evidence, and Eva did not once look at Zoe.

It didn't help us that the prosecutor was a woman who you'd like to make godmother to your children. She led Eva down a gentle path of questioning that was devastating to us.

'Were you with your brother Jack when he got a drink for Zoe?'

'Yes, I was.'

'In your view did Jack add anything to the drink that was alcoholic?'

'I poured the drink myself, so I know he didn't.'

'Did you pour the drink from a bottle?'

'Yes, but I had to open it.'

'So you don't think the drink was spiked?'

'No. I saw him carry it to the room they were in. If he spiked it, he would have had to do it in front of her.'

I saw the panic on Zoe's face during this testimony and I willed her to stay calm, because of course the story that she'd told the court directly contradicted this.

'And did you see Zoe taking a drink earlier in the evening?'

'Yes.'

'And what did she drink?'

A tiny stumble in Eva's composure here, but it could easily be read as grief by the judge.

'She drank,' Eva said, 'vodka and coke.'

'Did you make that for her?'

'No. She made it herself. And she was generous with the vodka.'

'And did you see her refill her glass?'

She pursed her lips, before replying, 'Yes, yes I did,' and Maria's gasp was audible throughout the entire courtroom.

And the prosecution hadn't finished there. Another girl, a friend of Eva and Amelia, testified to the same thing and there was nothing we could do to contradict it. It was their word against Zoe's, and they were in the majority.

SUNDAY NIGHT

After the Concert

TESSA

As I drive away from Chris and Maria's house, I feel absolutely wrung out. It's eleven o'clock at night and I need my bed. I send a text to Sam, who I hope isn't waiting up for me, to say that I won't be coming round because I need to go home and sleep. We didn't have any sort of definite arrangement, but he knew I went to the concert alone, and that I might have an opportunity to visit him afterwards, so I feel I owe him the courtesy of letting him know at least.

I always feel guilty when I see Sam, and that's never easy, but I don't seem to be able to stop myself going back to him, because, although I love Richard, I'm tired of his joyless existence.

We've tried everything to lift Richard's spirits: a chemical cosh, a course of therapy, a holiday, hobbies, a different diet, exercise, and more. And we've tried all kinds of different combinations of the above, but, in the end, none of them have worked.

Richard's black dog is his constant companion, and he leavens the intensity of their relationship with alcohol. If I have a role in his life any more, it's to make sure that while he's in the teeth of the dog, the rest of his life doesn't disappear. I do this because I hope that his depression will lift one day. If it never does, I've made a very bad call. His addiction will have got the better of me. It's ironic, really, as it's my life's work to cure and to rehabilitate.

It means that I dread going home. I dread it every day. I dread the monotony of his despair and the way that he can leach the colours from everything. I dread his inability to enjoy even a hot cup of tea or the smell of a freshly plucked mint leaf. I sympathise with his feelings, because I understand depression, or at least I think I do, but I dread it too, with every cell of my body.

It was why I was extremely happy for Maria when she met Chris. She was in the teeth of the black dog too up until then, put there by Zoe and by the shock of the loss of their world on the farm in Devon. You don't think of farming families imploding, or I never did. There's something about the continuity of their way of life that makes it seem, from the outside, more stable than the choices the rest of us have made. But clearly, I was wrong. So when Maria met Chris, and things between them developed, I was glad for her, and I was glad for Zoe; in fact, I was unbelievably relieved.

Richard hasn't found that thing which will allow a slice of light to pierce the darkness in his head yet, and if I'm honest I'm not sure why the darkness ever fell so completely. He had disappointment at work, for sure. He was passed over for a prestigious appointment, which should have been his, because he was never good at playing the politics in his department, but others have survived that kind of thing without succumbing to such a complete breakdown.

I sometimes wonder whether our childlessness has deprived

him of what might have been a source of happiness. Would the Richard who worked so enthusiastically in his department, who loved to travel, who decorated our house, and so carefully planted up our garden in the early years, and dreamed of blooms and sunshine in the summer, have been saved by becoming a father? Would that have made the difference? Or would I have spent my time explaining to our confused offspring why Daddy wasn't getting out of bed today, or hadn't smiled even though it was Christmas.

I'll never know; it's just something I wonder about when I'm looking for reasons. Alone, I'm not enough to anchor Richard in the present, and so of course I wonder if a family would have been.

So many 'what if's. It's something that must roll around Zoe's head too. What if I hadn't got in the car that night? What if I hadn't gone to the party? When Zoe was in the legal process, surrounded by lawyers and court papers, and police reports, the thing that got to me was how her case bowed every head. Sam would talk about that too. How the police handled her with kid gloves, how everybody around her was sunk by the misfortune of her situation.

Maria would have felt the 'what if' factor then too. What if I hadn't tried to save face? What if I'd let her plead guilty in the first instance? What if …

I park in the driveway of my house and, when I let myself in, I find that it's completely quiet, though a light glows from the landing upstairs.

Richard is in our bed, on his back. He's asleep and his snoring is loud and persistent. The bedroom is clear of bottles, but I find one stuffed into the poky dark area at the bottom of his cupboard. The neck of the bottle is still damp and smells of fresh wine. My heart sinks because it probably means he stashed it there before passing out on the bed, and that probably means that his bladder is full but he'll be too drunk to feel it. I sigh because it means I'm going to have to wake him.

I spend a good ten minutes shaking him into a state resembling consciousness so that I can persuade him to pee. He manages it, unsteadily, lurching along the landing like the drunk he is, words slurring and sliding out of his mouth, as clumsy as his physical movements. When he's done, he passes out on the bed again, exactly the same as before, and I'm left with aching arms and a pounding heart from supporting him down the corridor, from talking him through what he's got to do, and from dodging the amorous advances that he always makes when he's this far gone, but which we both know won't amount to anything once he's horizontal again.

Down in the kitchen I clear up the mess he's made heating and eating the lasagne and I lock the back door, which he's left wide open to the stifling night air.

Then I sit at the kitchen table, now scrubbed as clean as my surgery at work, and think about the conversation that he and I will have in the morning, an old conversation, where we both know our lines off by heart. It's a conversation about going to rehab, and how I want him to, and how he doesn't feel it's necessary because he feels he can get better on his own, and when I think of that, and of Tom Barlow, and all the things Maria will be having to explain to Chris tonight, weariness and loneliness saturate me and make me cry, just for a moment or two. And suddenly I crave company, not sleep, so I do what I shouldn't: I try to phone Sam.

SUNDAY NIGHT

After the Concert

ZOE

A short time after Tessa has gone, Lucas comes into the sitting room where I'm lying with my phone watching his PDF fail to download quickly. He tells me that we're all going to talk in Chris's study. He's changed his clothes and his hair is wet.

I start to say to him, *How do you know about me?*, but he puts a finger to his lips.

He holds out a hand to pull me up and I get a frisson of electricity when I touch it. I wonder if this means he's my friend, or my boyfriend, or neither, but I don't dare ask him and now isn't the moment anyway.

When I was in the Unit I made friends with people who I can't tell my mum about; actually, I can't tell anybody in the Second Chance Family. In the Unit, I sometimes felt like it was easier to make friends than at school. You have crime in common, after all, and I know that sounds stupid, and it doesn't make things easy always, but it does 'level the playing field', as Jason the Key Worker used to say.

My friends in the Unit were Connor (breaking and entering, repeatedly) and Ellie (common assault, three strikes and you're out). They were what Jason called 'Revolving Door Cases'.

'You're categorically *not* a Revolving Door Case, Zoe,' he said. 'Cat-e-gor-i-cal-ly not.' He pronounced each syllable separately to make his point. Jason didn't have much apart from verbal tricks to make his points. And laser eye contact. No PowerPoint presentations for him. Just me and him, in a room with a barred window to the outside, and a reinforced sheet of glass in the door, and a table and two chairs, which were bolted to the floor.

I would be wearing my lovely Unit attire of green tracksuit bottoms and top and Jason would be in jeans and a T-shirt. Unless it was winter, when a little line of snow rimmed even the barbed wire coils outside, until a sharp wind dispatched it into soft whorls, and then blew it into every crack and crevice in the building. Then Jason might wear a short-sleeved jumper over his T-shirt which, if I'm honest, made him look like a sad nineties pop star having a quiet night in.

'Put the f*****g heating on,' shouted Ellie from her cell, all night for the first night when it was got cold. 'Turn up the f*****g heat you f*****g c***s I'm freezing my f*****g tits off in here.' Her language was so bad it fully made me blush.

She banged her door too that night, an ear-splitting rhythmic pounding with a metallic edge that made me press my hands down hard on to my ears. You could make a good racket if you banged the door with a tin cup. The next day we got extra blankets, which had 'HMP Dartmoor' printed on them and were thin and grey and made me wonder who had slept under them before, and whether they were Revolving Door Cases who'd revolved all the way into an adult centre. You only have to be eighteen to go into an adult prison.

The reason I wasn't a Revolving Door Case, according to

Jason, was because of my family, which meant that I had a chance when I got out. My mum, he said, was determined to make a fresh start for me, determined to help me. I also had a talent, he said, with my music, my mum had told him all about it, and they had agreed that they couldn't think of any better way to rehabilitate me. Revolving Door Cases had no chance. They would go back into lives of abuse, and deprivation and neglect, and they would be reoffending and back in court before they knew it, their families watching dully, looking drowned by the inevitability of it all, if they bothered to turn up at all.

Lucas's PDF still hasn't downloaded by the time we all troop into Chris's study. It's on sixty-five per cent with five minutes remaining. I'm thinking that because Chris's study is where our WiFi hub is, that it might download a bit quicker once we're in there, but I forget all about that as soon as we get into the room.

It's not a room I normally go into. It's Chris's sanctuary; it's where he talks to Lucas when they need to 'chat'. Lucas never looks happy when he's going in there. My mum goes in there sometimes, but usually only when she's bearing a gift of some sort for Chris: a cup of tea, or coffee, or a Tom Collins if it's after six o'clock. I've been in once or twice and when I do I usually look at the frame that's on the wall behind Chris's desk. It's a black frame, about 12 inches square, and in the middle of it, mounted on a black background, is a single computer chip. Chris invented it and it's the reason he's minted. Chris was like Midas when he made that chip; it made everything turn to gold.

Not that you'd think that from the look of his study, because it's really plain. My mum always wants to decorate it, and sometimes she brings swatches of things home: new fabrics for Chris's sofa, or for curtains, but he always refuses. The sofa he keeps in there is one that he had in his office at work when he invented the chip back in the day. He says he's 'not a sentimental man' but he 'can't let go of that sofa'. It's a lucky sofa for him.

I get that, because I have a lucky hair ribbon that I wore at my first piano competition. I don't wear it any more because my image has moved on, but I always have a little feel of it before a competition, or a concert. I touched it before the concert tonight, not that that helped me much. The ribbon is black, and velvety, it looks like nothing much and the ends are a little frayed now, but the feeling of it is a lucky thing for me.

Beside the rank sofa, Chris has two club chairs, which my mum did persuade him to buy, because she said he ought to be able to have meetings in the home office without it looking like an Ikea showroom. Opposite the rank sofa, against the wall of the room, Chris has a big long desk, which is surrounded by bookshelves where there are tons and tons of books about computer coding and stuff like that, including three books that he has written.

Chris is very, very clever, my mum told me when she came home after her first date with him, and a basic knowledge of genetics will tell you that that is probably why Lucas is too. Lucas once told me that his mum was clever too, though she never got a chance to show it before she died, but I couldn't really have that conversation with him because it made me think too much of Gull.

'A student with exceptional potential,' the prosecution said about her in their summing up, 'a bloom cut down before it could flower,' which I thought was a bit much, but that was definitely something I was not allowed to point out, though I think if Gull had heard it she would have snorted, definitely. She always snorted like a pony on a cold morning when she heard something blousy like that.

I sit first, on the sofa. The cushions tilt backwards so I have to perch on the very edge of them if I want to preserve any kind of what my mum would call 'suitable decorum'. I'm careful to cross my legs at my ankles, not my knees, and I tug down the skirt of my dress so that it's covering as much of me as possible. Unfortunately, that does make the top of my dress ride down a bit so I have to wriggle a little to cover myself up as best as I can, and I can tell that Chris's eyes are on me under a frowning brow.

Lucas sits on one of the club chairs and, as he settles into it, I see a resemblance to Chris that I don't always notice. Lucas's looks mostly favour his mum, that's obvious. There are no photographs of her anywhere in our house apart from Lucas's room, but I've been in there and I could see how much they look like each other.

Chris is holding Grace's intercom and, as he puts it down on his desk, he jogs the mouse of his computer and the huge screen comes to life. On it, frozen in super-high definition, is an image of Lucas and me, sitting at the piano, in the church. Lucas is looking towards the camera and I'm playing, bent over the piano, one of my hands poised over the next note, the tips of my hair brushing the keys.

In the foreground is Tom Barlow, or rather the back of him, and it's him that Lucas is looking at.

It's the moment it all started to happen and, as my mum comes into the room, she gasps at the sight of it.

MONDAY MORNING

SAM

The judge didn't accept Zoe's Special Reasons plea.

He found against Zoe, he stated, because he simply didn't believe that she would have been monitoring what she drank that night. No matter that we'd explained that she was a conscientious person, a good student, that she'd had a piano competition the following day. We might not have convinced him anyway, but Eva Bell and her friend's testimony, which so strongly contradicted Zoe's claim that Jack Bell had spiked her drink, certainly put the knife in Zoe's back, and twisted it too.

Zoe stood up in the courtroom as the judge spoke to her.

'I find,' he said, looking at her over a pair of reading glasses, 'that as you were only fourteen years old on the night of the party, there was no reason for you to monitor closely how much alcohol you were able to drink before driving, because you were not legally able to drive a motor vehicle. I find that you did drink freely during the course of that evening and that you don't actually know how much you had to drink. Therefore, regrettably, I find that whilst you might not have known exactly how much you had to drink, you knew you were too drunk to drive that car.'

He sentenced her to an eighteen-month detention and training order. It meant that she would probably serve nine months, or thereabouts. I felt that wasn't too bad in the circumstances, but her family would never get the satisfaction of proving that Zoe had only done what she did because she was unwittingly drunk. She met nobody's eye as they took her down.

My goodbye to her mother was muted and painful. Tessa was there too, because I remember them standing together outside court looking desolate. Zoe had no other supporters with her that day.

It took me a while to get the trial out of my system. I felt a sense of failure in some ways, because I wondered whether I should have insisted more on a simple Guilty plea at the first hearing. It could have resulted in a more lenient sentence. In the end, we took a legal gamble and lost, and Zoe paid the price. I wondered if she took any satisfaction afterwards from knowing that she did, at least, tell the truth, or whether it was a regret or, worse, something to resent.

It wasn't until two years later, after I'd moved to Bristol to broaden my criminal practice experience, that I ran into Tessa by chance. We recognised each other immediately, and met for coffee the following week. Things developed from there. Until we reached last night.

Now, as I watch Tessa ease her VW into the Monday morning traffic outside my apartment, on her way to find out how and why her sister is dead, it's clear to me that things might just become very complicated indeed.

SUNDAY NIGHT

After the Concert

ZOE

It goes weirdly well. You wouldn't think it, looking at Lucas, who's got a face on through the whole thing like he's about to have a medical emergency on a TV daytime drama.

Once my mum has got over seeing Tom Barlow, and me and Lucas, frozen on the screen, she takes control in a way that I think is totally impressive, considering.

She isn't wearing her normal Second Chance Family clothes when she comes down. She's in a pair of leggings and a loose T-shirt. Maybe that's what makes me relax a bit, because she's dressed more like she used to dress, before it happened and when we still lived with my dad: still pretty, still nice, but way more casual. She's taken the make-up off her face and tied her hair back. The short, soft sleeves of the T-shirt make her arms look fragile and thin, and without foundation the dark circles under her eyes resemble small bruises. My mum, I realise, is very tired.

As she stands in the doorway, Chris gestures towards the chairs and the rank sofa. I think she's going to sit down beside me, but she doesn't. She takes the club chair opposite Lucas and Chris is left with the spare sofa seat. When he sits down, the weight of him makes the sofa cushions sag heavily and I become even more extra self-conscious about my bare knees and shoulders.

'Sit up, Zoe,' is the first thing my mum says as she looks at me with eyes that are red-rimmed and empty of everything except the bottomless look she had permanently for a long time after the accident. 'You're hunching.'

I notice that Lucas adjusts his posture too, when she says that, but my mum's oblivious. She focuses her whole being on Chris, like he's the last animal of his kind on earth.

'Thank you for listening,' she says. 'Zoe and I do have some proper explaining to do, we owe that to you both and I'm grateful to you for listening ...' Mum does a bitter-looking swallow then, and tears begin to slip from her eyes, though she doesn't pay any attention to them. It makes me want to cry myself and I have to work very hard not to.

Mum doesn't notice that though. She's sitting ramrod straight in the chair and she fixes Chris with her eyes, which I once heard him tell her were beautiful.

Chris doesn't do poetic description – 'I'm just a computer scientist!' he sometimes says, when Mum is asking him to make a decorating choice. 'You're the creative one!' – so 'beautiful' was probably an adjectival stretch for him. I could add to that description. Mum's eyes are pellucid, arctic blue. The blue is washed pale inside the eyes with a darker rim around the edge and, if you look closely, a fleck of hazel lies within one of her irises, like an intruder.

She tells Chris and Lucas the full blow-by-blow story of the accident, of my fall from grace, the way we told it at the trial. It's the version of the story where I'm as much of a good

209

person as a bad one; it's the version where I think I'm doing the right thing when I decide to drive the car. It's the true version.

Chris stands up when she's finished. He hasn't said a word while she talked. On his computer screen the image from the church is still freeze-framed, like Munch's silent scream. She tries to reach for his hand as he walks away from her but she's too slow. Mum doesn't look at me, she just folds her hands into her lap after that and waits, and so I copy her.

I look at the lights that are on in the room, because it's dark everywhere else now. Chris's desk lamp is dumping a tired circle of yellow on to the surface of his desk, and the glass wall lights that are sculpted to look like flaming torches are glowing, as is the bulb that shows off Chris's famous, framed computer chip. Between them, there's gloom.

'Maria,' Chris says, 'I'm glad that you've told me. Thank you.'

Mum's lips disappear inside her mouth. The tears roll down her face faster now. Chris doesn't look at me. He doesn't look at Mum. He's looking at the computer monitor, as if he's mesmerised by it. He leans forward and uses the mouse to click on the play button, and the film begins to move.

'Travesty!' Tom Barlow shouts. 'It's a travesty.'

On the screen, in the movie of myself, I finally notice Tom Barlow. I stare at him, then I get up, and I bang my leg against the piano, as I run out of the frame. I look like a fairy tale girl, fleeing from a wolf. Lucas just stays staring, and then my mum is standing up at the front, turning, and she says, 'Mr Barlow, Tom …' and Chris clicks pause.

'I'm just finding,' says Chris, 'the fact that you lied to me *twice* difficult to accept.'

That's therapy-speak, that 'difficult to accept' stuff. I've

210

had enough therapy to know it when I hear it. 'It's better to describe your emotions than display them,' Jason would repeat patiently at our Monday meeting when I'd raged or sobbed my way through the weekends at the Unit, 'then people can help you manage them instead of feeling as if they're bearing the brunt of them.'

Chris keeps talking and I think that if his voice were a cat then it would be padding quietly and unstoppably towards my mother with unblinking eyes.

'You lied to me about Zoe's history, and I suppose I can understand it, I think I can. What Zoe and you have experienced is obviously … well, I'm at a loss for words to describe it just now. You should have told me, but I understand why you didn't, it was a lie by omission. What I cannot understand, what feels like a slap in the face, is why you lied to me earlier, when you denied knowing that man. That was an out and out lie and you know how I feel about lying, and I'm finding that very difficult to accept.'

'I'm sorry,' my mum says. She stands and walks towards him.

'He came to my house!' Chris says. 'He's unstable. He needs managing, and he came to this house!'

'I never wanted to lie to you,' Mum says.

'You know how I feel about lying. You know it must not happen in my house.'

'Our house,' I say. I don't know why. It just slips out, because twice he's said 'my' house, but I should have kept it in my head.

'You! Stay out of it.' He doesn't look at me because he's watching Mum, but his arm shoots out and he points a finger at me while his gaze is locked on to hers.

Mum goes right up to him. She looks smaller than usual against him because she has bare feet. She slides her arms around his waist and rests her head on his chest. He's too angry to return the hug so his arms stay in mid-air, actively keeping distance between him and her. She looks up at him, like some kind of supplicant, trying to bathe her face in the light of him. 'I'm so, so sorry,' she says. 'I panicked. I should have trusted you. I was very stupid, I was insecure.'

Mum's arms snake further round Chris until her hands are linked and I can see his body soften a little at her touch. I marvel a bit at that. Beside me, Lucas is staring at them too but he feels my eyes turn to him and he looks back at me briefly, and I wonder if I have that power, with him, or if he's in charge.

Chris unpeels my mum's arms from his body and holds her hands in his, between them, as if they might pray together.

'It's going to rain,' he says, and he's right because I'm suddenly aware of a sharp, cool breeze that makes the open window rattle and we can hear the foliage shifting outside. 'Let's clear up and go to bed.'

'Chris.' There's a desperate note in Mum's voice that makes my heart tear, because I can tell that she still doesn't know which way this is going.

He hears her desperation too. 'We'll talk more,' he says, 'upstairs.' He tucks her hair behind her ear.

'Let's talk here,' says Lucas, 'all together.'

Chris looks at him. 'This is probably something Maria and I need to discuss alone at this point.'

I agree with him, although I know Lucas doesn't want us to leave them, but I don't understand that, and I want Mum to have a chance, so I say, 'I'll clear up,' and, as rain begins to smatter on to the windowpane, I stand up.

'I'll do it, you go to bed,' I say.

When I reach the doorway I turn and I look for a moment at them both standing there and I say, 'I'm sorry, Mummy and Chris.'

SUNDAY NIGHT

After the Concert

TESSA

One of the tube lights under my kitchen cabinets is flickering silently. It needs replacing.

Sam doesn't answer his phone so I leave a message to ask if I can come over, although I wonder if he's asleep. I apologise for potentially disturbing him. We're very polite to one another, Sam and I, though it's not formality. I think it's fear that we'll lose each other.

I put my phone down on the kitchen table and watch as the screen dims to black. I roll my shoulders back to ease the tension that's grabbed them in a pincer grip.

The room is stuffy and the smell of Richard's lasagne still lingers; it's cloying and it feels as though it will make the back of my throat catch. I get a glass and turn on the tap at the sink, waiting for the warm water to run through until it's cold before I fill it, and then I drink it all in one go. I look out into the darkness of our garden, and see the shape of Richard's shed at the end of it, and remember how I found him there earlier in the day.

Even though I know that the homes and the streets of Bristol will be full of people having normal, comfortable

214

Sunday evenings, I feel as though I'm the last person on earth.

And suddenly I can't stand to be in my house any longer. I grab my bag and leave. I'll just take my chances and go and turn up at Sam's flat, because there's nowhere else I can bear to be.

I'm halfway there, and about to pull over and try to phone him again to give him some warning, when I remember that I've left my phone at home, on the kitchen table, and I just can't face going back to collect it, not now that I'm nearly at Sam's.

No matter, I think. It won't do Richard any harm to not be able to contact me for a while, to understand how it feels to have a spouse who is utterly unavailable for support. It won't do him any harm to feel frightened in the morning because he has to cope with the unreliable actions of the person he's supposed to be sharing his life with. If I go straight to work in the morning I can manage without it, and Richard can always phone there to track me down. I'll tell him I stayed at Maria's, or with a friend.

I surprise myself a little with these sharp feelings of spite towards him, but the thing is, you need energy to cope with an alcoholic spouse, and I have none tonight, so the malice creeps in.

Rain begins to fall as I drive. It's not heavy, but it's persistent and my windscreen wipers creak noisily across the glass.

The city centre is empty and I find a parking space easily near Sam's apartment building.

Before I go up to Sam's flat I sit in the car for a moment and I wonder whether I should go back to Maria's house and check on them, before I remind myself that she's an adult and I mustn't interfere.

I wonder what Tom Barlow is doing, or thinking. I wonder if he's lying awake beside his wife and stewing, or whether he's online, searching for more information about Zoe, and her new family.

Raindrops spatter on the roof of the bus with a tinny persistence, like a fusillade of toy guns. My thoughts have become exhausting enough that I decide I've had enough of sitting in the car. I step out and run across the wide pavement that separates the road from Sam's building and I don't stop until I'm safely under the partial cover of the meanly proportioned porch, and I press the buzzer for his apartment.

SUNDAY NIGHT

After the Concert

ZOE

Outside, the surface of the pool has gone crazy rough with the rain that's coming down. Under the table there's a fox gulping down bruschetta that he must have pulled off the table. He runs away when he sees me. First thing I do is mostly close the big doors to the kitchen because the rain has come into the room and run all over the stone floor and it's slippery as hell. I grab as much as I can from the table and bring it inside, tripping through the rain and getting soaked.

Lucas is standing in the doorway to the kitchen when I turn to make a second run into the house, and now the rain's falling hard enough that it pings off the plates and back up into my face. I'm not unaware that this could be a romantic moment, that it could be the point where the soaking wet heroine is caught and embraced by the hero. But that doesn't happen.

'We mustn't leave them alone,' Lucas says.

'Can you help me?'

'Come back in.'

'I said I would clear up.'

I want to do just this one thing right tonight. I'm going to make the kitchen sparkle for my mum, and then, I've already thought of it, I'm going to go and lie with Grace again so that Mum isn't disturbed in the night.

'Why aren't you listening to me?'

'Because you looked deranged,' I say, though that's not precisely true.

I put the plates down by the sink, and I'm hoping Lucas might help me but he just stands there.

'How did you know? About me?' I ask.

'I played piano at a competition in Truro once,' he said. 'You were there. You beat me. I remembered you.' A crooked smile.

'When?' I try to remember because there's a competition in Truro that I entered most years throughout my childhood, but I have no memory of Lucas.

'It was years ago. You beat me so I remembered your name and I thought I recognised you. I got the rest off the internet.'

'But my name wasn't allowed to be reported.'

'You can piece it together if you look hard enough.'

It makes sense that he remembers me from piano. Except for the children we saw year after year at competitions, I only ever remember the kids who beat me, which is probably why he recalls me, but not the other way around.

'But Chris?' I ask.

'I was just with my mum at the time. We were spending a week on holiday, and it was bad weather so we entered the competition on a whim, for extra performance practice.'

'Oh.' I let that hang there because I don't know what to say because Lucas never talks about his mum. Then I think of something.

'How did you know about panop?' I ask.

'I saw you had it on your phone. It wasn't difficult to find your account.'

He must have had a look on my phone one day. I'm always leaving it on the piano by mistake, where it's hard to spot against the black shiny wood. He could easily have seen me put in my passcode too.

'It's what they used to send me messages on,' I tell him. 'The people at my old school. They bullied me.'

'I'm sorry,' he said. 'I only wanted to get your attention. I thought if you knew I'd kept your secret you'd believe in me.'

'Did you read the old messages that people sent me?'

'No. I couldn't do that.'

I'm grateful for that.

'Believe in you about what?' I ask, because that was a strange thing to say.

'The script.'

'You didn't need to do that. I would have read the script anyway.'

I feel like he's being really weird and kind of selfish about the script with everything else that's happening.

'I'm sorry,' he says, but he sounds a bit impatient when he says it and that annoys me too because the messages he sent really scared me. 'Come in. Let's go upstairs.' He catches my arm, and I try to shake his hand off but his grip is quite tight.

'You go. I'll come when I've finished.'

'Zoe!'

'What? I want to do this for my mum!'

He looks like he wants to reply to that, but what he wants to say is too difficult, so instead he drops my arm, although his fingers have pressed into it by now, and it hurts.

'Fine,' he says, and he goes upstairs.

By the time I've finished clearing up, all is quiet and the lights are off everywhere in the house. As I pass Chris's study I can see the steady green light of Grace's intercom, and I realise that they've forgotten to take it up with them, which means there's all the more reason for me to sleep with Grace.

Upstairs, the lights are also off in all the bedrooms and in the hall and landing, and I hear nothing. If the butterfly is still there, it's gone quiet. Only the rain is loud, still hissing and spattering on the glass skylight at the top of the stairwell.

Downstairs, I've laid out all the breakfast things and made everything perfect. I've put my mum's favourite cup out and a tea bag of Earl Grey tea neatly beside it with a spoon. I've put a mug for Chris beside it with a tea bag of English Breakfast, because that's what he likes.

In my bedroom I change out of my wet dress and put on a T-shirt and pyjama shorts. I dry my hair with a towel. I take my iPod from my bedside table. One rule in this house is that Lucas and I must listen to recordings of the repertoire that we're playing before we sleep. It helps us to remember the pieces, imprints the detail of them on our minds.

I creep into Grace's room. She's lying in her cot, on her back, head to one side. Her little fists are loosely clenched. She's got one of them in her mouth, and the other is just touching the mad soft hair on the back of her head. It's how she always sleeps. She's very quiet and I know I shouldn't but I pick her up and bring her into the bed with me. I place her between me and wall, so she won't fall out. She doesn't stir at all and I inhale the smell of her.

Carefully, I put my headphones in, and start the music playing on my iPod. Chopin. A nocturne.

As the music swells, I think about my baby sister beside me and think that if there's one way that I can pay back the world for what I've done, it's to take care of her as much as I can, to make sure that she doesn't make the mistakes that I did, to help her not to hurt people. It's a vow that I made when I first met her in the hospital, and it's a vow I repeat to myself all the time.

I settle down and cover myself in just a sheet because it's still warm in her room, and right before I fall heavily asleep, with the Chopin relaxing me through my headphones, I notice on the clock beside the bed that it's a few minutes after midnight, which means it's Monday now, not Sunday any more, and I hope that Monday might be better.

SUNDAY NIGHT

Midnight

TESSA

Sam and I watch a Hitchcock film and I relax. I curl up into him once we go to bed. After the events of the evening I feel as if I'm finally in a safe place, a place where I don't need to be a carer, or a supporter, or anything to anybody else. I can just be me.

As Sam's breathing settles into the rhythms of sleep, I lie awake a little longer and think about the evening and about how I'm glad I'm away from Maria's house because it's not my life after all, it's Maria's, and she is, after all, an adult who's made her own decisions.

I haven't mentioned what happened earlier to Sam because I didn't want to sully our time together. I wanted the few hours we spent in each other's company tonight to be simple and lovely, and unmarred by the imperfections that have spread like stains across other areas of my life.

But even with the warmth of his body beside mine, and the cocoon of his company sheltering me from reality for a while, I shed a tear or two before I sleep; just one or two.

SUNDAY NIGHT

Midnight

ZOE

I'm hardly asleep when I'm awake again and I hear screaming and for a moment, in my confusion, I think it's me.

But it's not.

The sound is coming from the front of the house and it's high-pitched, and frightening.

There's shouting too, and then commotion in the house. Feet pounding.

With Grace in my arms, I run on to a deserted landing, where all the bedroom doors are open and the lights are on, and down the stairs. The front door's wide open too, and I go out and then run-walk across the gravel, feeling the slippery sharp stones digging into the soles of my feet. Katya and Barney Scott stand beside the wooden shed that houses our rubbish bins and they're both drenched with rain, sopping with it, their clothes sticking to them like cling film.

They're looking at the door of the shed, where I can see that Chris is standing in boxer shorts and a T-shirt and has his hand over his mouth.

'Call an ambulance,' he shouts. He turns to Katya and

Barney. 'Give me your phone,' he says to them. 'We need to call an ambulance.'

Grace begins to grizzle in my arms because it's dark and wet and there's shouting and she doesn't know why she's awake. She uses her fists to try to brush away rain that's getting into her eyes but grinds it in instead.

'Keep the baby away,' Chris says to me, but he's fumbling with Barney's phone so he can't stop me when I walk past him and look into the shed.

On the floor of the shed, lying as motionless as the grave mounds at the church, blood soaking the side of her pale angel hair, is my mother. Her eyes are open wide and they stare at nothing at all.

I am still on my knees beside her when the emergency services arrive. They've taken Grace from me long ago, but they couldn't move me from my mother's side. I have sunk my face on to her neck, her chest; I have taken in the living smell of her for the last time. I have stroked the soft, soft skin on her temple, just like she did to Grace and me. I have whispered things into her ear that I want to tell her. And while I did all that her eyes still didn't move.

When one of the paramedics leads me out of the shed, and away from my mum's body, I see Chris, and Barney, and Lucas standing there. Katya is in the doorway of the house, holding Grace.

I see an ambulance in the driveway, its back doors wide open, and I see a police car whose lights are slowly flashing. I see that the rain has eased so the droplets of water look like nothing more than fine dust motes in the air, swirling and shimmering, lit up blue against the black night.

I try to run back to my mother's body, to be with her a while longer, because I'm not ready to let her go, but they don't let me do that.

MONDAY

ZOE

I sit in a circle with the others in the sitting room of our Second Chance House and I feel as if I would break if somebody touched me. I feel as if my skin and hair are brittle, as if my teeth will never unclench.

There are some pieces of music I've played which got under my skin and made me feel this way, but that feeling went away after I lifted my fingers from the piano keys.

This feeling doesn't. It sticks, and it reminds me of before.

'Grief blooms,' Jason said to me at the Unit in therapy sessions, when they were trying to make sure that I wouldn't have Unresolved Grief over the three deaths I caused. And he was right, because the pain of losing Gull and the others did unfold like a new bud at first, and it took for ever before it began to wither.

I have names for all those feelings because Jason told them to me. Adults like to put a name on everything you feel, as if a name can neutralise it. They're wrong though. Some things settle under your skin and don't ever go away, no matter what you call them.

Today, what I'm feeling is even bigger than before. After my mum's death, the grief doesn't just bloom, it bursts out. It creates a mushroom cloud, instantly. It fills the sky that night and envelops us all; it's towering and toxic. It's off the Richter scale.

I feel it.

Chris feels it.

Lucas feels it.

Grace does not. Because she doesn't understand what's happened. She carries on being a baby and we all watch her, passing her from arms to arms, not able to explain to her.

We all sit in the sitting room of our house together like in an Agatha Christie novel.

We are four teenagers, one baby and Chris.

And a police officer sits with us, and stares at the floor, but she's listening to everything we say. I know for sure that police officers always listen.

I want Tessa, and they want to contact her too, to tell her, to get her to come and be with us, but nobody can find her. She's not answering her mobile and her landline rings and rings over and over again, and Uncle Richard doesn't even pick up.

Outside, the drizzle has stopped and so have the flashing blue lights, though the police cars are still there, and we see them as the sun rises up in a hazy, too-bright dawn, which also coaxes our faces from the shadows and shows them sagged and doughy as if we've all been slapped senseless with the shock.

Yellow tape is stretched out across the entrance to our driveway and around the shed where my mum's body still lies.

At first, one of the policemen asks us if it could have been an accident, whether my mum had been drinking.

'I don't know,' says Chris. 'I just don't know. She'd had a bit of wine, but we'd all gone to bed. We were all asleep.'

Chris is upset and flustered, but he's the first to accuse somebody else.

'It was that man,' he says. 'Tom Barlow. You need to go and find a man called Thomas Barlow.'

The police officer encourages Chris to sit back down, tells him that he'll pass the information on, and that Chris will be interviewed in due course, but for now, if it's OK, they'd prefer it if we all stayed where we were.

Lucas begins to sob, and the sound of it is painful and loud. It makes Grace crawl over to him and put her hand on his leg and pull herself up, and he reaches down to stroke her small fingers and sobs some more. She watches his face with an open mouth until it makes her cry too, and then she thumps back on to her bottom on the floor and is full of despair of her own.

Barney Scott's dad arrives and stands in the doorway and says, 'I'm so sorry,' and takes Barney away after a talk with the police.

Everybody is talking. I remember it from before. Always the talking, and the building of cages with words.

Katya is tear-streaked and squashed out of her arrogant shape and she sits by me and looks like she might want to hug me like you see on TV reports where women cling and wail, but I feel nothing for her and I'm used to feeling things on my own so I edge away to make sure that she doesn't touch me at all.

Later, when dawn has just become proper morning, they ask us if we mind being moved to the police station. They say that the house has become a 'scene', and I'm straight away transported back to court where they kept repeating 'scene of the accident' over and over again. I look around instinctively to see if Mum has had the same thought and then I remember: she's gone.

The police come upstairs with each of us in turn to pack what they fully pedantically specify as 'a small overnight bag'. We all do except Grace who ends up with a bag busting with stuff, which I pack myself because I don't want Katya to do it.

Standing on the gravel, waiting to leave, feeling the heat start to push back into the day as if nothing out of the ordinary has happened, as if there had been no blue dust rain, and no broken body, I concentrate on the feel of the sharp stones pushing at the soles of my Converse, to try to keep myself solid. But even doing that I can't help myself glancing at the shed, and wondering if my mum is still in there, because the ambulance has gone. A policeman stands in front of the shed door and looks at his phone, and when I ask the question out loud, somebody else tells me that Mum's going to be moved very soon.

'Doesn't she need the ambulance?' I ask, but nobody answers.

They use two cars to drive all of us away from the house but not before Chris has got angry when he tried to get Grace's car seat out of Mum's car and it got stuck. Normally, Mum moves the car seat. After he finally yanked it free, Chris cursed and threw the car seat on to the gravel and stones kicked up and hit the side of the police car, but nobody mentioned that. Instead, I picked up the seat, and put it in the car, and so now I'm holding Grace's fingers tightly as we ride together in the back seat and Katya sits on the other side of me with the bag of Grace's stuff on her knees.

In the car, the police driver tells me that they've finally

managed to get in touch with Uncle Richard, Tessa's husband, and he'll meet us at the police station.

As we drive away from the house another policeman lifts the tape at the end of our road and somebody standing on the pavement with their dog stares at us, and my stomach is carved out with the feeling that the only thing I want is Mum, and my head is collapsing round an imploding feeling that my life is shattering again, and I begin to cry. Katya doesn't see because she's looking out of the other window with a face like an Easter Island statue and Grace is fully occupied playing with a piece of gravel which she must have picked up when we were at our house.

And, on top of everything, and through my tears, I feel guilty about that because I think Mum would have noticed it long before Grace might have had a chance to put the stone in her mouth, and I quickly take it away from her before she does.

And alongside that thought, which my mixed-up head is giving space to, my fear is beginning to unfold as fast as my grief did.

Two questions are pushing to the front of my mind and they're frightening me to the point where I start to shake.

One: what if my mum's death was revenge for what I did and they're going to come after me too?

Two: what if the police think I did it?

I'm a convicted killer, after all.

TESSA

When I arrive at Maria and Chris's avenue I'm not allowed to drive down it. I park on an adjoining street and run until I'm held back by the raised arms of a police officer who's guarding the strip of crime scene tape that sags across the entrance to their road.

'I'm family,' I say. 'It's my sister.'

He begins to explain why that's not a good enough reason to encroach on the 'crime scene' but I can't stand to listen, because I need to see, and so I duck away from him and under the tape and run the hundred yards down the street until I'm standing at the entrance to Chris and Maria's driveway taking breaths that scorch my throat.

I'm just in time to see a body bag being carried out of the shed, and placed on a gurney. Faintness almost fells me and I have to lean against the golden stone column at the entrance to the driveway. It's the realisation that this is true.

Maria's my younger sister; she was always a sprite compared to me, a waif, she was my shadow when we were younger, the one who could make our dad beam even when he was supposed to be cross with her, and now she's gone. Your younger sister is not supposed to die before you, it's not right. As I have no child who I fear will predecease me, this upsets the natural order of things for me in a way that's unexpectedly shocking. Our parents are both dead, but I didn't feel orphaned until now, because I had Maria.

As I watch the men carry her, I imagine how it feels to them, because I know the weight of a dead body. I've hauled an animal corpse out of the back of a car, or off a surgical table, on more than one occasion. When all the tissues are lifeless and the heart has stopped pumping, the weight of death is extraordinary. If someone brings a dead animal to us, when we prepare to move the body from our surgery car park into the building for cremation, we usually wait until passers-by have gone, to spare their feelings, but the folks with the gurney outside Maria's house take no such precautions. They're not paramedics, because there's no need for paramedics now. These are men whose jobs are rarely advertised, because they collect the lifeless bodies. They wheel the gurney towards the back of a van, which is unmarked. There's no need for an ambulance now either.

The policeman is by my side, and he guides me away, but he's kind enough to support me too and to explain gently that Maria's body is in the care of the coroner now, pending a post-mortem investigation, and a murder inquiry has been launched.

And as I take my last look back at their house I think something that I've thought before: 'What a waste.' And even my sceptical soul can't help but wonder if our family is somehow cursed.

ZOE

I feel safe in the police car in a sort of way because if Tom Barlow hurt my mum then he can't get me here, but I also feel afraid, because being in the police car feels like it did before.

It's not cold, or dark, and I'm not in my party clothes with shards of glass in my hair and cuts on my face, and I'm not over the limit, but it is a police car and I am being transported.

That's when I get the idea that I need Sam.

I know he's in Bristol now because Tessa told Mum once that she'd run into him and that he lives here now too, like us.

'That's a funny coincidence, don't you think?' she said to Mum, but of course Mum didn't want to talk about it so Tess had to keep her little smile at the coincidence just for herself.

The only person who can take me to see Sam is Uncle Richard, but I can't mention it to him at first, because when he meets us at the police station he gives me a too tight hug, but then all he does is try to tell the police that Aunt Tessa didn't come home last night. Nobody listens to him at first, but after he's told them like a thousand times eventually one of them asks him if Richard has any reason to fear for her safety, or if he thinks Tess might have had a reason to have argued with her sister.

'No!' Richard shouts in a too dry voice that lurches up an

236

octave. 'No she bloody hasn't. How dare you?' Uncle Richard is always fierce about Tess and my mum says that's because he loves her so much.

I want Sam, because of what I did before. I need him and his advice because I'm scared people will put the blame on me.

I hold my head together enough to put my plan into action because I'm able to put my grief in a box and put my thinking cap on. Jason at the Unit taught me how to do that. 'Imagine your grief as a flower that has bloomed,' he said in one of our sessions and I was like, 'You already said grief blooms.'

'Bear with me,' he said. 'Imagine it.'

So I shut my eyes and did; I made my grief into a peony, big and blowsy.

'Now convert that flower into something made of paper.'

I opened my eyes when he said that. 'What?'

'Hang in there. Do you know what origami is?'

'Of course. Japanese. "Ori" means "folding" and "kami" means "paper". First clear reference to paper models is in a 1680 poem by Ihara Saikaku.'

Jason leaned back and looked at me. 'Zoe-pedia,' he said and this encouraged me to say: 'The poem is about butterflies, in a dream, and they are made from origami. Traditionally, they would be used in wedding ceremonies.'

I drew breath because there was more I could have said. I thought that I could probably tell him the line of the poem in Japanese because I read it phonetically once, but Jason interrupted me:

'So imagine an origami flower.'

In my head, the peony I pictured morphed from a mass

237

of bloomy petals so soft that they could suffocate you, into something made of sharp folds and symmetry.

'Now, fold that flower up tight. Fold the blooms back in.'

I saw it in my mind. The collapsing of the flower, the neatness of the package I could make it into. It un-bloomed.

'Now imagine that you're going to stow that folded-up flower in a box. You'll take it out later, and you'll let it open out again, but for now we're going to fold it away and keep it safe, and see what happens when it's gone for a little while.'

It didn't happen right away, but once I'd practised these thoughts, and finally believed Jason when he said it was OK sometimes to step away from the grief, and the guilt, I discovered that I got my concentration brain back. That's the brain that lets me memorise anything that I see, the brain that connects with the music. It's the brain that Granny Guerin said was like our family's laundry basket: always packed to the brim, always overflowing, you could never keep everything stuffed into it and close the lid.

So on the morning after my mum dies I'm using Jason's advice, and putting my grief for her in a box. I know it can't stay there for long, because it's too big, but I also know that it's essential to do it, and to have my wits about me. I ask Richard to take me to Sam; I tell him we have to because of what happened to me before. I tell him that Sam knows Tessa from back then so he might be able to help us find her.

Richard looks at me and says, 'Well, he can't be any more useless than they are here, come on then, let's give it a go.'

Uncle Richard finds Sam's office address really quickly on the internet on his phone and when they don't answer his call he says it's probably because it's too early and it's best just to go there.

At first, we have a bit of a problem persuading the police to let us go, because they act like they don't know what to think about it, and Chris and Lucas and Katya just stare at us like they're in shock that we're abandoning them. But Richard is clever, and he knows that the police can't keep us at the station because we're not actually arrested, so they can't stop us leaving, especially if it's just for a little while. He tells them that Sam is a family friend as well as a solicitor and it would be a great comfort to me if I could see him.

The policeman obviously doesn't like it, but when it seems like he's made all the objections he can and Richard has answered them, all confident, he just asks Richard if he thinks he should be driving. Richard makes a nervous look at me like people always do when drink driving is brought up, and then assures the policeman that he's going to call us a taxi which is how he arrived at the police station in the first place. I can tell the question hurts his pride, but he's trying not to be too indignant or cross, because he wants them to let us go.

When we arrive at Sam's office there are people just opening up, but we have to wait for a while because it's Sam's day off, which I didn't think of, and some of the people stare at us a bit as they walk past in their smart business suit clothing while Sam's secretary phones him.

'He's on his way,' she says after she's spoken to him. 'You're lucky I could get hold of him.'

Once Sam arrives it's much better because we can be private in his office and I feel a surge of relief because Sam is somebody who knows every detail about what I did. With him, there's nothing to hide, and I don't have to pretend to be somebody else.

Sometimes, I think I'm more happy when I'm with people who know about it. In the Unit, all of us were there because we'd done something bad so it didn't make me different from anybody else, and that was relaxing in a way, it truly was. And with Sam, I feel like he doesn't judge me, he just helps me. I can say anything to him. With the Second Chance Family it wasn't like that. There was so much that I couldn't say, so much that I had to be ashamed of, even though the verdict at the trial was unfair to me and the idea of that twists and turns inside me every single day.

Sam sits, and we sit too, and in his hot, dark office with a scratchy carpet and framed certificates wonky behind his desk, I know I'm ready to tell him everything that's happened.

SAM

It's déjà vu: Zoe Maisey sits in front of me, and once again she's white with shock. The only difference is that there's no glass in her hair this time, and no hospital outfit. She's wearing a teenage-girl tracksuit-pyjama-type outfit, covered by a flimsy cardigan, which she's wrapped around herself tightly. She's shaking.

Beside her sits her uncle. He's red-faced, sweating and he stinks of alcohol. I hope he hasn't driven Zoe here because I suspect he's probably still over the limit, but I reassure myself that surely somebody in this family would know better.

But the worst thing is, that in spite of the bloodshot eyes and the oily, widened pores, and the untended shock of hair that's just starting to grey at the temples, he's quite obviously a very nice and also a good-looking man. His manner is lovely and gentle, though he's surprisingly posh. I never imagined Tess with a posh husband, but I can see instantly why she married him and I have to stop myself from hating him for this. I must not make comparisons between us. Jealousy would not be appropriate.

'She really needs her aunt,' Richard says to me. 'My wife. We've been trying to get hold of her for hours, but she went out somewhere last night and left her mobile at home and we don't know where she is.'

I know his name, but he doesn't know that I know it, and I must be careful what I say.

241

I extend my hand to him. 'Sam Locke,' I say.

'Richard Downing.' His handshake trembles, and his palms are clammy. He gives a two-handed shake, and his wedding ring, identical to Tess's, clashes with my knuckle when he encloses my hand with both of his. 'I'm sorry to turn up like this, but I know how much you helped them before. My wife, Tessa, told me about it, and Zoe was desperate.'

I wonder why he never came to court in Devon, why he and I have never encountered each other before. I've no time to consider this, though, because he's speaking urgently, almost furtively.

'The thing is, I'm worried about her,' he says. 'I don't know where she is. I'm sorry, I know it's nothing on top of what happened last night, but it's so unlike her. What if she's come to harm too?'

He's wide-eyed and genuinely worried, but I don't want this conversation.

I glance at Zoe who's looking at me with glazed eyes; I don't think she's taking in a thing that we're saying.

'I'm sure your wife will reappear,' I tell Richard, rather shortly, because how can I reassure him that I know she's OK. 'Perhaps she stayed with a friend last night?'

He begins to respond but I absolutely can't let this continue so I turn to Zoe and I ask the question that's been bugging me since Jeanette called me: 'Why have you come to me?'

'Because it feels like before,' she says. 'It feels like before.'

She breaks down into such awful, terrible sobbing that it's as if the sound of it alone could wound you. But what I'm wondering, even while she vents her grief, is whether Zoe knows something and knows that she needs protecting.

Richard tries to comfort her. He puts his arms around her and her head falls on to his shoulder. He looks as though he's feeling like death, and when our eyes meet his expression is one of compassion and confusion with a 'help me' in there too.

'Why is it like before?' I ask Zoe when her tears ebb a little. 'Do you feel responsible in some way?'

Richard says, 'Now hang on!'

'I need to ask.'

'She's just lost her mother!' Saying it chokes him up.

'And I'm on her side, but I need to know why she wanted to come here.'

Zoe is emotionally and socially immature, but she's also exceptionally intelligent. All the reports on her at the trial stressed this. She has the processing capabilities equal to any judge who might sit on her case and she has experience of the system too. Yes, she's in shock, yes, her mother has just died, but she's come to me for a reason and I need to know exactly what that is.

She peels herself from her uncle's shoulder, which is now wet from her tears, and says, 'Because I'm afraid.'

'Afraid of what?'

'Afraid of Tom Barlow.'

I remember him from the trial.

'Why Tom Barlow?'

'They're saying he disrupted the concert yesterday, and came to the house afterwards,' Richard explains, as Zoe fixes me with deer-in-headlight eyes.

'Do you think he hurt your mum?'

'I don't know. He's nice.'

She always said that at the time: Amelia Barlow is horrible, although her mum and dad are really nice.

'The police say they're going to talk to him,' Richard adds.

'If the police know about him then you mustn't worry,' I tell Zoe. 'They won't let him hurt you. What?'

She's shaking her head madly. 'But what if they blame me?'

I sigh. Zoe's mind has raced ahead down the path of somebody who has a victim mentality. I take a tough line with her in response: 'Is there anything to blame you for, Zoe?'

'Oh dear God, you poor child.' Richard rubs her back. 'You don't have to answer that.'

In her eyes I see she understands that I have to ask this, and that she's ready to answer. It's not the first time we've discussed her responsibility for somebody else's death. Zoe and I have trodden these boards before and it doesn't faze us, although Richard looks as though he might puke.

'No,' she says, 'I was asleep. I fell asleep with my baby sister, my new sister. I went to sleep with her in her room. I didn't hear anything because I had my headphones in.'

I'm about to reassure her that if that's the case, then she should have nothing to worry about, and that there's surely no reason for the police to think she would harm her own mother, but Richard interrupts me.

'Tessa went to the concert!' he blurts out, as if the memory is a big fish he's suddenly managed to hook out of the empty lake of his booze-addled brain.

'And she came to dinner with us afterwards,' Zoe tells him. 'She was there.'

'Yes that's right,' Richard agrees, as Zoe reminds him of

Tess's movements, his neurons firing their way out of his hangover now, and putting last night into some kind of order. 'She went to the concert, and we spoke afterwards and she said she was staying for dinner, but I didn't see her after that.'

I did, I think, but I can't say it.

'We had bruschetta,' Zoe tells Richard and tears still fall fatly down her cheeks. 'But the police are there now, we're not allowed home.'

While I often think of her as having a head that's far too smart for her age, in front of me today she is very much a child and I feel slightly guilty for taking a hard questioning line with her, though really I had no choice.

What I realise is that I'm well beyond my professional remit here. This feels like more of a personal, not a professional visit, and that makes me feel extremely twitchy. If Tess had been with Zoe, she wouldn't have let her come.

I stand up, look out of the window. I need to order my thoughts.

Various half-formed ideas scud across my mind: Zoe's going to need huge amounts of help, but not the kind that I can give her. She's here because she's afraid, that's all, not because she actually requires legal assistance. My gut tells me that she's not involved in this as a perpetrator, and my gut is usually right, though not always.

But what floods me with apprehension, on top of that, and makes me try to wrench the window open further, hoping for a gasp of fresh air from the dank gulley separating our small building from the towering block beside us, is the newly forming realisation that, even if I wanted to, I couldn't possibly help Zoe in this, in any of it, neither in an official capacity, nor a personal one. This is because the fact that I spent the night with Tess means two things: firstly, that I'm a potential witness, and, secondly, that our relationship is bound to become known.

I need, I think, a way out.

ZOE

Sam stares out of his office window at the building opposite for a long time, while I sit and lean against my Uncle Richard who smells strangely sweet, and I think about the men who are probably in the Second Chance House now, examining it for clues. I imagine it just like the wreck of the car in Devon: taped off, Property of the Police.

I wonder if the butterfly is still crouched in a high corner of our landing ceiling at the Second Chance House or if, in the darkness, its wings open and shut enough times that it used up its energy stores, and fell to the floor. I wonder if the men in white suits will find a small pile of powdery scales and a spindly-legged carcass on the cream carpet of our landing.

After a while, Sam clears his throat, says that he needs to make a phone call, and leaves the room. Richard and I stay where we are, and first he scrolls around his phone a bit, and then he puts it on the table, but he keeps picking it up again to check it and I can tell he's willing Tess to ring.

I just stare at the view that Sam was looking at.

The windows on the building opposite are like little boxes, each one showing you a glimpse into somebody else's day. I watch a lady at her desk neatly slitting envelopes open with a knife, before getting out the letters and unfolding them and then whacking down on to them with a big stamp. I can't hear her, obviously, but my brain provides the soundtrack, and the whump of the stamp as it hits the paper is loud in my mind, as well as the sharp sound as the knife slits the envelope, and the slurp each time she sips from a takeout coffee cup. The sounds alternate in my head, crescendoing, building up like the panic I'm feeling, until Sam returns.

I was right to panic, because he's betrayed me.

'I've phoned your dad,' he says. 'He's on his way.'

'No!' I totally and absolutely don't want my dad. He didn't cope with me before, so how is he going to now that it's even worse?

'Don't be angry, Zoe,' Sam says. 'You need somebody to look after you.'

'You don't know!'

'I do know.'

He's nodding at me, as if that makes him more right, which it doesn't, and I want to argue about it more, because I'm sharp scared of how my dad will be with me.

I'm staring hard at Sam, thinking of what to say, when Richard's phone rings and Richard lunges to grab it off the table where it's skittering around on the shiny surface as it vibrates even faster than his tremor hands.

'TESS MOBILE' it says on the screen.

'Oh God, it's you!' he practically shouts, once he's fumbled hitting the screen to answer it. 'Thank God! Thank God! Where the hell have you been?'

She's speaking to him urgently; you can hear that down the line, but not her actual words. Richard's face goes slacker as he concentrates on what she's saying.

Eventually, he says: 'I'm so sorry, darling, I'm so sorry about Maria, I just can't believe it and I just thought you … no, don't worry, I thought something might have happened to you too,' he says, and his hand is on his chest, but he fully lies when he says, 'God, Tessa, no, I'm not crying, no, I'm not, OK, yes,' and then gets back on track when he says, 'We're at the solicitor's place, Zoe's solicitor, do you remember him? … Because she wanted me to bring her here … of course we told the police where we were going, honestly they were in chaos, it doesn't inspire one with confidence … no, I didn't think of it like that … no, sorry, no, perhaps I should have, but there wasn't time to think … yes, she is … OK …'

He passes his phone to me. 'Aunty Tess wants to talk to you. She's OK.'

I can't talk to her at first. The sound of her voice, and the way it's strangulated and strange, makes me sob again.

'What happened?' she says.

It takes me a few moments to get my breathing under control, and Richard's arm wraps around my shoulders as I do. 'I don't know. She was in the shed. She never goes in the shed.'

'When? What time?'

'We went to bed. We all went to bed and Katya woke us up when she got back.'

'Did Katya find Mummy?'

'Yes!'

'Zoe, you've done nothing wrong, so don't behave as if you have, whatever you do. I think you should come away from Sam's office and come back to the police station to be with the others.'

'I don't want to be at the station.' Like the courtroom, the station is a vipers' nest, a place where I can trip myself up, say the wrong thing, dig my own grave, put myself behind bars.

'I know, I understand, but I'm coming now and I'll meet you there and then we'll find out what's going on and take things from there. You don't need a solicitor. You've done nothing wrong.'

'I don't want to be with the police.'

'But you don't want them to suspect you've done something either, do you?'

Sometimes people say things to you straight and I like that. I didn't think that coming to see Sam might make me look worse, but I see suddenly that she might be right.

In her silence, I ask, 'Where were you?'

'I stayed with a friend. I left my phone at home. I'm sorry I didn't come earlier.'

'Will I live with Daddy now?'

She sighs before answering, and it's a hollow sound. 'Honestly, I don't know what we're going to do, let's take one thing at a time. Zoe? Are you there?'

'Yes.'

'Don't worry about that now. We'll take care of you, OK? I promise.'

Sam is nice to me as he walks us out of the building, all of our feet thumping down flights of stairs.

'I don't think I've ever had a client just turn up before,' he says. 'It's very unusual really.'

Maybe nobody has ever needed you as much as me, I think. We're standing on the steps of his building now, and the soft early morning shadows are already getting shorter and more brutal, as the sun rises and starts to superheat the city and turn every surface into a glare.

'Don't be afraid, Zoe,' he says. 'The police will protect you until they know what's happened. They'll do a better job of it than me.'

I'm actually shocked that Sam, who saw how wrong things went for me before, could even think that, let alone say it to me. Until now, he's never been in the category of 'adults who don't understand', but he earns his membership badge right there on the steps, and I feel sick with disappointment.

On the drive back to the police station, my mind stays so blank with it all that I notice nothing apart from the fact that the air conditioning in the taxi is broken and his sweat is making half-moon shapes under Richard's armpits.

TESSA

I arrive at the police station at the same time as Richard and Zoe. He practically falls out of their taxi in his haste to embrace me, but it's her I want to feel in my arms first, because she's my flesh and blood.

'Where've you been?' Richard says, as I clasp her. 'I was so worried.'

I'm shot through with irritation at this, because I don't feel as though his concern is for me, but for himself. I'm already cross with Richard anyway, for taking Zoe to Sam. Cross because that's risky for me, but also because it feels risky for her. She doesn't need a solicitor. Why would we compound this desperate situation by publicly seeking legal advice for her? It makes her look suspicious. Richard has no common sense; he shouldn't have given in to her request.

'Later,' I say. 'For God's sake!'

I don't meet his eye, but from the way he falls in behind Zoe and me, bringing up the rear as we walk towards the entrance to the police station, and then scurrying past us to hold open the door, I think: He doesn't know about me and Sam, and for that, right now, I'm grateful.

As a uniformed officer leads us down a corridor within the police station, we hear Chris before we see him. As we round a corner, his voice is loud, and almost uncontrolled, as he explains to somebody that enough is enough, and the family can't stay at the police station.

'Why are you incarcerating us?' he asks. 'What are you doing that's in any way useful?'

We arrive by an open doorway that leads into a small room where Lucas, Katya and the baby are seated on sofas around a long, low table. Grace's face is tear-streaked and Katya holds her while wearing the expression of somebody who's both physically and mentally exhausted. Chris is standing beside the doorway remonstrating with a female officer who appears cowed by him.

'We're just in the process of opening up the investigation into your wife's death, sir,' she explains in a sentence where the words sound very carefully chosen. 'If you could bear with us while we do that, we will, of course, keep you updated on everything that's happening. It's a complicated—'

Chris interrupts her. 'I understand complexity. What I don't understand is why we're being held here. Why are we *camping* in your police station? What is the plan?'

His voice is louder now and it sets the baby off again.

'You could come to our house,' I say. 'If you'd like to?'

Chris notices us for the first time, but he barely glances at Zoe.

He looks back at the officer. 'Is that allowed?' he says. 'Or are we under suspicion?'

She's careful with her response. 'You're not being held here, sir, we simply wanted to offer you somewhere to be while your house isn't accessible to you. We thought it might be easier to conduct interviews while you were here as we'll be needing to speak to everybody soon.'

Behind Chris, Grace is having a low-level whinge and Katya is bumping her on her knee in a desultory way, which only makes Grace's mouth hang wider in despair. Zoe slips past Chris and goes to the baby, taking her into her arms.

'I have a baby!' says Chris. 'And children I'm responsible for. This isn't right! Look at them!'

They are a sight. Their bags are dumped all over the place, and baby paraphernalia has spread everywhere, including a pushchair, a nappy-changing mat on the floor, and a half-eaten jar of purée beside a bundle of wipes.

They need help.

'Officer,' I say. 'They can come to my house, if that's allowed? It's just over in Stoke Bishop.'

'I'll check,' she says. 'I expect they'd prefer you here just for now, but I'll ask.'

Only when she's moved away up the corridor do I step towards Chris and, almost as if it's an afterthought, we embrace awkwardly. Chris's grief hasn't weakened him physically; he feels as taut as the skin of a drum.

The police agree to us all going back to my house, and so we make the journey in an assortment of vehicles.

I regret the offer when we arrive there, though, because the reality of having Chris in my house, and the baby, and Katya, and the teenagers, is suddenly overwhelming. A Family Liaison Officer has come with us too. Between them, they make the space feel incredibly claustrophobic even though my home is a good size by anybody's standards. They leave no room for my grief.

Richard notices how I'm feeling; perhaps he's feeling it too. 'Go upstairs,' he says. 'Take a few minutes to yourself.'

It's as I'm heading up the stairs that I hear him add, 'Take a shower,' and I realise that I'm still in the clothes I wore to the concert. He surely won't remember what I put on yesterday, but he's not stupid either and I wonder if his shower comment is supposed to have a subtext, or if I'm being paranoid.

As the new fact of my sister's death reverberates around my mind, I take a hard line with Richard: if I cheated, you deserve it. You drank me to it.

I turn on the water in the shower and run it until it's almost too hot to stand. I hear shouting from downstairs, and the baby crying loudly, but I don't want to leave the shower until it's unbearable to stay in it any longer, because there's a part of me that can't cope with any of them, and doesn't want to look into a single one of their faces.

I think of Sam, and of my night with him, and want nothing more than to be back there in his flat with him, where the river is our soundtrack and our view, and it's just about us, and Richard is reliably drunk, and my sister and Zoe are OK in their new life and there are no more complications.

And beyond that, as the water streams down my back, and tears stream down my face, I feel only numbness.

ZOE

We never went to Tess's house much after Mum met Chris, but I love it.

'Every house is a world of its own,' Mum said when she and Chris were deciding on all the finishes for our Second Chance House. Mum had so many samples sent, for so many different things, and she would lay them out on the table and move them around like jigsaw pieces, looking to see which ones fitted best together.

We had fabric, stone, wood and paint samples in all shades of tasteful. Mum went for muted colours and expensive stuff and everything was strokeable. She loved her choices. She would smile to herself when each new thing was delivered and looked just right and Chris would say, 'You have such a good eye, Maria.'

In the end, the world she made looked like a magazine. She loved it and Chris loved it. They never stopped talking about how much they loved it. Grace puked on parts of it and I told them I loved it, but mostly I missed our farmhouse. Katya, when she arrived, took a look around every room in the house and, when we got back to the kitchen, she said, 'You have luxury lifestyle,' and looked very pleased about that.

Lucas never mentioned it, he just moved quietly around the different parts of the house and when he settled down anywhere it reminded me of a dark shadow cast over a patch of white sand.

Tessa's house is really different from the Second Chance House, but I properly love it. It tells lots of stories about Tess and Richard.

The main one it tells is that when they were younger Tess and Richard travelled around a lot, and they collected things. Their house is like a display cabinet for all the objects they brought home with them, but it's not posh. It's warm and friendly, and full of pictures as well as objects, and you can pick everything up and hold it if you want to and splat down on their sofa, which has blankets and throws on it, and sometimes a dog that Tess is fostering for work. There are rugs all over the floors too, which you have to be careful not to trip over, because nothing's perfect in their house, so they have curled-up edges and threadbare patches. Bookshelves clamber up most of the walls in the sitting room and the books are arranged in a higgledy-piggledy way, all different sizes and all different heights all over the place and nothing in alphabetical order at all. They're mostly travel books, and science and vet books, but there are lots of novels too and stacks of DVDs.

Tessa goes upstairs when we get back, and Richard tries to make tea for everybody, but nobody wants any, and Chris paces round the place until he stops and shouts at Katya.

'Stop the baby crying. Can you stop the baby crying?'

'Baby has lost mother!' Katya shouts back at him with surprising force. 'It is not time to make her be quiet.'

Richard looks from one of them to the other and says to Chris: 'Say you let me help on this front, what do you need?'

'Baby needs somewhere to sleep,' Katya says. 'And milk.' Richard's kind manner softens her tone though she still glares at Chris with intensity. I wish I dared to look at him like that, but I wonder what he'd say if I did.

'Are you up to giving me a hand?' Richard asks Katya. 'Shall we see what we can fix up?'

She responds by hoicking Grace further up her hip and following Richard in a huffy way.

Chris turns to me. 'Did you actually go and see a solicitor this morning?' he asks me.

I nod. A headache is bringing tears to my eyes, and, because of what he said to me last night, the question feels like a threat.

'Why?'

'I don't know.'

'You must know.'

I feel my hands start to shake, and I don't know what to say. I'm not ready to talk to him about that stuff yet. It's been secret for so long that I feel like I don't really have a vocabulary for it any more.

'What?' he says, even though I didn't think I said anything.

'I wanted Sam to help me. I know him from before.'

Chris is standing in the centre of the room, with his arms folded and his hair sticking up because he's run his hands through it so many times this morning. He considers me like I'm an interesting painting.

'There's a lot I don't know about you, Zoe,' he says and I bow my head to break eye contact with him.

In the Unit, I shared my room with a girl who told me how she always did that to stop her dad beating the crap out of her. *It sometimes works*, she said, *but sometimes it doesn't, but it doesn't cost you to try does it because they just want to feel like they're the king of you.*

It works on Chris, confirming my view that most people are members of the fully paid-up schizophrenia club. They act one way, until they don't. Just like that. Even Jason was all one way around me until he suddenly wasn't.

Chris sits down on the sofa in between me and Lucas, and he reaches out a hand to take one of mine and one of Lucas's, like we're going to pray.

I don't like the physical contact with him but I force my fingers to wilt into his hot palm.

'We're still a family,' says Chris, and he chokes on his words, 'and I want you to know that I'm here for both of you now.'

He squeezes my hand hard, and then he stands and leaves the room without another word.

Lucas and I look at each other. We've not been alone together since it happened.

'I'm sorry,' he says.

'Why was she out the front of the house?' I say. 'What was she doing there?'

'I don't know.'

He bows his head, and that makes me feel angry because I want more from him. I want the connection we had last night.

'It's all going to kick off now,' I say, and he rises to my bait.

'What do you mean?'

Sometimes when I'm angry I want to throw all the awful things that I know at people; I want them to feel all the horrible things that I've had to feel.

'You can do that,' Jason said to me once when I described the way that Amy Barlow's eyes were open but dead and her

259

ear was ripped half from her head in the back of the car, 'you can try to pull me into that scene, and wound me with it, but we both know that it's a space that only you occupy, Zoe, and my job is to help you move on from that safely, not to join you there. It's not my horror. You're punishing yourself if you inflict this stuff on other people because it will only push them away from you.'

I ignore Jason's advice this morning and I try to punish Lucas with my knowledge.

'Do you actually know what they're going to do? They'll take us in, they'll question us, they'll take our phones, our computers, they'll make us wait, they'll lock us in a cell, the investigation will go on and on and so will the trial. It never ends, Lucas. No matter what you do afterwards, it never goes away.'

'We were all asleep,' he says. 'We don't know anything.'

'Were you? Were you asleep?'

'Me and Dad were asleep!' he says.

'I was asleep too. I didn't hear anything.'

The thought that I slept while harm came to my mum is a torment to me, because I think how it could have been different if I'd not put my headphones in. Then I might have heard Mum go out, and maybe stopped her, called her back into bed with me and Grace instead. I could have done it, I could have pretended I had a headache, or a tummy ache, or something. She would have come, I think.

I begin to cry again, but Lucas doesn't move, he just stares at the tufted rug, which has repeating geometric patterns on it that draw your eye round and round in a whirl, and even when my tears stop, we stay silent and I look at a line drawing of a building, which Uncle Richard has framed and hung over his wood-burning stove. It's spare, and perfect, with orderly black lines on white like musical notation paper, and a thought occurs to me.

'Do you think she went outside to see Mr Barlow?'

'I don't know,' he says. 'How do you know they'll take our phones?'

'Because it's what they do.'

'But we're not under suspicion.'

'I will be.'

'Why?'

'Because of what happened.'

They tell you that in the Unit. If you've been done once, they'll do you again even quicker. Makes life easier for them. Everyone in the Unit feels like life's a conspiracy against them.

'It's not,' Jason said when we talked about it. 'Although some people do get stuck in a cycle of crime and punishment, it's true, but that doesn't have to be you, Zoe. It shouldn't be you.'

'My verdict was unfair.'

'I know you believe that, and it might or might not be true …'

'It's true.' I think about it every day, the feeling of being cheated at my trial, the helplessness of nobody believing me. In the Unit I still felt very angry about it, and although I still feel that way deep down, I've learned to hide it, because nobody wants to hear it.

'Let me finish. Regardless of whether your verdict was the right one, or not, you now have to look forward, and you have both the support and the opportunity to escape the cycle.'

261

My support was my mum, and my opportunity was music, which was organised by my mum, so what do I have now?

Lucas says, 'It doesn't make sense that they would automatically suspect you.'

'It doesn't have to make sense,' I tell him.

'It's paranoid.'

I'm not going to give him an answer to that. There are things that only I know about this kind of thing. Lucas has no experience.

'Zoe, can you do something for me?' he asks after he's worked out that I'm not going to rise to his comment.

'What?'

'Delete the email I sent you. The script.'

'Why?'

'Did you read it?'

'Only the first part.'

'Just delete it. I'm deleting it from mine.'

He has his phone out now and he's scrolling through it, probably deleting it from his 'sent' box.

'Why?'

'It doesn't matter any more. It's stupid.'

'What?'

'Pass me your phone, I can do it.'

'No.'

He scoots along the sofa, closer to me, and he puts his hand on my leg, which sends a jolt of something through me, but it's not the same feeling I had last night when he kissed me, it's stranger than that somehow.

'I'll delete it for you. Please. It was just a stupid thing. It feels wrong now. Please, Zoe. I lost my mum too, remember ...'

But he struggles to find more words to explain what he means by that, and it frustrates me when he fails.

'What?'

A pause, as his eyes search mine, reading my impatience, then: 'It's complicated. It's personal.'

'You're doing my head in,' I tell him, which is something everybody at the Unit used to say. Then I ask him, 'Have you ever seen a counsellor about your mum dying?' because I wonder if I'll have to. I don't mind, if they're good like Jason kind of was, but I do mind if they're just patronising and give me sad eyes.

'No.' I feel like he's lying when he says that though, because his eyes sort of dart.

'Why not?'

'I don't know. Dad, just … Dad said we could help each other, that we'd be better on our own. It was fine.'

I can see that it wasn't, though, because of the way he bites his bottom lip, and then when he holds his hand out for my phone again, and says, 'Please, Zoe?' I hand it to him, because I'm soft. He taps away at it before giving it back to me and, when he does, I say, 'They can find anything you delete, you know that, don't you? They'll find the panop messages you sent me.'

I say that even though I know that it doesn't really matter if they do, because they'll know about my history anyway, as soon as they put my name into their computers, and sending a panop message like the ones Lucas sent isn't a crime, but for some reason I still feel like having a go at him a bit. He doesn't get a chance to reply to me though, before Uncle Richard interrupts us.

'The police are coming,' he says. 'They want to talk to everybody again.'

We talked to them a little bit this morning, but as a group, not one by one, which is what I know they like best.

'Initial accounts,' I say. 'That's what they want.'

RICHARD

Keep Calm and Carry On.

It's a slogan you see everywhere these days, it's even printed on one of the tea towels that's draped over the radiator in our kitchen. It might have recently become part of popular culture, but that slogan has its roots in wartime strength and self-sufficiency, and today I vow to be its living embodiment, because Maria's death is a tragedy that has thrown our family into crisis, and somebody needs to keep their head.

My head is actually gripped in a vice of white pain, the worst kind of almost-migraine hangover, and I'm as parched as if I'd trekked the Kalahari, but action has always been a better kind of pain relief for me than anything you can buy from the chemist. It helps keep feelings of shame at bay too.

The bereaved family has only been in our house for about an hour, but already it's the baby who is proving most difficult to handle, so I've decided to take charge of her.

She's a gorgeous creature, utterly charming, and I'll admit to feeling quite fond of her already. The au pair was tending to her but she's rather uselessly gone to bed, though the poor girl did look beyond exhausted, and I suspect that she and I are possibly suffering similar symptoms from the after-effects of alcohol this morning, although I have the benefit of having slept.

Tessa didn't come home last night. It's a very heavy thought because you'd have to be born yesterday not to work out that it's likely she spent the night with another man. If she hadn't reacted so defensively, I might have believed that she'd crashed out at the house of a girlfriend. She's in shock, of course, and that will have modified her normal behaviour, but she and I dance such a game of accusation and recrimination that I know guilty and defensive behaviour when I see it. I'm an expert in it myself, after all.

As I cradle her baby daughter, my thoughts keep travelling to Maria, and the secret knowledge that I never warmed to her. She was a beautiful woman, like both her girls, but I found her prickly and, if I'm honest, shallow.

Tessa disagreed fairly strongly, so we didn't discuss it for fear of a row, but I didn't like the way Maria and Philip pushed Zoe so relentlessly on the piano. As far as I could see, the poor girl never got to climb a tree or feed a chicken on that farm if she could have been practising her arpeggios. Philip wasn't as bad as Maria, but he was guilty of it too. I don't know why Tess excused her sister and Philip this behaviour. My best guess is that she carried around guilt about being the high-achiever, the good girl, and she felt happy because Maria might finally have a chance to match those achievements, albeit via her daughter.

The invasion of our house is strange. Where yesterday I lost the battle with the urges, compounded by the silence of the place, today I find my self-control is performing fairly well. Odd, given the circumstances, and the levels of tension that are prevalent, but welcome nevertheless.

When I take the baby upstairs to attempt to change her nappy, I waste three of the damn things before I get one on to her. It's not easy to fit a clean outfit thing on those slippery limbs either, but I rather like the way she grabs my hand as I try. It stops the dratted tremor.

On the way downstairs, I pause by the bathroom door. I have a bottle or two of vodka stashed under the bath in there, tucked away behind the cladding. My throat wants it, my lips want it, and my head wants it. It has even stolen my heart.

As I prevaricate, the baby puts her fingers in my mouth – she's obsessed with doing that, for what reason I cannot guess – and I pull her hand away and lick my parched lips. Come on, Richard, I tell myself. Pull yourself together. Somehow, it feels wrong to drink with her in my arms. She's the antithesis of my grubby pre-owned path in life; she's fresh and new and unspoiled and I will not sully her.

I move on past the bathroom and down the stairs.

Later, when Tessa is up to it, we must talk, she and I, about where she was last night, and the conversation will no doubt be as sad and bitter as so many of our others, perhaps worse.

In the meantime, I shall try to be of practical use.

'Most Gracious Grace,' I say to her, 'would you care for something to eat?'

As we arrive in the kitchen, I feel strengthened by the fact that I resisted taking a drink, and I make some firm resolutions. I shall look after this baby so that the others don't have to. I shall try to resist asking my wife where she was last night, because she has just lost her sister.

I will not let this bereaved family down, and I will not let my wife down.

I have my first small success when Grace appears to relish eating mashed banana.

SAM

As soon as Zoe Maisey and her uncle Richard have left my office, I shut the door and look at my watch.

I have a scan booked at 11.30, and a bit later an appointment with the consultant to discuss the result. This is what they've described as a 'fast-track' service, which was not what I wanted to hear.

I can walk to the hospital from my office, so I have plenty of time to make a phone call, even though I shouldn't.

I take a deep breath as I flick through the contacts on my phone and find Detective Sergeant Nick George. He's an old school mate, and I'm wondering if he'll do me a favour. I can't ring anybody else, because I shouldn't be doing this at all; I'm a potential witness.

Before I dial, I decide that this call is best made outside. As solicitors we trade in discretion, but walls have ears, and this isn't a phone call that should be overheard.

On my way out, my secretary says, 'In or out for the rest of the day, Sam?'

'Out,' I say. 'Definitely out.'

'He works too hard,' I hear her say to one of the other admin staff as the doors swing shut behind me. 'It's supposed to be his day off today.'

They don't know about my appointment, nobody at work does.

Nick George works in the Criminal Investigation Department in Bristol. We met for a drink when I first moved here and I heard about how he'd got married and had twins via IVF and how his wife had struggled to cope with the babies when he worked nights. We'd got on well at school, never close, but friendly, and both of us ambitious. Secret swots. Our paths hadn't crossed through work yet, but that was probably just a matter of time.

Outside, the streets are already hot. I try Nick's number as I'm walking through the city centre, keeping to the patches of shade beside by the buildings, and he calls me back a few minutes later as I'm wandering along the edge of the canal and looking for some prettiness in the smooth surface of the water, but instead being distracted by bits of rubbish lapping the concrete edges and reflections of the corporate buildings around me.

'What's your interest, Sam?' Nick asks me.

I come to a stop in the shade beside a waterside bar, where the pavement is sticky from the drinks that were spilled the night before. Next to me, a huge area has been cleared in preparation for some sort of building project. A couple of shallow puddles linger in its centre after the rain, but mostly it's a vast expanse of dust and rubble.

'I know them.' I think it's best to be forthright with him from the outset, but I suppose I'm not entirely honest, because I don't tell him that I might be a witness.

'Not much I can tell except that the body was found outside the front of the house, in some kind of outbuilding.'

I'm relieved to hear that, because I understand immediately that it's a scenario that could throw up a vast number of suspects, both from inside and outside the family.

269

It's important to me that it could be somebody outside the family, for obvious reasons. I want to ask a thousand other questions, like if he knows the cause of death, but that would be definitively crossing a line, and I mustn't do it.

'You close to them?'

'I know the sister of the woman who died.'

'Oh dear, sorry.'

We both know the conversation is over and that it probably shouldn't have happened at all. I ask after his wife and kids and just as I'm ready to hang up, he says, 'I heard that you weren't well?'

'From who?'

'My mum.' His laugh is a bit embarrassed. 'The Bideford grapevine is still thriving.'

I did tell my parents about my symptoms and about the doctor's suspicions. They're the only people that know. Or the only people who I thought knew. They've obviously been talking.

'I'm OK.'

'Is it true?'

And suddenly, looking out over the empty site beside me, and missing Tessa, I feel like telling somebody.

'I have a scan today to help confirm the diagnosis. It's complicated.'

'Is it likely?'

'They're pretty sure.'

'I'm so sorry, mate.'

'It's OK.'

'Will you carry on working?'

'For as long as I can.'

He clears his throat. 'Drink soon?'
'Sure. Look I've got to shoot off, I'll call you.'
'Make sure you do.'
I probably will call him.

TESSA

Richard's carrying the baby. He's walking around the house with Grace on his hip as if he was born to it, and I'm not sure how I feel about that.

It's been a while since our friends had babies and we would occasionally carry them, and I don't think Richard has ever had Grace in his arms before. He's transformed into the image of a benevolent uncle and, because I've wronged him, I resent that he's a spectacle of goodness today. I almost feel he's taunting me with it.

I try to reject that thought, though, because I know that grief is a strange and unpredictable thing, and I recognise that it's provoking great surges of anger in me. If I'm honest, what I really want is for Richard to be looking after me, and me alone.

Or do I want Sam to do that? I'm confused, and the truth could be that at this moment I want them both.

'Katya's resting,' Richard says. 'The poor girl was just about finished. I think she's had the baby all night.'

He's pretending not to be feeling the effects of yesterday's binge but I've seen the empty ibuprofen packets in the bedroom.

We have a moment to ourselves, apart from the baby.

'Where were you last night, Tess?' he asks me.

'I needed some time alone.'

He lets this comment settle, visibly hurt by it. There are

arguments that we've had so many times that he knows the score: he's an alcoholic, therefore I have the moral high ground. Almost always. So he makes a submissive response.

'I was worried,' he responds eventually. We stare at each other across the room, and Grace tries to put her fingers in his mouth.

'Oh don't try that again,' he tells her, waggling her fingers. 'You'll find some ancient fillings or some other kind of horror in there.'

She tries again. 'Stop it!' he says, shaking her hand, and he laughs. Only a little, but the sound of it and the look of amusement on his face jolts me because I'm not sure when I last heard Richard laugh.

When the detectives arrive at the house, the atmosphere changes immediately. Where before we were roaming the rooms like lost souls, and the Family Liaison Officer busied herself locating the kettle, and the tea, like a mother hen, now we all become constricted, nervous, hyped up and we feel under scrutiny.

Chris responds to the detectives by putting on as good a version of his professional self as he can manage under the circumstances. Shaking hands, trying to find the words to ask practical questions. But he reminds me of a faulty robotic toy: you can see what it's meant to be doing, but it just can't manage it properly.

The detectives ask if there's a suitable room that they can use for interviews.

I install them in our dining room.

In the sitting room, Zoe is curled up in a corner of the sofa, her eyes watchful and guarded behind that hair.

Beside her, Lucas looks catatonic.

Richard has taken Grace upstairs to try to settle her for a nap in our bed; I can hear him singing a nursery rhyme that I didn't even know he knew. Katya has passed out on one of the beds in our small spare room, from shock, or exhaustion, or from an excess of whatever she indulged in last night, it's hard to tell.

I clear the dining room table to make space for the detectives. My work had been spread out all over it, mostly admin from the surgery, and I push all that to one side, as well as another of Richard's models-in-progress, this one at least partially constructed with all the precision and care he can be capable of.

I offer to make the detectives tea, as if they're plumbers just in to service the boiler. They decline. They're very business-like: crisp shirts tucked into shiny leather belts. Short back and sides for both, and one with salt and pepper speckles around the ears. They remind me of the Jehovah's Witnesses who sometimes come to the door in all their smartness.

They ask to speak to Chris first and we all wait nervously and almost silently with the Family Liaison Officer, as their voices grumble away indistinguishably for forty-five minutes, separated from us by the hallway and the shut dining room door. When Chris finally emerges, he looks strained.

They ask for Zoe next, but she doesn't move; those eyes, which belonged first to my sister, look at me instead.

'I want Sam to be there with me,' she says. 'Please can we phone Sam again?' and I understand that I'm her go-to person right now, and the responsibility of that makes my stomach lurch.

'You don't need him, love. You really don't.'

Still she won't move from the sofa. I wonder if the police have powers to manhandle her into the dining room to answer questions.

'Why don't you just have a little chat with the detectives,' says the Family Liaison Officer. She's a dumpy woman who has a bit of a wheeze going on that I'd want to treat if she were an animal. 'As soon as they've heard from you they can crack on and get to work finding out what's happened to …' She tails off. Zoe's stare is ferocious.

'It won't do any harm,' I'm trying to be reassuring but it's a struggle.

'Just do as you're told on this occasion,' says Chris and his words interject sharply like the crack of a whip. 'It's not negotiable.'

Zoe stands up abruptly, and her clothes hang off her in a ghoulish sort of way for a moment or two before she wraps her arms and her garments tight around herself again and shuffles towards the dining room. I see her slump into a chair opposite the detectives and then one of them gets up and walks around the table to shut the door behind her.

ZOE

Mum was my protector. Even when she got it wrong you could never fault her for trying. I knew that, and Jason banged on about it all the time. She wouldn't have let them interview me without Sam.

Mum was a bit taller than me, and had shiny blonde hair, which everybody admired and which she gave to me and Grace.

When I was little, she was cuddly and firm and soft, and she smelled of wood smoke and cooking. In the flat we lived in after the accident she smelled of cigarette smoke and in the Second Chance House it wasn't a smell, but a scent, and Chris gave it to her in posh bottles that she kept in a row on her dressing table. Her frame was thinner by then too. Not cuddly, like it used to be, but she looked great because it was *so slim*, everybody said so.

On the floor of the shed her body looked and felt cold.

Now, I just have my dad, and I have Tess, and I have Richard, I have Sam and I have Chris. But I'm very much not sure of Chris; in fact all I'm sure of is how much I don't really know him when Mum isn't here to be a bridge between us. The only thing I'm sure of is that he called me a slut yesterday evening, and that there was darkness in his eyes.

Tess and Richard love me but they won't defend me the way my mum would.

Sam doesn't think I need him.

My dad isn't here yet, and I don't want him to come anyway.

So when I sit down in front of the investigating officers I decide that I must protect myself, and I know what I'm going to do.

The policemen look exactly the same as each other, as if you'd popped them out of a PEZ detective dispenser. I've met a lot of police, and these two are definitely the most businesslike. They remind me of some of the men who come to the house to meet Chris: you want to unwrap them out of their perfect suits to see if they've got real beating hearts and breathing lungs underneath.

'We're very sorry for your loss,' one of them says.

I don't reply at first, because I'm thinking about the Unit.

When I got to the Unit, I thought everybody was going to be thick, and I was right in a way for many of them, but only if you're just talking about exam success. Second Chance Family type of success.

The kids on the Unit weren't thick at all if you're talking about being smart. They knew stuff about police interviews and legal advice and courtrooms that nobody tells you in your before life.

Right now, I'm not being charged with a crime; I know that.

But even though I'm not being charged what's ringing in my head is what the kids in the Unit said about giving 'no comment' interviews. It's the best strategy for not letting yourself get stuffed up by something that you say. What nobody tells you is that even if you're not under caution, even

277

if you're just 'having a chat' with the police, you can make what they just have to decide to call a 'significant statement', and then they can ask you about it later in a proper, recorded interview, and that interview can be quoted in court.

Ergo: no chat you have with police is a 'safe' chat.

Ergo: I decide to run my own 'no comment' defence.

Because then, even though they'll tell me that this could be seen as uncooperative behaviour, and it could be frowned on, etc., etc., all scare tactics, I'll avoid the trap of delivering myself into their hands, because a 'no comment' interview dumps the burden of proof on the police if they want to charge you.

Why am I giving so much weight to what the kids in the Unit said? Partly it's because as well as finding out they were cleverer than I thought they would be, I also liked and trusted them, a few of them anyway, though not all obviously, because some were proper psychos. It's also because there's one more thing nobody ever talks about in my life any more, and that's how totally screwed-up unfair my verdict was.

Eva Bell robbed me of a chance at getting the 'Not Guilty' verdict my mum wanted because she lied to protect her brother. At the time, my mum sobbed and said, 'It's a miscarriage of justice,' and Sam looked white and said how sorry he was, and my dad accused Mum of persuading me to make the wrong plea. In the Unit, I talked to Jason about it a bit but it was never a long chat because everybody in the Unit basically believes that they've been screwed over in some way so the key workers are fed up of hearing it.

When I first got out of the Unit, and we were in the flat, my mum used to talk to me about it and she was still really bitter, but since she met Chris I was never allowed to say how it was wrong. It was time to 'put it behind me', Mum told me. The 'miscarriage of justice' had no place in the Second Chance Life because it didn't exist there. It was erased, even though the unfairness of it had burned inside me since the trial, and still does.

What I can do right now, though, is to use what I've learned from it; and what I've learned is that you can't be too careful and you can never trust the system. Never.

It's difficult to do what I've decided to do, I know that from before, because early interview is the softly, softly stage, when you feel like the police are your friends, that they understand, and it's so tempting to talk, you even want to talk, and after the accident I told them everything, and I didn't realise that each word was another scoop of the shovel in Project Digging My Own Grave.

So I tell myself to be strong and I put my strategy into action straight away. When the detective says, 'We're very sorry for your loss,' I reply: 'No comment.'

There's a pause before one of them says, 'You're not being charged, love, we're not taking a formal statement from you. All we're hoping is that you can tell us a bit about what happened last night, just give us an initial account.'

When I hear that I think: Knew it, knew they were going to say 'initial account', but all I say is: 'No comment.'

He puts his notebook down on the table and drops his pen on to it. Then he leans towards me. 'You don't need to reply "no comment" in an interview like this. We're not asking you to account for yourself, it's just a chat.'

'No comment.'

'Can you at least tell us how old you are?'

'No comment.'

'We gather you played the piano at a concert last night,' says the other detective.

'No comment.'

His eyebrows shoot up his forehead. I'm not always good at knowing when I'm annoying people but I can tell that I'm royally pissing him off now.

'You're very good at the piano I hear?'

'No comment.'

'It's quite a thing to publicly perform at your age, isn't it?'

It's harder than you think to run a 'no comment' interview. The urge to reply, especially when questions are friendly, or flattering, is very strong. The normal answers to their questions form in your mouth but you have to swallow them back, and instead spit out the two words that they have to pretend don't frustrate them.

'No comment.'

'Would you say you're a prodigy?'

'No comment.'

'Do you enjoy playing with your brother?'

That one is especially hard not to reply to, because they've got it wrong, and I hate it when people get things wrong. 'Step. Brother.' I want to say, and in my head I would add 'imbeciles'. Jason didn't like me correcting people, but my mum and dad never minded. It made them laugh.

'No comment.'

I can see that I'm annoying the quiet one as well. He keeps trying tactics on me. He smiles, and then does a hard stare, and then looks quizzical as if he can't possibly understand why I might be saying 'No comment'.

Now he clears his throat and says, 'You do know, Zoe, that we're just trying to get to the bottom of what happened last night, don't you? It would be for everybody's good if you tell us what happened last night, because then we can focus on really finding out what happened to your mum. You'd want that for her, wouldn't you?'

'No comment.'

He tries not to be frustrated but a little twist of his lips tells me that he is and I have to bite my own lips so I don't smirk.

In the Unit, if you get to smirk at the expense of the police, you would get an A star, or a sticker on your chart, or a shiny trophy, or whatever.

I don't think the detective notices my lips twitching though, because the door of the room opens suddenly enough to make me jump and there is my actual, real dad.

TESSA

I'm standing just beside Philip Guerin when he and Zoe first come face to face, and my impression is that they might as well have the Grand Canyon between them because neither of them seems able to move at first, but when he finally opens his arms to her she gets up from the chair and runs into them, and the force with which she does that makes him gasp.

The first thing he says is, 'Why is Zoe being interviewed without an adult present?'

The detectives stand up and the one on the left says, 'We understood that Zoe is seventeen years old.'

'It's a grey area,' says her father, 'and you know that.' He says this wearily, as if the knowledge he has about the rights of children in the legal system is something he doesn't really care for, which is probably the case.

'It's perfectly acceptable,' the detective holds his ground, 'particularly as she's not being charged, this is just an informal interview; and you are, sir?'

'Her dad.'

Philip Guerin has aged since I last saw him, terribly. I heard from Maria that he hadn't done well since the accident, that his elderly mother was turning up at the farmhouse to cook for him, and you can see that despair in the way the lines on his face have set, and his defeated posture, though that is, perhaps, also a result of the news he's heard this morning.

In spite of that, I can't help feeling a substantial twinge of resentment towards him because he abandoned my sister and Zoe, claiming that the outcome of their shared existence was too much for him. He absolved himself of blame, hurled accusations of hothousing Zoe at my sister, but I'd seen him do it too. I'd heard him use the full armoury of parental weapons to encourage her to play the piano: threats, copious amounts of praise when she'd done well and buckets of emotional blackmail – 'You don't want to let your teacher down, do you, or your mum? She's given up so much so you can perform.'

The detective holds out his hand, says he's sorry for Philip's loss and they shake awkwardly, and introduce themselves formally, with Zoe's body still sandwiched against her father.

'I don't want you to think we're getting ahead of ourselves here, Mr Guerin,' says the detective. 'I understand that Zoe's had previous experience in the justice system, but I want to reassure you that she's not under suspicion at this time, and we're just trying to get her account of what happened last night, so we can start to get to the bottom of it.'

And from her father's chest, her voice distorted by his clothing, Zoe says, 'I was asleep.'

Philip lifts his hands as if to say, *There it is, she's told you everything*, but he doesn't then clamp them around his daughter. As she clings to his chest with what I can only describe as ferocity, his arms simply drop to his side in a gesture that looks a whole lot like defeat, and I have a terrible feeling that he's not going to be much help to Zoe at all.

SAM

Nick George calls me back unexpectedly, as I'm sitting down in the waiting room at the hospital. They're running late so I'm killing time by looking up the news on my phone to see if there's anything out there yet about Maria.

'BODY FOUND AT STOKE BISHOP HOME' it says on Bristol 24/7.

The only development on that is on the police breaking news website, which identifies the body as female, and in her thirties. They haven't released Maria's name yet, but it will surely be soon.

Nick doesn't bother with pleasantries this time. 'Look,' he says, 'I'm only going to tell you this one thing, and I shouldn't even be doing that.'

I put my finger in my other ear because the receptionist is talking really loudly to an elderly man whose head is sagging, revealing the topography of the vertebrae in his neck.

'What?' I ask.

'Forensics found evidence of blood spatter in the house.'

'No!'

'I can't tell you any more than that, and it'll be days before they can ascertain for certain whose blood it is, or get any other results, but I thought you should know.'

'God.' I let this information sink in. The police forensics team does a simple test that shows up blood and semen at a scene instantly, even if it's been cleaned away. It's the only test that gives a swift result. Everything else must be sent away to be examined in the lab.

'I've got to go. I hope it's not going to get too bad for the family now.'

'Where was the blood?'

'You know I can't tell you that, I shouldn't be telling you any of this at all.'

I want to mine him for more information, but I don't want to push my luck. 'Thanks, Nick. I appreciate it.'

'It's OK. I'm sorry, you know.'

I understand that it's my health he's referring to, not Maria Maisey's death. This was a sympathy call, his way of stroking my brow, a nod from one man to another man's misfortune.

Somebody taps my shoulder. It's a nurse, holding my notes and a hospital gown.

'Sorry, Nick, I've got to go but I appreciate it, mate, I really do.'

The nurse shows me into a miniature cubicle where she hands me the gown and tells me to change into it. There's a locker in the corridor, she says, where I can leave my stuff.

I get changed and, before I put my things in the locker, I try to phone Tessa but it goes straight to voicemail. The nurse hovers. The radiologist is ready for me, she says, we should hurry up.

TESSA

When it's my turn to sit down with the detectives my hands shake. The adrenalin that got me through the last few hours has crashed and I sit with my hands under the table, on my lap, where they keep up their involuntary motion. It occurs to me that this is what it must be like for Richard.

On the mantelpiece behind the detectives I notice a drooping vase of flowers, which I've forgotten to refresh. They were given to me by a grateful family at the surgery, but now they've become carcasses, with papery petals and shrunken stalks. Beside them hangs a watercolour that Richard and I brought back from Hong Kong, and have always cherished. Elegant and simple swathes of colour describe two pears on a branch and a small bird. The serenity of the scene is a world away from the mess we're in.

The first thing the detective says to me is something kind: 'We're very sorry for your loss, Mrs Downing,' and so then they have to wait until I stop crying. It's usually me doing this in the surgery, waiting for the grief of others to subside after I've offered them a kind word in a horrible situation, so it feels strange that the tables have turned. It embarrasses me.

'I'm sorry,' I say. 'I'm so sorry.'

'Please,' says the detective who first spoke, 'take your time.'

They stare at their notepads while I wipe my tears away and, after a decent interval, when I've stopped snivelling loudly, they ask if I'm ready.

'How was she killed?' I ask them.

'Ah, so, at this time it's hard for us to say for sure, but your sister's body has been taken into the care of the coroner for tests so we can establish exactly what happened,' the slightly shorter detective replies. He has kind eyes.

'In due course,' adds his partner, as if I might be unreasonably expecting a fast-track service.

Of course I'm thinking then of the morgue, of shiny stainless steel, of bodies in drawers, of the clank of surgical instruments on a metal tray and the bloodless cut of a post-mortem incision. My sister is too beautiful for such treatment. I always had a protective instinct towards her, however much she resisted it, and even when she chose her own, fiercely independent path through life. I felt that instinct every day of my life, until today, when she's managed to elude me with absolute finality.

'Could you give us your account of what happened last night?'

'From when?'

'From whenever you feel you'd like to start.' They're exuding patience, and they're purposely not leading my answers. This, I can tell. The account I give is up to me.

'I went to Zoe's concert,' I say. 'It started at seven-thirty but I got there at about six forty-five to learn how to use the video camera because it was my job to record the children's performances.'

'And did you go alone?'

I nod, hoping he won't ask me why, and am relieved when all he does is make a note. The other man has his arms folded and his head slightly cocked to one side. He's just listening and watching and I find that unnerving. Sam flits briefly through

287

my mind because it occurs to me that this is his world, and I've never glimpsed it before.

'Can you tell us about the concert?' says the detective who's writing.

Memories come to me vividly, and in sharp focus. I tell all. From the detectives' responses I can hear that they already know about Zoe's past conviction, and I think that either they've run background checks on us very quickly, or Chris has told them, and I reckon it's more likely to be the latter.

More note-taking, then they ask me to continue talking them through the evening.

My words flow until I get to the part when we're all back at Chris and Maria's house, because this is private territory, and I am, just like Maria, a private person. The invasion of our family's privacy was one of the hardest things to bear, for all of us, after Zoe's accident.

'Will the press report what happened?' I ask the detectives.

'They will report that there's been a death,' the listening one answers, 'and they'll report the progress of the investigation.'

'What about Zoe?'

'We won't be broadcasting Zoe's history.'

'Can they?'

The answer is in the expression in his eyes: it tells me that there's a point beyond which he has no control over what the press do.

'We'll do our best to make sure it doesn't happen if it could prejudice a trial,' he says eventually and the other man gives him a sharp look and says, 'Let's not get ahead of ourselves.'

'What?' I don't understand at first, and it's a thump in the gut when I realise that what they mean is that Zoe could be a suspect.

'Let's move on. Can you tell us about when you first arrived at the house?'

So I try, but my natural instinct to remain private means that I falter over my words and descriptions. I feel guilty when they ask me to pause while they take time to note down my words about my conversation with Tom Barlow. When they ask me why I followed him I also feel guilty when I say, 'Because I didn't know what he was going to do,' and then the guilt is compounded further when I think of him at the doorway to his home, with his wife and child.

The things I'm saying about him go against my instincts that he is a good and loving man, but they also feed a suspicion that I know Chris shares: that Tom Barlow could have hurt Maria. I wonder if she met him outside the house and tried to persuade him not to publicise Zoe's actions? Did she provoke a rage in him that he couldn't contain after a long, hot night of despair and frustration? That is surely the version of events that looks most likely right now.

I also feel as if I need to defend my sister – old habits die hard – and so to an extent I gloss over Maria's poolside scene by saying that she began to feel under the weather after a glass of wine, that she was tired from being up with the baby, and she never coped well with the heat, and I tell the police that I went home after Maria came out of the pool.

'And how did things seem with the family at this point, when you left?'

'I think everybody was tired, and a little rattled. The concert, and the revelation, had been difficult for them all. It was a complicated night.'

'Do you think her husband was angry with her?'

I think about this one before I answer, mostly because I'm not sure. 'I think he was upset, but he loves her, you know.'

I remember Chris wrapping his arms around her, enveloping her in a towel. I remember her burying her head into his chest.

'He loved her,' I say.

'OK.' He notes something down, but, as he does, I wonder whether I'm sure of that.

'Do you have something to add?' The detective watching me notices something in my expression.

'No.'

My sister had a good life, I'm sure of it. It's what we all wanted for her, after everything, it's what she deserved.

'Just one more thing,' he says. 'We're asking everybody who was at the house if they would mind letting us have their phones. Just to help us crack on with ruling things out; speeds up our inquiries. Would that be OK?'

I think of all the texts between Sam and I on my phone, and all the emails too, but I try not to let those thoughts show because the officer is watching me.

'No, that's fine,' I say and I get my phone out of my pocket and pass it to him.

He hands it to his colleague, who puts it in a bag, and writes my name on the outside of it. I see they already have Zoe's.

'Have you arrested Tom Barlow?' I ask them, because I feel as though they should be more interested in what he did.

The detective looks at me as if he's assessing me in some way. Then he says, 'Mr Barlow has been interviewed, but he has a solid alibi. He did not murder your sister.'

ZOE

Me and Dad sit in the garden. There's a bench there which my mum would have had pressure-washed because it's got lichen and bird mess on it, but we ignore that and we sit on it anyway.

Dad is wiping his eyes because tears are leaking out of them slowly and oozily, the way tar used to seep out of the old railway sleepers we had in the yard at the farm. I know he's crying because of Mum, but I'm also used to the sight of it because it's what used to happen after the accident when he sat for long hours at the window of our farmhouse, and looked out towards the fold in the landscape that allowed you a small glimpse of the ocean.

Nobody spoke to us, you see, in the village after the accident. Even though some of them had known Dad since he was a baby. We were shut out of all the communal arrangements too. Nobody bought our produce, shared costs for oil, or anything like that any more. That's what really broke my dad, Granny Guerin said. Not what I did but how other people treated him after it. It tore the soul out of him.

'I can't believe it,' he says. 'Out of the two of us, I never thought she'd be the one to go first.'

He's thinking about Mum, but I don't know what to say to that because it feels irrelevant to now, to the problem of now, which is who killed her and how scared I feel.

291

'Amelia Barlow's dad came to the concert,' I tell him. 'We didn't know there was a stone for her in the churchyard.'

'I know what he did last night but that man's not a killer,' my dad says.

'How do you know that?'

'Because I know his family.'

'How does that tell you anything?'

'He's from good stock, Zoe.'

'Why? Because he's from Devon? What difference does that make to anything? Reality check, Dad, I'm from Devon and I killed people, but you never stand up for me!'

I've snapped. It doesn't happen often but when it does I feel like I'm exploding with anger at all the people who won't accept that what I did was just an accident, and I should never have gone to jail, and I get frustrated that people who are supposed to love me can't keep up with all the things in my head, and I get angry too with the ideas themselves, the strength of them, the way that they race around and multiply and keep me up at night.

When I'm angry I am, according to Jason and my mum, my own worst enemy.

I'm standing up and facing Dad now and I know I must look ugly because I can feel that my face has contorted out of shape. If my mum were here now she'd hold my shoulders and look into my eyes and tell me to calm down, and tell me to count to ten with her and try to access my techniques for keeping in control of my emotions.

My dad just buries his face in his hands and I can't stand it so I start to hit him. I don't hit him hard, but my hands slap at his shoulders and the top of his head, and they keep slapping until he stands up and catches my wrists and bellows: 'Enough! Zoe! Enough!'

And I feel my knees crumple until I'm down on the brittle grass on Tess's lawn and it's spiking into my shins and my forehead and my hands, and pieces of it get into my mouth.

I don't want my dad with his leaking eyes and his permanent look of disappointment and defeat that I know I caused. I want my mum.

Out of the corner of my eye, I can see the twin trunks of Dad's legs as he just stands uselessly over me, and then I hear the voice of the Family Liaison Officer saying, 'Is everything all right, Mr Guerin?' and my dad says, 'No, it's not, I don't know what to do with her,' and then they both help me up, but I keep my body as floppy as possible at first, because sometimes that's the only way you can keep protesting how you feel when people have resorted to manhandling you.

RICHARD

Zoe is making a scene in the garden. I notice it happen from the kitchen window and the detectives in the dining room see it too, because one of them interrupts the interview with Tessa and calls for the Liaison Officer woman to go out and help. Grace and I are struggling somewhat to find something else suitable for her to eat, but we settle on a biscuit, which she seems to enjoy hugely, and somebody has put a bottle of her milk in the fridge so I heat that up the way I saw the Russian do it earlier: small saucepan, water heating, bottle floating in it. I feel quite professional when I squeeze some of the milk out of it on to the inside of my wrist to test the temperature, as I also observed.

'It's perfect, darling,' I say to Grace and she stuffs it into her mouth even before I've got us settled down properly in the sitting room, and guzzles it with the rather unnervingly greedy intensity of a lamb at the ewe's udder.

We disturb Lucas. He's looking through my collection of DVDs, and he jumps out of his skin when we enter the room, as if I'd caught him with his hand in my wallet.

'You can borrow one if you like,' I say, to put him at ease. 'I mean, not today, but when things are more … although if it helps to watch something now, then feel free.'

'No, thank you, I was just looking.' He sits back down, plunges his hands into his pockets.

I'm not really sure what to say to him, though I feel sorry for him. He probably had become fond of Maria, had maybe even come to love her, and to bear this in addition to the premature loss of his own mother is going to be hard, *is* hard. I'm also at a loss for words because I mostly only talk to other scientists at work and to Tess at home. My friends have long since slipped down the cracks between my infrequent attempts at keeping in touch. I should probably say something reassuring, or comforting, but all I can come up with is, 'Do you like film then?'

He nods. The movement is economical, the eye contact only fleeting.

'What sort of films do you like?'

He glances back at me, and then at the door, as if he's not sure either that we should be talking like this, but I think it's OK, especially if it keeps his head above water, reminds him that somebody is interested in him.

'I like some old films.'

'Such as?'

'Um. *Apocalypse Now* is a favourite.'

I'm surprised that he's been allowed to watch that in their closeted household, but I try not to let that show.

'One of my favourite opening sequences,' I say.

He sits up straighter, engages with me with startling intensity. 'I know, it's incredible. The montage is quite confusing at first but it gives you the whole scene, how it starts off with the slow rasp of the helicopter blades, which comes in and out like an echo, and you fade in to the palm trees with blue sky above, and then you see the yellow smoke and the helicopters coming across the trees and then, boom!, the explosion, which is so intense, and then there are loads of images overlaid on each other so you see his face in the hotel room over the images of his memories of Vietnam and then the fan above him becomes the helicopter blades and you've got "This is the End" playing over it which is so intense when you see his eyes, and his pupils are like pinpricks and then the camera goes to the window and you're in Saigon. And the voiceover starts. It's incredible.'

He comes alive as he delivers this speech and I'm astounded because I've never heard this boy talk so much. Granted, I've only spent time with him on a handful of occasions, but he behaved as if he was mute then, and Tessa has made the same observation about him.

'I love the scene where they brief the main character,' I say, wanting to keep Lucas talking, thinking that it's good for him.

He fixes me with eyes that seem slickly alive, like black treacle. He says, in a slightly strange accent: "'Because there's a conflict in every human heart between the rational and the irrational, between good and evil … Every man has got a breaking point."'

'What?' I say, feeling rather unnerved, before I appreciate that he's quoting the film, and in fact the scene I just mentioned. In truth, I have very scant recollection of it, but I don't want to discourage him, so I say, 'Oh sorry, yes! Bravo, Lucas. Yes, very good. It's a very dark film, I think.' That, I do recall.

'I think it's his best film,' he says.

'What is?' Chris has crept up on us, but he makes no move to take his daughter from me. The poor man looks absolutely shattered.

'Can I get you anything?' I ask him. 'Cup of tea?'

296

'Just keep doing what you're doing.' He gestures towards Grace, who hasn't really reacted to him, because she's still too busy sucking at the bottle, which is nearly empty now. 'I hope you're not being a film bore,' he says to Lucas, rather harshly I feel, though everybody is, of course, under pressure.

'No, not at all. He was very helpfully answering a question of mine.' I brush it off, while Lucas reverts to staring at the floor.

We're distracted by the sight of Zoe being led in through the hallway, and escorted up the stairs. She's leaning on the arm of the Liaison Officer and her father is in their wake. They ascend extremely slowly and we watch.

'She's a bit overwhelmed, I think,' I say to the others, because I feel the need to excuse her behaviour, perhaps because she belonged to us before she belonged to them, and even though Grace chooses that moment to finish her bottle and try to heave herself into a sitting position with the last gulp of milk drooling from her lips, it doesn't escape my notice that Chris is looking at Zoe with an expression that I would struggle to describe as either friendly or caring.

ZOE

They bring me upstairs and tell me to lie on the single bed that's in Richard's office. The bedding smells of a man and it's creased as if it's been used, but it's soft and comfortable, and I feel sleep taking hold of me like it sometimes used to do at the Unit: more of a cosh than a slipping away, as if your body has decided that you need time out and that's the end of the matter.

At the Unit they used to tell me it was shock that made me into a virtual narcoleptic for the first couple of months.

As I shut my eyes, I feel the weight and sag of my dad sitting down on the end of the bed. As I slip away, I hope he's not doing that staring at me like he'll never be able to work me out thing, but, by the time I wake again, he's gone and I'm relieved.

The waking is sudden, though: it comes via a deep, sharp intake of breath, and a sudden urge to be sitting up, as if the covers were about to choke me, and then the knowledge that my mum is no longer here flows back into my conscious mind like water coursing through the holes in a colander.

The digital clock on Richard's bedside table tells me that I've only been asleep for about twenty minutes. I can hear voices downstairs but they're faint and indistinguishable.

I let my tears fall silently because I don't want anybody to hear me sobbing and to come with sympathy eyes. I don't like people to see me cry because that's ingrained in me since

298

I was little. 'Don't cry if you lose a competition, Zoe, that's called being a bad loser,' or 'If you keep crying, your practice will take twice as long as it needs to.'

Not crying publicly could be seen as a little tribute to my mum.

It's also a tribute to the Unit where prolonged sobbing could make you a target. It keeps other people awake, you see, and they shout at you that you're fucking with their heads and that they'll give you something to cry about if you like.

So my tears fall silently and I think about how my mum has always been there to tell me what to do, and now I don't know who's going to do that.

I think of Lucas, who lost his mum too, and that reminds me of the email that he deleted, and I decide that I want to read the rest of the script. The first part was kind of soppy and strange, but there must be something more in it or he wouldn't have asked me to delete it if it was just like a love story all the way through. I know it's not on my email any more, but it will be on my mum's account still, surely, because it wasn't just me he sent it to.

I don't have my phone any longer because the detectives took that, just like I told Lucas they would, so that once again they can comb through my private world and then pretend in interview that 'internet experts' have told them what all the text speak abbreviations stand for.

They'll see the panop messages that freaked me out earlier, but I don't mind that too much, because it wasn't illegal for me to use panop, just 'not recommended' by Jason, and I can explain that Lucas found out about me and he sent them to wind me up.

At Richard's desk, which is just a few feet away from the bed I'm lying on, I click the computer mouse and his monitor comes to life silently. There's some of his work up on the screen, but I want the internet so I carefully reduce the windows he has open and go online. No passwords are required at any stage, and that is so different from our house where everything is password protected because of 'the importance of internet and personal data security'.

My mum's email is easy to access. I haven't done it often, but just sometimes because I saw her password once and that makes it very tempting. Her password is ZoeGrace and some numbers.

Her email account is very boring, though. She mostly emails her beautician and hair salon, she gets loads of shopping order confirmation emails, and she talks to some piano people, and baby group friends, and sometimes she and Chris have incredibly boring conversations by email about paint colours or when the man's coming to trim the tree or stuff like that.

It's easy to find Lucas's email and I see that it hasn't been opened yet, so I click on it. He's sent my mum the exact same thing he sent me – it's near the top of her inbox, just above an email from Chris with the title 'Appointment on Wednesday' as if my mum's his secretary or something.

Richard and Tess must have super-efficient WiFi because the attachment that Lucas sent opens immediately and I start to read on from where I left off.

'WHAT I KNOW'

BY LUCAS KENNEDY

ACT II

**INT. CHRIS AND JULIA'S NEW HOME.
DAY.**

JULIA is up a ladder, hair tied up,
overalls on, in the middle of a lovely
room, which has gracious and generous
proportions. She's painting the
intricate plasterwork on the ceiling
rose.

> DYING JULIA (V.O.)
> My marriage was lovely at first,
> and my only sadness was settling
> down so far away from my mother,
> so I wasn't able to be with her
> when she died. I hadn't really
> had time to make many friends
> in Bristol before I met Chris
> and our life together sort
> of overwhelmed me, so I threw
> myself into making our marriage
> a wonderful place. We renovated
> a beautiful house, which Chris
> bought for us, and very soon we
> discovered that we were expecting
> a baby.

We see JULIA pause in her painting, rub
loose strands of hair from her eyes, and
put a hand to her stomach. She has felt

302

a twinge, and we see in her eyes that she knows.

INT. KENNEDY HOUSE, CHRIS AND JULIA'S BEDROOM. DAY.

The room is beautifully decorated and a lined crib sits at the end of the bed. Sitting in bed, her newborn baby in her arms, is JULIA.

> DYING JULIA (V.O.)
> The pregnancy went swimmingly. I was healthy and energetic throughout it. And on a warm May day, my baby was born. We named him Lucas. Chris chose the name.

We see the baby close up. He's beautiful.

> DYING JULIA (V.O.) (CONT'D.)
> The problem was, Chris never bonded with the baby.

As the camera pulls away, we see CHRIS standing at the end of the bed. He's looking at his wife, who is entirely absorbed in her young son, and the expression on his face is blank. He feels nothing. He turns and leaves the room, and JULIA, lost in her son's eyes, is oblivious. It's only when the door closes behind him that she raises her head.

> JULIA
> Chris?

INT. CHRIS AND JULIA'S HOUSE, SITTING ROOM. DAY.

It's Christmas Day, a few years later. We see a lovely tall tree, and a fire in the hearth. The Christmas decorations are tasteful, restrained and conservative.

> DYING JULIA (V.O.)
> After Lucas's birth we still gave the impression of being a happy family, and we often were. But something had changed.

CHRIS, JULIA and LUCAS are opening presents. It's not an especially warm scene, there's too much formality about the little group for that, but they're

going through the motions cheerfully
enough, although the three-year-old
LUCAS seems to be rather a quiet,
guarded child. When he's given a present
he looks to his father for permission
before opening it.

> DYING JULIA (V.O.)
> The problem was that since Lucas
> had been born, Chris had become
> prone to losing his temper. At
> first it wasn't too bad, but as
> the years went by, it got more
> serious, and more frightening.

LUCAS has opened his present and is
looking at it on the floor. JULIA is
on a chair beside him and she too is
opening a gift from CHRIS. She gasps
when she unwraps it as it's clearly a
very expensive ring, bigger and more
flashy than her engagement ring.

> CHRIS
> What's the matter?

> JULIA
> Nothing's the matter. It's
> beautiful. I'm just shocked, in a
> good way, of course, that's all.

                    CHRIS
You don't like it.

                    JULIA
Darling. I love it. It's just so
much more than I was expecting.
It's wonderful, really.

She takes the ring out of its box and
tries to slip it on to her finger, but
it won't fit.

                    JULIA (CONT'D)
Oh dear!

She pulls it off and tries it on another
finger but the ring is too small. She
laughs nervously. CHRIS is watching her
like a hawk. LUCAS plays on the carpet,
oblivious.

                    JULIA (CONT'D)
Do you think they might be able
to swap it?

                    CHRIS
Put it on.

                    JULIA
     Darling, it's just a little bit
     small, I'm sure if we asked them
     they would be able to loosen it,
     don't you think?

                    CHRIS
     Put it on. Not on that finger.
     Rings don't go on little fingers.

JULIA glances at LUCAS, and then back
at CHRIS, who gazes at her impassively,
arms crossed.

                    JULIA
     Don't you want to see what I got
     for you?

                    CHRIS
     I want to see you put the ring
     on.

We see from JULIA's face that she knows
there's no point in arguing with CHRIS,
that she fears an escalation. CHRIS
watches without flinching as JULIA
forces the ring over the knuckle of
her second finger. It takes time and
JULIA's clearly in pain as she does it,
though she stays silent, so LUCAS will

                    307

not notice. When the ring is finally
on, JULIA holds a trembling hand out
to CHRIS to show him. CHRIS takes her
fingers and turns them a little from
one side to the other to examine the
ring. It's impossible to ignore the red,
scraped and bruised skin that bulges
around it.

CHRIS (CONT'D)
It looks beautiful. Well done.

CHRIS leans in to kiss JULIA and she
submits to this with an attempt at a
smile.

DYING JULIA (V.O.)
I kept the ring on for a week
before going to hospital to
have it cut off and receiving
antibiotics for the infection
that had crept into the broken
skin underneath. When Chris found
out, he pulled a clump of hair
out of the back of my head and
told me I was lucky that was all
he did.

**INT. KITCHEN IN THE KENNEDY HOUSE.
EVENING.**

Six-year-old LUCAS is finishing his
supper while JULIA prepares something
for herself and CHRIS. LUCAS and JULIA
exchange a smile and we see that the
atmosphere between them is sweet and
lovely.

> DYING JULIA (V.O.)
> Chris didn't always behave like
> that. In fact he was mostly very
> generous and loving, but there
> were triggers. And, as time
> passed, I learned to recognise
> them.

The peaceful scene is interrupted by
the sound of a car pulling up outside
and then the slam of a car door. JULIA
glances anxiously at the kitchen clock.

> JULIA
> Oh! I think Daddy's home early.
> Lucas, do you think you could run
> and play in your bedroom while I
> finish making supper for him?

The dinner she's preparing consists
of piles of chopped ingredients. It's
nowhere near ready, and we see that
makes her nervous. LUCAS gets up and she
ushers him out of the room and into the
hallway.

> JULIA (CONT'D)
> Well done, poppet, I'll be up to
> give you a kiss later.

> LUCAS
> Will Daddy?

> JULIA
> I don't know. He might be a bit
> tired, but I will, I promise.

She's speaking urgently now, time is
running out. We hear the back door open.

> CHRIS
> Hello? Julia?

> JULIA
> (whispering)
> What do you need to remember to
> do?

                    LUCAS
Put my story CD on.

                    JULIA
Good! And what else?

                    LUCAS
Lock my door.

                    JULIA
Well done, darling. You're a
clever boy.

When JULIA is sure he's gone upstairs
and she's heard the lock of his door
sliding into place and the beginning of
a story CD playing, she straightens her
outfit and her hair and goes back to the
kitchen.

               JULIA (CONT'D)
Hello, darling. How are you?

                    CHRIS
Where were you?

She shuts the kitchen door behind her.

                    311

**INT. KITCHEN IN THE KENNEDY HOUSE.
NIGHT.**

It's just an hour later and there's
carnage in the room. Food and glasses
have been overturned and it's clear that
something violent has occurred.

> DYING JULIA (V.O.)
> But even as things escalated,
> after every act of violence,
> Chris was sorry.

CHRIS and JULIA sit on the floor, both
in disarray. JULIA's blouse is ripped,
her cheeks are flushed high with panic
and her hair is very tousled, but she
and CHRIS cradle each other, though he
grips her more tightly than she does
him.

> CHRIS
> I'm sorry. I'm so sorry. I love
> you so much. I don't know what
> I'd do without you.

> DYING JULIA (V.O.)
> And every time, I forgave him
> because, if I'm honest, I could
> see no way to leave him. I was

afraid of what he might do to us
if I did. And I felt shame. Oh,
the shame I felt. Shame kept my
lips sealed.

Unseen by CHRIS, we see the desperation
on JULIA's face as he strokes her hair.

INT. PRIVATE HOSPITAL, CONSULTANT'S
ROOM. DAY.

JULIA and CHRIS sit together on one side
of a desk, and a DOCTOR on the other.

> DYING JULIA (V.O.)
> The problem is, that a life lived
> in fear takes its toll on you, so
> by the time I had a diagnosis of
> a brain tumour, five years later,
> all my confidence, and most of my
> strength had sapped away.

> CHRIS
> Is there anything that can be
> done?

                    DOCTOR
We can try to treat the tumour,
to control it, but we can't cure
it, and surgery is far too risky.

                    CHRIS
How long would she have, with
treatment?

                    DOCTOR
It's hard to be precise.
Treatment could extend life
by one month, or maybe even as
much as three. But, and it's a
significant but, treatment can
have some extreme side effects.

There's a beat while CHRIS and JULIA
absorb what this means.

                    JULIA
So it's a quality of life issue.

                    DOCTOR
Yes.

                    JULIA
Be treated and be very sick
for more months and then die
anyway, or turn down treatment

and die more quickly but more
comfortably.

                    DOCTOR
That's probably what it boils
down to.

                    CHRIS
Is it worth getting another
opinion? Are you sure?

                    DOCTOR
You're most welcome to get
another opinion but I will put my
reputation on the line here, and
tell you that I'll be absolutely
staggered if you're told anything
different.

EXT. A HOSPITAL CAR PARK. DAY.

CHRIS and JULIA get into the car, each
in their own world.

                    DYING JULIA (V.O.)
We got another opinion anyway,
it wasn't as though Chris
couldn't afford it, and, as the
first doctor predicted, it was

identical to his. Chris didn't
take the news well.

We see CHRIS thump the steering wheel of
the car, and we see him turn on JULIA.
He grabs her hair in what looks like a
familiar routine, and goes to smash her
head against the passenger window, but
stops just before it makes impact, and
holds it there, less than an inch from
the glass.

                    CHRIS
What am I going to do?

                 DYING JULIA (V.O.)
And, for the first time in my
life, I stood up to him.

                    JULIA
Just this once you are going to
let go of my hair, and you are
going to drive us home and we are
going to break the news to Lucas
together.

We see surprise on CHRIS's face, and
then we see that he is hugely tempted
to bash her head against the window even
harder than at first, but he lets go and

the hard expression on his face cracks.
He starts the ignition.

Camera stays on JULIA's face as they
drive away, the car lurching too quickly
as CHRIS reverses and then speeds out of
the hospital gates.

                    DYING JULIA (V.O.)
          I don't know why it worked when I
          stood up to him for the first and
          only time that day. He drove too
          fast, as usual, because he knew
          I hated speed, and he continued
          to bully me in small ways. But
          he never touched me again. Maybe
          it was because he feared that the
          medical staff would work out what
          was happening now that they had
          ownership of my body.

We see JULIA sneak a glance at CHRIS,
searching the desperate expression on
his face for clues.

                    DYING JULIA (V.O.)
          But, you know, in the end, I
          think it was a fear of death, of
          death's power. Death was going to
          take me so he couldn't have me

any more, so perhaps that meant
I wasn't worth bullying. Or maybe
it was fear that if he touched me
again I might somehow infect him,
bring him into death's orbit.
I didn't dwell on it though,
because the bigger question was
this: in a family like ours, how
could I ever leave Lucas?

As CHRIS and JULIA arrive home they see
LUCAS, looking out of a front window.
He's obviously been waiting for them.

ZOE

I am fully freaking out by the time I've read this bit of the script. I feel sick to my core. I want to read on, I'm desperate to, because I can see that there's another section, but I'm suddenly aware that the Family Liaison Officer is peering around the door.

'Zoe, are you OK to come downstairs to be with the others?' she says, but then she sees that I'm on the computer, and she moves across the room in a solid sort of way that reminds me of a Henry Hoover: round and squat and sort of gliding, and with a fixed expression on her face.

The next thing she says is in an *I'm-handling-you* tone of voice. It's the voice they use at the Unit before they get shouty.

In the Unit there was a progression of voices, and it went like this: first, *I'm-handling-you-calmly* voice, then *don't-mess-with-me* voice, then *I'm-warning-you* voice, then *shouty* voice, and by then the key workers would have gathered in numbers and they'd go in with the restraint holds, the ones where kids who don't have enough sense or have too much panic end up getting throttled just because they've kicked off.

It happened to one of the boys just before I arrived there. Everybody kept talking about it in my first few weeks.

The Family Liaison Officer's *I'm-handling-you* voice is quite a good one, but it doesn't manage to lose that holier-than-thou tone that people have when they think that they're more sane than you.

319

I can't deny that I'm online because she's probably not stupid, but I have managed to click off the windows my mum's email and the script were on, and even do a quick browsing history delete before she gets close enough to bother getting her reading glasses out of a top pocket and peer at the screen. I'm quick, you see, at covering my tracks. There are so many rules in the Second Chance House that you have to be.

'What were you looking at, dear?' she says.

'Just YouTube.'

We're having a different conversation with our eyes to the words that we're speaking. Underneath a disapproving forehead that's collapsed into wrinkle lines above her nose, hers are saying, *What the hell were you looking at?* and mine are saying, *There would have to be a planetary collision before I tell you that.*

'Anything special on YouTube?'

'I was looking for a recording of a special piece of music.'

'You don't need to stop it because I'm here.'

'It's a piece my mum loved. I don't really want to share it today, if you don't mind.'

In spite of, or maybe because of, all the lectures about not crying in public, since I was little I have been able to turn tears off, but also on, and on this day it's even easier than usual because they're lurking anyway, in a real way.

I snivel my way out of this one and she escorts me downstairs, saying, 'Oh, pet, it's not easy this, is it?' although I know she's not dumb and I think this is a definite attempt to get me to 'open up' but there's more of a chance of me becoming Henry VIII's seventh wife before I do that.

TESSA

My interview seems interminable, the only respite when we notice Zoe laying into her dad in the garden and one of the detectives asks the Family Liaison Officer to intervene, but it moves on relentlessly after that.

They question me at length about any relationships Maria might have had outside the home and I feel hotter and more tired with every question. When one of the detectives' phones begins to buzz I feel like it wakes me up a bit, before he silences it.

But then his partner's phone starts to buzz too. They exchange a glance and his partner says, 'Excuse me, please,' and slips out into the hallway, answering with a curt statement of his name before the door has shut behind him.

He leaves a newly created sense of tension, or perhaps it's expectation, behind him like a wake. The man interviewing me glances at the door once or twice before resuming his questioning.

'Did you know who your sister socialised with outside the home?'

I open my mouth to reply, but actually I realise that I have no idea, because Maria never mentioned friends. After Grace was born, I asked her if she was going to join any mother and baby groups but she told me in no uncertain terms that she'd done all that with Zoe in Devon and had moved on. 'I'm in a different place now,' she'd said, and I'd thought how that was true in many ways, but of course I didn't articulate that because her well-being was so precarious at that time.

'I think she might have belonged to a tennis club,' is the best I can manage. 'Maria sometimes played on a ladder there. It was in Clifton, I think, the club in Clifton.'

But even as I say it I'm not really sure, though I think I recall seeing Maria in tennis whites one day. 'Chris or Katya, the au pair, will have a better idea than I do about what she did day to day,' I say, to cover up my embarrassment at knowing so little about my sister's life. There was a time when I knew everything about her, because we shared a bedroom, clothes, secrets, everything. But that was when we were teenagers.

'And I think she might have belonged to a book club,' I say, as another memory comes to me: Maria in her kitchen, dressed in figure-hugging jeans and a silk shirt, heels on, putting cling film over a plate of hors d'oeuvres, issuing instructions to Katya and to Zoe, and telling Lucas that his dad would be back in an hour or so. Me following her down the hallway and saying: 'Sorry, I was just passing, I didn't know you were going out.'

'I'm dreading it,' she said, as she wedged the plate of food into the back of the car. 'Do you think that's going to be OK?'

She didn't wait for an answer. Maria never liked taking my advice.

As the boot slammed shut, I said, 'Why are you dreading it?'

'Because the book we're supposed to read is really long and *really worthy*, and I couldn't finish it.'

'Will they mind?'

'Yes! They will! And I don't want to humiliate myself.'

'Do you have to go?'

'It's run by the wife of one of Chris's colleagues. It's good if I go.'

'Oh. Have you read a synopsis?'

'I'm not as stupid as I look.'

She winked, and smiled, and I knew she'd be OK that night. It was a typical Maria comment to make, a brief flash of her feisty, much younger self, and the kind of thing she'd probably never have said in front of Chris. For him, she smoothed away all of her insecurities, and appeared fresh and calm and purposeful and content.

'I'll phone you,' she said and I waved her off before clambering back into my own car and wondering what the book was, before remembering with a smile the dog-eared copies of Jackie Collins and Jilly Cooper novels that we'd once shared.

I didn't report that conversation to the detective, of course, because it was irrelevant, but he told me, with one of those annoying sniffs that jerk the side of people's mouths up, that Chris had already told him about the book club, and given him names.

Our interview got no further because his colleague returned and beckoned to the detective interviewing me, from the door.

'Would you mind if we resumed this later?' he asked me, a veneer of professionalism barely masking an urgent tone.

'No,' I say. 'Of course not.'

I'm relieved they haven't got around to asking me where I was last night.

Once I've gone out of the room, I realise the interview has

left me feeling thoroughly jangled; I feel as if I'm starting to question everything I ever thought.

I want to phone Sam and I go to use our landline, which is a useless, old-fashioned thing that's not even cordless. It lives in our kitchen, but I find Philip sitting in there.

He still has his mobile and I guess the police aren't bothered about taking it because he wasn't in Bristol last night. He's talking on it now, in a low voice. When he sees me, he mutters an apology to whoever he's speaking to and ends the call.

Philip always did wear all his emotions on his sleeve – I think that was one of things that attracted Maria to him in the first place – and now is no exception.

The emotion he's displaying now is guilt, and there's a certain neediness there too, which is typical of him. That quality of extreme emotional availability and the urge to share and talk that made him attractive in his youth hasn't developed as he's aged, but rather lingers as a sort of immaturity which I know is about to annoy me beyond measure.

'I'm not sure what to do tonight,' he says.

'None of us are sure what's happening tonight,' I say. 'But if you need somewhere to sleep I'm sure we can muster up a duvet and a few sofa cushions at the very least.'

My irritation levels are swelling because I don't want to deal with domestic trivia like sleeping arrangements at this moment, and they increase further still when I see from his face that that wasn't the answer he was hoping for and I suspect he might have had something else in mind.

'You can't drive home tonight,' I say. 'What about Zoe?'

'I'm not sure what I can do for her.'

'You're not sure what you can do for her?'

'Well, what can I do for her, Tess? We're estranged. What comfort can I offer her?'

'You're her father!'

My hands are plunged into the hair on either side of my head. I've forgotten the advice of every people-handling seminar I've ever sat through for work. I am beyond being reasonable or understanding. Philip Guerin's attitude is absolutely inexplicable to me and if he doesn't respond properly, right now, I'm not going to be responsible for my actions.

'I'm sorry,' he says. 'I'm sorry. I just don't know how to be her father! How can you be a father to somebody like Zoe?'

I slap him.

I hit him hard, across the cheek and his head snaps to one side before he steps away from me and stands with his hand to the hurt cheek.

'You deserve it,' I say.

'It's how I feel.' There's a wobble to his voice, the sound of self-righteousness bubbling up and demanding attention, but I am absolutely unrepentant.

I believe that if you are lucky enough to have a child then you should love them, whether or not society labels them as flawed, whether or not you label them as flawed.

'You have a duty to your daughter,' I say.

'I've met someone new,' he tells me. 'I don't know if we can have Zoe.'

My heart sinks. Philip, like Maria, has embarked on a new life, and he obviously thinks that damaged Zoe constitutes a threat to its success.

'Are you serious?'

His head bows.

'Then the least you can do is tell her yourself, but not today, Philip, not today.'

'All right,' he says.

'And I don't know who you think she's going to want to be with. Have you even thought about that?'

'You?' he asks, and I can hardly believe my ears.

'Is everything all right?' Chris speaks from the doorway. He looks from one of us to the other, searching our expressions for clues as to what's going on. I have no idea how long he's been standing there, or what he's heard.

I want to lash out at Philip, to say something that will shame him, to ask him what is wrong with him, to tell him that he must have lost his mind and his daughter is his responsibility, not mine, but what stops me is that Chris is the father of Zoe's sister.

Whatever happens, Zoe is a child whose future we must consider, and Grace must be a part of that future, because she means the world to Zoe, and even emotionally retarded Philip Guerin would be able to recognise that if he'd seen them together before this day. Relationships with Chris, then, need to be managed. I know it's what Maria would want.

'It's difficult for everybody,' I say.

I wonder how much Chris knows about Philip. I know that Maria told Chris that they had a spectacularly messy divorce, which is why there isn't much contact between Zoe and her father. But that was before the concert. Chris might have more thoughts on that particular version of events now.

Chris says, 'I understand,' but before we're forced to continue like this Richard enters the room with the baby.

'Could I give her to you for a bit, old man,' he says to Chris, handing her over. 'Just need to pop to the bathroom.'

I hate that phrase when it comes from Richard. It can mean anything from the truth, that Richard's bladder is full, to a euphemism for the bottle of something alcoholic being dragged out from the 'hiding' place under the bath and slugged back, at top speed, before a redundant flush of the loo tries to disguise the onset of the inevitable fumy breath and strained veins across his face.

Chris takes Grace, who gives him a look of surprise as if to say, *Fancy meeting you here.*

He sits her on the crook of his arm in an easy motion and they look at each other.

'So like your mother,' he says. He buries his face into her neck and she responds with a squeal of delight and wraps her arms around his head. Grace is good at hugging. They are intense, baby hugs, but all the better for it.

'Thank God for you,' Chris says to his daughter, with tears in his eyes, and I feel a bit of a lurch in my stomach, as I understand that Grace, who has my parents' blood coursing through her veins, might live a life that's very separate from our family now, and that thought is, if I'm honest, terrifying.

Will Chris raise her and Lucas together in that big house? And where will Zoe be? Will Philip accept that he needs to raise his daughter, or will she be better off with us, or even with Chris, so she can be near her sister?

'We have a lot to discuss,' I say.

'I know,' says Chris.

But neither of us can bear to start the conversation just then, and so we move away from each other, to the safety of different rooms. Philip stays sagged in his seat.

327

SAM

I can't do up the strings of my hospital gown because they've got lost round the back of me somewhere. I'm humiliated by having to shuffle along holding it together to avoid everybody being able to see my underwear.

The MRI scanner looks familiar to me from television but I'm not prepared for the noise once I'm inside it, or the discomfort of staying still for such a long period, my hands held above my head.

Amidst the darkness of the machine and the thumping sounds that penetrate in spite of the headphones they've given me, I try to think about what Nick has told me and what it means for Tessa and Zoe.

It means that unless somebody broke into the house, the chances are extremely high that somebody in Maria's household murdered her, and the police will adjust their investigation accordingly. I think back to Tess's arrival at my flat the night before, and her silence, and I wonder what it was she didn't tell me.

I think of Zoe in my office this morning and I hope to God that she was telling me the truth.

I think of the magnetic waves that are passing through my body.

I think of all the people in the waiting room and how almost all of them had family with them, or a friend, somebody to hold their hand, or at least to talk to. Self-pity creeps in and ratchets up the feelings of desperation and claustrophobia I'm experiencing.

My relationship with Tessa is the best thing and worst thing about my life. I want nobody else, but while she stays with Richard I can't have her.

There is nothing I would like more, at this moment, than to know that she would be there when I emerge from this machine.

It's a terrible effort to keep still, but I tell myself I must because the very last thing I want is for this scan to have to be repeated.

A voice comes through the headphones I'm wearing and tells me that they're moving on to my spine now. The scan of my brain is complete.

I wonder what the radiologist can see.

ZOE

The Family Liaison lady, who tells me to call her Stella, is everywhere I go. She has what she calls 'just a little word' with Richard, even though it's more of a bursting fishing net of words if you ask me. She tells him that I was online on his computer and then says to him and to me, like twenty times, that it's probably a good idea if I don't go online at the moment because I might read something that wouldn't be good for me to see.

But I know that's not just what she means. I know she's watching me for signs to see if I've done something. And the thing is, I'm desperate to read the end of Lucas's script.

My dad's in the kitchen and even though I'm still angry with him I figure he's my best chance of reading the script because he still has his phone. He's sitting in there on his own at Tess's little kitchen table, which looks like it should be in a diner, with a cup of tea in front of him that he's not drinking. He raises his eyes slowly and looks at me like he's afraid that I'll go off on one again.

'Can I borrow your phone?' I ask him.

'What?'

'Just for a minute.'

He takes a deep breath, and I think he's going to say 'no', but instead he says, 'Zoe, I think it's best if I stay in a hotel tonight, so it doesn't put too much pressure on Tessa.'

'Can I come with you?' It would be good to get away from here, from the police, from Chris, and Richard, and all of the people. It would be good to be just me and Dad.

'I don't think that's a good idea. You should probably stay with the others.'

'Why?'

He can't seem to answer that even though I'm standing right in front of him waiting for him to say something.

'Why, Dad?'

'Well …' he says eventually, but I'm fit to burst by then because sometimes I feel like I can read his mind, and I know what he's going to say, so I shout at him.

'I didn't do anything! Honestly, I swear it, what do you think I'm like?'

'That's not what I'm thinking; but there are other things to take into account if we're talking about you coming back to Devon,' and that sounds like he's getting ready to tell me that he doesn't want me, and it makes me feel as if some big heavy teeth have sunk into me.

I try to blink back tears, and to focus only on what I want, which is his phone. I've already made a sore patch inside my mouth from the biting and I dig my molars into the soft, sore tissue there again and pull myself back into togetherness. Jason would be proud.

'Can I borrow your phone, please?' I ask him again. 'I just want to look something up.'

He hands his phone over to me, because he feels obliged now. Guilt is a good way to leverage people. Jason didn't tell me that; nobody needed to tell me that. I learned it because my guilt about what I've done makes me bend the

331

shape of myself to fit what other people want every day of my life.

In the hallway I meet Stella, who reminds me of the sheepdog on the farm, always trying to round everybody up.

'I'm just going to the loo,' I say. I've slipped Dad's phone under the waistband of my trousers, and my cardigan's wrapped over it.

I walk up the stairs, dragging my hand up the banister purposely slowly, so that she doesn't think I'm rushing.

I lock the bathroom door behind me and sit on the toilet.

I can't get on to Tessa's WiFi on the phone because I don't know the password for it and the phone doesn't log in automatically like the computer did, but that's OK because my dad is getting a 3G signal here so it takes no time to log into Mum's email and access the script.

The ending is so sad.

'WHAT I KNOW'

BY LUCAS KENNEDY

ACT III

INT. LUCAS'S BEDROOM. NIGHT.

JULIA is sitting on LUCAS's bed, reading him a bedtime story. She is very unwell.

> DYING JULIA (V.O.)
> At first, I lied to Lucas about my prognosis, because it was too painful to tell him the whole truth. I simply told him that I was unwell. But Lucas is a clever boy, and he very quickly worked out that it was worse than that.

> LUCAS
> Mum?

> JULIA
> Yes.

> LUCAS
> Are you going to die?

> JULIA
> Well, sometimes people who have this disease do die.

> LUCAS
> Can you get medicine to make you better?

                    JULIA
        I have some medicine.

                    LUCAS
        From the doctor?

                    JULIA
        Yes, from the doctor.

                    LUCAS
        And will it work?

                    JULIA
                 (struggling)
        No, my love, it probably won't.

They look at each other. JULIA is
willing LUCAS to understand but wishing
he doesn't have to all at once.

                    DYING JULIA (V.O.)
        He didn't reply to me, but he
        never wanted to leave my side
        after that.

INT. CHRIS'S OFFICE. NIGHT.

CHRIS lies stretched out on his sofa,
staring at the ceiling. We see from

the clock on the wall and the darkness
outside that it's very late.

> DYING JULIA (V.O.)
> Chris took it hard too. But
> instead of sticking close to me,
> he withdrew. My illness repulsed
> him. He spent every hour possible
> out of the home.

INT. HALLWAY OF THE KENNEDY HOUSE. DAY.

The doorbell rings and LUCAS runs to
answer it.

> DYING JULIA (V.O.)
> This left us with a problem.
> Because, as a result of Chris's
> behaviour, and in spite of the
> excellent nursing help that he
> organised, it was Lucas who
> inevitably became my main carer.

LUCAS opens the door and a NURSE is
there.

> LUCAS
> Hello, Annie.

336

                    NURSE

Hello, my friend! How's she
doing?

                    LUCAS

She's a bit sad today. I think it
hurts.

                    NURSE

OK, let's see what we can do
about that, shall we?

Upstairs, LUCAS stands at JULIA's
bedroom door and watches as the NURSE
greets her gently and begins to work
around her.

            DYING JULIA (V.O.)

And the fact that Lucas was
seeing and doing things that
he was too young for became
unbearable to me. As was the fact
that he was old enough to realise
that Chris should have been there
with us, caring for me too. So
I decided that something had to
change. I could think of only one
thing to do, and it took all my
strength to do it. It was time to
be cruel to be kind.

                    337

INT. THE KENNEDY FAMILY KITCHEN.
MORNING.

CHRIS is waiting in the doorway, holding
a set of car keys and watching JULIA and
LUCAS. JULIA is sitting down and LUCAS
stands in front of her while she adjusts
his uniform. JULIA's arms and wrists
look frail.

> DYING JULIA (V.O.)
> I forced him to leave me so that
> his life could be as normal as
> possible. It was the only way I
> could think to show him a way to
> go forward. He didn't want to.
> He wanted to stay at home from
> school, to crawl into bed with
> me, spend every one of my last
> minutes with me, but I made him
> go to piano, to sports clubs, and
> to school.

> LUCAS
> (tearful)
> I don't want to go.

> JULIA
> You have to go.

                    LUCAS
Please.

                    JULIA
                   (snaps)
Lucas, don't argue with me!

LUCAS is shocked and hurt by her tone of
voice. He turns and follows his father
out of the door wordlessly. The door
shuts behind them and we see JULIA,
alone in the room, utterly crushed.

              DYING JULIA (V.O.)
And it broke my heart to do it.
But I knew that if he was going
to survive life with his father,
he had to be strong, and so I had
to force him away. And I knew,
too, that things couldn't carry
on like this.

INT. CHRIS AND JULIA'S BEDROOM. DAY.

JULIA is in bed, looking even worse
than before. The NURSE is in her room,
unpacking medication.

                    JULIA
Could you do me a favour? Could
you get me a pen and paper and
something to rest on. You'll
find them in my desk drawer,
downstairs.

                    NURSE
You going to draw me a picture?

                    JULIA
          (smiles, though really
      she's too tired for jokes)
No. I want to write a letter.
Could you get me an envelope too?

                    NURSE
Of course I will. Do you need a
stamp?

                    JULIA
No.

                    NURSE
How's Lucas?

                    JULIA
He went to school today. I didn't
think he would.

NURSE

That's good. First time I've had
to let myself in I think, so
that's what I was hoping. It's
not good for him to be here all
the time.

JULIA

I know.

NURSE

He'll be all right, you know.

JULIA

(we see her pain)
I hope so, I really do.

NURSE

He's a good boy, bless him.

JULIA

He is.

INT. CHRIS AND JULIA'S BEDROOM. NIGHT.

JULIA is propped up in bed, alone, and
we see her finish writing something.

DYING JULIA (V.O.)
I wrote the letter. It was my 'Do
Not Resuscitate' order.

JULIA seals the letter in an envelope,
carefully, and then laboriously places
it in the top drawer of her bedside
table, an action that costs her a large
amount of effort. Inside the bedside
table there's a box, which she takes
out. When she opens it, we see it
contains a large number of pills.

DYING JULIA (V.O.)
And I counted the pills that I'd
been hoarding, to make sure I had
enough.

Satisfied, she replaces the box in the
drawer, beside the envelope, and turns
out the light.

**EXT. A STREET NEAR CHRIS AND JULIA'S
HOUSE. MORNING.**

LUCAS is walking to school. It's a
different day and he's wearing a hat and
coat. The camera follows him on his way.

DYING JULIA (V.O.)
After that, it was a matter of
waiting for a school day.

We see LUCAS sitting in a lesson at
school, unable to concentrate. He
stares at his book while the TEACHER
drones on.

DYING JULIA (V.O.)
It was a harsh thing to do, I know,
but I saw it as a way of releasing
him from the last few weeks of
my life, saving him from seeing
me wracked with pain, and out of
control of my body. I wanted our
parting to be cleaner, tidier, and
easier for him to bear.

We see LUCAS in the school dining hall,
picking through his lunch box, rejecting
everything in there. He checks his
phone, sends a text to JULIA, and waits
for the reply.

DYING JULIA (V.O.)
But timing is everything, and
Lucas texted me just after I'd
taken the pills, and lain back
in my bed, and placed the letter

on my chest. And, when I didn't
answer, he sensed that something
was wrong.

LUCAS stares at his phone. Then he tries
to call JULIA on her mobile, and on the
landline. There's no answer. LUCAS runs
from the school dining hall, and out
of the main school doors and starts to
sprint home.

> DYING JULIA (V.O.)
> I don't know how he sensed it,
> but he did.

LUCAS bursts into the house, and pounds
up the stairs, and tries to enter
JULIA's room, but she has locked the
door. LUCAS calls to JULIA, he bangs and
kicks the door and then throws his body
weight against it. When that doesn't
work he gets out his phone and dials
999.

> LUCAS
> Yes, hello, ambulance, please,
> yes, and fire brigade. Please
> come quickly. It's my mum.

INT. PRIVATE HOSPITAL ROOM. VERY WELL APPOINTED. NIGHT.

We find everything exactly as it was before, in the first scene. LUCAS and CHRIS continue their vigil by JULIA's bedside.

> DYING JULIA (V.O.)
> I didn't want Lucas to find me. The idea was that it would be the nurse who discovered my body, and that I would be dead by then. But even this is better than the lingering weeks of decay that Lucas would have had to endure otherwise. My end in this hospital will be as controlled as possible. And it will be soon. But, before I go, I understand that there's probably a question on your lips right now. How could I leave my son with his father? With the man who isolated me from people, who pounded my head against walls and reduced me to putty in his hands. My answer: I had no choice. My only solace: Chris had never touched Lucas. Yet. And I hoped, I prayed, that

345

if my son understood he must be
strong, then Chris never would
touch him. It was all I could do.

The machines suddenly begin to beep
again, and NURSES and a DOCTOR rush in.
CHRIS and LUCAS are ushered away from
the bed and can do nothing but watch
helplessly as JULIA slips away. The DNR
order prevents intervention and her end
comes quickly, and we know this because
the NURSES and DOCTOR step away from her
bed.

> DYING JULIA (V.O.)
> I had tried my hardest to give
> my son the best of me, broken,
> bullied, mocked, little old me.
> My attempt at suicide, and the
> DNR order, well they were a final
> act of love, and the hardest
> thing I've ever done, and I did
> it because the end, after all,
> was inevitable.

LUCAS watches blankly, in shock, as
the DOCTOR records the time of JULIA's
death, but CHRIS's face collapses into
grief. CHRIS puts a hand on LUCAS's
shoulder, almost as if so surprised by

the strength of his own feelings that he
needs supporting.

But LUCAS steps away from him.

THE END

RICHARD

I should be fighting my demons by now.

Usually, my emotions when I'm sober consist mostly of a cocktail of anger and desperation, garnished with emptiness, and they feel as if they're embroidered into every cell of my body, as integral to me as my DNA.

And when I feel like that, alcohol is the only cure I know, the only thing that can wash the misery away. I think of alcohol as being like a slick waiter, clad in black and white, weaving his way through a crowd with a silver tray held aloft, bearing upon it a generous helping of respite, and oblivion, just for me.

Who could refuse?

Not I. Not on a normal day, when all I want is some peace; when I would do whatever it took to escape those emotions. Any choice made on a normal day would be a choice to drink. To have a drink seems necessary, unavoidable. The taste of it might not appeal, but the feeling as it goes down your throat is oh-so-good, a physical numbness that anticipates luxuriantly the imminent longed-for dulling of your mind.

But today, with the baby in my arms, I feel something different. I feel invigorated.

It's such an unusual feeling for me that I'm careful around it, especially as this would be the most inappropriate moment conceivable to tell Tessa that I'm feeling a bit better.

When somebody arrives from the police station with DNA testing kits and they call for us to come and be swabbed one by one, the others look appalled, so I get to my feet and announce that I'll be happy to be the first.

The newly arrived officer has a bad shaving cut on his jawline, which I notice as he pulls on blue plastic gloves and scrapes a sponge on a stick around the inside of my cheek. He winces a little as he does it and I feel a tad self-conscious that my breath might be slightly on the rich side.

When I'm done, Tessa goes in, after passing the baby to me like a relay baton, and Grace and I make our way upstairs to wake Katya, who they want to include.

She's asleep face down in our spare room, and doesn't take kindly to being woken.

She descends the stairs and enters the dining room with her chin held high and it takes just a minute or two before she re-emerges with an expression of distaste on her face.

She's just in time to hear Chris say to one of the detectives, 'I take exception to being asked to take an invasive test without an explanation of why,' and as the detective begins to talk about 'routine investigations' and 'helping with our inquiry', Katya exclaims loudly: 'I am giving mouth swab even though it is not in my contract, because of deep situation.'

Chris is momentarily taken aback, and she takes the opportunity to shoot a few more barbs:

'People must do right thing. You must do right thing. You are always business talk yadda yadda yadda, and you never put arm around son.'

I look at Lucas. He's watching them anxiously, and his leg is jiggling up and down.

'Make test!' Katya is shouting now, and pointing towards the room where the young officer sits with his pile of plastic-wrapped kits.

A dark cloud passes over Chris's face and I think that this can only end in tears. What man could lose his wife to violent death and then hear this?

Zoe's mouth is agape too and I imagine that this shocks her because it's an outburst the likes of which she probably hasn't seen before in this new family of hers, where everything seemed to be buried all the time, emotions included.

'Katya,' I say to her. I put my hand on her arm because even her stance is confrontational, and, as I do so, the baby leans towards her, arms outstretched. Katya can't resist this. She turns and takes Grace from me. Behind her, Chris sits back down, a tactical withdrawal that I'm glad to see.

'We're very grateful to you, this is a horrible situation,' I tell her. 'Please know how much we're sorry that you have to be part of this.'

'I want call my agency,' she says. 'I have talk to police, I have make mouth swab, and now I wish to leave and stay somewhere else because sadness is making a strong feeling in my heart.'

She presses her fist to her breastbone as if in some kind of salute, and Grace puts a clumsy finger to a tear that's dropping down Katya's cheek.

Thinking that she's probably right, that it's a good idea if she goes, and that I've more or less mastered the basic requirements of the baby so we can do without her, I usher her out of the room, and direct her to the phone, taking the baby back from her as she lifts the receiver.

351

Behind us, Lucas says: 'Dad, are we going to take the test?'

I can't resist a quick look back to see Chris respond with a tight nod.

Crisis averted, my secret satisfaction grows just a little.

TESSA

I give the DNA swab, but I want to know why they're doing this and why my interview was interrupted so suddenly earlier.

It wasn't a dramatic interruption exactly, but there was certainly a frisson of something – suppressed excitement perhaps – amongst the police.

My mind's racing like a greyhound out of the gate, and I think that I really need to phone Sam now, more than ever, because he might be able to interpret the situation better than me.

Once Katya has finished speaking to her agency, Richard ushers her back upstairs as if he's a mother hen, and I take the opportunity to try to get through to Sam.

He doesn't answer. He has a day off today so I can't imagine why not. I try a couple of times and eventually leave a message saying that I'll try him again later.

I try not to feel upset with him for not answering, but part of me thinks it would have been nice if he was on standby, in case I needed him. It's not like he doesn't know what's going on.

As I replace the handset, I notice that Richard is in the doorway.

'Who are you phoning?' he asks.

The best lies are those that are closest to the truth. This is a thought that pops into my head, though I'm not sure from where. I don't consider myself dishonest, in spite of my affair. My infidelity is the only thing I hide; in all other areas of life I'm squeaky clean.

'I was phoning Zoe's solicitor,' I said. 'Because I wanted to know why they might be taking DNA swabs from us.'

'What did he say?'

'He wasn't there. They said he's out.' I think quickly enough to pretend that I phoned Sam's office, not his mobile.

'He was very hard on Zoe,' Richard says. 'Very hard indeed.'

'They know each other well enough for that I'm sure,' I tell him. Richard was learning to consume alcohol in previously unimaginably large quantities during the time of Zoe's trial, because he had only just discovered that his professional status had fatally stalled. He never once came to Devon to support them. He never witnessed any of it. That is, of course, yet another source of resentment for me.

I hold Grace while Richard begins to heat some food from the fridge for her.

'Katya told me she likes this stuff,' he says, showing me a teaspoonful of intensely orange goo.

Grace is watching him intently. I can tell that she likes him, and he makes faces for her that make her giggle, but I can't share the moment because all I can think about is the fact that Grace probably won't even remember Maria, and may not even be part of our lives in the future.

'I hope we get to see Grace,' I say.

'What?'

'Well, she'll go with Chris, won't she?'

Richard stands, aghast, looking at me. 'Will she?'

'He's her father! What did you think?'

'I hadn't really thought about it.' He turns around to stir the purée, and I notice his shoulders have fallen.

'Well, hopefully she can come and stay with us when she's older,' he says. 'And how will Chris cope?'

'I don't know.'

'Will Zoe go with them?'

'I very much doubt it. Why would she do that?'

He catches my tone of irritation.

'Give Grace to me,' he says. 'I can do this on my own. You take some time.'

I'm feeling tetchy because all of this will need to be worked out, and it will be complicated and painful for the children, and probably for us too, and I can't deal with it now.

I can't ignore either the small doubts about Chris that have begun to tug at me. It's dangerous to let my mind wander down this path, I'm very conscious of that, but I'm beginning to reassess some of his behaviour; in particular the way he folded my sister up in a towel and ushered her away at the end of the evening. To me, that looked loving at the time, but in the light of what's happened I can't help but put a more sinister reading on it now. Was it loving, or controlling? His aggression with Tom Barlow at the house, and his treatment of Lucas, the way he told him off in front of us all, would certainly edge me quite firmly towards a more negative reading.

I want to ask Richard what he thinks, because in spite of everything he's a good judge of character, or he used to be, but we're interrupted by the doorbell.

'That'll be the au pair agency, I expect,' he says.

'I'll get it.'

He tries a small spoonful of Grace's purée and winces. 'This is too hot,' he tells the baby, 'we might need to wait a bit.'

'What was the number of the solicitor's office?' he calls after me, as I leave the room. 'I might try him again, I think you're right to ask his advice.'

'Oh, I don't remember offhand,' I say.

'No problem,' he calls, as I reach the front door. 'I'll just do redial.'

Before I can stop myself, and as I'm opening the front door, I shout, 'No!' at him, because I know the call will go through to Sam's personal mobile. The representative from Katya's au pair agency gives me a quizzical look, as does Richard.

'Sorry,' I say to her.

She offers me her hand. 'Tamara Jones, West Country Elite Au Pairs. We always aim to respond to emergencies immediately.'

Behind me, I can feel Richard's gaze on my back and, as I take Tamara Jones upstairs to find Katya, I can see that he has the baby in one arm and the phone in the other.

ZOE

I don't want to be near Chris after what I've read.

I don't want him near me, and I don't want him near Lucas and I never want him near Grace again.

I wish he'd never, ever been near my mum, because I have a horrible feeling creeping over me that he might have killed her with his violence.

I'm struggling really hard to stay calm with that thought filling up my head. I desperately want to talk to Lucas about the script, to tell him that I understand now why he wanted me to read it so badly, and to say how I'm so sorry about what happened to him and his mum. But Lucas won't even look at me right now. All he's doing is sitting, and staring at his fingers and picking at the red skin around his bitten nails.

I also want to tell somebody else, I'm desperate to, so they know what Chris is really like, but I don't know who to choose, because I don't know if they'll believe me. Right now, I'm not one hundred per cent sure that Lucas would want me to share the script, because I can see that Chris can be very bad, but he's also Lucas's dad.

While I'm trying to think about it, we're all sitting together on the sofas: me and Lucas and Chris and Tess and the Liaison Officer who's eating a sandwich that stinks of fish, and nobody is speaking. Richard's feeding Grace in the kitchen. My dad's gone back out into the garden with his phone. When I came down and gave his phone back to him I tried to tell him about what I'd read in the script but he said, 'Not now, Zoe.'

The detectives have gone for now, but they said they'd be back later to 'have a bit more of a chat'. Katya has just gone too; she was collected by a lady from her agency. I'm sad and also not sad about that. I don't like her, obviously, but her going made everything feel even more real, and even more final. It made it all squeeze around me just that little bit tighter.

That panicky feeling is rising now, making me want to scream out what I know, and to flee from the room so I don't have to sit near Chris, so I'm looping a bit of advice from Jason in my head: 'Don't always react to everything the instant it happens, Zoe. Think before you speak.'

The problem is that I'm afraid I might not be able to hold any of it in any longer, so I go for the person I think is safest to tell.

'Aunt Tessa …' I start to say, because I want to ask her to come out of the room with me, so I can tell her about it in private, because I think she's the best person, the one I trust most. I feel like I blurt out her name when I say it, but my voice must have actually been quiet because Tessa just turns to look at me as if to say, *Did you say something?* and, before I can explain, I'm interrupted by Chris, who says: 'Can I use your phone, Tessa? I think it's probably sensible if I book a hotel room for us tonight.'

'Us?' she asks him.

Chris frowns, as if that's a stupid question, and then says, 'For Lucas and Grace and I.'

358

'You're welcome to stay here,' she says.

'It might be easier if we got out of your hair.'

'It's fine, really.'

'No, I won't hear of it. You've done enough already letting the police in here, and having us all.'

'Well, do you want to leave Grace here?'

'She's my daughter.'

'But it might not be easy looking after her in a hotel room. Very cramped. We're happy to keep her here for now, with the garden, and Richard is enjoying looking after her, I know he won't mind.'

'I plan to book a suite. We'll be fine, thank you.'

It's a pretty final statement.

'May I use your phone?'

She waves her hand towards the kitchen. 'Go ahead.'

She looks as gutted as I feel, and I wonder if her heart is pumping as fast as mine is and I think that if it's not now it definitely will be when I tell her what I know about Chris.

I don't get to talk to her about it though because Richard appears in the doorway just as Chris is about to leave the room. He's holding Grace and she's covered in orange purée. It's on her face, her clothes, her hands and in her hair. It's on a lot of Richard too.

'Bit of a catastrophe,' Richard says.

Chris looks at Grace. She shows him the palm of one of her hands, which has food all over it, and then she squeezes it into a fist, demonstrating how the orange goo squishes out between her fingers. She's delighted. Grace loves mess.

Chris makes no move to take her from Richard, but I get there in two strides from the sofa.

'I'll take her for a bath,' I say. I look at Chris. 'You can't take her like this.'

Because he mustn't have her.

'Take her where?' I hear Richard asking, but I don't hear the answer because I carry sticky Grace up the stairs and into the bathroom as fast as I can, and I lock the door so it's just me and her, and I turn on the taps of the bath and I let her help me squeeze some bubble mixture in. When that's done we sit on the mat on the floor together and I say, 'Grace, you are so gross,' and I imagine that my mum would have laughed if she could have heard me say it.

And I wonder how long I can keep us locked in here so that Chris can't take her away.

RICHARD

Zoe grabs that baby out of my arms as if the house is burning down and they must flee. She pounds up the stairs and we hear the bathroom door slam shut.

'All right if I use your phone then?' Chris asks Tessa.

'I said go ahead.'

'Lucas,' Chris says to his son before he leaves the room, making the boy's head snap up, 'go and get your stuff together, and Grace's.'

'Where are you going?' I ask Chris, but he doesn't hear me, or pretends he doesn't.

'Where are they going?' I ask Tess in their absence.

We're alone. The liaison woman has gone somewhere or other, doubtless roaming the house like some kind of shady private eye, as she's been doing all day, and Lucas shambled off obediently in response to Chris, in that way he has, as if he's embarrassed by the mere presence of himself in a room.

'To a hotel.'

'With the baby?'

'She's not our baby, Richard.'

That annoys me. I might have my weaknesses, but I'm not an imbecile, and I've been trying to be patient with Tess.

'I phoned the solicitor. On redial. I left a message,' I say.

She blinks rapidly. 'Oh?' she says, but I can tell that she knows what I'm going to say.

'Funny thing though: it was a mobile phone number. It went to a personal voicemail message.'

She's breathing heavily through her nose as she looks at me. Her face is masterfully still but I can read panic behind it, however carefully hidden. Her mind must be racing but all she manages to come up with is, 'Are you sure it wasn't a wrong number?'

I start to quote the message: '"Hi, this is Sam, please leave me a"—'

She interrupts. 'I know his number from before, OK? From the trial?'

'You remember his number from, what, two and a half, three years ago?'

'Yes!'

'So why did you say that you phoned his office?'

'I said it wrong. It's not the best day for me this, in case you hadn't noticed.'

I don't appreciate that. 'What are you hiding, Tess? Where were you last night?'

'Not now, please. Not this, now.'

We sit in silence, and I try to sort out in my head whether her explanation is a plausible one. It definitely could be. It definitely might not be. I think that I may be too tired to tell.

Tess moves from her chair opposite me to sit beside me. For a moment I wonder if she might be going to express some physical affection towards me, and my heart beats nervously in anticipation, for it's been a long time since we offered each other that kind of solace, even with a simple touch, but she leans towards me instead, and whispers: 'I've been thinking.'

I wait for her to carry on, but before she does she gets up

ZOE

Grace's bath doesn't take long to fill up, because she doesn't need it very deep. While it's running, I try to persuade her to lie down so I can take off her clothes but she won't, so I have to improvise and undress her first while she sits, and then while she stands and bangs the soap dish against my back. She's so chubby without her clothes on, and her thighs are almost thicker than my arms.

I put her in the water and then hang on to her tightly because there's no grippy mat in Tessa and Richard's bath to stop her sliding around, and she's like a slippery otter. We have a few dodgy moments when she slides under water and I have to pull her back up, though she doesn't even notice the danger she's having so much fun.

I work out that I have a problem when the water goes cold, and she's splashed every bit of me and the bathroom. It's finally time to get her out, and I need a towel to lift her, because her skin is so smooth that her body is totally slimy from the bubbly water and I'm afraid I'll drop her without one, but I can't see one anywhere. The towel rail is bare. I can't let go of her and leave her unattended in the bath even for a second while I find one, because she keeps trying to stand up, and I know she would fall and hit the taps.

So I shout for help. I shout for Tessa, but it's Lucas who

comes, and I can just about reach over to the door to unlock it for him while I'm hanging on to Grace.

I hope I don't look at him funny, though I probably do. It's because I need to tell him I finished the script, but I'm not sure how to bring it up, and at the same time I realise I'm changing in my head some of the things I thought about him before I knew what Chris was really like.

I tell him what my problem with the towel is and he leaves the room and comes back with a bedspread.

'I couldn't find a towel,' he says, and I'm thinking that my mum would never have had no towels in the bathroom, in fact I can hear the 'tsk' noise that she would make if she could see us now, but here we are, and I think the bedspread will do fine.

Lucas drapes it over his arms and reaches down into the bath and gets Grace.

She thinks the bedspread is amazing because it's so big. When Lucas gently lies her down on the floor on it she plays with it, shaking the edges around and nuzzling it on to her head as if it's catnip and she's a kitten. We sit on either side of her and watch her; it's almost as if we were her parents.

I get up, and I lock the door again, because I know that I have a chance to talk to Lucas right now, and my heart begins to pound when I tell him: 'I read the script. All of it.'

He doesn't look up at me, but I can see that his face goes sort of still. He carries on pushing the bedspread over Grace's face and then pulling it back in a sudden movement. It makes her give a throaty giggle. He says nothing.

'On my dad's phone,' I say, in case he's wondering, and so he doesn't think I'm making things up.

When he looks at me it's as if a layer of secrets has been

peeled away from his face, and showing in his eyes is the deepest, saddest expression I've ever seen.

'I wanted to warn you,' he says, 'and your mum. I wanted you to know what he's like.'

I find that I can't reply, because I feel like my worst fears are true, but it's OK because he keeps talking.

'Because if my mum or me had told somebody about him, it might have stopped him, and then she might have stayed alive for longer; she wouldn't have done what she did.'

'Did he kill your mum?' I hardly dare ask it but it sounds like that's what he's saying.

'No. My mum killed herself, and she was dying anyway, but if her life was better, if he hadn't ruined her life, and hurt her, she would have stayed alive for longer, she would have fought the disease better. I know she would have.'

I feel a cold shudder run over me, from the crown of my head to the very tips of my toes. It's a ripple of revulsion and sorrow, fear and, I think, certainty.

I say, 'Do you think your dad killed my mum?'

TESSA

Philip Guerin has crept in from the garden, his face flushed from the heat, and joined us in the sitting room. The Family Liaison Officer is in the kitchen washing up teacups.

Philip has overheard Chris booking a hotel and wants to know where they're going to be staying, and wonders out loud whether he should do the same thing.

'There's plenty of room for you here now,' says Richard, but Philip pushes on, asking Chris questions of utter pointlessness, about where the hotel is located and how far it is from here.

Chris tells him the name of the hotel and I know as soon as I hear it that Philip Guerin wouldn't be able to afford to stay there in a million years. I can see that Chris knows that too. He seems irritated, his answers short and his mind clearly elsewhere, though Philip doesn't seem to be picking up any of these cues. He drones on and on about a hotel that he stayed in once on a trip somewhere else, and it's the most boring kind of small talk. I want to scream at him to shut up because I'm trying to think. I'm also trying to be normal around Chris, which suddenly isn't easy, because all I find myself able to do is wonder what he's capable of.

Our landline rings. It's always an unfamiliar sound these days, though Richard tells me that cold calls are a frequent annoyance during his long days at home, and I have to bite my tongue to avoid making a sarcastic reply. He doesn't have much else to do all day, let's face it.

As the phone trills, my eyes meet Richard's.

'That's probably the solicitor,' he says.

Chris is alert. 'What does he want?'

'I'll get it,' I say, and I bolt from the room. I don't know whether that will look suspicious to Richard, but I don't care. I need to hear the calm warmth of Sam's voice; I need somebody to offer me respite from my family. I want his advice, yes, but right now I also want his affection too.

By the time I get to the kitchen, the phone has stopped ringing, and the Family Liaison Officer is replacing the handset.

'That was Sam Locke,' she says. 'He says to tell you he didn't have time to speak because he's going into an appointment, but he'll call back later.'

I feel bereft, unreasonably so probably, but I can't help myself. Annoyed too, because what appointment could possibly be so important that Sam wouldn't at least take the time to exchange a quick couple of words with me. I pick up the phone and hit redial and pray and pray through the first few rings that he's going to answer.

'Sam Locke,' he says eventually, and I hear caution in his tone. Probably he's not sure whether it's Richard or me phoning.

I wait a second or two to reply because the Family Liaison Officer is carrying a plate of biscuits out of the room.

'Hello?' Sam says.

The Family Liaison Officer moves very slowly, as if she wants to hear what I'm saying, but I wait until she's gone and I ease the door shut behind her.

'It's me,' I say to Sam.

'Richard phoned me.'

'I know, I'm sorry, we wanted your advice.'

'I'm really sorry, Tess, I've got to see somebody in a minute, I haven't got long.'

'If the police are taking our DNA, do you think that means we're under suspicion?'

There's a pause, and then he says, 'They've found evidence, in the house, so yes, I think family are under suspicion. I shouldn't tell you that, Tess, so please don't say that I did.'

'Oh my God. What evidence?'

'Blood. That's been cleaned up. It's the only thing that would show up this quickly, and there might well be more evidence down the line, it's just that the other tests take time.'

'That's why they're taking swabs from us,' I say.

'That would seem likely, yes,' he says. 'They'll want to know whose blood it is.'

'It'll be hers,' I say.

'Be careful of making assumptions at this stage.'

'Well, whose else could it be?'

'All I'm saying is that we won't have confirmation of that for days.'

He sounds a bit distant; his tone seems more professional and less reassuring than I would like, because I feel very afraid. I want to tell Sam that I'm feeling increasingly certain that Chris has hurt Maria but I'm afraid that if I talk in here, Chris might overhear me.

I think of Philip's mobile phone. The one he's been anxiously passing from hand to hand for most of the day, as if it's

370

puckering her so smooth forehead. A tear falls from his cheek-bone on to the fabric, and darkens it.

A strange expression crosses Lucas's eyes as he gazes at our sister, and it triggers an impulse in me to snatch the bedspread away in case he plunges it on to her face and smothers her, but before I act he lowers it gently down so that it's within her reach and Grace's reaction is practically ecstatic.

Lucas says, 'I was trying to protect her.'

'Your mum?'

'No. Your mum.'

'What?'

'I'm so sorry,' he says. 'I just need to tell you it was a mistake. I killed her Zoe, but it was by mistake.'

My eyes are brimming hotly now and I feel my lips and chin collapse hopelessly and the muscles in my body seem to dissolve, and I find that I have nothing in me, no words at all that I can give back to Lucas.

'I'm sorry,' he says again. 'But it was an accident, I swear it was, and I've decided I'm going to tell them everything.'

I find myself choking with sobs, convulsed with them. I cover my mouth with my hand to mute them because they're so violent.

Lucas picks Grace up and holds her close to him, and he sobs too. We sit there like that for what seems like for ever and then he hands Grace to me and says, 'I'm going to miss her. She's so perfect.'

His cheeks and upper lip and forehead are glistening with tears and snot and sweat from the heat of the day, and he stands up.

373

And, as he reaches for the door handle, the phrase that circulates around my mind, and makes me hold my sister to me as tightly as I possibly can, is this: 'Lucas killed my mother.'

SAM

The consultant sits behind a desk that he's clearly using just for the purposes of this clinic, because he's opening and shutting drawers crossly, picking things up from the desk and slapping them back down. I'm afraid that his actions might dislodge the rimless reading glasses that are balanced precariously at the end of his nose.

'They put things in a different place every time,' he says. 'Take a seat, please.'

'Sam Locke,' I say and we shake hands just before I sit.

I'm not used to being on this side of the desk in situations like this, and I feel as if I need to show him somehow that I consider myself his equal, even if it's just with a handshake.

I chide myself immediately for the feeling though, because it's not going to change anything he's going to say to me; it's no more than a futile attempt my pride is making to assert myself as a fellow professional, and, anyway, the doctor seems oblivious to it. He must see this twenty times a day. To him, I'm just a patient, somebody to keep at a safe professional distance, just as, I suppose, my clients are to me.

'I only want a pen,' he says, eyebrows raised. 'Ridiculous, isn't it?'

I hand him a pen from my own pocket, and he scribbles something on a fat, dog-eared set of notes, bursting out of their cardboard wrapping, before he puts it to one side.

'Right! Sorry about that. They always show everybody in too quickly. Always rushing.'

He takes a slim brown folder from a neatly stacked pile. It's pristine, and on the front of it is my name. When he opens it, I see a letter from my GP, a referral, and only one or two other sheets of paper.

'Aha,' he says. 'Yes. You've just had a scan.'

I nod.

'So we need to take a look at that.'

He begins to tap at the computer keyboard. He has to watch his fingers to find the right keys.

'Let's hope the system is going to be kind to us today,' he tells me. 'There are many hurdles we can fall at when we want to access scans.'

I'm silent, I just watch him. I must not dislike him, I think, because this man is going to be looking after me. On his head there's just a shadow of hair around the back and sides, cropped extremely close, and petering out on the crown, where there's a shine that I suspect he wouldn't like if he could see it. His suit is an expensive one, and his tie is extravagantly knotted, and certainly made of silk; there's a thick gold wedding band on his ring finger and an expensive watch clamped ostentatiously around his wrist. I suspect he has a lucrative private practice.

He must be feeling the heat in all that finery, I think, because I am.

'Ah yes! Here we are,' he announces finally. 'Got it.'

And I see his face collapse into a frown as he studies it and I feel as if I'm watching a piece of my world detaching itself and falling into a void.

ZOE

I want to tear Lucas's eyes out.

But I want to hold him too.

Grace is still in my arms and I have squeezed her so close to me that she has started to cry. Lucas is still standing over us, looking down at us, not moving, though his hand is on the bathroom door handle.

'What were you trying to protect my mum from?' I ask.

'From Dad.'

'Why?'

'Because he was about to hurt her, and I tried to get her out of his way, because I could see him coming for her. I pushed her, because I didn't have time to do anything else, but we were at the top of the stairs, and she fell down and hit her head. I didn't mean it to happen, I was trying to help her. It was an accident; I swear it, Zoe. I'm sorry.'

And before I can say anything to that he unlocks the door, turns the handle and he's gone, and the movement of the door sends a hot barrage of air into the room. I'm left sitting there in all the wet that Grace has made, just holding her while she grizzles. The force of what he's just told me makes it feel difficult even to breathe, let alone to try to understand what's happened, but I must.

Lucas says he's tried to protect my mum from Chris, and he's killed her instead. He said the same words to me that I said at my trial: 'It was an accident.'

'How are you getting on?' It's Richard, standing on the landing; it's like he's appeared out of nowhere. 'Are you all right, lovey? Have you been crying again?'

'I don't want Chris and Lucas to take Grace,' I tell him. I blurt that out, because it's how I feel, but also because something tells me not to tell him what Lucas just said, and I think it's because I don't want it to be true.

Richard is looking at me a bit oddly, and for a moment I wonder if he was listening at the door before, whether he heard what Lucas said.

'Is Lucas OK?' he asks.

'He's fine. He was just helping me.'

He stares at my face for a second, and then his eyes fall to Grace.

'I understand why you don't want her to go,' he says. He strokes Grace's head and she reaches out her arms to him and he takes her from me.

'I want to stop them.'

'I don't really think we can.'

'But Grace belongs to me and Mum. She always has.'

'Listen, I know it's really, really hard, but Chris is her dad. There's nothing we can do.'

'Help me. I want her to stay here, just for a bit.'

Uncle Richard looks even more red and sweaty than he did this morning. He sits down on the side of the bath, holding Grace on his knee.

'What if we offer to keep Grace for the day, just until they've checked into the hotel and got themselves sorted out?' he says. 'Then we can take her over there later.'

'She needs a nap.'

'Then I'll say that. She can nap here before she goes.'

I look at Grace. She doesn't often settle down quickly or quietly, and if that happens then Chris might just take her anyway. He's never patient about that kind of thing.

'I'll put her in the buggy,' I say. 'If we push her around she'll fall asleep.'

Grace has a buggy that's padded like an emperor's chariot. When she's tired, she never lasts five minutes in it before nodding off, because it's way too comfy and Mum says she likes the feeling of being in motion.

'Can you tell Chris?' I know he won't listen to me, and I don't want to say even a single word to him.

'Leave it with me,' Richard says.

He puts a hand on my shoulder and I feel like I can trust him, and that he's on my side, and I suddenly understand that there's something even more important that I should be doing: I need to find Lucas before he talks to anybody else.

The stairs make a sound like thunder as I run down them and I'm lucky because I find Lucas straight away. He's standing in the hall, in front of the sitting room door. There's nobody else there, and the door is semi-closed. He looks like he's steeling himself to open it, and tell everybody what happened.

I take his arm. 'Come with me,' I whisper.

He shakes my hand off. He's psyched up.

'I have to do this.' His words sound as if he's having to force them out from between his clenched teeth.

'I need you first. Please.'

I take his hand again and pull it to my mouth, and put my lips on the back of his fingers, just very gently. It's the only thing I can think to do. I want him to feel my touch because after my First Chance Life ended I felt like nobody wanted to touch me because of what I did, because I wasn't worth it.

They all talked and talked to me and at me about what I did and how to 'move forward' and guilt, and reparation, and sentences served, and future opportunities, and I understood all of that; but the reason I never felt encouraged by it, or strengthened was partly because I was sorry for what I did, so sorry that it hurt me every day, and partly because I was angry about what happened at my trial, but mostly because I felt I would never be worth anything, ever again.

'Your self-esteem,' Jason told me, 'is at rock bottom, and I don't like to see it that way.'

'Go figure,' I said back to him. It was at the end of our second to last session, it was nearly the last conversation we ever had; the last nice conversation, anyway.

Lucas starts to shake, and his fingers relax against my lips.

'Once you've told them,' I whisper, 'they'll take you away, straight away and we won't ever get to see each other again for a very long time, maybe never. I just want to talk to you one more time before you tell them, please.'

He looks nervous of that. Or is he nervous of me, and of what I might do to him now I know what happened.

'I want to hear your story,' I say, because that's the other thing I never had, the chance to tell my story without people always lecturing me around it. Sometimes I think I would have liked to tell my story to the mums and dads of the children I killed, that they might not mind so much if they heard it from me, away from court and judges and solicitors.

'Bad idea,' Jason said. 'Reparation justice does recommend

meetings between victims' families and prisoners in some situations, but this doesn't qualify as one of them.'

'Lucas,' I breathe the word on to his hand, terrified that we'll be interrupted, or overheard, that I'm too late. 'Please.' My breath feels hotter than the day even as it spreads across his fingers.

His shaking intensifies. I play my final card. I put down my ace.

'I understand,' I say, 'I promise.'

I hope I can keep this up. My impulse to punish him, attack him, rip him to shreds, bend and break his body like the kids who were in the car with me is strong, and it's fighting a hard battle with my sensible head.

'Where shall we go?' he says just when I think all is lost, and he'll confess and go to prison and Chris will disappear out of our lives with Grace, and I'll have nothing.

I exhale with relief and tell him that there's one place I can think of.

TESSA

Chris and Philip and I are sitting more or less in silence, as the Family Liaison Officer makes many and varied attempts to engage us in small talk, or any kind of talk. She talks about cups of tea, she talks about the process of grief, she talks about the structure of police investigations, and she talks about the weather.

Chris is managing to offer her a few responses, which she leaps on to as if they were scraps thrown to a dog. I think she must have been taught to try to engage with us, to become our friend. I want to tell her that I don't give a fig's leaf how many times a day she has to water her geraniums in the heatwave, but instead I manage to zone her out, so that her words become a wall of white noise, against which I try to think.

Philip is in our most comfortable armchair, head back, mouth open, snoring gently. The drive, he told us, and the early start, have worn him out. I have no words to describe my anger at his selfishness.

I watch Chris out of the corner of my eye as he talks to the Family Liaison Officer. I wonder if I should say something to her about my suspicions and, if so, what. If I make them known to her, and Chris guesses who has done so, and if I'm wrong, we'll never recover from that, and I don't know if I'm sure enough to risk that.

In a way, I'm grateful that Chris wants to go to a hotel.

It'll give me a chance to speak to Richard about him, and to get advice from Sam. And besides, Chris isn't behaving like a guilty man; he seems devastated.

I also can't deny that I crave the space that he and Lucas and the baby will leave in my house, because it might give me a chance to mourn my sister, and give Zoe a chance to mourn her mother.

So when Chris stands to look out of the window, to see if his taxi has arrived, I find that I'm willing it to be there.

'Any sign?' the Liaison Officer asks him.

'No,' he says, and then, 'Oh wait, yes, I think this is it.'

It occurs to me then, as he begins to move to answer the door, that if he is guilty of something he might flee, but that immediately seems a wild, stupid thought, and something for the police to be concerned about, not me. This is not television, I tell myself, where people can just disappear in an instant, especially not with a successful business that needs running, a reasonably high public profile, and a baby and teenager in tow.

'Lucas!' Chris calls up the stairs. The three of us are gathered in the hall now, though there's no sign of Richard or the kids.

'Lucas!'

None of them answer.

'I'll find him,' I say.

Chris opens the front door and there's a driver there, smart in a crisp open-necked shirt and chinos. It's definitely not the usual comfortable attire of the shift taxi driver, and behind him I glimpse a sleek black vehicle. Chris has called one of his work drivers, I realise; 'taxi' wasn't quite an accurate description. It reminds me once more how little I've understood about the life he and Maria have been leading.

I run upstairs to the bathroom to see if anybody is still there with the baby. There are signs everywhere that Grace has been bathed: water on the floor and bubbles gathered around the plughole, but the room is empty of people.

'Zoe?' I call. 'Richard?'

Again, no answer.

'Lucas?'

I see that his backpack has been slung on to one of our spare beds, all zipped up.

Then I glimpse them through a window; Lucas and Zoe are out in the garden, and it looks as if they have the baby in the buggy. They're patiently pushing her backwards and forward in the shade of our patio.

It's a lovely sight, as if they've come together to form surrogate parents for Grace, and I know Maria would be happy if she could see them. I watch as they peer at Grace together, under the sunshade, and then, carefully, they begin to walk up the garden with her, although the uneven slabs and the tufts of tough, desiccated grass that protrude between them make it slow going.

I hear talking in the hall and make my way down.

'She just conked out,' Richard is saying, 'absolutely blotto in my arms after her bath, so we've put her in the pushchair, and we thought you might prefer to go on ahead to the hotel and get settled in and come and collect her later. Or we could bring her to you?'

Chris doesn't look happy. He checks his watch impatiently.

'I don't want to be going backwards and forwards later on so how about I send the driver to work to pick up some things for me, because I need to do that anyway, and by the time he gets back she should have had an hour or so of sleep. Do we think that would work?' he says.

'Of course,' I say. That sounds like a fair plan to me and, besides, I'm flat out of the energy required to make any other kind of response.

ZOE

I lay Grace down, cover her with the sunshade and tilt back her chair. After that it's just a few turns around the patio and she's out like a light. She puts her hands up above her head, a fist by each ear, and looks really sweet. Her tummy is bare and the whole of it goes up and down as she breathes.

Lucas and me walk her down to the end of the garden, pushing the buggy carefully over the bumpy bits and we park it in the shade underneath a leafy tree that's grown tall beside Uncle Richard's shed.

I beckon to Lucas to follow me into the shed. It feels boiling-point hot inside, and it smells of wood shavings and paint and glue. I shut the door behind us anyway.

There's a workbench along one side with tools and stuff on it and above that is a shelf where Richard's models are displayed. Mostly, they're aeroplanes made out of balsa wood, but there are also Airfix models up there, painted really perfectly, and some complicated-looking Meccano type things with engines and wires. Some of the plane models are hanging from the ceiling on transparent threads and they turn a little after we come in.

Lucas doesn't look at any of it, instead he sinks down so that he's sitting on the floor and then looks up at me. 'What do you want?' he says. 'Don't you hate me?'

I kneel down, right up close to him. We don't have much

386

time before one of the busybody adults finds us and wants to know what we're doing.

'Lucas,' I say, and I take his hands, one in each of mine and I squeeze them because I want to make him concentrate on me, completely and entirely. 'This is really, really important.'

'I'm ready to tell them everything.' The sobbing begins again. 'I'm so sorry.'

'No!' I say. 'No you mustn't. Not yet.'

'I have to,' he says and his sobs are so choking that I shake his hands to try to make him snap him out of it, but nothing works, so eventually I slap him as hard as I can across his cheek. It really stings my hand, that slap, and it knocks his head from one side to the other.

'Lucas,' I say. 'Listen to me. Stop crying.'

His eyes are bloodshot and there's still dampness around his lips and under his nose. He looks wrecked. His expression has so many things going on in it, but I'm super-focused and I block everything out except for the thing that I want to say to him.

'Does your dad know what you did?' I ask.

'Yes.'

'What does he say?'

'He says we have to protect each other. We both have to say we were asleep, and we know nothing. Nobody can prove otherwise.'

'Tell me exactly what happened.'

'After we went to bed last night, I couldn't sleep. I heard you come up, and then I was lying in my bed for ages, until I heard them arguing in their bedroom. It sounded like he was bullying her, and I was afraid he was so angry about the lies you both told him that he was going to hurt her, so I got out of bed and I went and opened their door because I wanted to tell him to stop. He had hold of her, but when he saw me he let go, but then he started coming for me, and he was very angry. I stepped back on to the landing to get away from him, but he caught me and he pushed me back against the wall, by the top of the stairs. And your mum … your mum came after him, and she caught him by surprise and managed to pull him off me just for a second. She was standing between him and me, but she turned her back to him, to check that I was OK. Behind her, I could see that he recovered really quickly and he was coming to get her, so I tried to push her right out of his way, on to the ground. But when I pushed her she hit the banister post at the top of the stairs, and she sort of bounced off it, and she fell down the stairs.'

I can see it all in my head; I can see her lying broken on the stairs.

'There was blood,' he says. 'She hit her head when she fell, and there was blood.'

And all this while I lay in my bed sleeping, with Chopin playing on my iPod, and Grace in my arms. That thought almost stops me in my tracks completely, almost robs me of my courage.

'He made me clean the blood up,' Lucas says, and he retches at the memory. 'He made me clean it up while he carried her outside. I didn't know he was going to put her by the bins. I'm sorry. She deserved so much better than that.'

It takes me a while to find the words to ask my next

question because it's the hardest I've ever had to work to keep my emotions under control. But I do it for Mum.

'Why did you want me to delete the script?'

'Because Dad said we have to cover up for each other. He didn't know about the script, but I thought it would make the police suspicious of him and then he might tell them that I did it. But I want to tell them everything because I can't take it any more.'

I'm so close to Lucas that I examine his face almost forensically, wanting to understand every line and curve of it. I look at every pore, I see the arc of his damp, clotted eyelashes and I recognise that the smell of him is the same one that hung in the air of the Unit sometimes.

It's the smell of fear.

'He hurt your mum too.'

'Yes.'

'Did he kill her?'

'No.'

'But she died because of him?'

'She killed herself because he made her feel useless.'

I know that feeling; it inhabits every cell in my body.

'But she was dying anyway?'

'She never fought the disease. She might have fought it if her life wasn't so shit. She had no reason to want to live. I told you that.'

I put my finger to Lucas's mouth. 'Shh,' I say.

I don't say, 'But she had you,' because sometimes I understand that it's best to keep things to yourself when they are a hundred per cent guaranteed to hurt others.

His breath smells sour, but it doesn't gross me out. I realise

389

that I love the way that only I can see into his soul. Lucas has been carrying a secret around with him, just like I have, and that's a powerful thought. It makes my heart begin to beat a little faster.

I press my cheek against his where the wetness of his tears seals us together, and then I rest my head on his shoulder while he cries, and cries again, like his sadness is never going to end, and all the time my mind is working, and my thoughts are becoming very, very clear.

Then he says, 'I filmed it on my phone. I filmed him hurting her when I opened the bedroom door, because I was going to show you what he's like.'

'Is it still on your phone?'

The police will find it there, surely, if it is.

'I deleted it at the same time as the script.'

It might take them a little bit longer, but they'll still find it. The thing is, I want to act quickly.

'But I uploaded it,' he adds, 'before I deleted it. In case I had to prove that I was trying to help her, because Dad was hurting her.'

He describes the film to me and, as he does, my thoughts crystallise. Perfectly.

I take Lucas's hands in mine, once again, and I take a deep breath.

Then I say to him, 'I forgive you,' because those are the words that I've always wanted to hear. I give them to him right here and now, because I know, even if he doesn't yet, that they're the greatest gift that I can give him, and I just hope that they're enough.

For, you see, I've suddenly understood something even

more important than knowing what Lucas did to my mother; I've understood that Lucas is my only chance of keeping Grace.

Because otherwise Chris will have her.

And he will hurt her.

I know it in my bones.

SAM

The consultant says, 'I believe you've had a conversation with your GP about what to expect today?'

'I have.'

'As we suspected there might be, there are lesions visible in your scan. They're in both the brain, and the spine.'

He swings the computer monitor around towards me, and I see an image of my skull.

'This shows you a slice of your brain,' he says, 'as if we were looking at it from the top of your head down towards your feet,' and with my pen he points at several different areas on the screen. 'There are lesions visible there, there, and there's one more, which you can probably see here.' He's pointing out small smudges, which are pale grey and look distinct from the rest of the scan, as if somebody had left several small, dirty fingerprints on the inside of my head.

'For me,' he continues, 'taken in conjunction with the rest of your symptoms, this goes significantly further to suggest a diagnosis of multiple sclerosis, but I would like to do a lumbar puncture to confirm it. Do you know what that is?'

I struggle for a second to find words because my throat has gone dry. 'Taking fluid from your spine,' I say.

'And we do that because we're looking for things called myelin proteins. If we find them, then your diagnosis will be confirmed. If we don't, it won't unfortunately mean that you

392

don't have the condition, just that there were no proteins in the sample, so we might need to repeat the test. But based on this scan, I think it would be sensible to prepare yourself for an MS diagnosis.'

He starts tapping on his computer again.

'I think the best thing to do now might be to discuss how we can alleviate the symptoms you're having. Can you describe them for me?'

An hour and a half later, after a long wait at the hospital pharmacy, I leave the building holding a bag of medication and an appointment card for a lumbar puncture for the following week, as well as the contact details of the hospital's specialist MS nurse who I've just met.

Out on the baking hot streets, I feel affronted by the bright glare of the sun, the way it glints off car bonnets and roofs and the windows of the surrounding buildings.

I'm told the medication should ease the symptoms of numbness and joint pain soon, and I'll be grateful for that because it makes me feel vulnerable when I'm out, especially in crowded situations, and it's becoming increasingly difficult to hide it from others.

I knew the diagnosis was likely, and, though it's not confirmed, I don't think the doctor would be advising me to prepare myself if he wasn't certain.

Even standing in the shade, I feel overwhelmed by the heat, and by the momentous news I've just received. I take my phone out. Tess hasn't called me back yet.

'Sorry,' I say to her even though she can't hear me, and I turn the ringtone to silent.

I approach one of the taxis that are waiting outside the

hospital and ask the driver to take me home. I don't answer any of his chatty questions and, in the silence that I've imposed, I see him glancing in the rear-view mirror, wondering what's just happened to me.

At home, in the empty flat, I wish more than anything that I had somebody who would come home to me tonight, somebody I could tell, somebody who would be with me through it, to the end.

ZOE

When your world explodes all the pieces of it shatter and spread, and you don't see some of them ever again, and nothing is ever like it was before.

I lost the world I had before the accident and my mum helped me to build a new one. Now that world has gone too, and I will never see my mum again, but I don't want to lose all the other bits.

Before I left the Unit, Jason taught me one last thing. We'd just finished our final session, two days before my release, and I asked him why all of us kids were locked up like animals when what some of us had done was just a mistake, or unavoidable, because we were stupid, or young, or had other excusable reasons for what we did like a witness who lied and a judge who didn't believe the truth when he heard it.

'Punishment is considered an effective deterrent,' Jason replied and he adjusted the neckline of his 'Bowling for Soup' T-shirt, which was a gesture he always made when he was feeling awkward.

'That's the theory anyway,' he added. 'Look, it's an imperfect system, and we know it is, but that's why these sessions are important, because they're when you get a chance to unpick what happened to you and understand the reasons for it, so that we can try to find a way forward.'

'I told the truth at my trial and they put me in jail anyway,' I said.

'Well, as I said, it's imperfect, but you know kids didn't even used to get therapeutic sessions at all, so you're lucky in that sense.'

The clock high up on the wall told both of us that our time was up. As a way to end our last ever session, it felt like a damp squib, because he'd said this stuff to me loads of times before.

It wasn't the final thing he taught me.

I stayed sitting because I wondered if Jason might be about to say something cheesy and nice as a goodbye, actually I kind of wanted him to, but instead he said it was time to go, and he started to walk me back to my corridor in the Unit as usual.

There were places in the Unit where the surveillance cameras couldn't see you. Most of us avoided them, because they could be frightening places to be alone in. You learned that very quickly after you arrived.

Jason stopped in one of those places, between two sets of doors, which linked separate areas. I was waiting for him to swipe his security pass and push open the next set of doors so that we could carry on as usual, but instead he paused, and put his hand on my upper arm. There was nobody else around, because it was a time when most people were in lockdown.

'Zoe,' he said. 'You're leaving in two days, and I think you've got every chance of not coming back here, I really do. I'll personally be very disappointed if you do.'

'I won't.'

I said it quickly because I didn't like the way his fingers were pressing into my arm. I stepped away from him but I couldn't move far, because the space was so small, and every muscle in my body seized up with fear.

It meant that I was frozen to the spot even when he released his so-tight grip, and he ran his fingers down the side of my arm, over the sleeve of my sweatshirt, and across my cuff until they reached my wrist. They made contact with my skin there, and I held my breath as they burrowed up an inch or two under my sleeve. The pad of his little finger rested lightly on my wrist bone and I wished my bone would dissolve away, because it was a sickening feeling.

'You're so beautiful, and so talented,' he said, and his voice sounded as if his tongue had grown thick. 'You don't belong here.'

His hand travelled up from my wrist to my cheek then, and it moved slowly and brushed against the side of my breast on the way there. I forced my head back even further and felt my face quiver when he ran a finger across my cheek.

His breathing was loud and unsteady.

'I'll scream,' I said.

'My word against yours, Zoe. Who do you think will win?'

There was no reply I could make, because I knew the answer to that. It would be him.

He brought his head towards mine and his lips grazed my neck and then he said, 'Your life will be like that from now on, and you need to remember it.'

He stepped away from me suddenly then, and swiped the door with his pass and held it open for me to walk through into the bright white lights of the communal area as if nothing had happened. I walked slowly because I felt as though I might stagger, and I hardly registered that Jason was saying hello to Gemma who was on duty, and asking to see his next person, because I was feeling as though I needed to gasp for every breath.

I went to my room and curled up on my bed as tightly as possible. I felt cold, and I was shaking, and the only thing that stopped me from ripping up the sheet and wrapping it around my neck was the thought that I only had two more days in that place before my mum came to get me, and then I would never see Jason again and I would be able to have another life, a Second Chance Life.

I remember pretty much every single thing that Jason told me when I was in the Unit, because I have excellent recall, but it was that final message that he delivered in that camera-less space that lodged itself most deeply in my mind.

I already knew that life was unfair, and that structures society puts in place to protect you don't always work, but what Jason taught me there and then is that what happened to me had marked me permanently, turned me into somebody who could be pushed and pulled around, like a toy for other people to play with, somebody without a voice, and without the right to a normal life.

Unless.

Unless I'm brave enough to take control.

In the baking heat of my uncle's shed, a perfect idea has formed in my head: I want to save Grace from Chris, and keep her with me, so I can make her into the girl that Mum wanted her to be able to be.

I look at Lucas and I try to assess whether I can make the idea work. It'll be a challenge, I know, because he's like a whipped dog so much of the time, and especially now. The

398

thing I'm thinking of can't happen without him though, so I desperately need him to be brave as well, and that's because I need him to lie about what happened.

I whisper it to him, the idea that I've had, but, as I feared, when I've finished telling him what we need to do he says, 'I can't.'

'You can.'

'No.'

'If you tell the truth, they'll lock you up, Lucas, like they did me. You don't know what it's like in there. And then your dad will take Grace, and he'll hurt her. And I might never see you again. Ever.'

I try to stand as tall as I can. I put my shoulders back and shake my hair down the back of my neck. I stand the way my mum stood when Chris and Lucas got back from the concert. I stand the way she stood every day during my trial, when she was strong. I stand the way I want Grace to stand when she's older, no matter what's happening to her.

The problem is that however strong I am, the fear in Lucas's eyes looks as if it has run deep for a very long time, and I'm sure that it has. I also understand that right now he probably feels the same as I did just after the accident: like a trapped animal, full of panic and pain and shock about what's just happened, but I have to make him snap out of it, and see as clearly as I do that we need to do this.

'Do you want Grace to have a life like yours?' I ask him. 'Living in fear of your dad?'

He shakes his head, but he says, 'What you're asking me to do is wrong.'

'It's not wrong if it ends up being right. Think about it.'

I'm starting to feel desperate now, because if he doesn't agree to do as I ask we'll lose everything we have left, both of us will. I think of the script and I know he must feel the same kind of anger deep down that I do.

'Anger can be a release,' Jason told me once, though he was simultaneously advising me not to display it quite as much as I did then.

In desperation, I snatch one of Richard's models from the shelf beside us and I hold it out to Lucas and say, 'Wreck it,' because it's the only way I can think to tap into the rageful feelings he must have inside him, and that might be the only way I can make him agree to my plan, right here and now.

'What? No!'

'Come on!' I shove it towards him, but he bats it back roughly, and in that gesture I think I can sense his anger starting to fizz, and I wonder if he has ever once let it out before. It's enough to convince me that my tactic is a good one.

'I'll do it then,' I say. 'I'm not afraid to.'

Right in front of his face, I hold the wing of the plane and bend it slowly, the tension in it ratcheting up incrementally beneath my fingers.

The model is intricate, and lovely. It must have taken hours and days to make.

'Don't!' Lucas says. He makes to snatch it out of my hands and I just give it up.

'Break it,' I say.

'No!' He's holding it as if it's fine porcelain, but his hands are shaking.

'It represents your life with your dad,' I say. 'Break it, and you'll be free of him. Break it for your mum. Break it, and we

400

can do what we have to do to get justice for her and for my mum.'

'Why are you doing this to me? I tried to warn you, didn't I? I sent you the script.'

'You sent it too late!'

He looks down at the plane in his hands.

I think of what Jason said to me with his hot breath buffeting my face – 'My word against yours, Zoe. Who do you think they'll believe?' – and I know that if Lucas doesn't agree to do this with me then I can't do it on my own.

'They'll believe us; I know they will. This is the only way now,' I tell him.

'But what about the panop messages I sent you? The police will find them on your phone.'

'They know about my past, Lucas, they won't care if you know too. Think about it. That's all the panop messages prove.'

The clarity I'm feeling is incredibly pure and I'm getting increasingly frustrated that he can't feel it too. It's like there's mud in his brain, and he's thinking about all the wrong things. 'They won't bother looking at our phones any more anyway,' I say, 'if we do this right.'

He says, 'Maria didn't deserve my dad. And nor did my mum. Nobody does.'

'Grace doesn't deserve him either.'

He moves the aeroplane around in his hands so that he's holding it by its wing like I did, and then, just as I think he's going to put it down and leave the shed and I'll have failed in this as well as everything else, he starts to bend it. I hold my breath as the tension in the wood builds and it begins to split.

Lucas gasps, and I say, 'Don't give up now,' and it's like that comment is a sort of release for him, as if all his rage has suddenly boiled over.

He snaps off the wing of the plane, and then its tail, and I have to step backwards because he starts to bash the aeroplane against the walls of the shed until it splinters and shatters into smithereens and still he keeps on bashing it until I'm afraid that he's going to break his hand and he's saying, 'I hate you. I fucking hate you,' and we both know he's not saying that to me, he's saying it to his dad.

When he's finally finished, he looks at the few shards that remain in his hand as if he's not sure how they got there, and I say, 'Will you do it?' and he says, 'OK,' and my heart flips in relief.

RICHARD

Once Chris has decided to stay for a bit longer while he waits for Grace to finish her nap, he asks to borrow my computer. 'I just need to tie one or two things up for work so they don't bother us for the next few days,' he says. His face is grim and stressed.

'Be my guest,' I tell him.

I take him upstairs and show him the set-up in my office.

Could he have done something? I wonder again as I leave him to it. I have to resist the temptation to peer over his shoulder. Tessa has her suspicions, clearly, but that could just be guilt talking, because she is somehow convinced that she could have saved Maria if she'd made more effort to remain close to her after the marriage.

I notice as I cross the landing that we all left the bathroom in a somewhat destroyed state in the wake of Grace's bath, and I decide that I'll tidy it up, to make it nice for Tessa. I mop up the spilled water with the already wet bedspread, and then put it out in the hallway with the idea of hanging it up to dry in the garden, and I wash the dried-out bubbles from the inside of the bath.

As I scrub, I begin to feel confused about something I thought I overheard when Grace was having her bath. I thought I heard Lucas say something about Maria's death, but I'm sure I must be wrong, or Zoe would have reacted differently when I spoke to her immediately afterwards.

I wonder if I'll be able to persuade Chris to let Grace stay here for her tea. He'll struggle to organise that in a hotel. I wonder if she eats soup. I wonder when she's going to start missing her mother.

It appears that Grace has played with every plastic bottle that was gathered neatly around the edges of our bath, and so I begin to retrieve them from all corners of the room and stand them up in their allotted places. We're not used to things moving around, Tess and I. Ours is a quiet life.

I'm kneeling on the floor to reach a shampoo bottle that has somehow got stuck behind the stand that the basin sits on when the craving hits me. First, a wave of exhaustion, then a rush of all the emotions that I cannot bear.

Beside me, built into the cladding that surrounds the bath, is a small door. If I push it, it'll open, and behind it there's a hidden bottle of vodka. Cheap, nasty vodka. Beautiful, anaesthetising vodka. Just one push of my fingers and I can have it.

But I try to be good. I sit there, on my knees, in our nice little bathroom, and think of that beautiful baby, and Tessa's broken family, and of our shambles of a marriage, and although it takes me every ounce of strength, I manage to leave the room without touching the bottle.

Walking away is so hard. There's some pay-off though, I can't deny it, because as I make my way slowly downstairs I force myself to acknowledge that resisting the bottle is also a triumph of sorts, however grim I feel.

TESSA

I'm pacing downstairs. The detectives have vacated the dining room for now and I walk around it as if it can give me some clues, or help me to think.

I'm too restless to stay there for long though and, as I go back into the hallway, I almost collide with Zoe.

It shocks her, and she gives a little scream. She seems pent-up and extremely agitated, and she won't meet my eye properly, which is unusual for her. She tells me in a nervous voice, as if she's finding it hard to breathe properly, that she wants to gather everybody together in the sitting room.

She wakes up her dad, and she calls Richard in from outside, where he's been checking on the baby. She gets Chris down from the upstairs bedroom, and she asks us all to sit down, though she saves a seat in the middle of the sofa, beside Chris, which she insists the Liaison Officer takes.

Lucas is there too, and he's doing something with the TV. He's turned it on and holds the two remote controls and he's navigating through a series of screens that look unfamiliar to me.

Once Richard arrives in the room he of course asks Lucas what he's trying to do, and offers help and expertise, but the boy brushes him off a bit brusquely. It's clear to me that he more than seems to know what he's doing, though undeniably he's giving off nerves in exactly the same way as Zoe is.

As everyone's getting seated, Zoe stands beside my chair and I rub her slender wrist. 'What's happening, Butterfly?' I ask her.

She doesn't look at me, and she doesn't reply; she's fixated on what Lucas is doing.

It reminds me of how she used to be at the time of the trial. It broke my heart, because she always seemed to be somewhere else in her head, as if the core of her had curled up in fear, and, though perhaps it shouldn't have, that did make her somehow untouchable to the rest of us.

'Zoe?' I ask again, because her behaviour is scaring me a little, but Lucas says, at the same time, 'It's ready,' and then, as if she's taking a cue from him, as if it's something they've rehearsed, she turns to everybody, and delivers a short speech in a voice so laconic it sends a chill running through me.

'Lucas and me were afraid. But now we've decided to tell you what we know. This is a film from last night.'

We all turn to face the TV.

Lucas seems to have got it to link to the internet, and it's displaying a video site. I wonder if it's the film from the concert that he's about to play, but it doesn't look as if it is.

The picture that suddenly appears on the screen looks just like the inside of Chris and Maria's house.

LUCAS

I filmed this on my phone, in secret, last night. I held the phone down by my leg and my dad didn't notice.

As we watch the footage in front of my dad, and all of the other people in Tessa's sitting room, the only way I can force myself to stay there and watch it again, and go through with what me and Zoe agreed, is to think about how, if I was going to shoot this scene for an actual film, I would do it differently.

The secret way I had to film, before I dropped the camera and all it showed was the ceiling, means that the footage has a kind of *Blair Witch/Paranormal Activity* feel to it. It's a kind of indie low-budget terror look, which might work. But I'd like it to be more stylised, so I'd do it like this:

First shot would follow me along the landing, a tracking shot probably, using a hand-held camera, and looking over my shoulder from behind me, so you could see that I was approaching my parents' bedroom door and you could see it from my point of view.

As I walk down the corridor, the soundtrack would be a long, low note – low strings maybe – like a drone. The muffled sounds of an argument would be audible through the closed bedroom door.

As I stop outside the door, and listen, the camera would swing around, to show my face, so you could see how I'm trying to be brave.

Cut to a close-up of my hand opening the bedroom door. The door swings open.

The drone of the music is mounting, but not too much yet.

We see into the room. It's lit up by a small bedside lamp only, so there are powerful long shadows reaching across the space, and they make my dad look terrifying, like the evil guy on the front of a comic book.

My dad is standing over Maria. He's holding her by her hair and he's pushed her head back against the wall so you can see the smooth stretch of her neck.

Then there would be close-up shots: the back of my dad's hand, Maria's hair poking out between his fingers, the skin stretched across his knuckles and then her face, her jaw tense with pain and fear.

The drone of the soundtrack builds, adding more strings, higher pitched and clashing, so that it sounds discordant now.

I would be happy with that opening, it would show everything exactly as it happened.

When he works out what he's watching, as we all sit there in Tessa's sitting room, my dad starts to make a lunge for the TV before all the people can hear what he's going to say on film. But Zoe's dad is sitting beside him, and so is the police lady, and Zoe's dad grabs my dad by the arm and tells him to sit down in a voice that is deadly polite. Zoe's dad has a wrecked face, but he's big and strong and my dad is no match for him.

We're reaching the bit in the film where everything happens very fast. All the people in the room are totally fixated on it.

The footage gets more wobbly here, because I was frightened, but again I imagine it in my reshoot:

Dad turns to me, sees me at the door. 'Get out,' he says, and I would be sure you could see the vein that's bulged red and angry on his temple.

I might show my face on camera then, the way that I'm feeling even more fear, but I'm trying not to let it drive me out of the room as it's done so many times before, so I stay where I am because I want him to stop what he's doing.

A close-up of Maria's face, as she tries to turn her head to see me, even though Dad's still holding her hair. Her eyes are full of messages that I can't read because I don't know her as well as I knew my mum. They fall shut as Dad lets go of her hair and she drops to the floor like a rag doll.

Another tracking shot, still with a hand-held camera, to show Dad walking towards me. I stay where I am.

Maria says, 'Don't touch him!'

'Shut up,' Dad says.

'It's over if you hurt him,' she says.

The music stops here too. A sudden silence would be effective, I think.

He stops, and then he turns to face Maria and laughs. We see her raise her chin defiantly, but she looks small and fragile in comparison to him, the same way my mum used to.

'Are you trying to threaten me?' he asks her. 'Is that what you're doing?'

I want her to keep staring him out, but she drops her gaze.

'And if it's over,' he says, 'where do you think you're going to go? Another city? Another filthy little flat? Are you ready to be on your own with your daughter again? With not a penny to your name? Or will you crawl back to Devon and live amongst those people whose children she murdered?

409

You'll never cope, Maria. You're not capable of doing it on your own.'

A close-up of her face would show that she's realising something.

'You wouldn't,' she says.

It's then that I understand what she's understood, which is that Dad is implying that he would take Grace from her.

'What I wouldn't do is let my daughter be raised in a home with just you and her,' he says. He looks at Maria in the same way he used to look at my mum, as if she was worthless, and could never be anything else in his eyes.

Then he turns back to me, and this time his face is so full of rage that I step backwards on to the landing. One, two, three steps.

On the TV in front of us, we see how the phone camera wobbles, and it shows the back of my leg as I hide it, and then we see only scraps of action, but everybody watching who knows our house can easily tell that I'm walking backwards towards the top of the staircase.

I don't want to be backing away from him, I want to be standing my ground, and to be shouting at him, shouting all the things that I see in my films. I want to tell him who he is and what he is and ask him why he is a monster and why did such a monster ever want a child? Two children? I want him to dance while I shoot bullets at his feet. I want him to sweat with fear when he understands that I'm not here to do a deal with him, I'm here to kill him, but he's like Colonel Kurtz in all his glory, a towering maniac, a power-riddled Goliath. He haunts my dreams with his violence, and my days with his softly spoken words that are full of menace.

But I'm afraid, and my courage has trickled away. And he has me now; his hand's on my chest, pushing me against the wall right at the top of the stairs.

Behind him, Maria begins to stand, though she has to drag herself up as if she feels mostly weariness, and there's only the faintest spark of defiance left to propel her. Dad doesn't notice. My eyes are on his eyes, and I can see that his other hand is balled up into a fist.

I don't know which to look at, his eyes or his fist, because I'm not sure if he's going to strike, because you see he never has struck me. Yet. He's pinched, and pushed, but mostly he's just used words to keep me subjugated.

What disgusts me most is that I've let him do it to me all my life, and I let him do it to my mum. He never left bruises visible on her though. Never. My dad was too clever for that. That's why none of the doctors who treated my mum ever got suspicious.

The guilt and anger at myself that I never stopped him hurting her is the thing that fills my mind all day and every day, the thing I hear when I play piano, the thing that echoes in my head when I watch films, and when I'm in school, the thing that never leaves me. Nothing makes it go away, except maybe Zoe. Because she is like me: she has bad secrets too.

I saw a counsellor at school. Nobody knew that I did that. The problem was, when I got to the meeting, I couldn't actually say what I wanted to, so I talked a load of crap about being stressed about exams. The counsellor gave me a ton of leaflets, which were useless, but she did say one good thing. She said, 'Why don't you write about what makes you anxious? As a diary maybe? It can help.' I told her I didn't want to write a diary, so she said, 'What about a song?' and I asked her, 'What do I look like, a boy band wannabe or something?' She said, 'Well, what do you like?' and so I said, 'Film.'

'Well, why don't you try writing a script then?'

The script is what I sent to Zoe and Maria. I put my heart and soul into it, I pieced it together from things my mum remembered, I pictured the scenes in my head based on stuff my mum told me about when she and Dad got together, and old photos, and I sent it to them because I wanted Maria to know that I knew what he was like, so she didn't feel alone.

I wanted to warn Zoe too, because my mum couldn't stand up to him alone, or even with me; you need more people than that and I thought Zoe could help me help Maria.

But Zoe was right: I sent it too late.

I don't look at Dad while the film is playing on the TV. I do stop thinking of ways I would have shot it and I look instead at the faces of everybody except him and I see the horror there, as they witness what I have witnessed all my life.

On the TV we suddenly lose the moving images. I dropped my phone right after Dad slammed my back against the wall, which was the moment just before Maria caught him by surprise and managed to pull him away.

All you can see on the film when that's happening is the ceiling of our landing, the chandelier glinting with dim reflected light from the bedroom.

But you can hear the scuffle as she pulls him away, and then she says, 'Are you OK?' to me, which is hard to hear because as soon as Dad has recovered himself, which only takes a second or two, he says, 'You little bitch,' and then there's the sound of movement from when I tried to push her out of the way, and you hear Maria gasp, and then there's the sound of her hitting the banister post, and then the fall.

I started to scream then but Dad put his hand over my mouth before I could make much of a noise, and we both watched the blood seeping out of the back of her head and pooling on to the varnished wood on the stairs.

Just a few moments after that, the film stops. I picked up the phone and stopped it recording while Dad clattered down the stairs to see if he could save her.

The really important thing is that you can't see that it was me pushing Maria out of the way of Dad that sends her falling down the stairs. To listen to the footage, it's exactly as if he has done it. It's the inevitable result of his violence.

To make that extra clear, just like Zoe told me to, I turn to the room and I look the Family Liaison Officer in the eye and I say, 'He pushed her.'

Then, for the second time in twelve hours, Dad advances on me with his hand clenched into a fist.

I put my hands up to protect my face and curl up in my seat.

He never hits me though, because Philip stops him in time.

'Don't you dare,' Philip says. 'Don't you dare!' He pushes Dad back down on to the sofa, and holds him there.

'Are you really going to do this?' Dad asks me. 'Lucas? Have you thought this through? Do you think you'd like to tell the truth?'

I have to look away from him then, and to force myself to do it, to keep myself strong. It's so incredibly hard not to reply, but I mustn't. Zoe said all we have to do is to stick to our story, and I will.

Zoe does her bit then, she says, 'I saw it. I came out of my bedroom when I heard Chris shouting. My mum was trying to protect Lucas, and Chris pushed her down the stairs. He pushed her so hard, and he hurt me too,' she says. She pulls down the side of her trousers to show the Family Liaison Officer a large welt on her hip. 'He pushed me too.'

The Liaison Officer separates me and Zoe from my dad then. She stays with him, and so does Philip, and we leave the room, and tell our story again, to Tess and Richard. They believe us, both of them do, and the relief is incredible.

When the detectives have arrived, and talked to Dad, which seems like only minutes after the Liaison Officer has called for backup, I'll admit that my stomach lurches when I see them lead him away.

I run to the open front door as they take him to the police car. I can't help myself.

'Dad!' I shout, but he doesn't turn around, or look at me at all, not once, until he's sitting in the back of the car and it's backing out of the drive, and then his eyes lock on to mine as he's driven away.

414

SAM

It's late when I finally phone Tessa back. I try her mobile but it goes straight to voicemail again, and I'm loath to phone the landline in case her husband answers.

Outside the windows of my flat, I can see that the evening crowd has turned out. They're on their way to the pubs on the riverside, or wandering home from work.

I sit on a chair on my balcony with a beer in my hand, but back from the edge, in the shade, where I can feel concealed but also watch the people below.

I'm in that frame of mind where your own life feels as if it has been sucked so hollow that every detail of the lives of others seems designed to wound you. I resent the pair who wander, holding hands, beside the water. I resent the young office worker who walks jauntily along, phone to his ear, chatting to somebody he's going to meet later.

I even resent the old woman who walks along with a small dog trotting in her wake. I've seen them before. They take the same route every day. The dog is never on a lead. It knows where they're going and they're happy to be in each other's company.

I'm shy. I'll never be the rowdy guy having beers in a big crowd at the riverside pub, like the one I can see across the water. I'll be the man in the corner meeting a carefully chosen friend, or my lover.

But will my lover want me now?

I was her refuge, but now I'll be a drag. There will be attacks of my disease when I may not be able to move, when my pain might be excruciating. They'll probably worsen over time, so what use will I be to her then? I'll be more like her husband, with his alcoholism, which drains her. My state of mind and physical capabilities will be no better than his in time, and will inevitably become worse.

I poke at the palm of my left hand, willing the numbness to be gone, desperate to be able to feel more sensation there, but of course nothing has changed.

I pick up the bag of medication that I brought back from the hospital, which has been sitting at my feet, and I peel away the sticker that's sealing it and peer into it.

It contains three different boxes of pills.

'Diagnosis is often the trickiest time for our patients,' said the MS nurse who I went to see after the consultant. She was heartbreakingly lovely. 'Do you have somebody at home with you tonight?'

'Yes,' I lied. I didn't want her pity.

She gave me leaflets with titles like 'Coping with MS' and 'Information for Patients'. Leaflets that I still believe are for other people, not me.

I drink my beer slowly and think about the frailty of life. I think of Zoe Maisey and her poor mother.

I must begin to take these tablets tonight. I must take careful note of dosages.

I must try not to wallow too much in how little I appreciated my life before the passage of time was marked by the popping open of pill packets, the rattle of a bottle full of tablets being picked up, and the tearing sound as a nurse liberates a new syringe from its packet, just for you.

I can't face taking the tablets yet. I will, but not just yet.

My parents will take this hard. They'll phone soon, to ask me what happened at the appointment, and I'll have to tell them.

I think of the other messages that were left on my phone, from both Tess and her husband; the ones they left hours and hours ago.

I wonder if the police have made any progress.

I look online, idly really, to see if anything has happened, because it would be pushing things too far to phone DS George again, and I sit up straighter when I read that an arrest has been made.

'The suspect has not yet been named, but he's believed to be a member of the family,' a news website tells me.

'He'. So it's not Zoe. Thank God.

Did I think it was Zoe? No. Do I work in criminal law and see what's possible, however little you want it to be? Yes. So I would never have ruled it out.

More internet searching turns up a grainy long-lens photo that shows a man in the back of a police car. I'm pretty sure it must be Chris Kennedy, Maria's husband. No surprises in a way; he would naturally be a prime suspect for the police.

Tess will be absolutely shattered because she thought that marriage was saving her sister.

I try her mobile, which goes to voicemail, so I have no choice but to brave the landline.

I don't know if I'm going to tell her about my diagnosis,

but I want to know how she is, and what's happening and I want to hear her voice, and tell her how sorry I am and that I'm thinking of her. And, if I'm honest with myself, I also want to know when she's going to be able to see me again, because I need her.

TESSA

We sit in the garden after everybody has left. It's evening, and it's still hot and we want to escape the confines of the house that's had us trapped all day, and which feels sullied now, as it's where we had to learn what Chris did to Maria.

There are some generous patches of shade that have appeared as this awful day has progressed and the shadows have inevitably lengthened, but the sun still pours across the garden fence in places and heats up our patch of ground.

I sit on the bench with Richard. Around my ankles the parched grass feels prickly and beside me on the bench Richard sweats, and is mostly silent. We are both profoundly shocked.

My sister walked into a new marriage to escape her old life. She was vulnerable and I should have protected her more.

I say this to Richard.

'She was also ambitious,' he says. 'And you weren't responsible for her happiness.'

'I should have done more, I should have known her better.'

'She didn't want you close, I think she knew what she was doing.'

'But what must she have been going through?' We're speaking very quietly because the children are in the garden with us, all three of them. 'It's such a high price to pay.'

'The highest,' he says.

The kids have spread out a rug in the shade a few metres away from us, and filled the washing-up bowl with water, and they're playing with Grace. Philip Guerin is sitting with them.

On another day, it would be a perfect scene.

Our apple tree is dying. The trunks splits into two near its base and, while one side has produced a decent crop of apples this year, the other is barren.

Philip Guerin is sitting close to Zoe, but not very close. I know he doesn't want her to live with him.

She shifts position on the rug and is backlit by the sunshine, her hair a cascade of white, which so reminds me of my sister when she was young. The golden light silhouettes and burnishes Zoe's delicate arms and slender shoulders, and makes the drops of water sparkle in the air when Grace splashes.

Something is bothering me, a detail.

I look at my lovely niece. I see her point out something to Grace.

It's a butterfly, the source of Zoe's nickname.

And, as I watch it, I work out what's troubling me.

It's the injury to Zoe's hip, because I am fairly certain that I remember her hip clashing with the piano as she fled from Tom Barlow in the church. Fairly certain, but not positive. I wonder where the film of the concert is, because that would tell us. I wonder whether I have the stomach to watch it, and whether I even want to know, because Zoe told the police that Chris did it, that he pushed her.

Amongst the evening midges, the butterfly flutters on, looking for somewhere to feed. I recognise it as a fritillary and I think that it's a beautiful creature. Its wings are patterned in shades of orange and black that look magical in the wash of sunlight and against the intense blue evening sky, which the sunset won't tint for at least another half-hour. Fluttering amongst the flaxen stalks of our dried-out lawn the butterfly brings to mind more exotic locations than this.

The lavender spikes along our garden path are mostly desiccated by now, but I know where the butterfly will go, and so it does. It continues on its path, crossing the grass. It flutters right up to the children, causing Grace to pump her arms with excitement, and then past them and towards the corner of our garden where a rogue buddleia seed has over the years grown into a huge, magnificent plant. It's bathed in sunshine. Huge sprays of dark purple flowers arc away from it, and it's covered with butterflies and insects.

I watch the fritillary approach the buddleia, its path undulating yet somehow preordained, and sure enough it finishes there, alighting weightlessly on one of the generous racemes. Its wings close, and it begins to feed.

It will bathe in the honeyed sunlight and feast on the nectar until dusk begins to nudge away the daylight, and then it will find somewhere to settle in the dark, close by, and it will wait there until the light rises again in the morning, warming its wings and its body, so that it can make a foray out into another day.

This is the way of the world, I think. It's the natural order of things that so fascinated me as a child, and still does. But there will be only so many new daybreaks for this butterfly. It has a short lifespan. Some species can hibernate through the winter, but not this one.

Richard puts his arm around me, and I let him.

And I think, if Sam told me he wanted me, would I ever be able to leave now?

I say to Richard, 'Philip won't have Zoe, you know.'

'I know,' he replies. 'I know he won't.'

Richard is crying; he does that a lot. His depression is severe.

Our telephone rings.

RICHARD

There's an image that feels as if it's just within my grasp; it's an idea that's forming and then wavering, threatening to disappear, as if it's a mirage floating in the hot evening air.

I have not had a drink today, and this means that the idea is real, even if I can't quite make it solidify.

The idea is this: that Tessa and I will take on these children. I've spoken to Philip Guerin and he wants to go back to Devon without his daughter. He's met a new partner and she's from the local village, close to the families who lost children because of Zoe. Their relationship will not work with Zoe in their midst, and Philip will not consider moving away and starting again.

I expect we could try to persuade him, but why would we, when an alternative might be available?

Mentally, I remove him from the scene in front of me and I reimagine it.

There is Tess, and I, on the bench. I have my arm around her and she has remained in her seat, and not squirmed out from under my touch, as usual. In front of us there are three children on a rug: two blonde princesses and a dark, clever boy.

They are two damaged teenagers and a perfect baby girl who will never remember her mother, and we are looking after them. They will fill our days and nights and we will fill theirs. I will cook for them and organise them, and drive the older kids to music lessons, while Tess works as normal. We'll give them patient care and love and help, and their lives will be as good as they can be. We'll give them ordinary, we won't be seduced by their talent or upset by their histories.

There's only one thing that makes this mirage shimmer, and threaten to dissolve into the air.

It's what I thought I overheard while Zoe was bathing Grace earlier.

It was Lucas saying, 'It was an accident,' and 'I'm going to tell them everything.' It sounded like a confession, but maybe he was just talking about what they witnessed. It must have been.

I won't mention this to Tessa, but I expect that if I did she would say, 'Well what does that mean? Are you sure you heard it right? Had you had a drink?' So I won't.

I've already cleared up the broken model that I found in my shed. If one of them smashed it they would be doing nothing worse than I've done in the past, when all the sadness I've felt has occasionally driven me to an act of destruction like that.

To make sure I'm fit to take on these children, I'll go around the house and take every bottle and tip it down the sink. I'll never buy alcohol again. I'll go to AA. I'll be a perfect father to them. Even if Lucas doesn't want to stay with us, he'll always be welcome here to see his sister Grace.

Today is not the day to say this to the children. Nor will tomorrow be, and perhaps not even next week, but it's the offer I want to make them as and when they're ready to hear it.

If Tessa will agree.

I'm willing to bargain.

If she'll agree to this, I'll not ask questions about how she knew, off by heart, the personal mobile phone number of Zoe's solicitor. I'll not phone her friends to ask if she stayed with them last night, because I think I know where she was. I think she was with him. It was her that told me, her defensiveness when I phoned him. I'm not one hundred per cent sure, I have no idea how it might have happened, but I can live with a little uncertainty. It's a lesser demon than the ones I've been cohabiting with for the last few years. Tess's infidelity is probably as much as I deserved, and it's certainly no worse a thing than what I've put her through.

This is what I want to say to the children, this is what makes me feel invigorated, strong, hopeful: *Stay with us. We'll look after you. We'll make sure no more harm comes to you. We can be your family.*

From inside the house, our landline rings and I feel Tess tense up beside me.

'I'll get that,' I say.

SAM

I try Tess's landline because I feel I have to. I don't want her to feel abandoned.

It rings and rings, and I'm about to give up when Richard answers.

I'm tempted to hang up, but that would be childish, and this is not a day for infantile behaviour.

'Hello,' I say. 'It's Sam Locke, Zoe's solicitor, returning your call.'

I say that because I suspect he doesn't know that Tess and I have spoken since he left his message.

He says, 'Thank you, Sam, but we don't need you any longer, the police have made an arrest.'

'Yes, I saw that on the news. I'm so sorry. Is everybody all right? It must have been a terrible shock.'

'It is a great shock, yes.'

He draws out his words as if there's something else he's thinking of saying and I'm suddenly alert to the fact that he might know about Tess and I.

'Well, I won't keep bothering you any longer, but if there's anything I can do please just phone me.'

'I think you've done enough, don't you?'

'I beg your pardon?'

'Don't contact my family again. Don't contact Zoe and, most importantly, don't contact my wife.'

'What?'

'I think you understand me very well.'

'I …'

'Leave us alone.'

'Sorry, I …' But my words fall into the ether because he's hung up.

I sit with my phone in my hand and wonder if Tessa has told him about us, if she had to tell him. I'm still sitting there many minutes later, speculating, and shocked at the ferocity of his tone, when my phone rings.

Tess, I think at first, but it's not. It's my parents, and I can't ignore them. Not today. My mother cries when I tell her that my diagnosis is one step nearer to being confirmed.

'How will you manage, love?' she asks. 'Will you move back home?'

'I don't know, Mum, we'll have to see.'

I've had no intention of doing that, but after I hang up I drink another beer and watch the river some more and feel the beginnings of what feels like mourning for Tessa, and then I'm tempted by my mother's suggestion. I'm tempted to walk away from this city and this life and this relationship that's brought me the greatest feelings of joy but also the most profound feelings of guilt. I'm tempted to nurse my sorrows elsewhere, to rethink my life.

If I take myself back to Devon where I'll still be in pain, and my condition will inevitably degenerate, and I'll miss Tess every day, there will at least be sea air, and beautiful country-side and people who know me and love me. It'll be a return, sure, but also another chance.

Because what is there for me here, now?

And these thoughts circulate as I watch the reflection of the setting sun burning brightly in the windows of the boat-yard opposite my flat, until it sinks down far enough that it disappears.

After that, the city lights, and their reflections on the water, have to work hard to pierce the darkness.

EPILOGUE

ZOE

I'm standing at the side of the stage waiting to go on.

Outside there's ice on the pavement and when we arrived Uncle Richard had to catch my arm because I nearly slipped over when we got out of the car.

Lucas is in the crowd, manning the video recorder. He doesn't perform in public any more, though sometimes he bangs out a tune. That's how he himself describes his playing nowadays. He's so into filming and that's his thing now. He spends hours watching films with Uncle Richard. Richard doesn't make models any more, he says he never really liked them; he gets into the whole film thing with Lucas instead.

Grace is here, but we don't think she'll last long in the audience.

Richard says that he wouldn't bring her along at all, but he's sure that she's got an unusual interest in music for a child her age. She's captivated by my playing, he says. He's sitting at the end of the back row with her so he has an easy exit and can take her home when she makes her first squawk. But he wants her to be here at the beginning at least. It's my first concert since Mum died, and I think we all know in our hearts it's a kind of tribute to her.

My piano was brought over from the Second Chance House and moved into the dining room at Tess's house. Richard has converted his shed into a kind of cinema and film room where he and Lucas edit films and watch them on a pull-down screen.

'It's tech heaven,' says Tess when she looks in there.

I tried to phone Sam once, at work, but they said he'd left, gone back to Devon. They said he was poorly. I tried to tell Tessa, but she didn't want to talk about it. She reminded me of Mum then, pushing a subject away, lips tight and holding back feelings that I couldn't read.

I'm playing a short programme tonight, but it contains some of Mum's favourite pieces.

Because of the cold I'm wrapped up warmly, gloves on, and a cardigan, and I've been pressed against the heater that's in the shabby little green room. We've been careful with the venue we've booked on this occasion, so very careful. It's not a church; it's a music club. The piano on the stage is a beautiful Steinway and there's seating for around eighty people. This time, I shall make my entrance from the side, not down an aisle.

In my head there's a mantra: This is your Third Chance.

I don't think I have nine lives, but I hope I have three.

I hear my name called from the stage and, just before I go on, in my head I send a message to my mum. This is for you, Mummy, is what I think, and I have to wipe a small tear carefully from my eye.

I take off my cardigan and my gloves.

I'm looking good, in a dress that Mum chose for me before she died, a black silk dress with a high neck and three-quarter-length sleeves. I've brushed my hair until it's silky, just how she would want me to. As I enter the room and mount the stage, there's a round of applause.

Before I sit down, I do a small bow to the audience, and then the clapping stops politely. Tess is in the front row and she gives me a thumbs-up. Behind her, almost all the seats are full. My reputation has preceded me. As Chris might have said, if he hadn't been sentenced to fifteen years in jail: No publicity is bad publicity.

I sit. I adjust the stool, controlling my breathing, and I place my hands over the keys.

The piece is a nocturne by Chopin. It's achingly beautiful, soul-pulling music, which can make your insides ripple. It's for my mother, and for Lucas, who doesn't want to perform any more, but loves to listen. It's for Grace too, because she's going to be just like me, I know it. It's for Richard and Tess, who are looking after us now. It's for my Third Chance Family.

As I pull the first note from the piano, I'm instantly lost to the music, trapped inside it, living every delicate, haunting phrase of it, and I feel like my mum is living it with me.

And I know it's going to go well, brilliantly, in fact.

ACKNOWLEDGEMENTS

A great deal has happened in the year since I started to work on this book, and I'm indebted to all the people who've supported me along the way.

A super-sized thank you must go to Emma Beswetherick, my amazing editor, who did so much to shape my first book and has given me the confidence and opportunity to write this one. Your extraordinary enthusiasm, tireless support, and your razor-sharp editorial guidance and clarity are all things I simply could not have done without.

Thanks must also go to some other fantastic folk at Little, Brown: Charlie King and Tim Whiting, whose support I greatly appreciate; Kate Doran and Aimee Kitson for brilliant marketing; Jo Wickham for gently easing me into the world of publicity, and Stephanie-Elise Melrose for taking over the helm with so much energy and creativity. Dominic Wakeford for all your work on the manuscript, and Ceara Elliot for a fabulous cover design. Kate Hibbert for finding my books a home at William Morrow in the US, where my lovely editor Amanda Bergeron and the rest of the team in New York have worked wonders with their edition. It's such a pleasure to work with you all.

Another enormous thank you to my amazing agent Nelle Andrew, who is always there for me with the right words of advice, and bucketloads of support. I feel very lucky to have you on my side.

Huge thanks also to the fabulous Rachel Mills, Alexandra Cliff and Marilia Savvides at PFD who have sent my first book out into the world with wings on. Lovely Rebecca Wearmouth completes the foreign rights team and it's been so much fun to work with all of you.

To all the international editors and publishers who took on the book: thank you so much, you've also given me the courage to throw myself into *The Perfect Girl*. It's been a joy to work with and to meet many of you over the past year.

Thank you to my writing partner Abbie Ross for being there every step of the way. Your tireless support, friendship and determination have kept me going and inspired me too.

Thank you so much also to Annemarie Caracciolo, Philippa Lowthorpe, Bridget Rode, Janie and Phill Ankers, Jonathan and Cilla Paget, Andrew Beck and Vonda Macmillan Beck for always being there with words of encouragement. Annemarie, you get the trophy for the best pep talks.

My two retired detectives, who helped me so much with *Burnt Paper Sky*, were once again extremely generous with their time and advice for this book, and in particular they helped me devise a crime scene and timeline that would work with the intricate plot that I had in mind. Thank you so much to you both.

I also undertook research in the worlds of criminal law and incarceration to support elements of this book. Rob Rode and Margaret Evans were both extremely generous with their time and knowledge in this respect, and I'm very grateful to you both.

Any legal or police procedure mistakes are mine alone!

On the home front, another massive thank you must go to my family who has been very patient with me while I disappeared into my basement office for days, weeks and months on end to tackle this book.

Jules Macmillan. Thank you for feeding the children, the dogs, and the fish while I wrote. Thank you for listening when I needed to talk about the book (which was pretty much all the time), and helping me reverse out of many a plot cul-de-sac, and for your brilliant and thoughtful suggestions. Thank you most of all for being unstintingly supportive of this book, and of me.

Rose, Max and Louis Macmillan. Thank you for everything. You've never once complained as your full-time mum became a full-time writer, and that's something. Thank you too for patiently answering all my questions and letting me feed some of your own interests into my story. And not forgetting, most importantly, a very big thank you to each one of you for making me smile every day. I'm so proud of you all.

THE PERFECT GIRL
Reading Guide

INSPIRATION FOR
The Perfect Girl

The idea for *The Perfect Girl* began to evolve in my mind a long time before I started to write the novel. Many years ago, I was told a true story about a teenage girl that I simply wasn't able to forget. The girl in question was from a good family and had every opportunity in life, but there was something unusual about her. One night she had made a very grave mistake and had done something that caused the death of one teenager and severely injured another. She was around seventeen years old when it happened, and as a result of what she did she was sent to jail, destroying her chances of finishing school and going on to have the 'normal' life that was expected. While incarcerated she began to take drugs, and by the time she was let out she had become dependent. In spite of her family's best efforts, she took to living in hostels and remaining on the margins of society. Her life never recovered its original trajectory.

I was shocked by the tale. I felt sorry for the girl and her family, and her story raised all kinds of questions for me. What would it be like, I wondered, if your chance of a 'normal' life was destroyed in this way before it had effectively begun, based on one rash decision? How likely would you be to get a reasonable second chance at life after such a thing had happened, and what would that second chance be worth to you, and your family?

These questions felt pressing enough that I began to develop the novel thinking that similar events might make a fascinating, if difficult, backstory, and that it might be even more interesting if the girl in question was some sort of prodigy, because that could raise the stakes even higher for her and for her family. The question of which talent to give Zoe – my perfect girl – was an easy one to answer, as one of my own children is an extremely good musician, so we've inhabited the world of competitive piano playing for many years. It's mostly a very sociable and fun world, but occasionally you come across a child or young person who you suspect might be intensively schooled to play and under tremendous pressure to win, just as Zoe is.

As the novel developed I felt that I wanted to use Zoe's character to explore the ways in which teenagers are often extremely emotionally developed and intelligent, yet very far from being in control of their own lives. Zoe's personality and life contain many similar contrasts. Her mind is brilliant and it races wildly and imaginatively, yet she has also developed extraordinary strength and discipline from her piano studies. She's spent time in prison, but now lives in luxury and privilege. She's developing a public profile as a pianist, yet that talent has also made her feel isolated from her peers. I was fascinated by those juxtapositions: what they could do to a young person, how they might affect her feelings and behaviour. I often thought of Zoe as a caged bird: lonely, brilliant, beautiful, brave and not to be underestimated.

I set the book over a very short timeframe and used just a few locations and a small cast, because I was hoping to give it the intensity and claustrophobia of a chamber drama – a format I absolutely love. I also adore films and books in which the actions of one person trigger another's and so on, causing events to spiral unstoppably as they do in *The Perfect Girl*. For this reason I also used a number of other narrative voices in addition to Zoe's. I hoped it was a device that might allow the reader to experience the story almost cinematically, as the characters move in and out of focus and the reader is able to see the action developing from the point of view of each of the main players. It was a device that should also, I hoped, reveal each of the characters in more depth, peeling back their public faces and laying bare their real motives and thoughts. I felt that letting the reader into the head of more than one character could only raise the stakes for each of them, and would show how their motivations interplay with Zoe's.

It was a daunting but exciting challenge trying to bring all the elements of this novel together, and I hope you've enjoyed the result.

READING GROUP QUESTIONS

1. What advantages do Zoe's abilities give her? Can you understand why Maria pushed her daughter musically? What responsibility do you think parents have to a child who shows strong aptitude for something? What is fostering, and what is pushing too hard?

2. Zoe makes a very difficult decision towards the end of *The Perfect Girl*, one that will certainly have significant and long-lasting consequences for both herself and others. Do you think she did the right thing? How much sympathy do you have for her?

3. To what extent do you think of Maria as a victim, or as somebody who is deliberately deceiving others?

4. What does the character of Zoe's solicitor add to the novel?

5. What is the importance of music and its redemptive power in the novel?

6. At the end of the book both Tess and Richard seem to have an inkling that Zoe has deceived everybody but they don't discuss this. Do you think they'll talk about it eventually, and work out what might have happened? If so, what do you think they'll do as a result?

7. Lucas is a quiet character. How do you feel about him? Do you think he'll thrive in his new family, or could he be in danger of ultimately remaining loyal to his father and telling the truth about what happened?

8. A number of novels deal with the burden of a deadly secret – how well do you think this idea is handled in *The Perfect Girl*?

9. Do you recognise some of the pressures that the family finds itself under more generally? Is that urge to keep up with others, to be a successful unit, and to put on a good show familiar to you?

10. 'My mother: who never talks about what really matters …' How far is this observation explored in the book?

11. The ending is both satisfying for Zoe and morally ambiguous. How successful do you think it is, and did Chris deserve what happened to him?

TEN BOOKS THAT INSPIRED
The Perfect Girl

While I was writing *The Perfect Girl* I wanted to read any books that did one of three distinct things. I searched for novels that featured a strong teenage voice, took place over a very short timeframe, or had multiple narrators. I read very widely in those categories, and more, over the nine months that I took to write the novel, but the following are ten of my favourites.

The Catcher in the Rye by J.D. Salinger

A classic, obviously, but there is undeniable power in teenage narrator Holden Caulfield's voice, and the insights into his feelings of alienation and his struggle to understand his identity that the book provides. I love the quirky stream-of-consciousness writing style that makes you feel like Holden's confidante, and the way Salinger brings his wild, powerful, and clever mind alive so vividly.

The Outsiders by S.E. Hinton

This is a classic coming-of-age story but also a wonderful, heart-breaking novel that perfectly illustrates the way in which teenagers can be victims of their circumstances. In yet another powerful first-person narrative the story is told via the character of Ponyboy Curtis. He's a character who has stayed with me ever since I first picked up this book. I still feel a pang of concern for him now, and I'm writing this a good thirty years since I first read it!

Special Topics in Calamity Physics by Marissa Pessl

Blue van der Meer is the clever, academic teenager who narrates this novel, and I loved her energy and the way her mind spills out all over the page as she tries to work out why one of her favourite teachers committed suicide. It's a smart, insightful story, full of challenges for the reader, and a great who-dunnit too.

We Are All Completely Beside Ourselves by Karen Joy Fowler

Rosemary is the narrator of this novel, and although she's not quite a teenager because she's at college, much of the book describes her early years and her fresh, quirky voice hooked me in right from the start and led me through the pages at a gallop. It's a witty, brilliant and unusual book in which the action grips but some very thoughtful and important themes form its heartbeat. I defy anybody not to have a richer understanding of love and family after finishing it.

The Fault in Our Stars by John Green

How I love Hazel Grace Lancaster, the teenage narrator of this wonderful novel. *The Fault in Our Stars* was originally written for teens, and passed to me by my daughter after she had read it. I'll admit I picked it up with some scepticism but once I had, I simply could not put it down. Hazel's wit, kindness and perceptiveness combined with the unusual perspective on life that her illness gives her, and of course all of her normal teenage vulnerabilities, make this a very lovely, if sad, story about family, and life, and absolutely essential reading.

As I Lay Dying by William Faulkner

This novel tells the story of the death and burial of Addie Bundren, who has been the matriarch of a large family in 1920s Mississippi. It's told from about fifteen different viewpoints in intense stream-of-consciousness narratives that intersect and almost seem to weave through one another. As the book progresses, each narrator reveals more about Addie's life and the lives of her family members, and others. It's a demanding read, and a bleak story, but it's incredibly powerful, compelling and, above all, humane.

Chronicle of a Death Foretold by Gabriel García Márquez

This short novel is a masterpiece. Set over just one day, it tells the story of the final hours of Santiago Nasar. We learn in the very first line that by the end of the novel he will be dead, yet are gripped by Márquez's extraordinary observation of both the ordinary and the extra-ordinary as we learn how, against the odds, death stalks Santiago through those hours until it finally catches up with him. It is a tour-de-force study of human nature, love, fate and revenge.

The Mezzanine by Nicholson Baker

This novel has the shortest timeframe of any that I discovered while I was developing *The Perfect Girl*. It takes place over a single lunch hour and we spend this time in the mind of the narrator, Howie, hearing his every thought. The extraordinary attention to detail is a marvel, as is the rendering of the paths our minds can wander along, and if nothing else the novel makes a virtue of the mundane. Not a book to race through, it's a demanding yet strangely relaxing read.

The Dinner by Herman Koch

This is a gripping novel. The action takes place over just one evening at an elegant dinner where the protagonist and his wife must meet his brother and sister-in-law to discuss what they should do about their teenage sons who have done something very shocking indeed.

Ordinary People by Judith Guest

This powerful novel inspired a film that is one of my all-time favourites. It tells the story of a well-off suburban family who is struggling to live normally again in the aftermath of two life-shattering events. Narrated by Conrad Jarrett, a teenage boy, it's a sensitive exploration of depression, love, grief and guilt, and it illustrates in painful detail the tremendous psychological strains of keeping up appearances when life is never going to be the same again.

ANORAK IN FENLAND

Retired teacher Martin Brady's interest in footpaths leads him to investigate a run-down Fenland farm – which turns out to contain illegal immigrants and to be linked to a national neo-Nazi Organisation. His amateur sleuthing (whilst his wife is away on a course) leads to his being shot at, but not before undertaking a hair-raising river trip, causing a spectacular plane crash and discovering a Bunker which contains a photo of a rather special U-boat.....

i

John Nicholson

Descended from the Nicholsons who farmed in the nineteenth century at Grimblethorpe Hall in North Lincolnshire, the author has lived for many years in the Fens where this tale is set. Retired now from a career in teaching, he has also worked for the Hong Kong Shanghai Bank, in Paris, and as a Second Secretary in the Foreign Office. He and his wife, Angela (a retired French teacher) have long shared a love of the culture and language of France.

After attending the Stamford Endowed Schools, their children, Patrick and Lucy gained places at the universities of Cambridge and Oxford respectively – he to read Russian and French, she History. Their present Golden Retriever, Toffee, would like to point out, however, that she is in no way related to or similar in character to Sherry, who figures in '**Anorak in Fenland**' – and that goes for members of the author's family as well.

Also by
John Nicholson

*

Contemporary Problems of Foreign Exchange and Trade
(Ginn & Co Ltd, 1971)

Modern British Economics
(George Allen & Unwin, 1973)

A N O R A K

I N

F E N L A N D

by

John Nicholson

WRITERSWORLD
A SELF PUBLISHING RESOURCE

Published by WRITERSWORLD

Copyright © John Nicholson 2002

Cover design Alan Taylor

The moral right of the author has been asserted

Printed and bound by Antony Rowe Limited, Eastbourne

ISBN 1-907181-03-2

WRITERSWORLD
15-17 Maidenhead Street
Hertford SG14 1DW
England

www.writersworld.tv

For
Patrick Brady Nicholson
Счастливого пути!

CHAPTER ONE

"Bloody Hell! These books get worse and worse." There was a thud as Martin's action thriller hit the floor.

"Do calm down, dear. I'm trying to finish this marking."

"But it's ridiculous!" expostulated Martin. "Here we are on page 18 and he's already fondling her small firm breasts, contemplating her flat buttocks and hard at it. He only met her on page 15! And the bloody book didn't start until page 10!"

"You don't *have* to read escapist rubbish all the time. Why don't you take up a hobby or do an evening class or something? Lots of retired people do."

"That's not the point," said Martin, picking up the book again. "The publishers insist on bad language and graphic bonking – I remember an article or an interview with Dick Francis when he said he had to write a few steamy scenes in, just for the sake of it. Those bits just stand out like... like... sore thumbs."

"I wondered for a moment what graphic image you were going to use," said Jennifer, whose mind had been broadened over thirty years of marriage and a few more of teaching. "Why don't you make a cup of tea, get my case down from the roof and make a list of what I shall need to take on this course?"

Martin's wife was shortly to leave for three weeks in France on a language refresher course, designed to better equip her – or, rather, better to equip her – to guide her reluctant students to ever higher exam grades, using the currently fashionable 'target language' approach. Whether, thought Martin (whose growing disenchantment and cynicism had led him to seek early retirement from his post of Head of Economics) the approach would still be approved of by the time she returned, was another matter. However, it meant that he would have plenty of time to catch up on his reading, and could at long last tidy the garage. He might even decorate the dining room, one of several items on the notional list, hopefully prepared by Jennifer.

"You're always on about footpaths," said Jennifer when the tea eventually arrived, after much banging and crashing from the roof and a lengthy search for the sweeteners, "so why don't you join the Ramblers or get up an action group?"

"Action? Round here? You must be joking – it's dead. The Fens used to be famous for eels and wild-fowling, but that was before the seventeenth century. It's gone down since then. All there is now is sugar beet, and rape – and even that's a far cry from what the Vikings understood by the term."

"Yes, well, while I'm away, I suggest you practise both defeatism and decorating – the dining room and the front bedroom both need doing, and the books need sorting, and...."

Martin hurriedly revised his negative approach at the prospect of endless useful tasks and interrupted to say that he had been thinking of writing to the County Council about the removal of footpath signs, the culprits being in his view more likely to be the landowners than layabout teenagers. The latter were much too busy fulfilling their output norms in terms of lager-swilling, drug-taking and copulating – the last being undertaken in remarkably draughty locations, if the evidence provided by used condoms was to be believed. During the ensuing conversation, Martin agreed that it was silly to suspect respectable farmers, and agreed that it was, in any case, none of his business, and that he would think about seeing whether they needed someone to patrol and effect minor repairs.

Jennifer had her mind on other things, such as the packing, her husband's feeding arrangements, emergency telephone numbers, etc., as a result of which she failed to register how unlike him it was to be so reasonable. In fact, Martin had just had a very productive thought, leading to an idea which he knew would not commend itself to his wife – especially when she was going to leave him on his own. The thought was related to the removal, or rotating, of footpath signs, and the fact that he did not know who was doing it – but it was not related to the notion that it was none of his business. Martin had decided to do some investigating, to try to catch the culprit(s) in flagrante whatsit – and to decide on a plan of action as soon as he returned from taking Jennifer to the station. It was a decision which was going to have far-reaching effects.

On his return from Peterborough, Martin made himself a coffee and contemplated irresponsible behaviour – thereby demonstrating (although the thought did not occur to him) that some boys remain at the 'difficult age' well beyond their teens. To be fair, Martin did not plan to confront any youths if he found them – indeed, he expected to confirm that they were not to blame. He intended to hide in the hedge near to one of the signposts which he had had to relocate a few weeks previously, on one or two likely nights, and use the lack of action as a form of 'evidence' to support the theory that those with the greater motive and opportunity – the landowners – were the most likely culprits.

Having taken their Golden Retriever, Sherry, for her walk earlier – and been reassured by a lengthy telephone call that his wife had arrived safely – Martin set off as dusk fell. He went shrouded in dark clothing, without Sherry and also without his face blacked, as he was afraid of looking silly if discovered. He planned, in such an eventuality, to claim a desire to look for owls and bats. He remembered to take the dog lead, however, which could enable him to appear to be searching for Sherry, a torch 'just in case' and a thermos of soup, as it could be a long wait.

Martin stepped out briskly, his gumboots making little noise, his senses more acutely aware than was usually the case, conscious of the sound rather like distant surf from the main road a mile or so to the east. The lights of an occasional plane or helicopter winked above, as much a part of the Fenland scene as the odd tractor, ploughing by headlights or the softly gliding owl and flickering bat. Having arrived at his chosen spot, Martin settled himself down well hidden in the hedge which bounded a wide track, accessible by car, with two 'suspect' footpath signs just visible by the intermittent light of the moon through the scudding clouds.

It was about 10 o'clock when they came, stepping carefully in single file, silent and watchful, only visible to someone at a lower level, causing the graceful beasts to be silhouetted against the backdrop of the lighter night sky. The small herd of deer disappeared almost as soon as Martin spotted them, however, put to flight by an approaching car. He sank back into his hiding place as the courting (for want of a better word) couple drove on past to the end of the track, from where, to his now heightened aural awareness, came the intermittent sounds of copulation in the cramped confines of a Carina. As Martin had suspected, neither party was interested in footpath signs, so he decided to wait about another hour before calling it a day – or rather night.

He settled down to consuming the soup, hoping to see a badger or a fox, and wondering whether he could, on subsequent such occasions, bring a personal radio if he kept it at a very low level. A few minutes after midnight, Martin decided to return home and set about gathering up his 'things'.

He was about to step forward onto the path when he heard a faint padding noise coming not from the direction of the lane along which had come the car, but from his right. To his amazement, three darkly clad, silent figures moved across his line of vision, proceeding at a brisk walking pace. There was something faintly menacing about the patrol (for such it seemed to be to Martin, perhaps on account of his own somewhat strange behaviour). The air of faint menace, however, gave way to one of a definite threat when, a few metres behind the main party, Martin heard the low growl of the sort of dog whose bite is even worse than its bark.

The handler paused, emitted a quiet but penetrating hiss to warn his colleagues, and, to Martin's horror, allowed the dog to lead the way. That way would shortly result in the discovery of a watcher who would find it difficult to convince this sinister group, particularly when speaking between the jaws of a less-than-friendly neighbourhood hell-hound, that he was only there because he was interested in nature and not at all in their nefarious activities.

As the dog pressed on, drawn by the scent of its prey, Martin could only crouch lower, unable even to think that he had every right to be where he was and would do better to go on the offensive, to step forward and confront them with their behaviour.

Somehow, even if he had had the time to reason logically, Martin perceived this group to be likely to operate outside the law. To the extent that he thought at all, it was to regret that he had ever put himself in such a dangerous situation. The dog growled again, now within a couple of metres of his hiding place, and Martin grasped the vacuum flask which had contained his soup, hoping to repel the beast for long enough for the handler to bring it under control – always assuming that he wish -shhhhhough!.... The explosion caused Martin to drop the flask, clutch himself and fall backwards. It also caused the dog to start violently, pulling over his handler, who let out a curse – just the sort of reactions hoped for by the pheasant, which had lain undetected for several hours and now made good its escape, having erupted out of the thicket with the maximum of momentarily paralysing noise. Anxious not to cause any more disturbance which might draw attention to the silent group, the handler pulled the protesting animal away, leaving behind an elderly gent whose heart raced and whose one desire was to get home and recover – but not until he was convinced that the coast was completely clear.

Conscious of his lucky escape, Martin waited until he had recovered his nerve and then emerged from his hiding place. As he was about to depart, his eye caught the gleam of a small object on the track. On a brief inspection it looked sufficiently interesting to take home, particularly as it had almost certainly been dropped by the handler when he was knocked off balance. He was not prepared to use his torch to check for anything else, but thought he might return in daylight, if he felt up to it. It was, after all, a public right of way, so there could be no problem in walking along it, especially if accompanied by one's dog.

Before going to bed, fortified by a bath and a large whisky, Martin had a look at the object he had picked up and found it to be a form of identity card bearing a three letter, three figure identification, a photograph and the letters H F C. Finally, despite his fright – and helped by the alcohol – Martin drifted off to sleep, vowing never to eat pheasant again and reliving the moment when the handler fell back, masking any noise that Martin himself might have made.

CHAPTER TWO

Martin felt surprisingly brisk in the morning – livelier, in fact, than had been the case for some time. Perhaps the surge of adrenalin had done him good, for he set off after breakfast with Sherry, to check out the spot where he had hidden and see whether the file of mysterious men (or, he mused, men and women) had left any other clues. The footpath signs had not been disturbed and there did not seem to be any other artefacts lying around. He wondered just how close he had come to being discovered, and found, as he peered into the hedge, a perfectly formed footprint, made, he thought, by a walking boot or trainer with solid notched grips. This was not surprising, given the silent approach and nature of the ground they had been traversing, but as it was under two metres from his hiding place, and the dog would have been about a metre in front of the man's foot.... it had indeed been a very near thing.

As these people were not a threat to his beloved signposts and had done him no harm, there was no reason whatsoever for Martin to concern himself with the two matters which now occupied his mind. These were, of course, from where the group had come and to where it was going.

Some form of 'night hike' was a strong possibility, but scouts did not normally move as quietly as that – and were most unlikely to be accompanied by 'Baskerville' and his blaspheming handler. The army, or young offenders? The alternative of other pensioners behaving just as oddly as himself did not cross his mind – and in any case they had moved sufficiently fluently to set him thinking on the lines of a younger, paramilitary probability.

The answer was to follow their route and try to find out their destination, to set off in an easterly direction and see what transpired. It was reasonable to assume that they had followed the track, but after a few hundred metres it came to a lane forming a T-junction, with no means of knowing which way they had gone. After casting about for a bit, to no good purpose, Martin decided to return home, get on with some of the chores, and consider what, if anything, he should – or rather could – do to discover more.

The list of jobs, suggestions for meals, etc., included fish and chips for lunch, and as he had arrived home, he had seen the travelling 'chipper' trundling down the road to the next port of call. Martin decided to cycle after it, partly for the exercise and partly because it was possible to take the odd short cut through a housing estate if one heard its electronic chimes calling the faithful. Having cycled in vain for about twenty minutes, Martin gave up and considered the best return route.

As he got his breath back, he saw a van turn out of a road to his right and proceed slowly to the junction ahead. With a burst of energy, Martin accelerated after the vehicle, having noticed that it advertised fresh fish daily – perhaps because 'fresh fish weekly' had less of a ring to it – and there was no reason why he shouldn't cook his own rather than rely on the considerably more fattening version, nice though that might be. Jennifer would be suitably impressed, he thought, as he banged on the side of the van to stop it driving off, and cycled to the driver's window. Martin heard the driver reply briefly to his colleague, before winding down the window to see what the elderly cyclist was on about.

It transpired that he had no more fish to sell and was just on his way home, so Martin broke off the conversation and wheeled his bicycle forward. Then it occurred to him that it might be useful to discover when they delivered and whether one could order in advance. As he turned back, however, he caught sight of the driver's identity card, lying just behind the windscreen. The driver wearily wound down the window again:

"Well?" he asked, none too politely.

"I – er – just wondered – er – whether one could ... that is. ...When do you deliver?"

Martin found himself sounding like some doddering old fool, an 'act' which the driver seemed to find entirely in keeping with his appearance, which was perhaps as well, for the real reason lay in the nature of that identity card. It seemed to be exactly the same as the one dropped by the dog handler the previous night! Martin did not pay much attention to the driver's somewhat unconvincing explanation as to why it was not possible to order, partly because he was both disconcerted and excited by having picked up the trail again – and partly because he was reading the company name, which was blurred by a film of dirt on the side of the van. He apologised to the driver (in that typically British way which leads one to apologise when one is trodden on) and withdrew, having deciphered 'H F C FRESH FISH DAILY', which left him little better off.

Martin returned home without incident, without fish, but with a growing unease concerning the company he seemed to be keeping. As he rummaged in the cupboard for a tin of baked beans, he wondered how many were involved in this..... whatever it was. There had been three or four on the midnight trail and the van driver did not look like the photograph on the identity card that was now lying on the table, so that made five – plus the colleague to whom the van driver had spoken..... unless he had been the dog handler, of course. It then struck Martin that on returning to the van he should have gained some impression of the passenger's appearance – young, old, the same as this photograph, male or female. He had, however, no residual impression, and it was pretty clear why that was so: because the passenger seat had been empty. That meant that the voice Martin had heard just after he had banged on the side of the van had come from the back..... and the most likely explanation of *that* was not a talking cod, but a clandestine human cargo. There was, indeed, thought Martin, something very fishy about the van – and about the firm H F C. Martin decided to see what he could find out, and resolved to start by raising with Jennifer, when she rang that night, the topic of travelling delivery men.

His wife was pleased to hear that he had tried to buy and cook some fish (as opposed to purchasing the ready-fried version) and explained that there were plenty of suitable beans, which only needed soaking overnight. Martin shuddered at the word 'only', but pressed on to see whether his wife had ever actually bought any fish from Messrs H F C. It transpired that she had not, as she was never in when they called round, but that she had heard quite good reports of them from her friend Alison, who understood that they regularly visited Wothorpe Castle (a large feudal establishment some miles to the north). Martin was not certain that being known as a 'supplier of fresh fish to the gentry' was quite the same as a good report, but he found the information intriguing and only just stopped himself from conveying that impression down the phone.

"Where do they come from?" he asked.

"Oh, they always come from Hull," replied Jennifer. "There was one a few years ago, but he stopped – said it wasn't worth it in our area. Now remember you promised to pop down to Mother's to see how she is while I'm away. When are you going? And make sure that Sherry doesn't get into the hall, she likes to lie on the carpet and she's moulting at the moment."

By the end of the conversation, Martin found he had agreed to go down to Essex the next day. He also, somewhat belatedly, and to the animal's evident surprise and indignation, moved Sherry from her comfortable spot in the hall back to the utility.

That evening, Martin considered his next move. He could stake out the Castle, and try to follow the fish van, if it came; he could try to find out more about H F C; he could return to his original spot – or somewhere near-by – where he could make an intelligent guess as to the route the mysterious group had followed. Perhaps the answer would be to climb a tree to avoid the attentions of the canine scout. He did not fancy another encounter with the dog, however, and it could well be that no-one came for several nights. In the end, he telephoned an ex-pupil who lived in Hull, asking him whether he knew anything about the reliability of H F C as a supplier of fish. He also wondered whether any other of his scholastic contacts, built up over many years, could be of use. The local representatives of the aristocracy were not included in that list, for they were socially out of reach, as were most who lived in the shire counties and came from families whose origins lay far back in history – so far that they considered the present Royals to be upstart Continentals and regarded the feudal system as having been merely modified, rather than abolished, by the various events over the centuries. The ex-pupil was not surprised to learn he had retired, as he recalled a man of 'very mature years' some twenty years previously (when, in fact, Martin had been under forty!) but he agreed to ask his wife..... and then rang back half an hour later, with the disappointing news that there was no such company listed in Yellow Pages.

CHAPTER THREE

The next day, Martin set off, with Sherry moulting happily in the back, towards the Great North Road – or A 1, as it was rather less romantically marked on the map – and thence south to the M 11. As he drove, he reviewed his progress – or, rather, lack of it – and resolved to try to find a way of forcing the pace, regretting his failure to capitalise on having spotted another H F C identity card in the fish van. This recognition of his feebleness on that occasion was still in his mind as he registered the presence of a white van, parked on the hard shoulder just south of Cambridge. He slowed, noted that the driver was in the process of changing a tyre – and noted, too, the name on the side, visible now because it had been washed. It read 'H F C' – or something sufficiently like it for Martin to feel once again the adrenalin rising, as he drew away down the motorway, wondering how he could follow it. He slowed down to about thirty miles per hour, feeling somewhat conspicuous as an even more elderly man, wearing a hat (a sure indication, he always considered, of a doddery driver) had to pull out to overtake him, his octogenarian wife showing a need not so much of Help the Aged as Help the (Road) Raged. The turn to Duxford was signalled ahead, so Martin decided to leave the motorway, lurk with the bonnet up where he could see approaching southbound traffic, and thus be in a position to follow whether the van turned off or not. This ruse worked quite well and he was soon in pursuit of the H F C van, whose driver (always supposing he had something to hide) could have no reason to be suspicious.

As the miles passed, Martin began to wonder how far he would have to go: London? Dover? Budapest? No, there was no GB plate, thank Goodness. The van signalled its intentions in good time to turn off as if for Stansted airport, but then took the A 120, going east towards Dunmow and Colchester. It was less easy to follow without alerting the quarry, particularly as Martin lacked the necessary training and had no 'back-up' team. Whether or not the driver was aware of being accompanied, he took no evasive action, presumably reasoning – if indeed he bothered to think about it – that it was not so surprising if another vehicle was going the same way as himself.

The trail continued beyond Colchester until it became apparent that it would soon have to stop – at the North Sea. Martin was not inclined to push his luck by following the van to its ultimate destination, but at Harwich it carried straight on at the turning for the cross-channel ferries, making for the old town. Martin, although wary of making himself conspicuous, followed, deliberately driving on when it turned left towards the church and the quayside. By this time, Martin was in fact intent on finding his own destination – the nearest 'Gents' – followed by a cup of coffee and a pause to take stock, consider his next move and concoct some suitable tale to explain his late arrival to his mother-in-law.

The last was not difficult. He invented a flat tyre and added that he would have to wait until it had been repaired before resuming his journey, thus giving himself time to do some sleuthing. Restored by the coffee and a filled roll, Martin asked the cafe owner for a local telephone directory and looked up H F C in the business section. There was nothing as such, but there were, not surprisingly, several firms with those initials: Harwich Flooring Co.; Hardman, Fletcher and Charles, Solicitors; Harwich Fishing Co.; Harwich Ferry Contractors ..... . There were a few others, but Martin decided to try the Harwich Fishing Co., given the supposed nature of the business conducted by the van's owners. The address was in East Street, the whereabouts of which Martin easily discovered by asking when he filled up with petrol. He parked well short of his target and set off on foot, accompanied by a sprightly Sherry, towards the quay.

The search was made easy, however, by the presence of the H F C van outside a run-down corrugated iron building which carried no identification. Martin walked on past, not merely to disguise his interest, but also because he found that he now had no idea what to do. There was no sign of activity – no sign of fish, for that matter – and he felt that to call in on some pretext might prove counter-productive, should he be recognised in the future. It seemed to be another occasion for his secret weapon – local intelligence – supplied, in this case, by an ex-colleague.

Stephen had spent three years in Martin's department, before going on to 'higher things'. He was now Head of an 11 to 16 Community College in Harwich, and, as luck would have it, could spare Martin half an hour or so before setting off on the 'night shift', as he described it. There was to be a Governors' committee meeting, discussing the curriculum, including an input from the Humanities department. Stephen reflected philosophically that the governors (for whose benefit this was supposed to be) would probably be out-numbered by the staff and expressed envy of someone who had 'escaped' before the era when the early retirement rules were changed, known cynically throughout the profession as 'taking prisoners'.

"So, what can I do for you, Martin – looking for some supply work? Or are you into selling a textbook designed for a syllabus which has since been radically altered?"

"Well, it's a strange request, really, concerning the Harwich Fishing Company. Do you know anything about them?"

"Such as what?" asked Stephen. "Two of their lads have been through the school. No great shakes academically, but no problem – and the father was very supportive."

Martin considered making up a tale about a 'scratch and run' minor vehicle accident, but then decided to put his friend in the picture, outlining briefly the reasons why he had gone so far as to follow the van to its destination. He left out the bit where he had hidden in the hedge, as it made him look even more ridiculous, but said he had found the identity card whilst 'out walking'.

"Quite the little Jack Slipper, aren't you?" laughed Stephen. "I'm glad to see you've not lost your sense of adventure – even if the sense of proportion is a bit shaky! No, I can't think of anything which indicates the Harwich Fishing Co. is up to no good."

Martin was conscious that he had taken up sufficient of a busy man's time, and felt a bit embarrassed as he contemplated the thin series of coincidences which passed for 'evidence'. The knock on the door provided a suitable moment for him to take his leave, so as Stephen called out 'Come in!', Martin gathered up his anorak.

The member of staff who entered was introduced as Harry Bartlett, the Careers Master and, to Martin's mild consternation, Stephen asked him if he knew anything about the Harwich Fishing Co., adding, with the facility for instant mendacity possessed by all good Heads, that Martin was doing some work on the history of the local industry. Mr Bartlett gave a similar vote of confidence in the firm, adding that one of the lads had done his work experience there, reminding his boss that when he had been to visit, he had gone, by mistake, to the building next-door, where a very surly chap had eventually opened the door, holding a vicious looking Alsatian on a short lead.

On an impulse, Martin fished the dog handler's identity card out of his pocket and showed it to Mr Bartlett.

"Yes. That's the chap! But how come you ......?"

"The less you know the better," said Stephen smoothly. "You've been very helpful. Martin is in fact involved in a bit of positive vetting for the Foreign Office and it looks as though this H F C and the Harwich Fishing Co. may have been confused with each other again."

"I don't know if it's of any help," said Mr Bartlett, who was clearly nobody's fool, "but after that reception, I did a little checking on the establishment with the dog. It seems to be known as H F C, thought to stand for the Harwich Factoring Co., but seems to exist in order to do a bit of fishing and a bit of diving – especially the raising of sundry artefacts, occasional gold coins, et cetera, from a Spanish armada wreck a few miles off shore. They don't find much, or don't declare much, but seem fairly innocuous – apart from what might be seen as an exaggerated desire to discourage casual callers. Oh! And they're ex-directory, as are, of course, many eminently respectable people.... including headteachers!"

After thanking the two men, Martin set off towards his mother-in-law's place in Leigh-on-Sea, pondering the new information he had acquired and revisiting his idea that he would have to make some positive move rather than rely on chance encounters, valuable though those had proved to be.

Shortly after arriving in Leigh, he set off with Sherry for a walk in Belfairs Park, earning black looks from other dog owners, as he was too abstracted to pay proper attention to the whereabouts of his dog in relation to others. He did manage, however, to decide on a course of action, which made him rather better company on his return to the meal which, several hours delayed, awaited him on the table. He had resolved to compile a reasonable imitation of the H F C identity card, substituting his own photograph, and pay a visit to the local seat of feudal power, which, his wife had claimed, was known to be visited by the so-called fish-vendor. It might not throw anything up, but it was possible.

Having completed one or two minor jobs around the house, Martin took his leave, gratefully loaded a cake and several pots of jam into the car and set off back to Lincolnshire.

CHAPTER FOUR

Despite having arrived very late the previous night, Martin was up early and, with the connivance of David, the caretaker, had used his wife's school's photocopier and a plastic wallet designed for student identity cards, to compile an effective-looking version of the H F C card.

On his return home, he had a cup of coffee, checked on the times when one could visit Wothorpe Castle, and then strode briskly in the direction of a stretch of woodland which should contain plenty of interesting smells for Sherry. From time to time, Martin whistled the dog in, a task made easier by the almost total silence within the wood, whose tall, bare trees masked the distant background hum of traffic and prevented the sound from being snatched away by the wind. The effect within the ancient woodland was either peaceful or eerie, depending on one's mood. In the past, on such walks, Martin had productively pondered the best way of explaining the Theory of Comparative Advantage to his older students, and the best way of outwitting the efforts of the younger ones to learn as little as possible.

On this occasion, the image of pupils past – whose falsely innocent faces and earnest lies had long been replaced by equally inaccurate assurances that the product they were now selling was ideal for the purpose – faded from his mind, as Martin considered how best to approach his forthcoming visit to a seat of inherited wealth. He was reluctant to face the obvious, namely that he would neither see, hear (nor smell in the case of the fish connection) anything which would give him a lead.

These thoughts were interrupted by the realisation that he was approaching the edge of the wood and ought to bring Sherry to heel. She was gathering intelligence via her nose at a thicket by the side of the track and as he bent down to slip on the lead, Martin noticed, just inside the brambles, a perfectly formed footprint in a patch of yellow clay. Two things could be described as significant about the footprint. One was that it was, if his memory served him correctly, exactly the same as the one he had found so close to his hiding place, when he had gone back to have a look on the following day. The other was that it was underneath the brambles in such a way that they had to have been placed there *after* it had been made.

Martin grasped the vegetation in his gloved hands and – rather as he had suspected – it came away easily to reveal a sort of tunnel through the undergrowth along which one could proceed at a crouch. It led to a deep ditch which ran across the fields at right angles to the border of the wood, showing distinct signs of fairly frequent use by various animals, including the two-footed variety which walked upright. Intrigued, Martin carried on for a hundred or so metres, feeling rather like a would-be tomb robber in the Valley of the Kings. The sight of a heron rising lazily ahead of him, long legs trailing, long neck carefully tucked in, dispelled the Egyptian image and substituted one of a mediaeval messenger to Hereward the Wake, hiding out on a remote island, surrounded by sky.

The dog still on the lead, Martin clambered to the top of the ditch and surveyed the bleak landscape. Had he been further west, on what passed for a hill, he could have seen as far as Crowland Abbey in one direction and the church tower known as Boston Stump in another. As it was, there was nothing apart from a collection of run-down buildings and an old brick-built farmhouse about a quarter of a mile away. To one side, the high bank of a river could be seen above the level of the surrounding land. From the other side, there ran a line of old-fashioned telegraph poles, along what was presumably the access road, and the ubiquitous high voltage electricity pylons cut across the fields, running north to south.

It was an isolated spot, sheltered to the east by a belt of woodland, and it was the only possible goal for those who chose to tread the route which Martin was following. Convinced that he had found the destination of the mysterious midnight walkers, Martin returned to the seclusion of the wood, regretting his lack of a pair of binoculars, and wondering where the access lane joined the main network of roadways. Once back at home, Martin turned his attention to making himself look respectable, and preparing lunch, prior to the afternoon visit to the Castle.

Having decided to leave the Audi and take their other car, an old blue Renault, Martin set off, thinking that at least he now had another lead if (as was only too likely) nothing transpired when he contrived to show his forged H F C card. He was quite pleased with the look of the card, and with the simple way he had been able to alter the number on the first photocopy and then re-copy the result. He had changed one of the letters, an E, to a B, by inking in the joining sections, and adopted the reverse technique with one of the numbers, using Tippex to convert an 8 to a 3. He was, however, to come in due course to regard that aspect of his forgery as having been a mixed blessing.

Martin drove up the gently curving, mile long carriage-way, towards the imposing, beautifully maintained buildings, parked near the stables (now containing a café and various 'museum areas' of transport and implements of a bygone age) and strolled towards the main entrance.

The average age of the other visitors was about forty, but Martin did not feel out of place, apart from being a man on his own, as the average encompassed about half being under seven and the other half over sixty. He hoped not to be noticed in one way, but in another he was conscious of attempting a bit of lion's tail twisting – or at least provoking some reaction to his H F C identity card. He had already practised removing a ten pound note from his wallet in such a way that the card fell face up and felt very happy with the way the manoeuvre was accomplished. He was disappointed by the lack of reaction, however, for the lady on the till welcomed him exactly as she had the others, asking whether he had been before and offering him a booklet. He replied, truthfully, that he had been before and, in answer to her further enquiry, expressed his admiration for the Grinling Gibbons carvings.

"Yes, I thought you might like those," she said. "You'll find a particularly interesting example in an alcove at the far end of the long gallery."

Martin thanked her, picked up his change, the ticket and his H F C card and set off for an anticlimactic tour, taking in the portraits of haughty ladies and, in this case, chin*ful w*onders, painted next to their much more intelligent and, if the truth were told, rather better bred, gundogs. Despite the real purpose

18

of his visit, Martin gazed with genuine interest at the many exhibits and felt uplifted by the magnificence of the proportions of the rooms.

As he was about to leave the long gallery, he remembered the ticket seller's comment concerning the woodcarvings executed by the incomparable Grinling Gibbons. He had already seen the one he remembered from his previous visit and turned back with interest to examine the alcove. As he peered at the panelling, he was amazed to see it move before his eyes, disclosing a narrow passage, leading to downward spiralling stone stairs, which appeared safe, if ill-lit, and were clearly part of the oldest section of the house. Intrigued – and not a little apprehensive – Martin stepped cautiously down until he came to a small door on his left, giving a choice between it and continuing down to the lower levels of the ancient spiral stairwell. He tried the door, which opened smoothly to reveal a small windowless room, lighted by two wall sconces, once designed to hold torches (in the more literal sense), now adapted for electricity. As he entered, a young man rose from behind a modern, utilitarian desk, greeted him briefly and asked him to be seated.

"I'm afraid I don't yet know everyone, as this is my first day on this job," he apologised, "so I shall need to make a note of your number."

He held out his hand, into which Martin placed – on the reasonable assumption that this was the number to which he referred – the forged identity card. To Martin's surprise, the young man practically sat to attention at the sight of the card, giving a low whistle of almost awed approbation.

"That's some number," he said. "Were you on it? Or on the other one?"

Martin tried to hide the fact that he was appalled that he had contrived to forge the one number which would guarantee he was remembered, and thought frantically how best to answer a question which meant absolutely nothing to him. Fortunately, the young man came to his rescue, apologising this time lest he be thought impertinent.

"With a number like that," he added, "I suppose you're used to us youngsters being impressed!"

Martin reassured him that no harm had been done and agreed that it had happened before. In fact, he was dying to ask what was special about the number (which at that particular moment he could not even call to mind).

"I presume you've come for these in place of 584," continued the clerk, anxious now to make amends for his gaffe. "He had some problem with the van on the way to Harwich, didn't he?"

Martin felt sufficiently confident at this point to agree that the van had had a flat and was not as reliable as it once had been.

"Yes, and I heard he thought he'd been followed by some old boy in a white Audi, all the way from the M 11 to the Shell garage where you turn off in Harwich."

Martin had just about recovered from his consternation when his number had caused so much interest, but this piece of information left him thinking it was high time he departed – with or without the package which was now being pushed across the table.

"Well, that was probably just a coincidence," he opined, hoping to damp down the Organisation's interest in both Audis and 'old boys'. "I must be on my way, anyway."

"Yes, of course, Sir. Follow me!"

This time the slight awe in which he was held had caused the 'Sir' to be slipped in, and Martin hoped fervently that it would prevent any further conversation or check on his bona fides. They emerged behind a hedge which enabled Martin to slip, unremarked by the other visitors, back to the car park. There he lost no time, albeit without making his mounting concern apparent, in setting off back down the long drive. Among several wildly spinning thoughts in his head, there arose that of his departure being watched on CCTV, combined with heartfelt thanks that he was in the old blue Renault, and not the Audi.

In fact, Christopher, for such was the young man's name, entertained no suspicions concerning his distinguished visitor, who had to be one of the top men to possess a number like that, and who was clearly taking the opportunity to check systems under the guise of standing in for Gerald. Should he say anything to anyone? To the Agent? Would it be better to pretend he had not noticed, and to get the credit later for being discreet? His desire to share the news vied with his desire to prove his reliability and ability to keep a secret and avoid gossip. The latter won the day, which resulted in Martin gaining a useful breathing space.

The real courier drove up to Wothorpe Castle, supposedly to enable them to restock with fresh fish, about 36 hours later. Another hour or two was wasted checking their story that the papers had already been handed over – and checking on the description of number 534, who had seemed so familiar with the procedures and the problems experienced by the van driver. Eventually, they were forced to the conclusion that the two 'old boys' must be one and the same and that they were under serious investigation, possibly by the security forces, or an enterprising reporter. Christopher was interviewed and questioned closely as to what had been said: in particular, what the impostor had said concerning the number 534. He insisted that the visitor must have been genuine and indignantly rejected criticisms of his gullibility when faced with what must have been a forged I D card.

CHAPTER FIVE

Meanwhile, lying low as the rain teemed down, Martin busied himself with some domestic tasks, while trying to decide what he should do. He had opened the packet and discovered three sets of documents, which he had concluded must be forgeries made for sale to illegal immigrants. Martin had recently read about this lucrative trade and rummaged in the pile of newspapers which were ready to be taken to the skip, to remind himself. The more he read, the more convinced he became that this was what he had stumbled upon. The Fenland connection was there in a reference to the illegal immigrants being found jobs with 'gangmasters' who supply cheap labour to farmers. This system was quite common in the seasonal horticultural trade, with mini-vans setting off from as far away as Sheffield, and a high proportion of foreign-born (although not necessarily illegal) workers. The deals resulted in would-be immigrants paying up to £10,000 for transport, forged documents, legal assistance and a job on arrival. An immigration minister was quoted as saying that there was increasing evidence that organised crime was heavily involved as the profits were greater than those from drugs and prostitution. The numbers slipping through the net were estimated as thousands and the wretched people were often held prisoner in this country until further moneys were paid over – or they were forced into bonded labour to pay off the debts. More ominously, reference was made to the prevalence of violence if debts were not paid. Kidnap and murder were not unknown; members of both Triads and the Mafia were included in the international ramifications which spread to Russia, China, Colombia, Turkey, Brazil, Nigeria and the Indian sub-continent.

With mounting concern, Martin read about a 'forgery factory' run by a Turkish group in Islington, a Derbyshire lorry driver jailed for trying to smuggle 24 Asians through the Channel Tunnel (claiming he was threatened at gun-point in Germany) and a Romanian family of 22 found wandering by police in West Thurrock, Essex, at about three o'clock in the morning.

Martin gazed thoughtfully out of the window at the pouring rain and considered his position. He could – nay, should – take the documents to the police and voice his suspicions, even if aspects of his own behaviour made him seem a little ridiculous and even if it meant that he would almost certainly never hear the full story, which, he reluctantly admitted to himself, would always be a nagging disappointment. Also, he continued to muse, what could he say about the isolated Fenland farmhouse, for which he felt certain the original midnight group was making? Was a footprint, now washed away, likely to be seen as significant? Perhaps the best thing would be to see if he could find out a bit more – and then decide what to do. This scheme commended itself to him as much for the fact that it put off any real decision as for the concept of keeping him in the hunt. He was reminded of a discussion he had had with his wife some years previously. It had concerned whether he should try to become a headmaster and the qualities needed. At the same time they had been considering where to go on holiday, something he tended always to leave until everything was booked. He recalled the thoughtful and essentially supportive way in which she had agreed that he was academically well qualified, relatively literate and numerate, willing to work long hours, and good with people of all ages, from stroppy teenagers to experienced governors (even if the greater need was an ability to get on with stroppy governors and terrifyingly experienced teenagers). Jennifer had then added that he had one other attribute which should stand him in good stead, namely that of flexibility and the ability to weigh the pros and cons of any situation. As they had returned to the holiday brochures, she had qualified this statement by saying that no headmaster she had ever come across had been able to take a decision and stick to it. Headmistresses, on the other hand..... .

Reasoning that he might have a little more time before the Organisation went onto full alert, Martin decided to stick to his earlier idea of checking out the isolated farmhouse. He did not fancy plodding through the mud to within effective range of his binoculars, so set off in the Renault to find a road which would get him as near as possible. There were several remote-sounding settlements marked on the map, such as Moulton Seas End, Gedney Drove, Tongue End, Marshland St. James, but the nearest minor road appeared to be called Marby Dyke Drove, off which there ran a thin line culminating in a small un-named mark near to the river Glave. It seemed likely that the mark was the building in question, so, uncertain just what he would do when he got there, Martin climbed into the Renault and set off.

Crossing the bleak, windswept terrain, Martin thought that one had to have drawn the short straw to find oneself earning a living in such a spot, fertile though it might be. There seemed to be little by way of a really significant windbreak, not merely as far as the eye could see, but right across the North European plain. The wind continued to blow from the south west, bringing the rain, but if it were to swing round to the east this would indeed be a grim spot to be exploring on foot.

The unmarked, narrow, pot-holed lane was not in fact difficult to find, but after four or five hundred metres, Martin came to an open gate with a weather-beaten, faded notice, which informed the reader that he or she was about to move onto a private road, the property of Hall Farm Cultivators. The addition of 'Trespassers will be prosecuted' did nothing to encourage a would-be customer, and the thought flashed across Martin's mind that, given what he suspected, it could be that 'prosecution' would be the least of an intruder's worries. The buildings were just visible from this point but they were partially hidden by the belt of trees which Martin had seen when he had first discovered the probable goal of the dog handler and his companions.

Martin drove on past until he ran out of road (as he had expected) at the edge of a vast stretch of land from which sugar beet had fairly recently been harvested. He made a pretence of studying the map (just in case he was under surveillance) whilst deciding where to spend a few hours observing, in the hope that a person or a vehicle would arrive or leave, thereby giving some indication of the nature of the inhabitants and their business.

This time Martin had brought his binoculars and as he drove back he spotted a likely piece of cover for himself from where he could keep the farm access in view. He had to leave the car further away and make his way back on foot, feeling slightly exposed, hoping to rely on the binoculars as evidence of an intention to birdwatch, should he be observed. After two hours, he was feeling stiff and cold, and bored. There had been some activity – a post van which stopped a short way along the 'private road' to leave the mail in a rusty box set on a post, and a figure wearing a non-descript anorak with matching accessories, who walked down to collect it. Admittedly, it indicated a desire to keep people away, if not even the postman was permitted to approach the buildings, but he had not been able to see the face of the person who collected, as he (for that much Martin assumed from the walk and general build) kept his head down, looking neither to right nor left. The other unsatisfactory aspect was his failure to get a good look at the buildings from this approach, for they had appeared to be quite extensive when he had seen them first – although on that occasion he had had no binoculars.

Martin regained his car and sat thankfully in comparative comfort for a few minutes, before setting off home. As he sat, he noticed a light plane approaching from the south. This was not remarkable in the Fens, where a number of wealthy farmers had their own airstrip; neither was it remarkable that it was flying low – around 1000 feet. What was remarkable, however, was the fact that it flew lower, and slower, until it disappeared behind the line of trees, which was all that Martin could see from this distance to mark the spot where lay Hall Farm.

Martin felt certain it had landed at the farm, and cheered up at having gathered further evidence that things were not all that they seemed. That such a derelict looking business had a landing strip (and possibly its own plane) was certainly of interest. It encouraged Martin to renew his efforts to get a better look at the place, and forced to the surface a thought which had been lurking in his mind, as yet unformulated: the best approach route had to be the river. Martin drove slowly back, mulling over the best way to use the river in order to get close without being observed. In the loft they still had an inflatable boat which had seen service on many a holiday when the children were small; it should still be usable and, if he could take advantage of a moon-lit night, it should be possible to allow the current to take him right to the spot. As the craft was rather unstable and likely to overturn if it hit a floating branch, Martin decided to be well prepared for everything by borrowing some suitable gear. As fishing was the country's major participator sport (a fact unknown to many) and as Lincolnshire was one of the major counties in which it took place, it would not be difficult to borrow a form of 'wet-suit', with waders which went up to the neck, on the pretext that he wished to bath his dog in the river.

At this point the word 'dog' reminded Martin, as he drove homewards, that he had a book on dogs in the car which he had promised to return to the people from whom they had borrowed it. A detour in the direction of Stamford would not take long, and it would mean that at least one of his many tasks would have been completed.

Unknown to Martin, the pilot of the light plane circling above, tailing the car whose presence he had reported on landing at Hall Farm, now radio-ed back to his base that he was still able to follow its progress, and might even be able to report where it came from without having to organise any back-up. Normally, Gerald Gridley, who ran Hall Farm, would not have reacted in quite such an alarmist fashion as to order the plane to take off again and check on a parked car, but they had just spotted a man walking near the edge of the property, so it seemed worth it. In fact it was very easy for the pilot to follow the car home, note that it had parked in the drive, and even see what he took to be the owner disappear round the back and enter the conservatory. He duly reported back that the car came from a house at the top of Lark Hill, circled for a few more minutes, then set off back to base.

Having established that his friends were out, Martin spent some time searching for some paper and a ball-point with which to write a brief note of thanks and then left the book in the 'lean-to', round the back. He was vaguely aware of a light plane moving away from him in an easterly direction as he returned to the car, but not, of course, of its significance.

The small van which set out shortly after from the nearby Road Maintenance depot arrived just too late to find the blue car which had been followed from the air. Neither the two men

26

in it, who waited for about an hour, nor those despatched to carry out surveillance throughout the evening, witnessed its return (not surprisingly, as it was by then in Martin's garage). That night a file of men, complete with dog handler and dog, set off purposefully from Hall Farm, following back lanes and bridle paths to the top of Lark Hill. Entering the property from the back garden, they searched the empty house (whose owners were away on holiday), finding nothing which was, from their point of view, suspicious.

There was, as it happened, a blue car in the garage, so they contented themselves with disabling it, and passed the name of the eminently law-abiding inhabitants back to their superiors for evaluation – and appropriate action. During the search (a detail which was not contained in the report) one of the men pocketed an attractive, but not in fact very valuable, brooch when the others were not looking, unable to resist the easy opportunity, and keen to build up some capital for the day when he was given his documents and allowed to disappear into society.

Unaware of his narrow escape, Martin busied himself at home with household tasks, reassuring telephone conversations with his wife.... and acquiring the necessary equipment to investigate Hall Farm. The weather forecast looked quite promising for the following night, so Martin set himself to plan the exercise – for he was coming to think in quasi-military jargon, unaware of just how appropriate it was, given the attitude of his quarry.

Having decided how to go, what equipment to take and where to leave the car and to join the river, Martin allowed himself the luxury of considering what he hoped to achieve, indeed *why* he was going. The idea of getting close was all very well, but if it was a night-time approach, he was not going to see the layout, and would find it difficult to decide where to snoop, apart from watching a lighted window (if there were one) which might give some idea of how many people lived there, and their nature.

Martin decided to delay the aquatic expedition and return to the spot where he had found the second footprint, this time with his binoculars, and then work his way round, still at a safe distance, to survey the establishment in daylight.

CHAPTER SIX

The next morning he set off early with the dog to give her a short walk before following, alone, his earlier route to the edge of the wood from where the farm buildings were visible. It was a bright clear day, and promised to stay the same overnight – excellent conditions for the river approach. He found the hidden pathway without difficulty, but continued along the edge of the wood for a hundred metres or so, until he came to an ideal angle from which to observe. The main building was constructed of brick, ground floor plus two storeys, with about eight windows at each level, indicating a substantial number of small rooms. The tiled roof was covered in lichen, the window woodwork had not seen paint for years and the doors looked as if they were seldom, if ever, opened. There were various open sheds, a long, low strawstack, covered in a plastic sheet, weighted down with old tyres, and some brick-built sheds with concave tiled roofs. The inevitable corrugated iron, both as a roofing and a walling material, blended with rusting farm machinery, sprinkled with old tumbled hay bales between which grew a selection of hardy weeds, docks, nettles, and self-seeded scrubby trees. The whole was not untypical of a certain type of Fenland property, although one which had an airstrip was normally a total contrast, well maintained, including smartly painted fences, gleaming silos and an environment in which a weed would feel extremely conspicuous. In the morning sunlight, the property looked shabby rather than picturesque, and little could be discerned behind the uncleaned windows, other than matching curtains. It could be said to lack a woman's hand.

As he studied the outbuildings, Martin suddenly noticed the figure of a man standing near the long strawstack, although he had not noticed him arrive. Presumably he had come from round the back, the side on which grew the belt of trees, which (Martin knew from his earlier surveillance) screened the landing field. The man walked, carrying what looked like a clipboard, towards the back of the house and was lost to view, so Martin swung his binoculars back, and concentrated on an interesting shape in one of the upstairs windows. It was a triangle, about head height and...... With some embarrassment, Martin lowered his binoculars, as it occurred to him that what he was looking at was a person looking straight at him, also through binoculars. The sides of the 'triangle' were the arms, and the apex was the face. Too late, Martin realised that the bright sunlight must have given away his only partly screened position, by glinting on his lenses. It could be argued that only someone watching out for 'spies' would have seen him, but this was no time for quibbling. Rather, it was time to leave.

Inside Hall Farm, the watcher, in fact the man 'on watch', for the Organisation had been sufficiently alerted by recent events to post a look-out, put down his binoculars and spoke into a 'walky-talky'. Very shortly after, two quad bikes fitted with containers for crop-spraying – and as such quite innocent tax-deductible farm vehicles – set off from a dilapidated barn, driven by capable, athletic, unsmiling 'labourers'. Their instructions were to catch up with the unknown observer and at the very least find out who he was and where he lived, but not to flinch from bringing him back to the farm against his will if his actions showed him to be sufficiently suspicious. The boss had added that if this person fitted the general description of the impostor who had called at Wothorpe Castle and the driver of the car which was thought to have followed the van to Harwich, he should definitely be brought in. With this last eventuality in mind, one of the quad bike drivers was armed, but warned that on no account must other, genuine, members of the public see or hear anything out of the ordinary.

In addition to the two men despatched swiftly to the place where the glint of binoculars had been spotted, Gerald mobilised other forces. A helicopter pilot was contacted to go immediately to take off from Peterborough Business Airport, about twenty miles away, to look out for anyone breaking cover from the wood, and another member of staff from the farm, accompanied by two reliable Asian 'customers', hidden whilst awaiting documentation, were sent to patrol the eastern edge of the wood. Through the Organisation's links with the local 'gentry', it was not too difficult to summon up equestrian assistance (mainly female, but none the less effective for that) to stand around at strategic corners, covering the western and northern edges, although very few could be in place in under an hour. They were told to look out for a lone anti-hunting saboteur, take a mobile phone with them and telephone in if they saw anything. This time, Gerald was determined to find out who was on to them – and neutralise the threat.

Martin had departed rapidly back the way he had come, but had not gone far before hearing the noise of motorbike engines, which he had no doubt were driven by people anxious to make his acquaintance. All the thrillers he had ever read or seen on film combined to conjure up packs of martial arts experts, nets placed among the leaves under his feet to close and whisk him up towards the canopy of tall trees – and silenced firearms which, on this occasion, might be aimed rather more effectively than was normally achieved by the average 'B-movie baddy'. After a few minutes, however, reason reasserted itself and Martin stopped to hear the sounds of pursuit sufficiently distant as to cause no immediate problem, providing he kept moving towards the wood's western boundary, which was well away from Hall Farm. He also persuaded his head to overrule his heart, reminding himself that this was the Fens, not Viet Nam or Eastern Europe, and that he was a respectable (not to say boring) retired teacher out bird-watching, who had every right to focus his binoculars on a run-down farmhouse if he so wished.

On reaching the edge of the wood, Martin emerged carefully and surveyed the open countryside. Apart from two people on horseback approaching from the west (a common enough sight), the coast seemed clear, so he moved off at a rapid walk away from danger. In fact, of course, Martin had allowed himself to be driven, like a deer or pheasant (but not a fox which was altogether much craftier!) by the 'beaters' towards open country. In this case, things were made worse because he failed to recognise the danger represented by the horse-riders, who had now split up, circling to cover the other two sides of the wood from which he had just emerged. On seeing a lone figure who fitted the profile she had been given, the horsewoman, who ran a local stables and regularly rode to hounds, acted calmly and cleverly. She stopped and turned away so that the fact that she was using her mobile phone could not be seen, and then continued slowly towards a different part of the wood.

Quite unaware that his goose was virtually cooked, Martin continued, somewhat relieved that there was another member of the public in the offing, as it would prevent his pursuers from trying anything physical. Not, of course, that they would, but one nev.... Martin's thoughts were broken into as he became aware of the unmistakable phutter-phutter-phutter of a helicopter which could now be seen approaching from the south, flying at about 500 feet. The coincidence was too great and Martin's earlier (as he had thought) wildly exaggerated fears of a hi-tec chase, reminiscent of spies coming in from the cold, returned and caused him to turn back in panic towards the comparative safety of the wood which, he now realised, he should never have left. As the report came in from the jubilant helicopter pilot, Gerald could only curse the element of 'over-kill' which had resulted in one searcher over-turning the good done by the other.

"You bloody fool!" he shouted into the radio. "You've spooked him now: we were just closing in and he thought he was safe. Get that noisy lump of iron down here before you do anything else stupid. You can at least help to search the wood."

"You asked for the bloody chopper," retorted the pilot, who had been less than pleased to be turned out at such short notice, and felt he had done all that was asked of him and more. "You didn't say it had to be invisible as well. What am I supposed to do? Make smoke?"

"Oh! Shut up and bring her down here. We can still get him: he can't get out once I've got everyone in place, unless he has the sense to wait until dark, and even then the dogs should be able to sniff him out."

Martin stumbled, gasping from the effort of running, into the short term safety afforded by the trees and undergrowth and crouched low in dense cover to get his breath back and allow his pulse rate to slow. What now? Should he try to get to the horse-rider and ask for help? If only he had brought his mobile phone, he thought, followed by the realisation that it would probably not work amongst the trees – and who should he try to contact anyway, the R A C?

31

Before he had managed to think out a sensible plan of action, he heard the sound of approaching voices coming from his right. It was clear that they had abandoned all attempt at stealth and were now openly communicating by their walky-talkies, guiding each other to his last known position. Martin crept deeper into the wood, hoping to lie low and let his pursuers move past him: there did not seem, as yet, to be any dogs nearby. Whether this strategy would have worked – or how the hunters would have acted had they reached the edge of the wood and realised he was lurking somewhere behind them – was never put to the test. Instead Martin, with growing horror, became aware, as he approached the main central footpath, of a line of people blocking his eastwards route. As he peered, still unnoticed, through the undergrowth, he saw that they were waiting for those in front, who were at a junction in the footpath system, to decide which way to go, consulting efficient looking maps. They appeared, at first sight, to be respectable to the point of total harmlessness – but that could have been said of the fish van, thought Martin, as he waited for them to make a move. The lead pair turned, after a couple of (agonisingly slow) minutes, and called back:

"Take the left-hand fork and keep going until you reach the edge of the wood. We'll pause there for everyone to catch up."

Martin was so intent on not being seen that he almost missed his opportunity, indeed almost failed to realise what he had found – a group of respectable ramblers all dressed (and mostly aged) exactly the same as he was. He stepped out onto the track and hurried after the last of the group, pulling a woolly hat from his pocket, and removing his glasses, hoping that this simple attempt at disguise would be sufficient to make it impossible for the Hall Farm gang to work out which one was their quarry. Martin also relied on the fact that not all those who had set out on that day's ramble would know each other, would realise that he had just joined them – or even mind if he had. After about two hundred metres, Martin had positioned himself fairly centrally within the line and had passed a few words with several of the walkers, thus enabling him, should it prove necessary, to engage in more animated conversation. In due course, they emerged from the wood, passing two young, 'unrambly-looking' men, whose eyes Martin was careful not to meet.

It was in this fashion that Martin escaped from the wood, finished the walk and departed for the nearest telephone box to ring for a taxi, a ride in which, he reasoned, would prevent his pursuers from spotting, whether by air or by horse or by car, one of the group who had to walk home a suspiciously long way, having no means of transport. Martin asked the taxi-driver to wait whilst he went indoors to get some money, having explained in response to his friendly interest, that he had developed a blister so did not feel up to walking all the way home. As he handed over a fiver, Martin thought that it was money very well spent, as was the additional 'price' of appearing to the taxi driver to be a bit of a wimp, having failed to complete a ramble which some who could give him at least ten years had found no more stressful, indeed less so, than a visit to Queensgate Shopping Centre in Peterborough, just before Christmas.

CHAPTER SEVEN

As Martin immersed himself in a deep, hot bath and began to take stock, things were much less tranquil across the Fens at Hall Farm. At each level the fear and insecurity of the superior resulted in the inferior(s) being blamed for their failure to discover the identity of the elderly investigator. When at last they got around to doing something more productive than blaming each other, they, too, took stock and called a conference, including the Area Commander, John Dalton, who flew in from Colchester.

Firstly, there appeared to be one person involved with no back-up. Secondly, that person seemed to be remarkably naïve and lacking in tradecraft, easily panicked, unable to conceal his actions. Thirdly, however, he had acquired the means to penetrate the Organisation and demonstrate considerable knowledge about its origins and activities and was now in a position to make a connection between the Fens and Harwich – and they did not know how far beyond those two 'cells' his investigations had taken him.

"He knew about the 534 and the 'Retter', so he knows our real allegiance."

"So he must know what's been going on at Harwich."

"And he knows about the illegal immigrants, because he collected the documents."

"He'd already made the connection with Wothorpe Castle, so he probably knows about the Scottish dimension – or can make a guess at it."

"And he probably knows about Thorpe Tunnel."

At this point another, less alarmist, voice joined the discussion, reminding the group of the other aspect of the enigmatic investigator, namely his naïveté and lack of professionalism.

"I am not convinced," said John, "that he has put all this together yet .... but I am convinced that if he were to retail it all to the wrong people in Intelligence, they would very soon put two and two together and make not just five but fifty-five. This old fool must be stopped before he does any real harm."

"When you say 'the wrong people' in Intelligence, do you mean we have some 'right people'?" asked Gerald.

"You would do well to forget you heard that, and have more sense than to ask," came the reply. "You know what curiosity did to the cat."

Gerald had merely been going to suggest that, if they did have sympathisers in British Intelligence, they could be asked to keep an ear to the ground so that any move in that direction could not only be headed off, but could also be turned to advantage in discovering his identity and associates. Faced with the thinly veiled threat from his superior, however, Gerald did not put forward this eminently sensible suggestion, reverting to the rôle of bumbling local commander who was not paid to think, just to do as he was told. The conference broke up on the more positive note that the 'old boy' was sure to try again and that his luck could not hold for ever. They were to be vigilant, swift to act and remember not to under-estimate an opposition which, to date, had eluded detection in ways which showed an element of resourcefulness, even if there had been a heavy reliance on what could only be described as very good fortune.

Blissfully unaware of the forces which were being mobilised against him and lacking virtually all the knowledge ascribed to him by the mysterious Organisation which he was discovering as he followed up his original quest for midnight footpath sign removers, Martin luxuriated in his bath, considering his next move. He had borrowed some gear suitable for a night approach to Hall Farm by river, which he planned to undertake as soon as the weather was suitable, and was considering how he could cause 'them' to make an expedition from Hall Farm which would lead him to the other destination – the place from where that original group with the dog handler had been coming. In addition, Martin ran over in his mind the strange conversation at the Castle. What had the young man said? 'Were you in it – or the other one?' And was he not deferential, almost reverential? Was there even more to this than a bit of illegal immigrant-running, presumably via the port of Harwich? Just how extensive was the organisation if it could call up light planes and helicopters, and get its forging done courtesy of the aristocracy? Where else did the fish van call, and what other rackets were they involved in? Martin got out of the bath, dressed and studied the map to determine the best point at which to embark. That was fairly obvious, there being a section of by-passed road which carried a bridge, providing a secluded spot where a parked car would attract little attention and a geriatric would-be member of the Special Boat Service could clamber unnoticed into his inflated craft. Martin had been turning over in his mind the best exit route after his reconnaissance – especially if a rapid departure seemed called for. To paddle upstream was not an option, especially as the river was in spate, although that same condition would help if he could carry on downstream. The answer was to leave one of the cars at a point two or three miles away, where a road came close to the river, return and set off in the other one. With appropriate timing it should be possible to walk a mile or so to a point where he could catch the local 'Delaine' bus back to near his home. His lack of a team – or at least a partner – was beginning to prove a problem (but who else would join him in such an escapade, other than someone who only had his straight-jacket removed at weekends?). Martin put away the map after spotting a single track 'drove' which ran to a point about fifty metres short of the river some three miles downstream from Hall Farm. He then climbed up into the loft to get the old inflatable which he hoped was still serviceable enough to carry him down the Glave to a point close to the farm buildings. The little dinghy proved quite easy to find, although it took longer to locate the pump and some time to inflate it sufficiently for test purposes.

Martin had taken the dog out and fed her and himself by the time his daughter rang to make sure he was not fed up and bored (bored!). He reassured her that he was coping quite happily, eating proper food, getting plenty of exercise and sleeping well. Putting down the phone, he decided on an early night in order to make a prompt start in the morning to set up the 'getaway' car, return and prepare for an early evening departure.

Having slept well, Martin rose full of keen anticipation. The morning's activities worked out satisfactorily. He parked the car, secreting a spare key under the offside wing in a magnetic holder which he had had for years and never bothered to use and stepped out briskly towards the main road after climbing up over the high bank and down to water level to mark the spot with a 'flag' made from an old dishcloth. Having walked back just over a mile to the main road, Martin only had to wait about half an hour before the familiar blue bus hove into view, precisely on time, to bear him westwards across the bleak Fenland countryside.

Once it was dark enough for his purposes, Martin stowed the half-inflated boat and paddles into the car, and pulled on the all-over waterproof fishing waders which he had borrowed, covering them with an old anorak lest he be noticed as he drove off. A thermos of soup, torch, elasticated tape (used when playing tennis) to stop his glasses falling off, spare clothing and a balaclava completed his equipment. After a final look at the weather, Martin set off to a point well up-river which was accessible by road. He had often taken the dog there for a swim, and as an afterthought once again included her lead, so that he could pretend to be calling her if discovered walking nearby. He felt that he might pass as merely an eccentric (how right he was!) to a passer-by, even if the dog handler and his friends were unlikely to be similarly impressed. Once again, the adrenalin was flowing and Martin's movements were more fluid and his senses (but not, it must be admitted, his powers of judgement) were sharper. He drove without incident to his chosen launch site, parked the car in a secluded spot and completed the task of inflating the plastic boat.

After several days of rain, the water was flowing very rapidly, and he had little need of the paddles, other than as a means of fending off from the bank as he sped effortlessly downstream, overtaking branches which rode lower in the water.

Although one could see more at river level from the light reflected on the water, the speed at which he was travelling made the spill inevitable: the boat bumped violently into a heavy, half-submerged log, tipped its crew overboard and moved off, gathering pace, into the night. The current was strong, but the river was still shallow enough to walk with one's head out of the water – except right in the middle, and

Martin had had the forethought to put his few supplies (the thermos, etc.) into a canvas bag which was attached to his wrist.

Hoping to catch up with his transport, Martin set off to wade down river, stumbling on the uneven surface and cursing his failure to attach a line to the boat against such an obvious eventuality. In the dark and with the high retaining banks cutting off the immediate view, it was difficult to work out exactly where one was, and had he remained on board Martin might well have been swept beyond the farm. As it was, he decided to climb the near bank in order to get his bearings. He was nearing the top when suddenly, less than fifty metres ahead, both banks were flooded with light. The surprise and fear of exposure felt by Martin, however, was as nothing compared to that experienced by the fox which had unwittingly triggered a hidden alarm. The unfortunate animal stood silhouetted on the top of the far bank, looking across (although from where he was Martin could still not see them) at the darkened windows of Hall Farm.

Suddenly the fox crumpled to the ground and lay there motionless. Martin raised his head cautiously above the bank and looked towards the floodlit buildings. The alarm triggered by the fox had done him a great favour, as he was well away from the light, invisible to them, but able to observe the inhabitants' reactions. As Martin watched, he saw an opening appear in the long low strawstack covered in old tyres. Light spilled out and shone on the figure of a man in his shirtsleeves, looking towards the river bank. Another man emerged from the house, carrying...a rifle. It was not possible to hear what was being said, but Martin had the impression from his gestures and the second man's body language, that the latter was the subordinate, being given orders to go and check up. The boss also asked for the gun and, as it was handed over, Martin could clearly see the telescopic sight and a wider shape at the muzzle which seemed strangely familiar and had to be (as he recalled the sudden collapse of the fox) a silencer.

"And raise the sensors while you're there!" Martin heard the instruction as it was called after the departing guard, who was striding towards the river. This last order made sense to Martin, as he could see that they would be keen to avoid a false major alert – still more, he suspected, unnecessary use of illegal firearms. Leaving the door into the strawstack open, the senior man went into the house, carrying the rifle, so Martin searched for a lighted window to see where he went. As he peered intently at the darkened building, he saw a slight movement at one of the top windows, which was open, making it clear where the shot had come from.

Martin now turned his attention to the riverbank. The first man was pulling himself across to the far side by means of a line attached to a small rowing boat – in effect, a sort of chain ferry. Once at the far bank, he climbed up, threw the dead fox into the river and then bent down among the bulrushes. He straightened and moved up river until he was almost opposite. This area was dark, but there was enough light to see him bend down again among the undergrowth. The sensors – that's what it must be, thought Martin, and he looked cautiously around. The man returned to the left bank and continued with the task of adjusting the height of the sensors. It was not until the final one, less than ten metres from where he lay just below the top of the bank, that Martin saw what he was adjusting. It was made to look like a bulrush – invisible to the casual glance (which is all the average person gives a bulrush!) – but, when you knew, could be detected as the only one in a clump which did not sway in the wind. Somebody had spent quite a lot on the security of Hall Farm, and was even prepared to arm a guard to keep out intruders. When that guard moved on round the remainder of the defences, Martin raised himself, being careful to keep below fox level, to continue his inspection of the premises.

Within Hall Farm, however, another person had been on the move. He had taken advantage of attention being confined to the area where the fox had been killed, and of the temporary absence from the strawstack bunker of the boss, to slip inside the open door. Somewhere in there, he was sure, could be found the papers he had been promised, for which his family had paid so much. He was fed up with being an unpaid – and effectively imprisoned – member of this organisation for which he was forced to work. He was expected to help to steal vehicles, moving by night from one hidden base to another either on foot or in a closed van, unaware even of his destination. Once inside the Bunker (as it was called), Ahmed paused to look for a filing cabinet or desk which might contain the papers. To gain access, he had gone down a short flight of steps into a small, bare room, containing only a desk, phone and three chairs. It took a moment to establish that there was nothing to interest him there, but his eye was drawn to the far end where another door, followed by a further, longer, flight of steps, led into a larger room containing a bank of television screens, one of which showed him a guard about to return from the far side of the little river. With mounting panic at the thought of being caught in the act, he looked round the room, taking in the red and black hangings, the black and white photographs of men in naval uniforms and, across one end, a blown up print of a warship moving rapidly through the water. Hurriedly, he pulled open drawers and lifted up piles of papers, hoping to find those vital documents. Choking down a cry of frustration at his failure to find what he wanted, he turned and scrambled up the steps, expecting at any moment to be confronted with his captors. His only thought was to get away – to where he did not consider – before they found out that someone had seen the inner room and tried to steal the documents.

On the long, often freezing journey across Europe, Ahmed had been in no doubt about the ruthlessness of those whose assistance he had sought. To stay now, he was convinced, meant death – a death easy to cover up, for officially he, like others before him, did not exist, and his family would assume that he had perished somewhere along the hazardous route. As silently as he could, bending low, he moved away from the buildings, seeking the cover of the dark and the undergrowth and praying that it would be some minutes, at least, before his escape was discovered.

Martin heard first, and then saw, a figure coming towards him. The furtive nature of his movement, the way he stopped to look behind and the lack of guile had he been trying to sneak up on the hidden watcher, convinced Martin that this was an escape in progress – an escape that was about to fall foul of the bulrush sensor which lay between the fugitive and the river bank. Taking care not to raise his body, Martin wriggled forward and whispered loudly:

"Stop! There's an alarm sensor near you."

Fortunately, despite the panicky nature of his departure, the terrified Asian froze. Martin crawled closer and whispered: "Follow me – and keep close to the ground. There's a sensor hidden in the rushes."

It was no time for explanations. Neither party knew quite what to expect of the other. One had little to lose and the other felt that anyone who feared the Hall Farm hierarchy deserved help – and might throw valuable light on the whole organisation. Slowly and carefully, they worked their way back to the level of the river, which Martin knew to offer their best chance of undetected escape. Martin lost valuable time persuading his new partner that the best route lay downstream, back towards the farm, but eventually they slipped into the water and half swam, half floated in the rapid current, expecting at any moment the sounds of discovery, which, they both well knew, could be followed by extreme action.

It took Paul, the guard, several minutes to complete his tour of the sensors, after which he reported back to Gerald, who had remained on watch at the upper window. The latter remained for a minute or two looking out at the night when he returned to the Bunker, then stepped inside. The howl of rage coincided with all the perimeter lights coming on as Gerald discovered the intrusion. All the inhabitants, illegals and legals (if one could use such a term for those who worked for the Organisation) were quickly mustered, resulting in the discovery of one significant absentee. Search parties were quickly despatched and the dogs were woken from their slumbers and provided with an article of Ahmed's clothing.

From his vantage point, Paul unconcernedly noticed what appeared to be a fairly large log floating past the 'ferry', considered taking a pot shot at it, but restrained himself, remembering the lecture he had recently been given on that subject, and continued to search the night for the missing Ahmed. The dog soon led them to the river bank, where the trail ended, calling into question the direction of flight thereafter.

"Which ever way he went, he can't get away quickly," reasoned Gerald. "It's dark and he doesn't know the area. More importantly, he's got no transport or contacts. He'll move more rapidly if he went downstream, but we can go round by road and have a good chance of spotting him if he tries to hitch a lift."

"He'll be sopping wet, too, so no-one's likely to pick him up," said the other assistant, Henry. "He'll look as if he's on the run, which'll help, too."

"He may be struggling upstream – more than likely, as he'd have had to come back towards the farm otherwise – so I'll take the dogs and see if we can pick up his trail where he comes out of the water. You drive round and work your way back up river from Moulthorpe Drove. Once it's light, we'll get the chopper airborne and I'll have a word with one or two coppers I know."

"If he does get away, surely he won't say anything? He won't want to draw attention to himself."

"There's a problem there," replied Gerald, grimly. "He got into the bunker while I was upstairs, and ...."

"You didn't leave the inner room door open, did you? You don't mean he knows about the ....?"

"No, of course not. He probably didn't even realise he was looking at a U-boat, still less what it was used for. But if he were to tell the wrong people, someone might put his two with their two and make five. I want that young man back, Paul, alive or....not."

CHAPTER EIGHT

In his all-over waterproof outfit with a balaclava, Martin was able to float past the floodlit section giving a good impression of a log, and contrived to shield his companion from the watcher in the top window. To their relief, they were swept along unnoticed (happily unaware of the passing thought of a casual shot by the guard who had shot the fox) and soon gained the safety of darkness. At a bend in the swollen river, a branch had stuck, and various items of floating debris were building up behind it, one of which was the inflatable dinghy.

Martin grabbed his companion's arm and pointed to the boat. They scrambled on board, not waiting to disentangle other flotsam which had attached itself to the line and rowlocks, for a rapid escape was essential. Once in the boat, they speeded up and, less than ten minutes later, Martin spotted the marker flag he had prudently planted near his parked car. There was no time to deflate the boat, so it was allowed to float off in the general direction of the North Sea, and the two men, wet, cold and not a little frightened, still crouching although there was no immediate danger, ran to the car. Ahmed (as Martin had discovered him to be named) was by now beyond being surprised that there was a get-away vehicle. He waited patiently while Martin searched for the key (which turned out to be under the offside rather than the nearside wing, as he had at first thought) and eagerly got into the back, changed into the spare clothing and crouched down on the floor as instructed.

To begin with, Martin drove slowly, without lights, but on gaining the main road, he speeded up and relaxed, allowing himself to start thinking of the implications of his virtually knee-jerk reaction in aiding the runaway – and remember to remove his balaclava. Occasional cars passed in both directions just after he joined the main road and then his headlights picked out a white van, parked in a lay-by on the near side. The quick glimpse he had of the letters H F C painted on its side as they swept past was sufficient to raise his heartbeat and it was all he could do not to speed up and draw unwelcome attention to himself. Fortunately, all that could be seen from the van was an elderly gent, driving soberly home, manifestly not accompanied (or likely to be accompanied) by an Asiatic on the run. His somewhat unconventional garb was not discernible, although it did make Martin think that he had better not take a route which caused him to stop at traffic lights (particularly in an area where he was known!). His mind ranged over the scenario of him explaining to one of his more bourgeois friends why he was dressed in a tight-fitting rubber suit, accompanied by a young semi-clothed Asian, who preferred to travel in a crouched position, next to a heap of wet clothing, both of them smelling of river mud.

In fact, they arrived home without further incident, and in due course had cleaned up, donned dry clothing and were facing bowls of soup which had arrived on the table by way of the freezer and the micro-wave. As the meal progressed, Martin listened with mounting sympathy to the story told by Ahmed, whom he now perceived to be quite young (eighteen, he claimed, but Martin thought that sixteen was more likely). Others with whom he had set out had not survived the terrible conditions, including, at one time, twenty hours in the back of a refrigerated lorry, next to boxes of frozen chips. His main worry was that in running away he had lost his chance of getting false papers which would enable him to get work, save and send money home to repay the thousands paid to the organisation which ran the smuggling – and make it possible for the family to survive. The tears of frustration, shame, anger even, flowed as he related the tale.

"The papers must have been there somewhere," he said. "I got right into the inner room but there was not much time – and if I'd been caught....." He shuddered and then turned to his rescuer: "Can you get me papers? I'll steal for you, work for you, I'll even.... ." His voice died away and he lowered his eyes.

"Even what?" Martin asked, thinking mainly that he needed to draw Ahmed out on the contents of the 'inner room' and other aspects of H F C and their wider connections.

"It was why I decided to go," came the reply. "It was because of Gerald. He... he....."

"He had it in for you? He made you work too hard?"

"No, no. It was the opposite – he liked me, he gave me extra food, and he wanted to ...."

"Bugger you, you mean," said Martin sadly, realising he had been a bit slow-witted.

"Yes. They told me when I left home that I could earn money this way, if all else failed, that I was only ...."

"Eighteen?" Martin interrupted, with a smile. "Never mind that – or stealing. You can help me by telling me all you know about the set-up, particularly in this area. We'll start where I started. There's a regular route through the woods, going west from the farm: where does it lead to?"

"To the other, much bigger, bunker. They call it Thorpe Tunnel and there's a hidden door, leading into a large underground area, with electric lighting, cooled air, telephones, and several locked doors we never go into. I think that's where they keep the stolen goods. They grow mushrooms there as well, and there are bags of something called 'peat' – explosives we think – and ....."

"Hold on, hold on. Is it an old railway tunnel, with a security fence and a road running over the top of it?"

"Yes! I thought it might be a good place to escape from – to get a lift. There's quite a lot of traffic."

Martin searched his memory for something he knew about Thorpe Tunnel. It had been built in the late nineteenth century and the line had been closed in the 1950's, but there was something about it ... . Yes, he remembered now. He had, for a brief period, been acting senior teacher some years previously and liaison with the Civil Defence had been delegated to him. As a result, he had attended a meeting called to familiarise everyone with the procedure when we received four minutes warning of the arrival of a Russian rocket bearing a nuclear bomb. The main concern of most of those attending centred on the list of people who were adjudged sufficiently important to the continued running of the country to be allowed into the nuclear bomb-proof Area Government 'bunker'. To some this might have seemed of little interest, given the nature of the devastation and the remote chance of finding oneself both within 200 metres of the entrance and in a position to receive the warning. However, it had soon become clear to Martin that the rules of precedence were extremely important as they reflected *status*. Was the Mayor of a small town more important than the Chairman of a parish council? Both were third tier authorities, neither had any significant power (unlike, say, their French equivalent) but neither was willing to be left out if the local Cadet Force Captain was allocated a place. Yes, Thorpe Tunnel – that was it: the bunker which, rumour had it, had started its 'clandestine' life as a base for the local (anti-German) resistance movement, during the second world war. Now *there* was a well-kept secret, thought Martin: all those poachers recruited to slit Nazi throats if *they* had won the Battle of Britain!

"Right! Thorpe Tunnel. Let's have a look at the map," said Martin. "Yes. Here it is – and there's Hall Farm, with the river running along to the south, and your cross-country route through the woods about here.... and along this track... here."

"You know the route well!" Ahmed sounded surprised. "If you are this chap we were trying to catch, they are making a mistake: they think you have not much idea. Gerald said you were a 'bumbling old busy-body'. What does 'bumbling' mean? Is it busy, like a bee? Are you a policeman – or a secret agent?"

Martin, privately thinking that Gerald was not far out in his assessment, tried to look enigmatic and avoided a direct reply to the lad's desire to improve his vocabulary.

"The less you know about me the better, young man. Carry on telling me what you know. You say you got into this 'inner room'. What did you see? You mentioned a picture of a boat: what sort of boat?"

It took several questions and recourse to an illustrated Encyclopaedia before Martin was satisfied that (a) it was a submarine and (b) it had a number rather than a name painted on the sail. This latter forced him to the conclusion that it was a German craft, for the English equivalent would have had a name, such as Ursula, Utmost, or Upholder. Further questioning concerning the red and black décor pointed to an interest in, if not an actual connection with, the Third Reich and the Nazis. Martin might not yet be at a point where he could make two and two make five (the development feared by the senior men in the Organisation), but he was beginning to let his imagination stray beyond suspicions of mere smuggling and forgery.

"And what is there at the farm? How many work there apart from those like yourself who have been smuggled in by this – er – the 'Organisation'?"

"I've only seen three, but Gerald is in charge – and sometimes, as happened recently, others fly in by plane or helicopter to see him. They make sure we don't meet those people."

"What else can you tell me?" asked Martin, eagerly. "What do they do? What happens to these stolen goods? What do you know about H F C, or visiting local country houses?"

At this point, a calculating look crossed Ahmed's face, and Martin remembered that, whilst the lad might be grateful to his rescuer, his main aim was to get the papers with which to obtain work – and money. It had clearly occurred to him that he possessed knowledge with which he might bargain.

"I can't remember anything else. They kept everything hidden from us," Ahmed mumbled.

Martin noted the mood of mulish stubbornness and reflected that, whatever cultural differences there might be between the continents, adolescents bore remarkable similarities. Was it not an ex-head of Eton who had said of the boys that they would either let you down or do you down? As he pondered how to use the potentially powerful weapon which Ahmed represented, in his investigation of the dog handler and his colleagues, Martin suddenly remembered the package he had been given so trustingly by the clerk at Wothorpe Castle. He had only glanced at it but now was the time to take a closer look. He made an excuse to leave the table and nipped upstairs to the drawer under the bed, where he had placed it, along with other important documents, such as passports, his will, etc. It took only a few minutes to discover that the batch he had been given included some for Ahmed – with a different family name, but bearing his photograph. The lad's opinion of the meaning of 'bumbling' would be even higher, Martin thought, if he was told that documents could be provided. More importantly, he would be willing to co-operate fully if, as a result, he received the papers. If he knew that they were in the house, however, there was a risk that he might try to steal them – even to the point of using violence to do so. Martin debated with himself the propriety of aiding and abetting an illegal alien. Should he not turn him over to the police, drawing their attention to the possibility of the presence at the farm of firearms, and of stolen goods in the bunker? Ye-es ..... but on the other hand he had not rescued him in order to turn him in and he was very conscious of the enormous sacrifice made by the Asian family. The main crime was committed by the Organisation which made hundreds of thousands of pounds, casually causing the death of many of the desperate human cattle whom they 'helped'. Ahmed at large (and believed to be still in the area, but increasingly fearful of discovery either by 'the law' or themselves) could be a potent weapon.

Martin returned to the kitchen, just in time to see Ahmed moving away from the telephone, holding a scrap of paper.

"What are you up to?" demanded Martin, his mind full of theft or betrayal. Had he been about to ring the farm to tell them where their persecutor was, he wondered?

Wordlessly, Ahmed showed him the piece of paper, on which was written Martin's telephone number.

"I'm s-sorry," he stammered. "I thought I might want to ring you in the future or..... ."

A thought suddenly struck Martin, causing him to interrupt:

"You will have done the same in the bunker. Is that right? You can give me that number in return for keeping mine."

He could hardly stop him remembering the number anyway – and it was not such a great crime. One could call it sensible and, a pound to a penny, he had done the same at the farm.

"I – er – I'm not sure I can remember it," said the lad, unconvincingly. "I think it was something like 3424, or 4324."

"Right!" said Martin, firmly. "Let's get something clear. I can get you some papers, but my bosses are going to need something from you. You've no money, but if you co-operate fully, and I *do* mean fully, I'll recommend that we help. Is that clear?"

To Martin's consternation, Ahmed burst into tears and flung his arms round him, promising he would do anything they wanted, and would be forever in his debt.

Pushing the young man gently down onto a chair, Martin cleared his throat, and renewed his quest for useful information. First of all, he asked for the number on the telephone in the farm bunker. Ahmed had written it down and went to get it from his pocket, before realising that the paper had become sodden during the escape by river.

"Never mind!" said Martin, seeking to calm the lad's tendency to panic. "Just take your time and imagine yourself back in the bunker. Now close you eyes and tell me all you remember: the furniture, the pictures, other doors, the floor – everything."

Other items in the inventory were not particularly useful, although he described a swastika in the midst of the 'red and black' mentioned earlier, and said that the local boss, Gerald, was one of the men on the U-boat. Martin was intrigued by this, but did not wish to break Ahmed's concentration, so he let him carry on. It did, however, seem unlikely that Gerald would be pictured on a vessel which was presumably destroyed either in battle or by scuttling over fifty years previously. By now in an almost trance-like condition, Ahmed continued reporting what his inner eye saw – including the all-important telephone number.

"I put the paper into my pocket," he continued, "with the keys, and then I turned and ran out, knocking over a pile of books. Then I got away from the house as quickly as I could, until you told me to stop – and helped me to escape."

"Very good!" said Martin. "You've remembered the telephone number. Now, can you remember the number of the submarine?"

Ahmed thought hard, but could only say that it was three figures and might have been 458: he had not paid it much attention.

"Not to worry. Is there another phone in the house, and if so, has it the same number?"

"No, I don't think there is: they used what they called 'walky-talkies' around the place."

"Yes, I know. It's a sort of phone with no wires," said Martin by way of explanation. "I keep one in the car."

To his surprise, Ahmed corrected him immediately:

"No. Not a mobile phone. These were different. You had to press a button to talk and it would only work over about a mile."

"Did you see mobile phones before coming to Europe?" asked Martin, as the boy seemed so certain.

"I had heard about them," came the reply, "and, of course, I saw Gerald using his. It had a leather case and bleeped as you...."

"Er, Gerald's mobile: you don't happen to know the number of that, I suppose?" asked Martin as casually as he could.

"Oh, yes. We all had to memorise it – but not write it down!" beamed Ahmed, writing it carefully next to the other one.

"This is excellent!" said Martin. "Just one thing more – unless any other ideas occur to either of us. You mentioned some keys; what did you do with them?"

Again the young man, intent on providing value with which to impress Martin's mythical bosses, tried to recall the exact sequence of events during his hectic few minutes in the bunker.

"I – I don't know," he sighed at last. "I think I must have dropped them when I knocked over those books, unless I put them in my pocket – with the scrap of paper I'd written the telephone number on."

"In which case," continued Martin sadly, "they are now at the bottom of the river. Oh well, you can't win 'em all – and I can't see myself nipping round there to try them out, even if you had kept them!"

"Have I told you enough?" asked Ahmed anxiously. "Will they give me my papers? Please tell them I have co-operated!"

"I think," said Martin, somewhat ponderously, "that you have a very good chance, but before we move you out of this area, I want you to help me to bamboozle our friend Gerald."

"What is 'bamboozle'?" queried Ahmed, "And Gerald is not my friend: I told you I would not let him ....."

"Yes, yes. Just an expression," assured Martin hurriedly. "I'll explain in a minute. Now, where do you want to go to? London?"

"They said they would get me fixed up in Leicester. It's a small town over in the west, with plenty of work and plenty of people of my race. Can you take me there?"

Martin had reservations about the availability of work in the 'small' town in question, but could see that it made sense. However, it definitely did not make sense to go to a place where they would expect Ahmed to go – and probably had several 'business partners'. It would be much wiser to go to another town with a substantial Asian population, such as Bradford, he explained. Then, noticing the drooping eyelids opposite, and suddenly himself feeling in the grip of fatigue, decided to leave the nature of his plan for 'bamboozlement' to the morning.

CHAPTER NINE

Andreas Ketels dozed gently on the settee in his expensive home in a much sought-after part of the Wirral. At the age of eighty, he was one of a steadily dwindling group who had formed the hand-picked crew of the 'Retter', each of whom had been personally briefed by Grossadmiral Dönitz in those far off closing days of the war. As Hitler's chosen successor, Dönitz wished to approve personally those charged with the task of carrying on the fight, of bringing about by whatever means presented themselves, the resurrection of the Third, or rather the Fourth, Reich.

"Germany has lost the war. You and many like you are charged with making sure that she wins the peace!"

Andreas still remembered the stirring words, of feeling proud of the bravery, not of himself and his colleagues, who were going to live and deceive and prosper in Japan, in South America or, as in his case, having spent many long school holidays there, in England....but of those who planned the whole scheme, yet stayed behind to face disgrace, hardship, death. It was nearly time for him to be driven to the monthly meeting of the 'High Command', but he continued to dream, to reminisce, to marvel at their success. He recalled the night departure from Lübeck, the last minute conference with the Captain of the XXI class 534 (who shot himself in '48, fearing, it was thought, that he would give away the secret if his mind started to get feeble with old age) and then returning, full of confidence, to supervise the loading of the 'Retter'. What a boat! If only we'd had a hundred of those in 1940 – or even in '43. The gold was already on board, he recalled, smiling to himself. Enough to fund their operations for ever, or so they thought. Why should the metal have broken the rule of centuries? It had half the buying power now of, say, ten years ago. The old man was dreaming now, seeing the precious human cargo, the young boys, fair-haired – just like so many in East Anglia, thanks to their marauding forebears a thousand years before – all excited, some tearful, all quiet, over-awed by the moment, as yet unaware that they were to be submariners and risk the horrible death experienced by so many of their fathers.

"Time to go!" He remembered hearing the order: "Time to go!... Time t..." Ketels awoke with a start.

"Time to go, Sir!" repeated the young driver-cum-bodyguard, whose father had been one of those children the old man had been dreaming about.

"Oh, it's you. I must have dropped off for a moment. What's that stuck in your ear, man? An earring? Get rid of it – and if you're wearing lipstick, take that off as well!"

Kevin Parrish flushed with concealed anger.

"Orders, Sir! We're supposed to look like everyone else, give no hint of our breeding by," he quoted from memory, "higher standards of dress, speech, deportment or lifestyle than that appropriate to our temporary calling."

"I see," replied the old Nazi, icily, "and do I take it that you have recently downed ten bottles of lager and watched a violent video in your avid pursuit of ethnic decadence?"

Without waiting for a reply, he rose from his settee, already regretting his peevish outburst and placed an arm in the sleeve of the coat held by the object of his sarcasm. The latter swallowed his irritation, reminding himself that his moment would come, that soon he could act like this old relic, but with real underlings, with the trappings of power and wealth, able to boast of his lineage. It would be, he thought, like those descendants in America of the Founding Fathers: they, too, had made a perilous journey by sea.

"Take me past the old 534," ordered the passenger peremptorily.

"Is that wise, Sir? We have been asked not to show too much interest in her."

"Just do as I say!" instructed the old man. "There is no reason why *I* should not show an interest. Unlike yourself, I have the honour – and cover – of having been a loyal servant of the Reich, who has served his time as a prisoner."

Without replying, Kevin turned off to take them past the Maritime Museum, outside which could be seen the wreck of U-534, raised at great expense from the Kattegat, where she had been sunk by Allied aircraft in May 1945, attempting to escape, like so many others. The old man chuckled quietly:

53

"They thought they would find gold and papers and important relics – and they found nothing! They'd got wind of the importance of the cargo, but they didn't realise her rôle! 'Proceed on the surface; fire your anti-aircraft guns if attacked. Draw them away: the 'Retter's' special covering should hide her from their radar, but we must take no chances. Sacrifice your whole crew, if necessary – and hint at your keel being filled with gold. Let them think they are the chosen ones. Draw them away as the hen partridge pretending to have a broken wing: don't let them find the fledglings'. Did I ever tell you about the 'Retter'? Hydrogen peroxide for fuel; nearly 30 knots under water; invisible to radar – 'stealth' they would call it now – able to stay under water almost indef....."

"Yes, Sir. You did – and so did my father. Shall we move on? It's getting late."

"If we'd had fifty Type XVIII's!" continued the old man. "The scientists at Eckernforde put all their efforts into developing them after those rockets failed to tame the British. Most of them were captured in Lübeck Harbour, before they were fitted out. They only needed a small crew, you see – and practically noiseless!"

"Which was the one which surrendered eight days after the capitulation, half way to Tokyo?" asked Kevin, deciding to humour his passenger, from whom he had heard the stories a hundred times.

"That was U-234! She was one of twenty long-range boats, taking the top-ranking party members to South America and Japan. They left it too late, of course....but some of us were successful."

Silence fell, as the old submariner relived that last journey. Off-loading the precious human cargo, including his own baby son, to be collected by English sympathisers just off Blakeney, in Norfolk. Then back down the coast to the final resting-place. It was the gold – they were right, it was the most expensive keel ever made – which had let them down. They'd salvaged it gradually over the years under cover of the wreck of a Spanish galleon, but now it had to be drugs or immigrants.. it was clever, the cover for that, declaring a little, and.. it was the keel, and she was built to stay down for ever... but the gold was falling, so they had to use other ways...and the rockets .... but the gold was f.... The old eyes closed, and Kevin drove slowly off.

"Time to go! Time to go, Sir! Wake up, Sir! We're there."

But this time there was no sudden awakening from a dream. The sleep was deep......and permanent. The High Command would have to choose a successor.

The meeting was cut short, the start having been delayed by the need to comply with the formalities associated with a sudden death. In this case, there was no question of foul play: Andreas Ketels had fallen asleep and died, essentially of old age. 'The best way to go', they all agreed, adding, in their private thoughts, 'better by far than the hangman's noose, or an SAS bullet'. The Chairman tapped lightly on the table:

"Can we make it brief, please, Gentlemen. Just confirm all is well or if there is a problem. I'll run down the list. Finance?"

"Gold may rise a little as a result of the slump in Far East share prices: it's a haven in times of trouble. We're watching closely, and will unload more if it rises enough."

"Right! International movements?"

"Immigrants are flourishing. There is pressure building to tighten the regulations, which should squeeze out some of our, shall we say, less well-connected, competitors – and enable us to raise the fee."

"Thank you, Alistair. Let's move on to those connections you mentioned. Police?"

"We're still keeping the women more or less in their place. There's unease about failure to deal with those known to be corrupt – to move to a less rigorous level of proof. On the other hand, we could find more and more people in quite influential positions willing to – er – supplement their income, as they fear for a future without state benefits as of right for the old."

"Thanks. Did you arrange this right wing government for us, Eric?" The Chairman paused for a moment to allow the laughter to subside, and then added: "Don't answer that! Just give us an idea of the political scene."

"The U S of E is looking more and more likely – and when it comes, no country within it will be able to match the influence of a united Germany!"

"Careful my friend: don't fall into the trap of under-estimating the British. Our predecessors did that!"

"We're well advanced with our referendum campaign, Malcolm. We shall be able to bring a whole new meaning to 'forecasting the result' by the time it takes place. The electorate here imagines that only blacks are capable of rigging elections. I can confidently forecast the result we want!"

And so it went on round the table. The Army would support a right wing coup, the Air Force to a lesser extent (but the move towards integration of command was making that less of a problem). Schools were more or less under control now, becoming accustomed to sudden, unexplained, changes of direction dictated by central government. The emphasis on the inculcation of basic values and state-approved religion was very helpful, making it easy to label those who questioned as woolly-minded left wing thinkers (or, better still, agitators).

"I still advise the Movement to change its policy on homosexuals: there is nothing left wing about the concept, and, indeed, it goes well with our approach to women. Many of our most loyal supporters are closet gays, frightened only of being denounced to – ourselves! Can we not....."

"I asked for a brief report, David. Bring this up next time. We could always 'fail to succeed with some manifesto items' – after all those who supported Clinton don't seem to have got much out of it!"

"But votes are not the point: I consider we should really put away our prejudice and...."

"Not now!" said the Chairman firmly, to sympathetic and, in several cases, hypocritical nods from the others. It was all very well for David with his reputation as an ardent womaniser, but for others, anything other than disgust, preferably expressed in a way which was technically illegal by the current law of the land, could spell the end of a promising career in the Organisation.

"Next please: the regions. Any problems?"

"Nothing too serious, Chair, but there is...."

"Can we dispense with these politically correct expressions, John. There is not going to be a female in the chair! You're a Rotarian, you should know better!"

"Sorry, Chairman," continued John smoothly, veteran of a thousand meetings, ready with the timely 'on a point of information', or the terse 'seconded'.

"I also operate at District level, school Governing bodies and, of course, the River Board. One finds oneself slipping into the... ."

"It sounds as if one had recently been talking to one's monarch," sneered the Chairman, to sycophantic smirks from some of the older members, "but do, please, carry on. What is the nature of this – ah – problem?"

Stung by the older man's patronising attitude, John Dalton, Leader-Designate of the Blackwater District Council (and Controller-Designate of one third of England, from Colchester to Newcastle, when the New Glorious Revolution took place), replied in what only he recognised as ageist terms:

"It concerns what my man Gerald describes as a 'bumbling old busy-body' who has been spying on their local base, Hall Farm, for several days, and the recent escape of a young immigrant."

John paused, to be rewarded with a curt request to continue.

"They nearly caught him in the woods near the farm, by enlisting the aid of a local riding school, who were led to believe they were rounding up a hunt saboteur.... but he evaded capture. Gerald blamed the helicopter pilot, and the unfortunate arrival of some ramblers."

"Shock troops indeed!" interjected the Chairman, who found himself entertaining inappropriately sympathetic thoughts about this slippery senior citizen. "And I suppose the aircraft carrier your man whistled up got stuck in the Forty Foot, or whatever the local waterway is called?"

The laughter at this point was general, but John continued doggedly:

"He also posed as a Veteran, using a forged Identity Card carrying the number 534, thereby persuading the Castle to hand over a complete set of documents destined for the latest batch of immigrants. In addition," he continued, by now to an audience no longer laughing at his expense, "he is thought to have followed the van to Harwich."

A babble of consternation ran round the table as the potential significance of all this knowledge in the wrong hands struck home.

"And what," demanded the Chairman after calling the meeting to order, "is 'bumbling' about that? This agent seems to be running rings round your man – er – Gerald. Why is he unable to deal with the matter? Should he be replaced – or does he need authorisation to resort to extreme measures?"

"Things may not be as bad as they seem," said John, but the resultant uproar prevented him from making a fuller explanation.

In fact, there was no reason to assume that the escape of the immigrant was connected, or that the elderly investigator had any notion of the real significance of the information he had (almost certainly unwittingly) uncovered. The meeting instructed John to deal with the matter personally, using any means he thought fit – and, once the threat had been neutralised, to consider carefully what to do about Gerald.

Before agreeing the date of the next meeting, the Council had one other item to consider, indecent though the haste might seem to be. Andreas Ketels had to be replaced, and as there was not even a pretence of 'democracy' about the exercise (for this was a self-perpetuating group) there was no time like the present. Seizing the moment, Edwin, another septuagenarian, recalled his instructions in such an eventuality, and moved with commendable (and unwonted) despatch:

"I propose Andreas's son. He's very sound – can be relied upon to carry on the good work," (This was said to propitiate the older clique), "and is in touch with the younger grass roots element in – er – in ..."

At this point it became clear that Edwin had absolutely no personal knowledge of the man in question, and he tailed off as John helpfully interjected:

"The Fens, in fact." He paused for effect. "You have just instructed me to consider carefully what to do about him."

There was an embarrassed pause whilst this intelligence was absorbed, followed by the Chairman asking for, but not getting, a seconder. In truth there had not been time for the lobbying and machinations which normally accompanied these occasions, during the period between the resignation, assassination, death or incapacity of the outgoing member and the next meeting of the Council.

"I have one or two excellent people to sound out," said the Chairman, "but I should have to be sure that they were willing to serve before moving to a proposal."

Whether anyone was fooled by this pretence that they would be lucky to persuade such talented and self-sacrificing people as he had in mind, it was difficult to tell, but they readily agreed, after the unfortunate experience of their colleague, to leave the matter until the next meeting.

On his way to the station, en route to London and thence to Colchester, John rang Gerald to tell him of the death of his father. He had already decided to confine that conversation to imparting the news, together with appropriate sympathy, merely adding that he would try to drop in 'in a few days' time'.

"I'll keep you posted about the funeral arrangements, but I'm sure you appreciate that it would be very unwise to attend: we don't want people putting two and......."

"Yes, quite. I fully agree, Sir."

Gerald wondered whether to raise the question of his father's successor. As his superior had had the sensitivity not to ask about the 'little problem' (which was still not resolved) he decided to follow suit and not mix business with bereavement. That 'sensitivity' on John's part extended to not telling Gerald that his whole future was under review (not to say his continued existence). By not, at that point, saying that he was about to take over the hunt for the troublesome detective – and would be arriving very shortly – John had also given the impression that Gerald had a few days to sort things out by his own efforts. It allowed him to think that there was no need to remain on the premises, awaiting a phone call alerting him to the imminent arrival of the top brass. Later, John was to regret that omission.

CHAPTER TEN

Martin was woken by the insistent ringing of the telephone. His wife, having failed to raise him when she had rung two or three times during the previous evening, was beginning to wonder whether he was all right. Partly because he had only just woken from a particularly deep sleep and mainly because he could hardly tell the truth, Martin's explanation of where he had been sounded, even to his own ears, somewhat weak. However, they re-assured each other that all was well; that the dog was well ('The dog! the wretched animal hadn't even been fed last night', thought Martin guiltily); that the plants had been watered; that he would get the dry-cleaning when he was next in Safeways.

Ahmed, who had gone to sleep wondering what it meant to be 'bum-boozled', and glad that it was to Gerald that it would be happening, came down to breakfast hoping that Martin would now agree to organise his papers. Promising her a really good walk that evening (but unwilling to leave Ahmed alone in the house), Martin let the neglected animal out into the garden, trying to ignore the air of cowed and injured misery which it (like all Golden Retrievers) was able to generate in the hope of being seen by a passing RSPCA inspector. Mentally adding another two years for cruelty to animals to the five he was likely to get for aiding and abetting an illegal immigrant, Martin settled down to plan the next move.

"As soon as I can get your papers, I want you on your way, Ahmed. It's not safe for you to be in this area and I can't keep you hidden from view here for long."

"I've told you everything I can remember," said the lad anxiously. "What else will they want me to do?"

Martin almost corrected the plural in the last sentence, before remembering that he was supposed to be the front man of a large and powerful organisation. If only that were the case!

"This is what – er – *we* require from you," he said firmly. "You will ring Gerald on his mobile, asking him to help you. Give him the impression that you are at the end of your tether, cold, wet, exhausted, nowhere to go; that you want to come back; that you will do anything – and you must stress *anything* – he wants if he will help you."

As Martin had begun, Ahmed had felt apprehensive, but as the plan unfolded, his eyes shone at the thought of his persecutor being 'bum-boozled' (Ahmed's version had a certain piquant appropriateness, in view of the lure envisaged by the plan!).

"Will you catch him in a trap – or shoot him as he arrives?" he asked eagerly.

"Don't concern yourself with the details." (Details – a casual shooting – what *was* he doing, for Heaven's Sake?). "I won't be there; you won't be there. We shall ring him from a distance, just to get him well out of the way and make sure he continues looking for you miles from where you actually will be," said Martin, appalled at the thought of tangling with this professional thug in person. "I also want you to record your story on tape, including the reason why you ran away. It will be useful to clobber Gerald with and will enable me to convince others about the whole set-up, as they may not believe me without any hard evidence."

In fact, Martin thought that he might be able to imitate Ahmed's distinctive accent well enough to fool someone who was expecting to hear him. The telephone always distorted the real voice to some extent. These tapes would also provide a useful learning resource.

"Right! Let's be on our way. I'll just check the car and see that the coast is clear, then we'll smuggle you in. It won't be very comfortable, I'm afraid, but you have, alas, experienced a lot worse."

As he was cleaning the back seat and floor of the car, Martin came across a brooch which he recognised as being exactly like one belonging to the friend whose house he had visited recently. Could Ahmed have got hold of it – and dropped it? Had he dropped anything else? A more thorough search did, in fact, turn up a very interesting item: under the passenger seat, Martin found the bunch of keys which the lad had taken from the bunker. He decided not to mention the keys, which he could still not envisage actually using, but thought he might ask one or two questions about the brooch.

Partly for evidence and partly as additional material to enable him to perfect his impersonation, Martin made use of a gadget he had purchased some years before to record from the telephone. Several staff had had nuisance calls and the idea had been to produce recorded evidence, although in fact it had never been utilised. It very quickly became apparent that Ahmed had quite a talent for acting. From his first tentative, whispered 'It is me, Ahmed. Is that you, Gerald?', he successfully conveyed a desperate, frightened, hunted, naïve boy, who saw Gerald as his one 'friend' – the only person to whom he could turn. As agreed, he claimed to be ringing from a call-box near to the old bridge at Crowland, which would divert attention well away from the A 1 and Bradford. Before ringing off on a note of rising panic at the supposed sight of a police car, Ahmed said he would make for Thorpe Tunnel and would ring again to arrange a meeting.

"Now let's be clear on one thing, you cock-teasing little bastard," said Gerald (and it had to be admitted that the first adjective was entirely justified by Ahmed's promises of doing *anything*, if only he could be given his papers), "if you don't show up, I'll personally wring your scrawny little ...."

"I must go! I am not safe here. You must come alone to the Tunnel: if I see anyone else, I shall run away. You must come alone – but please come, please!"

As he flipped his phone off, Gerald smiled grimly to himself and murmured:

"Don't you worry, sonny, I'll be alone!"

He found that the thought of killing the troublesome young Asian, after taking advantage of his trusting nature, stimulated the very satisfying erection which had increased as the telephone call progressed. Such was his condition that he had to remain seated for some time when his assistant came into the room to ask for instructions.

"I think we'll concentrate our hunt round here for that fugitive," he said. "Call in the vans. Ahmed will have run off across the fields and be hiding in a shed somewhere. I'll get stuck into the search myself, too. You can cope here. Don't ring me unless it's urgent – and I may have to switch off if I'm stalking him. Understood?"

"Well, ye-es," said Henry doubtfully. He did not like responsibility and, although he was quick to criticise everyone else in authority, lacked confidence in himself, should there be a problem and no-one to contact (and thus blame if anything went wrong). "What if one of the others goes walk-about? Or suppose someone turns up from H Q? I'm not sure I know how to work the radio link with the plane."

"You'll be fine. You've seen me work the radio, and if someone just 'turns up', tell them to wait. I've got a man-hunt on my hands: I can't hang around on the off-chance that John, or someone, will want to drop in to count the socks."

Gerald spoke these high-sounding words, designed to indicate that he was not afraid of the hierarchy, safe in the knowledge that John had made it clear that he would not be around for 'a few days'. He was also confident that by then he would have dealt with Ahmed.

Admittedly, the problem of the elderly snooper remained irritatingly unresolved, but so far there had been no repercussions from his acquisition of the false papers, some of which, ironically Gerald thought, had been destined for the wretch who was now on the run. It was just as well those two had not got together! Probably the old fool had realised he was batting out of his league, had been badly frightened by his narrow escape in the woods, and would never be heard of again.

Buoyed up by the thought of his forthcoming sexual gratification, to be followed by that exercise of ultimate power, the deliberate taking of life, Gerald set off, supposedly to scour the countryside with the aid of his dog, in fact to await the call on his mobile which would guide him to his unsuspecting prey.

After that, he reminded himself, it would be time to see what could be done about taking his rightful place on the High Command. He had always understood that his father had someone primed to propose him, but presumably he had failed to do so – or the equally doddery colleague entrusted with the task had forgotten! They were all past it, that generation, content to wait for ever. Even he, Gerald, was over fifty now: they needed to get a move on, force the pace. If they waited much longer for the 'ripe plum' to fall, he would be too old himself! For a moment, his mood of gleeful anticipation was overturned by the thought of spending all his life under cover, hidden away in obscurity in places like Hall Farm (what a dump that was!), only to be passed over when the moment came, or die of old age if cautious counsels were to prevail much longer.

"They say there's always someone worse off than yourself, Nero," said Gerald to his four-legged friend. "And that someone is about to get his come-uppance."

At the sound of his name the dog raised his head and gazed, amber-eyed and uncomprehending as his master laughed and shouted:

"His 'come-uppance', Nero, now there's an apt expression for you! His come-bloody-uppance!"

****

The twin objects of Gerald's lust and derision sped north up the A 1 towards Bradford. In order to maintain the fiction of an extensive organisation, Martin had claimed that the papers would be passed to him at a Service Area en route. After about thirty miles, he told his passenger he could sit normally in the back and get to know the nature of the scenery – so different from that of the Fens. Martin also took the opportunity to tackle him about the ring he had found on the floor of the car. As he had suspected, it had been stolen from the house visited by Martin on his return from viewing the farm. It had been given to Ahmed by Gerald, presumably in an (unsuccessful) attempt to gain his friendship. Martin said he would take it back to its rightful owner and asked Ahmed whether he knew why they had targeted that particular house. It was with not a little surprise that he learned of his narrow escape.

"Weren't they taking a risk of being caught by the police?" he asked.

"Caught by the police! They often act as lookouts for them. Gerald boasts about his contacts with the police and the River Board and a firm of builders who were very useful, too."

"What was the name of the builders?" asked Martin eagerly. "Did you see their van, or know which town they came from?"

It soon became clear that Ahmed was only repeating something which was talked about amongst the immigrants. It could be a rumour designed to prevent anyone from 'shopping' the Organisation to the authorities. It seemed highly unlikely that they had many police on their side, but one could not rule out the odd one or two, for there was plenty of money to be made from the immigrants, not only 'up front' as a fee, but also as willing accomplices in theft – one of the services Ahmed had offered in an attempt to persuade Martin to obtain identity documents.

Eventually, having joined the M 62, Martin pulled in to the Services, where he made a pretence of entering the 'Gents' in order to be contacted and emerged carrying a packet which in fact he had taken in with him. Fearing another extravagant display of gratitude, Martin waited until they were back on the road before passing the papers over his shoulder.

"Here you are, Ahmed. I think everything's in order. Take a look."

Forcing himself to be calm, the delighted recipient carefully opened the packet and sorted through the contents.

"It is all there – just as Gerald said it would be!" Then, remembering that these were not from that source, he hurriedly added. "But I think these are probably much better – and you have not had any money for them. I – I don't know what to say. Thank you so much!"

To Martin's relief, the young man lapsed into silence, gradually coming to terms with having attained his goal. For weeks he had endured great hardships, had come close to death, seen others succumb and forced himself, against all reason, to believe that the money his family had paid would not be wasted. What would the future bring? Might he still be caught and sent home? In fact, although he did not realise it, thousands who had no papers and were in theory waiting for their case to be investigated succeeded in 'disappearing' somewhere in the U K – usually in London. Ahmed's chances of getting away with it, thought Martin, were good, unless the sinister organisation he had stumbled across were to make it their business to find him. If they found Ahmed, moreover, they could make him tell them how to find the 'bumbling busybody'.

As they neared the dropping off point, having turned off at Junction 27, Martin felt a touch of fear. He had, by any reasonable standards, been a bloody fool – and it all stemmed from that damned footpath sign!

"Well, this is it, young man. You're on your own now," said Martin as they arrived in Bradford. He nearly added the trite 'Don't do anything I wouldn't do', but realised not only the hackneyed nature of the phrase, but also the wide scope it offered, given the sort of things he had in fact recently been doing!

"No emotional goodbyes, now!" he admonished, noting a certain wetness around his companion's eyes. "Just wave and wish me luck – and here are your final instructions. Memorise the contents: we don't want this to fall into the wrong hands."

With that, Martin handed over an envelope and drove rapidly away. The car was almost out of sight by the time Ahmed had opened the envelope, wondering what more was expected of him. The tears flowed then, as Martin had feared they would (hence his rapid departure) for the contents were a brief message and five ten pound notes. The note read: 'Good Luck! Bamboozle the lot! Martin'.

It was an uneventful journey home. As he drove, Martin considered his next move, hovering between the gung-ho and the lie-lo, but much of the time he felt too drained to do more than concentrate on his driving. It was, in short, a tired old man who turned into his drive to find the house lights on and his daughter's car parked accusingly in the driveway. Normally, he would have been delighted to see her, welcoming her stimulating conversation and enthusiasm and the way in which the house seemed to come alive again and glow – literally, in the sense that every room in the house would have the light on! There was also, however, a sense in which he was a bit frightened of his children: they were both more successful and cleverer than him and absorbed new ideas in a tenth of the time he needed – even when he was capable of doing so. On this occasion, of course, Martin had every reason to be apprehensive, for he knew he had been making a fool of himself and Elizabeth would not be fobbed off with bland comments. Such tactics were all very well on the phone but would never survive a face-to-face encounter.

He had not taken any trouble to hide away the evidence of his recent activities. (Try explaining a 'wet-suit', a house which had hardly been touched in terms of cleaning, to say nothing of strangely worded tapes, if she happened to have pressed the 'play' button!). No; the game was up. Wearily and above all guiltily, Martin climbed out of the car to commence the dialogue with a somewhat shifty:

"Hallo! This is a nice surprise: I wasn't expecting you! Is everything all right?"

CHAPTER ELEVEN

Elizabeth had been about to have a go at her father concerning the state of the house, the fact that he never seemed to be in when anyone phoned and her mother's concern lest he were unwell. However, the forced joviality, the tiredness bordering on exhaustion and the rather pathetic air of a small boy caught in the act, disarmed her – and alarmed her. Perhaps the old boy was unwell, or was going through some sort of mid-life (well, fairly late-life) crisis. There was something else different about him, too, but she could not quite put her finger on it. Being both a practical and a sensitive person, she recognised the need for food – and affection – before questions and explanations, if the latter were likely to be forthcoming.

"What's more to the point," she said, giving him a kiss, " is how *you* are? You look all in. Tea? Or something stronger? Then I'll get you something to eat and you can tell me how you've been managing without Mother. Er – you're not feeling unwell, are you?"

The restorative effects of a strong cup of Assam, combined with sympathy, bacon and egg and his own need to confide in someone, caused the strange tale to emerge. Despite trying not to stem the flow by appearing too critical, Elizabeth could not repress an exclamation when it came to the waterborne incursion along the little River Glave, scene of childhood boating trips on hot summer days, when the only possible danger she could recall was a large, severe-looking swan, sailing majestically towards them, very clearly convinced that it had right of way. Similarly, being 'buzzed' by a low-flying, hostile object brought to mind, not a helicopter gunship, but one of the larger dragonflies, which her father had always referred to as 'four-engined jobs'. And all the time, there lurked unseen this gang of homicidal smugglers!

As the tale unfolded, Elizabeth's concern about her father's health diminished. His colour returned, as did his general animation – and she discerned the 'something about him' which had eluded her when he arrived. He was less bored – or was it....? No; he was less bor-ing! Elizabeth had never consciously thought of her father as being boring – indeed he was quite an out-going type whom her friends always found it easy to talk to – but he led an essentially boring life (as he would be the first to admit). Now that he had recovered from the 'down' of having delivered Ahmed and a long drive with nothing to eat, she could see that his adventures had caused the adrenalin to flow and sharpened him up. He looked thinner (probably on account of his inadequate diet, it had to be said) and if not actually younger, a more 'with-it' version than the last time she had been down, when the similarity to Victor Meldrew was beginning to be worrying rather than funny. The report requested by her mother was going to be difficult to compile – very difficult – but she could reassure her concerning the old boy's physical well-being.

"I suppose your mother suspected something, did she?" he asked eventually. "I didn't think I sounded entirely convincing last time we spoke.....but I couldn't tell her the truth, now, could I?"

At least, thought Elizabeth, he had got that bit right. A fraction of this lot would have made her mother jump on the next plane back. Remembering a canoe-ing trip on the Vienne many years before, her mind ranged over the thought of her father, armed to the teeth, surging down the river, intent on rolling back the jack-booted invaders. A dreadful pun on 'Jerry-actric' rose to the surface of her mind, as she wrenched her thoughts away from phantasy to – something not a whole lot different – the barely believable reality.

"I'll think of a way to stop Mother worrying. What's more to the point is what to do about the H F C gang. Incidentally, Hall Farm is nearly H F C, too!"

"You know, you're right! We must look into that – in fact, I think it's....."

"Hang on, Father, hold it! *We* are not doing anything, and that includes you. These people are too dangerous and too numerous. We need to think how best to alert the authorities, so that someone can find out the scope of the Organisation and its aims."

"I suppose," said Martin reluctantly, "it had better be the police. I did consider it before, but I wasn't sure if they would believe me."

"More importantly," replied Elizabeth, "they might be working for the other side, if your Asian friend was right about the help they sometimes got. No. I think I might give Patrick a ring and see if he has any brilliant ideas."

"But your brother's in Poland or somewhere, translating poems. What on earth could he do?"

"Well, let's say he doesn't only translate poems. He has certain contacts – and we know he's on our side," replied Elizabeth enigmatically. "Yes, the more I think about it, the more I think he might be very interested."

"Good God! You mean he's a – a 'spook'. Well I'll be damned. And all this time, I've been thinking of him poring over an abstruse manuscript, discovering the Magyar equivalent of spondees and dactyls. He never said he was in Intelligence!"

"The whole point of being a spy is that no-one should suspect you of being one!" said Elizabeth. "And make sure you forget you were ever told anything."

"Well, I'll be damned, Patrick a spy. Who would have thought it? I wonder where he gets it from?"

"You're a fine one to be asking that," replied his daughter with some asperity. "The only reason you've survived the last few days is because no-one could possibly imagine that an elderly retired schoolteacher with an interest in footpaths was the deadly agent they were all looking for. Your camouflage," she added, with a distinct edge to her voice, "could be described as 'impenetrable'! But I rather suspect you've been enjoying it all, and here and there, it has to be said, have shown some talent."

Martin felt he was on ground too weak to permit of a riposte to this last rather patronising remark, so he offered to turn in whilst she contacted her brother.

"Yes, O.K. I shan't have a lot to say, and he may be busy. I think I've a fair idea of the overall picture."

Martin had recounted nearly everything, although he had not wished to compromise Ahmed, so, in his account of the visit to the Castle, he had said that the forged documents were not quite ready. He had nearly owned up when Elizabeth had pressed him about his parting with Ahmed, however.

"Did you hand anything over before you drove off?" she had asked. He had hesitated over the direct lie, his embarrassment being noticed by his daughter, who had added, resignedly – for it was clear that he had risked a lot for the lad who probably saw him as a 'soft touch':

"Come on. How much? How much did he con out of you?"

Martin had lowered his eyes, not (as she had thought) because he was ashamed of his naïveté, but to hide the relief which would have been apparent and replied in a suitably shame-faced (and entirely truthful) way:

"Er – only fifty pounds. I couldn't let him go off without a penny to his name."

"You'll never learn, will you – and have you checked the silver?"

"The silver!" her father replied disparagingly. "You're looking at it, over there: the place is barely worth turning over – and not everyone can afford to adopt high principles."

Once upstairs, Martin checked again that the other documents were still there, then, relieved that he was no longer on his own, fell rapidly asleep.

The conversation between brother and sister, both being mindful of the need to maintain security, was brief and to a previously arranged pattern. It resulted in several other international calls, as a result of which a competent, experienced Intelligence agent was to find himself Lincolnshire-bound the following morning, charged with the task of contacting Martin, establishing the nature of the emergency and deciding what, if any, action should be taken.

Before going to bed, Elizabeth played over the tapes of Ahmed's story and noted his clear expectation of getting papers from her father's 'organisation'. Had he omitted something when telling the story? Surely, the young man couldn't long survive without them? Or would he come back to try and get them? Perhaps the Intelligence Service could come up with something.... which reminded her: someone should be making contact fairly soon, but until then they needed to keep the Hall Farm mob busy. She groaned inwardly at the realisation that that would mean an early start the next morning, put the lights out and went to bed, but not immediately to sleep, as her mind was full of the series of events related by her normally entirely predictable father. Sleep only came after she had decided on a simple – and safe – ruse for keeping Gerald occupied. She would discuss it with her father in the morning. After all, there was no harm in encouraging him a bit, now that the matter had been reported.

CHAPTER TWELVE

Gerald was awake early, having passed a less-than-satisfactory night trying to sleep in his van, which he had parked in a lay-by on a minor road not far from Thorpe Tunnel. On two occasions Nero had woken him, growling to be let out to see off a fox which could smell the supply of dog food inside the van. The cramped conditions, overpowering canine odour and lack of a handy shower, combined to make him wonder whether the prize was worth the rigours of the race. Today should bring the expected call from Ahmed, however, and he would make the little sod pay for all the worry and discomfort he had caused. He drove off to the anonymity of the fast food outlets on the A 1 to have a wash and a desperately needed cup of coffee.

Elsewhere, others were stirring. Gerald's assistant, Henry, had not slept well either – but that was worry, not physical discomfort, for his lack of confidence in himself was entirely justified. He was right: he *was* inadequate, prone to panic, unable to take a decision and stick to it. Why had Gerald gone off and left him? Surely, as leader, his place should have been back at base, not farting around the countryside with that bloody great dog? His train of thought was interrupted by the insistent tones of the telephone. About time, too: he hadn't heard from Gerald for hours. He lifted the phone. Perhaps he had succeeded in getting his hands on that wretched little ......

"Hallo Gerald, where are...?"

"John Dalton here. I want to speak to Gerald."

Henry froze, staring moronically into space as the phone squawked again: the unthinkable had happened. What should he say? The answer was not, in fact, very difficult. All he needed to do was to say that Gerald was not there and offer to take a message, but the information conveyed to John was that he was in the hands of a stuttering incompetent, who seemed unable even to contact his own boss.

"Have you found those two, yet? Is all under control?"

"Er – yes, or rather no. Gerald's out looking and mustn't be disturbed. There's only ......"

73

"Mustn't?....I'll decide who should be 'disturbed'. Get him on his mobile now and tell him to contact me."

"But he may be stalking Ahmed and the noise will give away his position. It'll be your responsibility."

Henry waited for the reply which would absolve him from all further thought, but the silence lengthened. John had rung off, unwilling to listen to any more drivelling 'buts' from this Fenland fool.

The phone rang while Gerald was in, or to be more accurate on, the toilet. Reception was poor, but Gerald gathered who was ringing and heard a reference to the Regional Controller. He agreed to ring back shortly, switched off and considered his position. Ahmed should have rung by now: he would give him a few more hours, but he couldn't stay out and stall H Q for much longer. Still havering, he moved outside to a point of better reception, where his next course of action was decided for him by the ringing of his phone. A slow, cruel smile spread over Gerald's face as he recognised the unmistakable and agitated voice he had been hoping to hear.

"Calm down! Calm down!" said Gerald soothingly. "Are you near the Tunnel? When do you want me to meet you?"

They agreed that it would be best to wait until it was dark and Gerald uttered appropriate reassurances about his desire to help and his willingness to arrive alone. He also noted the increasing desperation of the fugitive, who would now be willing to submit himself to *any* indignity in order to get his papers. The wait and the discomfort of the night (to say nothing of the risks associated with failing to 'jump' when contacted by the Regional Controller) were all about to pay off!

Now for that call to the farm. Henry would have to stall John, explain that Gerald was following up a recent sighting of the runaway and was confident of catching him in the very near future. He would try to ring in occasionally, but was not to be contacted unless anything really significant happened – such as one of the others finding Ahmed or the meddlesome old buffer. In fact, thought Gerald, as he gave his instructions to his protesting assistant, where he would be most of the time his mobile would be out of range – and he wouldn't be telling them he was at the Tunnel until he'd had a few hours fun. It was a pity he couldn't keep the lad locked up for a month or two, but he had to be seen to be dealing with the matter effectively, so Ahmed's permanent silence was needed. The Movement had retained the Nazi attitude to homosexuality, so he would not take any chances of being expo.... er.. found out, especially at a time when there was a strong likelihood that he would be put up for the High Command.

Replacing the phone, Henry turned to Paul, who was just about to issue forth, accompanied by one of the immigrants, to scour a few more highways and by-ways.

"I'm not taking the rap for this. If that John rings again, I'm not covering for Gerald. He should be here to deal with all that."

"Yes," replied the other guard, "and I'm not sure whether we can trust these other buggers: they're beginning to think Ahmed got away. It's a short step from that to deciding to scarper themselves."

"What? With no papers? They'd be caught and sent home: they won't risk that."

Paul lowered his voice:

"What papers? Christopher up at the Castle told me they'd given them to some real high up, who was checking up on the system. Gerald did his nut when he was told!"

The sharp, intrusive ring of the telephone cut short the two underlings' conversation. Mouthing 'Good Luck!', Paul left the 'strawstack bunker' to continue the search, and Henry cautiously raised the receiver.

"Henry here," he said, wondering who it was this time.

"Still no Gerald! Did you contact him as I told you?"

"Yes, Sir. He was following up a lead and rang me back later to say – er – that he – er – was following up a lead and ....."

"You just said that, man! What did he actually say? Just tell me his exact words: is that asking too much?"

Henry was not up to dealing with this bullying approach, and had already decided he would drop Gerald in it if he got any aggro from H bloody Q. The stutter disappeared, the tone became studiedly neutral – that of a mere reporter of facts.

"He instructed me to stall if you rang again. He was only to be disturbed if someone else found either of the two we're all searching for – Sir!"

Henry braced himself for a tirade, but was pleasantly surprised.

"Thank you. You have been most helpful. I'm glad someone is acting sensibly. What did you say your name was?"

"Henry, Sir!" replied the guard, by this time standing to attention, relieved at last of the burden of responsibility.

"Right, Henry. I shall be along later in the day. I shall also organise some reinforcements. There's no need to bother Gerald with all this. He's obviously too busy. Just keep it between the two of us – O K ?"

"Yessir! Right, Sir! As you say, Sir! Can I....."

"I'll be in touch later. Goodbye!" John allowed his fury to surface as he cut the connection. "What a moron! And who the hell does Gerald think he is? I'll give him stall. Roger!" He called to his assistant and issued a series of instructions. The Fens and these two troublesome civilians would soon be sorted out – and Mr High-and-Mighty Gerald with them!

Elizabeth grinned at her father as she put the phone down after her conversation with Gerald:

"Well, what did you think? How did I do?"

Martin knew his daughter had always had a talent for mimicry – the 'musical ear' inherited from her mother – but he had been staggered by this performance, the fruits of listening to Ahmed's tape.

"Fantastic! Ahmed's own mother would have thought it was him! We can keep this character Gerald – and anyone else at the farm – running round in circles for ever!"

"What a repulsive man. You could hear him gloating – and I was getting worried he might want to go into specifics about the nature of the 'anything' I was offering to do for him!"

"Oh, I'm sure you could have coped," said her admiring father, without thinking.

"Really? With my experience of sexual deviancy, do you mean? Thanks very much!"

"No, no. I meant you would have the intelligence to think of a way of – er – getting him off the subject. You know quite well what I meant. You're just trying to wind me up."

"It's not difficult!"

"Yes, well...what do we do now? We've got Gerald nicely out of the way for several hours."

"We do two things: we wait for someone to come to help us – sent by Patrick – and I , which means not you, ring Mother."

"You won't tell her about all this?" asked Martin anxiously. "She'll only worry," he added solicitously. "You know what she's like."

"Oh, yes. I know what you mean. It *would* be silly of her to worry over such trivial matters as you being chased round Lincolnshire whilst organising the escape of an illegal immigrant from the clutches of Boris Karloff!"

"I don't think that Boris and Gerald are of the same – er – sexual orientation, in fact," objected her father mildly.

"You know perfectly what I mean! Don't quibble over unimportant details. That man is dangerous and you are – well, you're *you*! "

At this point, Elizabeth broke off as she realised from the look in his eye that it had been her turn to be 'wound up'.

"You're impossible – and you know it. However, your James Bond days are now over, so I can truthfully tell her you are in good health, that she has no need to worry and I'm preparing some suitable nourishing dishes, as you were being rather unadventurous in.... your culinary habits," she finished firmly, in response to his raised eyebrow at the word 'unadventurous'.

While his wife's 'agent-in-post' was reporting the agreed, bowdlerised, version of the condition of dog, house and husband (in descending order of importance), Martin made a cafetière of drinkable coffee and browsed through the local paper. He nearly missed the small item on one of the inner pages, his eye in fact being caught by the somewhat fanciful heading 'Fox Overboard'. A dead fox, ran the report, had been found entangled in the mooring rope of a small inflatable dinghy, found near Spalding. A police spokesman said that a local angler had noticed the boat, but there had been no reports of children missing, so it had probably just been swept away from its mooring by the strong current. They urged parents to be careful, as recent heavy rains had swollen some normally placid rivers, increasing substantially the dangers which always applied to some extent. It was claimed that the police agreed with the reporter's suggestion that, as far as the fox was concerned, 'fowl play' was not suspected.

"Well, well," thought Martin, turning his attention to the Telegraph, "if only they knew!"

There were, as usual, several items concerning the strength in certain areas of Europe of the neo-Nazi movement, which now intrigued Martin, and reminded him of the still unexplained interest of Gerald in the war-time U-boat service. He was still reading the Telegraph, studiously avoiding any articles on education in order to maintain the equilibrium of his blood pressure, when Elizabeth finished her lengthy telephone call and there came a knock on the door.

CHAPTER THIRTEEN

Kenneth, the agent from British Intelligence, had had a pleasant, traffic-free drive, broken by a very acceptable 'Early Starter' at a Little Chef near Wansford, having considered calling in at The Haycock, and decided it might look bad on his expenses claim. He was looking forward to a day in pleasant rural surroundings, well away from his boss, with plenty of time to file a brief report, having reassured this member of the public that everything was now in good hands. The lightness of spirit associated with his anticipation of the day became even lighter when the door was opened by an attractive young girl. He didn't quite say: 'Hello. Is your Daddy in?'.... but he came close.

"Good morning, Miss! One thing's certain: you're not Mr Martin Brady – and he's the one I've come to see!"

The 'vision of loveliness' spoke, pointedly not opening the door for him to enter.

"I will enquire whether he wishes to see you. Whom shall I say it is?"

Even the insensitive Kenneth sensed that somehow he had got off on the wrong foot, but never-the-less he continued to march out of step.

"I think it's best if I tell him that myself, my dear. You'll find he is expecting me."

It was the 'my dear' which triggered the cold hard look, accompanied by a curt response that if he failed to produce suitable identification within ten seconds, she would phone the police and have him locked up. It was, therefore, with some relief, a minute or two later, that Kenneth found himself talking to an amiable old boy, very few of whose genes seemed to have found their way into the D N A of the fiercesome female whom he had (presumably) fathered. The story was complex but the clarity with which it was told caused Kenneth to have grave doubts about its authenticity. Would these two quintessentially pampered middle class citizens react so calmly if it were true? What evidence was there to show that 'Ahmed' had ever existed? Even the rubber boat had disappeared, and one could hardly build a report for action of any sort on the existence of an I D card for a firm called H F C. Not only that, thought Kenneth, mentally starting to write that report behind his bland exterior, the man is even a Telegraph reader! Leaning back, he dropped the I D card containing Gerald's photograph onto the kitchen table – or, to be more precise, onto the opened newspaper.

Life is full of coincidences, and the section of the paper on which it fell contained several obituaries, one of which concerned the life and times of one of the survivors of a force which suffered 80% losses in World War Two, namely the German U-boat service. Andreas Ketels, former officer in the German Navy, it reported, who spent several months as a prisoner of war, but later made his home amongst his former enemies, etc., etc., had died peacefully in his chauffeured car. There was more interesting detail but the coincidence in question related to the accompanying photograph – and its immediate proximity to that of Gerald. The likeness was immediately apparent, for the photo was many years old and was almost certainly the one which had caused Ahmed to say that he had noticed that Gerald had been one of those standing on the U-boat.

"I expect you're wondering whether we have any hard evidence to back up our story?" asked Martin, as he carefully aligned the I D card with the photograph in the newspaper.

"Well, old boy," replied Kenneth, relieved that the point had been made for him, "no-one doubts you of course, least of all myself, but some of the people I report to are going to say just that. I realise you have the tape, but they would say that it could have been made by anyone. Th....."

"By me, for example," interjected Elizabeth, in tones which belied any suggestion that she had meant to be helpful.

"Well, since you mention it, yes..... not, of course that I am for a moment suggesting that you....."

"You have just given us some evidence, my friend," said Martin, not being above the odd patronising expression himself. "There it is. Look! They're father and son: it stands out a mile. Not only that. If you read the text, you'll find the U-boat connection. Ahmed was right!"

"Ye-es," said Kenneth reluctantly. "You may have a point there, I agree, but one can't always believe what one reads in the newspapers."

Hurriedly, he added that he would have it 'checked out', in response to the beginnings of a contemptuous curl of the young lady's lip. Martin continued to look thoughtful, searching his mind for something triggered by that remark about not always being able to believe what you read. What was it? Something he'd read recently.

"The fox!" he shouted, causing a temporary alliance between the two younger members sitting at the table, both of whom wondered whether the pressure had finally got to him. "It was in the Local. Where did I....? Here we are, under here, somewhere in the middle of the paper. Yes, look!"

In triumph, he pointed to the story about the discovery of an inflatable boat.

"Yes, this does, to some extent, bear out your story, I agree," said Kenneth reluctantly. "You could go and identify it, perhaps."

"No. Not the boat, you fool! The fox! Don't you see? The bullet might still be in it – a bullet, not shot from a cartridge. That guard had a silenced rifle. I saw it in silhouette although it was dark. Very like a Heckler and Koch G3 fitted with a noise suppressor..... I'm not sure, but whatever it is, it's illegal, so we've got them!"

"And since when did you become an authority on firearms, Father? Had discipline at that school broken down to the extent of the staff being issued with personal weapons?"

"Since you ask," said her father, restoring her faith in his predictable respectability, "I remembered it from a project done by one of my Third Years on the resurgence of the German arms industry. He was quite a bright lad, father worked for ....."

Kenneth thought it was about time he took control, as the only professional present, apart from which, that part of the story had always struck him as being particularly weak. Probably, the old boy was a bit hard of hearing, or had his ears blocked with mud, so just hadn't heard the shot (always assuming he had been there in the first place!).

"All right! I'll get the police to check the cause of death – that's if the carcase is still around – and if it *is* a bullet, we'll pay a visit to your farm, claiming we've had a report that they've an illegal weapon on the premises."

Privately, Martin had his doubts, not only concerning the availability of the carcase, but also about the advisability of just 'visiting and asking' at the farm. It might only alert them to the continued threat of discovery, and it would be easy for them to deny having any weapons: they would hardly keep them hanging on the wall for all to see. On the other hand, it was the first time that the man from 'Intelligence' had shown any inclination to take any aspect of the story seriously.

"We can continue to keep Gerald away while you call at the farm, if you like," offered Martin. "That would weaken the opposition. In fact," he added, warming to his theme, "I could organise a diversion while you go in and search."

Repressing the phrase 'God save us from gung-ho senior citizens', Kenneth diplomatically thanked him and pointed out that he was not going in as might a drug-busting squad, merely in the capacity of a Home Office Firearms Licensing Officer, accompanied by a member of the local police force, in pursuance of a report from a member of the public. He also reminded the two civilians that using the telephone system for purposes of deception was an offence – unless, he added hurriedly, to Elizabeth's retreating back – it was on official Government business. He reached for the phonebook to obtain the number of Spalding Police Station, pretending not to hear what had sounded uncommonly like 'pompous prick' as the door closed behind her.

The telephone call from Kenneth, using his Home Office 'cover', caused some consternation within the police force as the fox carcase had been disposed of, there being more interest in the possibility of a boating accident than in the exact manner of the animal's demise. After a couple of hours, however, it had not only been located, thanks primarily to the forgetfulness of one of the cleaners, but also examined. The cause of death was found to have indeed been a bullet, fired (to Martin's smug satisfaction) from a Heckler and Koch Gewehr 3, in all probability fitted with a silencer. As the probable time of death matched that claimed by Martin,

Kenneth's request for assistance in approaching the inhabitants of Hall Farm was readily agreed, and P C Carradine was instructed to help the 'man from the Ministry'.

This information was rung through to Martin's house by the duty sergeant, whose call, unfortunately, was overheard by another member of the force, who realised its importance and passed it to his contact, who in turn rang Hall Farm.

"Are you quite sure you don't want us to organise a diversion, now that you realise they're armed?" enquired Martin. "They've got sophisticated intruder sensing equipment – and a lot at stake, you know."

"Ah, yes. The electronic bulrushes," said Kenneth, who had placed little credence on that part of the story. "Just leave it to the professionals. This is merely a verification exercise. They'll have no idea why we're coming and no reason to regard us as intruders. I doubt somehow that the person who reads the electricity meter has to lay down a creeping barrage in order to approach in safety!"

Kenneth paused after this (as he saw it) witty exposé of the situation and then threw the old boy a bone in the form of a request that, if he did wish to be of assistance, he could cut along to a point near Thorpe Tunnel to see whether Gerald was on his way back. At least, he reasoned to himself, it should keep them (for Elizabeth insisted on accompanying her father) out of mischief.

Reference has already been made to it having been 'unfortunate' that the sergeant's telephone call had been overheard by one of the Organisation's police contacts. What made it disastrous, rather than merely troublesome, however, was the absence of Gerald.

"George here. Clear the decks. The police are on their way with a chap from Intelligence. They know you've got a rifle and will be with you any time now!"

"Christ!" exclaimed Henry. "That stupid bugger Gerald's gone off and left me! What am I supposed to do?"

"Not my problem, old boy. I'm just paid to pass on info. What ever you do, you'll have to do it fast, though. I shouldn't let them find your – ah – 'guests', if I were you....and remember: this call didn't take place!"

Henry gazed panic-stricken at the receiver, as his caller cut the connection. Where was John's number? Should he call Gerald? No: John didn't want him to know he was coming. What was an Intelligence agent doing – and how the hell did they know about the rifles? He would have to do something – they could be here any minute and those illegals must be hidden away. Two of them, who had been out all night, and Paul, were asleep upstairs in the farmhouse. They might wake up and panic!

In fact, Henry was doing enough panicking for all of them, torn between contacting HQ and warning the others at the farm. Still cursing the absent Gerald, he ran upstairs to wake Paul, warned him the police were coming and then dashed back to the bunker to telephone for instructions and help. As he entered the hidden door in the 'strawstack', he heard, this time with relief, the urgent ringing of the telephone.

"Thank God!" he gasped as he snatched up the receiver. "Henry here: who's that?"

It was with a mixture of anger and fright, but above all relief that he heard the answer he had prayed for:

"Gerald here. What's the matter?"

"Everything bloody thing's the matter, for Christ's sake! The police are on their way – with a bloody Intelligence man. H Q are taking over the whole operation ... Oh Christ, I was told not to tell you that ......there's reinforcements coming – and John – and I don't know what to ......"

The rising note indicated a man close to breakdown, on the verge of tears, capable of any misjudgement:

"You've got to get back. Bugger that Asian – or the other guy. Get yourself back here now!"

The reply was terse and failed to reassure Henry:

"Now, get this! I'm on my way and I'll ring again in about ten minutes. Do not on any account ring H Q. I'm not having them take anything over. Just stall the police: say you've only got a shot-gun, or something. And don't ring me. I'll ring you."

A few miles away, Martin switched off his 'mobile' and looked triumphantly at his daughter.

"Well! Didn't I do well!"

"Rory Bremner has nothing to fear," she replied, "but you got away with it. I winced at that southern 'gun', mind you. Only six for artistic impression, but nine point three for effort."

As he set off to brief his colleague, Henry heard the bleep of the furthest sensor and glanced at the VDU: a car was approaching slowly. By this time feeling physically sick, Henry ran across to the farmhouse and shouted up the stairs:

"They're coming! Get down here, all of you! Paul, you take these two and shut yourselves into the bunker. I'll stall these people until Gerald gets here."

"What if the.....?"

"No time for questions. Just do as I say!"

CHAPTER FOURTEEN

Although the man who met them seemed rather out of breath, there was nothing out of the ordinary to be seen by the time Kenneth and his police assistant drove into the ramshackle farmyard.

"How do you do, Sir? Are you the owner of this place?" said Kenneth, taking in the general air of neglect, the rusting machinery, old overgrown hay bales and tumble-down outbuildings.

"No, he's on his way – er – should be back soon," mumbled Henry. "If you'd like to wait in the kitchen, I'll get on with my – er ... ."

"Oh, I'm sure you can help us, Sir. While we're waiting, you won't mind answering a few questions, will you?"

It had not escaped Kenneth's notice that the man was agitated, wanted to get away – and, perhaps most surprising of all, had not asked who they were or why they were there. It could merely be that he was unused to visitors, better with sheep than people, a bit shy and awkward..... or it could be that the visit had been expected. As his young, inexperienced colleague, 'on loan' from the police, was not in uniform and looked more like a member of a school Sixth form than part of a two-man hit squad, the absence of curiosity as to their identity was, well – odd.

"I expect you're wondering why we're here, Sir? Here's my identification, and this is P C Carradine. No need to be alarmed – we're just following up a report, which may well be mistaken, that you have an unauthorised fire-arm on the premises."

Henry glanced at the proffered I D cards and mumbled that he didn't know anything. It would be better to wait until his boss came, as he would know all that.

"Yes. We'll wait, but just for the record, do you know if any guns are kept on site? Legal ones, that is?"

Remembering his most recent instruction from Gerald, Henry replied that they had a shot-gun, for the rats, rabbits, etc.

"Good. Quite understandable," said Kenneth, soothingly. "Could you get it for me, please? Then I'll get the owner to show me the licence. I expect everything's in order."

"I – er – don't know where it ....," muttered the hapless Henry, sweating profusely now, unable to meet his questioner's eye.

"Is that it hanging on the wall?" asked Kenneth, pointing at an old 12-bore, the presence of which Henry had forgotten, largely because it was never used, did not work, and was there only as a form of 'decoration', as were the old cooking pots and horse brasses, designed to look harmless and bucolic.

"Oh! Oh, yes. I couldn't remember where it had been put," said Henry lamely.

"You use it to shoot rats, I believe you said. Have you shot any recently?"

At this point, Henry remembered that when one was being questioned, it was a good thing to say as much as possible that was true. With relief, he replied reasonably accurately that, as it happened, his mate – who was also out – had recently had to shoot a fox which had been after the chickens.

To Henry's surprise, his visitor showed considerable interest in this use of the gun, although it was easy to answer the questions: when, where, what had happened to the dead animal.

"And have you any other guns around the farm?"

"No. That's the only one – at least, as far as I know. You need to ask the boss – and he should be here any minute."

Kenneth walked over to the wall and lifted down the old gun. It took no more than a minute to confirm that the relic had certainly not been fired recently – probably didn't even work.

"I don't think," he said, fixing Henry with a penetrating stare, "that you are being entirely frank with us, Sir! This gun is not in a fit state to be fired. Are you sure there is no other weapon – one which fires a bullet, rather than a cartridge, possibly fitted with a silencer?"

The wild-eyed look, the gasp of horror, the stumbling denial, all combined to make Kenneth realise not only that there was almost certainly such a weapon, but that the rest of Martin's improbable story could well prove to be true.

"I think you'd better get in touch with your superiors, Constable. We shall need a search warrant and we shall need to ask this gentleman's 'boss', always assuming such a person exists, a few questions!"

Inspector Green had been worried about the interest shown in the goings on at Hall Farm, but he had decided to co-operate, whilst passing on a warning to his contact. He had long been on the pay-roll of the Organisation as one of a small, but influential, proportion of the uniformed force, who found their shared membership of the Masons a useful cover for far more sinister purposes than mere self advancement and occasional favours or 'blind eye turning'. When he received a call from the young P C whom he had selected as lacking in initiative and unlikely to ask awkward questions, he realised that this Intelligence chap could be about to make waves, big waves, the sort that cause people to drown, especially if those people could be criticised for allowing things to get out of hand.

"Right, Matthew. You get back here. Leave our friend at the farm, keeping an eye on this fellow, and we'll see about how best to follow things up."

"Should I arrest him first, Sir? Or bring him with me?"

"Arrest who, lad? The bogus Environmental Inspector or the farm labourer? No, you can't arrest someone for not firing a gun at a fox, especially as the owner is out! That Intelligence chap isn't carrying, is he?"

"What, a gun, do you mean?"

"No, a loaded banana, you fool. Of course I mean a gun! These people are a law unto themselves – create more trouble than they're worth, half the time."

"No, I don't think so. I'll ask him."

"Never mind. Just get back here," said the exasperated inspector, anxious to get the nosy agent on his own and well away from any direct connection with the forces of law and order. How they dealt with the chap was none of his business, except in so far as he would expect a substantial bonus for buying them time and opportunity.

After the departure of the young policeman, Kenneth and Henry eyed each other speculatively.

"You'll save yourself a lot of trouble – not to say a few years inside – if you come clean," said Kenneth.

"I've nothing more to say," said Henry, who seemed much calmer now, even though he must know that the game was virtually up.

The silence lengthened. Kenneth tried again, acting on the assumption that all of his elderly informant's information could well be correct:

"What about these illegals?" he said casually. "We shall be picking them up and getting them to give evidence before sending them back, to stop anyone else using you and your mates as a route to the West. Are you sure you don't want to tell me about it?"

Henry maintained a sullen silence, but he was not the only person who had heard those last words. The other was Issed, who had been sent from the bunker by Paul to find out what had been happening when the security V D U showed the visitors' car departing rapidly, presumably to summon help as it only contained one person. Having heard the visitor's intentions towards himself, Issed nipped smartly back to the bunker, prepared to follow any instructions designed to prevent Kenneth from carrying out his threat.

There was no longer, it appeared to Paul, any point in pretending there were no weapons on site, so, armed with two hand guns (one for Henry), he and the two Asians emerged from the bunker and moved silently, knowing every inch of the ground, towards the back door of the farmhouse.

"Are you going to tell these people to give themselves up," asked Kenneth, after another silence, "or do I have to search the cellars, the attic, even the....Bunker?"

This sally was rewarded with a look of surprise from the taciturn Henry.

"Ah! I see you thought we didn't know about that! Perhaps now you see that your only hope is to tell me everything you know. Let's start with these smuggled immigrants. Where are they at the moment?"

It was with some quiet satisfaction that Henry was able to answer that particular question:

"Two of them are right behind you!" he said, as the trio entered the room noiselessly. "Don't try anything! Well done,

Paul. Give me that shooter – and don't be afraid to use yours if he tries anything. We can just say he left after a bit, so no-one will ever be able to prove anything."

"I thought you said the police were here? Who's this chap?"

"This, my friend, is a member of Her Majesty's Secret Service – a Mr Black, so his I D card would have us believe. Somehow, I doubt whether he'll be around for much longer, though, so I shouldn't bother getting on first name terms with him."

"You won't get away with this!" expostulated Kenneth, rising from his seat. "You'll spend the rest of your life in prison if anything happens to me."

"Grab him! Get some rope and tie him up – and slug him if he doesn't shut up."

Kenneth struggled in vain as the two wiry immigrants held him until Paul returned with some rope.

"What shall we do with him, Henry? Drop him down the old well?"

"Not a bad idea, but we'd better let H Q decide. In the mean time, if anyone asks, or the police come back, say he went off to look round just after that gormless copper drove off. I don't somehow think our friends in high places will enquire too closely. Lock him up in the brig – he seems to know all about the Bunker, so he can spend his last few hours in it!"

"How come he knows that?" said Paul. "Do you think they caught Ahmed and sweated it out of him?"

"I don't know, but I've no doubt John will persuade him to say! Right! Paul, you'd better get upstairs on look-out. And you two, get him over to the Bunker. I'll come with you. Gag him just in case anyone happens to be in earshot until he's locked up in that inner room. He can shout all he likes there, or scream, if it comes to that!"

The sound-proofing qualities of the bunker were demonstrated as they opened the door, for the last two or three rings of the telephone (which had been trilling its request to be unhooked for the last two minutes) could then be heard.

"Let's get this chap locked away safely, then I'll see who that was," said Henry, taking a bunch of keys from his pocket.

"And check those bonds. We don't want him to think he's in a hotel and start ringing for room service!"

As the door clanged shut behind him, Kenneth could see why his guard had referred to it as 'the brig'. There was no light, no heat, no furniture – and nothing on the damp concrete floor. He had no doubt that he would be missed, and no doubt that Martin and the police knew where to look for him. They would have to move quickly, however, for he also had no doubt that these trigger-happy gangsters had everything to gain from silencing him. Permanently.

He knew too much – and yet he knew too little. Who, or what was H Q ? Was there an absent 'boss' as Henry had claimed? Judging by the regalia, decorations, hangings and photographs he had glimpsed on the way to his 'prison cell', Martin's ideas about the neo-Nazis were anything but fanciful after all.....but were there really people in 'high places' who would protect them.... or even encourage them to go further? Kenneth was no fool, was, indeed a 'professional' as he had rather patronisingly (he now realised) pointed out to Martin. He set about trying to free himself from his bonds and think how he could bargain for his life and/or escape. Surely someone in this organisation would have the sense to stop their underlings from making a terrible mistake. Why in Hell's name had he been so contemptuous of the help offered by Martin and his daughter? What would he not give for a 'diversion' now!

CHAPTER FIFTEEN

The area round Thorpe Tunnel was quiet and peaceful when Martin and his daughter arrived there, having (like Gerald, whom they could not see) left the car some way away. Training jets from R A F Cranwell passed carefully overhead, in long curving sweeps and occasionally evil-looking 'tank-busters', from a more distant American air-base, appeared silently and were gone, to be followed a second later by the explosive thunder of powerful engines. The wild life continued to graze, hunt, buzz or bleat, according to its nature, but mere mortals ducked in fright, thankful that on this occasion the aircraft had all contrived to miss each other.

Having found a suitable vantage point, they settled down to wait and watch, taking it in turns to scan the area with the binoculars. Various vehicles passed below them, but none stopped at the tunnel itself, although a lay-by a few hundred yards away, next to an area of woodland, seemed popular as a 'comfort stop'.

"That place seems to be well manured!" said Martin, somewhat crudely, earning himself a withering look. "There goes another – the furniture van. Where's it from?"

"I can't quite see from this angle, but the telephone number looks like 01428, wherever that is," replied Elizabeth, sweeping the binoculars round to the left. "Oh! what was that.....?"

"It's probably down south – someone will be making a packet, selling there and buying up here."

"Well, well, I think I must be looking at the famous Gerald!" exclaimed Elizabeth. "There's a man standing up, looking at something through binoculars."

"Careful! Don't let him see you – the sun on the lens can give you away. I know: it's what gave me away, I think."

"Don't worry. It's how I came to see *him*: the sun's behind us. He must have moved as I swept past him to look at that furniture van."

"Let's have a look!"

"Hang on. I think it's the van which interests him – enough to make him forget and break cover to get a better view."

"Perhaps the driver's taking his trousers off! If it *is* Gerald, he'd want a good look, or," he hurried on, forestalling criticism, "perhaps the driver looks like Ahmed?"

"He doesn't and... Now, that's funny! There are two other men now, just inside the wood: they can be seen from up here. Where on earth did they spring from?"

"Let me have a look at your watcher: I'll recognise him from his I D photograph, if it is. Thanks ..... yes, it's him all right. He's putting the binoculars down to get something out of his pocket. Hell! It's his mobile phone. If he rings the farm, he'll find out I've been impersonating him!"

"And he'll find out about the....."

"Reinforcements!" they both exclaimed, brains racing to take in what was happening.

"They're being dropped off from that van!" said Elizabeth, getting there just ahead of her father. "And Gerald must have recognised the vehicle as one of theirs, so he....Give me that phone!" she concluded. "I'm going to stop him getting through to the farm."

"But they ....."

"Shush! Ahmed has seen the reinforcements, too, and....."

Martin, watching through the binoculars, saw Gerald pause and press a button on his mobile. During the course of quite a lengthy conversation, Elizabeth managed, the accent never slipping, to convey to Gerald that Ahmed was near-by, had stolen a mobile phone (the number of which he did not know) and had taken fright at the sight of the other men whom Gerald had brought with him – despite having said he would come alone.

Gerald was torn, once again, between duty and 'pleasure'. He tried to reassure 'Ahmed' that he knew nothing of the extra men, that he was trying to find out and could still meet him, as agreed, in Thorpe Tunnel.

"I'm not going down there to be caught by those men. They're probably going there, too. I know where you are. I can see you from here. I'll come to you. And don't use the phone to tell them where I am. If I hear or see you using it, you'll never see me again!"

Elizabeth stopped, cut the connection, and let out a long slow breath.

"That was brilliant!" said Martin. "Let's hope it works. It should give us ten minutes to think what to do. The pace is a bit too much for my creaking mental faculties!"

"It depends mainly on how things are going with our revered professional spy," said Elizabeth, adding in a slightly exaggerated version of the real thing: "No need for you to worry your pretty little head about that, my dear!"

"Time for Gerald to ring in, I think," said Martin.

"I thought you were expecting to gain ten minutes," said his daughter, focusing the binoculars.

"Rory rides again! Here we go – and I'll watch those flat Fenland vowels, this time!" Martin keyed in the relevant numbers and waited for the ringing tone.

"Engaged! Blast it. I wonder who it is. Is it.....?"

"No. He's still sitting there. Just looked at his watch. Now he's looking at the furniture van. I can almost feel the anxiety from here!"

"Ah, at la(h)st! Sorry – last. I'd better get in character!"

Over at the Hall Farm bunker, Henry heard the phone start to ring again....and, down in Essex, John's assistant turned to his colleague.

"They're not answering. I've rung for about three minutes."

"Could be out of order, or there's a problem. Either way, John's not going to like it. I'll ring the plane. He can sort things out when he gets there. Charlie should be there with the reinforcements any time now. Talk about a sledge-hammer to crack a nut!"

"From what I can gather, this chap they're after *is* a bit of a nut!"

Henry had intended to key in 1471 to see who had been trying to get through, but managed this time to pick up the receiver in good time.

"Sorry! We were a bit busy, but all's well now."

"Gerald here. About time, too," grumbled the voice (well nearly) of Gerald, adding: "Put me in the picture."

Elizabeth observed, rather than heard, the conversation. Her father said very little – just the occasional grunt to encourage Henry to continue – but the widening of the eyes and the odd grimace made it clear that the monologue was

94

something more than a detailed run-down on the current state of the Common Agricultural Policy.

"Yes, I see," Martin said eventually. "You've all done very well. You haven't told H Q yet, have you?...No, never mind. Leave that to me. Don't harm him in any way until we get instructions...The well, yes....but no drastic action until they give the word.... Oh, just to double check, which number did they ring from before?... Good, good..." Martin signalled to Elizabeth to write the numbers, ".....2131. O K . I'll be in touch shortly."

Martin was about to ring off when he had a sudden thought.

"One thing more, Henry. It's occurred to me that young Ahmed might ring the farm, or even get someone to ring pretending to be one of us!...Yes, that's right... well, let's agree a simple code. We can change it as often as we like. If the person ringing asks what you should put on a stinging nettle rash.... and the other answers 'buttercups', then we..... Yes, yes, I know that dockleaves are the thing – that's the whole point of the code! An impostor – someone pretending to be one of us – would say 'dockleaves', but we will say 'bu.....' Yes, you've got it! Right. I'll be in touch, so don't ring me!"

"Buttercups!" said Elizabeth scornfully. "Why choose something with a 'u' in it? You could have said 'hollyhocks' or, or … oh, never mind. What did he have to say for such ages. I'm dying to know!"

"Unfortunately 'dying' could be one of the options," began Martin as he related the disastrous outcome of Kenneth's reconnaissance.

"You've got to do something, Father. You can't just let him rot. Surely they wouldn't kill him in cold blood. They'd never get away with it!"

"Working backwards, no they wouldn't get away with it, but that's of little interest to Kenneth if he's dead; yes, they might – in cold water, to be more exact. Bear in mind that the racket they're in is shared with Triads, Mafia, drug cartels – you name it. And as regards your first point, who was it who recently told me my James Bond days were over?"

"I didn't mean charge in, showing true grit, for God's sake! Think of something. We could ring the police!"

But even as she said it, Elizabeth realised the problem: those friends in high places on the one hand and incredulity on the other.

"Or," she continued, "we could ring his Intelligence people..... yes, I know: we might get the wrong person. Well, I'll get on to Patrick anyway. Give me that phone."

They both knew really that Kenneth could have minutes rather than hours to live; that 'the man from H Q' was on the way; that a group of perhaps half a dozen men had joined the hunt. Moreover, a humiliated Gerald was about to find out what was going on – and could well take precipitate, violent action to make up for his absence at such a crucial time. The logic of the situation, reinforced by Elizabeth's encounter with an answering machine in response to her call to Poland, pointed to the need for a 'cunning plan'.

Martin coughed apologetically and looked anywhere but at his daughter:

"If – and I only said if – we could arrange a diversion, I've got Gerald's keys back at the house," he began hesitantly, "and if I could get to that strawstack, I think I could find the door .... and one of his keys might...."

He tailed off and waited for an outburst of scorn and derision, references to his lack of experience and training, and similarity to 'Q' rather than even the lowest 'field man', let alone 007.

In fact, Elizabeth regarded him thoughtfully and merely said:

"And what, still speaking purely hypothetically, did you have in mind by way of a diversion? Not, of course, that I should let you attempt anything like that on your own, even if there were any possibility of action on the lines you propose."

Martin had, in fact, given some thought to what amounted to a diversion for some time. His reason for getting Ahmed to tape his story had been partly in order to get Gerald out of the way. He had vague plans of driving into the farmyard to have a really good look round, aided by the set of keys which Ahmed had snaffled and believed to be at the bottom of the river. If enough vehicles, all at once, were to converge on the farm, it would be well-nigh impossible for them to deal with an intruder hidden in the middle. The sort of vehicles he had in mind were fire engines, gas detector vans, Anglia Water, the police, the River Board, an ambulance, perhaps – even the odd T V or newspaper reporter. If all or most of those were telephoned and told there was an emergency (leaking gas, electricity pylon collapsing, water flooding out of the raised river bank, etc.), there would be total confusion in the farmyard. One more person, claiming to be, say, an environmental, health or animal rights inspector also called out on (appropriately for the Fens) a 'wild goose chase', would never be noticed, let alone suspected.

Although she had not seen it, Elizabeth could envisage the narrow Fen road, the cramped, muddy farmyard and the confused and inadequate Henry.

"Hmm! You've given this some thought haven't you? What were you like at school, I wonder? It might work at that – the diversion, that is, not you as the White Knight."

"I know what you mean, but one can't involve some innocent by-stander in this. Your young athletic friends for example, or ex-students I could rustle up. One might even contact a member of the opposition by mistake!"

"If only Patrick would ring back," said Elizabeth. "He could pull the right strings and send in someone more – er – well not you , anyway!"

"The only trouble is," said Martin thoughtfully, "the roads would be too blocked to get Kenneth out. Perhaps we shouldn't call quite so many?"

"Now hang on! Nothing has been decided yet. I know you. You'll be hiring a helicopter next and getting me to read you the flying instructions from the handbook!"

"That would be the answer, though, wouldn't it? A helicopter! If only we could get hold of the right people quickly enough."

Conscious that time was running out, they racked their brains for a solution. It boiled down to wondering whom they could trust, for just as some elements of the police were thought to be dicey, so might be others, such as the military, or their M P, or even members of Kenneth's Intelligence organisation itself.

"Did you tell Patrick to ring on this machine, by the way, or," he added, seeing the reply in Elizabeth's face, "is there at this very minute a message on the answerphone at home?"

Quickly, they got to their feet to return to the car.

"Just before we go, is Gerald still sitting there waiting 'goodly'?"

Elizabeth focused on the relevant spot: "Yes. Is it worth another smoke signal to keep him sweet?"

"Wrong type of Indian, but yes. Talk as we hurry along: it'll sound more authentic."

As they made their way back down the hill, 'Ahmed' could be heard pleading with Gerald not to go and leave him, explaining that he had had to double back because of the extra men who had emerged from the furniture van. The aim was to make Gerald think that he was playing a fish on a long line, gradually winding him in, but always risking, by too sharp a 'jerk on the line', that it would snap, resulting in the loss of the catch. In fact a better analogy might have been that of the line being reeled in to yield up an old boot – or even, given events unfolding back at the farm, 'fishing while Rome burned'.

Father and daughter were back home by the time Gerald decided to ring the farm to see if there was any news, so they did not see him shouting, puce with rage, engaged in a pointless discussion of the merits of nettles and dockleaves with Henry, who appeared to have 'flipped' under the strain!

In fact, Henry did well, once having established – by means of the 'stinging nettle code' – that he was in direct communication with the impostor whom Gerald had warned him about. Without giving him any useful information, he discovered where the man was ringing from, including the fact that he had seen the Haslemere Furnishing Company van unloading its complement of 'troops'. The fact that the 'real' Gerald had been told earlier about the expected reinforcements, whereas this one clearly had no knowledge of that conversation, convinced Henry utterly that he had a 'wrong'un', probably the man they had all been trying to catch for several days. In other circumstances, his request that Gerald go down to the Thorpe Tunnel bunker to help issue them with arms would have been seen as a master-stroke, for a bogus Gerald would have crept near to get a good look at the place.

The real Gerald found it altogether a sensible request – something to hang on to in the welter of waffle about improbable herbal remedies. He replaced the phone into his pocket, seething with anger at having been 'stood up' by that wretch Ahmed, who had cost him a very uncomfortable night and delayed the hunt for the elusive bearer of I D 534. As the incident involving a false I D card came into his mind, he recalled that he had mislaid his own. He had been reluctant to ask for a replacement, thinking it would 'turn up', as it would have made him appear inefficient. He had wondered if he had dropped it that night when Nero had put up a pheasant, but he had gone back the next day and there had been no sign of it. He would have to come clean soon – make up a story about dropping it down the well by mistake, or something.

Occupied with such thoughts, Gerald was caught totally by surprise when he was suddenly thrown to the ground and sat upon by two burly men, who proceeded to tie him up whilst preventing him from uttering a word, then gagged him efficiently and hustled him towards the bunker. Apart from breaking his mobile phone, they did no damage and regarded his pop-eyed attempts to convey outrage with contempt. Nothing could be more obvious than that this was the man who had been unmasked by Henry, whose subsequent call to H Q had resulted in their instructions to lock him up after searching him and leave him to the tender mercies of John, who was arriving shortly by plane at Hall Farm airstrip. Had their search revealed his I D card, of course, it is possible that they would have given him a chance to explain himself. There was, to be sure, a set of car keys, but no visible vehicle: that was parked well out of sight, in a spot where the odd bark from Nero would not attract a lot of attention.

Having locked Gerald away, they settled down to await the arrival of ... that same Gerald, meanwhile congratulating themselves on a job well done. There was one small doubt raised by one of the men, though:

"He looks a lot younger than we were told: ugly looking customer, mind you – and he stinks of dog!"

Behind the gag, Gerald strained to tell them what bloody fools they were, but their stupidity did not extend to the tying of knots. In that respect they scored ten for technical merit.

CHAPTER SIXTEEN

There was, indeed, a message waiting when Martin and Elizabeth arrived home.

"It'll probably be the bloody library telling me the book I ordered is now ready for collection," said Martin, as they waited for the mechanism to work its magic. On this occasion, however, his pessimism was unjustified.

"Hi! Dad – it's me. I've got a few days spare so think I'll pop home. Can you meet me at the usual airport? It'll be handy if you want to fit in a visit to Gran. Oh, and would you let Adrian know as soon as possible on 763291 – same code as Gran funnily enough. He can probably help with that other query you had. I'll ring again to let you know the flight number. Cheers!"

"Well, well. He must be worried about being overheard – those friends in very high places, I suppose," said Martin.

"Yes, thank God he's coming: this is getting a bit beyond us two!"

"Can you remember that number, or shall I play it again?"

"Yes, but do you know Gran's code?" replied Elizabeth.

"Easy: it used to be O S O 2 – S O for Southend, in the days when telephone numbers had proper letters."

"And for half a groat you could get drunk, go to the cinema and have a newspaper full of fish and chips. I know! Now, what .. is .. the.. code?"

"And," continued Martin smugly, "before they added an extra '1', so the code is 01702."

"At last! Now let's find out what the limp-wristed Adrian has to say for himself!" said Elizabeth, keying in the number and handing it to her father.

"Don't be so judgmental. He can't help what his name..... Oh – er – can I speak to Adrian, please?"

"What was the name again, Sir?"

"Adrian...A.. D.. R...."

"Yes, I'll put you through," said the Intelligence Service operator after he had verified the significance of the codeword.

The duty officer had some idea of Kenneth's mission, but as the latter had set off having little notion himself of just what was involved, it took some time to brief him on sufficient of the background for him to make sense of the urgency of the immediate situation.

"Right! Leave it with me. I'll get someone down there as quickly as possible. Stay by the phone – oh, and don't tell anyone else about this. As you've gathered, not everyone is trustworthy, however respectable they might seem."

Martin put the phone down with some relief and turned to his daughter:

"Perhaps the diversion won't be needed, after all!"

"Yes – pity in a way: I'm sure it would have worked, and I thought of another type of firm to send in: Dial-a-Pizza..... or Indian or whatever."

"Yes! And a certain poetic justice if the Taj Mahal Take-Away could come to the rescue!"

"I think we ought to ring the farm to get an update. They've probably rumbled us by now, as Gerald will have been able to prove he was the real one after a bit."

"He probably thought buttercups *were* the best treatment for stinging nettles – he's stupid enough!" said Martin, ringing through, ready to get in character.

Martin started to establish his bona fides by means of the 'stinging nettle' code, but was cut short by Henry.

"No need for all that now," he said cheerfully. "The lads have caught that other chap. They've got him locked up at Thorpe Tunnel. In fact if you're still near-by, you could cut along there and 'interview' him. Although," he added hastily, "I'd rather you came back here."

"Yes, well put me in the picture about Ke...." He managed to turn the name into a cough before giving away that he knew it, and continued, "about this chap from Intelligence and John, etc."

Kenneth was no problem, it seemed, and still in the land of the living, but John was expected to land at the farm airstrip in about an hour and a half, depending on head winds.

"Good. With any luck, I might have Ahmed by then. If so, I could get those characters to guard him, too, with that interfering old fool."

"John said that he wanted an 'accident' organised for the Intelligence chap very quickly, so that the time of death would look right for him having wandered off round the farm."

"Must go. There's someone coming!" said Martin, cutting the conversation short following this reminder that any rescue attempt would have to be carried out within the next hour, preferably before the arrival of John.

A series of rapid phone calls established that a helicopter (in preference to a Harrier, the arrival of which might have alarmed his neighbours) would land shortly in Martin's back paddock to collect Gerald's keys. For reasons of later 'deniability', it was agreed by 'Adrian' that Martin and Elizabeth should organise the diversion, enabling two S A S men to drive into a farmyard crowded with unnecessary vehicles, and 'spring' Kenneth from the bunker. There would be time to pick up Henry, his mate and the 'illegals', together with John and company, later. It was essential not to panic Henry – or Gerald if he had managed to get himself accepted by then – into killing Kenneth.

Although well aware of the serious nature of the whole affair, Elizabeth and Martin, one on the regular phone, the other on the 'mobile', quite enjoyed themselves ordering sufficiently expensive quantities of various goods and services to ensure efficient service, all to arrive promptly in one hour's time.

"Here we are! 'Take away food'," said Elizabeth, opening the Yellow Pages. "I could jam the A 15 with these, never mind that narrow Fen road. I'll start with Ali's Kebab House in Bourne, then Eastern Balti in Spalding – they claim 'Local fast free delivery'. By the way who's going to pay for all this?"

"Never mind that. The Intelligence Service should value Kenneth sufficiently to stump up for the odd curry! Rip out that sheet and give me the book. Now, who do I contact to fix that strong smell of gas? Here we are 'For any gas emergency... call free' ... 0800 111 999. That'll save the tax-payers' money!"

Soon taxis, pizzas, the RSPCA ('That reminds me, I must take that dog out!'), the gas, electricity, water emergency services and one or two others, were geared up to descend on

Hall Farm. The keys had been collected and passed to three tough-looking characters, carrying authorised weapons, stun grenades, etc., who were waiting in an anonymous looking van, two hidden in the back, ready to slip into the 'convoy'. One thing was certain: those stuck out in that Fenland backwater, unable to go back on account of the continuing flow of vehicles, would not want for sustenance – or lack the sound of colourful language.

"I'll just gild the lily by telling Henry that I've ordered some take-away food to be delivered, so that the party from H Q can be fed," said Martin. "It might gain a few precious moments if they're expecting something, even if they do think it's a bit odd."

Henry did indeed think it odd, as such a thing had never happened before: indeed no tradesmen called, although suitably agricultural looking vehicles came and went from time to time. He was also surprised to receive a call, about twenty minutes later, from their contact at the River Board, asking what the problem was. It would have been better had Martin not included that organisation in his list of 'emergency call outs', for it had been heavily infiltrated right across the country. Messages began to flow. Henry was instructed to check back with Gerald concerning his unprecedented and out of character decision to invite a delivery of food.

It would also have been better had Martin not (as he had indeed described it) sought to 'gild the lily' by ringing to say that a van was on its way, for on receipt of this, to him strange, message, Henry sent Issed on a 'quad bike' to intercept the delivery at the main road. About twenty minutes later, a little ahead of time, the first of the vans, bearing a Pizza from Crowland, pulled up to consult his map and was approached by Issed.

The 'hit squad', waiting in a handy lay-by, were less than pleased to see an altercation taking place about a mile from the farmyard, as they realised that there was a danger that the crucial element of surprise could be lost. Fortunately, apart from having no money (hence the altercation), Issed did not have a mobile phone, so was unable to let the farm know why he continued to wait, despite the departure of the delivery van.

Paul, as look-out, was concentrating on the delivery van, so he did not see what happened when another van drove up and parked alongside. He reported this to Henry, who was in the bunker waiting for a call from the plane bringing John.

"Keep watching!" he told Paul. "Gavin from the River Board just rang to ask what's up. Apparently Gerald rang them, too."

"O K. Wait....the second van's moving off, now. Yes, so's the first one. I can see the word Pizza on the side. Good, I hope it's got salami.. I ... Issed's getting back on the bike.... Can't see any package. Did you give him any money?"

"No, I did *not*. Gerald can pay. I've only got a tenner. That's his problem. I can't think what the silly sod's doing anyway. What's happening now?"

"Issed's having trouble starting it. I bet he's forgotten to put his foot right down on the clutch, the dozy berk!"

In fact, Issed, minus his anorak, gloves and crash helmet was tied up and terrified in the back of the S A S van. Those same garments now adorned one of the soldiers who knew perfectly well how to start the bike, but was playing for time, well aware that he was likely to be under surveillance from the farm. Accustomed to taking the initiative and adapting rapidly to changing circumstances, the S A S team had established from Martin that he had informed the farm of the impending arrival of a fast food delivery (unspecifically, as it depended on which one got there first). Martin had been suitably contrite, but as it turned out it made it possible for the bogus Issed to stop and talk to each new arrival, in full view of the farm.

"There's another van coming!" Paul informed Henry excitedly on the intercom. "Issed's got off the bike and is stopping it.... and there's a bigger van starting to slow dow....."

"There's something funny going on, Paul. Send Akbor on the other bike to help keep them there. Hell! The pilot's calling from the plane now....."

Henry put down the intercom and cursed as he struggled with the unfamiliar equipment.

"Where the sodding hell are you when you're wanted, Gerald? Hello! Hello! Come in you stupid bastard!"

His frantic fingers sought to make the connection, each time getting the sequence wrong. The intercom buzzed again. "For Christ's sake! I can't get through to the plane! Can you work this gadget, Paul?"

"There's a string of yellow flashing lights now. I think they're all coming here. What do we do? Shall I drop a couple of 'em? They must be...."

"They must be after that bloody man tied up in the brig. I don't know what to....Christ! The plane's circling: I can see it on the monitor. It must be a trap. I ....."

Once again the intercom cut off, leaving Paul gazing appalled as the two quad bikes sped back towards the farm and the plane, which had failed to get an answer to its request for confirmation of clearance for landing, came in on its final approach. The occupants did not notice Paul waving frantically from the top window of the farm, nor did they notice the quad bikes approaching at speed. The pilot, however, did hear from Henry, who managed at last to get the sequence right.

"What the hell are you doing?" cried John as the engine screamed angrily and the small plane levelled off and started to climb. The pilot, however, heard only the panicky screeching of Henry in his ears:

"Don't land! Abort! Abort! For God's Sake don't try to land. There's a....."

But neither the pilot nor John, nor his assistant ever knew what the problem was, for the straining engine failed to gain sufficient lift to clear the tree line at the edge of the airstrip. The landing wheels caught the top of a tree, lowering the nose that all-important fraction, so that, as they climbed from just above the river beyond, a wing caught the highest of the four overhead wires looped between the pylons which stretched northwards for mile after mile back to the main electricity supply plant and south for the industrial and residential needs of Peterborough. The explosion was spectacular and the flash from the stricken plane was the more visible as it coincided with the instant failure of every light in the area.

"Now that's what I call a diversion!" said the leading S A S man, as he skidded to a halt in the farmyard and called out, relying on being mistaken for the Asians, to establish where the opposition was.

It was unfortunate that Paul had been thinking about 'dropping' someone, for as a result he had his rifle raised to upper chest level as he leaned out in response to the call from what he believed to be Issed. He died instantly in a brief burst of silenced fire.

Armed with the knowledge of the approximate position of the strawstack door, Kenneth's rescuers had little difficulty in unlocking it with the aid of the keys provided by Martin. Rapidly donning gas masks, they opened it and hurled in a small but instantly effective gas grenade.

Neither Henry, who was just taking in what he had done, as the lights and monitor screens were extinguished, nor Kenneth, unaware of the whole scene, knew anything of the entry of the gas-masked soldiers. Having now been joined by the third member of their group, the party of six – three standing, three inert over their shoulders – slipped out into the yard. They went unnoticed by the occupants of the various emergency vehicles, taxi-drivers, etc., who had been proceeding in an orderly line towards the farm when they were stopped by the aerial drama and its shocking, mind-numbing result. It came as no great surprise to them, therefore, to see a low-flying olive-painted twin-rotor helicopter suddenly appear (in response to the call from its S A S colleagues on the ground) and hover close to the buildings. They might have been surprised, had they thought about it, by the speed of response, but then the same could have been said for the emergency services who were on the scene 'almost before the plane had ceased to burn' as one impressed reporter later put it.

CHAPTER SEVENTEEN

Apart from the phone call to elicit the fact that Martin had alerted Hall Farm to the imminent arrival of deliverers (in the more literal sense of the word!), he and Elizabeth had had no further contact, so had the same reaction as everyone else to the sudden failure of the electricity – shock and irritation. It did not occur to them that it might be connected to their own recent actions. No electricity, so no T V.....so no evening news bulletin containing brief details of the crash of a light plane, understood to have 'got into trouble' en route to Hull. The telephone, however, was still working, as a result of which Martin was preparing to set off for Stansted Airport (in response to a brief call from Patrick) still unaware of the success – one might almost say 'devastating success' – of the operation.

They had decided that it would be best if Elizabeth stayed, in case her mother rang, and to discover anything the authorities thought fit to tell them about the operation at Hall Farm, especially the well-being of Kenneth.

"Are you going to take the H F C identity card to show him?" she asked. "And what about the tapes of Ahmed?"

"Those tapes need to be kept safe. Put them in the freezer. I seem to remember that being used in some book I read, so that no-one would find them."

"Unless they'd read the same book, of course," said Elizabeth drily. "I'll get the card, then. Is it upstairs?"

"I think I put it in the basket on top of the fridge. Have a look."

"Now that's much safer. No-one can ever find anything there! Is this it – oh, no, that's slimy old Gerald. This is more like it. An international super-spy brilliantly disguised as a doddering old fool, I D number S U B 534. Why did you choose that num....Hey! That must have been why the chap at the Castle reacted to it – S U B...sub-marine! And we know Gerald was keen on U-boats and," she rushed on, pursuing the train of thought, coming perilously close (from the point of view of the 'High Command') to adding two to two and making five, "....and that old boy we think was his father was in U-boats during the war."

"Yes," said Martin, having caught up at last. "I asked Ahmed if he could recall the number on the U-boat in the photograph, but he couldn't. I think he said there was a 5 in it, but....."

"But it doesn't matter!" said Elizabeth impatiently. "We can get these S A S people to go and get the photo!"

"Well, yes, but for all we know they may have blown it up by now."

"Fusing the lights the while?" said Elizabeth facetiously, and then stopped short. "Actually that... Oh no, it was just a coincidence – I hope! To change, or rather revert to, the subject, why *did* you choose that number?"

"I just altered Gerald's. His was S U E 5 8 4, and it was easy to alter them by erasing or inking in parts of letters. It might be interesting to find out about U-534, I suppose..... if it existed. I must get going, though, or I shall get into trouble for being late."

"Yes. Given the sort of people Patrick seems to be able to conjure up, he'd probably have you shot for dereliction of duty. Leave the research to me – reading history at Magdalen may not have fitted me for much, but for that, I think I can say it did."

After her father had gone, having left instructions concerning the dog and a request to give his love to her mother when she rang, Elizabeth gave some thought to the nature of the conspiracy, or if not that, criminal organisation, which her father had stumbled upon. How widespread was it? Clearly Gerald looked elsewhere for instructions – and had contacts at the Castle and among the police. There was a branch in Harwich; the men who were dropped off by the furniture van came from somewhere, possibly from wherever the telephone code served; a helicopter was available from a nearby base at very short notice, and there seemed to be several H F C vans around; surveillance systems and loaded rifles implied that they had plenty to hide. Was their secret the traffic in illegal immigrants, or were they just one aspect of profitable business engaged in by..... by what, or whom? Perhaps Patrick could throw more light on it – could and would? Would he have pulled those strings in order to bring to justice minor criminals? Well, perhaps, to protect their father, who was clearly way out of his depth, even if the old devil seemed to be coping quite well, and was far from being intimidated. Indeed, it would be better if he *were* more frightened, she thought, hoping that the Hall Farm lot would never find out who had pretended to be Gerald and created the spurious 'stinging nettle' password.

"Now," mused Elizabeth, "who do I know who's a walking authority on U-boats?"

Martin set off for Yaxley to join the A 1 with a spring in his step. He always enjoyed the hassle-free experience of meeting his son at Stansted. It was an easy drive on the recently improved A 1, followed by the A 14 and then that least used of motorways, reminiscent of the best French autoroutes, the M 11. As the sign to Duxford came up, he was reminded of his wait on the bridge when he tracked the H F C van to Harwich. It was only a few days ago, but so much had happened it seemed quite a long time. What, he wondered, drew them to Harwich? Probably to arrange to process more unfortunates like Ahmed – those who survived that far. And what was *he* doing now? Had he managed to get a foot on the ladder – or had he landed on a 'snake'? He would have enjoyed hearing about Gerald, tied up by his own side! Martin continued to run over recent events and speculate about the success or otherwise of his diversionary tactics, until he saw the turn off for the Airport and concentrated on getting into the correct lane, to proceed, still unpressured by traffic (what a contrast with Heath Row!) to the car parks set aside for arrivals. He had a good hour to wait, as the flight from Prague was slightly delayed, so he rang Elizabeth to let her know he had arrived and see if there was any news. The modern, spotlessly clean, uncrowded concourse had a calming effect, so he was brought up short by his daughter's excited greeting.

"It's all happening here!" she began, somewhat to his alarm. "Did you hear the news on the way down?"

"No – I....."

"You didn't? The plane crashed, killing all on board – that's why we've still got no electricity. Julian rang to say that....."

"Julian? Who the Hell is Julian?"

"Oh, you know who I mean! Adrian! Anyway he rang to say 'mission accomplished', but I've no other details. Except one: he said the S A S asked to have a special word of thanks passed on to whoever had organised the diversion. Apparently it went like a dream – or a nightmare, depending on whose side you were on!"

"So Kenneth's all right? What about Gerald and his mates?"

"No details. All too secret, it seems, but he must be O K if 'mission' was accomplished. Anyway, well done us, eh? Tell that fat slob of a son of yours that with time and good leadership, his men could have a lot to offer!"

Martin found it difficult to take in the latest events, and could not imagine how or why a plane, presumably the one bringing the Area Commander, had crashed. However, there was more to come from Elizabeth:

"Also," she continued, "I've been busy on the U-boat front. I rang a friend in Sussex – more on that in a moment – who is an authority on such matters. Apparently one can walk round the old 534, if one is so inclined!"

She paused for both effect and breath.

"Walk round it?" The response was satisfyingly astonished.

"Yes. It's at the National Maritime museum at Birkenhead, having been raised from where it was sunk in 1945. It was thought to have important Nazi relics, gold, etc., as well as top party officials. They were all trying to escape from the Baltic, or Kiel, or somewhere at that time, but this one didn't make it."

"Didn't make it? Were there any survivors?"

"Yes. They nearly all survived, it seems..... and the official line is that there was nothing superspecial in the wreck when they brought it up. Mind you, if you believe that, you'd believe anything! I'm going up there to have a look."

They exchanged a few more words on the subject and then Elizabeth returned to a remark she had made earlier.

"There's one other thing, which might interest Patrick, if he doesn't know it already. You know I rang that friend?"

"Yes, the authority on....."

"Yes, Gareth. Well, he lives in Haslemere....and the code for Haslemere is 01428 !"

"Ye-es," said her father, wondering whether he was being particularly thick.

"Don't you remember? That was the code on the furniture van which brought the reinforcements! So it was probably the Haslemere Furniture Company – which is H F C!"

"Well, yes, but there is such a thing as coincidence, and you can't be sure it was called that."

"And is it just coincidence that Hall Farm is H F – probably followed by C for Company?"

"'Cultivation', in fact, if I recall the sign correctly," said Martin, "presumably to go with the mushroom beds over at Thorpe Tunnel. You could have a point, but not all H F C's can be bent."

"Maybe not, but they're suspect. What about these from the Yellow Pages? Holbeach Floor Covering; Hacconby Farming Company; Health Food Centre – that's Boston; Hereward Freight Company; Huntingdon Football Club....."

"Come off it. Every town beginning with 'H' that has a Football Club can't be helping to smuggle immigrants in order to balance the books! I'll pass on the tip, though. I suppose it would be convenient for vehicles to move from one area to another without exciting interest....like a Hull or Harwich Fishing Co. lorry going to Hall Farm. It'd be taken to be a local one at each place. Anyway, I must go. Take care!"

Martin replaced the receiver and, before setting off in search of a cup of coffee, sat down to ponder this latest intelligence.

He wondered whether the S A S had shot the plane down with a hand-held ground to air missile, but it seemed a bit strong and might have been seen by all the 'visitors' – always assuming they had arrived. Presumably they had, as the diversion was said to have been very effective. He had been a bit concerned when they had rung to ask whether he had told the farm. It had sounded as though something was amiss. Then there was the U-534: no wonder the young man at the Castle had asked respectfully if he was on it, when he saw the I D number. Mind you, one would have to have been well over 70 – the Germans were dragging in very young men by the end, but not, as far as he knew, under 5! The recruiting age was getting down to primary school level in some of these African countries these days, mind you..... and it was all too literally true that modern weapons were so light and easy to use that a child could master them. There was something else that the chap at the Castle had said. What was it? Something which related to the submarine – although he hadn't known about it, so the comments went above his head at the time. Probably didn't matter, anyway. Back to the present; time to go to the arrivals area.

"Might even," thought Martin, setting his wristwatch alarm, so as not to appear too geriatric by being still asleep when his son arrived, "doze off for a few minutes...." And he did, allowing his adrenalin-laden, overloaded system to calm down.

He was woken half an hour later by the insistent bleeping at his wrist, a bit stiff in the neck and feeling in need of a thirst-quenching drink, but otherwise far better able to face the world. The drink and a 'wash and brush up' would have to wait, however, as the Prague plane was down and the passengers would shortly be clearing customs. Eagerly, he scanned the arrivals, remembering the many times over the years that he had sat in the same spot, welcoming one of his children, or a foreign exchange student (most of whom seemed to exhibit an almost total unwillingness to communicate in any language, particularly English). In due course Patrick strode round the corner, instantly recognisable by the confident, almost loping walk, although the clothes marked him as 'Euro-man', along with the hair-cut.

To Martin's faint surprise, he waved from a distance and smiled, calling out 'Hi! Dad' from a short way away and putting down the shouldered bag in order to shake his hand. Having expected the usual British reserve and comparative difficulty in getting his son to communicate general gossip and small talk, Martin found himself surprised, given recent events, at the banality of their conversation. This was explained in the midst of what could only be described as a welcome, almost conventional, interest in the welfare of his mother, sister – and even the dog. Seeing the look of puzzlement on his father's face, Patrick continued the

113

catechism, but inserted an instruction to act normally, and not let this look like anything other than a holiday visit. Martin realised then that he was a form of cover for his son, who presumably thought they might be watched, or overheard.

"And don't look round!" added Patrick out of the side of his mouth. "We'll talk in the car....So, how are things? Still enjoying retirement – getting some of the decorating done?"

"Oh – er – yes, thanks. I've been using my new PaintMate: it's really good on ceilings. I've nearly finished the dining room and....."

"That sounds par for the course – nearly finished. You haven't lost your touch, then – nothing like nearly completing something!"

"I'll nearly finish you in a minute!" said his father, joining in with what he feared sounded like false laughter, but hoped was good enough to convince 'them', wherever they were.

In fact, he need not have bothered as the two shared sufficient features and mannerisms for there to be any doubt as to the meeting being genuinely father and son, as opposed to an occasion for 'clandestine business'. The hidden watcher contented himself with a quick photograph and then lost interest.

Still uncharacteristically discussing the merits of PaintMates and paper-hanging, they proceeded towards the parking ticket machine (without, to Martin's regret, having stopped for any form of refreshment) and joined the numerous people making their way to their cars. Martin had for years found it difficult to keep pace with his son (mentally as well as physically) but he found himself tending to move ahead as they emerged from the lower level.

"It's over there," he said, leading the way.

"Don't rush, Dad. I don't want to catch up those two ahead. Just take it steady."

"Are they spies?" whispered Martin, thinking it safe to refer, at least obliquely, to recent events which had presumably resulted in his son deciding to return to sort things out.

"Good Lord, no. The Honourable Anthony Laurence Burton-Latimer would be most insulted to be taken for a spy! He's just obnoxious, filthy rich, spent four years patronising those who were not from the top rank schools when we were at Cambridge – and less than happy when I got a First and he didn't!"

"What does he do, now?"

But Martin's question remained unanswered, as the object of their discussion turned, caught sight of Patrick and came towards them with a beaming smile of recognition.

"Paddy, you old devil! How's the world treating you? Still raking in the royalties on those poems?"

Patrick replied civilly and explained that he was taking a short holiday at home.

"I thought life was one long holiday for you – academic Poland can't have the stress endured by those of us who toil in the old 'Mille Carrée' – or have you moved into other fields these days?"

Was it his imagination, or was there a slight edge to that last question, wondered Martin, as he allowed his hand to be grasped in a probing, but unrequited, Masonic handshake, and debated whether to ask if the pompous twit of a merchant banker worked in Takeaway Catering. ('Meal Carry' indeed! – or perhaps it was a 'caff' called the 'Square Mille', he continued silently to invent whilst exchanging conventional banalities).

"And are you a Cambridge academic, too, Sir?"

"No, L S E actually," he found himself replying. "I've recently retired – from teaching."

As Martin imagined, both the first reply, and certainly the second, were sufficient for him to be dismissed as of no further interest to Burton-Latimer, who parted from them in a haze of easily resistible charm and expressions of the desirability of the two young men 'getting together some time'.

"I see what you mean!" said Martin as they smilingly waved farewell and Monty (as he reprovingly reminded Patrick that he was known to his friends) rejoined his companion who was obviously the chauffeur. "I was tempted to ask him if he was related to Joyce Grenfell's 'Lumpy Latimer', just to see his face! And as for the 'Square Meal': I ask you!"

"I could almost feel the mutual disdain!" said Patrick. "But he's big in the City – or so he would have us believe."

As they were leaving at the same time, it was not surprising that they found themselves a few minutes later side by side at the traffic lights which controlled the big roundabout at the junction with the M 11. Glancing across to his left, Martin was reminded of his daughter's suspicions.

"If Elizabeth were here," said Martin, "we'd be following your aristocratic chum! He's travelling in a suspect vehicle!"

"A Renault Espace? Isn't that carrying francophobia a bit far?"

"No, the name on it – Harlow Ferry Cars....H F C! She has this theory that the reinforcements were probably dropped off by the Haslemere Furniture Company – and Hall Farm is really Hall Farm Cultivation and....." Martin continued his explanation as they moved round to the next set of traffic lights.

"Can you pull over for the Services, do you think? I could do with a coffee and there's nothing on the M 11."

"So could I. I thought you were in a hurry to get to – to wherever you want to go. Is it home, by the way? Oh God, these South East drivers. Can't the bloody fool see I want to get across?"

Patrick laughed, to the surprise of the driver of the articulated lorry, whose face was suffused with incipient road rage caused by his encounter with the bucolic 'Sunday driver' who had got into the wrong lane.

"You haven't changed, I see! Just go on round again – it was my fault. I should've told you sooner. I ought to make a phone call and you haven't got the mobile."

"Me, too. I'd better ring Elizabeth. When shall I tell her to expect us?"

"I'll let you know after those calls. I might want to stop off in Cambridge – but not for long. You sit over there, Dad. I'll join you in a few minutes."

CHAPTER EIGHTEEN

In fact, Patrick was nearer twenty minutes and returned with a wry smile on his face.

"I've been brought up to date on certain of your recent activities," he said, having first made sure that no-one could overhear them. "As your son, I am appalled, but in my – er – other capacity, I should like to congratulate you...and ask for your further assistance."

He paused and then added:

"Before we go any further, we should like you to sign the Official Secrets Act, to which end I have arranged for a brief meeting at my College with an appropriate person. Is that all right?"

There was no doubt in Martin's mind that it was not as a parent he was being addressed, that he had little option but to co-operate and, even after the forthcoming ceremony, would only be told as much as it was good for him to know. Facing him was not only a formidable intelligence, but also a steely resolve and – yes, that was it – the habit of command.

"Well, yes, of course; whatever. Are you going to pin a deputy's badge on Elizabeth, as well? She's au fait with everything, and has a much better memory than me."

"Don't worry about that, Dad. It's not a problem. Now let's....."

"You mean she's already signed it, don't you? Bloody Hell, I've been living in a nest of spies all these years and never....."

A dreadful thought occurred to him:

"Don't tell me your mother is at this very moment inserting a hatpin at the base of some Third World dictator's spine?"

"Far more likely to be undermining our own government's attempts to achieve a favourable Balance of Payments, if I know Mother...and I haven't said that any of us is a 'spy' as you so indelicately put it...any more...." he stifled his father's objection, "any more than *you* would be if you were to do your civic duty by continuing to help to investigate what could well be an aspect of neo-Nazism." ·

117

Put like that, there was little more to be said, so, at the latter's suggestion, Martin handed the keys to his son and settled back to get another half hour's recuperative slumber on the journey to Fitzwilliam College. He came to in time to marvel, as he still did each time he saw them, at the mediaeval splendour of the colleges as seen from 'The Backs'.

"Lifts the old spirit, doesn't it?" grinned Patrick, noticing that his elderly parent had surfaced.

As they drove along, he had glanced across from time to time at the nodding head, the hair even thinner – and certainly greyer – than he had remembered it and silently wondered how the Hell the old boy had managed to outwit such a murderous scheming bunch.

"The Backs? Yes, it sure does. When I'm here, I can't imagine how people can rave about Oxford....until I go there again!"

"Oh, Oxford certainly has something," said Patrick turning into the car park at the front of Fitzwilliam, "but not as much as Cambridge!"

"Don't let Elizabeth hear you say that!"

"The poor, deluded soul. Right. Now leave this to me. The College has put my usual room at our disposal, so I'll leave you to wait a few minutes in the Porters Lodge while I brief these people. Then someone'll come and get you, to be 'sworn in'. That O K by you?"

"I'll give Elizabeth a quick ring; I forgot to do so at the 'Services'. Then I'll wait in the chapel. I shall feel a bit less 'spare' than standing around, looking like everyone's grandfather. Shall I say we'll be there in – what? Two hours?"

"Make it two and a half, then she won't worry if we're a few minutes late."

About ten minutes later, Martin was collected, warned about the significance of his actions in signing the Act, and was then, at last, ready to engage in an in-depth discussion, which was really a form of interrogation, interlarded with some explanations and many more references which went over his head, as the little group hammered out the way forward.

"To keep our options open," said Patrick, "I gave instructions that the guy who was in the bunker – the one who told the pilot not to land – was not to be allowed to regain consciousness for the time being. He was in an inner room, so never saw the S A S open the main door. He was suddenly rendered unconscious by the gas grenade, so we can feed him any story we like, bring him round where we like.....or," he nodded at his more 'hawkish' colleague, "we could stop him coming round at all."

"Surely he's not high enough up in the Organisation to lead us to anyone. We already know his boss: he's trussed up, oven-ready, in this Tunnel place. He'd've been taken out if he'd offered any armed resistance, so ....."

Martin tried to keep all expression off his face as they debated the fate of the wretched man, for in his capacity as the spurious Gerald, he had come to regard Henry almost as a colleague – a bit simple, unable to cope when things got difficult, but surely not so evil that he had to be exterminated. However, Martin knew it was not he who was going to be taking that decision: he waited in silence.

"I agree he's of no great consequence (although doubtless his mother loves him), but you're quite right, Bernard, to home in on the one who really matters – Gerald, who's suffered the indignity of being captured by his own side."

Martin recognised the technique of making the person whom you intend to persuade believe that he it was who had thought of it first!

"Haven't they worked that out yet? They only had to get the farm to ring the relevant mobile number, then, when the one at Thorpe Tunnel rang, it would be obvious who was the real Gerald and who was the impostor."

"I have been advised," replied Patrick," that when they entered the Tunnel bunker, using Gerald's own keys, of course, they found him still tied up, next to his inoperative mobile phone, which must have got broken at some point. There were no signs of the famous reinforcements, who must have just abandoned him to his fate. I gave instructions that he was to be told nothing and kept there until we decided how to deal with him."

"I think he should get a taste of his own medicine. Drop him down a handy well: he was quite happy to see Kenneth go that way!"

119

Once again the 'hawkish' approach was advocated by Bernard, and once again the voice of reason, or perhaps it should be called 'guile', raised the intellectual level – not that that was difficult, in Martin's view, with Bernard around.

"No, we'll stick to your original idea, Bernard, and use Gerald. He could be very valuable alive and working for us."

"Out of gratitude? He'd be too frightened of the Organisation to stick to any bargain he made with us and if they just left him there, they can't regard him as too much of a security risk. Presumably he doesn't know anything really worthwhile, but I agree he should be kept for us to sweat out of him what he *does* know."

The last few words caused Martin's scalp to tingle at the thought of being 'sweated' by Bernard, whose ancestors probably worked over Guy Fawkes in order to unmask the other plotters.

"I haven't crossed all the 'T's' yet," said Patrick, ignoring Bernard's failure to realise that – from *their* point of view – it was not Gerald who had been left by the 'reinforcers', "but I think we can persuade Gerald to work for *us*. I think we can ensure that, from his friends' point of view, he comes out of this smelling of roses."

"But the man is an absolute liability!" expostulated Martin, unable, despite his earlier resolution, to keep quiet. "He was conned into effectively deserting his post, failed to keep in touch, left his incompetent assistant to carry the can, as a result of which the regional boss, or whatever he was, has been written off! He smells more like the stuff you put *on* roses: they'll crucify him!"

"I'm glad to see that *someone* in the family can see the main picture," said Bernard. "Welcome aboard!"

Martin was struck with an instant feeling of contrition at having let down his son, and disgust at finding himself lining up with the bloodthirsty and, to put it mildly, unsubtle Bernard.

"I only meant..... "

"And you were quite right, Martin" said Patrick, using his father's given name for, as far as the latter could recall, the very first time.

He carried on, mildly amused by the look of surprise, which owed as much to the 'Martin' as to the endorsement of his father's expression of dissent. "That is our lever – his fear of his present bosses finding out what really happened. Our other lever is his love of his fellow man, or, as the Greeks might have put it, homophilia. Again, he won't wish his superiors to be made aware that the plane crashed because he was trying to entice young Ahmed to the Tunnel for his own sexual gratification."

Patrick paused while his slower-witted audience took in the beauty of the scheme.

"It could be said," said Martin, relieved that his outburst had been turned to advantage, "that you have him by the short and curlies!"

"Yes, it might work," said Bernard grudgingly, "but only if you could produce any real evidence."

"But we can, Bernard, and we can persuade Gerald to provide us with some more, too. No.....," Patrick hurried on, as he saw a gleam in his colleague's eye, "not by wiring him up to the light, but by getting him to enunciate certain appropriate phrases, out of context, and then getting our tame Ahmed impersonator, or rather impersonatrix, to provide suitably incriminating questions. The technical boys should be able to construct something which would ensure an instant death sentence for Gerald."

"No court of law would convict him on that sort of evidence," said Bernard authoritatively, drawing on his knowledge of police procedure. "You'll have to do better than that!"

Even Martin, however, could see the obvious, but it was the fourth member, Ralph, who spoke, almost for the first time.

"It's not the courts who would have to be convinced, but the neo-Nazi High Command, and they won't be quibbling about the 'burden of proof'. Not only that, we only have to convince Gerald. Providing he thinks his colleagues would believe the tape, he'll work for us. Yes, it's brilliant. Let's get to work crossing those 'T's'!"

'T'-crossing revolved around the construction of a scenario which would explain the destruction of the plane, the escape of Kenneth (without Henry being aware of it) and the death of

Paul, whilst preserving, or rather enhancing, the reputation of Gerald. At this point, Ralph took over and quickly set in motion the brainstorming session.

"First of all, some easy bits. The immigrants must have taken fright and disappeared, followed by Paul, who has to be the person who fouled up."

"Yes. He must have rushed into the bunker, knocked out Henry (who therefore remembers nothing and is a bit confused), given dud instructions to the pilot and then......"

"..... fled, realising he would have to answer with his life for killing the occupants of the plane."

"The only trouble is that Henry wasn't hit; he was gassed," objected Bernard.

"If we decide on that story," replied Ralph, "we make sure he gets a hefty clout before we bring him round: if it genuinely causes concussion, so much the better. Now, what about Kenneth? Did Paul let him out – or overpower him when he burst in to finish him off?"

"One of the Asians could have freed him – before running away, that is," suggested Martin, tentatively.

"Possibly," said Ralph encouragingly. "Keep the ideas coming: any other suggestions?"

"We must remember," said Patrick thoughtfully, "that Gerald himself does not necessarily have to have been jumped by the reinforcements: that could have been (as the two who locked him up thought) the person impersonating him. Bear in mind that Henry thinks he was talking to the real Gerald most of the time. That could be useful in developing a story which puts Gerald in a good light and is backed up by Henry."

Martin made the occasional contribution, but most of the time he struggled to keep up as Ralph and Patrick rewrote history, searching for a way to divert any blame from Gerald, whilst ensuring that Henry, if questioned by Gerald's superiors, would confirm the tale.

"Henry would never stand up to a professional interrogation," said Patrick, "so we have to make sure that he believes the tale which Gerald will spin him – and feels indebted to him, loyal to him, flattered when asked by Gerald to be his personal assistant in his new job."

"What new job? He'll be lucky to keep the old, never mind a new one," exclaimed Bernard, dead on cue.

"I think," said Ralph slowly, "that Patrick is ambitious for our new friend – wants to see him get on in life. Am I right?"

"We said earlier that we wanted him 'covered in roses'," said Patrick mildly. "We can't predict the course of his career, but we can do our best to get him trusted – even twist things so that the recently deceased Regional Controller is seen as trying to take over Gerald's operation and, in the process, causing a monumental balls-up."

"Including his own death," said Martin. "Talk about poetic justice!"

"If the story is that the real Gerald was riding to the rescue, who are they to think is (as far as they know) still tied up in Thorpe Tunnel? And who do they think that *we* think he is?"

The discussion continued too rapidly for Martin, who was still trying to get his mind round the implications of Ralph's questions when he became aware that all three were looking at him.

"Sorry! I was just trying to work that last bit out. Did I miss something?"

"Yes!" said Bernard nastily. "Your death!"

Martin stared at the grim-faced trio in astonishment (mixed with some alarm and the beginnings of anger)."My what! Come off it. I've managed to stay out of their way – and in any case...."

"Don't worry about it, Dad," laughed Patrick. "We'll find a stand-in on the night. The point is that Gerald can report to his superiors that, on opening up the mushroom farm, he discovered someone tied up – and then acted decisively to get rid of the evidence."

"But surely I – that is, this person – would be missed. There'd be relatives. Some explanation of why he he'd been watching the farm would be needed."

"It is never," said Ralph, "difficult to convince someone who *wishes* to be convinced. They thought all along that they were dealing with an amateur, someone who just happened to be nosy, was working on his own, but, by sheer luck – his own bad luck, it will now appear – started to peel back too many layers of the onion."

Ralph continued to develop the scenario. The man knew too much to be allowed to live and, under Gerald's skilful questioning, gave away the fact that he had told no-one what he was up to. His only relative was his sister, who lived in Canada, and his neighbours in a large faceless estate in Peterborough thought he went off bird-watching (as, indeed, had been his habit until he started taking an interest in Hall Farm). He had (Gerald would report) grown quite animated when he explained how he had followed the H F C van all the way to Harwich, where he had lost it. Gerald would be able to add, with the superior smile of one of the Gods, that the brief excitement afforded to the poor old bugger probably made up for the curtailment of his existence, which was unlikely even to be noticed until Christmas, when he was in the habit of making his annual telephone call to Canada.

As he drove steadily home from Cambridge, Martin ruminated on the disturbing similarities between the fictional 'busy-body' and himself, the real life one, whose neighbours also thought he went dog-walking (and bird-watching) and whose boring life had likewise been injected with excitement. He, too, could have had 'bad luck', been caught by Gerald and quietly disposed of. He shuddered and glanced across for reassurance at his son, who lay back, eyes closed, running through a series of ingenious scenarios to explain how Gerald, the resourceful, dynamic master planner, had reacted to finding Kenneth locked up at the farm. Had he already been released by the bungling Paul? Had he still got him locked up, planning to claim to the police when they came looking for him, that he must have wandered off and fallen down that well? Behind the closed eyelids, the formidable brain created and rejected, wove webs and summoned legends with which to confuse his opponents, only too aware that the passage of time would very soon start closing off options.

CHAPTER NINETEEN

An emergency meeting of the High Command had been arranged to take place two days later: it was going to be a sombre one. Their number had been reduced by two, the first by natural causes, the second in an unexplained plane crash on a routine flight to one of their outlying units somewhere in the Fens. Moreover, they knew no more than could be gathered from news reports, in addition to a comment from a police sympathiser (unconfirmed) that a member of the Intelligence Service had visited the farm just before the crash. They knew, too, that John had arranged for a van-load of reinforcements to travel north, only to be recalled, having achieved little, as soon as the nature of the disaster had been discovered. Word had also been sent to Vienna, who had already arranged to send a man to check on certain rumours concerning the British section.

The information had been passed to the unit on Mersea Island, near Colchester which, like so many others, used as its hidden base one of the government underground bunkers, known only to a very select few since the early nineteen-forties. Those few had been approached to form the core of the 'resistance movement', set up to carry on the fight after the expected German invasion. This particular outpost consisted of a large garage, built ostensibly to house a single-decker service bus for what became the Eastern National. Although quite large, its size was more than tripled by the extensive underground chambers, reached from a hidden trap door in what appeared to be an inspection pit. Ownership of this building had passed to the River Board in the sixties and the secret of its hidden accommodation had been passed from father to son. It was, perhaps, paradoxical that the present guardians of that secret, just like their equivalent in the Fens, and throughout much of the land, now owed allegiance to a structure dedicated to the re-emergence of that same German National Socialist organisation it had originally been designed to combat. Hitler, of course, and his senior colleagues, would not have seen anything odd about this, for all along they had cherished hopes of an accommodation with the U K. Right up to the end, with Russian armies within striking distance, they continued to hope that the British would realise that the real enemy of Europe lay to the east, that they would abandon the foolish pact with Stalin and help to drive them back. The common enemy was Communism, and there were those who sympathised among the British aristocracy, including, many thought, not only the recently dispossessed monarch, but also those who had been entrusted by a gullible government with the task of setting up, and commanding, the embryonic resistance movement. Who could be less suspect of being in command of a bunch of poachers than the landowners who were their traditional enemy?

By the nineties, of course, many such subterranean complexes, having been first decommissioned then re-arranged as (still secret) local seats of government in the case of a Russian nuclear attack, had been sold off to a 'suitable' bidder. One such was Thorpe Tunnel, owned quite openly by Hall Farm Cultivators. Others, like Hall Farm itself – and the old bus garage at East Mersea – remained secret, and actively engaged in the long-term service of those who still schemed to bring about one Europe under the leadership of a strong, re-united right wing Germany.

It was to this area that Vienna's man 'Larry' (Monty to his friends) was driven, after his encounter with Patrick and his elderly uninspiring father. He, too, like Patrick, had sat back in silence, running over in his mind the events which had caused him to return hurriedly to England. There had been some faint suggestion that Patrick Brady was not quite what he seemed and had it not been for the obviously genuine nature of the father/son meeting, Monty would have been extremely suspicious. He had, in fact, arranged for a photograph to be taken of the person who met him – although in the event that had been a waste of effort. He had long been aware that Patrick engaged in the odd bit of low level intelligence work for H M G, under cover of his (very genuine) academic pursuits. Monty, himself, did likewise, gaining useful contacts thereby, but there had been disturbing reports coming to him that someone, somewhere, was getting together a task force to

126

investigate aspects of the neo-Nazi Movement which could result in them being panicked into unwise action.

The H F C car swept on towards Colchester, where it turned off onto the B 1025 to Mersea Island. As so frequently happened – twice a day in practice, depending on the height of the tides – they were brought to a halt at the Strood, where a line of vehicles waited for the flood tide to subside and render the Island accessible. An impatient man by nature, Monty looked up in annoyance as the car slowed, but was reassured to some extent when his driver pointed to a man moving towards them from a River Board Landrover which was parked on the other side of the road.

"Good! They may have a message for me: I'll stroll along and have a word as if I'm asking about the tides."

Remembering to point occasionally at the causeway and the marshland surrounding it, the two men spoke for rather longer than was required to establish whether the tide was still coming in, for there was indeed a message, bringing news of recent happenings. 'Monty' Burton-Latimer returned slowly to his car and sank into the back seat, plainly a worried man. He was shocked to hear of the death of John, one of the most able members of the Council in his opinion, and worried by the escalation of interest in Hall Farm from that evinced by an elderly busy-body to the involvement, however tentative, of the Intelligence Service. Could there be someone pulling strings in the background – or were these strands unconnected? Of more immediate importance, what should be done to ensure that the secrets of Hall Farm be kept, despite the presence of police, crash investigators, reporters and even T V cameras?

The sea water having now receded from the roadway, it was possible to continue the journey, ostensibly to the motor cruiser 'Python', which Monty kept moored in a channel just off East Mersea, for his local cover was that of a wealthy 'winter sailor' (as those who seldom ventured forth were disparagingly known to the natives). In his absence, an eye was kept on the boat by a firm from West Mersea which was home to hundreds of such vessels. It would not have amazed Elizabeth that the firm was called 'Henry Farley Chandlers' and made use of vehicles bearing the letters H F C.

As soon as he had rowed across to the well appointed craft, Monty set about communicating with a number of influential members of the Movement, using his link to the powerful transmitter set in the 'Garage Bunker', a few hundred metres away on dry land. However, no-one either knew exactly what had happened, or had much idea of how to proceed, apart from hoping to hear from the local unit commander, always assuming that person (name of Gerald, apparently) was still both alive and at large.

"What's this chap like, Malcolm? Is he up to dealing with a situation like this?"

"Well, I don't think John was very impressed: he wasn't in favour of his replacing Andreas when Edwin proposed him. In fact, he was on his way to take over as things seemed to be getting out of control."

"A bit early to be organising a replacement wasn't it? The old chap was barely cold!"

"Yes it was, Larry, but I think Edwin had been asked to put him up, as a favour to an old friend, handing down, father to son, you know!"

"Oh! He's the son, is he? Well, well. Now's his chance to show what he's worth – if he's in a position to do so, that is. I have one or two connections in the area; might make a social call and contrive to meet this chap. We can afford to write off that set-up. The important thing is to make sure no-one gets wind of the Harwich operation."

"John wasn't too worried about that, but there was some report about one of our vans being followed. They suspected the same chap they saw checking on the farm with binoculars – very amateurish, just nosy."

"When was that?" asked Monty, far from totally reassured.

"About a week ago, I think. One of their immigrants went walk-about around the same time."

"Any connection?"

"No. No question of that, but as far as I know they hadn't found either of them by the time of the plane crash."

"Which, again, had no connection, I presume?" asked Monty whose inclination was never to rely on coincidences being quite what they seemed.

"Well, hardly old boy! Bird-watching snoopers and stateless lads living rough are unlikely to be operating ground-to-air missiles. This Intelligence chappie *might* have put a spanner in the works, but it would be a bit, shall we say, unsubtle and more likely to *stop* them finding things out than ......"

"There's no question of our own people having caused the crash, I suppose?" asked Monty. "To do just that – stop H M G from finding out what we're about. Was the agent killed at the same time?"

"You're always looking for conspiracies! Planes *do* crash from time to time – and I shouldn't let your opinion of the leadership be too widely known, or we might be reading *your* obituary!"

"Which is another way of saying that you agree with their, or rather, *our* capacity for ruthless action when needed!" replied Monty. "I may be various things, but naïve I am not, nor squeamish. Such action might, for all I know, have been entirely appropriate. I shall therefore be just as suspicious as the opposition if it transpires that their man conveniently perished before he could make a report. We desperately need more information."

Having not yet worked out just what he was up against, 'Monty' Burton-Latimer failed to appreciate that what he did not need (but was likely to acquire) was a large portion of disinformation. He was not, however, one to let the grass grow under his feet, so made further phone calls to arrange his transportation to and accommodation at Wothorpe Castle. The current owner, like his immediate predecessor, enjoyed a substantial subsidy from the proceeds of the neo-Nazi Movement for doing little more than provide a respectable front and condone various dubious, not to say downright illegal, activities. This both ensured his current high standard of living and promised a position of power, wealth and influence when the long-planned unification of Europe took place – not under a weak, vacillating democracy, but under firm, efficient leadership, patriotic in the real sense, able to move on the world stage with the confidence of the Germany of 1940.

In the mean time, to keep the great ideal alive, money was needed, to buy continued loyalty as son took on the torch from father, especially as those who took over became distanced from their forebears by time. They were held together by the secret they shared rather than by blind obedience to a 'führer', or by pseudo-religious concepts which sought to continue the fight pursued by the 'chivalrous' in the mediaeval Crusades, against the race deemed to have put to death the Son of God. They had become, of course, little more than a secret society, akin to the Mafia, or the Triads, seeking to benefit themselves by the age-old methods of theft, intimidation, blackmail and assassination. The anti-gun lobby had their full support; they championed those who suffered from the freedom of the press; they looked with approval at the reduction of local democratic influence in favour of powerful regional assemblies; they looked forward to the minor twist which would be needed to make the National Curriculum an effective means of child indoctrination. All that was needed was 'enlightened' leadership, the emergence from the shadows of those who had grown from the seed sown so effectively in the very last days of the Second World War. That seed had been carried under water and nurtured by the many who sympathised with the Great European Ideal, which had foundered against the unholy alliance of the then leadership of America and Russia – two of the small group of bullies in the world playground.

Thus thought the likes of Monty, John (whose light had gone out when his plane struck the Fenland pylon), the current Lord Wothorpe, and others on whom Patrick was engaged in foisting the corrupted (in more than one sense) Gerald. The latter was incapable of appreciating anything other than his own personal situation, caring little for ideals, whether 'Great', 'European' or related to ethnic cleansing, but was none the less dangerous when wielding a gun. He would not be the first member of a ruling group, if he could become accepted, who lacked the intellectual powers required for efficient discharge of his duties, however. History could show many examples of the lunatics being given the keys to the asylum.....and some examples of those lunatics being ultimately controlled, for a few years, by a woman or man who was, in all senses of the word, 'rational'.

As he sped westwards from Colchester towards the M 11, Monty came to feel that his short term aim was to meet this Gerald and form a view concerning his competence. Someone had to take over from John, but on the face of it, this fellow's experience was very limited, even if he was the son of one of the 'founding fathers'. His present command was little more than a muddy outpost, boasting a permanent staff of what? Three plus a few 'illegals'? On the other hand, he was acquainted with the set-up at the Castle, well to the north of the region, and regularly visited the all-important operation at Harwich. He was in a position to call up helicopter support – although one wondered whether he had botched that manoeuvre, just as one wondered to what extent, if at all, he was personally responsible for John's plane crash. Had he managed to do anything about the visitor to the farm, whom their police sympathisers had identified as an Intelligence agent? Which reminded Monty: a bonus payment should be made in that direction, to ensure continued loyalty to the cause.

Subject to his being unexpectedly impressed by Gerald as a result of meeting and talking with him, Monty thought it would be better to appoint Roger, John's deputy, to command the Eastern Area. There was, however, no reason to raise him to the High Command, a post for which he, Monty, was far better fitted, although it would increase the risk of his being rumbled, and, in any case, he had his eye on even higher things. No, on the whole he preferred to manipulate the Council members, be the puppet master, so to speak, maintaining his ability to move in diverse circles, including the Security Service itself, at present only at the lower levels.

At Wothorpe Castle, Monty was greeted by the butler, shown to his room and told that, as requested, an office had been put at his disposal. The Agent for the Estate, Philip Proudfoot ('Another possible contender for preferment within the movement,' mused Monty), was away, as was His Lordship. The latter was in fact a distant cousin who, whilst being his host and the ostensible reason for the visit, did not get directly involved. He was not expected, thought Monty wryly, to 'dirty his hands' in the day-to-day business of murder and mayhem. As a result, only the young assistant, Christopher, was available to run errands.

Monty visited the Castle rarely. Despite having some good shooting, first class venison and salmon flown down from the Scottish estates, it was, in his opinion, uncomfortable and inconvenient. One had to keep disappearing into secret passages to avoid the paying public, and his host's I Q was only, in Fahrenheit terms, marginally above the far from stifling temperature deemed suitable for the well-being of the fabric: neither managed to rise much above sixty.

Duty called, however, and Monty settled down to catch up on various items of business, including the latest on Hall Farm. The only additional piece of information came from the police contact, who could give a welcome reassurance that the bunker had not been discovered. As the disintegrating plane had brought down the telephone wires, it was quite possible that one or more of the staff (including the odd 'illegal') might be inside, unable to emerge as the failure of their surveillance system made it too risky, and unable to communicate with the outside world by telephone. They hoped to restore telephone communication fairly soon, but as there appeared to be no-one at the farm, it was not possible for the police to exert pressure to get the matter treated with any urgency: only the owners of the farm, or their 'friends' could do that. Monty was not worried about the survival of anyone trapped in the strawstack bunker: it was built for that very purpose and kept provisioned against any eventuality. He had not expected, however, to be faced with the communication problem.

"We'll see what we can do about restoring the telephone link in the morning," he told Christopher. "In the mean time, I must be told immediately we hear from Gerald, or anyone else on his staff. Get me a link to Northern Area: I'll get them to send someone who can pretend to be an insurance assessor. Have you got any spare keys for that 'bunker'?"

"No, Sir – at least not as far as I know. We didn't go there at all. In theory they just supplied us with fish; not, that is, from the farm, but they went there as well and brought us the passport photos and then....."

"Yes, yes, I see," said Monty. "There must be one of them somewhere who will have the sense to get in touch shortly. I'll ring round one or two people to see if they know of any spare keys. If the worst comes to the worst, we'll have to get hold of a J C B and dig them out on some pretext or other, but we'll give it twenty-four hours and hope something turns up."

CHAPTER TWENTY

Unknown to either, the two high-powered young men who had met and sparred verbally at Stansted a short time before, were now only a few miles apart. One, Monty, hoped to receive some information, the other, Patrick, was working hard to provide it. On arriving in the area, Patrick had dropped his father off at his home and gone on to Thorpe Tunnel, where a by now very apprehensive (and, it has to be said, rather noxious) Gerald was still tied up, just as he had been when left by the two who had apprehended him. They had been rapidly withdrawn when the whole operation ran into the ground with the fatal plane crash.

Awaiting Patrick in the Tunnel bunker was Kenneth, fully recovered from his experiences at Hall Farm and bearing no great good will towards Gerald (not that the wretched man had had any part in his treatment, or even knew who he was). Patrick had instructed that Kenneth bring with him a discreet two-way communicator so that, despite controlling the course of the interview, he could ensure that the only visible contact was Kenneth, who would do the talking. The fewer who knew that Patrick was more than an international academic, the better – and in that context he had wondered whether the condescending (but, he acknowledged, far from stupid) Burton-Latimer had heard that he might have 'branched out'. As Patrick knew, Monty himself had on occasion been helpful to the Intelligence Service, so would have a few useful contacts.

The hand which Kenneth was asked to play was a strong one, but he played it well, only occasionally needing a prompt from his hidden mentor, via the tiny speaker inserted into his ear. Having been carefully briefed by Patrick, who was situated in an adjacent room to monitor the proceedings, Kenneth moved in on Gerald, who was appalled to discover that he was now in the hands of the opposition. Whilst he required some evidence (newspaper report, photographs, etc., of the plane crash) he readily grasped that one of the options open to his inquisitor was, quite literally, to do *nothing* – to walk away and forget about him for a week or two. All the forensic evidence, and their own belief, would confirm that he had been left to die by the two members of the reinforcement team. In due course, they might work out that they had killed the wrong person, even if they failed to discover how, as Henry had been captured also (so could easily be made to 'disappear') and Paul was dead. Only if H M G could see a very positive advantage in keeping Gerald alive would they do so. He, Kenneth, who brought total realism to his expression of anger on this point, would be more than happy to mete out to Gerald the fate the Organisation had been prepared to arrange for *him*. There was, after all, little difference between being dropped down a well and being left to moulder in a mushroom farm.

A by now terrified Gerald offered to change sides, inform on all his contacts, give them all he knew about the immigrant-smuggling operation – anything. He would never have suggested killing a member of the Intelligence Service had he been put in the picture, but that fool Henry had only gibbered on about stinging nettles, and obviously had failed in the simple task of arranging the landing of the plane. He would make sure that Henry paid any price they wanted if they would only let him, Gerald, go free and carry on working for them. He could give them contacts in places they would never have *dreamed* of.....At this point, Kenneth languidly responded that he presumed he was referring to the Castle and that Gerald had really very little to offer which they did not know already, unless he could provide fuller details on the submarine connection.

It soon became apparent that Gerald was wary of telling them all he knew, lest he then be considered expendable, and be left quite literally to rot. Responding to the instructions passed to him, Kenneth now pointed to the cassette recorder which had been, quite openly, registering their conversation.

"What do you think your superiors would say if they were to receive a copy of you agreeing to work for the other side?" he asked his prisoner.

"They'd kill me, but why should you want to tell them. I can be more use to you on the inside than....."

"No, they wouldn't," said Kenneth. "They would regard it as something said under duress – and start feeding us dud information. You could convince them that your true loyalty still lay with them, and then go on to prove it in some appropriate way."

"Well, I – er – I wouldn't. I mean it wouldn't.....my loyalty, that is. You could rely on me to...."

"To do anything to save your foul-smelling skin!" Kenneth completed the sentence threateningly. "No, *that recording* will not ensure your continued co-operation with us..... but *this* one," he paused to insert another cassette, "should do the trick."

Any fight that had still remained in Gerald evaporated as he heard Ahmed's voice, and his own setting out in graphic detail just what the lad was expected to do in return for the older man's help. He could imagine only too well the combined effect of a revelation that he was not only homosexual but had, in effect, caused the death of John Dalton and compromised the entire operation in order to indulge his, to them, unacceptable passion.

"How – how did you...? He said he was....." Gerald's voice died away and silence fell in the room as the tape came to an end.

"Just leave him to stew for a bit," came the instruction to Kenneth. "You've done well. He'll do anything you tell him in the future. Leave him and come next door so that we can plan the next phase."

Kenneth emerged from the interrogation room, shutting the door firmly behind him on the thoroughly dejected and demoralised figure still tied to his chair, sitting miserably in his own excrement.

"Whew! The smell in there!" he said, removing the tiny speaker from his ear. "He's ripe for plucking – do you want to take over, now?"

"No. You're doing very well. I don't want him to see me, as we might meet at some time and one cannot rely on a fool like that not to give the game away. Give him a few more minutes, not longer as we have to get him moving, and then this is the plot."

Patrick proceeded to set out the 'life-line' which Kenneth was to offer. It was, in many ways, an attractive proposition. In return for selling his soul to the devil (incarnate in the form of Kenneth), Gerald was to report to H Q in terms of a scenario which bore about as much relation to fact as an incorrect choice in the T V panel game 'Call My Bluff'. If presented persuasively and in a transparently honest manner, it had a seductive ring of truth about it.

Patrick made Gerald and Kenneth go over and over what was supposed to have happened, and was not satisfied until he heard Kenneth report (with some disgust) that Gerald's swagger was returning. Gerald now enjoyed seeing Kenneth's discomfort as he described the latter's cringing whine as he was lowered into the well, head first. Kenneth (he would claim) had later recounted the sensation of pounding in the ears, bulging eyes and the last thoughts as he struggled to hang on to the life-retaining breath. Gerald even embellished slightly, describing how he had drawn the attention of the emergency services away from the yard by telling them he had seen a figure staggering towards the river, thus enabling him to slip unnoticed inside the strawstack.

By this time, Gerald had come to half believe that he really had shown that cool resolve and instant grasp of a dangerous situation expected of someone worthy of promotion. He had got over his surprise at being told that they already knew who his father had been (although he had the feeling that some of his contribution concerning the numerous children, like himself, who were brought over by submarine at the end of the war, came as news to them). After an extensive wash and a change of clothing, with the sentence of death lifted and the prospect of his re-instatement, Gerald was not only ready to play his new rôle, he was looking forward to it.

"The big factor in our favour," said Patrick as he settled down to listen off-stage and, if necessary, pass instructions to Kenneth concerning the response required from Gerald, "is that they won't wish to believe that their organisation has been penetrated to the extent that it has. That renders them – or most of them – essentially gullible. The interpretation of events which we are feeding them is one which will be music to their ears, music designed to lull them to sleep, or at least encourage them to relax their guard."

The star of the forthcoming show acknowledged the signal from his erstwhile tormentor, who had now become his 'control' and reached out purposefully for the telephone.

"H F C. Can I help you?"

"Gerald here. Put me through to David."

"I think he's rather tied up at the moment. Can I pass on a message?"

"No, you can't. Untie him, and put him on the phone NOW!"

The new Gerald was drawing on histrionic talents never before suspected. His eyes shone, his voice crackled with command and, despite himself, even David (who had been privy to John's less than complimentary comments), was impressed. As the tale unfolded, David realised he was out of his depth. Someone more senior needed to hear all this, and decide how to proceed. That lah-di-dah so-called banker who had just flown in from Eastern Europe was the best person to pass this particular buck to.

"Hold on, Gerald," he interrupted, "I'll get in touch with our Larry. He's somewhere up your way at the moment. Do you know him?"

After a fractional pause, Gerald replied that he didn't know him, then added for good measure:

"Is he reliable? I don't want some cock-eyed cowboy who imagines he can ride in and put the world to rights knowing sod all about it!"

David winced at this scarcely veiled reference to his late boss – and both Patrick and Kenneth tensed at this show of aggression, wondering if Gerald had gone too far.

"If you're referring to John, I'll have you know he....."

"John's out of it!" snapped Gerald. "I asked you about this Harry. Can you, or can you not vouch for him?"

Battered by the bullying treatment, anxious to pass the matter on and appalled by the callous attitude of the caller, David backed down, becoming if not servile, certainly acquiescent.

"It's not Harry, it's Larry – and yes, he's reliable. He reports direct to the High Command. I'll get him to ring you. Are you at the farm?"

"No, Thorpe Tunnel. And tell him to get a move on."

"I'll inform him," said David, without inflection, adding, as the phone went dead, "and I hope the tricky bastard stuffs one of those bloody pylons right up your Fenland fanny!"

Back at Thorpe Tunnel, Kenneth and Gerald, partners now in deception, whooped for joy.

"Bloody marvellous! You sounded like everyone's pet hate: a right little shit on the make. I can think of a few like that on *our* side!"

A strange look passed over Gerald's face: not 'hurt' exactly, but … reproof.

"But I am on your side now," he said.

Patrick, listening in the next room, smiled and said quietly to himself:

"I do believe you are and so do you! Now for the big one – this Harry/Larry."

CHAPTER TWENTY–ONE

There was rejoicing, too, at the Castle when the news came through that Gerald was not only all right but seemingly had everything under control.

"He insists on meeting you, apparently," said Christopher, who had taken the message from David.

"Really!" said Monty. "And how is it he's heard of me – still less knows I'm here?"

"David thought you were the best person to contact in the circumstances – and Gerald was acting pretty high-handed."

"Was he? Do you know him, by the way?"

"No," said Christopher. "I've only been here a short time, but the others do. They haven't said much about him. He usually calls in the van to collect papers and....."

"Unless he sends an elderly fraudulent stand-in?" interposed Monty, enjoying the younger man's embarrassment.

The latter had been going to say that his colleagues had also said that Gerald was normally very quiet and that he was amazed to hear that he had been 'uppity' with someone from H Q – and equally surprised to hear that he had sorted everything out, rather than wait for 'them' to tell him what to do. As it was, this information, which just might have rung a warning bell in Monty's mind, was not conveyed, for Christopher, crushed by the reminder of his gullibility, stood in red-faced silence.

"Well, as it happens, I want to see *him*," said Monty, after a brief pause, "so you'd better set it up."

Christopher paused, wondering whether he wanted Gerald to come to the Castle, or would prefer to go to him.

"Well, get on with it. I have other matters to attend to before I fly back. I have no wish to spend another night in a freezing cold, crenellated cubby-hole!"

Monty's experience of the mediaeval delights of the 'Old Tower', a room whose only merit lay in its total inaccessibility by members of the paying public, had not left him in the best of moods.

Christopher hurried off, reflecting that however high-handed Gerald turned out to be, he could hardly be worse than this miserable sod. He duly rang Gerald at Thorpe Tunnel Bunker and agreed with him that 'Larry' (the name used by Burton-Latimer within the Organisation) would be there in about two hours. He, Christopher, would bring him in his own car, a white Honda Civic, and call back for him later.

Acting on Patrick's instructions, Gerald was very calm, reasonable and efficient – just the sort of person for whom Christopher would like to work, in fact.

"Things are a bit hairy around here at the moment," concluded Gerald, "so if you hear anything interesting, give me a buzz."

"Will do!" replied Christopher, flattered at being paid the compliment of treatment as an equal, especially from someone with a reputation for not being afraid to tell H Q to get off their backsides.

In fact, 'Larry' was far from pleased at being expected to crawl around in some damp mushroom-ridden cave and demanded to know why Gerald was not coming to *him*.

"Because, *Sir*," replied Christopher, "you did not ask me to arrange that; you left it to me, and I've agreed it with Gerald. He won't be happy to have the meet altered, and there's not much time, anyway. I said I would bring you, which I trust is to your liking."

Christopher paused and then, fresh from his confidence-boosting encounter with Gerald, added:

"The bus service is not very good out here in the sticks."

"Let's remember one thing," snapped Monty. "I do the jokes around here – and next time check before you make arrangements. How far is this – er – tunnel?"

"It'll take about twenty minutes – and it's a bit muddy," said Christopher, eyeing the highly polished Italian ('poncy' was the adjective which occurred to him) footwear sported by Larry. Perhaps, he thought, homophobically confusing the meaning, the name was short for Lothario, a name he recalled having looked up in a dictionary and found to mean a 'gay seducer'.

The timescale made possible a small amount of rehearsal, the setting up of recording, photographic and video equipment, all available in the Bunker, and the agreement between Gerald and Kenneth of a procedure in the case of a tricky line of questioning. The ploy agreed was that, if he could not think of a good answer, Gerald was to flap his left hand. The gesture would be seen by Kenneth, who would be watching on CCTV. He would contrive a noise, such as would give Gerald an excuse to leave the room to investigate, gun in hand, closing the door behind him.....and Patrick would provide instructions on how to respond.

The other aspect of the arrangements concerned the preparation of that lethal Ground Control Approach operative, Gerald's assistant, Henry. He, along with the body of Paul, and the comatose Kenneth, had been bundled out of the strawstack bunker by the S A S team and helicoptered away.

In accordance with Patrick's instructions, Henry had been kept unconscious until this moment, as a result of which it was possible for him to be brought round by Gerald and told that he had been carried from the bunker over to Thorpe Tunnel, where he had remained out for the count. He had been given a suitable bash on the head to give credence to the notion that Paul must have unaccountably decided to take over the landing procedure after rendering Henry and Kenneth unconscious. As would be expected, Kenneth was under guard and able to confirm to Henry that he was now working for Gerald.

Henry was full of admiration for his immediate superior (whom he had earlier criticised for having left him to stew on his own) as he learnt of the problems he had encountered, and his cleverness in 'springing' his colleague and the prisoner from the bunker under the very noses of the emergency services. He was also impressed by the casual way in which he related the despatch of the elderly snooper, whose body would eventually be found somewhere near Cromer, believed drowned off the north Norfolk coast whilst looking for a lesser-spotted shrike. He it had been, apparently, who had made the hoax telephone calls before being so efficiently unmasked by Henry – and left to die by John's bungling group of thugs. Gerald (supposedly) had elucidated the fact that the old fool had told no-one what he had discovered, but had denied all knowledge of the documents, even when subjected to 'persuasion'. It was to be Gerald's conclusion that the visitor to the Castle was a different person altogether. At present this was left unexplained, but Patrick had plans for Gerald to evolve a plausible theory later. The odd 'loose end' was not to be wondered at: it often occurred in real life.

Monty arrived in good time and fastidiously negotiated the muddy path down to the level of the old track, from which the rails had long since been removed. Watching on the closed circuit T V, Patrick let out a low whistle as the image of the person known to them so far as 'Larry' registered on the screen.

"My old man was right. He *was* travelling in a suspect vehicle!" whispered Patrick to Kenneth. "That's none other than our old friend 'Monty' Burton-Latimer. No wonder he's so filthy rich. He must be quite high up in the Movement – and he's quite well connected in our own Intelligence circles, too. He's no fool, so we'll have to be careful."

"Shall I nab him – sweat him a bit?"

"You sound like another colleague of mine! No, not for the moment. We want to find out all we can first, see where he leads us and, with any luck, get him to support Gerald for the post of Area Commander."

"These pictures and the voice recordings should be all we need to reel him in when we want, anyway," whispered Kenneth, to Patrick's approving nod and signal for silence as the encounter began.

Monty listened for some time in silence, making notes and observing Gerald, who was well aware that if, on reflection, his story did not hang together, it was unlikely that he could be protected from the long arm of the neo-Nazi movement. Eventually, Monty signalled him to pause and then asked him to go over certain items:

"Just so that I can brief the Council without looking a complete ass, old boy, could you go over your encounter with Paul? They'll want to be quite sure why you felt it necessary to kill him."

"I had an option, of course – let him kill *me*! As I let myself into the bunker, he came through from the inner room. I could see Henry slumped over the radio and started to ask what was going on. Then Paul turned his gun towards me....." Gerald stared straight ahead, seemingly reliving those few seconds.

"He shouted: 'I've fixed Henry and now it's your turn!' I just stood there for a moment, flabbergasted. I had no weapon, facing a madman, the outside crawling with people. Paul had the Intelligence man lying on the floor in front of him, still tied up and, like me, expecting a bullet at any moment."

"And then the lights went out?" queried Monty, glancing at his notes.

"Yes. I suppose I owe my life to the pilot's failure to clear that pylon. I was able to jump Paul, wrest his gun off him and then, sensing that he was about to open the strawstack door to escape, got in a lucky shot in the dark before he gave the game away to those outside."

"Did you fire a burst, or just one shot?"

"What is this? A murder enquiry? I....." expostulated Gerald, frantically waving his left hand in order to gain time – time during which a noise was heard, in the fashion pre-arranged.

"What was that? Stay here! I'll go and investigate."

Gerald drew his gun and moved fearlessly (not difficult, given what he knew about the noise!), showing coolness, determination and the ability to take over when it was needed. Despite himself, Monty was impressed. There were certain aspects on which he would like to question Henry, especially on the period before the unwelcome visitors. He wondered whether it had been sensible of Gerald to leave Henry to cope. Also, should he have been aware that Paul was so unstable? On the other hand one has to delegate....hmmm.... Perhaps a chat with Henry, who sounded a fairly simple soul, might throw light on the sort of chap that Gerald was. It was a pity that....

Monty's train of thought was broken by the return of Gerald to report that it had only been the Intelligence agent, knocking over a pile of boxes.

"Now, where were we? Accounting for the possible waste of ammunition, as I recall. Well, the empty shells in the bunker should give a fair idea: I didn't check very closely before disposing of him down the old well, but I doubt whether more than one or two struck home."

"Never mind about that!" said Monty (whom Gerald had to remember was 'Larry' as far as he was concerned). "I didn't realise you had that chap here: I'd welcome a word with him while I'm here."

As Patrick had calculated, the realisation that Kenneth was available to corroborate details and check for new-found 'loyalty to the cause', deflected the course of the debriefing. The next move had been planned, too.

"Not wise," stated Gerald firmly. "I don't want him to know too much about the Organisation – and it's better if he doesn't know who *you* are. He'll work to me only: I'm the one with the drop on him, and I shall vouch for him."

Gerald raised his hand, still holding the (unloaded) gun:

"And, should it prove necessary, I will personally take care of him," he added, menacingly.

"Do stop waving that thing around," said Monty, deeming it wiser to accept what was, on reflection, good advice. "Is Henry available, by any chance?"

Gerald smiled: "I have to find him first. Then you're welcome to chat to your heart's content."

"But I thought you said you'd rescued him?" queried Monty, starting through his notes, with the beginnings of a frown of irritation.

"It's complicated, isn't it?" laughed Gerald easily. "Both he and the agent, whose name, by the way, is Kenneth, have to be 'found' as far as Her Majesty's Government is concerned. I shall search an out-of-the-way barn over by the airstrip, aided by my trusty hound Nero....and lo! having sought, I shall behold those two, trussed up by Paul, beginning to despair of being found."

"You seem to have thought it out very well," conceded Monty, "but make sure you don't get the stories mixed up."

As in fact there were two other versions of 'the truth', Patrick, listening to the exchange near-by, heartily endorsed Monty's warning.

"You'd better run over this interfering busy-body again," said Monty. "He's somewhere in the North Sea at the moment, isn't he?"

"Running over him is not such a bad idea!" said Gerald. "No, he's in fact awaiting onward transmission. I haven't had time to give him a maritime burial. In fact, you might be able to help me there. I've no authority over that bunch of 'enforcers' sent by John and I don't want to involve more people than necessary. Could you get the two who actually *saw* the old boy to come up here and transport the body to the coast?"

"Yes, certainly. Good idea," said Monty. "There's a bit of a vacuum in command. Will be until they appoint a successor to John, which needs to be soon."

He paused, wondering whether Gerald would propose himself, whether he had been trying to impress with a view to such a move. After all, he was the son of one of the recently deceased members of Council. Gerald, however, had been prepared for this situation, so he merely shrugged and replied that the obvious move was to confirm the deputy, David, in the post. As far as Gerald knew, he seemed to be quite sound. ('Nothing like damning with faint praise', Patrick had said).

"Right!" said Monty. "I'll report briefly to the High Command that you have everything under control here, then some time I'd like a few words with your assistant, Henry. Can that be arranged?"

Both Patrick, listening in and Gerald himself, noted the tone – not deference, but not arrogant bullying either, more one of acknowledging the authority of the commander on the ground, who knew better than him (Monty) just what was possible and the implications of actions by outsiders. In that last attitude, Monty was more correct than he realised. Gerald knew *much* more about those implications: things were far from being as they seemed.

Monty, however, was very relieved. Secrecy had been maintained. The police could be told that Henry had had no idea that Paul had acquired a rifle until he had threatened the Intelligence agent. Gerald was equally astonished and none of them knew what had happened after the plane crash. They could only assume that Paul had fired at the plane, as he seemed to have gone berserk, causing the pilot to take fatal avoiding action. When this scenario had been explained to Henry by Gerald, the former (anxious to forget his own descent into panic) had been delighted at the blame being doubly fixed on Paul. The 'true' version (as Henry believed it to be, and as it had been told to the Organisation) blamed Paul – as did the 'fictitious' version given to the local police

146

inspector, who was only too happy to make token efforts to track down the missing farm labourer, whilst accepting uncritically the innocence of Gerald and Henry.

CHAPTER TWENTY-TWO

A couple of hundred miles to the north-west of the Fens, a hastily summoned meeting of the Council which oversaw the Organisation in England received with relief the preliminary report from 'Larry' and agreed to meet again the following evening to enable that gentleman to report in person. On the agenda was the Fen Affair in general, and the matter of replacing recently deceased members, in addition to that of the appointment of a new Area Commander for the Eastern Region. The Chairman was known to have a 'favourite son' – not in this case an expression denoting an actual family relationship – and Edwin was understood still to be attempting to peddle his candidate, although respect for the very able and sadly missed John (who had been killed whilst attempting to sort out the mess which had developed in the Fens) made it unlikely that the remainder of the Council would accept Gerald, however well connected he might be.

Meanwhile, Patrick was reviewing the forthcoming meeting between Monty and Gerald's assistant, who was still a bit groggy from having been kept drugged into unconsciousness until it had proved expedient to revive him, a condition not helped by a hearty knock on the head, designed to give credence to the tale of an attack by Paul. He was, however, in a fairly suggestible state, grateful to Gerald for having rescued him from the strawstack bunker, supported his unconscious body in the water as they floated down the river Glave, and brought him to the safety of Thorpe Tunnel. ('It might sound unlikely, but it could actually happen!' Patrick had said). The mythical river trip had (so Henry had been led to believe) been made even more difficult by having to ensure that Kenneth, whom Gerald had had to render unconscious lest he cry out, also be kept from drowning. This feat of initiative and strength (carrying the inert bodies to the van and from it to the bunker at Thorpe Tunnel) greatly impressed Henry, who had completely forgotten his earlier sentiments concerning Gerald, from whose fundament – in Henry's opinion – the sun now shone brightly.

Given this state of mind, it was not going to be difficult for Monty to be fed a form of corroboration of events leading up to the crash, devoid of references to Gerald's unsupportive, and, as it turned out, fruitless, absence and failure to respond to his superior's order to get into contact immediately. Henry had also been primed to refer to John's insistence on horning in on the exercise, resulting in their frightening away Ahmed, just as he had been about to give himself up to Gerald.

Monty, having concluded his debriefing of Gerald, asked if he could make use of the bunker's toilet facilities, so he was out of the immediate area when the phone rang. Patrick got Kenneth to fetch Gerald to answer it, attaching a small listening device to monitor the call simultaneously. It proved to be a very excitable Christopher who, on driving back to the Castle, had spotted what looked remarkably like the chap who had claimed to be a member of the Organisation, and to whom he had trustingly handed the batch of forged documents a few days previously. He had followed him, and his dog, across several fields, having abandoned his car, and was now keeping watch on his house. By this time, Patrick knew what the address would be: that of his own father, who was now in deadly danger. Hurriedly, he wrote instructions for Gerald, who continued the conversation appropriately.

"Well done. Keep watching. Follow him if he goes out again. But on no account approach him, or do anything to harm him. For one thing he may well be dangerous, and for another, we think it's probable he was reporting to John, was in fact sent to check on operations in this area."

"Oh no!" bleated Christopher. "I rang the Agent before ringing you – and he said he would take care of him. I was to stay here to keep a look-out while....."

"How long ago did you ring him?"

"About five minutes. I'll tell whoever comes not to take any action – on your instructions."

"Do that! I'll get over there as quick as I can. Don't let him out of your sight, and be careful!"

Gerald cut the connection as instructed by Kenneth, who ushered him hurriedly back into the other room so that Patrick could ring his home number.

"Dad? Now listen carefully, don't ask questions and do exactly as I say."

"Right! Well, what do you want?"

"Put on that dreadful yellow-coloured anorak and take the dog out. Go towards....."

"But I've just got back from taking her – and why *that* anorak? It's in the...."

"I said 'Don't ask questions'. Trust me: it's important. Get moving NOW! Go down the lane and across as if you were making for Thorpe Tunnel. No violent hurry; your usual pace, but keep moving. Right?"

"Well, you know best, I suppose. Shall I...? O K, O K, I know: no questions. I'm on the way!"

"Whew! Thank God for that!" said Patrick. "Now let's get hold of the S A S! They can earn their pay."

As Patrick started to put through a call to R A F Wittering, Ned Swinnerton and his assistant, Brian, were setting off from Hadding, a village not far off the A 1 near Wansford, in response to a request from Philip Proudfoot, the Agent at Wothorpe Castle. Ned was a big man by any standards, who claimed to be descended from Will Scarlett, 'second to none for strength and sturdye limm', whose attributes were attested to on a plaque above the west door of Peterborough Cathedral. Like the man from whom he claimed ancestry, Ned was a gravedigger in addition to running the local smithy, Hadding Farriers, and was often to be seen in or near the churchyard at Fotheringhay. The connection with the long gone sexton of Peterborough Cathedral was enhanced by the fact that one of the 'two qveens.. hee had interd', Mary, Queen of Scots, had been beheaded at Fotheringhay. The castle was now little more than a mound, and of the extensive buildings of the Abbey, there remained only the western half, the Parish Church. The magnificent collegiate church, rebuilt in the 1440's on a massive scale, shrank to half its size following the destruction of the eastern half and the College in 1575. By then all the chantry priests, whose task had been to pray for the souls of Richard II, Henry IV and Henry V, had been dispersed. It was not until the 1920's that excavations took place, but even they did not discover everything that lay beneath what was now a grassy platform situated between the present church and the river.

Handed down over the ages, perhaps from the days when it was an important centre of support for the House of York, was the secret of the underground chambers and narrow tunnel which emerged close to the present course of the River Nene, its mouth covered by some tumble-down stone-built farm sheds, which housed the tools of the grave-diggers' trade. It was from there that Ned had extracted the tools of his other trade – that of an active 'soldier in the field' for the Organisation. He and his father before him had followed the lead given by a member of the local 'gentry', allegiance to whom they put higher than that to God, Queen or Country (believing that all three would, if they only knew what was good for them, welcome such action). The array of hand guns, rifles, ammunition and explosives was impressive, although the selection carried by Ned and his assistant – and their mien – appalled Christopher when they caught up with him, guided by his 'mobile'.

Not long after his second call – to Gerald – Christopher had been surprised to see his quarry, sporting this time a bright yellow anorak, set off again with his dog. Keeping in touch from time to time by phone, Christopher followed him warily, finding little difficulty in keeping the gaudy garment in sight, until joined by the massive blacksmith and his smaller, but sturdy, cold-eyed assistant. Thinking that 'Central Casting' could hardly have done a better job if asked for two murderers, Christopher demanded, and was shown, their H F C identity cards (which, in their case, related to Hadding Farriers Castings, the name on the van).

"Where's he gone?" said the big man, who, like his sixteenth century forebear, could be described as being 'of mighty voice and visage grim'. "You're too far back here: he's given us the slip."

"Don't worry. He's easy to follow...Yes, he's in sight again. Look out for the yellow anorak....and there's the dog. He's following the footpath signs – obviously comes this way often. Hey! You're not supposed to shoot him! Put those things away! Gerald said he might....."

"Just shut up, sonny. I know who I take orders from – and it ain't you, or yer precious Gerald. Right Bri! Take this – and drop 'im if he starts to make a run for it. And, that goes for you, too, if you get in our way!"

Christopher quailed before the venom and the vicious-looking rifle onto which 'Bri' was carefully fitting a telescopic sight.

"And you can give me *that!*" Ned snatched the mobile phone with which Christopher had started to warn Gerald.

Frightened and completely out of his depth, Christopher followed, willing the elderly walker not to speed up, wishing he had never spotted him in the first place.

It was then that nature took a hand, in the form, once again, of a game-bird. This time, however, it was not a pheasant, whose intervention had earlier saved Martin from discovery, but a partridge, which scurried across the path of Sherry, causing her to set off in hot pursuit, still attached by the lead to her master. The movement of the dog could not be seen by the two men who were stalking Martin, but the sudden rapid movement of the yellow anorak was all that was needed for both to come rapidly to the firing position, Brian slightly ahead of his boss. The sharp cracks of high velocity bullets rent the air, one puncturing the yellow anorak and felling its wearer, another speeding over the falling body into the thicket beyond. The sound of shots and subsequent effect was heard and seen by Kenneth and Gerald, both of whom broke cover from about two hundred metres west of the fallen figure.

"Christ! They've shot him!" exclaimed Gerald. "And all I've got is this piddling revolver, which," he added, in mounting disgust and sudden fear at his exposure to superior fire-power, "isn't even loaded!"

He dropped flat and turned to see Kenneth zig-zagging rapidly across the open field, brandishing a small hand-gun.

"Don't be a bloody fool! Drop flat. For Christ's Sake! No! Drop!"

Kenneth, however continued unharmed towards the fallen man, oblivious even of a tall menacing figure, now visible at the far side of the field, rifle in hand, holding by the arm another who gazed as if mesmerised at the crumpled yellow garment, its motionless contents and the two lifeless farriers.

From his uncomfortable position in the thick hedge, Martin raised his head cautiously. He had been frightened into staying down by the two rapid shots, fired from just above his head by his burly captor, who had first held him whilst his mate removed the yellow anorak, and then sat on him, enforcing total immobility and silence. Shocked and bemused by the sudden ambush, Martin took in the scene and tried to summon the energy and will to escape whilst he had even half a chance. One moment he had been proceeding as instructed, accompanied by..... now that was another thing. They'd taken the dog!... And then wham! He was thrown to the ground, not a word spoken, his anorak and bobble hat removed and, quite literally, sat on by a muscular lout with a rifle and hard grey eyes. They had remained like this for a few minutes until..... Yes, hadn't he heard two more distant shots, fractionally head of the other two? He watched as his recent assailant led another man rapidly towards the crumpled yellow shape.

Corporal Charlton growled at Christopher to stand still, then went forward to speak quietly to Kenneth, who was removing the tell-tale anorak after checking for a pulse.

"Where'd they get him?"

"No problem – slap bang in the middle of the back. The body armour did its stuff, but the force of the bullet knocked him down. It looks as though he hit his head on a flat stone. Ah! He's starting to come round now."

"He'll live....which is just as well for that silly little prick over there!" muttered the corporal. "Keep him looking dead!"

The corporal moved towards the terrified Christopher, narrowing his eyes mercilessly:

"I get the feeling you're about to attempt to escape, or make a sudden movement which unfortunately will look to me just like someone drawing a gun!"

"No! No! Don't shoot! I tried to stop them. They – they – wouldn't..... I said Gerald had told me to just follow. You've got to believe me! Ask Gerald. Oh God! He's not... I mean..... Whose side are you on? Gerald said he might be one of ours after all. It was the Agent's – Proudfoot's – fault: he sent for those two. I only......"

"You only set him up, is that it? Don't worry: he's dead so you'll die too, along with Proudfoot," said the corporal dismissively, as he was joined by Kenneth who was satisfied that the other soldier had now recovered sufficiently to stay 'dead'.

"Please! They all told me he was a spy. I said he was genuine. Was he working for H Q – or for Dalton? Was he..... right at the top?"

"Be quiet, man. The less you know the better," said Kenneth, watching the corporal move back and bend down close to his now fully conscious mate, as Christopher collapsed in self-pitying tears.

"So it works – the flak jacket? " he murmured quietly, making sure that Christopher could not hear. "Not a bad test! You all right, Pete?"

The other S A S man, who had substituted himself, as instructed, ('earning their money', Patrick had called it) for the elderly 'non-professional', grinned ruefully and replied quietly, without moving:

"Yeah. I'm O K. A bit sore and I've got a headache, but nothing that'll stop me from sorting out whoever set up this scam! What happened to the chap who shot me?"

Corporal Charlton drew a finger meaningfully across the throat of his supine colleague.

"And the other one? He fired, too, I guess....God! You've been busy. Are you in the clear?"

"The guy running this'll fix it. Probably it never happened!"

At this point, the 'wet work' being – for the moment, at least – at an end, Kenneth decided to take charge and called out to the corporal:

"Can you go over and tell that 'rambler' we don't need any help, please? I'll keep an eye on this lad."

Kenneth had noticed that Gerald was starting to make his way towards them and realised that it was essential that he should not be seen by Christopher, for whom Patrick had 'other plans'.

As much to Kenneth's surprise as any one's, the corporal raised his rifle and sent a bullet spinning into the grassy slope just beyond the advancing Gerald. With gratifying rapidity, the latter threw himself to the ground as the supersonic crack sounded inches over his head.

"That should curb his curiosity! Now, what do you want done with this worthless little shit?"

Charlton turned towards Christopher, only to see him crumple to the floor.

"Well, would you believe it? He's gone and fainted. Was it something I said?"

CHAPTER TWENTY-THREE

Kenneth gave a resigned sigh at the thought of rebuilding Gerald's faith in the good will of his new masters after having had a gun turned on him, and got out his mobile phone to report the success of the recent exercise – and the body count – as he walked towards the spot where they had left Martin. Although he did not show it, Patrick was appalled by the turn events had taken, not least by the danger to which his father had become exposed. There seemed little doubt that the pair from Fotheringhay had set off intending to exterminate the impostor, on whose orders it was not quite clear. It might have been a 'Thomas à Becket syndrome', with his father cast in the rôle of 'turbulent priest'..... but who had been the Henry the Second? The Agent, Philip Proudfoot? His intellectually challenged employer? A central, so far unknown, figure? The only suspect with the perfect alibi was the slippery Burton-Latimer, who was about to return to the Castle, where they must be surprised at the cessation of reports from Christopher.

"Give me a minute to think this through, Kenneth. Meanwhile, see how my father is. From the sound of those two S A S men, he may have been a bit shaken up: they don't sound the nanny type and will have had to act quickly. Ring me back in, say, five minutes – and don't let Gerald or, of course, Christopher, see Martin. I'm not sure if it's safe for him to go home yet. That depends on who's running the show, if anyone, from their end."

Kenneth rang off and trotted back to Martin, to find him looking his age, feeling the cold, and still shaking from a form of delayed shock

"Here, take my coat. You look frozen. Sorry about that. We had to move quickly when we heard they'd sent someone to follow up a sighting by that young lad you saw at the Castle. Their team consisted of two blacksmith-cum-gravediggers..... and ours (apart from me and Gerald who arrived just after the shooting) consisted of two members of the S A S. As you'll have gathered, one of them shot the two from the Organisation, who'd come hell for leather in a van from

Fotheringhay, as soon as they opened up on what they thought was you!"

"S-s-sorry. C'can't s-stop sh-shivering. Must be getting old! W-where do you want me to go, now?"

"I'll have to check with Patrick. Can you stand, walk about a bit, flap your arms? We'll get you in the warm as soon as we can – but....."

"Wait!" said Martin. "Where's Sherry? She may have been frightened by the bangs and taken off. I'll call her."

Motivated by concern for his dog, he struggled to his feet, trying to control the shaking.

"She'll be all right," said Kenneth reassuringly, although now that the animal had been mentioned, it occurred to him that it hadn't been around for the last few minutes. "I'll just check with Patrick, then I'll round her up."

Patrick had thought through part of his strategy, but still had no knowledge of the extent to which the Castle had been in touch with any higher authority. He should be able to get an accurate idea from Gerald, but that needed time – time to tell Gerald what to say, what line to take, and then time for him to pass the information back.

"Tell Gerald to get on the phone to the Castle, saying he's heard from you and asking for Burton-Latimer – that's 'Larry' to them. He may not be there yet, so Gerald's to insist on them getting hold of Proudfoot. He's to take a tough line with him. 'Who the hell authorised this? Three people dead; Christopher scared shitless (that bit's true, anyway) and will have to be got out of the country pronto; when H Q realise what's happened, the life of whoever was responsible won't be worth a nickel, as they've shot this important agent; papers on him show he was working for the very top brass, checking on efficiency; etc., etc.'. When we let him, Christopher can claim he reported all this, but was told he was an idiot..... that sort of thing; O K?"

Kenneth assimilated the instructions as fast as he could, explaining that Gerald was about three hundred metres away – and probably pretty scared, as was, he reminded Patrick, his own father.

"Oh God, yes. Poor old boy. Put him on the line... Hello, Dad! It's all under control now. Sorry you had such a fright. How are you feeling?"

"Well – er – a bit sort of groggy, you know..... not quite up to 'Shoot out at High Fen', I suppose..... but we're worried about Sherry: no-one's seen her since the – er – incident. She's got a tag on, but....."

"She'll turn up, Dad. The point is how are *you*? Can you cope on your own for a few minutes... while Kenneth gets things moving for me?"

"Yes, O K," said Martin, who was beginning to feel a little more human after hearing the familiar voice. "I'll start looking for Sherry."

"Don't you go and get lost, too! Keep the others in sight, so that we can get you home as soon as I'm sure it's clear. Take care!"

Back at the Thorpe Tunnel bunker, Patrick cradled the phone and looked down at his notes. There were getting to be too many loose ends, too many 'disappearances', which might make someone suspicious. The supposed body of the impostor would have to disappear; the two S A S men who had implied to Christopher that they were members of some Organisation hit squad would have to disappear – with no clear indication of who had summoned them; Christopher would have to disappear, lest he once again see Martin – but not before he had (more or less) explained how the Fotheringhay farriers had met their end. Possibly the Organisation could be relied upon to put about their own story, prompted by Gerald. A shooting accident? Surely not both of them at once? A vehicle accident – but what about the bullets? They could have been shot by rival drug-runners and left in the van: something like that had happened a few years before in south Essex. What about his father – did he need round-the-clock protection, or would he have to 'go on holiday'?

The priority was to get Gerald accepted by the higher echelons of the Organisation. For that, the key was that wretch Burton-Latimer, who must have finished talking to Henry and now be beginning to agitate at having been left incommunicado, without transport. Time to get Gerald and

Kenneth back here, to Thorpe Tunnel – the quicker the better. He stretched out a hand to the phone:

"Kenneth? Those soldiers came on motor-bikes, didn't they? Good. Well I imagine they left them pretty near...Right, one of you on each: it's only about a mile cross-country to here. Get Gerald to explain to 'Larry' that Chris, as instructed by the Agent, had gone after the 'impostor'....and that a bodyguard appeared from nowhere when the guys sent by Proudfoot shot him....Yes, that's right – and that he said he would take care of the bodies.....What..? No, four in all. There's a dead 'rambler' as well from Chris's point of view! Get him to tell Proudfoot to organise transport for Larry – and tell him just to say that Gerald's man is on his way to report...and that he, Chris, is getting the hell out of it, as it's all gone wrong.....Yes, then tie Chris up and blindfold him thoroughly. I don't want him seeing the so-called dead come back to life....Yes, he might not come round from that faint!...Then tell the corporal to take him to the Fotheringhay van. I'll get a couple more blokes from Wittering to meet him there.....Oh, and tell the other soldier to give me a lift back to my old man, who's fussing about the dog! See you shortly!"

After a, quite literally, hair-raising journey on the back of the two motor-bikes, Gerald and Kenneth arrived back at Thorpe Tunnel, the former having been briefed by Kenneth as they jogged and scrambled the final fifty or sixty metres. Patrick met Kenneth, who had arrived, as arranged, just ahead of Gerald after slipping out unseen by Monty and Henry. He reminded him that Gerald was to say he had given Kenneth instructions to advance across the field and find out what had happened from Chris (whom he had seen standing with the man who had fired the shots). If Chris were questioned later, he wouldn't be surprised to hear of Gerald's mistake – nor, given his own doubts as to whose side the assassin was on, would he be surprised that Kenneth had not said Gerald was hidden in the hedge on the far side of the field.

"Is that all?!" gasped Kenneth, as he struggled to take on board the rapidly adjusted scenario.

"That's the best I can do in the time available!" said Patrick as he set off. "If Gerald gets asked who his helper was, he's to say it was the Intelligence man, who had thereby proved to his satisfaction that he was loyal to the Cause... and that he then sent him to look for Chris's car. That'll explain his absence, although in fact I want you in the inner room, near the phone, monitoring what goes on. I'll be in touch."

Patrick set off rapidly to rendez-vous with the motor-bike, which, after a short, exhilirating run, dropped him close to the spot where Martin had been 'bush-whacked'. To his surprise – and concern – there was no sign of his father, who should surely have heard the approaching engine, even if he had moved some distance away during the previous ten or fifteen minutes. Wondering whether the old boy had fainted or something, Patrick set off to look for him in the immediate area, sending Pete down the track in case he had decided to go home.

Having been told not to let the others out of sight by his son, Martin was surprised to see most of the party suddenly disappear on the motor-bikes, leaving only a gagged, bound and blindfolded figure propped up against the far hedge. After getting enough strength back into his wobbly legs to start moving, he set off, warmed by Kenneth's anorak, to search for Sherry. Not liking to whistle or call out in case he drew unwelcome attention to his presence, he walked on, following the route taken by his substitute. A few minutes later, he heard the first motor-bike returning and hurriedly dived for the hedge, uncertain who was friend and who foe. He watched him load up the blindfolded figure and set off down the track, then cautiously started to raise himself upright to continue the search. He failed to complete the movement, however, not because he was aware of the advent of the second bike, but because his eye was caught by the familiar brown feathers of a partridge, eyes closed in death, facing him from the ditch. The cause of death might well have been fright, or shock: the agent, however, was patently clear, for the bird's tail feathers were firmly clasped between the rigid jaws of the elderly Golden Retriever. Against all the odds, for the first time in its life, the dog had managed to catch its life-long prey, but there was no smile of success in the eyes, no slowly wagging tail, sure of receiving the benediction of 'Goo-d Doggy' and the instruction to 'Drop it!'

As he slowly examined the motionless animal, his recently regained equilibrium draining away, Martin realised what had happened. The first bullet having pierced the yellow anorak, the second had passed over the falling body and struck the dog just as its triumphant jaws clamped themselves round the fleeing partridge.

It was thus that Patrick came upon the 'elderly busy-body', scourge of the enemies of the State, gazing fixedly, seemingly more shocked by this tableau than that of the recent human slaughter.

"Oh, no! Poor old Sherry," he said, bending down close to his father. "Are *you* O K, though?"

"She's never caught one before. I hope she knew. I shouldn't have let him take her: she tried to help me – but I couldn't......"

"It wasn't your fault. It was the only way to save you. We heard too late to do it any other way. Sorry, Dad. They spotted you, and followed. Those two thought it was you they were shooting: you'd found out too much and someone panicked. Thank God we got there in time!"

But Martin could only think of the unfairness of the thousand-to-one chance of the second bullet striking the innocent animal, merely doing the job it was trained for. He sat there, stroking her head, and muttering:

"Poor old girl: you caught it. You really grabbed it that time..."

Suddenly, he broke off and looked up, appalled by the thought:

"What about your mother? What do we say? She asks about the dog every day...and she's always telling me off because Sherry's so trusting when I talk to her and say I need a new pair of gloves – or....."

"Yes, I know, you old fool....and ask the animal if she's read the menu: 'Roast Dog'. Never mind Mother for the moment: how are *you*? You've been roughed up, found... this, and....."

"I should never have accepted those documents, that's what must have done it. I bet someone from the Castle recognised me and wanted to get the rest of the documents back. It was just a game then and I wanted to know what he meant by 'the other one'. Yes, that was it, that's what he said. It must have been the other submarine! Tell Elizabeth: she..... Oh, hell! I'd better get Sherry home. Give me a hand up, old boy!"

With the help of the S A S men, Patrick got his father and the stiffening dog, still clasping its feathered prize, back home, where a message from Elizabeth awaited them to say she was on her way back that day and wished to be met at Peterborough. He also got them to place the dead gravedigger and his assistant in the back of their van, having rung his immediate superior in the Intelligence Service for clearance for a simulated 'drug gang assassination' (two gunshot victims to be discovered in a burnt out van in a local quarry). Of the blacksmith's long remembered ancestor, it was recorded 'no doubt his sovle doth live for aye in heaven'....but one had to be less confident in Ned's case.

CHAPTER TWENTY-FOUR

Monty's patience had been sorely tried by the time Gerald got round to dealing with the matter of transporting him back to the Castle – achieved by a brusque phone call which resulted in one of the estate workers who was not 'security cleared' arriving in his Lordship's Landrover. Monty and Gerald travelled together, unable to talk beyond a whispered: "The shit seems to have hit the fan good and proper, Larry. I'll put you in the picture as soon as we get there. Proudfoot's cocked it up: Christopher got in touch with me....."

"What the hell's going on?" asked Monty, when at last they could talk in the Agent's office.

Gerald explained all he knew (or rather all he was prepared to lay claim to by way of knowledge) to 'Larry', while Proudfoot, to whom Gerald had spoken earlier on lines laid down by Patrick, stood, his eyes assuming a hunted look as the catalogue of disasters unfolded.

Monty grew increasingly nervous as he realised his proximity to the 'field of battle'. It was not his habit to lead from the front; indeed he took great care never to be directly involved with the nefarious activities which provided the funds to keep alive the long term aims of the pan-European neo-Nazi movement, a substantial sum from which found its way into his own pocket.

"Right! Well, this is not the time to apportion blame. The main thing is to inform the High Command. I need to get over to Liverpool as soon as possible." He turned to Philip Proudfoot. "When's the next train from Peterborough?"

"Er – it's – that is, you might do better from Grantham. I'll get Christo.....Oh, no, of course. I'll see what I can....The train, that's it, the train......"

Gerald, who seemed to flourish as a 'double agent', saw his chance to re-inforce his dynamic image.

"I can whistle up a helicopter within half an hour – much better than...." His pitying look was more effective than finishing the sentence, which could only have continued on the lines of: '....waiting for this silly bugger to organise anything!'

163

Monty accepted thankfully, anxious to get well away before anyone started investigating the recent spate of violent deaths, and also keen to advise the High Command that the Eastern Area, bereft of a leader, was flying apart in a series of unco-ordinated, even mutually destructive incidents. There was no longer any doubt in Monty's mind who was the best person for the job: Gerald. While they were waiting, Gerald discussed with Monty the best way to get Christopher out of the country, both wondering, but not articulating the thought, whether it might come to removing the young man in a more permanent sense.

"Are you sure that old boy was working for John Dalton? He didn't tell me – and we worked pretty closely together," said the Agent. "You thought he was a spy," he added accusingly, turning to Gerald. "That's why you were hunting him....."

"No, no!" said Monty, impatiently. "They caught that chap. Gerald's got him stashed away somewhere, waiting for the two that caught him to come and dispose of the body. That's right, isn't it, old boy?"

"Yes, Larry. There was a period when it looked as though it might have been the same chap.... but John was, well, from my point of view, interfering – from his point of view quite legitimately checking on all of us. He didn't tell me – and he didn't tell you, Philip. I'm sure the High Command will understand why you had him shot; it's always a risk when the left hand doesn't know what the right hand's doing. Don't you agree, Larry?"

Proudfoot winced at the confident use of the first name by this – this – *peasant*. He had nurtured hopes of moving higher in the Movement, saw himself as an obvious candidate for John Dalton's job, and eventually, perhaps, a seat on the High Command....then, who could tell: a regional governorship when they made their long-awaited move?

"Yes, yes. I'm sure they'll understand," said Monty, with palpable insincerity, adding enigmatically: "I'll see they're fully briefed, with everybody's contribution recognised."

The helicopter was about five miles away when the phone rang again and was picked up by the Agent.

"Proudfoot. Who's speaking?... Christopher! Where have you b... What do you mean? Yes, he's here, but he's not your.... You cheeky little devil! Make your report now – and to *me* or I'll see you....."

"One moment, Philip. Let me have a word.....Hallo, Chris. Larry here. Can I help? We're fairly well in the picture, but your own perspective would be most valuable."

Charm and authority oozed from the well-fed smoothie, but Christopher was adamant.

"I don't trust Proudfoot. Those vicious killers of his threatened me when I told them we suspected the chap in the yellow anorak might be working for the top brass. They gunned him down before anyone had a chance to question him – and now I want Gerald to get me out of the country. Put him on the line. There's something else I'm only telling him."

"Over to you, it seems!" said Monty ruefully. "You seem to inspire the lad with confidence – and we need his report."

The last phrase was by way of an explanation to Proudfoot, who saw his authority being usurped by, as he saw it – with much justification – the gormless nonentity, Gerald. A dreadful thought struck the tall, competent-looking confidant of his Lordship, to whom so many owed their livelihoods: this 'Larry', who had the ear of the High Command might recommend.... He, Philip Proudfoot, reporting to Gerald? Doing his bidding, even accepting a lesser job? Stuck in that Fenland slum, ferrying immigrants....Never! He sat down, defeated, to contemplate his fate when it became known that he had had one of the most senior men in the Organisation killed: that bloody Ned and his.... Proudfoot buried his head in his hands as Gerald took over the phone and calmly reassured Christopher that he would be kept hidden for a day or two until arrangements could be finalised.

"You've got them there! The bodyguard....Yes, I gathered they found conclusive evidence....Yes, quite, but they gave you the..... Oh, I see. Hang on a minute!" Gerald turned to Monty with a grin. "The chap who was the 'minder', who shot these two from Fotheringhay, has various documents which he'll give to Christopher as soon as he has clearance." (Patrick had instructed that time be gained to forge something suitable). "Apparently," Gerald continued, relaying

165

Christopher's words, "our man had expected to hand them to John, so had to keep them when the plane crashed. The bodyguard's done well to realise the importance of these documents – although he failed to protect his charge, so has to face that music, of course. One other thing: Christopher will only give them to me. I ought to hand them to John's successor. Can you get someone to give me instructions – and perhaps you have contacts across the Channel I can liaise with concerning young Christopher?"

"Yes. Good!" said Monty. "Something's going right for a change! Hang on to those documents when you get them. Who knows? You might be needing them!"

"O K Christopher," said Gerald, returning to the phone. "Stay where you are. I'll get across as soon as possible and we'll take it from there. Don't worry; you're in the clear!"

Gerald contrived to look blank, as if the significance of Larry's reference to the possibility of his 'needing' the documents had been lost on him. Neither Monty, nor Philip Proudfoot, the Agent for Wothorpe Castle Estate, was fooled, however. The latter, indeed, rose slowly to his feet and, muttering that he had a few things to see to, left the room just as the clatter of the approaching helicopter called a halt to the conversation.

"I suggest you hang on here for the time being," said Monty, casually, "just in case I need to confirm any details."

The same insouciant charade was played out, this time without the mute participation of the devastated, disillusioned and, by now, clinically depressed, Philip Proudfoot.

As soon as he was alone, Gerald availed himself of the direct line to communicate with Thorpe Tunnel. He permitted himself cautious optimism concerning the outcome of the 'election' of a successor to his father – and even more confidence concerning his imminent elevation to controller of the Eastern Area.

"It's becoming very clear that someone needs to be appointed to stop us – or rather 'them' (just a slip of the tongue, sorry!) – from pulling in several directions at once, and indulging in more mutual annihilation!" Gerald concluded.

"I hope," said Kenneth, with a hint of steel in his voice, "that the slip was not Freudian – for your sake."

"Don't worry, you've got enough on me to ensure my loyalty, which I think has already been amply demonstrated. Even your 'controller', whoever that is, couldn't have stitched up Proudfoot like I've just done. I know which side my bread's buttered..... and, like Christopher Robin, I *do* like a little bit of butter on my bread!"

"I think you've got your ditties in a bit of a twist there," said Kenneth, "but talking of Christopher, have you managed to arrange anything?"

"Larry has agreed to put me in touch with one of his Continental cronies – and I imagine we can work the immigrant route in reverse, or just send him conventionally under a false name."

"O K. Well done. I expect we'll be in touch again, soon. Where will you be?"

"Waiting here for good news – then wherever they send me.....but I'll keep you in the picture."

****

The agenda of the special meeting of the High Command, in Liverpool, had the receipt of Monty's report as its first item, together with discussion of appropriate action, followed by the appointment of a replacement as Controller for the Eastern Area of England ... and then the appointment of two Council members.

Death, assassination, removal of evidence, torture and blackmail were no strangers to the hard-bitten group, who followed the twists and turns – including the 'turning' of the Intelligence Officer known as Kenneth – with interest rather than horror.

"Has this chap Gerald got firm evidence of his double agent accepting our money?" asked one.

" Yes. Apparently the chap co-operated fully – was anxious to prove how we could 'fix' him if we wanted to. Gerald's got photos, tape recordings, the lot! He played hard to convince, kept saying H M G would never believe it, so he might as well kill the chap.... making him work desperately to suggest more and more damning evidence against himself! I was impressed, to be honest – didn't expect to find any signs of intelligent life in the Fens at all, let alone a man of his calibre!" replied Monty, staking his reputation on his protégé.

"Well, he comes from good stock!" said Edwin. "I propose we...."

"One thing at a time, please," said the Chairman firmly. "We shall be coming to that under item 3. Can I take it we're agreed, then? Larry's man to take over the Eastern Area with immediate effect. No dissenters? Right! Now for the next item...."

"Excuse me, Chairman," said Monty. "May I break off to inform him, please – or would you? It really is essential that someone gather up the reins before the wagon crashes into the ravine!"

"Go ahead, Monty.... I mean Larry, sorry! Not that I'm giving away anything unknown to all of us, as I'm sure you appreciate! We don't need you for the next item in fact, so I know I speak for all of us in saying a hearty 'Thank you' for sorting out this mess, for coming back so promptly..... and," he added, a little archly, "should there be any need for support for any project which affects you personally in the future, you can rely on us."

To nods of approval and a broad, conspiratorial wink from Edwin, Monty rose from the table and paused as the Chairman added chillingly:

"This new chap has our approval to deal with – er – Proudfoot in any way, and I do mean *any* way, he thinks fit. Do I make myself clear?"

Monty nodded, gathered up his papers and left to telephone Wothorpe Castle, hoping he would encounter Gerald rather than the disgraced Proudfoot.

He need not have worried. As the phone was ringing, Philip Proudfoot parked his car on a farm track not far from the Mallard public house at Little Bytham. The name owed nothing to the frequent sightings of wild duck in the area, for the sign depicted the famous steam engine which had hauled trains at over 100 miles per hour in the 1930's along the nearby length of track, the fastest stretch along the whole of the King's Cross to Edinburgh line. The driver knew there was no point in even *trying* to stop the Intercity in the thirty seconds which elapsed between the man stepping onto the track and the slight bump he felt as the engine fulfilled Philip Proudfoot's desire to end it all. He slowed whilst he reported the incident and got clearance to continue south, accelerating to well over the 1930's record speed in order to arrive on time at Peterborough.

CHAPTER TWENTY-FIVE

Peterborough station was also the destination of Patrick, in his case by road, en route to meet his sister who was travelling back from Birkenhead after the completion of her research into U-534. Her tour of the rusty hulk, refloated some years before, had been interesting, but it was the small museum which had proved of greatest value, in particular an aerial photo, taken by one of the planes which had sunk her. The picture showed the boat speeding defiantly on the surface, anti-aircraft guns firing (to good effect, it might be added). As she gazed at the old black and white print, it came to her. The U-boat was making no attempt at concealment; rather it was inviting attack by the planes....it was drawing them to itself.... leading them, leading them *away*. Yes, that had to be it! Leading them away from the real prize – the *other*, invisible, submerged U-boat, with its precious load. The U-534 was a decoy; the stories about its cargo of high Nazi officials, gold and 'sacred' emblems had no truth, as those who laboured to refloat it found to their disappointment.

Excitedly, she related the tantalising tale to her brother, whose habitual flippant cynicism was stilled as he recalled the recent remark made by Christopher to his father: '.... the other one, were you on the other one?'

"Brilliant!" he declared. "But how did it elude the enemy? Our radar was pretty effective by then, and what seemed to be all the others were eventually caught on their way to Japan or South America."

"That's the point! I'm sure this one didn't go that far! I. G. Farben are known to have been developing a protective screening – what we would now call a 'stealth' covering – to make it invisible in all senses. Not only that, the latest U-boats could travel fast under water, possibly, in a successful prototype, nearly 30 knots – and they could travel in virtually complete silence at 2 to 3 knots. I think they brought a more precious load than gold, although that as well, doubtless." She paused for effect.

"Go on, go on!" said Patrick, his mind racing with the possibilities of her theory. "Spit it out!"

"They carried *children*. Yes, children, like your friend Gerald, who must have been inserted into the community by sympathisers at all levels of society (and God knows there were plenty about, from the highest in the land downwards). They've bided their time, built up an organisation, turned to crime for finance, and Father, meddling old fool that he is, stuck his walking-stick into the ant-hill, or whatever simile you like!"

At this point they turned off the main road and Patrick broke off from speculating on the possible survival of Nazi 'water babies' to explain his concern about their father. His sister was shocked by the story, and dashed in to see him as soon as they arrived back at the house (observed by one of the hidden S A S soldiers, whom Patrick had arranged as protection for all of them 'just in case').

To the concern (and irritation) of both of his children, Martin, as soon as his son had departed to collect Elizabeth, had left the warm room, the whisky and the comfortable settee, to go out into the drizzle, dig a large hole in the orchard and carefully lay both dog and partridge therein. He had just finished the gruesome task as the car turned in and appeared, gaunt, tired, wet and miserable, covered in mud – and stubbornly guilty.

"You, you... Oh, Father!" said Elizabeth, torn between delivering the comfort he needed and the tongue-lashing he so richly deserved. "Why couldn't you leave it? Come on; you'll make yourself ill. Take those wet things off. Patrick! Run a bath and talk some sense into him!"

Between them they got Martin into a bath and outside some hot soup, but a series of ominous sneezes showed that recent events had combined to render him *hors de combat* – and make it impossible to provide a reassuring bulletin for his wife when she rang for news. Even half the truth was enough to start her talking in terms of returning home early, a course deplored by her son as he would have to provide protection for her as well.

"Try to get her to stay there!" he whispered. "Things could get very nasty if they happened to discover I'm involved, or who Dad is. There are too many loose ends to be absolutely sure we're fire proof."

171

To himself, Patrick added that if Burton-Latimer ever paused for real thought, he could start asking some very awkward questions.

"Come on, Dad, let's get you out of those wet things. And by the way, what did you mean when you said you shouldn't have taken the documents?"

There was a pause while his father sipped a hot Lemsip, then he looked almost sly and said:

"Can you keep a secret?"

"Oh come off it! You know I can... now, give!"

"Well, I gave one set to Ahmed... I know it was illegal, but he had had such a rough time and....."

"What documents, Dad?" asked Patrick, his patience beginning to wane. "Where did they come from?"

"From the Castle. I didn't mention them before because I shouldn't have kept them, or given them to......"

"Kept them? Where are they now?"

"Upstairs, under the bed. There are two other sets. I suppose it'll all have to come out now..... but I want Ahmed kept out of it."

Patrick dashed upstairs and opened the package with growing delight. He rushed past his father, calling out:

"You're brilliant! Any more little secrets like that? I'll just set these up so that they were 'found' on the body of the dead 'you' – that is whoever one assumes was wearing the yellow anorak – and strengthen Christopher's hand when he's negotiating his escape from the country! I got him to say there were important documents, which I was going to have forged. Now we've got the real thing! I'll be right back. You've done really well!"

The praise did more for Martin's morale and general well-being than any drugs, baths or blankets, and he clambered thankfully out of his sodden gear as his son began to brief his 'troops'.

The telephone call with France did not go well. Torn between telling the truth, concern for her father, loyalty to her brother and a desire not to worry her mother, Elizabeth failed to reassure, admitting first that the dog was not in the best of health, then that it had unfortunately been shot by mistake when pursuing a partridge, finally that her father had been

172

rather shaken and had a bit of a cold. Given that it had been like getting blood out of a stone to arrive at what was presumably the truth concerning the dog, Jennifer half expected that her husband's 'slight illness' would turn out to be terminal by the end of the conversation. There seemed so much opposition to her returning early from the course that she resolved to depart with as much despatch as possible (whilst appearing to agree to wait a day or two to see how he was feeling).

"He dotes on that animal really," she said. "She's his only companion now that I'm working and he's retired. They commune together and he walks her off her feet. He'll be thinking it was his fault; I know him. Is he having her cremated, do you know?"

Elizabeth had stopped short of telling her mother about the burial scene and had implied a 'normal' shotgun incident, with the dog getting in the way of pellets intended for the partridge (which was the 'authorised version' for the neighbours). She was, in fact, concerned about her father's tendency to cover up his feelings, but recalled that his main worry had been that his wife would be upset, so should not be told, lest it spoil her 'holiday'.

After conveying strict instructions that she was to be told immediately if Martin's health or mood deteriorated, Jennifer rang off and straight away contacted the British course leader to say that she would have to leave the next day as her husband was unwell – and the dog had been shot. They were very understanding and offered to make all the booking arrangements for her – although regretting that she would have to pay the full fare herself, virtually the same as the cost of a return ticket, as she mentioned to her hosts that evening. They were a French family, the Cazaux, whose daughter had been an 'exchange student' with Elizabeth some years before.

"They ought to pay in the circumstances. I'll have a word with them if you like," said the husband.

"Oh, don't worry. It's only money....and a dead dog hardly counts as a 'bereavement', does it?" said Jennifer, so the Frenchman shrugged his shoulders, and rose to refill the glasses, the conversation turning to a discussion of pets and their foibles.

****

Mrs Pateman had worked at the Castle for about eleven years, ever since her husband had been killed in a road accident. He had worked as a general labourer and driver, helped with the 'shoots' and earned good money, some of which, he had once told her, was 'for keeping me mouth shut – and you'll do the same if you know what's good for you'. This had been in response to a question she had put when he had been called out late at night and had returned with a badly bruised arm and ripped jacket. After his death, they, or rather the Agent, had been very good to her, fixing her up with a job collecting money at the front desk.....with a substantial bonus for 'extra duties', the performance of which had thrown light on her husband's advice, and, very recently, had caused her to discuss the carvings of Grinling Gibbons with an old chap who had contrived to show her his H F C identity card. She was sharp-witted and could remember his face quite well enough to recognise it again when, as now, she found herself staring at his photograph.

The tragic suicide of Philip Proudfoot, who had been so good to her, had thrown the staff at the Castle into a flat spin, but after all those years, Mrs Pateman had become his unofficial personal assistant in matters to which most of the staff were not privy. She therefore took it upon herself to open an envelope addressed to him containing the 'deliberate error' in the spelling of his name as Proudefoot, indicating that this was Organisation business. The envelope contained three photographs and a note saying they were to be passed on to 'Larry', as he had requested. They had been taken a day or two previously at Stansted Airport, and showed the subject (Patrick) talking to another man, agent number 534, whom she knew had caused Mr Proudfoot a lot of worry, possibly to the point of driving him to take his own life.

Mrs Pateman rang her contact number and was rapidly connected to Larry, whom she had met during his recent brief stay at the Castle.

"Could you describe this photo to me, Mrs P?" asked Monty breezily. "It's two people, you say, one of whom looks a bit like the chap whom you passed on to Christopher. Is that right?"

"It doesn't look a 'bit' like him, Sir," said the lady, bridling at the over-familiar 'Mrs P' and remembering she hadn't taken to this lah-di-dah chap, by whom she sensed her Mr Proudfoot had felt in some way threatened. "It *is* him – but I don't know the young man with him."

A dreadful thought was creeping unwillingly up on Monty at the mention of a young man.

"Did you say the note mentioned Stansted Airport? Does it give a date as well?"

It did – and the description of the young man fitted perfectly.

"Bloody Hell!" ejaculated Monty, as a cold feeling gripped him, only to be succeeded by a hot flush of fear and anger combined. "The tricky little bastard!"

"I beg your pardon!" said Mrs Pateman starchily. "I'm only trying to be of help. There's no reason to......"

"No, no. You've been *most* helpful, Mrs – er – most helpful. I didn't mean to be....you just took me a bit by surprise. Now please don't mention this to anyone else. I may ask you to do a little investigating for me, for additional – er – that is a generous expense allowance. Could you manage that, do you think?"

In mentioning money, Monty had pressed the right button, for Mrs. Pateman's widowed mother seemed to be a constant drain on her resources, and she still suspected that this old chap had in some way 'done the dirty' on Proudfoot.

"Well, that depends, of course, on what you want. I mean I'm not, well, I'm not normally one to pry into other people's business, but....."

Despite his anxiety, Monty could not repress a slight smile as he recognised the phrase of the inveterate snoop. This one, he thought, could be a very useful pair of eyes. They agreed that she should commence immediately to find out all she could, starting from an assumption that his surname was Brady, he lived somewhere a mile or two east of Thorpe Tunnel and had a son called Patrick – the one in the photo.

"I shouldn't go to the actual house after you've discovered it," said Monty. "I don't want to risk alerting them." (And there might be a body-guard, he thought, but decided not to mention it to his new colleague).

"I expect that man from the Fens would have a good idea where they live. Shall I....?"

"No, Mrs Pateman, I think we'll leave him out of it – for the moment, that is. One other thing. Don't be surprised if you hear he, that is the father, has just gone away, or is in hospital, or has recently met with an accident. Any background would be useful, though."

In the event, one did not have to be Sherlock Holmes (or Miss Silver, for that matter) to locate the house: the local telephone directory showed Brady, Martin as being the only one in the immediate area, at 57, Southorpe Lane. Half an hour after her conversation with Burton-Latimer, Mrs Pateman was on the way, rehearsing in her mind a series of questions to put to householders at the *other* end of the village.

It only needed one friendly, garrulous person, and Mrs Pateman struck oil at the third house.

"Oh, no! Mr Brady is *much* older – he's retired now, used to be at the Grammar. It might be his son you want, but he's away most of the time. They did very well, went to....Yes, there's a daughter as well.... Gracious me, no. *She's* still teaching. I saw her only the other day when she called round for some eggs...."

Mrs Pateman thought at this point it would be a good idea to prolong the conversation (not that it seemed to be difficult!) by asking if she, too, could buy a dozen....if that was possible. It was, but it took time, during which Monty's personal spy was deluged with information, some of which she found time to commit to paper whilst her source broke off to answer the telephone.

Among the trivia (as they appeared to Mrs P) she learnt that Mrs Brady – a very nice woman, who.....etc., etc. – was away at the present, in France, on a course. That was why she had been stocking up with eggs, for her husband.... . Mrs Pateman agreed that she 'knew what men were', and established that her talkative friend did not know where in France, had, indeed, only a rather hazy idea of 'France' as a concept. She also established that Mr Brady was on his own this week and – this as a result of the telephone call which had interrupted the flow

– her friend Mrs Chadwick had just heard that the dog had died... so he wouldn't be out walking it if she called round... but her friend had seen the son, so he wasn't on his own after all, which was nice, as it's always upsetting when.....

Mrs Pateman, who now knew everything except the colour of underpants her prey was wearing, agreed that Mr Brady would be unlikely to be taking the dog out in the circumstances, and extricated herself, accompanied by Mrs Tolliver, the jolly gossip, who insisted on carrying the eggs to the car.

Unaware of the explosive nature of the information in her possession, Mrs Pateman took her time – a little shopping, some carefully set out notes – before contacting the man whom she knew only as 'Larry'. She reasoned that it would not do to make the task look too easy: that might reduce the amount she could expect for 'expenses' (which, she reminded herself craftily, could include those eggs). Also, she had no knowledge of the nature of recent events which had led up to the suicide of her boss.

The information that (although Mrs Pateman had not actually *seen* him) the subject of the photo was still alive, was going to galvanise the Organisation into action, and the news of the dead dog came as useful confirmation to Monty when he received the report. However, the fact onto which he latched was the absence on a course in France of Patrick's mother. Posing as a researcher from the Department for Education and Science, he soon found out from County Offices which establishment they used for their residential language courses; also that there was a (mixed) party of secondary teachers there now. International directory enquiries led to the secretary at the 'Institut Pédagogique'. She had herself made the booking and confirmed that Mrs Brady was on her way home, via Stansted Airport. As a result, she could not speak to the 'education officer' who needed to check certain details in order to process her expenses claim.

"Right, clever Dick, let's see what use your first class degree is when you hear we've, or rather 'they've', got your mother!" said Monty to himself, as, still based in Liverpool, he prepared to set up the abduction of Martin's wife, preferably before she left the Continent, but with a fall-back at Stansted

177

Airport, where, he assumed, she would be met by a member of the family.

CHAPTER TWENTY-SIX

Christopher, the Agent's assistant, was by now in hiding in Thorpe Tunnel Bunker, a move organised by Gerald. However, when the latter heard from Larry that he was to assume command of the Eastern Area, he rang the Bunker to inform the young man (who congratulated him warmly) and say that Larry had agreed to take care of arrangements for his, Christopher's, untraceable departure from the country. This was to be followed by 'adoption' by, probably, the Dutch branch, where an Englishman loyal to the Cause would be a useful asset.

"I shall be a bit busy," said Gerald, using the understatement to demonstrate his ability calmly to take the pressure, "so I'll have to leave it to you to liaise direct."

Christopher duly rang the number which Gerald had given him and asked to speak to Larry:

"Speaking. Who's that? ..Ah! The chappie who 'always said that the man he gave the papers to was genuine'?"

"Er – yes. But I can quite see why ....."

"And saw him ruthlessly gunned down by our own men?" continued Monty, who had just discovered that some form of switch and/or pantomime must have been played out among the hedgerows.

"Yes. I reported all that to Gerald," said Christopher. "He said you would get me out of the country. Why are you....?"

"All in good time, laddie," came the reply. "First of all, tell me *exactly* what you saw....then I will tell *you* that you were the audience for a little playlet, written, produced and directed, I have no doubt, by an old Cambridge acquaintance of mine, who works in his spare time for British Intelligence!"

"I – I don't understand," said the hapless Christopher. "I saw him fall... and.. were the other two pretending to be... ?"

As he asked the question, Christopher felt the vomit rise in his throat at the recollection of the two bodies, heads damn' near blown apart, blood, brains and tissue exposed on the bright grass.

"They were dead I tell you. Dead!" Christopher's voice rose to a shriek.

Recognising the unwisdom of having wound the young man up when he was too far away to control his actions, Monty sought to calm him down, saying that he, Larry, had found a way to control the opposition and was expecting a call from some friends in France in the very near future by way of confirmation, at which time he would organise the Continental end of Christopher's translation.

"In the mean time, sit tight and don't breathe a word of all this to *anyone*."

****

The two 'heavies' who had been sent to Charles de Gaulle airport to kidnap Jennifer were disappointed when the announcement failed to bring a middle-aged English lady called Mrs. Brady to the information desk. They had no photograph, so had hoped to 'flush her out' by that means. They did not despair, however, as presumably she was leaving it to the last minute, had been delayed, or – just possibly – had passed through the gates before they got there.

"What about that one?" asked the junior of the two. "She's on her own, looks English – we can check by reading the labels on the case – and is about the right age."

"But why didn't she respond to hearing her name – if it *is* her?"

"Perhaps she's a bit deaf, or was in the toilet or something. I'll get them to try the announcement again; you watch her carefully, and wander near to look at her cases."

This time, the message included the first name of the target, Mrs Jennifer Brady, and had the gratifying result of making the lady stop, listen hard and start towards the Information desk, only to change her mind and join the crowd moving forward, as the flight was called immediately after. The reason for these movements was that she had intended to go through and then check on the announcement, which had not sounded quite like her married name (not surprisingly, as it was Radley) but was definitely Jennifer.

'Heavies' are not known, in whatever country or cause, for their finesse or ability to analyse, plan and stalk their victim. Jean-Paul was no exception to that generalisation and he had been told to watch for signs of recognition when the announcement was repeated.

Mrs Radley was able to dine out for many months on the strength of the story she had to tell of being asked to accompany the burly French 'customs man' to a back room, where she was told to empty her bag and show her passport. She stood there, worrying about missing the plane, wondering why they thought her name was Brady and listening to the muttered conversation between the two, after which one departed, presumably to ring his superior. He then returned twenty minutes later, wild-eyed, to indulge in excitable French which she was unable to follow. It was at this point in her telling of the story that Jennifer (Radley) still recalled her indignation, for, without a word of explanation, still less apology, the two men 'really rather rough-looking, one would never have taken them for Customs officials in *this* country!'... had literally thrown down her passport and run from the room! And that, the story continued, had not been all..... .

****

"Not to worry!" said Monty on being told that, because of the mistaken identity, the real Mrs Brady must have slipped past them at the last minute. "We'll pick her up this end, at Stansted. It may be all for the best. The secretary was quite sure she'd checked out. She'd made the booking herself, the day before. If she doesn't turn up at Stansted, it'll mean she was warned – in which case we'll have to unmask the source. Tell your men to hang on and see if someone like her, *exactly* like her this time, arrives late. Meanwhile, I'll double check with the Institut and the airline."

The virtual collapse of the chain of command in the Eastern Area meant that it was extremely difficult to get hold of any operatives. Monty tried to contact Gerald at Thorpe Tunnel, but was told he was 'not available' by Christopher, who answered the phone:

"He said he'd let me know where he was, once he'd managed to take over his new job. He was off down south somewhere. If you locate him, can you tell him to get in touch as two blokes are on their way here and I don't know what to do with them."

"Really!" said Monty. "They must be the two who 'arrested' the impostor. Gerald asked for them to come and dispose of the body ......but as he isn't there, they can do a little job for me while they're waiting for his instructions. I know Gerald would approve. Give me the number of their mobile!"

Explaining that they would have to get their skates on to arrive before the plane, Monty sent the two members of the reinforcement team from Haslemere back down the A 1, across to the M 11 and on down to Stansted Airport with instructions to abduct Mrs Brady. They were travelling in a fast car, so he considered it should be possible to get there in time, as in fact proved to be the case.

Monty was delighted when they reported that they were in position and that the plane was due to land shortly, about eight minutes behind schedule. He had, by this time, checked with the Institut Pédagogique, who confirmed the lady's plans, the flight number, etc., and had spoken to the Departures desk. There a bored young man, unimpressed by any Englishman, even one who (for a Customs official) spoke excellent French, glanced down the passenger list and confirmed the presence of a Mrs Brady.

"Mais, bien sûr, prénom Jennifer.... elle a failli de manquer le vol, mais....."

As it happened, acting on different information a little later, Patrick was told the same thing, this time by a different, but equally unimpressed young man, who read the notes made by his colleague, finding them most useful in saving time – time more profitably spent applying himself to the much more rewarding task of chatting up an attractive blonde who claimed to have mislaid her ticket.

As a precaution, Patrick arranged for two armed agents to observe his mother's arrival and give the 'all clear' to Elizabeth, who, still unknown to Jennifer, was meeting her. Thus it was that four athletic-looking men (two from each side), all carrying guns, all prepared to abduct, maim, kill, disable, and then disappear, found themselves waiting and watching in the arrivals area at Stansted Airport. Also there (but aware of only two of the four) was Elizabeth, who had come to meet her mother, with strict instructions to do as she was told by the body-guards, who had made themselves known and were in direct contact by phone with an anxious Patrick.

The reasons for Patrick's concern had begun when Elizabeth had popped out, having seen the state of the fridge, to get some eggs. It was a short step, given the communicative skills of Mrs Tolliver, to discover that someone had been asking questions about the family. Moreover, the sharp-eyed lady was able to add that the enquirer worked at the Castle, there being a staff parking permit on the windscreen, exactly the same as the one her daughter's boyfriend's uncle had on his – and he had worked there for.....Elizabeth had cut short the conversation and rushed home to report the disturbing news to Patrick.

"Somehow they're on to Dad," he decided. " Never mind for the moment how. If it's Burton-bloody-Latimer behind this (and I must assume it is) we've got major problems. He's a nasty bit of work – won't stop at anything – and he's no fool. I'll double the guards on this place and we'd better get Mother back here."

"Surely they wouldn't......" Elizabeth's voice betrayed both shock and fear as the perils of their situation opened before her.

"Too damn' right he would – if he found out where she was, which is highly unlikely, mind you."

But Elizabeth recalled the garrulous Mrs Tolliver, as she expressed surprised pleasure at seeing her. 'As I was only saying just now, it was nice your brother was around, what with your mother being in France and the dog and everything. Men are not very good on their own, I always say and that lady from the Castle said the same thing. Funny them not having any eggs up there, though.....'

"I think they'll know by now," she said, sadly contemplating the significance of the phrase 'as I was only saying just now'. "What *have* we got into?"

In a flurry of phone calls, Patrick set up as much protection as he could, including a team to intercept his mother at Charles de Gaulle Airport, which arrived too late.

"We have one advantage," he told Kenneth. "It's safe to assume they don't yet know that *we* know that *they* know that I – and my father – are involved. I've had no warning from Gerald, though, which could mean he's changed sides.... I agree, I agree, but it *could*. It could mean that Burton-Latimer suspects that Gerald is working for us, so has deliberately left him out of it....or it could mean that B-L arranged for this woman to ferret about and report direct to him. Let's hope it's the last scenario."

"Why, for God's sake? Surely the whole point of having an agent in place is to get prior knowledge of what they're doing? If this Latimer chap leaves Gerald out of it, we've had it!"

"I know what you mean," said Patrick, " but in the longer term we don't want them to suspect Gerald, so if he *hasn't* been told, and we know anyway, we're better off. The trouble is that Burton-Latimer may take a long hard look at the fable he's been fed, and suspect practically everyone."

"The trouble is he may grab your mother. Never mind the long term," Kenneth grimly reminded Patrick, who fell silent, fingers surreptitiously, and uncharacteristically, crossed.

****

Mrs Radley had enjoyed her flight. A fuss had been made of her on account of her unpleasant treatment at the airport, which had caused her nearly to miss the plane, being ferried out to the runway just before it took off and then upgraded to First Class. The large gin to steady her nerves, followed by two glasses of wine, was more than enough to induce a mood of theatricality, so it was with glee that she swept down upon her staid and astonished husband: an audience at last!

"You see before you," she proclaimed in ringing tones with a suitably expansive gesture, "Mrs Jennifer Brady! New wives for old! Pick up the car keys... I'm yours for the price of a....."

But details of the tariff were never vouchsafed, to the short-lived relief of her embarrassed spouse – and disappointment of most of those within earshot. At the mention of the name of the person they had come to abduct, the two Organisation 'foot-soldiers' exchanged a quick glance and then closed on their prey.

"Mrs Brady? Would you accompany us please, there's been a mix-up with your ....."

A second such approach was too much for the unfortunate lady, however, who let out a piercing shriek and swung her hand-bag to such good effect that the bogus official, caught completely unawares, fell to the ground. In the process, his mackintosh opened, rather like the classic 'flasher', exposing his weapon – metallic rather than phallic, but none-the-less alarming to Mrs Radley, who shrieked at full volume:

"He's got a gun! Stop him, Oliver! Help! Help! Kill him - he's ... No! Don't shoot. Ahhhh!"

And with that Mrs Radley crumpled to the ground as the panicky gunmen started to run for the exit, one loosing a shot into the air to ensure a free passage.

As luck would have it, the stray bullet struck a child's helium-filled balloon which had lodged in the steel 'rafters', causing a sharp crack which the two men took to emanate from a hidden sniper. Both turned, guns at the ready, as they realised their chosen route led to the lifts rather than the loading area outside.

The men sent by Patrick to prevent such an approach were in two minds, for no word had come from the daughter, watching out of sight on closed circuit T V, to the effect that this Mrs Brady had emerged from behind the screens. Also, they were loath to declare themselves to the extent of drawing their own firearms. Frustrated and irresolute, they could only observe the rapid departure of the opposition, thankful that the attempted kidnap had failed.

Stansted, however, is regularly patrolled by security police, armed with sub-machine guns, alert for any terrorist threat. It was towards two such men that the bungling pair had turned, on finding their route blocked and (as they believed) under fire from above. They were in no state to react sensibly to the appropriate shouted warning, the result being all too predictable. They were cut down by a burst of automatic fire, each receiving several bullets in the chest. One was pronounced dead on the spot, the other, Gordon, underwent a successful operation at the East Herts General Hospital, Harlow, after which he was placed in a recovery room, still asleep.

The two British Intelligence agents had been in danger of making themselves conspicuous by *not* joining the crowd which thronged towards the scene of the recent action. They, like Elizabeth, had continued to watch the emerging passengers, hoping that the real Mrs Brady could be got away as soon as she had collected her luggage, under cover of all the excitement...... but they were disappointed.

CHAPTER TWENTY-SEVEN

At the start of the news item concerning a 'shoot-out' at Stansted Airport, Gerald was only mildly interested, there being no reason to connect it with the Organisation. When photographs of the two 'terrorists' appeared on the screen, however, he found himself gaping like an urchin with its face pressed to the sweet shop window, for there they were, the two who had held him captive in the Bunker!

"Couldn't have happened to two nicer guys!" he murmured to himself. "Saves me from having to do the same thing, but what in Hell's name were they doing there? And who sent them without consulting me?"

A telephone call to Thorpe Tunnel, answered by Christopher, brought him up to date – and made him realise how close Larry was to unravelling the web of lies in which he had been enmeshed by Kenneth and his unobtrusive behind-the-scenes manipulator.

Monty, for his part, although he had never seen them, had little doubt that the two dead men in the news were his 'hit squad' and even less that Patrick had acquired an informer within the Organisation which had enabled him to keep one step ahead. Mrs bloody Brady must have been warned, so had never got on the flight, which had been booked as a decoy. Somehow they had got to the K L M / U K Air clerk who had misinformed him – or hacked into their computer and altered the information. Who, then, was the traitor that bastard had 'turned'? Monty reviewed the events of the past few days, trying to sort impeccable fact from the illusionist's patter. What could be relied upon? He knew that the man in the yellow anorak had not been Patrick's father. So who *had* he been – and was he *really* shot...by whom? Had any of that ever happened? Who had actually witnessed the events....or, more relevantly, *claimed* to have seen them happen? Monty forced himself to face the worst possible scenario – that the traitor was Gerald. If that were so, he, Monty, would have to go back to the High Command, before whom he had argued so forcibly for Gerald, indicating clearly his support for an appointment, not just as Area Controller, but to that august body itself. Surely it wasn't? No, it couldn't have been him: he didn't know about Patrick's father; didn't know about the move against his mother at Charles de Gaulle; didn't know what sort of brain he was up against. At least he hadn't cocked things up like that fellow Proudfoot, thought Monty, continuing his train of thought, which led to the ghastly conclusion that the Agent had walked under a train because he believed he had ordered the killing of one of the Organisation's top men – a man who had probably never existed, had never been killed, and had certainly not been a member of the Organisation!

Who, then, knew enough to warn Patrick and give him time to spirit his mother away, minutes ahead of her would-be abductors? Mrs Pateman? Hardly. She it had been who had discovered the vital facts. Not, of course, that that was conclusive: that 'knowledge' had resulted in two more deaths – on the wrong side. Christopher? Could be... in fact... Monty ran the events past his mind's eye casting this time Christopher in the rôle of double agent. By Heaven, it is! Only Christopher knew in time to warn Patrick. It had been Christopher who had supposedly stood by the assassin as he gunned down the Fotheringhay pair – or, more probably, tied them up and removed them from the scene. After all, who had actually *seen* them dead? Gerald? No, he'd been shot at to keep him at a distance! The Intelligence agent whom Gerald thought he'd 'turned'? Yes, perhaps. He'd better warn Gerald not to trust him until they were sure, and get his help in eliminating that bastard Christopher before he could do any more damage. Or, wait! Perhaps he could be used to pass on dis-information until Patrick realised his man had been rumbled.

The 'Fen Affair' had taken up so much of Monty's time since his return to England that he had so far had no opportunity to carry out the main task with which he had been charged by the group to membership of which he aspired, the Grand Central Council. Based in Vienna, they controlled national High Commands throughout the world and had recently become concerned at reports from Britain of impatience amongst those who served in humble circumstances – the Geralds of the movement, facing retirement and contemplating the dubious benefits of having waited and waited, for about forty years, for the coup that never came. For years they had been held in check by their fathers, who had held high rank and enjoyed authority (if only briefly) at a very young age. As a generation, they had gambled and lost – but at least they had 'lived'. Now it was the task of the next generation to keep in check the young firebrands, to make them serve in lowly positions as drivers, Water Board labourers, clerks, foremen, etc., buoyed up by their secrets, additional income and the promise of wealth, respect and power over the colourless ordinary people. Always that promise – one that those under thirty could see had proved illusory for their fathers... the middle generation, who would never personally benefit, a significant number of whom wished to return to the gaming tables and gamble all, once again, on a right wing revolution. Monty had been told to weigh up the situation and influence thinking towards caution, to discourage Britain from going off at half cock, thereby alerting society to their existence, and setting the Cause back another thirty to fifty years.

The Continental view was that there was no need to undertake any risks – that the course of history was with them. They noted the re-unification of the two Germanys, the collapse of the great enemy, Russia, the compliance of France and the surely unstoppable emergence of a United States of Europe. They noted too the clumsy democratic systems which could easily be subverted by men of vision, for whom the end of the eventual fulfilment of the great Nazi dream justified any means. The growth of support for the 'Right' would easily lead to the emergence of politicians loyal to the Cause, of which there were many (either by genuine conviction or under some form of duress). The pressure on jobs, houses, welfare, etc., caused by the inflow of Eastern or Middle Eastern peoples was already being turned to the advantage of the heirs of the Third Reich....despite their involvement in that traffic as part of their criminally inspired money-raising activities. Just as there is no stronger supporter of law and order than the retired bank robber anxious to protect his ill-gotten gains, so the policies of these bandits bristled with Draconian measures against crime, with deportation, with death or disfigurement for 'offences against the state', with the creation of sub-classes such as women, only tolerated if needed to render some service and with simplistic loyalties to flag, symbol or physical fit. Those who were not for them were deemed to be against.

Monty forced himself to consider the advisability of immediate and unannounced departure, to avoid being dragged into the swirling waters as the British – or, at least, the Eastern Area – ship foundered, betrayed within and weakened by a series of small, but spectacularly unsuccessful encounters. On the other hand, to return having accomplished nothing, and possibly be seen as having failed to prevent (or worse still, helped to bring about!) a major disaster, would put paid to his hopes of ...... No. He would have to get in touch with the High Command before leaving the Liverpool area. His new protégé, Gerald, would have to win his spurs by stabilising the situation. Once he had been alerted to the danger represented by Christopher, he should be all right.....and Monty would make sure he got the credit for the unmasking by passing the information through the High Command.

The Chairman agreed to a meeting, but was far from happy to hear that the Fen business was still not under control. There seemed always to be a development which would solve everything – followed by news that matters were now worse. It was encouraging however, that Larry had now pin-pointed the rotten apple responsible for the latest debâcle so things should run more smoothly. As regards the hawks versus doves debate, it was, the Chairman cautiously admitted, true to say that there were plans to use the forthcoming national referendum to generate a climate more suited to a pro-active approach. Well, yes, to effect a transfer of power to a group dominated by sympathetic..... Yes, yes (crossly by now) one could call it a form of coup – but only once there was no risk of failure.

Monty, mindful of his brief, which did not include the transmission of direct instructions, forebore from pointing out that phrases such as 'no risk of failure' could be seen as the product of complacency. Parallels of a sort could be drawn with the Maginot Line, the defoliation bombing by the Americans in Vietnam, the Bay of Pigs escapade and the Argentinian decision to occupy the Malvinas, safe in the 'knowledge' that there was little which Britain could actually do about it.

"You plan to fiddle the result, I gather?" said Monty.

"Let us say we expect it to be a very close result – and that as 'Chairman' I shall need to exercise my casting vote," came the reply, delivered in a distinctly repressive, but confidently amused tone, for this was becoming too much like an interrogation for the speaker's liking. "If you want details – and nothing is absolutely final yet – I suggest you request a copy through channels, so that the High Command may deal with it appropriately."

In fact, the plan was for the result to be a larger 'No' than could easily be believed, followed by the exposure of the many unsuspecting minor agents who had followed instructions to act in a fraudulent manner. This in turn would lead to a crisis situation which could only be resolved by a second referendum. Those who had helped to uncover the first 'fiddle' would be held in reserve to do a similar job, should it be needed, but all their projections had pointed confidently to there being no need to intervene. Not only would there be a resounding (genuine) 'Yes', but also the mobilisation of right wing groups, hitherto opposed to European Union – and their consequent success at the polls on a tide of righteous indignation against the 'moderates' – would ensure sufficient 'democratic' voting power to bring in martial law. The latter would be needed to stabilise a situation which the British neo-Nazi movement had plans to thoroughly destabilise. Aspects of that, thought the Chairman, smiling to himself as he saw his ambitious, scheming colleague prepare to depart, would make paratroopers dressed as nuns seem very small beer! And then there was the 'Retter'... but after over fifty years would it really still work? John had sworn it had been meticulously maintained..... .

"I don't want that Christopher taken care of for the moment," said Monty, interrupting the older man's train of thought. "He'll be useful as a channel of dis-information. Can you let Gerald know he's not safe, though?"

"Gerald? Oh, yes, I shall be briefing him fully on the 'Retter', now that he's to be on our committee, so I'll pass on your suspicions."

"More than suspicions: I'm certain," said Monty, nettled by something in the tone of the last remark... and not happy with what amounted to a refusal to be open about the plans to force the pace. "That was a quick decision on the appointment, then?"

In reality, despite his claim to certainty about Christopher having been 'turned', Monty was aware of a niggle at the back of his mind which told him that, with Patrick involved, he would do well not to believe it had been snowing until he was living in an igloo. However, he was pretty sure of Gerald – and to admit now to this pompous old fool that he might have been wrong was more than he could stomach.

"Yes," said the Chairman. "Your recommendation won the day. He wouldn't have been our first choice had John been – er – available: he didn't think a lot of him, in fact. Gerald's come well out of this mess, however: seems to be able to command respect from the younger element, which we need."

Yes, thought Monty, with another frisson of worry, including friend Christopher, which was not as great an endorsement as he had thought! But he held his peace.

****

Martin's wife, Jennifer, had still not been located by the Organisation, which was convinced that British Intelligence had been warned and was keeping her in a safe place. The latter, however, were convinced that, despite the shambles at Stansted, some section of the Organisation had kidnapped her – possibly on her way to Charles de Gaulle Airport, possibly from the Institut – and were keeping her as a trump card.

Patrick was wary of showing his hand. He knew that Monty was a spy, but he had to be able to prove it to his superiors, not all of whom he could trust. Moreover, because of the presence of traitors, everyone was to some extent suspect – including himself. If accused, Monty would try to put together a case to prove that he, Patrick, was the real spy and either succeed or at least gain sufficient time to counter-attack. If he could gain leverage by threatening his mother, as he certainly would if backed into a corner, Monty could still turn the tables.

Both Patrick and Monty, mobilising their considerable resources, continued to search for a (genuinely) harmless middle aged school teacher, who remained blissfully unaware of her predicament, recalling, as she sped along the autoroute to Calais, the way the previous evening had ended. Henri Cazaux had been some time refilling the glasses, whilst his wife and Jennifer discussed pets. In fact, realising that his English guest was worried about the extra expense incurred by returning from her course ahead of time, he had been busy.

"It's all arranged!" he had announced when he eventually returned. "You stay here this evening; we go now to collect your luggage; you leave with our good friends, Marc and Georgette Loriot, first thing tomorrow morning!"

"But Henri....perhaps Jennifer would rather....." demurred his wife.

"Would rather pay for a plane ticket? Of course not: it would be ridiculous when they are driving to England and would enjoy her company. Do you not agree?"

He looked to Jennifer for approval and received it, noticing that she bit back the comment which had risen to her lips. "And don't worry about the ticket. I have a friend who works there – and he has promised to arrange a refund. These things can be done if you know the right people. Shall we go and get your luggage?"

Hélène apologised for her husband's high-handed action, but reassured Jennifer that the Loriots were very 'sympa' and would take her wherever she wished to go. Did she wish to telephone home to explain the change of plan? As Jennifer had been at pains to keep from her family the fact that she had decided to return, that was not necessary.

They did not see anyone when collecting her things and her room-mate, Miss Priscilla Plant, did not notice their absence when she returned at two in the morning to fall, fully clothed, onto her bed, where she slept as for dead (dead drunk was nearer the mark) until after ten the following morning. Miss Plant, when capable of mental effort, assumed that Jennifer had left as previously arranged to catch her plane. No-one asked her if she had left the night before, and if they had, they would have been no better off, for her memory of the entire evening was a blur. She recalled that Jennifer had talked of visiting friends, but had no idea who or where they were, whether she had in fact gone to see them or at what time she had departed in the morning. Miss Plant explained that she was a 'heavy sleeper' to the course director, who felt quite light-headed from the alcoholic fumes which remained behind as she, suffering the unaccustomed effects of a hang-over, carefully left the room.

And so it came about that Jennifer, very fortunately for her, eluded the attentions of predators and protectors alike. By nine the following morning, she was on her way, still expected on the midday flight for, in accordance with the well known Irishman's law, Henri Cazaux's airport friend had put his back out, bending down to pick up his brief-case and had spent the next few hours in agony, failing, therefore, to take the appropriate action concerning Jennifer's change of plan. During what became a crucial period, she remained booked in. This inaccuracy was compounded by the desk clerk misinterpreting a note concerning the apparent success in locating the lady, resulting from his observation of what he took to be Jennifer being escorted to an interview room by men who had claimed to be security officials, when getting him to put out a call for her.

The procedures for double-checking operated effectively, but the actual people who dealt with the phone calls from Monty – and, indeed, from Patrick – failed to pick up the error. When more stringent checks were made as a result of the failure of Jennifer to arrive at Stansted, the foregoing became apparent. Both sides knew she had not travelled KLM / UK Air, both suspected the other side had her somewhere..... but neither had a clue as to her whereabouts.

"They *will* be surprised when I turn up!" said Jennifer brightly, as the helpful French couple approached King's Cross station, having driven up from Dover. "It'll give Martin something else to think about, in stead of brooding over the dog. I do wish he would get out a bit more. Life in the country can be rather, well, 'humdrum', as we say. Thank you so much! No, I can manage, really. I'll ring from here and get someone to meet me at Peterborough. Now remember: you're always welcome! 'Bye!"

****

"Mother!" exploded Elizabeth. "Where have you *been*? We've been....Wait!....I – er – there's someone at the door," she invented desperately to gain time to consult and consider, calling out to the security guard with her hand over the mouthpiece. "It's my mother on the phone! She seems to be all right, and is, I think, at King's Cross. What shall I tell her? Where the hell is Patrick when he's needed?"

Lazing upstairs in a foot of herb-laden hot water, unaware that his wife had been told that he had caught a cold and was cast down by events, Martin heard the note of concern in his daughter's voice, and reached for the cordless phone which, as a matter of routine, he always took with him when having a bath.

"Hello, dear! How are you? Not long to go now – how's it going?"

"Martin! Where's Elizabeth gone? And never mind me..... How are *you*? I was so sorry to hear about Sherry..... Look, I can't talk now. The train goes in five minutes..... Can someone meet me at Peterborough in about an hour? If not, I'll get a taxi."

At this point, Elizabeth raised the receiver once again, realising that she would have to decide whether to tell her mother about her pursuers (always assuming she was still unaware of them) and whether to persuade her to stay put, get on the train..... or what.

"Oh, Hell!" she said despairingly to the guard, who had come running, revolver at the ready, on hearing her shout. "Father's on the other phone. That's all we need!"

She was just in time to hear her father swallow his surprise at hearing that his wife had returned early, manage to avoid delving into the murky waters of what she had been told and merely reply hurriedly:

"No. I mean no problem...... we'll be there..... see you soon."

"Elizabeth! That was your mother! Did you tell her to come back? I said I didn't want her bothered. I'm quite O K and..... anyway, I must get dressed and collect her."

"I think, Sir," said the Intelligence agent entrusted with ensuring their safety, "that she is the one to worry about. There have already been two attempts to abduct her. Let's hope she gave the opposition the slip just as much as she did *us*! The best thing – if you feel well enough – is for you and your daughter to drive in to the station with a couple of us following. That'll leave two to keep an eye on this place. Meanwhile, we'll try to get in touch with your son."

Shocked by the news that there had been attempts to kidnap his wife, Martin did as he was told and, on the way to the station, listened without interrupting as Elizabeth put him fully in the picture.

"Bloody Hell! They must have a Hell of a lot to hide. How on earth did she avoid them? Where can she have been if the people running the course haven't been able to find her?"

"At least that murdering bunch of Nazis haven't been able to either," said Elizabeth. "But what shall we do if she's not on this train?" she added, voicing everyone's concern as she swung the car round the roundabout and headed back to the station.

"Ten bloody minutes," said Martin, glancing at the dashboard clock. "Those two over there could be the opposition – or, more likely those!"

"Stop being silly!" said his daughter. "What about the two who have just drawn into the car park?"

"Yes, they look pretty tough.....but aren't they our two lads?" objected Martin. "Oh, all right, you win! If anything happens to Jennifer, though, it'll be all my fault. I should never have poked my nose in....." His voice tailed off and he turned away to hide the tears of worry, of regret ....of love.

"Come on, you old fool," said his daughter, placing a consoling hand on his arm. "Let's go and meet her – and don't let her see you looking like that. Your job is to look cheerful, brisk, surprised, but *pleased*, to see her; not too cast down about Sherry..... just a few minor local difficulties. Nothing to worry about. O K?"

Martin responded well to the advice, almost literally shaking himself out of his gloomy mood.

"You're right. Thanks. As regards the dog, it won't be difficult. I'm ashamed to say that all this with your mother has completely driven Sherry from my mind....."

"I should damn' well hope so, too!" replied Elizabeth, leading her father firmly into the station.

CHAPTER TWENTY-EIGHT

As the new Eastern Area Controller, the order should have come to Gerald to arrange the murder in hospital of Gordon, the surviving half of the hit squad which had come to grief at Stansted. He could at least have tipped off Patrick, even if refusing to implement it would have been too compromising. In fact, it was given by Monty direct to the local commander at Haslemere, (who was also worried about being linked to the Lincolnshire killings) with a request to make *absolutely* sure by using someone who could recognise the victim.

"One other thing," added Monty, "have you heard about that Christopher – the lad at the Castle? No? Well, he's the one who's been tipping off the opposition. I want to interrogate him: the Chairman asked me to organise someone to pick him up. Can you cover that as well?"

"We'll take care of that, Larry," came the reply, "providing we can despatch the bastard slowly and painfully afterwards: he's caused the death of one, shortly to be two, of my best men."

"O K – but let the Chairman know," said Monty. "And no balls-ups on this one: there's been enough mistaken identity recently. Let's get it right for a change!"

Monty's remark was not well received, as the 'Mrs Brady fiasco' had been orchestrated by this same 'Larry'.... but a recent recruit whose record appeared to be suitably scruple-free (and could recognise Gordon) was duly despatched to perform the grisly task before Gordon could pass on, whether willingly or under the influence of drugs, information which might incriminate others. As one of those 'others', Monty was particularly keen to guarantee the man's permanent silence.

Masquerading as a hospital porter, the assassin, one Kevin Goode, gained access to the relevant area with ease (aided by a consultant loyal to the Cause). Whilst there were advantages in the fact that Goode could recognise Gordon, the converse proved counter-productive. Gordon gave the appearance of being asleep when his murderer peered in the window, but in fact he was surveying his surroundings through half closed eyelids... and recognised him. He also noted the man's expression, which, combined with his knowledge of the way in which the Organisation operated, forced him to the unpleasant conclusion that he was about to be sacrificed. He was still unable to talk, but rage and fear combined to create readings of pulse, brain activity, etc., which caused the nurse who came to check on him to scribble the results hurriedly, dropping her ball-point pen in the process, before departing rapidly to get help.

By the time his system was found once again to be stable, Gordon had made up his mind. He would write a 'confession', hoping thereby to get lenient treatment (including a new identity). After all, they hadn't in fact killed anyone, and surely information about the body in Thorpe Tunnel Bunker, and this chap 'Larry' who had set up the attempted kidnapping, would be sufficient to bargain with. The trouble was there was so little time if, as he suspected, the fake porter had instructions to silence him....and though he had the ball-point pen dropped by the nurse, he had no paper, and could barely move.

Kevin Goode had to work a long shift before seeing his opportunity – the brief descent into slumber of the policeman detailed to sit on guard outside Gordon's room. His attack was swift, silent and lethally effective: Patrick had lost a vital link in his quest for clearly demonstrable evidence of Monty's real loyalties.

That was the bad news, but it was more than outweighed by the good, when it was flashed through to Patrick: his mother had been found – or, rather, heard. Somehow she had evaded Monty's agents. The other good news was that Mrs Pateman had been located – not difficult with Mrs Tolliver's excellent description, combined with the type, colour and number of her car, including the tell-tale parking permit for the Castle. She was 'singing' loudly about 'Larry' whose description fitted Monty perfectly, even down to the rather prominent ears (which he was more than happy to have compared to those so often highlighted in caricatures of the heir to the throne). The only link needed was proof that the 'Larry' who could be identified by Mrs Pateman, if that lady were shown Burton-Latimer in a 'line-up', was the same person who had arranged

199

the attempted abduction. Patrick still hesitated to make his denouncement, knowing what he was up against. It had to be water tight, and it had to be soon or the traitor would 'do a Lucan' – probably aided by some of the same people who had helped that gentleman to evade arrest.

Patrick was right: Monty was on his way back across the Channel, by train to Leeds, thence to London (King's Cross), by Underground to Liverpool Street and from there by the boat train to Harwich. By one of life's weird coincidences, he was walking across the concourse just as Jennifer put down the phone and hurried to catch her train to Peterborough. She was looking ahead, searching for Platform 3 and ran straight into him, her own modest weight boosted by a substantial suitcase on wheels.

"Sorry!" said Monty, quintessentially English, displaying that nation's absurd habit of apologising for someone else's clumsiness.

"No, my fault. I – I must dash..... The train....." panted Jennifer.

"Wait!" said Monty, rubbing his knee. "You've dropped your paper."

Jennifer smiled her thanks at the nice polite gentleman with the protruding ears; what a difference from those rude Parisians! And so the two passed in mutual ignorance, hunter and hunted colliding and splitting apart like atomic particles in a chemical reaction. Perhaps Patrick's superstitiously crossed fingers had worked after all – or may be, for once, the devil had failed to look after his own.

On the other hand, Monty's luck held in respect of Gordon's failure to get hold of any paper to complement the ball-point pen found tightly gripped in his stiffening fingers. The body had been wheeled to the morgue prior to the performance of an autopsy to determine the cause of death. Patrick had little interest in the result of that examination, for he had no doubt that the gunman had been murdered by his own side, the method being of purely academic interest at this stage. He was equally uninterested in the bed-sheets which surrounded the corpse. In that, however, he was making a big mistake, for, by a superhuman effort, the wounded, almost immobilised, patient had contrived to scrawl upon the starched white cotton sufficient key words to link together 'Larry', Thorpe Tunnel, Gerald, Mrs Brady, H F C and the neo-Nazis. Gordon's determined effort to revenge his death deserved better than to be bleached into obscurity in the hospital laundry – and so it proved. The orderly whose task was to strip away the bedding noticed the biro marks and looked more closely. As he deciphered the writing, he grew both excited and nervous. The guy was thought to have been 'got at', so the writing would probably help to find the assassins, but whoever drew attention to it might well find themselves in deep water (literally, wearing the proverbial concrete overcoat).

By a happy chance, the porter had not long before read an article drawing attention to the decline of the word 'secret' in the Secret Service, citing as evidence the publication of the name of the head of the Service (a far cry from 'M') and the provision of a telephone number, available through Yellow Pages. It even quoted the number, going on to 'rubbish' the idea by means of an imagined conversation which began 'U K Export/Import, Boris speaking.....'. He placed the sheet where it would not be disturbed on finishing his shift and went home, resolved to ring if he could find the article but too nervous of being identified to risk Directory Enquiries.

Whilst this delay gave Monty more time to make himself scarce, it was unfortunate for him that the porter had to post a small parcel – for it was while waiting in the queue at the Post Office that he saw a poster giving him the very information he required. Careful to disguise what he was writing, he copied it down: 0171 930 9000. Then, having posted the parcel, he made for a vacant telephone. In fact, it was just like ringing any other business answer phone:

"This is the M I 5 Phoneline. If you have information which you want to give to the Security Service, please hold the line and an operator will speak to you."

No pressure was applied for him to identify himself and at the end (having only related the contents, implying that it was written on paper and being vague about the author), he was thanked and asked if he would either give a number where he could be contacted or, failing that, ring again in about an hour. The call was timed and its location deduced as being a public phone booth near the East Herts Hospital, at Harlow. There were sufficient keywords in the message for its contents to be rapidly conveyed to Patrick, for whom the location – close to the hospital to which the two gunmen had been taken from nearby Stansted – was the clincher.

"Could he have written something before they got to him?" he asked the ward Sister when she came to the phone.

"Well, it's true he had Nurse Macaulay's biro gripped in his hand when we pulled back the sheet – but he couldn't have got hold of any paper without asking, and he never regained the power of speech, so...."

"What about the bed-clothes? Did you check them? Or, rather, would you please do so?" he asked, with mounting excitement.

The public-spirited porter rang back as requested, to find that all seemed to be known except the actual location of the sheet, which he gladly supplied.

Knowing the difficulty for his superiors of being confronted with a denunciation by one member of the Service of another – deciding which one is the traitor before taking positive action – Patrick had been waiting until he had some 'proof' which he, personally, could not have manufactured: this was it. The Director was convinced, and the hunt for the Honourable Anthony Laurence Burton-Latimer was on.

****

Monty rubbed his knee where the clumsy woman had rammed her overloaded suitcase into him and contemplated the spreading urban sprawl of Colchester as the train left for Harwich. He had considered leaving the train and taking the bus to Mersea Island to get aboard his boat, but felt he was too well known in the area for safety. No; a rapid, anonymous departure was required before the Department grew suspicious – encouraged by that fellow Brady. If only he'd managed to get his hands on the wretch's mother – doubtless just as dreary a person as the father.....and how the hell had *he* run rings round Gerald? He'd better ring Vienna to get fixed up with somewhere to lie low until they could stabilise the situation. They'd be worried by the hawkishness he had detected amongst the British leadership, especially if they intended to activate the 'Retter'. The bloody fools! All they had to do was sit back and wait. Look at the recent successes of the National Front in France: extra payments to 'racially pure' parents, even! And all in the precious name of local democracy. There was plenty of time to make the odd telephone call before passing through passport control to the ferry......but the reflective calm of the moment was shattered by the information thereby gained. Monty learned that he was, without realising it, 'on the run'. Had he continued and boarded the ferry, he would have suffered a similar fate to that of Crippen, and been caught by a radio message and detained on board ship.

"I'll get back to my launch and sail her across," declared Monty, wishing he had followed that course an hour earlier

"Too risky," came the reply, "and as you seem to have failed to bring the British round to a policy of patience, there is a little job we want done before you leave."

"Before I leave!" expostulated Monty, recognising the criticism implicit in the reference to his 'failure'. "You've just said I could be picked up at any moment. I'm sure John Dalton's replacement can organise something this end – he's only just down the road and we've been working together lately."

"Yes, that should make it easy. He's the one you're to contact. Get him to hide you for a day or two on the 'Retter': tell him you know more about it than he could learn from a visit, despite what he will have found in John's safe, which is true – or will be shortly. He's sure to be interested enough to come to Harwich. Now, listen! This is what you are to do."

****

With the office door locked, and instructions not to disturb him, Gerald settled down with a large mug of coffee and a few biscuits. By applying the combination of numbers, number of clockwise and reverse turns of the dial – and the all-important pause after the third and fifth digits – he was able to open John Dalton's safe. He noted the substantial amount of money and wondered whether it was accountable, skimmed through the notes on staff (including a far from complimentary comment on himself which, presumably, had not been given a wider distribution!) and lifted out two fat files. The first contained a large number of short typed notes and cuttings of varying length taken from a wide range of publications, going back over many years. They were numbered with the prefix R P, followed by a letter, two numbers and then another one, two or three numbers. Given the contents, it was not difficult to work out that the letter referred to the country – F for France, for example. The next two numbers gave the year and the final series the identification. Key words were highlighted, so that B 98 64 was presumably cross-referenced to 'bunker' and ran as follows:

'Bunker sale. A nuclear bunker buried 300ft below ground at R A F Ash, near Manston, Kent is close to being sold. The bunker has two control rooms, a fire station, sewage works, accommodation and a maze of corridors.'

A slightly earlier item contained several words deemed worthy of cross-referral and was a letter to the Times, again from Kent, which ran: '..... at Referendum Party functions is the fear that if Britain enters the E M U, which Helmut Kohl advocates, it will mean the surrender of all control over fiscal and social policies.....'

The last section was underlined in its entirety and read: '..In effect Britain will become a province of an undemocratic European Union dominated by Germany.'

The other file contained very different material, all neatly typed and bound, with the prefix S T T. They were a series of plans, all designed to create civil unrest, the latest relating to the forthcoming Referendum on European Monetary Union. Gerald read on, fascinated, while his coffee grew cold and his biscuits remained untouched. The extent to which the leadership appeared to be able to call on sympathisers was an eye-opener. Key positions throughout the Kingdom were in their hands – in our hands..... no, dammit, in *their* hands, for clearly he, Gerald, was held in such low regard that he would never have gained the recognition his abilities and breeding demanded, had he remained loyal to the Cause. Kenneth, he mused, would be delighted with this! He read on, noting references to the 'Retter', to plans to sink a ferry, having issued a warning supposedly from the I R A, to an attempt (which was planned to fail) to blow up the House of Lords on November the Fifth. Again the aim was to manipulate public opinion by making them believe the worst of other (especially left wing) terrorist groups, to observe the incompetence and weakness of the legitimate government of the day..... and then to be receptive to firm action, especially the imposition, 'temporarily', of martial law.

In all cases, there was an army of adherents, each small group unaware of more than a handful of like-minded people, throughout the land. The pattern of Hall Farm, the Castle, Fotheringhay, the helicopter near Peterborough, was repeated nation-wide, with similar units... at East Mersea, in Essex, for example and, of course, Haslemere in Sussex. Infiltration of the police was a feature, as was that of the River Boards, Water Authorities and Sea Defence Boards. It was clear, too, that extensive use had been made of the secret depôts set up in the 1940's and the 'Resistance Freedom Fighters', whose expertise and potential for murder and disruption had never had to be put to the test against the expected German conquerors. Everywhere, it seemed, could be found facilities such as those at Hall Farm (the strawstack bunker), Thorpe Tunnel and the ancient passages at Fotheringhay, the secret of which had been lost with the sudden death of the two blacksmiths and their immediate superior, the Agent at Wothorpe Castle.

Constant reference was made to the 'Retter', and Gerald turned with mounting interest to the relevant Appendix. Although he had picked up parts of the story over the years – hence the large photograph of a submarine in the inner room at Hall Farm Bunker – he was fascinated by the account, only his eyes moving as they scanned the yellowing pages. He had been part of it, over fifty years ago, one of the babies loaded on board this triumph of advanced engineering, incorporating all the latest technical refinements which came just too late to win the war.

Capable of staying under water indefinitely, of high submerged speeds, silent running at 2 to 3 knots and shrouded in a radar resistant 'stealth' material, the Retter (the 'Saviour'), boasted a keel made largely of gold and contained boxes of documents designed to put pressure on British collaborators. It also had torpedoes, of course, and even the ability to fire rockets from a submerged position. There had been three major technical hopes as the war turned against Hitler – rockets, submarines and the destructive potential of splitting the atom. It was clear from these documents that in the 'Retter' they had developed two of these to form a powerful threat: a threat which, it appeared, still existed.

"Of course!" murmured Gerald to himself. "Just off Harwich: the gold didn't come from a 16th century wreck at all. I must pay a visit – go back to the womb, as it were!"

He returned the files to the safe, having made a few brief notes for his report, and emerged, stretching, to be told that a person identifying himself as 'Larry' was very anxious to make contact.

CHAPTER TWENTY-NINE

As he listened to Monty's insistent request for sanctuary on the 'Retter', Gerald started to feel out of his depth. What line should he take? It was not practicable to ring his 'control' from the office, so he decided to set up a meeting some way away in order to give himself time to unload his information and get guidance on how to cope with Larry, who had not given a return number – not surprisingly as he was ringing from a (very) public booth in the Stena Line waiting area.

As it suited both parties, Gerald quickly got Larry's agreement to meet at Harwich, Parkeston Quay in about an hour and set off, clutching his mobile phone. After about ten minutes, he pulled off into a well-screened lay-by and set about the task of tracking down Kenneth, who told him to drive on, ready to pull in again, to get instructions before meeting Larry. Kenneth debated whether to warn Gerald that they were officially aware of Monty as a spy, but thought it best to leave the timing of that as a decision for Patrick.

In due course, briefed by Kenneth on Patrick's instructions, Gerald drove into the Harwich International Ferry car park, where he was rapidly joined by the harassed, sweating Larry, who urged him to get him out of sight as quickly as possible.

"Vienna told me I was blown," he gasped. "That bugger Brady, it must be. Those incompetent fools made a total *balls-up* of snatching his mother. You've got to hide me on the 'Retter' until they can set up a safe route. Are you in the picture about the sunken sub., over there?"

Monty flapped his hand in the general direction of the open sea, hoping his protégé would accept what amounted to instructions without counter suggestions or too much checking back with his High Command. Monty's orders from Austria were to immobilise the Retter's 'weapon to end all weapons' (as it had seemed back in 1945). The first step was to get on board. Thanks to his relationship with Gerald, that was going very well.

Patrick had correctly foreseen that Monty must have been warned that he was being hunted, but had been unwilling to take the excellent opportunity offered of picking him up, lest it point too clearly to Gerald as the source of information. In fact, they had completely lost Monty and feared he had managed to quit the country. "Tell Gerald to see what he wants," had been his instructions to Kenneth. "If he wants to be hidden, O K. They'll have several places in the area, and Gerald will know where he is, so there should be no real problem. Gerald can get advice from his local staff if he's not yet fully au fait with all their codes, local commanders, etc."

In fact, Gerald had often visited the H F C establishment in Harwich Old Town, towards which he now took Larry, although only since examining the documents in John's safe had he realised the full depth – in every sense of the word – of that operation.

Back in 1945, the un-numbered U-boat known as the 'Retter' had sailed with U-534, escaping under cover of the diversion provided by the sinking of the latter. It had voyaged as far as the North Norfolk coast, where it had unloaded the precious human cargo before returning to a pre-determined spot a few miles off-shore from the port of Harwich. That spot was not far from a flashing marker – a small light-ship in effect, easily visible from the cross-channel ferry as it wound its way slowly down the narrow channel in the estuary. Many years before, about four hundred, in fact, one of the supply ships of the Spanish Armada had foundered at the spot, sinking a surprising depth, for there was a sort of underwater ravine into which, by chance, the stricken ship had finally fallen, together with its cargo. The right to dive and retrieve treasure had been acquired before the war by a local landowner who had been sympathetic to the Nazis.....and the sleek, fully operational, gold-laden U-boat had been carefully manoeuvred to lie alongside the ancient wreck, enabling comings and goings to take place as if for the purpose of salvaging the 16th century remains.

Entry to the submarine was effected via the rocket-firing 'port', for the boat (a fore-runner of the much more powerful Polaris) was able, or so the scientists claimed, to despatch rockets from beneath the sea. All this Gerald had gathered in theory as he perused the secret documents. Now he was about to see it, courtesy of Clarence, whom he had known for years to be in charge of the salvage operations which (supposedly, as it turned out) produced a steady trickle of gold, coins, cannon balls, etc.

The arrival of the car (which appeared to contain only Gerald) was monitored by one of Patrick's men, placed near the H F C offices after the place had been identified as 'dodgy' by Martin. This was convenient, as Gerald had not been able to break off and report his movements whilst with his 'guest', who was presumed to be crouching on the floor in order to escape detection.

Shortly after their arrival, Gerald and Monty boarded the sea-going launch used to 'service' the salvage operation, their docking at the diving platform being photographed by a hastily routed reconnaissance aircraft.

"Now we give old Klaus a buzz," said Clarence to Gerald as they made fast in the centre of the substantial concrete platform, covered not only to keep out the weather, but also prying eyes, so that it resembled the process of docking in one of the old Channel port U-boat pens (which had influenced the design). "Your friend can step out now. He'll not be seen."

"Klaus? I thought his name was Stanley," said Gerald, recalling the details in the file. "How long does he stay here at a time?"

"He's Stanley the same as yon toff is Larry – but there's only four of us come here regular, and he's Klaus to us. You'll see!" he added with a knowing laugh.

"And who relieves him – you?"

"Hardly! I'm a respectable fisherman and antique dealer, aren't I? No, there's no relief for old Klaus..... and you can take that whichever way you like. Here we go!" he added, as an answering buzz came from the depths. "One at a time. I'll have a quick word on the old ship-to-ship so he knows what's up, then you go first. I'll stay up here."

Clarence stepped across to the intercom, from which emerged a crackle of noise concluded by a sharp word and a muttered:

"Cantankerous old sod!.... He's ready," said Clarence.

"But not 'willing and able'?" asked Gerald who had heard the tenor but not the words of the exchange.

209

"You could say that – but he'll do what he's told. Can't say I blame him, the life he leads. Just step in and spin the wheel to make the seal tight..... then press the down arrow and wait until you see a green light. That'll mean you've arrived and are secured to the airlock. You unbolt the hole in the floor – and provided all is well, you climb down to the good ship 'Retter'!"

Feeling extremely vulnerable, Gerald stepped inside the small 'bathysphere' and turned the locking wheel. In due course, a green light appeared, which he took to mean it was time to press for 'down'. Apart from a slight rocking, there was little sense of movement as the chains which raised and lowered the globe moved slowly, powered by electric motors top and bottom. The bump as it met the casing of the last of the ill-fated German submarine navy caused Gerald to fall against the side, bruising his head and adding that discomfort to the mounting claustrophobia and the chill which had crept over his under-clothed body as they descended.

"That miserable bugger could have kitted us out for this," he grumbled to himself as he bent to release the hatch, pausing to wonder whether the equipment was still safe.

It was with considerable relief that he stepped down to the warmth of the submarine and took in his surroundings. The shining gauges, brightly lit and quite spacious interior, with its table containing the remains of a meal for one, the flags and badges of the long gone military might of Hitler's Germany..... all this he barely noticed, for the scene was dominated by the single shining eye of the septuagenarian? – octogenarian? – whose bent frame and pale visage confronted him.

The stream of sailor's German which issued from the twisted mouth was too rapid for Gerald to follow, but the foul stench of the Ancient Mariner's breath and the spittle as the tirade continued, caused him to push the old ruin away and move past to gain breathing space. So this was Stanley, he thought, servant of the 'Retter', the 'Saviour', who must have been here for – surely not since.....? God, it was possible! His thoughts were interrupted by a buzz from up top which caused the noxious creature to turn to move slowly up the ladder to make secure the hatch in the sphere. Presumably that was what the old wreck had been on about, thought Gerald: one was supposed to secure the base of the craft before entering the submarine.... again poor briefing by Clarence. There seemed to be scope for tightening up on John Dalton's staff, thought Gerald, conveniently forgetting that that was precisely what the wretched man had been doing when he met his end. Steeling himself to cope with Klaus's company in the confined spaces of the aged submarine, he indicated a desire to use the intercom and spoke to Clarence.

"I'll take a look round with – er – Klaus, then I'll come up and Larry can return..... yes..... a few days, I said, not a few hours. We can't organise his escape that quickly. No; it's a bit cramped down here, so I think it's best if I come up first....He says what? He'd rather do it that way? Good – about ten minutes, I imagine. Will you have a word with Stanl...with Klaus? My German's a little rusty. Oh, does he..... well, have a word all the same, will you. Here he is."

Gerald passed the receiver to Klaus and removed himself to the other end of the immediate area, while Clarence carried out his wishes. He found the meaningful (uncomplimentary) glances and the knowing cackles extremely irritating, as they clearly arose from comments far from appropriate concerning their new boss. The sooner he was out of here, the better, gold or no gold, he thought, as the conversation concluded and the aged caretaker signalled him to follow.

There was no doubt that the engineers had built well. Some repairs and strengthening had been carried out, but everything appeared to be in working order. It seemed unlikely that the torpedo tubes were clear of external obstruction, and one had no way of knowing how easy it would be to reconvert the rocket firing arrangements, should plan S T T 4 be thought desirable. Indeed, after so many years it would surely be unwise to risk the shock of actually firing a rocket. Gerald noted the markings on various boxes which appeared to contain warheads, and did his best to reproduce in his notebook what looked like Russian and Arabic letters on six much newer boxes. The freezers contained plenty of food, a small desalination plant took care of drinking water needs and there were both an air-line and a power cable leading to the diving platform.

Before leaving, Gerald noted that the firing mechanism for the rockets was protected by a form of combination lock, akin to a wall safe. Klaus indicated that he did not have the number, much to Gerald's relief, for the man was not fit to be trusted with a bow and arrow, never mind an untested, archaic and probably highly volatile underwater version of the 'V 2', with God only knew what in the warhead! H M G would have to decide what to do about this threat to the environment parked at their back door – and the sooner he passed on the information, the better. Time to return topsides for fresh air, dry land, and instructions.

Monty had been trying to think of a way of getting Gerald out of the way to have the 'Retter' to himself, so he was delighted when it was proposed that he go down and Gerald come up. He heard Clarence say a few hours, but did not hear the correction from down below. Clarence, for his part, did not *forget* to make this clear to 'Larry' – he had his own reasons for quite deliberately allowing him to continue to think that his sojourn in the 'Retter' would be only a matter of hours.

Gerald sniffed the air appreciatively as he stepped from the deep sea 'lift', and allowed Monty to seal himself in.

"See you to-morrow," he called as the hatch closed, adding to the sound-proof globe, "Good Luck with Klaus!"

"On the run, is he?" said Clarence. "You can always tell.... had one years ago, poor bugger. Klaus was younger then..... He's matured with age, just like a ripe Camembert!" He laughed unpleasantly as he saw Gerald's nose wrinkle with the recent memory. The very thought of spending a whole day in the company of that...that...crone was enough to cause a nauseous shudder.

"Heard the forecast?" asked the boatman, continuing with evident glee. "By this time tomorrow they reckon Force 10: you'll not be seeing yon toff while next week."

"Did you tell him?"

"Not bloody likely! We never do... had one chap – very upper class – bit like 'im. Only lasted two year; less than that in 'is right mind."

"Two years! Down there on his own? Surely he...."

"Oh, he'd have been all right on his own – books, letters, videos, we even put bets on for them. No, it's Klaus: they can't stand 'is 'abits, you see. When 'e eats, 'e....."

"Spare me. I'd rather not know. You can't get up-wind of someone in a submarine. Doesn't anyone try to do something about him?"

"Are *you* going to? No, it's too late... he's just rotting away, and mad as a hatter. Lives, if you could call it that, for the 'Retter', thinks of himself as a sort of High Priest."

"He's certainly 'high'," agreed Gerald. "Larry'll be upset if we don't get him away to the Continent pretty soon."

Clarence's chuckle was suppressed, emerging as a cross between a snort and a bark. He'd seen it all before..... like the other fella he'd been talking about..... just disappeared one night. They could come up for a breath of night air when no-one could see them....but there was always the risk in daylight of a distant telescope, or aerial photo's. There'd been a plane overhead earlier – often was round here – and they couldn't risk being seen when they were on the run. Mind you, the price was high.... high, yes!

Shortly after returning from the Retter, Gerald left Harwich old town and stopped after about two miles to phone in his report, only to be told to drive on and pull in at another, better hidden, lay-by where Kenneth was waiting. In due course, all the details, including the reproductions of the markings on the newer rockets, were made available to Patrick, together with Gerald's brief summaries of the contents of the two fat files from John Dalton's safe. The information was dynamite and Patrick instructed Kenneth to get hold of the complete details as soon as possible.

From information already supplied, however, it was clear that the Organisation had, mainly from the former Soviet Union, obtained modern rockets, almost certainly now armed with a powerful nerve gas or, perhaps, droplet-spread anthrax germs. Whilst the original rockets were unlikely still to be usable, these new ones, if the projection facilities were intact – represented a significant threat, or last ditch weapon. It was one of Patrick's staff who came up with the probable reason for the prefix S T T which applied to the scary scenarios involving chemical warfare directed at London – and always blamed others in order to create chaos, suspicion and mistrust of the legal authorities. It was, she suggested, short for 'Shake The Tree'.... and was contrasted with the evidence of steady success throughout Europe. Those items justifying a waiting game, showing that history was on their side, were given the prefix R P; surely that must be 'Ripe Plum', she had added, to general agreement.

It was not quite so easy to decide what to do about the underwater arsenal, however. If faced with a direct threat, it would be better to blow it up to prevent a missile launch, but no-one could be sure that such a move might not seriously contaminate the ocean, risking the creation of that very civil panic which the Organisation hoped, in the S T T plans, to turn to their advantage.

"We have to assume that they wanted to get Monty on board," said Patrick. "He could've got away, but we know he deliberately missed the ferry and then contacted Gerald. The question is: why? What's his mission? Remember, he must have been sent over here. By chance, he and I met at Stansted, both very much on 'business', both claiming otherwise."

"Surely he could just have been warned he was rumbled – and didn't risk being caught on the ferry? The 'Retter' was the obvious hiding place: we'd never've known without Gerald."

"Perhaps," said Patrick, "but he was ahead of us, and good intelligence from our own Secret Service was, indeed still is, available to him. The other point is whether he was deliberately misinformed by his own side, frightened into running to Gerald for help, and whether Vienna was unimpressed by his contribution to the British scene... to the point of giving him last minute instructions concerning his mission whilst he's under the waves. The crucial thing – and we've nothing to go on – is whether Monty is there to make it easier to 'shake the tree', or to remove the effectiveness of that ultimate weapon, lest it be misused by the British leadership. Time may tell – in the form of instructions to Gerald from Vienna and Liverpool."

"We may not have time," said Patrick's chief. "I want a strike force ready at a moment's notice – but I want it to appear to be an accident. How about a rival submarine? No-one would know what had happened if we ran a night attack."

"Daytime is better," opined Patrick, "for an accident. Oh, yes, it is... something on these lines: three planes on a training flight; one gets into trouble. The pilot gallantly stays with it long enough to clear the populated area, ejects just before it crashes into the sea..... at the very spot where there is an insignificant treasure-seeking operation on a 16th century wreck."

"A wreck loaded with bugs and modern high explosive?"

"Easy! We load up the sacrificial plane with bits of Second World War mine casing...... then those bits will be found, and appear to have caused the massive explosion. What a happy chance! Another miracle, better than the parting of the waters of the Red Sea."

"It could work!" said a colleague, whilst another added drily: "It wouldn't be the first time a plane has crashed conveniently. With modern guidance techniques, the hero could bail out several miles away."

"Or never have been on board at all!" added the Chief. "Get it set up ready to go, using some suitably obsolescent fighter plane."

"Are you implying, Sir," interjected the only military man present, "that we have any other sort?"

CHAPTER THIRTY

Christopher and, to a lesser extent, Henry were feeling abandoned. Monty had promised to organise the disappearance of Christopher from the area and to contact his Continental colleagues to find a suitable position.... but he seemed to have gone to ground himself. Gerald was too busy, perhaps too elevated, to concern himself with low grade operatives. They couldn't stay indefinitely at the Thorpe Tunnel bunker: their absence from the Castle and the farm, respectively, would soon look very odd.

"Why don't you come with me to 'suss out' Hall Farm?" said Henry. "If the coast is clear you can stay there. Give me a hand around the place.... perhaps drive down to get the next batch of immigrants."

"I can't be seen around here!" said Christopher, appalled at the thought of settling down for a lifetime of obscurity in the Fens, playing second fiddle to Henry, "but I might try my luck down south. Is it Harwich you go to?"

"Yes, but you'd have to be *told* to go down. You couldn't just drop in. If you wait a few days, Gerald'll get things organised again. Surely it's worth having a look..... but stay here if you prefer. I'll ring you if the bunker's untouched."

"And suppose they're waiting for you – what then? I shall be sat here wondering what's happening."

"So come and see! I know a cross-country route, along paths and through the wood. You can get quite close to the farm without being seen.....Good, let's get moving. Use those spare gumboots: it's quite muddy in places, but take your shoes as well."

And so the two young men set off in an easterly direction towards Hall Farm, carrying a basket of mushrooms as 'cover', a modern day version of the wolf striding out for Little Red Riding Hood's grandmother (for the basket contained Henry's gun in addition to the innocent fungi).

Playing, quite unwittingly, the rôle of the far from street-wise maiden in the same fable, Martin had set off to go into town. Much as she loved him, Jennifer had found him a bit of a nuisance 'under her feet all day', and had urged him to go for a walk to get some exercise, even though it was not made necessary by having to take the dog. They had compromised on his walking into town to go to the cash machine and get his hair cut. With the virtual incarceration of Monty, Patrick had removed the permanent bodyguard, although they had a number to ring if they saw anything suspicious. So it was that Martin, having been put off by finding four people waiting at the old-fashioned 'barber' he insisted on patronising (despite the lack of appointments and uncompromising nature of the styling), found himself in effect committed to being 'out' for the next two or three hours.

It was not surprising that his steps took him towards the wood, but he didn't *have* to carry on to the 'secret path' which led to Hall Farm. Given the operation of 'Sod's Law' on such occasions, it could be said to have been almost inevitable that he was just about to remove the false brushwood screen when Christopher and Henry caught up with him. He turned at the noise and the obvious mutual recognition precluded the possibility – by either party – of a muttered greeting and departure.

"But you were....I saw..." Christopher lapsed into open-mouthed silence, but his colleague had his pistol out in a second, for it was clear that this was no chance encounter with a genuine member of the rambling public.

"Stay back!" Henry commanded Christopher. "You'll be in my field of fire. Now, I don't know how you know him, but I'm pretty damn' sure he knows too much."

"Put that away for God's sake!" cried Christopher. "We don't want another balls up like last time: this is – er – one of our most senior people. He's....."

He turned to the petrified Martin, who was conscious only of his stupidity in failing to stay away from danger: no bodyguards, no-one knew where he had gone, no hope of playing the innocent old fool, the rambling rustic..... and no convenient body-armoured stand-in.

"You must believe me!" continued Christopher, who was in fact overjoyed to see that 534 was alive and well. "I'd no idea they were going to shoot: I tried to stop them, but they threatened me. They wouldn't believe you were genuine.... I told them... and then the others found you were bringing a report! Old Proudfoot was shattered.... he walked under... but you must know all this! I'm so relieved. You see they blame me, too, and I suppose they're right, but *please*," Christopher ignored his colleague's firing angle and actually fell to his knees before the astonished Martin. "I swear I meant you no harm!"

"That's all right. I understand. All in the line of business," said Martin, keeping a wary eye on Henry, who did not seem to be a fully paid up member of his newly founded fan club.

"Er – what are you two doing here?" he asked, reasoning that by taking the initiative he might forestall the same question being put by one of *them*.

"We're on our way to the farm," said Henry, who had still not lowered his gun. "And how come if he saw you shot, you're not dead?"

Blasphemously, Martin recalled that he was not the first person to be asked to explain himself in such circumstances. 'Good question' came to mind, along with 'Doubting Thomas' and 'Ye of little faith'..... but, after a barely perceptible pause, during which his brain raced like a ship's propeller as it rises clear of the water, he replied:

"You've heard of body armour? Plus the fact that they didn't get a second chance; we were expecting some such move. Now, you get on your way – and take care. Report what you find in the usual way.... and do you think you could point that thing somewhere else? I'm somewhat under-dressed for the occasion!"

Martin smiled in what he hoped was (literally) a disarming manner, and bent down to give a helping hand to his chief (and possibly only) disciple.

Christopher grasped the proffered hand eagerly and stood to look his generous, brave, truly *venerable* leader firmly in the eye:

"Tell me what I can do to make up for it. Let me prove my loyalty!" he exclaimed, melodramatic in his appreciation.

Martin had great difficulty in reciprocating the direct gaze, and was spared the task of formulating an appropriate response (being, as a schoolteacher, unused to praise of any sort, let alone the fulsome variety), by the interjection of Henry, who had at least postponed sentencing of Christopher's idol for the gathering of medical and psychological reports:

"That'll keep! We're off to the farm, and you're off to... wherever you sprang from. Got a vehicle somewhere?"

"I tend to use public transport whenever possible," said Martin loftily. "It's better for security. There's a bus due along that road shortly, so I'll wish you two lads good luck and – er – keep up the good work!"

"Do you live round here, then?" asked Henry.

"Good Gracious, no," said Martin. "I, well, I get around. Back to London, now. We may meet again, of course, but my work takes me to various places."

If only he had said 'Bristol' or 'Worksop', rather than 'London', thought Martin a moment later, for the delighted Christopher almost yelped his request:

"London! Let me come with you. Larry said he would arrange for me to get clear of this area – of the country, even...... but *you* could do that. I mean, I could help you, work for you, if..... that is ....if you'll have me."

The lad was so genuine and Martin, like many in his profession, was essentially an optimist where the young were concerned, so found himself assuring Christopher that he would do what he could. Realising that he had to explain how he came to be walking, with no car nearby, Martin claimed to be about to catch a local bus to Peterborough and thence by train to London, King's Cross; if he wished, Christopher could accompany him. He was, he felt, being sensible (rather than just pushing his luck) as in this way he reinforced his credentials as a member of the Organisation. He should be able to make an excuse to use a public phone before too long and then warn either Gerald or, better still, Patrick what was happening. Being accompanied by Christopher, Martin thought, would ensure that he was not attacked by other members of the Organisation.

In fact that was not quite the case. Thanks to Monty, Christopher was a marked man and at that very moment, two thugs from Haslemere were on their way to South Lincolnshire, charged with the task of bringing the young man, preferably but not necessarily in one piece, to a spot where he could be interrogated. The Chairman had been contacted by the Haslemere commander and had agreed to let him send his men to deal with the traitor whom Monty had unmasked: for such people the Organisation had no mercy.

The first opportunity for Martin to telephone one of the 'very important people whom only he knew' occurred at Peterborough station. Handing Christopher fifty pounds, he told him to join the queue for tickets, whilst he used the phone to make suitable arrangements for his reception in Holland. With relief, Martin turned towards the phone booths, only to pause as he realised that he was unable to remember any of the most suitable numbers – not that for Gerald, for Patrick nor for their special security guard. Cursing this evidence of advancing senility, Martin rang his own home, hoping against all the odds that it would be one of his children who answered. In the event, he was faced with his own answering machine and prefaced the rather alarming message with an instruction to get the information to Patrick, or Elizabeth, or the Security Service guard as soon as possible. Although his wife was very efficient at checking for messages, he had no means of knowing when she would return to the house. He emphasised that he was in no danger and requested that someone with instructions on how to deal with Christopher meet the next train at the London terminus. Should there not be time to arrange things by then, he would go on to Liverpool Street, where he would take the next available train to..... Harwich. Surely, he reasoned, that should give enough time, even if his message did not get to the right place for several hours.

Christopher was in the queue for some minutes, during which – as luck would have it (good or bad, depending on one's viewpoint) – he was spotted by Harvey, whose colleague from Haslemere, Michael, had gone to collect the pre-arranged Avis rental car from the nearby office. Surreptitiously, Harvey studied the photograph, hoping that Michael would soon return to confirm his opinion and decide whether to snatch him, follow him, or ring for further instructions. To his surprise, Harvey saw Christopher purchase the tickets and then move to rejoin a travelling companion – an old boy with a worried look who had just finished telephoning. The worried look transferred itself to Harvey, however, as he saw the pair converse briefly and then move through to the trains, just as the public address burst into life announcing the imminent arrival of the G N E R non-stop service to King's Cross.

"Come on, Michael, you dozy bastard!" said Harvey to himself. "They'll have gone in a minute and we ought to be on that train – and we need instructions about the other chap, who's probably Christopher's controller. How the Hell can I let him know?"

The noise of the incoming train galvanised Harvey into action. Desperately, he scribbled a few words on a scrap of paper and turned to a fairly 'with it' looking middle aged man who was waiting to meet someone.

"Excuse me Guv'nor, but my mate, name of Michael, has been delayed. Could you give him that when he comes looking for me, please? He's a tall dark chap, wearing a green anorak, long sideburns, earring in his left ear, heavy brown boots and a tattoo on the back of his right hand. That's my train! Can't wait. Can you do that, please? Gotta dash!"

Michael completed the formalities at the Avis office, strolled over to look at the vehicle, dumped his anorak, containing the papers, in the back and then returned to the forecourt to collect Harvey – who was nowhere to be seen. He nipped through onto the platform, which was virtually deserted, nearly everyone having piled onto the recently departed London train.

"Where the ... oh, the 'Gents', I suppose,' he muttered. But he wasn't there, nor in the cafeteria. Returning, somewhat puzzled, but not yet alarmed, to the forecourt, Michael started as he was accosted:

"Are you Michael, by any chance?"

"Who wants to know?" came the aggressive reply, as Michael continued to stare with mounting frenzy around the waiting area.

"Sorry! It's just that I thought I saw a tattoo on your...."

"Now look here. I don't know what your game is, but I'm busy and if you don't want a tattoo where it hurts most, you'd better make yerself scarce. Savvy?"

"Well, really, I was only....." spluttered Harvey's outraged courier, as he retreated, deciding he would think twice before approaching anyone else, even if they fitted the description to a 'T' (including an anorak, which this unpleasant lout, it had to be admitted, did not seem to own). He stuffed Harvey's hastily scribbled message into his pocket and sat down to wait for his brother, aware of the continued presence of the tattooed man, who, he related later, buzzed backwards and forwards (by then wearing a green anorak and talking urgently into a mobile phone) for about ten minutes like the proverbial blue-arsed fly.

On the journey to King's Cross, Martin was regaled with the life history of Christopher, whose father had been killed in a boating accident when he was about three, after which his mother (helped financially by the Organisation) had brought him up on her own. At the age of sixteen, she had taken him to see two men who had told him that his father had been brought as a baby to England in a German submarine, that he was a member of a 'master race' and was assured of a steady well paid job, and eventual power and wealth if he was willing to take the oath of allegiance to the Organisation. In exchange for following orders, he was installed originally in an insurance office and then, when his mother died of a brain tumour, was invited to join the staff at Wothorpe Castle. Clearly, the Organisation, his only 'family', enabled him to keep faith with the memory of his father, and seemed to offer much in return for very little. The recent incident involving Martin had been the first time that Christopher had come across the really seamy side of the Organisation. He had obviously been badly shaken by the violence, bloodshed and manifest illegality of that occasion. He knew the theory that the ends justified the means, that once in power they would abolish crime and make the land safe for all to travel in, but the reality of maiming and killing was a very different thing.

Forged passports to help Asians could be seen as a valuable service if you wished to delude yourself, rather than a criminal racket, thought Martin, with a feeling of moral superiority, which quickly gave way to one of guilty understanding as he recalled his own recent dealings with Ahmed!

The young man enjoyed his work at the Castle, referring with pride to the important people who had visited over the three months he had been there, most of the time fetching, carrying, driving and running messages. As someone who had taken the oath, he was trusted and picked up a lot from conversations behind him in the car, from telephoned messages and faxes. Many of the names he mentioned surprised Martin (and many more would have caused a ripple in Intelligence circles). He was anxious to progress in the Organisation, to prove his willingness to die, if necessary, for the Cause – or, more specifically, for ......

"What should I call you, Sir? I mean we use first names mostly, as you know, like Philip for Mr Proudfoot, and our Area Controller is – er – was John... but I can't really use your I D number....."

"As you will have gathered, Christopher," said Martin gravely, "I operate outside the usual network. Only a handful at the top, the very top, know me and know my name. I should like to look on you as...as a nephew in a sense. There may be occasions in the future when I shall call on you to do something for me as I feel I know you and can trust you."

"You can, you..."

"No. Let me finish," continued Martin, warming to his theme, "Others will merely know me as '534'. If you discover that they also know my full name, you will know they have, like me, a special rôle within the Organisation. You might come across me using other names, but I have decided to include you among that small group who know me. My name is Charles – Charles Hastings: on occasions such as this, call me Charles, but don't let on that you know the rest. All right?"

The young man was, well, delighted, flattered even, but something more. They had been talking quietly, insulated from the others in the half full carriage, but, mercifully, Christopher managed to restrain himself from carrying out the act that he felt was appropriate – to kiss the signet ring which shone dully on the 'papal' finger. In stead he relapsed into silence for the last ten minutes of the journey, contemplating his good fortune and sensible of the great honour which had just been conferred upon him.

Their arrival at King's Cross was somewhat anticlimactic. There was no sign of a bodyguard, a courier or even a placard. Martin ambled along the platform, hoping to be approached by a representative of H M G, unaware that he and his companion were being followed by the similarly disappointed Harvey, who was expecting the back-up *he* had requested in the note to his colleague, Michael.

"I'll get a taxi!" said Christopher, helpfully, noticing that his idol was obviously tired as he was walking so slowly. He dashed off, giving Harvey the problem of deciding which one to follow and returned in triumph five minutes later. By that time, Martin had worked out that he should have taken the opportunity to do a vanishing act, as opportunities during the onward journey to Harwich would be difficult to engineer. Panting after Christopher, trying to keep out of sight, came Harvey, uncomfortably aware that if he were to lose the young man, his life would not be worth living.

"If I ever see that old bastard I asked to pass a note to Michael, I'll murder him," he thought. "He *must* have come looking for me. You can't rely on anyone these days."

As he watched the two walk towards the approaching taxi, Harvey realised that 'make your mind up time' was here. Had Christopher been on his own, he could have taken him – killed him if that was the only way – but he couldn't be sure about the old boy with him. Could he be from the Organisation? Doubtful. From M I 6? If so, they must have been let down, as someone had clearly been expected.... but not by Christopher, come to think of it. Could he force himself upon them – 'Mind if I share your taxi, gents?' – and then hi-jack the cab? In the end, he decided to risk relying on their declared intention, easily overheard, of going to Liverpool Street. The risk proved justified and it was with relief, prompting him to give a substantial tip to the driver, that he arrived in time to see the pair, fortunately still walking slowly, as they moved towards the queue for the ticket office.

Martin was getting worried. What could he do if they arrived and there was no one to meet them at Harwich? It would be easier to disappear here in London – pretend to go to the toilet and then, once out of sight, just 'take off'? The same ploy would have no chance of success at a small station. On the other hand, it would be a pity to throw away his special relationship. Perhaps Patrick could make use of it? In addition to that, he was loath to disillusion the young man, to say nothing of putting him seriously at risk. No. He couldn't leave him to be 'disposed of' by the S A S, for Martin realised that now that Christopher knew him, he might, if allowed to roam freely, see him again. He might see him with Patrick, with dire consequences. Surely Jennifer would realise the importance of passing on his message – unless.... his blood ran cold. Supposing she had been in a car accident, was unable to get home, was at this very moment in intensive care?

"Are you feeling all right?" asked Christopher solicitously, for the old boy was looking distinctly grey around the gills. "I'll get the tickets; why don't you go and have a cup of tea or something?"

And so it was that both Martin and Harvey decided there was just enough time for a quick call, whilst the object of their surveillance, unaware that he was on the Organisation's hit list and relying for his safety on what amounted to a phantom agent, stood unconcernedly in the queue for tickets.

CHAPTER THIRTY-ONE

"I'm back!" called Jennifer as she opened the front door, expecting that her husband would have returned and could give her a hand unloading the car, which was groaning with supplies from the local Sainsbury's.

"Oh, well, at least he's getting some exercise," she thought, moving into the living room to check for messages on the answerphone. Jennifer sat down part way through, took some notes towards the end – and then played it over again to make more notes. Although a born worrier, for some reason she reacted only with calm efficiency to the astonishing contents.

Somehow, over in France, she had known she ought to get back and now she realised what they had been keeping from her – or part of it. She had been right: he had sounded shifty..... and was obviously much more deeply involved than she had been led to believe. Could it be, she wondered, that Patrick had returned to help, rather than 'happening to be taking a few days off'? We'll see, she decided, finding the contact number referred to in her husband's message and dictating the contents of his plea for help.

By the time an S A S man arrived, Jennifer had put the frozen goods into the freezer, packed an overnight bag and was in the process of gathering a change of clothing for Martin.

"Sorry about all this, Madam," he said. "There's no need to worry: we're following up the message and can get someone to your husband very soon, now."

"Good," replied Jennifer. "Too late to catch them at King's Cross, though?"

"Well – er – yes, but plenty of time before they arrive at Harwich. Can I give you a hand with....."

"Yes, you can as a matter of fact. I must just finish packing, so can you get the rest of the groceries out of the car before we leave?"

"Before we lea... Er, where were you thinking of going?" asked the soldier, by now feeling pressurised by events, and picking up the plural pronoun with distinct unease.

"I am not *thinking* of going anywhere. I intend to go to Harwich, and thought that you might prefer to come, too, if you have been assigned to be my 'minder'.... but I'm quite happy to go on my own. I shall be ready in about two minutes. There's a phone in the kitchen: leave the stuff in the car if you prefer."

"Now hang on, Miss. You can't go rushing off to Harwich. It's – well it might be dangerous and...." Corporal Johnson was used to calling the shots but he quailed before the onslaught:

"Firstly, young man, it is not 'Miss', but Mrs Brady. Secondly, I was unaware that I had been placed under house arrest..... and thirdly it is precisely because I realised that my husband was in danger that I decided to go to Harwich to be of assistance. It was also why I would have preferred to have you along, but by all means stay and guard the house if those are your orders. Now, if you will excuse me, I'll finish getting my things."

"Bloody Hell!" said the corporal, but very quietly, under his breath. "Women!"

He moved into the kitchen, rang his section leader for instructions, and was told to accompany the lady but keep in touch. Perhaps she had a 'mobile'? The vital piece of equipment was visible on the kitchen table, so Corporal Johnson reassured his contact on that point as well as on the enquiry as to how the 'little lady' was taking the news.

"Oh – er – very well...."

"No hysterics – you don't need a female to...?"

"No, no. Quite the reverse: enough already if you know what I mean!" replied the Corporal, raising his voice to conclude the conversation as Jennifer came down the stairs. "That's all agreed, then. We'll get going and you'll contact us en route." Smiling encouragingly, he turned to Jennifer:

"That's all settled, Mrs Brady. I'm to accompany you – if that's what you wish, of course – and they'll keep us fully informed. Shall I carry that?"

"Thank you!" Jennifer smiled sweetly. "The name's Jennifer, by the way, and *you'd* better drive as we need to get a move on. I'm really quite looking forward to this with you to protect me: I was dreading having to go on my own!"

The corporal accepted the car keys, the flattery and the change of personality with relief and they set off towards the A 1, Jennifer calmly reminding 'Jacko' that his superiors would not have the number of her mobile, so she had better let them know while he concentrated on his driving.

"Yes, that's right, the Audi.... the A 14, yes.... Newmarket. Yes I'm fine and Jacko is an excellent driver. Yes, I'll tell him. Bye!....Your friend asked me to say the sun is shining down there and the driving conditions are very good," Jennifer said as she put the phone down and settled back, outwardly cool, calm and collected, apparently to enjoy the ride.

Slightly flushed with embarrassment, Corporal Johnson, who could recognise sarcasm when he heard it, made a mental note to thump the afore-mentioned 'friend' when he got back.

A short time after his mother had telephoned through the contents of Martin's answerphone message, Patrick was considering its implications. He wondered briefly how it had happened that his father had 'bumped into' Christopher and another man (who had to be Henry) and then set about analysing the new situation. As he was well aware of Monty's present concerns and location, he was not surprised to learn that Christopher felt abandoned. Indeed, he himself had forgotten the young man who was now, Mrs Pateman and Monty having been 'neutralised', the only person who knew enough to work out the family connection between 'busybody' and Intelligence Officer. He had relied on Monty and Gerald between them to get Christopher out of the country, as much as anything to avoid having to take more drastic action to remove him from the local (and possibly even global) scene.

Even as Patrick contemplated the advantages of continuing to string the chap along, allowing the Organisation to install him in Holland, whilst keeping in reserve the ability to manipulate him, Kenneth telephoned. His news was that the Haslemere unit had despatched two thugs to deal with the traitor, Christopher, one of whom had been left behind for some reason at Peterborough station. The latter (Michael) had rung Henry at Hall Farm, who had, fortunately, rung Gerald as Area Controller. There was, Kenneth added, an old boy with Christopher, who (Gerald had said) sounded just like the one who had collected the documents from the Castle! What, Kenneth concluded, should he tell Gerald to do?

"For now," said Patrick, "tell him to send a couple of men to shadow them. Presumably, they now know, or will shortly from this other guy from Haslemere, where they are. I've just had that confirmed as Liverpool Street station. I want Gerald to appear to be co-operating fully in the search. I'll organise one or two things this end and then put you more fully in the picture."

Patrick was right: the Organisation did now know where the pair had got to, thanks to a call made by Harvey. Both sides just managed to get a team of armed operatives to Liverpool Street in time to follow both Christopher, who had no idea he was under surveillance by either side, and Martin, who hoped he was being joined by his own.

****

Gerald's two men had no reason to suspect that their presence was known to the Security Services, for whom they believed Christopher to be working, together with (almost certainly) his elderly companion. One positioned himself where he could keep an eye on their 'prey' whilst the other, furnished with a helpful description, set off to make contact with Harvey.

Patrick's three men had hoped to be able to identify the opposition with reasonable confidence but the presence on the train of Army personnel returning to their barracks at Colchester made the task extremely difficult, although they found them useful as 'cover'.

"We've got to find a way of getting Martin away from this Christopher," said Patrick's boss. "The other lot could move at any moment."

"They won't move until told to do so by Gerald," said Patrick, "and we can control that. I don't want to spoil the hold that Martin seems to have managed to get over Christopher if I can help it: there could be a useful long-term asset there."

"Well, it's your father, so if you think it's worth the risk....."

"I agree we should separate them. I'm trying to think how best to do it, not taking risks," said Patrick, rather more sharply than was perhaps appropriate when speaking to one's superior, a sign that, despite the outward calm and logical approach, he was feeling the strain.

"At least your mother's in good hands," said the Chief's personal assistant, seeking to lower the temperature slightly. "She's got an excellent bodyguard and there's no way the opposition can know where she is."

"True," said Patrick. "They can't be that far away from Harwich by now, with Johnson driving.... In fact. Yes. I've got it!"

One usually pays attention to an announcement containing one's own name (or that of a close relative) and Martin was no exception. He was paying careful attention when it was repeated:

"Will Miss Elizabeth Brady, believed to be travelling with Mr J C Carrier, please come to the Customer Service Manager's Office, which is situated at the rear of Coach B."

Surely Elizabeth was not on the train? And her companion J C..... Not for nothing, it turned out, had he wasted so many hours doing crosswords. It had to be Christopher, the carrier of Christ, of J-C; in other words – J. C. Carrier. Slowly, Martin rose to his feet, smiled at his companion, to whom the message meant nothing, and, saying he'd be back shortly, strolled towards the rear of the train. There he found one of Corporal Johnson's three colleagues, who introduced himself as 'Dave' and said:

"Well done, Sir. And to reassure you that you can trust me, I'm told to tell you that Candy Island sounds much better."

Martin grinned at this reference (which only someone in the family could know) to his father's unshakable belief that this was the name of the location near Southend which everyone else knew as 'Canvey' Island.

"Good!" said Martin. "What are my orders, then?"

"You return to your seat and tell sonny boy he's to carry on to Harwich, where he will be met by 'the man from Hall Farm'. I hope that makes sense."

"Yes. It sounds O K. That way, Ger – er – that man won't see me."

230

"Not only that, Sir. You'll be out of the way if there's any unpleasantness."

"Oh, yes," said Martin casually, sensing there was some aspect of this which he was unaware of, "are you expecting much trouble?"

"Well, Sir, with three of them on the train, all out to get this lad and three of us told to protect him – and you, of course – things could get quite lively!"

Martin's mind raced. For some reason 'they' were after Christopher – must have followed them onto the train. But surely Gerald could protect him? Unless he didn't control these men, or would attract too much unwelcome attention if he called them off and allowed Christopher to escape.

"Well, I must get moving," said Martin. "Have you identified these three, yet?"

"We're pretty sure about two of them, but haven't pinpointed the third yet. It should be easier after all these soldiers get off at Colchester. Mind you, *we'll* be more obvious, too, if they're looking out for us."

Martin returned thoughtfully to his seat and leaned forward confidentially towards Christopher.

"There's been a new development," he said. "As you know, Proudfoot sent two men to kill me. We foiled that attempt but I've been told others in that group are still trying and at least two, possibly more are on this train. No, don't look round. There are a lot of military types on board at the moment so it's impossible to spot them. I shall get off at Colchester, which should divide their forces, but as you've been seen with me, and are known to have been present when their two, those 'blacksmiths', were gunned down, suspicion has fallen on you, too."

"I feared something like that," said Christopher, "so did Gerald and Larry. That's why they were going to get me out of the country. Can't I come with you, Charles?"

"You're most in danger, at the moment, near me," replied Martin. "Carry on to Harwich and don't trust anyone except Gerald. If he's not there for some reason, mingle with the crowd, make a dash for it and go to ground. Then ring this number," he added, handing over that for his own mobile phone. "Identify yourself as – er – Mr Bearer and I'll send help. Just leave a message if it's switched off."

Christopher gripped his hand in silent thanks as he palmed the piece of paper, realising he might never see 'Charles' again, but could always count on him as a powerful friend in a very high place.

The train drew in to Colchester, where a large number of passengers alighted, including Martin, whose departure was seen by Corporal Johnson's colleague with relief..... and by Harvey with indecision. Should he abandon Christopher to the other two and follow the old man? Or should he stick to his orders which related only to the traitor in their midst, whose actions had cost the lives of two of his mates at Stansted? He had little time to decide, for the train would soon move off, there being only a handful waiting to get on. In desperation, he moved forward to speak to one of Gerald's men who had joined the chase at Liverpool Street.

Harvey's obvious interest in the elderly agent and subsequent actions were observed by Dave, who was now confident he knew all three of the opposition. The next move, however, came too quickly for Dave even to think about countering it. Just before the whistle blew, one of Gerald's two men ran to the nearest door and jumped down onto the platform. Dave gave his colleague the pre-arranged signal, and he moved past, giving the impression that he had just joined the train, to the seat opposite Christopher.

"This seat taken, mate?" he asked the wary looking young man, who shook his head and resumed staring out of the window, wondering if his new companion would turn out to be his executioner. In the mean time, Dave slipped his mobile phone from his left-hand pocket – the one without the loaded pistol – to warn his superiors by text message.

Patrick had sent instructions to his father to descend at Colchester, go to the Cafeteria and wait to be picked up by someone who would identify himself by a reference to 'Candy' Island very early in the conversation. It had seemed straight-forward enough, and Corporal Johnson was even now on his way (his route to Harwich taking him very close to Colchester). The message from Dave, however, that his father had been followed by one of the thugs from the Organisation, was received with considerable alarm. Shortly, both his mother and father would be at Colchester station, potentially exposed to violent action. The odds were much too even for Patrick's liking: one against one, both armed.

"Put me through to Johnson, now!" commanded Patrick.

"Johnson! It's H Q. The subject got off the train as arranged, but he was followed. I'll give you the description as soon as I can but he's almost certainly armed and probably believes subject to be working for us. Extreme sanction authorised if necessary, bearing in mind the safety of the general public. Got that?"

"Yes, I think so, dear," came his mother's voice. "I am sure Jacko will be able to deal with it. Er – E T A approximately six minutes. Any instructions for – er – 'subject' when we meet him?"

"Mother!" exclaimed Patrick in exasperation, startled out of his careful anonymity. "You – you're – for God's sake take care! This chap won't do anything other than keep the old boy under observation. Tell Johnson we're sending a back-up team; he'll know the priorities. And Mother!"

"Yes, dear."

"You're something else!"

"Thank you dear.... I have the impression that you are, too. Shall I give 'subject' your love, when I see him?"

"Er – yes, of course," said Patrick, to the amusement of his hard-bitten colleagues, "and tell Johnson to identify himself by referring to – oh God!", he paused in further embarrassment at having to parade a family joke with his mother in her present mood, "...'Candy Island' at some point."

"Is that both God and Candy Island, or just Candy Island, as in 'Swansford' for Wansford, dear?"

"The latter, Mother! Now just do it.. please!"

"Wilco. Over and out!" came the reply, eliciting a spontaneous burst of clapping round the table, which drowned Patrick's incipient apology for his parent's 'mili-ternal' style. By this time, Jacko, despite the forthcoming danger and the need to concentrate on getting to the station as quickly as possible, had given up trying to keep a straight face as he thought of the incident coordinator's embarrassment at finding his own mother on the line, unable to prevent her from putting him firmly in his place.

"Don't worry, Ma'am. Your husband'll be all right."

Jennifer did not trust herself to reply and tried to stop her hand from shaking as she severed the connection.

CHAPTER THIRTY-TWO

The Chairman was distinctly worried. Various reports he had been receiving concerning the Stansted incident made it clear that H M G had been just as puzzled by the non-appearance of this woman whom Larry had been pursuing as had the Organisation. It transpired that she had received a call from her daughter the night before she vanished (this information had been expensive to obtain, and was thought to be accurate), as a result of which she had decided to go home to her husband who was upset about their dog, of all things. It seemed the chap was a bit inadequate and unable to look after himself when she was away. Bloody effete English, he thought scathingly. Need proper leadership – always have. If only..... But back to the point, he reminded himself. She had not been 'tipped off' any more than had H M G..... in which case this young man whom Larry had told him was leaking information was in the clear, or at least should be given every opportunity to establish his innocence. It looked as though this Monty/Larry chap sent over by Vienna had made a balls up and tried to blame it all on this young lad. The trouble was that the Chairman had authorised what amounted to a death warrant. That Haslemere lot could well ignore Christopher's pleas and protestations and.....and the slow and awful death would be *his* fault. Well, partly his fault – in fact not really anyone's except that chap Larry, who seemed to have disappeared off the face of the earth. Larry seemed likely to have contacted that new member of Council, thought the Chairman.... and put in a call to Gerald in Colchester.

Despite having to be patched through to Gerald on his way to Harwich, it was no time at all before the Chairman was utterly convinced of his error in ordering Haslemere to go after Christopher, and fully in agreement with leaving Monty in his submarine timeshare until the whole matter had been resolved. It was one thing, however, to take the decision to call off the troops and quite another to make it effective. The two from Haslemere had been split – and Harvey did not have the mobile phone. Unless and until Harvey called in, he could not be given fresh orders and might well go so far as to shoot Christopher if he thought he was about to flee the country. To compound the communication problem, the man who left the train to pursue Martin took the mobile phone, thus making it impossible to contact *his* partner, who continued, with Harvey, to follow the 'traitorous' Christopher.

****

Martin had been less than happy to leave the train, although he could see that it made sense. Despite the fact that the young man had been instrumental in setting up an attempt on his life, Martin felt responsible for him. It was bad enough to allow him to believe that he was some sort of Nazi messiah, risen from the dead, omni-present, omniscient, omni-every-damn-thing, who only vouchsafed his name to his chosen people. To then abandon him to the S A S or, worse by far, his own people who believed he was the traitor in their midst......that was, well, sacrilege. As he mused on these lines, standing in the queue for refreshments, Martin was unaware that yet another employee of the Organisation had him in his sights (not literally, fortunately, but that might be only a matter of time).

Barry, the afore-mentioned employee, had had little time to consider his recent move, for, whilst their orders had been to follow both men, nothing had been specifically said as to what they should do if they split up, or, indeed, what they were supposed to do when they all arrived at their destination. The answer was to ring in for instructions, so he nipped outside to gain sufficient privacy, and was still deep in telephonic conversation when Corporal Johnson came running down the platform.

Such was the speed of events that the corporal had dashed from the hard-driven car just before H Q (a different voice this time) rang through the description of the Organisation's agent who was pursuing Martin, to enable him to identify the opposition.

Although not by nature what one might call 'agent material', Jennifer in defence of her husband was proving a formidable threat to the forces of misrule and disorder.

Realising the value of the information she had just been given, she hurried from the car after the recently departed Jacko.

Armed with his description, it was not difficult for Jennifer to spot Barry, who was in the process of explaining on his 'mobile' that he could not tell his partner that there had been a re-think on Christopher as they had become separated. He was also having difficulty in getting sense out of Gerald concerning the elderly chap whom he had followed into the Cafeteria.

"Hang on!" he said, desperate for precise instructions, "He's talking to a chap who just dashed in – could be one of theirs, or ours, if it comes to that. He's obviously not pleased to see him, doesn't trust him, is moving away..... the other chap's following. The woman on the till looks bothered: she's.....Oufff!"

Gerald took the phone from his ear at the sound of its hitting the ground and turned to his assistant:

"Something's gone wrong. The phone's dead and Barry was on about some chap who'd just dashed in. I need a full team at Harwich, and I don't want another Stansted episode at Colchester station. Is there someone nearby you could send to find out what's up?"

"Well, there's Mrs Banstead: she lives quite near and does the odd bit of work for us, but she couldn't help Barry if he's in real trouble."

"Fine!" said Gerald. "Right, do that, then join us at Harwich. Barry may have just dropped the phone for all we know!"

In fact, the Organisation's operative was in considerable trouble having been sent sprawling by eight stone of concentrated venom, after being disorientated by the inhuman screech which drew Jacko's attention to the fracas just outside the door of the Cafeteria. Jennifer, who seemed to have inflated herself like a cat arched and spitting to repel its canine opponent, was attempting to render the unfortunate Barry sightless by means of a wicked-looking weapon, which she had removed from her foot. Dazed by the attack from such an unexpected direction, Barry was no match for Jacko, who emerged to protect the 'defenceless female' from his depradations.

"They sent his description," panted Jennifer, "and he was on the phone, telling them all about you. Then he was going to shoot you both.....so I... Oh Martin! Are you all right? This horrid man was....."

"I never bloody touched her," gasped the indignant Barry. "She came at me like a – like a mad thing. She ought to be locked up: she's barmy, that's what!"

"We'll let the law decide that!" said Jacko, sitting firmly on the battered and indignant thug.

He was pretty confident that a search by the police, who had been called by the lady on the till, would rapidly reveal the presence of a concealed, unauthorised hand-gun. That, combined with Jennifer's claim that he had attacked her, would be sufficient to ensure that this particular member of the Organisation took no further part in hostilities for some years to come.

For his part, Martin was quite speechless as he and his now trembling wife clung together. After a few moments, he led her gently to a table, to which the helpful assistant, the one who had called the police, brought both tea and sympathy.

"That dreadful man!" she said. "And your husband was having trouble with another one just before. I think they must be rival gangs, Mafia or those Chinese: no-one's safe nowadays. It's the drugs – they're all on them, killing each other and Goodness knows what. Would you like anything else, dear? A whisky, or – or do you need a doctor?" she added, solicitously.

"No. No thank you. I'll be all right..... now," replied Jennifer, finding her voice at last and holding Martin's hand tightly as much, one felt, to stop him going off somewhere as for the feeling of comfort.

"I think I'd like a whisky, please," said Martin, beginning to recover from the trauma of being approached by someone with the wrong codeword, for the whole point of it was that it was *not* 'Canvey' as Jacko had said..... but *Candy* Island. That difficult situation had suddenly changed into what had appeared to be an attack on his wife, who had no business being there at all but had certainly caused the resolution of that phase of the affair in no uncertain fashion.

"That'll be two pounds, please. Any ice?"

"Er – no thanks.. I seem to have....." Martin had handed all his money to Christopher, who had had to spend most of it on tickets, the taxi, etc., and found (not for the first time) that he had to turn to his wife for help.

"Here you are," she said with a resigned grin, raising her eyebrows expressively at the assistant's words as she accepted the coins:

"Men! They're all the same!"

By the time an S A S back-up team arrived, the police were dealing with Barry and a helpful, but shrewd, woman officer was taking a brief, unrevealing, statement from Jennifer, supported in its inaccurate detail by both Jacko, who 'happened to be passing', and Martin, whom she had arrived to meet in the family car ('just outside in the short term car park, Officer').

Mrs Banstead arrived unobtrusively and observed Barry's predicament. There were various other people about, including a tough looking character, whom she took to be one of the opposition, an elderly couple who appeared to be understandably shaken by the goings on and several other on-lookers like herself. The best source of information, she decided, was the lady behind the counter who had obviously been there all along and seemed to be quite enjoying the excitement.

"Oh yes, dear," the latter replied to Mrs Banstead's enquiry. "I saw it all. That dreadful man suddenly attacked that poor woman just outside the door and..... No, he came in here and ordered a coffee – which is still on that table over there, untouched!"

It was clear that not drinking the dubious beverage was seen as another sign of anti-social behaviour on Barry's part by this witness, who continued to explain how she had thought he looked a bit odd ('on drugs, obviously, like so many of them these days!'), although she had been keeping an eye on the other one at the time.

"Oh!" said Mrs Banstead, hoping to hear something which made some sort of sense. "Did he have an accomplice?"

"No, dear, he must have been from a rival gang, the other one, because he broke off from attacking the old man who was sitting on his own over there, when he heard the shrieking."

"Good Gracious!" said the bemused Mrs Banstead. "What a time you've had! Was the old man hurt?"

"Nothing much. He managed to get away from his attacker and comfort his wife, who ......"

"His wife?" interjected Mrs Banstead, too sharply, forgetting she was supposed to be a passing customer. "You said just now he was on his own!"

"No need to take that tone!" said her informant huffily. "I'm quite sure she was his wife, because he didn't have any money when it came to it .... and that'll be eighty pence, if that's all you're having."

Despite apologising and purchasing a distinctly un-Scandinavian looking 'Danish', Mrs Banstead was unable to make much more sense of the affair and her report was not going to convey any useful information whatsoever, failing in particular to mention the apparent inconsistency of the impecunious old man and his wife departing trustfully together with the former's erstwhile 'attacker' driving their car. In pursuance of her orders to find out all she could about the older man who had accompanied Christopher, however, Mrs Banstead did manage to prise one piece of valuable information out of the Cafeteria lady. She had distinctly heard several references to a place with which she was familiar in South Essex, namely Canvey Island. In addition to this, the Organisation knew from Barry that the S A S man who had held him down until the police came was not welcomed by this man (a fact confirmed by the Cafeteria lady). Despite – or, in reality, because of – its lack of clarity and reliance on the fanciful utterances of the Cafeteria lady, Mrs Banstead's hopelessly confused report was later accepted by the regional boss (Gerald) and, to her surprise, she was complimented on its depth and helpfulness.

In accordance with his orders, and their wishes, Jacko had set off to drive the by then calm and content couple home. He was able to report that after about ten miles they were both sleeping peacefully in the back, which made it possible for Patrick (after asking a colleague to contact his sister and suggest that she return home as soon as possible) to give his full attention to the situation at Harwich, Parkeston Quay, where the London train had now arrived.

Trailing 'minders' from both sides, in addition to the still out of touch Harvey, Christopher descended from the train and moved with the crowd towards the International Ferry departure area and, he hoped, sanctuary in the form of the familiar face of Gerald.

CHAPTER THIRTY-THREE

Still hoping to be contacted, Christopher joined the queue for passport control, as did his leech-like companion, Mike, who could feel the tension building as they neared the young, sharp-eyed, though seemingly casual, Passport Control Officer.

As the only 'General' present, Gerald should have realised that failure on his part to make a move would result in precipitate action by Christopher. Without a 'script', however, Gerald was useless under pressure, so he had still taken no action by the time Christopher found himself three places from the front of the queue. Still hoping to be contacted, Christopher fumbled in his pocket, muttered something to the effect of having forgotten his passport and walked rapidly to the nearest exit.

Feeling that all eyes were on him – which was not so far from the mark, as Gerald had brought two more to help shepherd the young man away from harm – Christopher approached the double doors, which slid open invitingly. Beyond lay the darkened platform, the rails straight ahead, to the right a few small offices, piles of boxes and empty trollies and to the left a yard, on the far side of which could be seen various storehouses and an alley leading up into the town. Even now, had he had the sense to walk along to the Stena Line offices and make some irrelevant inquiry, Christopher might have retrieved the situation, but the urge to get away was too strong.

Turning left, he broke into a trot along the deserted platform, about fifteen metres ahead of Harvey, who, having followed casually through the sliding doors, turned to his right, moved behind a pillar and swung round, bringing his gun to bear. At Gerald's shout of 'No! The plan's changed!', Christopher turned, relief at hearing the voice turning to shock, as he took in the levelled gun and felt the impact of the bullet penetrating his chest.

Even as Christopher fell, Gerald shot his killer, moving out from behind the pile of boxes to do so, then making good his escape before anyone could take in just what had happened.

The first person to reach the fallen Christopher was one of Gerald's men, to whom Christopher gasped:

"Tell Gerald that 534 was genuine. He's one of our top men and....."

He coughed as the blood welled in his throat and the fear showed in his eyes as he realised he had been fatally struck and fell silent.

By the time the ambulance came, the Organisation men had all disappeared, leaving Mike, as the dying man's supposed travelling companion – and a priest who happened to be just behind in the passport queue and had been alerted to the probability of trouble by the young man's evident fear as he waited. Just before he breathed his last, still in the speeding ambulance, Christopher seized Mike's arm in a fierce grip and said:

"My money: it's.... give it to... I owe him... tickets....and tell him..."

"Tell who? Who is it?" said Mike urgently.

"Charles," came the reply, clear and distinct. "Tell Charles. He'll....."

"Charles who? What's his other name?" asked the priest, realising the end was at hand. But they found the reply, though clear enough, puzzling, as was the almost sly, knowing look:

"You don't know! They don't know; he was right! Charles said they......" And, strangely content, knowing he had kept faith to the end, the young man died.

There was no reason for the media to link the unprovoked attack on a middle-aged teacher on Colchester station with the shoot-out between 'rival drug gangs' at Harwich, but they soon discovered that the (unarmed) victim had been a colleague of the Agent at Wothorpe Castle. A spokesman for the feudal seat claimed that they had no explanation of either event, and no reason to link them – although the younger man had not reported for work for several days.

The very public nature of the two incidents, and their relative propinquity, made it inevitable that connections were sought between the Stansted and Harwich deaths, but the more significant connection between Sussex and Lincolnshire was not picked up. Mrs Jennifer Radley might have drawn attention to the fact that a Mrs Jennifer Brady – surely *the* Mrs Brady – had been attacked elsewhere in Essex, had the report she read not referred throughout to Mrs Jackie Brady and described her as 'middle-aged', an epithet clearly (in Mrs Radley's view) inapplicable to someone who could be mistaken for herself.

Malcolm, the Chairman of the British High Command, was furious, a sentiment intensified by his personal guilt at having sanctioned the pursuit of Christopher. He communicated his feeling in unequivocal language to the Grand Council in Vienna, pointing out the trail of deaths and confusion that had followed wherever their man, Larry, had seen fit to meddle.

For his part, Larry remained unaware of the drama played out so close to his temporary maritime residence, the seas around which had been too rough to permit Clarence and his friends to return and deliver him from the malodorous Klaus. The task required of him by Vienna had been to de-activate the missile launcher permanently and render harmless all the rockets, torpedoes, nerve gas shells and any other explosives which the British High Command might be stupid enough to consider using in order to hasten the moment when they could take power. He had done his best, but was out of his depth when it came to the more recently imported weaponry of Russian origin. However, they would have to decide what to do about that when he reported in. In the mean time, having little better to do and anxious not to give his companion any opportunity to make conversation, he passed the time looking through files, boxes of papers, newspaper cuttings, etc., which was how he came across the photograph.

"Klaus!" he shouted. "Come here....Stop! That's near enough. What do you know about this?"

At the sight of the black bushy moustache and arrogant stare depicted in the photo, Klaus started to cackle uncontrollably, inserting between these bursts of hilarity phrases which appeared to imply that this person had spent two years with Klaus before departing. For someone who was himself a raving lunatic, to make signs implying that the person depicted went round the bend was, to say the least, distasteful – especially as he looked remarkably like......

"Oh, clear off, you cretinous old ruin!" cried Monty, pushing the spindly arm away as it quivered towards the photo. Klaus fell backwards, failing to prevent himself from striking his head sharply on the edge of a protruding strut.

The silence, though welcome, seemed to be deeper, and longer, than Monty would have expected.

"Klaus! Come on, get up and tell me who thi......Klaus? Oh, Christ, now the old fool's died on me! Trust him to..... Oh, well, at least he's stopped that bloody cackling."

He had, but Monty soon found that whilst Klaus alive could be said to be aromatically challenged, the stench of his maturing corpse in the confined quarters surpassed description. Not only that. Monty had not yet found out how to operate the 'bathysphere' from below, which prevented him from getting a breath of fresh air even though the heavy seas were now subsiding, making it safe to use.

"Gerald!" he shouted at the steel cavern. "Where the Hell have you got to? Get me out!"

****

"It's me Mother. I can't be long now. I'll be down later on – give you a ring from King's Cross then. Anyway... how are you?"

Jennifer was delighted to hear her daughter had managed to get away, not least because she was a bit worried about Martin:

"I'm fine, dear. No ill effects, at least...."

"At least what? Did you get hurt in the brawl – not having nightmares or anything? Why not take a 'tranque': it'd calm you down if....."

"No, nothing like that... it's your father, really. He was fine yesterday; well, a bit quiet, perhaps, but considering he'd been kidnapped by that awful man, that wasn't surprising. I think he may be worried he'll be back, but we're very well protected, so....."

"Worried the chap'll be back? Didn't you see the news? If he'd gone on to Harwich, Father might've been caught in the cross fire! Incidentally, the awful man, as you call him, didn't kidnap him the way I heard it – and anyway, he's dead!"

"Dead? Oh good! No, we went straight to bed without looking at the T V. Well, well; that should set his mind at rest."

"Ye-es," said Elizabeth, "but don't you think he might just be upset about Sherry, still? He's a sentimental old so...er.. so-and-so. Not that," she added hurriedly, "We aren't all very sorry about it, of course."

"Yes, it could be that, I suppose," said her mother doubtfully, "but he seemed to be better last night, tired but not, well, as deflated, if you know what I mean. Anyway, I'll tell him as soon as he comes in from the garden. Now, how long will you be staying? It's just that there's nothing in the house, so I've got to go shopping. Is there anything you fancy?"

They discussed menus and other practicalities for a few more minutes then arranged a probable meeting time.

"Martin!" called Jennifer, as she returned to the kitchen, "Mar..... Oh, no! Where's he gone, now?"

She bent over the hastily scribbled note to find that he had come in from the garden while she was on the phone and decided to go for a walk 'up the hill'.

"He'll be worrying himself sick," she thought, "and then he'll go off like last time with one of those bandits, or something."

Fearing the worst (whatever that turned out to be) Jennifer rushed upstairs to look out of the window and saw with relief that her husband was returning down the 'hill' (which was little more than a gentle incline, although it gained in stature from the flatness of the surrounding countryside).

"Thank Goodness!" she thought. "He's coming back. We'll have to get another dog. I think Elizabeth was right when she said he was still upset about Sherry; probably blames himself."

Jennifer, however, was only half right. Martin did blame himself, but it was the death of Christopher which had exercised him, ever since he had got up early, read the account and seen the pictures in the morning paper. He had said nothing, but lapsed into near silence, giving rise to his wife's concern. To have claimed to be the great 'Charles', Christopher's protector, a power behind the scenes on whom the young man could call in time of trouble, had been deceitful, taking advantage of one of life's victims. Had he, even at the end, clung to the belief that 'Charles' would avenge him? As he walked, Martin ran over in his mind his recent encounter with Christopher, and as he walked and thought, he remembered the young man's naïve trust, his horror at coming into contact with casual murder and his relief when he realised that the person he had so cleverly followed had not, after all, been killed. Martin dwelt, too, on his own success in gaining a hold over a member of the Organisation. That could have been a useful asset. It would have made Martin himself of value as Christopher's contact......and that puffed up, patronising hyphenated swine had, quite wrongly, accused the lad of being a traitor and set him up to be gunned down within yards of sanctuary. Moreover, that same Burton-Latimer, he strongly suspected, had run to Gerald for help in evading the law – and was almost certainly hidden in the submarine which Elizabeth had deduced when investigating U-534.

"Oh, there you are!" said Jennifer brightly. "Nice walk? ..... Elizabeth rang, and do you know what?" She hurried on, not waiting for a reply. "Apparently it was on the news last night. That man who recognised you's been shot! So you needn't worry any more. There was a gun battle at Harwich and....."

"Yes. So I saw. Lucky I got off at Colchester, given what happened. Actually my man was pretty harmless, but when bullets start flying about they're no respecter of persons. Are you off out, then?"

"Yes. Elizabeth's coming down later and the stocks are a bit run down, so....."

"She's coming, too, is she? That's nice."

"Why? Is Patrick coming? No-one said! I'll get enough for four in that case. When did he say he was coming?" asked Jennifer, adding with some asperity. "I'm only the cook; no need to tell me!"

"Oh – er – I thought *you* said he was coming. Perhaps it was him. I'm not sure," said Martin, who had only very recently decided to ring his son to get him down to bend his ear on the subject of Burton-Latimer. To be more accurate on how best to make sure the said B-L suffered the torments of

Hell, rather than succeed in using his many well-connected acquaintances to wriggle his way to a cushy billet.

Jennifer was pleased to find that her husband seemed to have cheered up after his walk and asked if he wanted to come shopping with her (secretly hoping he would decline, as she was looking forward to being a bit extravagant and taking her time browsing round Queensgate).

For his part, Martin was keen to set up a meeting with his son to discuss certain proposals, so welcomed the chance to ring him in his mother's absence.

"No, thanks. You carry on; I've got one or two things to do, the first of which is to make some coffee and finish reading the paper."

"You're feeling better for that walk," said Jennifer. "We could see about getting another dog soon; what do you think?"

"Well, they get you out, I suppose, but they're rather a tie. I'm in no rush, really. Anyway, you get cracking: it's perhaps as well if one of us is here in case Elizabeth rings."

As soon as his wife had gone, Martin seized the phone and rang his son.

"Oh! It's you, Dad. Everything O K? How's Mother?"

"We're both fine, thanks. She's just gone to Peterborough, so I thought I'd......"

"She must be feeling better, then! A spot of retail therapy, is it?"

"Not entirely. Elizabeth's coming later...and if you do, too, she'll be cooking for four, so..."

"Me? I'm a bit tied up at the moment. There are still quite a few loose ends, as I'm sure you realise, but I could probably manage to get down in a few days," said Patrick, thinking of the can of worms he had caused to be opened up by denouncing Burton-Latimer.

"Yes, quite," replied his father steadily, "which is why I'd like you to come down. I have some information – and some thoughts – on the subject of our hyphenated mutual acquaintance which would be best conveyed face to face .... mine to yours, to be more precise."

"Well, I didn't say which particular loose ends I......" demurred Patrick, with perhaps just a hint of irritation in his voice.

"No, you didn't; nor did you say 'full fathom five he lies' for that matter," persisted Martin. "I should like to pass on a few....."

"How the Hell did you know where he .....?" asked Patrick, surprised out of his customary care concerning the transmission of information.

"I didn't, well not to be absolutely sure, but I do now!" replied Martin, triumphantly, "But more importantly, you may recall that I spent several hours with Mr Bearer recently, during which time I ...."

"Mr Who? And please don't use tricks on me like that last one, by the way .....Oh, yes, I follow – Mr Bearer. Why? Did he say anything particularly revealing?"

"It's not for me to decide what is or is not 'revealing', which is why what I have to pass on needs to go direct to you: why I need debriefing and am requesting a 'meet' to that end," continued Martin, his tone altogether crisper, quietly persuasive, not to say insistent.

Reluctantly, Patrick agreed to come down, adding that if his father considered there was a degree of urgency and that what he had to say might bear directly on certain matters of which they were both aware..... he would find the time. What he meant was: 'It had better be worth my while'.... as they both well knew.

"I'm back, dear!" called Jennifer. "Can you give me a hand with these?"

'These' referred to the vast pile of groceries she had abstracted from Waitrose – whose share price, Martin was wont to declare, started to rise whenever she was spotted entering their car park.

"Right!" said Martin moving to the back of the overladen vehicle. "Did you get enough for Patrick? Oh! Silly question: there's enough here to feed the five thousand!"

"Don't be silly – and anyway, surely the whole point was that it only needed a few loaves and fishes? Is he coming? Any particular reason?"

"Oh, I think he just wanted to make sure you were all right," her husband replied. "They worry, you know!"

****

"Would you say, Mother, that your firstborn and his father are, shall we say, not in full agreement about something at the moment?" asked Elizabeth later that evening.

"Well, I know what you mean," said Jennifer, who, like her daughter, had been hearing sounds of verbal strife from the other room. "Do you think I ought to go in and....."

"No! I do *not*! Leave them to it," replied Elizabeth. "In fact, it's not Father who's getting het up. Come to think of it, he seemed different to-day: more positive, sharper, not quite so – er – more ....purposeful."

"You're right, dear. I've known him like this before. I remember once I thought we should be walking the streets by evening: he set off to take issue with his Head about one of his students. This lad had been very rude to another member of staff (a 'self-important pseud', in your father's opinion) and they were talking of rewriting his University entrance reference. Martin was furious, but he kept himself under control, demanded to see the Head – almost forced his way in – and argued logically, calmly and...implacably. He's got quite a good analytical mind, really – or he had, anyway. He's seemed a bit like that all day – well since he went for that walk, this morning. He was quite different before, verging on the depressed, which is why I rang you."

"Well he hasn't got any students, now – unless that dog had assumed tutee status, that is!" said Elizabeth, distractedly operating the remote-control to indulge in a bit of 'channel-hopping'.

"You owe me!" said Martin. "The department owes me.... No, you listen! I didn't ask to join your mob... well all right.... but I didn't answer an advert: I was persuaded, as a responsible citizen. I've given you a lot of names, some of which clearly surprised you, and I tried to set up an 'asset' in Christopher, only to have him assassinated by his own side because of this fellow Burton-Latimer's casual, lethal, incompetence."

Patrick sought to 'set the record straight' by reminding his father that they had set out to deceive Monty, and had succeeded; that the aim – insofar as there had been one, when it came to the involvement of the phantom agent 534 – had been to wrong-foot the Organisation, to get them chasing their own tails as it were. The story, one could say, was more one of H M G's success (including, he added by way of diplomacy, Martin's own contribution) than of Monty's incompetence.

Martin, however, was not to be deterred. He had decided that morning to avenge his trusting acolyte: an eye for an eye would do fine, a plus being a slow and painful eye if attainable in Monty's case. He was well aware, however, that the Intelligence world had no time for sentiment, including revenge. The plan he proposed was supported, therefore, by recommendations such as 'value for money' (the taxpayers), deniability, and continued security. It steered clear of any form of 'deal' with Burton-Latimer, whatever knowledge or influence he might have.

"We don't want him being made Keeper of the Queen's Pictures, do we?" Martin had asked, maintaining a calm persistence, countering argument with reason, practical advantages against the risks associated with later discovery.

Eventually, Patrick offered the nearest he was prepared to come to a concession to his implacable parent.

"Right!" he said. "If, and only if, they agree, I will try to get the Task Force to listen to your plan.... with *you* presenting it. They may take the view that we owe you that, and this material you've just given me should help your case, but it must be understood that the whole procedure is covered by the Official Secrets Act, and that you will not be involved in the decision-taking. Don't expect me to help you; don't blame me if you get a verbal mauling."

"Done!" Martin thrust out his hand: "Sold to the old fool in the wheelchair! When will it be?"

"Hold on, Father, hold on! They may not even agree to hear you out: don't get over-excited. On the other hand ..... it's not a bad plan, so marshal your arguments, stick to what you know – which is not, I have to say, absolutely the full picture – and, well you'll know you've done your best for this Christopher, even if he did try to have you neutralised!"

"It's not a question of....." his father started to protest, only to be firmly sat on.

"Come off it! I know you. But you're dead right not to admit it, and that secret will be safe with me. Let logic prevail!"

Jennifer and Elizabeth were relieved to find that the two men seemed to have resolved their differences, and noted the friendly, but business-like, exchange as Patrick left early the following morning:

"I'll be in touch then, Dad. Be ready to make yourself available, but .....well, you know!"

"Don't worry, I've got the message..... and Patrick!"

"Ye-es?" said his son cautiously.

"Thanks!"

"You may not find much to thank me for, if it comes to it," said Patrick, thinking of the ordeal which lay ahead if his father were called to make a presentation before his hard-headed, high-powered, uncompromising colleagues, "but...... Good Luck!"

CHAPTER THIRTY-FOUR

"And what," asked Elizabeth, once her mother had departed to take her son to the station, "was all that about?"

"Oh, nothing much: I've agreed to go to London for a debriefing, if they want me to," replied Martin.

"You seem to have taken a lot of persuading!" replied Elizabeth, making it abundantly clear that she knew a good old-fashioned lie when she heard one. "Was my brother in the business of 'pulling rank'? He really is a bit much!"

"No, I wouldn't say that," said Martin. "More a matter of presentation than substance, one might say. In fact, I must get on with putting together a report. Apparently they might want me to present it in person."

"Can't he do it? You're, well.... a bit – er – out of practice, aren't you?" said Elizabeth.

"The phrase you're looking for is 'past it'," said Martin cheerfully, "and cocky Sixthformers can be pretty daunting, too, believe me: I'll survive if it comes to it."

Elizabeth surveyed her father, and recalled that he had kept his cool and continued to exude an air of competence, and the thought struck her that the boot just might have been on the other foot – in which case.......

"I'm beginning to think you might, Father. Will we all be walking the streets in the near future?"

"Be what?" said Martin, settling down with a pad of A4.

"Oh, nothing; just something Mother mentioned."

It was as well Martin had decided to get cracking on his presentation, for the summons came late that night. He would be met at King's Cross station, near the 'Arrivals Board' at 10.30 the following morning. The driver would know his name... and would ask if he wished to go to 'Candy Island'.

"I suppose," said Elizabeth scathingly, on being told the ridiculous codeword, "the whole encounter will be captured on 'Candied Camera'! You're enjoying this, aren't you?"

Some might have called Martin's smile enigmatic; the word which occurred to his daughter, however, was 'smug'.

"I think you look very nice, dear. Nothing like a clean white shirt, I always say. Have you got a hanky?"

"Oh, Mother, really. He's not trying to get a job. One thing you will need, though."

"What?" asked her father, falling into the trap neatly.

"Your 'Old Person's Railcard' – no need to bother about proof of age!......and Good Luck!"

"Have a nice day, dear, and don't go off with any more strange men this time," said Jennifer, giving him a farewell kiss.

"At least that leaves me free to pursue strange women!" replied Martin as he reversed out of the driveway.

"Well," said Elizabeth to her mother as they both watched Martin depart, "at least he's no longer depressed. I only hope he's up to presenting this famous report....."

"Oh, he'll be all right," said Jennifer, confidently. "It's only to Patrick and one or two friends, apparently. It'll do him good to have a day in London, and the ticket's paid for!"

Elizabeth debated whether to voice her suspicion that the 'friends' in question were likely to be the type that are only ever referred to in inverted commas and might not be all that amiable, but decided not to spoil her mother's day, contenting herself with:

"So you're not worried about the 'strange women', then?"

"I think," replied Jennifer, with feeling, "that Olga will need more than a long cigarette holder and a split skirt to get your father going!"

****

"Good of you to come, Martin," said the Director. "You probably know most people here, so let's get straight to the main business. The floor is yours."

Martin glanced round the room and recalled the advice his first Head of Department had given him: 'Don't give the buggers an inch or they'll run you ragged'. To his relief, the easy habit of a thousand such encounters had not totally deserted him, as he found when the door opened to admit a latecomer, who looked round to find someone sufficiently senior to receive his apology.

"Seat over here," said Martin briskly. "You've only missed the warm-up act. No harm done! Now, give me two minutes without interruption to set out the bare bones, then I – or, I hope, one of you – will respond positively to those who express doubts, reservations and good old-fashioned ridicule."

The group relaxed slightly, recognising that Martin had seized the initiative and was making it clear that the floor was indeed his, however briefly. The Director smiled slightly to himself, thinking that one or two of his colleagues might live to regret it if they tried the last of the possible reactions the speaker had listed: this Martin might be out of his depth, but he'd learnt to swim in some quite rough seas and had no intention of drowning unaccompanied.

"As I see it," began Martin, "the best way to protect the duplicity – in its literal sense – of Gerald is for it to be absolutely clear to the Organisation that H M G has no idea where Monty is. Looking at this from their point of view, the best way to prevent Monty from being found and 'encouraged' to implicate many others...." At this point, Martin glanced at Bernard, whose one track mind caused a predictable flicker of interest to show in the carefully blank attitude he had elected to adopt, ".....many others, would be to eliminate their Honourable colleague rather than allow him to testify, or do some form of deal. The next best thing to *that* – for I have to assume that, unlovable though he may be, he has friends in high places – would be for H M G to be hoodwinked into believing that he had died. In such circumstances, it would be respectable for us to cease searching for him. Instructions to Gerald could be to organise a suitable scenario whereby Monty, attempting to escape the long arm of you lot, comes to, if not a sticky, certainly a fairly public, end. As we would in fact be prepared to believe anything, including his being eaten by a python whilst visiting the zoo, the incomparable Gerald should gain even more Brownie points and confound anyone in the Organisation who suspects he lacks star quality. Having successfully achieved Monty's official death, the Organisation can keep him hidden in some suitably remote spot – for ever more."

At this point, Martin paused and took a sip of the water thoughtfully provided by his son, both to revitalise the 'vibes' with which he was willing the group to accept the logic of his argument, and to allow the picture of Monty the submariner to swim to the surface of all those who knew where he was at present......which meant everyone except, in theory, himself.

"For Monty to be kept incognito," Martin continued, "under what would have to amount to some form of 'house arrest', would mean that the Organisation rather than the British taxpayer would cover the cost of his keep: a saving of, say, £50,000 a year in an open prison, or more if he's guarded from ex-colleagues bent on ensuring his silence.... to say nothing of the probable costs and possible embarrassment of a trial."

Martin paused again, consulting his notes.

"There's another aspect of Burton-Latimer, however: he's no fool. I met him, disliked him, was dismissed by him as a 'nobody', a rôle I have spent years perfecting," (a slight lightening of the atmosphere, even the odd chuckle, greeted this self-deprecatory interjection) "...but thought him a dangerously able adversary ....."

"May I ask why you considered him, well before he was found to be an active neo-Nazi, to be 'an adversary'?" interrupted the suave career Civil Servant, who had been less than enthusiastic when told that the meeting would start with an address by a 'very recent recruit who had special knowledge to contribute', and had not liked the lack of respect shown to him when he had arrived a couple of minutes late.

Martin found a pause helpful, partly to rest his throat, which was beginning to feel the strain, and partly to remind the meeting of his opening 'contract' of two or three minutes to develop the structure *before* the barbed comments. He regarded his questioner thoughtfully, the pause just long enough for both the Director and Patrick to wonder whether the interruption had stopped the flow, even disconcerted the old boy to the point of reducing him to silence.

"I had hoped to complete the case for the prosecution before the onset of a very proper and necessary descent into detail," Martin continued calmly, "so I would ask you, for the moment, to accept the relevance of my answer, even if it escapes you. He left Stansted Airport, turning east at the main roundabout, in a taxi owned by a firm called 'H F C' . I pointed this out as making him 'suspect' to the member of the Security Service with whom I was travelling at the time."

Patrick smiled broadly, as did Ralph (whom Martin remembered from the meeting at Fitzwilliam College) and the group, including the now even sourer-faced questioner, remained silent as he finished developing his proposals.

"Monty, I assume, is no fool. He thought Christopher was working for *us*. As soon as he finds that all is not immediately well, despite the young man's assassination, he will start to examine the whole series of supposedly unconnected events – and suspect Gerald. He already knows about the Brady family, of course, but the key to the whole affair is Gerald: he must be protected. The best way to achieve this is for Gerald to be Monty's keeper, thus ensuring total censorship of any letters he might wish to have sent to the British, or European leadership. It would be preferable if the arrangement had the full agreement of Monty's Continental masters. Should problems arise, such as Gerald having to hand over to a 'genuine' subordinate, Monty would have to be silenced to prevent him from getting word out to those above Gerald in the hierarchy. In short, Gentlemen, although not exactly an apologist for Mr. Burton-Latimer, I propose he should not be brought to book by H M G, despite the considerable evidence of his real allegiance. Get the Organisation, specifically Gerald, to be, in effect, his gaoler. Get *them* to foot the bill for his food and housing, and pretend to believe whatever smokescreen is put up to cover the official disappearance of this much-respected and very smooth operator."

Martin sat down, fighting to control the tremor in the hand that reached for the glass of water, as the Director rose to his feet.

"Thank you, Martin. Succinct, logical, perceptive, persuasive ......but as you are not fully au fait with all the aspects, there may be problems not yet taken into account. I think I should clear the air, or rather expand Martin's security clearance, to cover the 'Retter'. You referred to the probable desire of the Organisation to keep Monty hidden. You were right: he is at present on board a World War Two U-boat, known as the 'Retter' (the 'Saviour', as you may realise, in German), which has lain submerged since 1945 – perhaps the longest maiden voyage on record! It is the reason for the depôt you discovered at Harwich – another H F C, of course.... clever of you to have spotted that so early on. The enterprise is under the control of Gerald, in his new job as Eastern Area Commander. Right! Other points, please .... Percy?"

Martin looked up to meet the far from friendly eye of the task force member with whom he had already crossed swords.

"I, too, am no admirer of Monty, but you seem to be condemning him to a lifetime, which could be suddenly curtailed, banged up in a steel coffin just off Harwich. His lawyers would argue that his crimes, though considerable, do not merit such an extreme penalty. What would you say to that, Sir?"

"I would say, Sir, that Burton-Latimer's failure to consult Christopher's lawyers before condemning him to immediate death absolves any of us from the need to apply Judge's Rules, or whatever safeguards apply in ordinary cases. I would also say that *we* are not doing anything. My proposal is that Gerald be given the kudos for suggesting something which any other member of the Organisation is likely to come up with, for as long as this odious creature is out of favour. He will, in effect, be not unlike Lord Lucan – missing, presumed dead."

"To reinforce that point," added Patrick, "Monty gained no friends in Sussex when he sent those two, without consulting their immediate boss who later had to have one of them murdered by his own man in the hospital. Added to that, I know from Gerald that the British Chairman wrote to Vienna complaining about Monty, as a result of which they are quite happy to have him left on the 'Retter'. He's run out of allies: no-one wants him around."

Martin was delighted with the way things were going: a few more minutes and he could relax. He could feel the dynamism draining away, realised why he had retired: dominating was too damned tiring!

"There is one cloud on the horizon, Toby," said Ralph to the Director, his voice quiet in a room suddenly stilled. Percy looked up, recognising an ally....and Martin's heart sank. Ralph was no fool: without his approval, the scheme was doomed, and he would for ever feel he had let down Christopher in death as well as in life.

"Not everyone is aware of Christopher's last words," Ralph continued, glancing across at the Director. "He mentioned another agent by name and until we can track that person down and find out what he knows, what Christopher told him, whether he had one of his men helping Monty, for example, we cannot be sure whether we are in fact one step behind. I have to counsel caution at this juncture – to consider, repugnant though we may find it, a deal with Monty..... his freedom for that name."

"Sorry, Martin," said the Director. "Need to know, and all that. Your scheme is grand. We even know now that Vienna want to check on the 'Retter', to make sure that Monty had defused the weapons. They'll find he has – or, rather, that by then *we* will have done....but the important thing is that they've no plans to bring Larry, as they know him, back with them."

Martin could feel fatigue creeping over him, but knew, too, that one more effort was required. He sat, head down, shoulders hunched, gathering his strength.

"Hrrmm!" the Director cleared his throat. "Well, I'm sure you would all wish to join me in thanking ......"

"If you were to locate this Charles.....," interrupted Martin, sitting upright now, speaking slowly but distinctly.

"I don't think," said the Director, glancing with disapproval at Patrick, "that I mentioned the name, which remains *highly* classified... but please carry on."

"You didn't Director, and what is more, neither did I, until now. So how do *you* know it?" Martin gazed accusingly at the great man.

"Just for the record, Director," said Patrick, "Martin did not hear it from me: it's the first time I've heard it mentioned. Perhaps we could ask him how....."

"Christopher said it in the ambulance," said the Director repressively, "but he said it in the hearing of only two people. Which one did you get it from?"

There was a shocked pause, as it dawned on those around the table that whilst they were aware that both the priest (who might even have been a Nazi sympathiser) and the S A S man had travelled with the dying man, only those two – and the Director, who had immediately put the highest possible classification on it – knew precisely what the dying man had said.

"Neither," said Martin with a smile, "but I'll offer 50 to 1 he wouldn't tell them the surname!"

It dawned on his son first.

"You old bugger!" he said. "It was you, wasn't it? You were 'Charles'. You couldn't just be 'Agent 534' all the way from Peterborough to Colchester! And only you know the surname, too!"

"Me, and, as poor old Christopher was led to believe, the very top level of the Organisation! So he kept faith to the end. I told him he might come across me using other names and he was only to trust, if it came to the crunch, another person who knew my *full* name. That's the relationship we had: that's what poor bloody hard-done-by Monty loused up. Christopher wanted something to believe in: that was the appeal of his neo-Nazi 'family'. I was pretty confident he wouldn't have divulged the other name, which, by the way, was 'Hastings'. To him it was .....sacred."

There was a different sort of silence now. They all recognised what it had cost Martin to explain, realised the depth of his anger and contempt for Monty, to whom the name 'Charles' would have meant nothing, although he would have strung them along with some tale or other as a bargaining counter. The Director's glance moved round the table. Wordlessly, each man present nodded briefly, Ralph making also a slight movement of his open palm, to signify the removal of his objection.

"Thank you, Martin. Please leave us now. You must be exhausted. My secretary will find you coffee, I'm sure."

Dazed, drained, yet somehow uplifted, Martin stood, gathered his papers and left, looking at no-one. He didn't even notice that they all stood as a mark of respect as he left, resuming their seats as the door closed behind him, and the Director said:

"Unless anyone has any further points to make, please signify if you are in favour of ...... 'Operation Hastings'."

CHAPTER THIRTY-FIVE

Monty did not find it surprising that the first return trip in the 'lift' was taken by Klaus, Clarence having instructed his assistant, Norman, to remove the body and wait for him to come up to stow it on the tender. After so long shut in, first with the ghastly Klaus alive, later with his decomposing flesh, Monty was desperate to be the second load. However, when Norman reported that a boat was approaching from the seaward side, he reluctantly agreed that Clarence would have to go next (as the two wily boatmen had calculated, before inventing a phantom 'visitor'). Monty's feelings, however, when Clarence then told him over the ship-to-ship that the danger had passed but they had no instructions to take him off, ranged from the incredulous to the murderous, the latter when he detected in Clarence's tone not only that he was enjoying the conversation, but that it was the first of many similar to come. Had Klaus, many, many years before seethed beneath the waves with impotent rage? And the man in the photo.... what was it the old ruin had said? Had he, too, suffered for weeks, months – even years, before..... before what?

Monty sat down to consider his options and do some serious thinking about the events which had combined to place him down here, out of favour, out-manoeuvred at every phase. The hand of that devious sod, Brady, was clearly behind it all, but surely, now that Christopher had been disposed of (that much was clear from the newspapers he had seen) the High Command should be able to move effectively. Why, then, were they – and that had to include Vienna – leaving him to rot down here? He deserved to be fêted, not forgotten; what had gone wrong?

It was some time before the awful thought struck Monty that he might be out of favour because he had been wrong about Christopher....and that for the same reason he was still being out-played, namely that *someone else* was the informer making it possible for Brady to act the puppet-master. He remembered then that he had originally considered and rejected the possibility that Patrick had 'turned' Gerald:

rejected it not because it was so far-fetched, but because it would have been so embarrassing to have had to go, cap in hand, to that pompous bugger, Malcolm.

"So where do you go from here, Monty," he asked himself. "Come on. You're brighter than that ..... that.....'nobody'. Just look at his father – what a *boring* little man!"

And so Monty hatched his plan. He would write to the Chairman, Malcolm, telling him that he now realised that someone else was the 'mole', not Christopher...and that he, Monty, would only divulge the name, together with some other important deductions concerning the happenings at Hall Farm, *in person*. The sealed letter was duly received by Gerald following the next maintenance visit, together with a report that Larry seemed very low, had asked when he was to be allowed to go, but didn't argue or shout, just sat, staring at nothing.

The same information caused Patrick to warn Gerald that Larry was not to be trusted and might try to escape if given half a chance. He also had a different letter written to be passed on to the Chairman, in which the Retter's 'prisoner' complained about his treatment, about the incompetence of the British High Command, hinted that he would be taking his view direct to the Grand Council and that he, Larry, was 'not without influence'.

"Monty's no fool," said Patrick to the Director. "He'll work out, when he either receives an unhelpful reply – or none at all – that his letters are being intercepted. From that he will strongly suspect Gerald, and be able to work out most of the rest."

"Perhaps another visit like the last, when we defused the weapons, only this time we don't bring him round again after injecting anaesthetic gas into the 'Retter's' airpipe?" suggested Bernard.

"I'm sorely tempted," said Patrick, "but he can't do any harm where he is, and his sudden death might alert the Organisation that we're on to them..... and cause them eventually to suspect Gerald."

"You have to admit he's dangerous while he lives. I bet your old man would want him snuffed out!" said Bernard, remembering the implacable venom which had led to Operation Hastings.

"Perhaps," said Patrick, "but no-one's asking him. *We* have to decide, taking, I hope, the long view and weighing the risks against the possible gains."

"All right," said the Director. "Are we all agreed to wait and see? But," he added, "let's agree, too, that if the situation deteriorates suddenly, as it well might, Monty is to be – er – 'snuffed out' by appropriately unattributable means."

****

The midweek maintenance visit to the 'Retter' – outwardly to the diving platform over the wreck of a 16th Century transport ship – was usually undertaken by Derek and Stuart. Clarence saw them off from the H F C office, with a reminder to take care on entering the submarine.

"Remember this guy could tip over the edge just like the last one, so be on your guard."

"Yeah, yeah. Bit before my time, he was. This one's more likely to top himself from what you said last weekend. ... but I'll be ready, in case."

Derek slipped a small automatic from his pocket to show his boss, and set off with Stuart at the helm and his load of fresh fruit, newspapers, videotapes and (Monty's special request from three weeks previously) an exercise bicycle.

There was no immediate answering 'buzz' on the intercom this time, however, so Derek tried again, looking meaningfully at his partner.

"D'you think he's ill?" Stuart enquired nervously.

"Could be. He's not out in the garden, that's for sure. I'll take a spare intercom unit in case the other's bust. O K, here goes; I'll let you know the score in a few minutes."

Derek opened the hatch gingerly, gun in hand, as he entered the 'Retter', calling out:

"Larry! Larry, where the..... Oh Christ! You stupid...."

As he had half expected, and had warned Clarence, Larry had had enough. He swung slowly to and fro, suspended from a strut at the far end of the section, an empty bottle of whisky on the surface which passed for a desk. Sadly, for he couldn't help feeling sorry for the guy, Derek pocketed his gun and moved to perform the gruesome task of cutting down the body.

"Dead on cue," thought Monty, moving out from behind his visitor and raising the heavy spanner to bring it down with all his strength on the back of Derek's unsuspecting skull. The latter fell, clutching onto the dangling, death-like scarecrow dressed in Larry's usual garb and causing the crudely made dummy to disintegrate in the process.

"Now for the other sucker!" muttered Monty, reaching for the intercom.

"Stuart!"

"Here... what's up? Is he..."

"Yeah, dead to the world, you might say. I'm sending him up first. Pull the body out and send the lift back down, then I'll come up and contact Clarence. Ready?"

"God, the poor bugger. After all that.... Yes, I'm ready."

Monty grinned evilly to himself as he cut the connection. So far all had gone according to plan, including his imitation of Derek, to whom he had listened carefully on earlier occasions. Between the impure sound and the nature of the news, he had relied on Stuart failing to notice the deception. He activated the 'bathysphere', checked the safety catch on Derek's gun, arranged himself suitably on its floor and waited, as it rose slowly through the water, for the unsuspecting Stuart to pull him out at the top.

It took about half an hour to shoot Stuart, return to the 'Retter', secrete Derek's body in one of the empty torpedo tubes (if only he had thought of that as a relatively smell-proof storage place for Klaus!), return to sea level, load Stuart onto the tender for later disposal .....and set off towards Holland. All he needed was time. The longer no-one knew just what had occurred, the better chance he had of getting to Vienna and telling his story in the right place. Set against his information concerning the 'turning' of Gerald (now in an influential position within the leadership), the murder of a couple of low-grade operatives would be seen as fully justified.

Back at the H F C depôt in Harwich, Clarence occupied himself with various tasks, including a bit of shopping, and arranging the clandestine receipt and resale of suitable artefacts (for the 16th century wreck had in fact long ceased to supply anything which could explain H F C's continued presence). On this occasion, however, he had told his men not to be too long as he was expecting a routine visit from the Health and Safety Executive, who would want to check all their equipment. It was not so long, therefore, before he became aware that they had not yet returned and activated his shore-to-ship radio link, only to be met with ...... silence.

A quick scan through his binoculars was sufficient to tell him the tender was not in view, and cause him to report the matter to Gerald before welcoming the H & S E inspector. The latter passed a somewhat inconclusive two hours with a very distracted man who kept breaking off to indulge in brief, uninformative telephone calls, which consisted largely of 'No, not yet. I'm busy with the Safety Inspector... No, I've no idea'.

****

Patrick was having a brief, but genuine, holiday at the family home when the news of Monty's escape came through to him, by which time the double-murderer-double-agent, sought for different reasons by both the organisations for which he worked, was well out into the North Sea, maintaining strict radio silence and, so far as he could judge, completely unobserved.

"Trouble?" asked Martin, as his son replaced the receiver gravely.

"No reason for you not to know, I guess," came the reply. "Monty's given them the slip and is on his way to Holland in their maintenance launch."

"Will he make it in such a small boat? Surely he'll drown – and good riddance!"

"Oh, he's got a pretty good chance: some crossed from occupied Holland to Harwich during the Second World War in much less suitable open boats. It took some time – and this one isn't fast either – but they made it. I *told* them to be careful: he's ruthless and intelligent, with nothing to lose."

"Why didn't he make for the Essex coast and get through to the senior men in the Organisation?" asked Martin.

"Because he's as far out of favour with them as he is with us, and if, as I suspect, he had to kill some of them to get out of the 'Retter'....they'll want to see him dead as much as we do!"

"Oh! We want him dead, too, do we? I thought he'd become a sort of protected species, kept caged up with the odd bottle of wine poked through the bars from time to time!"

Patrick ignored the dig and replied quietly:

"If he gets through, we, as a family, will be prime targets of the Organisation, second on their list after Gerald. We have to get to him first....and, yes, the Director ordered that he be 'rubbed out' – no, 'snuffed out' was the term used by Bernard, if I remember correctly – if there were any development such as this. Don't worry: they remain convinced by your eloquence and concern for the Privy purse!"

"Bernard! That moron! Monty would run rings round him. Can't we do anything?" asked Martin.

Patrick noted, but didn't comment on, the plural pronoun, for he found it helpful to talk through ideas with someone, and there was no time to convene the full task force. Positive action was needed now.

"Can't you just scramble a fighter, armed with air-to-sea missiles – an Exocet or something..... or send a fast patrol-boat after him? He can't outrun them, or even reach territorial waters, can he?" suggested Martin.

"The trouble is that we're not supposed to know what's happened. As far as we know, Burton-Latimer died in the wreck of his boat – the Python, strangely enough, given your reference to us being prepared to believe an accident at the zoo! That means that if we go after him, his objective would be achieved, namely, the unmasking of Gerald. No, he's in more danger from his own people, who believe they've everything to gain by having him killed."

"I presume you got Gerald to organise the decoy boating accident? So," continued Martin, as his son nodded in confirmation, "why not get him to propose an Exocet? They must have access to weapons like that, surely?"

"Well, yes, probably," said Patrick, "but it'll be dusk shortly, and some innocent seafarer might see it skimming over the ocean, followed by the flash on impact!"

"Hmmm! Yes, it wouldn't be very discreet. I see what you mean ..... but if it was carried out by 'terrorists' – which is what they are – and on the High Seas, H M G wouldn't be involved. It's better than doing nothing!"

"True," said Patrick, "but we have a little time to try and improve on it. Remember we need to turn a blind eye, which means not going after Gerald. If he's too involved and the attack on an innocent British boat is too obvious, we might have a problem."

"Couldn't the 'Retter' set sail for one last glorious mission? Bags of poetic justice there!" said Martin. "Even if the torpedoes didn't work, they could ram this tub, then scuttle the sub!"

Patrick recognised the suggestion for the flight of fancy it clearly was, but even as the thought crossed his mind that the ancient warship had in fact bristled with modern rockets (now defused by both sides!) he remembered their provenance: they were Russian. That meant that someone in the British Neo-Nazi High Command had contacts who could, perhaps, purchase not just a weapon, but its use – could buy Monty's assassination, in fact.

"You've given me an idea! Thanks Dad. I'll need to get on with it now, or Monty will get clear away. You won't be needing the phone for a bit, will you?"

Martin took the hint and left his son to plan Monty's second fatal boating incident, remembering the 'need to know' principle which meant he would be excluded from these high level matters, which included arranging for an AWACS plane from near Lincoln to pinpoint the target as it battered its way across the North Sea.

In a short time, Patrick's instructions to Kenneth resulted in a proposal from Gerald to the Chairman of the British High Command.

"Surely a Russian pilot or ship's captain could be persuaded to go after Larry, Malcolm," said Gerald. "I have no personal contacts, I'm afraid – not much call for them in the Fens – but those rockets on the 'Retter' covered in Cyrillic lettering must have lined the pocket of some high-up in Georgia, or wherever."

"Good point, Gerald. I'll get on to them. We can't have this chap appearing suddenly in this boat of yours: open up a right can of worms.... to say nothing of his having murdered its crew. What happened?"

"We don't know any details yet, but Clarence's men must have got careless and allowed Larry to overpower them; I did warn them he was a tricky customer. The main thing is to make sure he never makes Holland – but discreetly. Have they got a fast ship in the area which could ram the bastard?"

"I'll check, Gerald. It could be expensive, mind you: these Ivans are hard bargainers.... but they deliver, with no questions asked. It's a changed world from my day. Never thought I'd be teaming up with the old enemy! Let you know how I get on. If it's no go, you should be able to rustle up a Harrier – at least, John claimed to be able to. Check his records."

****

Monty was enjoying himself. After his spell in the 'Retter', to feel the wind on his face and experience the thrill of deep sea travel was almost magical. Perhaps the laugh which escaped his lips might have been described (had there been anyone nearby to do so) as a touch unbalanced, but six hours out from Harwich, he could permit himself a little mild hysteria.

"The game's up, Patrick!" Monty shouted at the waves. "Gerald's goose is cooked – and thanks to that dreadful Mrs P, I can tell the exterminators *where to find your dreary little parents!*"

Even as he roared this challenge from the darkened cock-pit, Monty felt his world almost literally turn upside down, his ability to reason nullified by the tearing crash as the reinforced sail of the giant Russian submarine, equipped to smash the ice beneath the polar seas, rose like the horn of a huge black sea-bull and tossed the tiny craft in the air. Gored from below, it sank beneath the surface of the sea in seconds, as did its hit-and-run attacker, several of whose crew considered it to have been the easiest way to get a substantial share of £200,000 that they had so far had the good fortune to come across.

Before accepting the commission from the neo-Nazi Grand Council, the Russian contact – who was not above hedging his bets – had checked with British Intelligence to establish the degree of displeasure the proposed action would incur. Their almost total indifference to the fate of what they claimed to be a drug-running vessel, crewed by members of the gang, came as a slight surprise. Perhaps, the Russian thought, extra money could be earned in the future by warning them about their 'enemy within'....but, for the present, it seemed that those on board had run out of friends.

Malcolm, the Chairman of the British neo-Nazi High Command, received the whole-hearted endorsement of all its members for his forthright action.

"Thank you, Gentlemen.... it was Gerald's idea, in fact. Well worth the money; completely discreet. And whatever may have gone wrong lately, we can rest assured that our operations can continue with our security completely 'water-tight'.... if you'll excuse the expression!"

Despite certain little local difficulties in Britain, the Vienna-based Grand Council, to membership of which Monty had aspired, were very content with the way things were going across Europe. They were convinced that their turn would come, confident that they appealed to sufficient young people to ensure the succession, as it were. They were pragmatic and ruthless, an attitude often euphemistically referred to as 'business-like', and conscious of the need to control the hotheads.

"Apparently Larry had already de-activated nearly all the weapons in that wretched submarine our British colleagues are so proud of. He'd done a thoroughly professional job, according to the team we sent in. They were most impressed," said the President. "Now we have a report that he shot his way out and tried to escape across the North Sea! It seems they managed to do a deal with the Russkies, who had one of their big subs in the area which made a detour and sank him. Perhaps our men should have brought him out when they went in to check?"

"Better to have let sleeping dogs lie, I think: he'd already been officially presumed dead, as you know, President – a 'boating accident' organised by our British High Command, which completely fooled the British Security Service. The last thing we want is to draw their attention to that set-up off Harwich. No, the re-appearance of Larry would have been a serious embarrassment to us, as he, himself, would have been the first to realise had he been in his right mind."

"Oh! Was he no longer.....?"

"Completely, President, I regret to say. Malcolm showed me an absurd letter he'd written complaining and threatening to contact you – and the maintenance team had reported him as being seriously depressed shortly before he made a run for it."

"I see what you mean. Pity. He seemed quite promising, might even....oh, well, these things happen. At least there was no breach of security and Malcolm's very impressed with the chap who took over the Eastern Area. Comes from good stock he tells me: breeding will out, I always say! Now, turning to other matters: this business in France. Can we agree our policy for the elections? It all looks very promising!"

****

The news that Monty had been 'sunk without trace' filtered back to Martin after a few days, but the violent events of the previous weeks had left little more than a slight scar on the flat, peaceful Fenland scene, in the form of a number of pieces of the light plane which were in the process of sinking beneath the fertile soil. In accordance with policy decided at the highest level, the many firms sporting the initials 'H F C' continued to trade, including those under new management such as Hall Farm Cultivation.

The footpath signpost which had proved so disastrous for the Organisation had not yet been interfered with again, but it was now checked daily by Martin as he exercised the new puppy. Quite often, however, his thoughts strayed, running over aspects of recent events.... regretting the death of Christopher, wondering how Ahmed had fared, recalling the success of the 'takeaway diversion'..... reliving the fear of discovery when he was spotted by the low-flying helicopter .....and .... and where had that dog got to?

"Here Jacko! Here! Sit-tt! Good doggy. Right; let's get back and see if we can get some decorating done, shall we? No more excuses now, are there?"

As he arrived at the back door and started to remove his gumboots, Jennifer came out to tell him that she had taken a phone call in his absence from a very high-powered lady who described herself as 'Sir Somebody Something's personal assistant'.

"Would you ring the number I've written on the pad, identify yourself and ask to speak to Ms Patterson – as soon as you return from your walk," said Jennifer, her whole being radiating a desire to know who these people were, whilst letting not one interrogative word pass her lips.

"Ah!" said Martin, provocatively. "The delectable Pattie: I wonder what she wants."

"Pattie!" exclaimed Jennifer scornfully. "I suppose her boss is 'Knightie' to you! Who on earth are these people?"

"I have absolutely no idea," said Martin, laughing, "having never heard of either of them. Like you, however, I can't wait to find out – but not before I feed Jacko, and make us both some coffee."

"La Patterson won't like being kept waiting, dear, to say nothing of the good baronet. I'll make the coffee then you can ring whilst it's brewing."

In fact, although he affected indifference, Martin was a little worried by the message. Had the Organisation tracked them down, rung only to set up a 'snatch', or to make sure they were alone? Should he check with someone before ringing back, or was he exhibiting paranoia?

"Right, dear," said Jennifer, "there's the number. Off you go!"

Warily, Martin waited for his call to be answered, wondering whether the boffins had managed to develop a supersonic note which could be passed down the phone lines and turn the listener's brain to mush, not that his was any great shakes these......

"Room 303; can I help you?"

"Yes, I hope so," said Martin. "I've been asked to ring this number and speak to a Ms Patterson."

"And you are....?" came the carefully modulated reply.

"Before we go into that," said Martin unhelpfully, "I should like to know to whom I am speaking, and the reason for contacting me."

"If you are Mr Martin Brady," said Ms Patterson coolly, "I explained to your wife that I am Sir Toby Hillman's personal assistant. Are you in a position to speak with him now?"

"What sort of 'position' would you consider appropriate? At present, I'm standing up – and still have no idea who you or your boss are, or, indeed, whether you really are who you claim to be."

"One moment, please," replied the P A, trying hard – well, quite hard – to keep the exasperation out of her voice. She reported the exchange to her boss, who was highly amused and asked to be connected direct to the Fens.

"Martin! Absolutely correct of you to want some confirmation of my bona fides, especially in view of your own success in imitating Gerald when talking to Henry! Toby here: I was privileged to be on the end of your recent presentation concerning B-L, and should like to pop down to see you if it's convenient, to discuss a small project which might interest you. Can you spare me a few minutes?"

"I – er – B-L? Oh, Burton-Latimer.... I see, so you're Toby... Are...?" But at this point the penny dropped and Martin's face flushed in embarrassment. "You must be the 'Director'. Sorry. My wife didn't quite catch the name; she thought your secretary said – er – something different," he finished lamely.

"Oh, don't mind Mollie: she probably gave her the full works; quite correct, but it just confuses people! 'Sir Toby Hillman' gets one a better seat in a restaurant, but it's of little use otherwise! Can you give me a few minutes, then?"

"Yes, of course. I can come up to London any time."

"Rather come down to you if that's O K – more discreet if you see what I mean. How about this afternoon, 3 p m? No need for any elaborate identification as we've met before."

"Yes, right. 3 p m. I'll be there – I mean here."

"Good. 'Bye for now." The Director put the phone down and grinned at his scandalised assistant. "See what I mean, Mollie? He has a way of disconcerting people without meaning to. I plan to make use of that talent – and the fewer of our people who know, the better!"

"Well, dear," said Jennifer, who had listened in exasperation as her chances of upward social mobility receded to zero, "you made a right hash of that! I'll get the poor man some tea when he arrives. Will you pop into town and buy a cake? And don't be wearing those old trousers when he gets here. It's interesting his knowing that nice Mr. Burton-Latimer. Such a shame he was killed in his boat the other day."

"What," said Monty cautiously, "do you know about Monty – er – about Burton-Latimer?"

"Oh, nothing really. I recognised his picture with the obituary. No doubt at all, with those ears. Definitely the same chap. Very polite, a real gentleman."

"Where did you meet him?" asked Martin, with mounting amazement.

"At King's Cross," came the reply. "I bumped into him, literally, as I was running to the train when I came back from France. I don't know where he was going – down to Mersea, perhaps, where he kept the boat. Of course we had nothing in common, didn't know each other. Just a chance encounter ..... but it's strange that Sir Toby happens to know him, too, isn't it?"

Martin could only utter a strangled noise of affirmation as he contemplated his wife's latest revelation and imagined Patrick's face when he told him. Mind you, he thought mischievously, it should be interesting to see how the Director copes with Jennifer mentioning that she bumped into Burton-Latimer when the resources of both sides were frantically trying to find her. What with ramming Monty with her suitcase and flattening their hit man on Colchester station, she made Rosa Kleb look like a dinner lady! Which made a change from one or two dinner ladies he could think of who looked like Rosa Kleb.....

"Now," mused Martin, "what was it ....? Ah, yes. Trousers and cake, then for this 'discreet' meeting. I hope the Director isn't disappointed: it may very well be kept secret from most of the Intelligence Service, but it's most unlikely to escape the attention of that worthy soul of indiscretion – our Mrs Tolliver!"

THE END